The Bells of Chugiak

Karla Fetrow

The Bells of Chugiak (Athabascan: Place of Many Places) is a fictional story based on true events, anecdotes, and activities.

The purpose is to illustrate how these people, who had grown up in a modern structure with the modern conveniences of energy power and lights, running water and instant communications, abandoned these and struggled with lawlessness, isolation, and natural disasters to become lawful, stable communities.

The characters in this book are not intended to represent anyone living or dead.

This book is dedicated to pioneer women. Many sacrificed their careers, sold all their belongings, and put their faith in men they barely knew to build communities in the wilderness.

ISBN: 9798840370216
(C) 2022 Karla Fetrow
Published by Subversify Press, located in Anchorage, Alaska.

Book illustrators, Regina Fetrow and James Hinton.

A special thank you to Lot Arangua , who makes all things possible.

Introduction

The Alaskan Homestead Act was passed in 1898 to encourage settlement in potential farmlands and within the fledgling territory of Alaska. However, interest in farming was low among Alaska's new settlers, with the larger number of migrants focused on fur trapping and gold mining. With mining camps scattered from the Knik River basin to Talkeetna, the need for food services soon became apparent.

In 1935, a farm colony was created in the Matanuska Valley, but pioneering interests didn't really occur until the end of World War II. By then, the United States had gone through the Great Depression. Farms had gone bankrupt. The returning workforce discovered the same jobs that didn't exist when they left for war, didn't exist when they returned home. Alaska became the hope of those who wished to start over.

Alaskan homestead claims followed the same policies for homesteading as in the Continental United States. Prospective settlers were expected to stake and pay a small fee for filing their claim with the land office. They were required to live on the land for a minimum of five years, live in a habitable dwelling more substantial than a tent, and cultivate one-eighth of their land.

The Homesite Act made it easier for war veterans who did not wish to invest in full-scale farming. The newly built army and air force military installation provided secure jobs in construction, heavy equipment, technical engineering, and clerical work. All they needed was a one-hundred dollar filing fee for a choice piece of Chugach land.

The five-acre parcels within the Cook Inlet area were quickly snapped up by war veterans and Civil Service employees intending to make Alaska their home. These family-oriented people formed strong communities that became the base of many modern Alaskan towns today.

What was remarkable about this population surge is that it did not settle tightly close to Anchorage or other population hubs, such as Palmer in the Matanuska Valley, which offered electricity, running water and road services, but into wilderness areas that had no official roads, no power and light services, and no territorial representation.

They were not alone in the wilderness, however. Existing communities consisted of Native Alaskan villages that had lived their solitary lives for centuries, Russian communities more than two hundred years old, isolated from the Motherland long ago, yet still seeped in Russian traditions, and a mixture of miners, traders, trappers, and long-term military personnel.

Neither were the incoming Civil Service workers of a common heritage. Although a large percentage of them had farm backgrounds or came from western pioneer stock, the post-war settlers represented not only the different demographics of the United States, but also US allies. Some allied veterans chose jobs with the US Territorial Civil Service, adding to the diverse mix, pioneers from Sweden, Norway, France, and England.

The satellite communities took pride in their diverse mix. In fact, one community took so much pride in its diversity, it adopted the name "Chugiak", the Athabascan word for "place of many places", which they claimed was a correction of the spelling and pronunciation of the Chugach Mountain Range.

Book I: The Builders

It was a blustery day; or maybe an ordinary day if ordinary can be used in terms of war - when a young seaman received a package from his sister. Maybe the waves were rolling thunderously, and maybe there was peril ahead, but memories blur in those brief moments of happiness. What the seaman knew was this. There were more dreary days than bright ones. Ship quarters were dark and cramped. Tragedy was common. Happiness lasts longer when it's shared.

Packages from home were like jewels discovered in a perilous cavern, like water in the desert. They were flying machines that transported the receiver for a few brief minutes, into a world where families did their chores together, sent their children to school, drove automobiles and attended social functions; a world with blue, quiet skies and green, unblemished pastures. The young seaman, who had stumbled upon the nickname, "Bruiser" at an early age, was ready for transportation into that nearly mythical realm and could think of nothing more practical than to invite his bunk mate to come along.

This practicality of close companions among very unlikely personality matches could only be found in times of war. Bruiser was much of what his name indicated; a large man both in height and bones, with block-sided shoulders and a lunchbox head. The head itself sprouted a vigorous forest of black, short curls, a thunderous brow and a broad, high-bridged nose. His light-colored eyes twinkled merrily, however, and his lips twisted with mirth.

"I'm Irish, by God," he was fond of saying. "And I'll bring you the luck of a leprechaun."

Frank Lamar, on the other hand, felt lucky enough only if he could tip the scales at one hundred, forty pounds. Stretching his body to its maximum height, he was satisfied that he nudged in just under five foot seven. He had slender, delicate piano hands, small feet and a narrow, quarrelsome face with a large nose. If he referred to his ancestry at all, which was rare, it was to bemoan the fact that his name was the French word, "Lemaire" and had been Americanized several centuries ago when his first ancestor crossed the ocean.

Frank didn't believe in luck. He believed in strategy and plan fulfillment. Spontaneous instances, such as being chosen to participate in a crewman's heaven-sent bonanza, were better explained as the grace of God, or on the more practical level, a case of "scratch my back and I'll scratch yours." Frank also had a sister; several in fact; and there was no reason to believe he would not be able to return the favor.

Bruiser closed the curtains to their cell. Although he knew what the package probably held - his enlisted duty had occupied his attention for nearly two years now, and without fail, Millie's packages had arrived once a month, containing chocolate brownies and oatmeal cookies- he wasn't at all sure there would be enough to go around to everyone who stopped by their door.

Frank, who had been lounging from the top bunk, came to immediate attention. "It smells good, Bruiser. You haven't even opened it and it smells good."

"I was getting to that," he said hastily. He pulled the curtains tighter. "Get down here with me. We'll tie my blanket to your bunk in case the smell is too thick when I open the box."

Frank flipped over the side of the bunk in a somersault, landing squarely on his feet.

If Bruiser had the advantage in a brawl with his large size, Frank had the advantage of being quick and nimble, and generally managed to wade through a fight without a scratch, which was far more than could be said for Bruiser who attracted the offended and the offensive like a magnet.

Calculating the best words for securing a generous share, Frank said hopefully, "My sister, Julie, promises to send figs next month, after they ripen."

"I don't like figs."

"She dries them very nicely and makes a candy with them. They come from my mother's yard. She has a couple of fig trees."

Bruiser had taken out his pocket-knife to run a straight, clean cut through the tape. "Candied, huh? Maybe I should try them. I wouldn't want to dishonor your mother's figs."

"Now, that's the right spirit. We've got cherry trees, too. When the war is over, you'll have to stop by our house and have a sample of fresh made cherry pie."

Frank began tucking in the sides of the blanket so that the bunk was completely closed in. Bruiser clicked on a flashlight and aimed it at his package. Cautiously, he slid back the wrapper and gently peeled it away from the box.

At the top was a letter and a photograph. Underneath was a smaller box wrapped in newspaper. The cunning girl had left the papers intact so that they smoothed out easily for reading. Frank folded and settled the papers back inside the box while Bruiser unveiled the container.

The tin had enough cookies in it to put five large men into a diabetic coma, but Bruiser still measured out his treasure with caution. "Three for you and three for me," he said, then made a small pile. "One for the commander and four for whatever beggars come around. That leaves a little over half a box for the rest of the week."

Frank sat with his back to the wall and his knees drawn up, one of the pages from the newspaper in front of him.

"It's kind of hard to believe that over there, life is carrying on as always. Look at this. Perry Como is coming to Seattle. Well, this is dated six weeks ago. He's been there by now. But see what I mean? People are still going to the theater. They still go to the movies. They stop to buy ice cream while strolling through the streets. I can hardly remember just strolling in the park and stopping to buy a hotdog or going on a carnival ride. I think I want to go on a carnival ride. I want to go on the Ferris wheel, and go up and down in a loop, over and over."

"Are you homesick?"

"Actually, I'm not. That's funny, isn't it? I want to see my mother and my sisters. I don't really care much for Southern California, though. It's the heat. It bothers my lungs."

Bruiser grunted. "Northern Idaho has a nice climate. Summers are as sweet as a woman's kiss. Winters will kick the devil out of you. I reckon when it's all over, I'm going to go there and get into the lumber business. Pop already has a homestead up there in the north country."

There was a knock at the wall behind the curtain. A very hopeful, and somewhat round face appeared in black-rimmed glasses and a short, brusque haircut. "I'm sure I smelled something delicious."

"Eddie, my man. Just the guy I want to see." Bruiser waved him inside. "I need a drink. No, I need two drinks. One for my mate here, but it's got to be your best stuff. None of that potato water." He held up two oatmeal cookies.

"I smell chocolate," accused Eddie.

Bruiser drummed his fingers. "Alright. Turn your head. Two chocolate brownies, but - I want the real thing. I know you have some of the bottled stuff. Two chocolate brownies on delivery."

"Let me see them." Bruiser held up the prize for inspection. "Oh, they're big. I'll be right with you."

As delicately as they were nibbling at their treats, they still had eaten one whole cookie apiece and part of another when Eddie reappeared. They completed the transaction as stealthily as thieves. As Eddie started to leave, Bruiser called out to him. "One more cookie in the morning if you make sure nobody bothers us tonight."

"How long do you think that will last?" Asked Frank as they settled back.

"Who knows?" Shrugged Bruiscr. "I can't be the only one who received a package today. Anyway, it's always good to rack up a few favors. Good drink, eh?"

"I do believe it's real whiskey."

"The little devil. I wonder how he does it?"

"Never underestimate the power of the grapevine."

"Now that's something an Irishman would say."

"The French have their moments of wisdom."

"Except when they settle in sunny California, eh?"

Frank cleared his throat. "I'd like to settle in the North."

"Do you now? There's still plenty of open land to settle in the northwest region."

"I mean far north. I've been there."

Bruiser appeared unimpressed. "Really? The first ship I served on was with the Kodiak fleet. I didn't like Kodiak very much. It was a wet, windy place. I have no idea why we were so fierce about protecting it."

"It's part of the strategy.Defend Alaska against Japan to keep them off the North American mainland. They're building an air force there as well. When it's over, that's where I want to go."

Bruiser scoffed. "Then you should meet my sister."

"Because she bakes incredible brownies?"

"Because she's always talking about seeing other places. She went to Pennsylvania once to meet her great aunt."

She couldn't have been more than twelve, but they packed her on the train with her own saved money, and off she went. She followed the fruit pickers all the way into California when she was just fifteen. Now, she lives in Seattle, while the rest of the family lives in Idaho, and she tells me she likes it there!" He said this in a hurry as though there was too much to tell about his sister and it all needed cramming into shorthand.

He began reading the letter privately to himself for a few minutes, then said, "This is just like Millie. This is why you should meet her. Now, she is finding fault with Seattle. It's too big. Too noisy. Everyone moves too fast. That's how Millie is. She's looking for something. You're looking for something. Maybe if you meet up, you'll both find what you're looking for."

"Do you think she would move to Alaska?"

"That woman? She'd hop a boat to China if she had the chance."

"But to live there? Become a pioneer?"

"You really are a lunatic, Frank. No more whiskey for you."

"I'm serious. It's the one thing I think about when I don't have to think about anything else. I was in Ketchikan. Down on the Panhandle. It was magnificent there. The mountains – they went straight up, and they clawed at the sky. And the solitude… It rained a lot. It splattered on your tent, sort of making its own music. You could hear wild animals snuffling around in the brush. There were eagles and whales. More than I had ever imagined. I have to go back."

"Hmm." Bruiser looked at the letter, then at the attached photo. "It's about my sister, mate. You know, I'm a bit fond of her and now you're telling me that if I introduce her to you, my very good friend, you're going to whisk her away into the wilderness?"

"Oh, she would never consent to running off to God knows where with a small, ugly man."

"That's the problem, right there! She probably would!"

"Then let me see her picture."

Bruiser held the photo tight for a minute before relinquishing it. "Understand she is my favorite. Millie never really was much like other girls. She was more like one of the guys. She could out-run, out jump, out fish any of us and kept plenty of opinions on the side. She keeps those opinions. That's why she's soured on Seattle. She'll let you know all about it if you think of writing to her."

Frank stared at the photo. To any viewer gazing at it, it was a snapshot of a pleasant young girl of perhaps twenty, with an oval face, dark hair clumped thickly about her shoulders, sparkling eyes, and a relaxed, confident smile.

What Frank saw must have been more detailed. The way her eyes slid just a little away from the camera. The restless turn of her head. Something secret and twinkling just below the curve of her lip. He stared for a very long time, then climbed up into his bunk. "Her name is Millie?"

"Millicent Snipes."

"Millicent Snipes. Say, Bruiser? That's the girl I'm going to marry."

Frank Lamar began his letter to Millie the next day. He folded it and tucked it in the envelope with Bruiser's message home. Two months later, a missive came for him, packed in the same box of cookies and trinkets she sent her brother. Frank answered promptly, and without waiting for an answer, began writing a new letter to Millie once a week.

Soon, she began writing back with the same regularity, although at times, three or four letters would be bundled together in the same mail delivery. It didn't perturb Frank.

He read them in order, according to the date stamp on the outside of the envelope.

The war continued its brutal affair. The seas boiled with blood between short stretches of calm. Memories of a peaceful world grew more distant, stirred vaguely only by a photograph and a few written words. Frank poured himself into words, using them to chase away the dark and dirty mornings, the sullied air thick with violence.

As Frank Lamar wrote, he began to dream. The silent mountains and emerald islands of a distant land became more real than the clatter of boots against metal, more vivid than the ocean spray breaking against the bow. His dreams decorated his letters, along with his longings for a peaceful existence and his cravings for family life. None of this was extraordinary. Many young seamen in their solitary days, yearned for the touch or voice of a young woman. Many acquired long distance sweethearts through a bunkmate's sister or cousin.

Most thought of marriage when they returned from the war to end all wars. Most, like Bruiser, thought of returning to their hometowns, looking up a sweetheart or a potential one overlooked when they first put on a uniform. They thought of returning to their jobs or of finding new ones.

But the words Frank and Millie wrote set them apart from the ordinary. They didn't want to pick up where they had left off before the war. Something had gone wrong. The peace they had been promised in the first war to end all wars had been broken by hunger and hardship. The world that was supposed to open like a flower with the marvelous inventions of machine travel and radio was hostile and distrustful. They needed to do something different.

Exactly what they needed to do differently, they were unsure of, but the only way to find out was with a clean slate. This placed them in a small group of people with the same disturbed convictions. This tiny handful were neither skilled entrepreneurs, nor forward-seeking opportunists. They had no missionary goal to unite them. In fact, forty years of hardship had left many questioning the wisdom of applying themselves to an organized religion at all.

They were dreamers, however. They were idealists. And they could build. As the war marched viciously toward a close, they cast their eyes on the last piece of unsettled frontier and its promises. It didn't matter that this handful of people had not met. It didn't matter that they hadn't truly defined their evolving beliefs. Their aspirations were the same.

Neither Frank nor Millie knew they had been set apart from the ordinary during the long months of their written exchange. Bruiser suspected.

Throughout his sister's correspondence with his best friend, he continued to insist that their desires were not normal. Despite his belief in their lack of good judgment, he brought it upon himself to assist the young couple in determining where they should live by bringing out maps, introducing fellow shipmates who had also served time in the north country, and generally doing his best to show Frank what a large and miserably deserted wasteland it was.Frank remained unimpressed.

The war ended abruptly, while they were still stationed in the Sea of Japan. Frank stared out at the blackened skies and could imagine no wasteland more horrible than the one in front of his eyes.

"I've applied for a clerical position at the new military base near Anchorage," he told Bruiser. "I think they're going to give it to me. They want more desk clerks."

"That's because no man with a halfway decent education wants to go there," said Bruiser, jabbing at Frank's greatest vanity, his academic record.

"Never-the-less, I am going. I have only to ask Millie if she will come with me."

Having exhausted all his arguments, Bruiser resigned himself to the fact that because he had shared his cookies with his bunkmate, he would now have to share his sister, and decided to make the best of it. It wasn't like anyone could tie Millie down. If not Frank, another man could sweep her away and carry her off to parts unknown. Or she could leave on her own. At least this way, Bruiser could keep tabs on her. She would let him know if she was unhappy and he would come and get her, come hell or high water.

"Didn't you write to her about your intentions?" Bruiser asked gruffly.

In answer, Frank took out his pipe and lit it, appearing unhappy in the way only Frank could, with that air that someone had greatly underestimated his abilities. "I did. I told her I would be receiving a position and find myself in agreeable enough finances to ask her hand in marriage."

"You told her all of that!" Said Bruiser, as though impressed. "And how did she answer?"

He fastened his eyes on the horrid waters floating with humankind's destruction. "She asked, 'shouldn't we meet first'. I am doomed."

It was true testimony to the kindness of Bruiser's heart that instead of using the opportunity to discourage his mate from galloping off with his favored sibling, he used it to console his friend and give him courage. "But that's good! That is so like Millie. If she wasn't interested, she would never request a meeting."

"Do you think... She will like me?"

"Ha!" Spat Bruiser. "She will meet you with bells on."

Frank hoped this was so. Three days after D-Day, having recovered its wounded and dead, the battle-weary ship began its course back to the mainland, that glorious place of blue skies and open arms that had become more a fantasy in the minds of the boat's occupants than a real place. He had no choice but to place his faith in Bruiser, his only solid connection to the woman of his dreams. He was convinced Millie was the woman he loved. Articulate, cheerful, clear-headed, and adventurous, she was precisely the lady he needed to take north.

He had no doubt he needed a wife to take north. Every long-term resident had advised it. If he wanted the closeness of a woman, if he wanted a partnership, a family, he would have to find one to bring one with him.

"It ain't easy finding a lady friend of your own once you go north," an old-timer in Ketchikan had told him. "Ten to one. The men outnumber the women ten to one."

The ship eased into the San Diego harbor to the cheer of crowds and the thrill of marching bands. The waterfront exploded in celebration.

From San Diego to the San Bernardino Valley wasn't far, only sixty miles or so. Bruiser dropped into the naval base city to celebrate, and through the obligatory duties of the buddy-system, so did Frank.

Fortunately for Frank, and possibly unfortunately for Bruiser, who may have entertained the thought Millie would find Frank less appealing if he demonstrated a weakness for drinking, there were limits to the number of days Frank would celebrate.

Forty-eight hours later, after reservedly accompanying his buddy through an amazing display of alcohol consumption and debauchery, Frank managed to shove Bruiser on a bus and off they trundled toward Los Angeles and San Bernardino, Bruiser more unconscious than conscious, and Frank watching a landscape go by that should have been familiar but was so lost between where he had been and where he wanted to go, it was just a series of meaningless pictures flying by his window.

Part I

Millie

One

The war ended with a bang. It ended with two mushroom clouds and a shudder that shook the earth. The world looked on, thunderstruck, and fell to its knees, numb. There came a silence so great, you could hear a pin drop. Then, a sigh of relief. It was over! It hardly even mattered anymore who had won, just that the carnage was over.

Well, thought Millie, *maybe it did matter they had won, or she might never have seen her brothers again, or the man who courted her.* This courtship had reached a critical point, one she could delay no longer. Her unseen lover had proposed to her.

It didn't shock or disturb her. The Northwest had a long history of mail-order brides, and the practicality of such an enterprise had not escaped her, but it did make her realize she would have to come to a decision, and it wasn't going to be easy. She read the latest letter again and added it carefully to the others tied with a thin satin ribbon and kept in a box with a small amount of potpourri.

For three years, she had lived in Seattle, helping to support the family farm in northern Idaho. She had always been independent.

Three older brothers had made sure of that, never sparing her a single lump that came from running with the boys. Before the war, she could have stayed home and learned the fine arts of being a housewife, but she didn't care much for it.

She had preferred to continue following the fruit pickers or find other means of outdoor summer work between her months of schooling.

During the war, there wasn't much question of staying home. Somebody had to find a job and Millie was the best qualified. Millie was studious. Millie could type. Millie found an office job. She was a career woman now, or she could be if she wished to stay.

It was odd that she hadn't thought that much past the war. Maybe she thought it would never end. Maybe she thought there was always going to be a gloomy mantle over their heads, and she would sit in a cubbyhole, wearing her fingers to the bone, avoiding the few men lurking in the streets who had by now turned into lechers and thieves.

She could go back to the farm now. It wasn't the worst place a person could live. Some would say it was downright pleasant. She could go back and stifle. She could live out a monotonous and predictable life, orchestrated to the satisfaction of her mother, Cora Snipes. Millie squeezed back the thought. She would not go back to the farm.

The ships were docking into port. She had seen it in the newspapers. It had been confirmed in wild phone calls and she had yet to hear from Bruiser or her would-be fiancé. One doesn't expect much better of Bruiser, although it would have been nice…She had wished…

Millie firmly returned the box to its place on the top shelf of the linen closet. Wish in one hand and spit in the other. See which one comes up full the fastest. She straightened her dress, put on her gloves, and left for work.

Thank heavens for telephones. Even greater than the joy behind the confetti throwing parades celebrating the end of the war, was the sound of the familiar voice bellowing with its usual robust energy, "Millie! Millie! There was a time or two I thought I'd never hear you say hello again."

Millie gripped the heavy black handle of the office phone in her hand, not feeling the least bit guilty at using company time. It was a party that hadn't died down in days. Messages flew by whatever means available and her availability was at her workplace.

"Where are you?"she demanded above the static between the phone lines and the commotion in the background.

"California! I'm making a delivery. I'm delivering your future husband to your doorstep."

She remained calm. Bruiser was a practical joker, which meant you never really knew when he was telling the truth.

"Then I suppose you're staying with Frank's family at the moment."

More static. "I am. You should see me. I'm swarming with Hollywood girls. They think I'm a naval officer. Once you put on that dress uniform, they don't know the difference. And with an eye patch, I'm quite rakish."

"And quite tardy!" She paused as his words hit home, then asked timorously, "An eye patch?"

"It's a magnificent accessory, I assure you. You should try it sometime. No, don't try it. I don't believe it has the same effect on women."

She counted the number of seconds needed in her head to take control over herself. It had been her brother's life-long obsession to poke at her, to tease and pry until she committed an emotional outburst.

Five seconds, or five breaths between the numbers, the same as it had been when he first answered the call to serve his country. Her patience hadn't improved much in four years.

Just to make him feel bad, she told him, "You should know, Raymond will be here this weekend and he is flying in from New York. Even Peter was thoughtful enough to drop a line. I expect he'll be home as soon as his paycheck finishes burning a hole in his pocket. His ship also came into the New York Harbor, but he says he's taking the bus to save money. Well, we know what happens when Peter's feet hit the road."

The voice crackled in and out, carried more by her brother's exuberance than any irregularities in the connection. "Good ole Peter. I heard he left a weeping heart at every port. Oh, he left them all right, but the only thing they were weeping about was losing their latest mark."

"You've always been mean to Peter."

"He's always deserved it. He wimped out on the hard work because mama said he was too frail, so the only things he ever learned to do were play cards and bet on horses. Admit it."

"He was frail. And he has vices, but I think, no more so than any other family member."

"Aw, Millie. We can't all be perfect. If I was home right now, I'd dust off your angel wings. It's our duty to have flaws so you can practice your forgiveness."

Dismissing his flattery, which was only meant to make her feel kindly, she scolded. "And I will in good time, but first please explain to me why you were not able to pick up the telephone and give me a call before now?"

"Now, don't start having a lover's quarrel with Frank before you've even had a chance to meet him. San Diego was more my idea than his own. It was only going to be one night, but somehow, three days later, I ended up here, somewhat indisposed. There was nothing left to do then, but to be polite and join in on their festivities."

"So, you forgot."

"It was them Californian women! You've got to understand about them. They get inside a man's head. Don't let him think. All golden legged and sunshine smiles. I hadn't seen women like that in two years! No. Maybe never. Say, don't you want to talk to Frank? He'll tell you I did my best to resist, and I visited only one Tijuana cantina."

"Oh, Bruiser. Tijuana? What were you thinking? Never mind. I don't want to know. Just tell me when you're coming home."

Instead of answering directly, she heard the phone shuffle. Then Bruiser said quickly, "Here's Frank. He wants to talk to you."

She sighed and pieced back together her composure as a stranger's voice explored her attention. "Miss Snipes? Millie? I've been looking forward to hearing your voice." The words rumbled deeply, cautious but not at all timid.

She gathered her thoughts, centering them around the letters that had become increasingly more candid over the months, and said in her best telephone voice, "And I've looked forward to speaking. Has my brother behaved shamefully or are you as accustomed as he to discovering questionable establishments and giving them customer support?"

With his strong bass voice emphasizing every word he spoke she was glad he had a controlled laugh. It rolled around in his throat a few seconds without exploding into the phone.

"I was warned that you have a sharp wit. I'm afraid I lost Bruiser when he went south of the border for a couple of days - but was finally able to recover him and deposit him at my mother's home, where he remained, as he puts it, somewhat indisposed. He seems to have recuperated, however."

"In other words, it has taken him this long to sober up."

"Well, it would have taken him longer, but he became motivated by the thought of seeing you again. Honest."

"Oh, I doubt that. He became motivated when he thought about how angry I would be if he didn't call shortly."

"But now he has called and wants you to know we'll be on our way to Seattle very soon and hopes you can forgive him."

Millie sighed. "Well, but it's Bruiser, you know. He has his ways. I would have disowned him a long time ago, but he has a good heart."

"I'm glad that you have not disowned him as his generous heart is what has allowed our correspondence. I have been sincere about everything I wrote. I'm only waiting for your answer."

Millie had her own set of beliefs that had to do with never agreeing to a deal, sight unseen. She had no problem with engaging in an overseas romance, believing much in the character of good letter writers, but it was no more practical than buying a house based solely on the location and a description. "How long until you are in Idaho?"

"I'm currently waiting on some official paperwork to confirm my position at Fort Richardson. As soon as I have it in hand, I intend to start moving north. My commander told me it would take about another two weeks, but the post has been secured. I'll be a working man."

"Ask me properly when you arrive. I still have some old-fashioned sensibilities."

"I will do so."

Such a long telephone conversation between the two dispersed states was bound to add up to a tidy sum, so they hastily said their goodbyes before the words dissolved into wasteful sentimentalities.

As Millie hung up, a small thrill she had not allowed herself to entertain for four years beganfrom the pit of her stomach and rose up until it tickled her throat and caused her eyes to glisten.

She returned to the workload on her desk, but her mind was roaming. Should she quit her job? It didn't really seem practical. What if once she met Frank, they didn't get along? It seemed doubtful, but it could happen. It wouldn't be the first time a brother had endorsed a candidate who really did not live up to her expectations. But Bruiser... Bruiser knew her best. He wouldn't bother dragging along a buddy over eight hundred miles if he didn't think the outcome was worth it.

What if when she returned to the farm, she didn't want to go back to Seattle? What if it seemed too far away and disconnected for this new feeling? *Everybody was coming home.* Everybody – and the memories she had stifled for years came flooding back. All the good times. All the family dinners, all the silly squabbles, all the mud fights, the wrestling, the afternoons fishing. They shouted with childish laughter and scampered on clumsy feet.

Just before five and the end of a somewhat unproductive day, Annabel Long breezed by the row of chattering desks and grasped Millie by her shoulders, squeezing them as she brushed her smoothly capped head against Millie's page boy curls.

"I have the most wonderful news. You remember Rodney Johnson, the boy I dated in high school? He looked me up! Millie, he proposed to me! Look at this! Have you ever seen anything so fine?"

She spread out her hand so Millie could appreciate the ring in all its jeweled glory. "I had no idea you were serious about him," she answered, surprised.

"Oh, I've been serious about everyone, but I invest my emotions with caution. Can you imagine losing your fiancé at war? I know the tendency was to be hasty and make promises nobody had any idea they could keep, but it opens the door to unnecessary heartache I always thought. I've had plenty of strong thoughts about Rodney but kept them guarded. There now. We can at last throw all caution to the wind. And what have you been thinking about, my dear?"

"Quitting my job."

"Now there is a bold move. Then he's proposed; and you are going to accept?"

Millie twisted one of her curls around her finger a bit uncomfortably. Annabel was a native Seattle resident, born and bred, very modern, very liberated, and casual about all manner of bedroom conversation. She often teased Millie for her old-fashioned reticence. Still, the question required an answer.

"I insisted on a proper courtship, but he has managed to get through two years with Bruiser without turning him into an accidental death, so he must have some redeeming qualities."

Annabel laughed and sat on the edge of Millie's desk, establishing their confidentiality. "My dear, a tolerance for Bruiser is not a true measure of virtue. His habits can be annoying, but not to other men. Men have the most marvelous ability for admiring all the things we find abhorrent and are endlessly surprised when we don't agree with their appraisal. Do you have a photo of him?"

"Yes," she said, smiling as she rummaged through her purse. She had already donned the finely tailored linen gloves that protected her hands and nails in public as well as adding a dash to her wardrobe; but removed them and smoothed them out next to the purse while she searched for the prized object. It had been slipped into an envelope to avoid being scratched, and she drew it out with as much care as she would use in handling a phonograph record. "He sent it in his last letter."

It was one of those standard head to bust photos they peddled by the thousands for students and military personnel. He was in his navy blues, with his cap tucked under his arm. Extremely close-cropped hair curled tightly to his scalp and retreated hastily from a high-ridged forehead.

"Oh," said Annabel. "He has a good chin. Never trust a man with a weak chin. They have no will power. At least now you know he's not hideous. He's rather scholarly looking. If you should decide to turn him down, I might take him into consideration."

"But you're engaged!"

"We do so many things in the heat of the moment," she said flippantly, then laughed at Millie's expression. "Don't look so fearful. I was only yanking your chain. I think you have a good catch, Millie. Now we should congratulate each other."

The end of the war was liberating. They could love again. They could plan for the future. They could hope as they had never been allowed to hope before. The men were coming home! They bustled into airports. They filled the streets. They charged the air with excitement.

Millie returned to her apartment, her hands shaking, her mind whirling. She should take a bus to Idaho this weekend. She would meet her returning brothers. It was only three hundred miles. It would take half a day to get there. She could leave Friday, after work, and be back in time to prepare for Bruiser and her prospective fiancé.

A strange word to her. She rolled it on her tongue. She had only thought loosely about marriage. Her dreams about her future were more wrapped up in her own possibilities than the possibilities marriage could bring her.

But the possibilities Frank brought with him were enough for both their yearnings and creativity.

Millie hummed to herself as she packed for her weekend and sorted through her clothing, deciding what she would keep and what she wouldn't if she abandoned her current dwelling.

Homecoming is always everything you dreamed, yet everything you hoped wouldn't happen.

Millie's brother, Raymond, flew into Seattle as he had promised, and joined her on her visit to the family home. Raymond was as large as Bruiser, but instead of dark, swarthy looks, Raymond was blonde and fair-skinned.

It was said, Bruiser took after his father's side, who was half Native American and so dark, he was nicknamed Blackie, and Raymond took after his mother, the typical, big-boned, fair-skinned Viking Irish. Millie loved Raymond. He was level-headed, hard-working, and honest, but she adored Bruiser. Raymond was the gentle light. Bruiser was the storm.

The bus trundled out of the station, lumbered unconcernedly past the soot-smeared downtown buildings shooting straight and tall, but offering no true shelter from a drizzling rain that would probably brood fitfully off and on throughout the day, then pour solidly for the evening, the gears squealing as it picked up speed beyond the city emptying out on the open highway.

The heavy clouds only covered the coastline. As they rounded the chubby foothills of the mountains pushing back against a roiling fog, orchards and fields blossomed out in dappled sunlight. Idaho farm country soon blushed and glowed under a noon day sun, the semi-idle fields slowly coming back to life as more returning soldiers stepped out to tend them.

Hayden didn't have a taxi. It barely had a bus station and what there was, served as a small café with three main specialties: eggs, coffee, and donuts.

Millie and her brother didn't need one. As soon as they stepped off the bus, there was her father, better known as Blackie, waiting for them in his expiring Model A, sputtering out grease and fumes as it always did, but ready to growl and lunge to its feet each time it stalled, with just a few cranks and a good kick to the front grillwork. It seemed he would have updated his vehicle by now, but it was her pa'sway. If something still worked, why give it up?

His philosophy extended to the home place. Just off the side of the front porch, a hand cranked water pump provided their water. An old Ford tractor fitted with a tin can replacing the top to the spindle, stood next to the barn door. A small shed sheltered a stack of firewood, most of it freshly cut in preparation for the winter.

Even though electricity had recently been installed, the house was dim. The darkly stained, unpainted walls absorbed the crackling energy, and the low ceiling evoked shadows along the floor. But it was kept up efficiently.

This was not because of her mother, Cora Snipes. Her mother had resigned herself to a bedridden life filled with grief the day her first son joined the military. As each of her three dutiful boys shipped off to war, her grief deepened. She had dreaded each passing day, each knock at the door, fearing the worst and expecting no good news at all. Even though the family had all come safely home, Cora was convinced her bed-ridden state was permanent.

It was because of her sister, Emma. Emma never let a speck of dust escape her, nor allowed a single smudge to disrupt the harmony of her kitchen. The coffee pot was always full, and the bread box was always packed with delicious loaves of freshly baked bread.

Emma was taller than Millie, with longer bones that found more than a few extra pounds of weight uncomfortable. She drew a longer shadow that flickered slowly as she moved about the kitchen, still cleaning, and sorting jars.

She wiped her hands on her apron, then quickly untied, and discarded it as Raymond walked through the door, her face bursting into smiles. "How often I thought we had lost you!" she cried, smothering him with kisses. "You should have written more. The silence was terrifying."

He half-heartedly held her back. "You know that when you are a Snipes, no news is good news. Only the women in our family know how to hold a pen. The rest of us are handicapped."

She slapped a hand limply in the air, letting it brush him because she never did know how to answer her brother's wit. Emma took things directly, stating only what she saw necessary and always was just a little puzzled as to why so many of the family members had to turn statements into laughing matters.

She knew no harm was meant by their silliness. Their idle words amused them, so there was nothing more she could do than be indulgent.

The weekend passed quickly. Raymond settled into the routine of helping Blackie with the farm work before Saturday could be called a full day, while Millie helped Emma with the household chores, and in trying to keep their mama comfortable.

This was a part of her sporadic visits that had become routine. Cora Snipes had a number of conditions for her comfort; primarily that her soup was neither too hot nor too cold, that her magazines remained orderly and in close reach, and that her pillows were always freshened and plumped, and her blankets aired.

"I suppose now that the boys are all coming home, you'll be able to quit your job." She said, her two chins quivering when she talked.

Millie hesitated as she tucked a quilt around the back of the sofa, cradling Cora's head. The sofa had been built for two, but with mama's girth and all her props, it only accommodated one. "I won't be living at home."

"Why wouldn't you? It's disgraceful to see a single young girl living alone. Why she might as well put out a red light and announce herself."

"I might not be living single. I have been considering a man's proposal."

"Humph." Cora shifted her weight and grabbed the corners of the quilt, rearranging them to her preferences. "You can't get married yet. Your sister is older. Properly, she should get married first."

Millie straightened and brushed at her completely stylish print dress to emphasize her words. "Things aren't done that way anymore. Besides, if she's not yet spoken for, but I am, why should I wait? I'm twenty-one years old. That's old enough to make my own decisions."

Cora was not impressed by Millie's nice clothes, the figure she cut, or even the cute little cap she was currently unpinning from her head. She sniffed loudly and pointedly.

"You are too opinionated. I never should have let you grow up as one of the boys. You always forget a woman's duties are to her home and kin, not to fanciful thinking. Marriage is out of the question until Emma marries. You could help her by staying home so she can go out and dance in mixed company. How are any of the young men going to see her if she's slaving behind a stove? You're obliged to give her an opportunity."

"And my opportunity? What about it?"

"You're a smart girl and not bad on the eyes. You'll find another opportunity if this one can't wait."

She turned fitfully, finding her pillows unpleasantly arranged and pumping them back into place. "And why couldn't it wait, I'd like to know? Is your young man's proposal so conditioned, or are you in the family way?"

Millie's offense was evident in the way she lifted her head and gave a sidelong smile. "I haven't even met him yet, so that wouldn't be possible. His proposal is conditioned because he has an appointment to keep. My young man is being fitted for a civil service position."

The mention of a position didn't impress Cora Snipes, either. "Bah. I don't want to hear anything more about it. You're getting all uppity, consorting with men who wear white collars to work. Simpering mama's boys who never knew a moment of hard labor in their lives. You believe you've found a good mate because he cansendcharming letters? Nothing but bad can come of it, mark my words. You'll forget who you are. You'll forget your roots."

Millie believed her roots were the last thing she would forget. They had a habit of digginginto her, making her do and say things that were not exactly reflective of a thoroughly urbanized, modern woman.

Her roots were what she would plant in new, fertile soil, and though she suggested this, mama's opinion, which was rarely openly opposed, completely discredited Millie's faith.

Millie returned to Seattle without ever explaining her intention to move north.

Two

Five o'clock in the morning is an ungodly hour to have anybody come calling. Millie rolled out of bed and groped for her footing, which could only be achieved after she had draped her robe around her and had shuffled into her slippers. She wobbled from her bedroom to the living room, her eyes heavy-lidded, and opened the door as far as the chain bolt allowed.

"Good morning, dear lady. I am here on behalf of True Hearts United, ready with our fabulous one-time offer. Guaranteed to achieve matrimonial bliss, here's..."

It was as far as the speaker got. The door slammed closed, the bolt slid, then the door flew open again and ejected a flurry of bobby-pinned hair, fuzzy night wear and very sloppy slippers on completely delighted feet.

"Aaron Bruce Snipes! I should hang you by your thumbs and beat you with an ugly stick, but here you are and all I can think of is how happy I am!"

"You aren't going to cry now!" Bruiser pulled back from the embrace just long enough to look in her face before jubilantly sweeping her around a few times. "You'll spoil everything if you cry."

"Spoil? How could it be more spoiled?" She drew back to look at him. "What is this? You are really wearing an eye-patch? You weren't pulling my leg, or are you pulling it now?"

He moved away her hand. "Now don't you go messing with this. It's a badge of honor. It's the best thing that ever happened to me. The women just want to cry when they see a man with an eye patch."

"Why didn't you tell me?"

"I did tell you! You just weren't listening."

"How could I listen? You were in Hollywood! How should I believe anyone calling from Hollywood?"

"It wasn't Hollywood! Just close enough for my eye to see the most scintillating bevy of beauties the world has ever known. I was thunderstruck, and I was going to explain, but now, Millie. You'll have to forgive me. All those months at sea. I'm only human. You know I am. I don't have your pass into the choir."

Her eyes flitted past his shoulders and noticed the stranger who was no longer really a stranger. "And you! What's your excuse? You couldn't pick up a pen while your friend lay dying on a hospital bed?"

Frank, who had been lounging in the hall, arms folded, came to alert with his best apologetic expression.

"I would have," he said. "If I could have found a moment of peace and quiet. It happened in Okinawa when the fighting was at its worst."

She was silent a moment, digesting this information. "What happened?"

"Artillery shell."

Her eyes blinked rapidly as she slipped several times between laughing and crying. "Oh! Look at me!" She finally said. "I am a disgrace." Beckoning them inside with one hand, she used the other to frantically pull the pins away from her hair and partially groom it.

"And this is not the way you'll look every morning of your married life?" LaughedBruiser. "Oh, he might as well get used to the devil behind the clever mask. Give the man a chair. We have been in bus seats longer than I care to remember, and one thing I have learned about Frank Lamar. He dearly loves to sit at tables."

Millie gave him a chair, or rather he chose one quite casually. Francis Jay Lamar had learned one strategy in life. Watch and learn but make yourself appear at ease while doing it. Frank had many tricks for acquiring this effect.

First, you locate the most comfortable spot available, which for him, was any place within the immediate vicinity he could claim personal territory.

He preferred corners he could lean back in with a full view of the audience and enough table space for his pipe, a newspaper and coffee.

The second thing to consider were the hands. Frank talked with his hands. If they were tied behind his back, they would be squirming each time he opened his mouth. Having an open area for his hands was important if he was going to engage in prolonged speech but having a place for keeping his hands occupied was crucial if he was silent.

He had a solution for his nervously twitching hands when he was quiet. Hold something. A paperback novel would do for waiting in lines and work breaks. Coffee cups were agreeable for social settings, and so was smoking his pipe.

Filling a pipe with tobacco was an art, from removing the kit from the inside breast pocket of the suit jacket, to lighting the small pile and inhaling the smoke. It was best performed at a table, as was reading, and drinking coffee.

For this reason, Francis Jay Lamar accommodated himself quickly, choosing a chair where he could watch his intended bride's interactions with her brother, and planting the corner-stones for his territory around him on the table, in this case, his pipe, the tobacco kit and the single ash tray.

Five in the morning is an excellent time to think about coffee, especially if it involves a reunion. Millie felt her new suiter's eyes on her back as she measured out some ground beans, placed them in the metal filter, filled the aluminum pot with water, and set it on the back burner of the stove. It was disconcerting. She was a firm believer in never judging a book by its cover, but she had no wish to be a misunderstood book.

She excused herself as quickly as she could, dashed to her bedroom, found a pair of slacks and a frilled checkered blouse to put on and ran a brush through her hair.

Now, casually dressed but with her curls all tucked in neatly under her chin, she returned to see how far along the coffee had progressed. It was perking nicely, the glass percolator top showing the color slowly changing from light yellow to a deep, chocolaty brown.

"I have heard," she said, taking her place at the table once the coffee had sufficiently perked. "Alaska is ripe for homesteading."

Frank leaned back in his chair. He had placed it sideways with the table, so he could stretch out his legs and cross them. It was also so he could lean one arm on the table and smoke his pipe. He puffed a few times before speaking.

"It is. I won't say people are moving in droves to settle, but the opportunities are great. The place that I've chosen, Fort Richardson, is close to Anchorage, but north of it is a whole wilderness just waiting to be claimed."

Bruiser snorted. "If it's a homestead you want, there's no better place than looking around right here, in the northwest. You're not going to be able to grow anything except snowballs in Seward's Ice Box," he cracked, chortling at his own joke.

Before Millie could provide an argument concerning the territory's poorly represented climate, Frank cleared his throat and said, "Actually, I'm thinking of just a small piece of land. Something that doesn't require clearing sixty acres and growing a crop. The Home Site Act sells parcels in five acre lots and the only requirement is to live there more than six months out of the year. That's just the right size for a garden, a few chickens, and a nice front lawn. I don't want to farm. I want to build."

"Do you see?" Said Bruiser, nudging Millie. "He's as nutty as you. You'll make the perfect couple."

Millie huffed. "You're the one who's not thinking straight. Frank has already been given his civil service post. If he changes his mind, he'll have to hunt for a job all over again. Do you think jobs are magically going to grow on trees? Three million men returning home and at least half of them don't know what they're going to do. I say, take the good jobs while they are there."

"Good jobs?" Bruiser set down his coffee long enough to fish around in his pocket for a cigar. He rolled it and tamped both ends. "Being sent to the remote edges of the wilderness is not usually classified as a good job. It's like being banished to Siberia," he said before popping the cigar into his mouth and lighting it.

He made a few smoke rings, then said, "show Millie your letter of recommendation, Frank. This is how enviable your fiancé's post really is."

Bruiser continued to wheedle until Frank laughed. "Oh, he has a sense of humor," he said, feigning self-consciousness. "I will. Just a moment. It's in my briefcase."

He set his pipe into the center of the ashtray, with the stem propped against the lip. He had prepared himself for this and was eager to present his credentials. He stood up, tucked in his shirt, and retrieved a somewhat weathered, brown leather case piled with his suitcases. He balanced it on his lap to snap it open and retrieved a letter from among a stack of certificates and other official paperwork.

"Here," he said, pushing it in front of her, then settling back to refill his pipe. "The history of how I acquired my post."

The letter began on a few notes of familiarity and continued in a casual and somewhat jovial vein to notify the receiver that he had been petitioned by one, Francis Jay Lamar, for a civilian post with the Army Corps of Engineers.

"You have several reasons to be thankful for this," said Bruiser out loud, standing with her to read the contents. "Francis served courageously, defending his team with the same vigor during the great rotten tomato fights on board that he displayed on the battlefield. He has managed to dodge nearly every practical joke and is the suspected perpetrator of at least a few."

Millie looked at the clock. It was nearly breakfast hour. Already her mind was planning out the day. She would have to notify work this would be her last week. Even if she changed her mind and didn't marry, the work decision couldn't be put off any longer.

She was beginning to understand now why a man like Frank Lamar and a man like her brother could be bunk mates for two years without strangling each other. They had the same sense of humor. They laughed gleefully at the words that mocked the platitudes of venerable society.

"Yes," she said, keeping her own voice dry, "I can see this is high praise."

"Very high," laughed Bruiser. "Read on."

Instead of joining them, Millie returned to the stove and cracked half-a-dozen eggs in a bowl, with a small amount of milk, scrambling them furiously before dropping them into the frying pan. Today was Tuesday. She would tell her workplace these were her last four days. The voices had gone silent. They were waiting for her return. Finding some cold ham slices to add to the eggs, she set them on the table and sat down.

Frank put his pipe away and looked approvingly at the breakfast but continued reading his letter first to keep the paper crisp and clean.

"As my clerk, I discovered that Francis not only knew how to type but was actually able to spell and could put entire sentences together using correct grammar and punctuation. As you know, clerical skills such as these fall just a half inch short of a miracle, especially in uncharted regions where such skills are needed the most."

The letter continued with a brief history of his military record and his previous experience with the Civilian Conservation Corps and ended in stating his pleasure that a man of equitable academic skills still had the lunacy to desire a post in the remote territory.

"Notice the last line," said Bruiser. "Even his commanding officer thought he was nuts. Life is easier here. There are plenty of options for a man of Frank's qualifications. Do you know who goes to Alaska? People who don't have any place else *left to go*."

Millie finished a piece of jam and toast daintily and brushed the crumbs away with a napkin. "Nothing you tell me, Bruiser, will make me change my mind one way or the other."

Bruiser's chuckles ended in his throat. "Are you saying you're not planning to marry him?"

"I'm not planning to get in the way of his goals."

Frank was returning his letter of recommendation to his briefcase. He snapped the case closed, sat back on the couch with his hands between his knees and asked, "Does that mean you will marry me?"

Her hands crept to her hair to tuck in her curls. "I'm going to work until the end of the week, then we are going to Idaho to meet the family. I'm not going to make your path that easy for you, Mr. Francis Lamar. But neither am I the kind of girl who will say one thing and do another. If I marry you, it won't be to trap you into a life of my own choosing. It will be to follow you and support what you've worked so hard to achieve."

"Don't court her too hard," advised Bruiser. "It's not going to be easy to tell the old folk."

She laughed at him, although uneasily. "I've already told them my prospects, just not where I would be going."

Although his hands were still pressed between his knees, Frank sat at rapt attention, his ears sticking out like antennae. "Astonishing," he said to Bruiser as though she wasn't there, then added to reassure her, "I'll be a complete gentleman. I'll come bearing gifts."

"Don't think you can make mama happy," broke in Bruiser. "Nothing can make her happy, but some things make her unhappier than others."

"Mothers are like that," nodded Frank gravely. Now that he had secured a trial period, he had cheerfully resumed his place at the table, surrounded by his items. He let a puff of smoke from his pipe waft toward the ceiling, as though he was reflecting on something regrettable but unavoidable.

"My own mother wasn't very pleased either. Their unhappiness can't be avoided. We either follow the lives they dreamed for us, only to discover it wasn't a good idea, or we follow our own dreams, which may also be a mistake, but if it is, at least it's of our own making."

"Then it's all a matter of what you can tolerate best," said Bruiser. "A muddle created by listening to another person's advice or having your mother say, 'I told you so'. Either way is unpleasant."

Their conversation continued all around and about her, but not really with her. She could easily have been invisible. That wasn't what bothered her. Men were like that. As soon as they recovered from their astonishment that they had things in common, men consorted with each other as though they were the only intelligent beings on earth. Frank and Bruiser had two years of consorting. That practically made them brothers.

She stacked the breakfast dishes in the sink, announcing, "I've got to leave for work. You're the clean-up crew, Bruiser.

There's an extra key in the end table drawer if you want to go anywhere."

She returned once more to her room, this time to change from her casual clothing to a wool skirt with matching, boxed jacket. She held her face close to the mirror, outlining her upper lip with red.

Cripe! She had sounded like a Puritan! All the time she had spent on the defense from the onslaught of her brothers and friends, and she didn't even know how to flirt. She really didn't even know how… she finished her lower lip and pressed the two together. She didn't know how to be with a man.

She had four days to learn how. She didn't really have anyone to go to for advice except Annabel, and of course Annabel made herself available with every lunch break.

Instead of remaining at her desk, Millie coaxed Annabel into the lady's room.

"You mean you've never dated?" Annabel asked in astonishment after Millie's confession.

"Oh, I have!" She answered hastily. "But not like that. If I go to a dance, I want to dance. If I go to the theater, I want to see the performance. I become intolerant when I have an octopus hanging onto me."

"You are saying you are a virgin."

Millie rummaged quickly in her purse for a comb to smooth under her curls. "There. You said it. What if he wants to kiss me? What if I'm not ready to have him kiss me?"

"Millie, he proposed to you! What do you think you will be doing when you marry?"

"That's what I'm trying to say! What shall I do?"

"Do you like him?"

Her frantic heart slowed its flight. "Yes. I do. He's funny. He's elegant, like a Hollywood star, and he's always performing."

"Performing?"

"Yes. He speaks and moves his hands like he's saying lines in front of an audience."

"Peculiar man."

"But I do like him. He's a gentleman. How many gentlemen do you find in these parts?"

A loud guffaw escaped Annabel's mouth before she muffled it. "A virgin and a gentleman. This ought to be lovely."

"Oh dear," said Millie with dismay. "I thought you could help me."

"Millie, sweetheart, I wish I could. Nothing would delight me than to help you. But you have only four days to turn into a sizzling hot tomato. You'll have to play it by ear, love. The only thing I can tell you is, if he makes any advances, don't slug him in the gut. Try to enjoy it."

"Try to?" Asked Millie weakly.

"Believe me, if you like him, it won't be hard."

Millie grew up in a house full of boys. Frank grew up in a house full of girls. If Millie was wise to the baser instincts of men, Frank was wise to the basic delights of women. When she arrived home that evening, the house was neat as a pin. A simple dinner had been prepared, and a bouquet of flowers flourished on the table.

"I thought we could take in a movie tonight," he said as greeting. "Bruiser says you like Spencer Tracy."

"I do not like Spencer Tracy," she said, forgetting to flirt. "He stars in horrible, depressing war movies."

Frank folded his arms and gave Bruiser a stern frown for delivering false information. "There is a Cary Grant movie. You wrote you like Cary Grant."

"Oh." Millie gave an involuntary sigh. "He's the cat's pajamas."

"There is one playing…Arsenic and Old Lace. You've probably seen it."

"But I haven't! I've been meaning to, but there never seemed to be time."

It was the right choice. If they had chosen a romance, Bruiser would have been noisy the entire time, nudging them every ten minutes and making inappropriate jokes. If they had chosen a war movie, she would have left in the first ten minutes. She couldn't abide them. It was over and she wanted to put away the memories of war forever.

What they had chosen kept them all entertained. Halfway through the movie, Frank put his arm around her shoulders. At first, she stiffened, then relaxed. Cautiously, she tried resting her head against his neck. It was comfortable. He shifted slightly to make her more comfortable and continued watching the movie.

The third day, she suggested going to Fisherman's Wharf when she got off work to pick up some fish and vegetables at the open market. It was an unusually pleasant day, with cotton candy clouds that stretched and turned to shades of amber and gold as the sun lowered over the ocean front.

She was getting used to Frank. She wasn't sure how it could be done in two days, but it seemed perfectly natural to tuck her arm into his and stroll the pier to its farthest point in the ocean. She leaned over the rail, trying to imagine herself on one of the tugboats puffing between the jeweled islands of the Puget Sound. If she half-closed her eyes and allowed her mind to drift, she could almost see around the next bend.

"It gets better," he said. "When you go up the coast, the islands become thicker and larger. The mountains on the side grow bigger and bigger. Glaciers calve and fall into the sea."

"But we won't be on a boat."

His arm tightened with the word, *we.* "No. I don't even know what it looks like from the air. I don't even know what it looks like beyond the Panhandle, but I know that it calls to me."

A wind blew down from the Sound. Wrapping their jackets tightly around them, the young couple turned away from its bluster, toward the marketplace. She huddled within his embrace for the added warmth. The sun was lowering and spreading out over the horizon, deepening the shadows. Toward the northwest, the islands turned blue-black under a violent flame, while on the docks, workers scrambled for the last bit of daylight.

There was a grim desperation in the men and women clamoring over the pier, bringing up their shrimp baskets, tying in their boats, bundling their catch for the day to sell at the market. The Depression was a dying beast whose labored breath still poisoned the air.

"I think it will be nice to start over," said Frank. "In a fresh place. Maybe we won't make so many mistakes. Seattle is young. San Francisco is young. All the northwest is young, but its cities are teeming over with people. I don't want to live in a city, but I don't want to farm, either. Those are the only two choices we have here."

She didn't know why. Perhaps it was the dimness of their surroundings reminding them of poverty-stricken years. Perhaps it was the strangeness of a relationship she was not trying to push away but that seemed to exist in a limbo of what she should be saying and what was her customary performance. She felt reckless and bitter.

"We can't pretend we aren't running away from something because we are. Look around you. What do you see under all the noise and celebration? Sad, tired people trying to patch their lives back together."

Their stroll was carrying them deeper into the shadows of tents, crates, and dubious vendors. "We're broken," she continued. "If we stay here, we are part of all that has been broken and needs to mend. Maybe we will mend. Maybe we won't. If we leave, we take all our broken parts with us. If we do that. If we take those parts with us, we're running away."

She could feel his hand squirming inside his pocket and squeezed his arm tighter. "Are you afraid to go through with this?" He asked.

She shook her head and struggled to find the words to express the feelings she had never allowed to surface. "I'm not. I'm more afraid of this. Of becoming like this."

In the evening, the marketplace smelled like fish, urine, alcohol run flat and mixed with street grime, stale tobacco, and the thick scent of marijuana. The people who occupied the night life were dark, shadowy creatures flickering under a string of poorly lit bulbs and crouched over both legal and illegal business.

They stopped near a stall selling tomatoes. "You can light your pipe," she said, trying to keep her voice light after her dark confession. His hands were twitching nervously inside his pockets, while his face looked drawn and thoughtful. She studied it curiously.

"You really haven't been in many places like this, have you?"

"I was raised in San Bernardino," he protested, drawing out his pipe.

A tight, bitter smile drew a straight line across her face. "It's not the same. This isn't a red- light district. It's waterfront trade but it's desperate trade. It's failure. I go to the market. I'm not afraid of it. Most of the people are honest, some dishonest but not dangerous. They try to earn an honest day's wages, but the Depression brought them down. The war brought them down. They gave up. It's what I can't accept, this giving up."

She purchased some tomatoes and an onion. "I guess we'll have spaghetti tonight. I have hamburger in the fridge."

Returning his pipe quickly to his pocket, Frank picked up the grocery bag. Millie nodded and continued, "I can abide by poverty and can understand the desperate acts of a good man, but I do not accept living desperately. I've seen many go down that road of despair and end up in places like this. I won't accept it."

"You won't accept despair?"

"I don't accept giving up. Once you do, you are not a part of anything. You said in your letters, you wanted to be part of something. So do I. I want to be a part of something I can believe in, that gives me hope. This life doesn't give me hope. I know it's early, but I look around me and all I can think is, they are going back to exactly what they were doing before. It's not going to get much different. That's what I fear."

"I don't give up."

She looked into his eyes for a moment. He wasn't performing. They were dark and sincere. She hadn't seen him drink much. Still, she wasn't to suppose the stack of empty beer bottles piling up in her kitchen trash all belonged to Bruiser.

"It's the vices that suck them in. They can't control their vices. They become abusive. They neglect their homes. I want a life of dignity, Frank."

Trying to appear gallant in these surroundings that encouraged neither chivalry nor pride, Frank told her, "There is one thing I swear to you. If you will marry me, there will always be a roof over your head and food in your stomach."

She didn't answer him right away. A block ahead, Bruiser was waving his arm and urging them to hurry. Among his remarkable traits, Bruiser had an ability to merge with his environment. When Frank and Millie were out together, Bruiser was always in the background, but completely invisible. He only reappeared when the couple's direction turned back to Millie's apartment. The thought of it as "the apartment" was a loose term, as there was little left to indicate someone was living there except for the collection of half- packed suitcases.

"I have it! I have just the deal for you!" Bruiser said excitedly. He took the grocery bag from Frank and pressed a piece of paper into his hand. "Take this phone number. Put it in your wallet and give him a call tomorrow. Man has a Studebaker he wants to sell for fifty dollars."

"You want us to buy a car?" asked Frank.

Bruiser was quick to correct him. "Not us. You. It will come out cheaper in the long run, with all our luggage, to buy the car so we can drive into Idaho instead of using buses and taxis."

"Cheaper for you," scolded Millie. "You won't have to buy a ticket."

"No! Cheaper for you!" Bruiser groaned. "How are you going to leave Idaho? Buses and taxis and hauling all that luggage again? How are you going to take your honeymoon? You are going to take a honeymoon, aren't you?"

Bruiser waited and Frank looked at Millie, unsure how to answer. "Yes, we are taking a honeymoon," she said.

This was a new threshold for Frank. He had not gone into the details of his planning stages beyond securing a wife and a position.

Now that both goals had been accomplished, he realized there were a multitude of gaps in his strategy, primarily in transporting his wife to her new domicile. As a single man, he would have simply boarded the plane with a suitcase and his credentials and landed in the hub of military familiarity.

As a married man, he had considerations. He wouldn't be able to bunk with other bachelors. He would need adequate housing, anda vehicle to get around town, take her shopping, anddrive to work.

"Maybe," he contemplated, reaching once more for the arm of his formally confirmed fiancé, "that's not a bad idea. We could buy a car here and drive it up the new highway. We'd be better prepared. They say you can't really get around in Alaska without a car."

Instead of taking his arm, Millie clasped her hands together and jumped up and down in unrepressed glee. "A car! We're driving a car."

Somewhat surprised by this child-like response, Frank mused gravely, "if we drive, we can bring more luggage, plus we'll have a car."

A transformation came over Millie. A car was a sign of serious commitment. It was property. It was shelter and transportation. It was their freedom. A man who would buy a car to transport his wife to Alaska was a man who valued his companion. It was a man who wanted to bring as much of home with him as possible. They weren't running away. They were starting over.

She laced her fingers into Frank's on the way home, barely listening to the conversation between her fiancé and her brother. When they reached the dimly lit entrance to the apartment, she lifted her face and let Frank kiss her. It was a nice kiss. It tasted like cherry tobacco and black coffee. He had a good scent - tooth paste, shampoo, and aftershave. She almost wished he would kiss her again.

Bruiser watched them holding hands in the living room and listened to them discuss what they should and shouldn't bring. "You guys are really going to do it," he said finally. "You're really going to get hitched and move two thousand miles away."

"You should come with us, Bruiser," said Millie lazily, still snuggled close to Frank.

"Neah." Bruiser lit a cigar and watched his smoke rings with a melancholy face. "By 'n' by, I might. Not right away. Got some living to do right here. I'm going to work the farm a while, then maybe take a job at the timber mill in Coeur d'Alene. I always did like that place."

"We'll miss you."

"No, you won't. You'll be too busy. But by 'n' by, I'll get to you."

They stayed up late that evening. Millie even shared in a few beers, which wasn't in keeping with her normal preferences that ran from an occasional glass of red wine to complete sobriety, but it was a special evening.

It was the evening brother and sister realized they really were letting go of each other to travel their separate ways. It was an evening for saying their goodbye's.

Three

For days, the scenery had been the same: flat, grain covered plains stretching for endless miles. The entire world must depend on the wheat harvests extending from Kansas, USA, to Alberta, Canada. There was little else to see other than wheat, corn, barley, and tall grain storage bins. Even the staggered houses, with their barns and sheds, were plotted out and built exactly like each other. If they weren't following a road that assured them, they were traveling north, Millie would suspect they were traveling in circles.

Millie stared out the window, letting the monotony roll over her like a wave of despair. It was probably too much to ask for the best to be a little better, considering they were only recently grateful to find each other still alive, but it would have been altogether nicer if things had gone more smoothly.

The Studebaker, for instance. It ran fine during their final days in Seattle, taking care of last- minute business, but they had no sooner passed the city limits of nearby Tacoma than it coughed, shuddered, and ground to a stop. Frank laced his fingers around one knee, Millie groaned and held her head, and Bruiser banged his hands on the steering wheel. "I should have known! I should have known! This is a town car. It's not used to the countryside. You know, it sucks gas and oil right out of the air and doesn't know how to travel long distances. Never mind. I can fix this. She just needs a little extra lubrication."

He tinkered under the hood a good two hours while Millie and Frank tried pretending they were unperturbed and thoroughly enjoyed standing next to a barbed wire fence, withthe scent of over-ripe apples wafting from a nearby orchard andtheir Sunday clothes fluttering lightly in the breeze.

Finally, it coughed apologetically, stuttered to a shaky rumble, then after some hacks and wheezes as it changed gears, continued carrying them down the road. It got them to the farm before breaking down again, and of course, youngest brother Peter, spoiled and favored by his mother, had returned to the family embrace before Bruiser had. He grinned gleefully when he saw his sister step out of the wheezing vehicle, although most of his joy was over their apparently failed investment and not with their family reunion.

"Who found the lemon?" he asked, shaking hands all the way around before it occurred to him perhaps a few hugs were in order. He did so briskly, giving each a solid thump in the middle of the back with his fist before breaking loose.

"It's not a lemon," objected Bruiser. "It just needs to develop its lungs. It's not used to long-distance running. Pa can fix it."

Peter cackled and danced about, sparring at the newcomer to their midst, his elbows close to his chest, his fists jabbing at the air. "You're the one bunked with Bruiser? Bet you feel like a sucker now, don't you? Fancy city boy hooked a big Irish girl and a broken-down car."

Millie's pa, who had gone by the name, "Blackie" for as long as anyone could remember, had just turned the corner of the house to investigate the disturbance and heard Peter's last words.

Grabbing him in a headlock, he held the lad down until he apologized. "Don't mind the boy," advised Blackie in a gravelly voice. "His ma dropped him on his head when he was little."

Blackie was a big man, bigger than Bruiser, a dark man, made even darker by his years in the sun. Who he was depended much on individual interpretation. When Cora O'Malley Snipes married him, she claimed she did not know he was half-Sioux, believing him to be a darker version of the Irish, which she said was Black Irish. What was important to her was that he behaved like the Irish, therefore he must be Irish.

Millie, Emma, her brothers, and probably the entire town, saw Blackie Snipes as a kind man, a quiet man who avoided conflict, and the most dependable mechanic in the county.

Blackie kept his hair cut short, wore bib overalls and lace-up boots, and attended every hoe-down; therefore, he was a man like any other in town, just with a better ability to tan.

Frank only nodded, having felt no real offense. He was more impressed with his future father-in-law's size and vigor, a sure sign of Millie's genetic disposition, than he was with Peter's lack of wit.

Frank was a believer in genetic dispositions. He was born with a weak set of lungs, inherited from his own father who wheezed with asthma. To seal his compromised condition, he had suffered the torments of tuberculosis as a child, spending a large part of it on the family farm in Kansas, swirling in a depression of its own.

He admired powerfully built men, even though he had never let his own size stop him from doing anything. Size didn't matter but a great set of lungs were an enviable asset.

Frank Lamar saw something different the first time he saw Millie's father. He saw a man who had been humbled. He saw someone who had surrendered half his heritage to comply with another. Why he saw this was a secret kept by Frank Lamar, whose family relished keeping certain parts of their long-lived American history, private. Frank's sensitivity became clear the evening after he had met all the family members and had a chance to speak with Millie in private.

"I don't believe I will call your father, Blackie," he told her.

She had turned her head to look at him in surprise. "What would you call him? Pa? You can't call him Mr. Snipe. He's your father-in-law."

"What is his real first name?"

"Aaron."

He had grinned. "Bruiser is a Junior. Yeah. I'll call your father, Aaron."

Blackie took one look under the hood of the car and nodded reassuringly at the anxious couple. He could fix it. In fact, bringing him an engine to work on was bliss. He liked nothing better than tinkering under a hood as it kept him away from the family feud that stayed rekindled on a regular basis with the assistance of Cora Snipe.

It had been a bad start, and it didn't really get much better. While Blackie worked on the car, Cora Snipe worked on Millie, determined to convince her that marrying Frank and moving to Alaska was the worst idea she had ever entertained.

After using every ounce of logic she could contrive, as well as some emotional illogic, Millie finally burst out, "There is nothing on earth that is going to make me pass up the opportunity to live in Alaska."

This was the daughter Cora understood, the one who was as immovable as the Rock of Gibraltar. The one who followed the fruit pickers, the one who set up residence in Seattle. Plumping her pillows and snuffling loudly, Cora sulked a few minutes, then picked up the box of chocolates Frank had bought her and began eating them. She was resigned, but not truly accepting.

The next thing to go wrong was their wedding ceremony. Cora Snipes was a Believer only when it was convenient. She never attended church, said prayers, or joined a charity drive, but she did celebrate Christmas, bought new clothes for Easter, and reminded her daughters of Christian principles whenever she suspected them of swaying.

Since Millie was currently under full suspicion, Cora felt entitled to find a preacher for the ceremony. After pronouncing the happy couple man and wife, he then confessed he was not yet a fully ordained minister, so their marriage might not be quite legal. Although discussions were not in order while they remained within the family circle as it would appear they were fault-finding the good character of Cora Snipe, Frank and Millie remedied the situation by marrying in front of a justice of the peace when they returned to Seattle to close the apartment.

Frank found humor in it. Frank enjoyed telling anyone who would listen, that he had married his wife in two states to make sure she couldn't get away from him.

Millie didn't find it quite as amusing. It was one more example of her mother meddling in Millie's life when she was quite capable of muddling her own affairs without assistance.

Their honeymoon consisted of a twelve-hundred mile drive down the West Coast to visit his family in San Bernardino. There were people, Millie knew, who found the long drive tedious.

They had already forgotten the Depression years, drifting from town to town, looking for work, or maybe they chose to forget. Millie chose not to. Some of her favorite memories were of riding in the back of the pick-up truck, not knowing where they were going, only following the fruit pickers wherever they were needed. And she liked picking fruit.

Inside her was a farmer, but there was also someone who liked to let the long miles slide under her feet. Traveling to pick fruit had satisfied her. She had not even been aware that the labor was a far step down from the ladder of what the family had once been. If she had known, it would not have changed the brightness of her youthful memories.

The honeymoon couple had taken the drive slowly, stopping where they pleased to admire the different moods of the coast. They stayed on Highway One and never saw a large town before San Francisco, only the amazing black cliffs slamming into the ocean, the sand beach coves, each sheltered pool a subtly different color from pale turquoise to deep blue.

She had been on the coast before, but this was her first vacation, and her honeymoon. Her first idle journey just to see the splendor of the Northwest. She was no expert, but as honeymoons went, she failed to imagine one that could have been more perfect.

As soon as they reached the Washington/Oregon border, she felt liberated. She was no longer the person her family knew: the good student, the capable bread winner, the sister who was more of a buddy than the youngest sibling.

She was no longer the person Seattle knew– career-minded, socially reserved, purposefully cultivating a taste for the arts.

She was becoming something new. She didn't blossom all at once, but over the miles. Each corner they rounded peeled back another layer of her old life, replacing it with something new and unexplored, but strangely familiar.

She was a woman with a life-time companion. Certainly, in her youthful dreams of what she would do when she grew up, she had included marriage, as she could not imagine herself a spinster without children.

Until her overseas courtship with Frank, she had considered her prospects for marriage unexciting. She had never doubted she could do more than her current life offered; she just hadn't considered there would someone who would open that door. Someone who would see things her way.

Frank was a patient man and he understood women. Four days of acquaintance had been enough to agree to his proposal. It hadn't really been enough to thaw out. Her brothers inhibited her. The farm inhibited her. Even her apartment in Seattle felt too sterile and uncommitted to welcome a lover's embrace. It changed once they left Seattle. Now she felt the years stretched out in front of her and how each day would be a taste of something different to shape out this new and different person.

They spent the first night of their honeymoon in the Redwood Forest. They rented a cabin in a secluded area where they could hear the ocean boom against the cliffs in the distance, and the giant trees surrounding them murmur in the breeze. Their honeymoon dinner consisted of steaks ordered from the nearby diner and a bottle of champagne.

"Are you happy?" Frank asked anxiously over the single candle sitting on the table.

The cabin was plain, the only furnishings a round, wooden table, two chairs, a closet, and a bed covered with a heavy quilt. The half-moon strained to send its light through the towering trees. The dark night whispered.

"Yes," she said. "I'm very happy."

Maybe it was the miles of shedding away her old self. Maybe it was the cabin and the champagne, sparkling like moonlight. She remembered the letters, growing longer and more tender, and forgot the busy chatter that had sought to influence her one way or another, hearing only her own voice stating what she really wanted.

He was a performer; some might say a show-off. He was flamboyant. Her heart said, charismatic. He loved her. She knew this with certainty. It wasn't a lust or a craving. It was still, patient and waiting.

Something opened deep inside her and made her whisper across the table, "I think I'm ready to be your wife."

The car hit a bump and Millie's eyes fluttered open. She hadn't realized she had dozed. She checked the scenery floating by outside her window. It was still unchanged.

Nothing but flat plains and mild apologies for hills had passed by until waving fields of wheat and oats bored into the mind, leaving it rolling over golden grain even when she was asleep. She settled to doze again.

Blackie had done a suburb job on the car. It purred like a kitten the entire time. At first, Millie had thought it was an omen that things would get better. Eventually, she resigned herself to the fact that it was just a testimony as to Blackie's skills.

Their honeymoon was perfect. Even San Francisco carried with it a perfection of its own. It was turning to autumn and the bubbling land mass decorating the Golden Gate Bridge shone with the colors of russet and gold.

They spent one night in a low budget hotel with a neon-sign as their night view and prowled the streets until they found a smoky nightclub dressed in black with dancers, bass guitars, and trombone players weeping over jazz.

They felt smart. They felt swinging. They knew how to cut a few steps of their own, but it was their honeymoon. They drank wine and watched the show, feeling contemporary and sophisticated.

Their fun ended south of Big Sur. Millie had never been so far south, so surrounded by a landscape deserted of all but prickly desert things, blazing white buildings, and busy, aggressive highways. The September sun of Southern California scorched her, and she wilted, sweaty and miserable in clothing too warm and a hat that did nothing to shield the blistering whiteness from her eyes.

She didn't complain. Frank said she would feel better once they reached his home and the comfort of the broad front porch sheltered from the sun's rays, but it wasn't the heat that eventually crushed her under its own weight. It was the distinguished opinions of Jocelyn Lamar, Frank's mother.

Jocelyn Lamar was not nearly as concerned about genetic dispositions as she was about pedigree. She was positive Millie's was lacking crucial prerequisites. Her tactic was to remind Frank of his potential and how much of it would be wasted by leaving civilized life for a barbaric country. She also worried that Frank's new wife would not be able to comprehend him.

49

"It has nothing to do with you," she had reassured Millie. "I can see you are studious and smart, but Frank comes from a competitive, scholastic background. We have the finest universities you know, right along with Harvard and Yale. But if he must insist on his Daniel Boone experiment, I suppose you are the best type of wife for him to bring along."

The sisters, at least, had been more supportive. They thought Millie's Seattle style of dressing was charming, although a little outdated.

"I suppose the heavy, stuffy suits are more compatible with cold weather," they sniffed.

"We don't wear wool, and all these dark blues and greens. Honestly. The funerals are over, my dear. It's time to brighten up and wear lace and floral prints. Oh, but you are going to Alaska! That will never do."

They also felt Alaska would be a grand adventure, although they had no desire to live there.

"Oh, no," they said simultaneously. The three seemed to twine together into single thought processes. "L.A. is the best place for prospects. We could find a movie producer or a wealthy oilman, even a millionaire businessman. Not that the money matters, but it's nicer, overall, and we could never live someplace so uncivilized as Alaska. I have heard they don't even have hair salons. Now, where would we be without hair salons?"

If they had returned on the coastline, they would have returned quickly to mountainous country on their way north. They hadn't done that. Conscious now of the dwindling season, they had traveled north as quickly as they could through the hotter, flatter inland area of California and Oregon, making a beeline for Hayden and saving four hundred miles off their trip.

They didn't stay long on the farm. The inland heat did not include the mountainous region of northern Idaho. The brittle, yellow days and cold nights were a constant reminder that winter was around the corner.

Instead of joy that they stayed on the farm resting up and helping with the harvest, Cora Snipes declared they had compounded her misery by having to say goodbye twice.

"You should be gone the first time," she said bitterly, but finally accepted the hugs from both her daughter and son-in-law when she saw they truly intended to leave.

It was so far away now, as distant as the prairie grass piling up behind them, then dropping from view. It had been three days since they crossed the Canadian border and not one thing had changed in the landscape. Not one thing.

Millie felt her legs twitch restlessly and sprawled them as far as she could in the limited foot space. "How many more miles is it to the next town?"

Frank's eyes traveled past the flat, Alberta fields, searching for the distant blue gleam of mountains. "The signpost back there said sixty-seven kilometers."

"What is that in miles?"

"Forty or fifty, I think."

"That's not so bad. From Edmonton, we'll hit the Alaskan-Canadian Highway?"

"A bit past, but it's close. Are you hungry?"

"It will wait for Edmonton." Her legs were restless, but she would stretch them in Edmonton. She reached down to knead the muscles. The last town they had stopped in had been Calgary, just a day's drive across the Canadian border. Calgary had the feel of an old west town recently tamed, yet the inhabitants were typical farmers, and the town itself, neat as a pin.

She watched the prairie fly by, the left- over grain past its prime and hanging dully in the early October sun. Flatland disinterested her. She liked variation. She liked layers of color. "Do you think it would have been wiser to just pack everything and shoot up through Vancouver after our honeymoon?"

He glanced at her, then back to the road. They had taken the long way to the Alcan by using the Idaho border, and it wasn't a scenic route, either. He assumed she was tired, bored, and second-guessing their wisdom. "Wouldn't it have looked silly to have this much stuff in the back of our car for a honeymoon?"

Still feeling cross, she folded her arms and sulked. "I don't know. Maybe it would have made me feel more like we are gypsies. I wouldn't have minded becoming a gypsy, Frank, but it was difficult saying goodbye to my mother twice."

"Well," he said cheerfully. "If that's what is bothering you. For the next two weeks, we will be living a full gypsy life. Will that satisfy you?"

Millie calculated the time they had already spent on the road against two weeks of uninterrupted travel.

It was possible her appetite would be fully satisfied once they reached their destination. She suddenly laughed.

"Now that we have a taste for it, do you think we will be able to settle down?"

"If not, I think we will have enough room for exploring."

He patted her knee and she scooted closer, laying her head on his shoulder.

There was plenty of room for exploring, and especially her new feelings. She had never been in love before. She believed she liked it.Increased traffic and sprouts of residential housing announced they were coming close to Edmonton.

Frank slowed his speed and checked his gas gauge. "Just in time, we're nearly out of fuel."

They stopped at the first large full-service station with a diner attached. Millie blinked in the bright overhead lights and got out of the vehicle, chasing the blood flow back into her legs. There wasn't anything else close by except a few fenced in homes and a store that looked like it had once been a house.

The attendant came out just as Frank opened his door. He was a nice- looking boy, no more than eighteen, with hair the color of the dying fields and freckles splattered across his face. He apologized for his tardiness, filled the tank, washed the windows, and checked the oil.

"You're a quart low," he told Frank, showing him the stick. "You're burning oil." He pointed to several locations under the hood that Frank was to assume were trouble spots.

"You should get a tune-up while you're here and an oil change," the boy advised. "You're headed up the Alcan, aren't you?"

Frank nodded his affirmative.

The kid wiped away at some grimy spots. "Those mountains are rough. If you break down, there won't be any help for miles."

"How long will it take to fix the car?" Frank asked anxiously.

The young fellow shrugged. "Probably no more than a couple of hours. Have you had any problems? Coughing? Stalling?"

"She coughs sometimes."

"Yeah. Let's find out what ails her."

Frank knew enough about cars to understand that losing a quart of oil was not a good sign. He also knew the vehicle well enough by now to detect differences in its performance. It was louder. The exhaust blew smoke. It shivered sometimes.

He had chosen this gas station because of its size and because it was busy and situated just three blocks from Main Street. It was a successful enterprise in a fair-sized city. That said something for it.

"Okay," he agreed. "Is it that easy to tell where we're going?"

The young man slapped a grease rag over his shoulder and shrugged. "United States license plates. Car covered with dust and loaded down. A bit easy."

Frank followed as the attendant eased the car into the garage and probably would have supervised the entire procedure except that Millie took him by the arm. "We'll just go to the diner and wait, maybe walk around a bit. Two hours, you say?"

The boy was already pulling out his tools. "She looks like she's in pretty good shape other than burning oil. Spark plugs and alternator look brand new. Two hours should do it."

The diner had the same successful look as the gas station. It was very shiny, with modest wooden tables and benches. The waitress had the same variation of wheat colored hair, tied back in a perky ponytail. She recommended the chicken and dumplings, which sounded very hearty and welcome after their long ride.

"We did alright, didn't we?" askedFrank while they waited. "It does sound a bit like backtracking to go south, turn around and go north again."

Feeling a little guilty for having been the first to question their sound judgment, Millie answered, "it was the last chance we had to see family members. We had to do it, Frank. We don't know when we can afford to see them again and you know they won't come see us. They won't do it."

"Bruiser said he would visit."

"He probably will, eventually. None of them are much inclined to get out much."

He watched her fold and unfold her napkin, a wrinkled little frown between her eyes. "It could have been better, couldn't it?"

She brightened up as the coffee came and dimpled a smile at the waitress. "They'll come around, but they won't come and see us."

"We can sleep in town tonight if you'd like. It's your last chance to see civilization in a long time."

Millie stared out at the brooding afternoon and the distant, neatly framed buildings growing closer together toward the center of town.

"No, I don't want to. I'm ready to let it go." She propped her chin on her fist. "You know, I didn't know the Alberta plains were so big."

"You've never been on the plains?"

"No. I think I have never been so far from mountains."

"We will soon see so many, you will be sick of them."

"I think that can't happen. I can already feel it, the mountain air. It smells differently than the plains."

"What you feel is winter setting in. It comes earlier in the north."

They dawdled, soaking up the steam coming from the kitchen and the food. They listened to the murmur of the radio and the chatter of customers as though they would never again know the sounds of modern life.

The waitress returned to check on them, swinging her ponytail and popping chewing gum. "Is Jeff taking care of your car?" She asked, noting on her pad they had asked for pie and coffee to go. "He's the young guy at the service station."

"Is he good?" asked Frank.

She snapped her gum. "Oh yes. His dad owns the shop. Jeff began twisting a wrench when he was seven. He gives everyone the cautionary speech but not everyone listens."

"He said it would take two hours," said Millie.

"Then give him three." She brought them dessert and their thermos of coffee. "It's good that you listened. The road gets really bad as soon as you start climbing and service stations are a hundred kilometers apart. Are you going to Anchorage or Fairbanks?"

"Anchorage," said Frank.

"Then you still have over seven hundred kilometers to go after you cross the Alaskan border. Fairbanks is closer."

When they finished their meal, they left a fifty-cent tip and gave another fifty cents for the extra coffee.

The waitress had filled the thermos to the top and even gave them a handful of breadsticks. "For the road," she explained. "In case you get hungry."

The afternoon had grown late. There was a marked chill in the air that seemed to come directly from the north. When they left the restaurant, Millie folded her arms, burying her hands in her sweater's bulk. "We'll have to dig out our jackets. We haven't hit the mountains yet and it's turning cold."

They walked back to the car still sheltered in the garage. The attendant was standing proudly beside it with a list of things he had replaced and the total cost for parts and labor.

The costs were all somewhat higher than they would have paid in the United States, but the parts were everything you would reasonably expect. He charged the standard rate for an oil change, and the labor was accomplished in a reasonable amount of time. Not only that, but the young, diligent mechanic had also washed down the entire outside of the car.

"We had to put her up on blocks to check the driveline and rotate the tires," he explained. "So, we had to take the load off the top. I thought I might as well clean her up a bit at the same time. You're going to need those headlights."

Frank thanked him, paid him in cash and added a two-dollar tip. Millie left the two discussing the car's maintenance and opened the trunk, hauling out their heaviest coats.

"I'd take out those blankets, too," suggested the young man. "It's going to get cold. Listen," he added, as the two climbed into the car. He propped his arm up on the driver's door.

"I see you've got camping gear on top of your vehicle. We have campgrounds, but this time of year, it can be rugged. Not so much here, but when you get in those high mountains. There won't be any real towns. Just an occasional gas station and store. Fill up at every gas station you come to. If you're out there in the wilderness and the weather turns bad, go to the nearest house. They'll let you in. Don't try sticking it out in a tent in bad weather, eh?"

Frank nodded. "Gotcha."

The youngster patted the hood of the car. "You're nice folk. Take my word for it. This is a bad time to be traveling. If you see a blizzard coming in, don't try sticking it out. Go to the nearest house."

He held out his hand, Frank thanked him profusely and promised to use wisdom while traveling. The young man watched them go as though he had just dispatched his best friend into the unknown.

"Friendly around here," commented Millie.

Frank had found the pause a good time to bring out his pipe and light the bowl. He exhaled casually to demonstrate his high degree of sophistication. "The new highway has brought them business. They want to please."

She fumed a little at his cynicism then said tartly, "oh, I think it's more than that. I think they liked us, and I know I liked them."

"Why shouldn't they like us? We're not criminals."

She laughed. "You don't think criminals are likable? I'm surprised Bruiser didn't teach you better."

He continued trying to appear worldly-wise. "I believe he tried. I don't have a knack for these things, I'm afraid."

"Did he beat you at poker?"

"Yes."

"Did he stick you with the bill at the pubs?"

"All the time."

Millie clasped her hands together and nodded her head as though she had won a major battle. "He's a criminal, Frank. He's a likable, shifty, underhanded criminal."

He drove another mile, then cleared his throat and said, "Millie, I know you're disappointed in the way our families reacted, but don't take it out on Bruiser. It's not his fault and he's not a criminal. He's just Bruiser."

She sniffed but hard as she tried, she could not control the tears that ran down her face. "I'm going to miss him. I'm going to miss all of them."

She dabbed at the treacherous drops, checked in her make-up mirror to help regain her composure, then added dryly, "the young man and the waitress probably liked us so much because you tip generously. It's a good way to encourage fond regards."

He coughed as though unsure whether she was complimenting him or displaying her brittle humor but considering he did not want her taking a dim view, decided it was probably all for the best.

"You receive better service when you tip," he said, explaining his behavior in the most practical sense.

The sun was beginning to set, discouraging their hopes of seeing the mountains before nightfall, but just when their hearts sank with a resigned sigh, the westerly slant of the rays lit up the far horizon, and a host of wavery blue lines grew taller and more distinct in the distance. Frank's foot pressed heavier against the gas pedal, zooming across the last of the great plain, the base of the thunderous heights looming closer and closer.

He pulled over to the side of the road and stopped at the first steep rise. They got out of the car to watch the sunset. There was nothing left of the red ball, only flaming colors that swept over the ridge and lit up the nodding fields. Behind them was the plain fanning out as far as the eye could see. In front of them were the stocky conifers, rocks and crags marking the beginning of their ascent. "Do you want to say goodbye?" Asked Frank.

"I already did," she answered.

Before returning to the car, she reached into the back seat and pulled out the blankets and coats. "It's getting colder."

Frank drove more cautiously now that it was evening, and they were on a steep, winding, unfamiliar road. They hadn't gone very far at all before their wheels hit gravel. The car jiggled over the washboard. "I think we officially hit the Alcan," he announced.

Millie sat up sleepily. She had settled into the blankets and coats and drifted off as soon as the stars appeared. "Really? It's dark as pitch. I can't see a thing."

"You'll see enough of it tomorrow. Sixteen hundred miles to go, Millie. We're good if we make it in six days."

"That doesn't leave you much time for settling in before having to report for work."

"It's enough. I don't report in until mid-November. That's over a month. From now on, Millie Lamar, all your worries are on my shoulders."

"Take your time. I have plenty for the two of us."

They abandoned the idea of camping the very first night. A light snow had fallen recently, and the wind picked it up, sweeping it over the gravel road. The cold seeped in through the floorboards, overpowering the car heater.

When they stopped for the night, they remained in the vehicle, burrowing deeply into their coats and blankets. At times during the night, and in the early hours of the morning, Frank would sit up and turn the car engine back on, warming the cab before shutting it down and sleeping again. Millie noticed in the fitful stirring between wakefulness and sleep that some of her worries did seem to lift from her shoulders.

They hadn't fully prepared themselves for the Alcan.

Physically, they had done the best any human can for the treacherous journey. They had plenty of warm clothing, boots, coats, and blankets to brave the plunging temperatures. Their automobile ran like a champ. They took the advice of the Alberta mechanic and stopped at every gas station along the way. Their maintenance record listed two flat tires, a tail pipe replacement, a broken headlight, an oil change, and a radiator flush during their climb through the mountains, but the attendants cheerfully said, that wasn't bad for the Alcan.

Nothing could have mentally prepared them for the Alcan. To say that it was twelve hundred miles of unpaved road was an understatement. The Alcan had hurriedly been punched through in the last years of the war. It was not only unpaved, but it was also barely graded. It was packed dirt that crumbled away at the sides, washed out in slide areas, dug through giant potholes, and humped over giant rocks. The occasional stretches of gravel were luxuries, despite the dust and jittering.

The solitude reared on white-capped heads, clean as the driven snow, deep as the sounds of thunder. It engulfed them until they were as tiny as mice, squeezing out breaths between the rumble of the giants. Higher they climbed, the world dropping below them, with only the gods looking down on their puny efforts.

At times, Millie was afraid. It wasn't the road itself, which squeezed around ledges without shoulders to prevent the abysmal drop into valleys thousands of feet below and connected by bridges so narrow, they had to wait to one side for the lumber trucks that groaned one by one in their perilous passage over canyons and gorges on to creep over the stocky crossings.

It wasn't the winter breathing heavily behind them, waking them to thickly frosted mornings. It was the solitude of the Alaska Range. The icy mountains shot straight up, piercing the sky like a serrated knife. They were a wall hiding a world no human was allowed to trespass. As wizened elders whose awakenings have ascended time and space, the enormous mountain tops gazed downward and wondered, "what are you doing here?"

It was at times like this that Millie would feel humble and afraid. She would curl close to Frank; her hands held prayerfully in her lap and feel relieved when she saw a house in the wilderness – evidence that they were not alone!

Twice in the high mountains, they stopped at a house for the evening because of the enveloping cold. Both times, the residents were already in bed, but the door was unlocked and there were two blankets on the couch. They added another log to the fire to keep the cabin warm and woke in the morning to a cheerful couple sitting down to breakfast with two extra plates on the table.

Frank fretted a lot. He had estimated three days of driving the Alcan. On the fifth, they were still on the Canadian side of the border. Very early in the morning of the sixth day, they reached pavement. It was erratic, old, and mended with tar, but it told them they were drawing close to Canada's border towns.

It was a sudden thump that registered more in the mind than in audible form as it was a transition from constant rattling to the quiet purring of the automobile. After hundreds of miles maneuvering violent terrain, it felt like they were driving on cushions. They were relieved, yet Frank fretted. They were behind schedule. He took advantage of every bit of smooth, level road to push his speed to the limit.

They finally did get lucky, although they didn't realize it immediately. They were just ahead of the real winter. It followed behind them, snapping at their tails, yet somehow, they managed to stay ahead of the major storms. By the time they arrived at the Alaskan/Canadian border, there was about the same amount of snow they had seen on the ground before they had reached the high elevations of the Alaskan range.

The border town didn't seem much different from Canada. It was perched on a high plain between two mountain ridges, with the arctic wind sweeping unheeded over the landscape. What houses there were, had been painted white over and over until they glistened in unblemished fortitude, the shutters and doors trimming them in bright green. Their yards, too, were spread out evenly on both sides of the houses, with a drive straight through the middle to a barn-like garage.

Millie thought they were unfortunate. They had spent seven days on the Alcan, which was one day more than they had hoped, but by taking the young man's advice, they had been cautious. They ate at whatever lodge or diner might be available. They listened to the reports on the road ahead and had taken precautions. They learned about the washouts and avalanche areas and how to navigate their way around them. They bought chains for their tires and used them on the icy, or snow-packed roads high in the Alaska range.

At the Alaskan border town of Tok, they were told, "winter is holding out". The red line measuring the temperature squatted just above zero, with a flat wind moving the frost like fairy dust.

The weather-burnished man who ran out to fill the car, his coveralls half unbuttoned, the flaps on his cap perky as dog ears, said conversationally as he washed the windows, "You've had a stroke of luck getting through those mountains. Winter hasn't gotten serious enough yet. The sky is still clear. If you push it, you can get through the last pass over the Chugach late tonight. A storm is moving in. You don't want to be in it."

Millie thought she understood. Having seen the high plateau and English-influenced domiciles, she began to model in her mind a place much like Alberta. This notion was rapidly dispelled. She soon became conscious that they had started to climb again, although not so abruptly.

The landscape spilled over with trees, rivers, and lakes on one side, and twisted, black mountains pointing straight up on the other. She realized she was in a cradle between two ranges - one violent, the other tumbling with wildlife.

What houses there were; and there were very few of them; were modest cabins set away from the road. Many of them were covered with antlers interspersed with bear skulls tacked to the eaves of the roof. Some had a handful of huskies tied out in the backyard.

The land itself seemed to change around each corner, with a different backdrop, a different lake, a different herd of caribou moving over the tundra, a different snow-capped mountain biting the sky. It was also one of the most difficult pieces of the entire highway. At the top of the range, the unpaved road dipped and buckled, dodging over melting permafrost.

As it careened downward, it heaved and twisted, bounced over potholes, inched over landslides, and hugged against the walls of giant ledges, while rivers crashed into canyons hundreds of feet below them.

Finally, they emptied out into a peaceful, gracefully spreading valley. Frank pulled over to the side of the road and consulted one of several detailed, hand-drawn maps he had been mailed by one of his new co-workers who had already taken the highway. He compared it to the official map.

"We're in the Matanuska Valley. Sixty miles and we're home."

Millie was still trying to catch her breath. Home! Her heart pounded. It had been terrifying at times; this swoop through some of the most dangerous country she had ever seen; the dizzying panorama that had changed with each bend in the road. "That was quite an adventure."

"It's only just begun."

Once again, they were losing daylight. It seemed they were always in a rush to get as far as they could before the black night descended, yet it always came on them just as they reached a milepost. Frank checked his watch.

"Not quite six o'clock. They say the daylight hours here get very short in the winter."

"Oh, they get shorter everywhere. Five-thirty isn't a spectacular difference."

"No, not yet. It wasn't in Ketchikan either, until November, and Ketchikan is farther south."

She thought about it for only a second. "Oh, I'm sure we will survive."

The Matanuska Valley wasn't like any she was familiar with; tame, wide pastureland with gently rolling hills.

Gorged out from the giant glaciers that had only receded a couple hundred years ago, the valley took on its own shape, roiling between the two giant ranges, snatching some of the heaving mountains, and grinding them down to rocky knolls and grassy hills.

A few farms sprang into view, with horses and cattle behind barbed wire fences, nibbling at snow powdered, short-cropped pasture. The pasture had been chopped away, cleaned, and groomed from the wilderness, while the open frontier snarled around them.

Fifteen miles into the valley, winter caught up with them. It blew in abruptly, with a flurry that battered at the windshield like millions of tiny, white insects. It roared into the valley. Millie clutched the map tightly in her hands.

There were two rivers to cross, fed from two different glaciers. The giant rivers had the same destination, dumping their turbulent waters into the Cook Inlet basin. Once they crossed them, the road would follow the inlet all the way into Anchorage. The closer they came to the two rivers, the greater the force of the storm that pounded against them.

In the storm, Millie thought she was hallucinating or perhaps had died and had started the journey to the other side. Only able to see twenty feet in front of them, Frank inched along the barely visible road while Millie served as the co-pilot, cautioning him if he swung too close to one side or the other.

They crept up on a substantially sized bridge. They started across. As the headlights peered to the far end, Millie almost cried out in alarm, but caught her tongue. The car appeared to be headed straight into a mountain.

There was no turning back.

The storm pushed against them, the bridge groaned and shuddered in the thrashing storm – the car crept forward as though of its own will. Both Frank's hands gripped the steering wheel as he stared desperately ahead, the rear of the vehicle swinging with each icy bump. They were drawing close enough to the flat-faced cliff to see the ridge of conifers at the top, crowding each other for space.

A wind gust lifted the snow flurry just long enough for the headlights to brighten the road a few seconds. That's when she saw the white painted guardrails and the sharp turn to the right that squeezed the road between the mountain and the inlet.

The storm continued to batter, but on this side of the inlet, it was buffered. The wind didn't rip and tear with the same ferocity. It sounded almost quiet compared to the pummeling they had taken in the valley. "I don't see any houses anywhere," whispered Millie.

Frank kept his eyes directly on the road in front of him. "We're not that far from Anchorage. As soon as we find a lodge, we'll stop and get our bearings."

Millie lost track of time and distance. They seemed to be caught forever in the snowstorm. She felt they had traveled a hundred miles before they saw a disturbed patch of light beaming through the swirling snow, although Frank assured her it had only been ten.

The lights spread over a cleared drive and spilled into the road. Sighing thankfully, they wheeled into the drive.

Two gas pumps stood side by side, their overhead lights blinking erratically. Behind them was a stout structure built from logs and supporting a plywood shelter squatting over a generator.

The generator made a loud, thrumming sound as they approached the lodge steps.

The interior was typical of most of the lodges they had visited in the high northern mountains. It had once been and still supported a trading post with piles of fur, Native crafts, hatchets, mackinaws, blankets, and grocery staples. It also contained a bar counter serving up beer, soda and coffee, a central dining area with a limited menu, and a few local people visiting.

The Lamars had developed a taste for the hearty meals served along the Alcan, often delivered with a markedly wild game flavor when the menu said it was beef.

All three tables in the dining area were free, so they chose the one closest to the fireplace.

A woman somewhere in her mid to late forties, set two cups of hot coffee down in front of them before even taking their order."Anyone who has been out and about in this weather needs it," she explained. "Special today is chili. Thirty-five cents a bowl."

Chili was agreeable. The woman called to the kitchen, "two bowls of chili, Zeb," then drew up a chair to sit with them. "Where are you headed?"

She shook her head when they told her their destination. "Not tonight, you're not. It's a complete white-out with a dangerous bridge up ahead. Do you have a place you can stay?"

The chili was delicious. It warmed up Millie right down to the toes. "We only just got here," she explained. "We don't even know where 'here' is."

"Well, here isn't anywhere, exactly." Since there were no other customers to wait on, Zeb had joined his wife. He grinned at the chance to talk to a newcomer. Perhaps a few years older than the woman, and about three inches shorter, he was round, but muscular, with a seriously weathered face and teeth turning yellow from tobacco.

He gestured around him. "We call 'here' Wolf Creek on account of the wolves in the area. I've got a couple of wolf dogs out back. They come as a result of the wolves sniffing around the huskies. The G.I.'s like them though. They come out every weekend to look at them and take pictures."

"We're picturesque," said the woman, plumping the ruffles on her apron. "That's what we were told. What's your business with Anchorage?"

"My business is with Fort Richardson," answered Frank with his best rumble. "I've been assigned to a post."

It's not known whether Frank meant to impress or was simply stating the facts, but his words had a positive effect on his listeners. "Military!" Zeb held out his hand. "I want to thank you for your commitment to your country."

"Thank you kindly. I'm no longer military, though. I've gone into Civil Service."

Zeb wasn't detoured in his enthusiasm. "Even better. We already have a few Civil Service living here. They don't spend a lot of money at a time, but in the long run, they are our best customers because they have steady work."

After a self-satisfied sigh, the proprietor leaned back, only to catch something out of the corner of his eye. "Betty Lou, get off the counter. Nobody wants to see you strip down."

What Millie had first believed to be a young man whose beard had not yet come in and who had very little fondness for bathing, called back, "Well, tell dingus here he just got beat arm wrestling a woman and I told him from the start what I was. Now he don't want to believe it."

"I told you before to leave the G.I.'s alone, now, go on. Show some manners. We've got some new folk, just come off the Alcan."

"Are you going to live around here?" asked Betty Lou, pulling up a chair and straddling it. On second glance, you could see the features were feminine, if a little strong and stubborn. Her jaw was square, her lips thin, but her eyes a very pretty shade of green. Her hair was poorly cut and worst for its lack of care, but it was possible with a good shampoo, the color would be light brown.

She was dressed much like a trapper, in knee-high fur boots, a few ermine skins hanging from a home-fashioned belt, and a fur-trimmed leather vest over a wool plaid shirt. Frank did his best to appear both cultivated and at ease with the uncultivated of the population. "We don't know where we will live yet. We'll have to look around."

"Well, I can tell you." She said, lighting up a hand-rolled cigarette. "You won't find no place better than here. I've been around. The whole Matanuska Valley. Up around Fairbanks and Delta Junction. They've got their good. They've got their bad. When you weigh them out, this area comes out with the most good."

"And Anchorage?" askedMillie, just a little fascinated by this wild west image come to life in the far north.

"Oh, Anchorage," sighed Betty Lou. She hiked up one leg and propped the ankle against the knee of the other. She leaned forward. "There are some that like it. Can't live without it. Me? I've got to go there sometimes to get wild. All them city lights and the music just blaring out. They make me drunker than a bear eating fermented berries. But some gotta have it all the time. The lights, the noise, the busy-busy. Don't know how they do it without going crazy, but it's a known fact. There's more that live there than in the whole territory put together."

"Maybe not all of it," objected Zeb's wife, who had finally introduced herself as Solace.

"I been around, and you haven't," said Betty Lou. "Unless they're hiding some place I don't know about, most these new folks been flocking into Anchorage."

"They like the electricity and the running water."

Solace got up to refill their coffee cups and brought them each back a piece of rhubarb pie. "Eat up. You can't go anywhere tonight. What Betty Lou says is true. No electricity, and we're the only place around here that's got a generator. You need it when you're a business. Our house is just across from the lodge. You can sleep in our living room for the night. Come morning, they'll probably have the roads cleared if it stops snowing by then."

"How far is it to Anchorage from here?" Asked Frank.

"Oh, around twenty miles or so. Fifteen to base. It will take you about a half hour to get there."

The storm was still swirling around as they walked the short distance to the cabin, but the fury was leaving. The wind whined and mumbled in fits. There seemed to be a touch of irony and a justifiable moment for pondering the significance of being chased by winter and having it catch up with them just twenty miles from their goal.

Her suspicions that all things happen for a reason were further provoked, when in giving them extra pillows and blankets to make themselves comfortable by the fire, Solace said, "next month, one of our hunting cabins will be free. It isn't much, understand. No more than a room with a pot belly stove, but if Anchorage doesn't suit you, it's like Zeb said. We've already got some Civil Service moved out this way. They're veterans, with wives, just like you two. They could help you settle in."

Four

The next day, the sky was leaden, but the storm had ended. A few tired snowflakes fell as the stragglers of the abandoned flurry and an occasional burst of air flustered the trees, releasing a part of their snowy burden. Zeb Grant was digging out the path between the house and the lodge, and trucks were trundling up and down the road with plows. Frank put on his coat and boots to join the older man.

Solace had gotten up early. She already had a large bowl of dough that she was kneading and rolling for bread.

"Why didn't you wake me?" Asked Millie, cleaning her hands and taking up a portion of the dough to knead.

"Oh! You looked too worn out. Imagine driving in that blizzard." Solace clucked her tongue. "I reckon you won't have any more trouble. Do you have chains for your car?"

"We had to buy some in Canada. There were spots on the Alaska Range we wouldn't have been able to cross without them."

The matronly woman listened with a look of satisfaction, nodding at Millie's account of her travels. "We've got a bad bridge a few miles up ahead," Solace explained. "It's at the bottom of a steep hill with another steep hill on the other side of it. The bridge is always icy in the winter, and you can't make it to the top of the hill if you're climbing without chains."

They were ready to leave by early afternoon. Solace made sure they ate a hearty breakfast, refused to take money until they left it on the counter and walked nonchalantly out the door, and followed them as far as the driveway, calling, "now you know where we're at. Come back again."

"It is picturesque," said Millie as they were leaving. She had turned her head to look back at the two wooden structures tucked against the slope of the mountainous foothills. It was on a ridge, with a fog lifting under it. As the fog peeled back, the flat, grey inlet rolled beneath it.

"We should come and look on a clear day," agreed Frank.

There were absolutely no improvements in this road over the one they had just traveled for nearly two thousand miles. From the dips, they could tell there were potholes and uneven structure under the newly packed snow.

The road twisted and turned conveniently, relying more on the ease of arriving from one point to another, than any practiced arts in surveying, grading, and leveling. Frank had wrapped the chains over the wheels as advised and discovered even before arriving at the bridge, there was much treachery for the unaware in this water-rich area with lakes, rivers, gullies, and trapped fog.

The ice lay smoothly just under the layers of snow and the shoulders of the road rolled away, slumping into deep ravines.

On the other side of the two enormous hills that had been split apart eons ago by the raging river below them, the foothills fell back, revealing a relatively flat stretch of land, and a wider, flatter road. Not only that, they were also beginning to see real signs of settlement.

There was an outpost sign and evidence of military industry behind the thinly scattered forest. There was more traffic, a few squatting houses that gradually came closer together. They saw an airport. Frank pulled into the parking lot and consulted one of his maps.

"Merrill Field. The rental my commanding officer found for us is somewhere in this area."

Millie helped him examine the numerous drawings and notes, finally agreeing their rental was a small house in a neighborhood of small houses wedged between the airport and the two military bases. It was a convenient, yet noisy location.

They only had to ask for directions twice before locating the landlord for the house promised to them. The prospective landlord was a military lifer who was satisfied with his captaincy and was looking forward to retiring at forty and a career in housing rentals.

He told them all about this while sitting in his home office on base, drinking hot chocolate and rifling through desk files.

"Yep. Twenty years next winter. You should have stayed with military, Frank. You could have had officer's housing. Now, you're stuck with me."

Frank looked around the small but comfortably modern room and out the window at the orderly streets. He sniffed, almost with disdain, or as though he would have shown disdain if he was not in front of a senior officer. "Not for long. The wife doesn't want to live in town. We'll be looking at homesites."

The captain chortled, shook his head, and leaned over his desk to give Millie a patronizing smile. "It's all wilderness out there. No conveniences whatsoever."

Lacing her gloved hands and placing them firmly in her lap, she gazed back, her chin tilted, letting him know with her expression, she was not at all intimidated by his manly wisdom. "As I've been made aware," she said. "I'm no stranger to hardship. I'm grateful you held this house for us, but I don't think we will stay long. We are already looking at prospects. I apologize if that's an inconvenience."

The captain dropped his eyes and shuffled through some paperwork. "Eh?" He said without looking up. "Happens all the time. At least you're straight up about it. We'll just rent this out on a monthly basis. We're working in the same building, Frank. You can pay me there. Just give me a week's notice before you leave because there is always someone else looking."

The deal was concluded with a handshake and exchange of money. Their new landlord drove with them out to the house, which was only three blocks away from the military border and handed them the keys.

It was more of a cottage than a house, among a row of different-colored cottages. It had a small, snow-covered yard, a picket fence, and a carport. It had one bedroom, a small kitchen and bathroom, and a combination living and dining area. The furnishings consisted of a table with two chairs, a bed, and an aging sofa. It was all they needed.

They unpacked the car, hauled their things in and threw the blankets on the bed. The blankets were thick with dust after their long journey, but Millie didn't care. She threw herself down on top. "Oh my God. I'd forgotten how it feels to lay on a bed."

Frank joined her, but instead of lying down, he sat up with his legs stretched in front of him, his back against the wall and lit his pipe. "It's not a bad place. It's close to work. It's close to shopping. You've got electricity, running water, oil heat. Maybe we should think of staying here until spring."

A low-flying plane roared overhead. "And there's the noise," said Millie. "You'll hear enough of it at work. Do you really want to hear it at home as well?"

"It would only be for seven months."

She rolled on her side and propped her head on her hand so she could look at him. "No, it wouldn't. The rent will eat over half your paycheck. We've gone through most of our savings, and we'll never be able to buy property if we stay here more than three months."

"You are thinking about one of the Grant cabins, aren't you?"

She rolled back over and looked at the ceiling. "Betty Lou told me, the correct name for the Chugach is Chugiak and it means place of many places. That's kind of neat, isn't it?"

"You would rather be a Chugiak woman than a Chugach one?"

"Yeah. It sounds better. It has a ring to it, like a bell, and Betty Lou likes it better."

"If you keep listening to her, you'll be wrestling grizzly bears by next summer."

She sat up and crossed her legs, bouncing on the bed. Her voice sounded almost wheedling. "It would save a lot of money and she said there were already four other Civil Service employees living in the area. You could help each other out."

He put his pipe away and smiled at her. At the oddest moments, something childlike came out in her, something that looked at the world as a shiny new toy. It was times like these when Frank was the most attracted to Millie and when she was the least conscious of her charm. He teased her, answering in an aloof voice, "I would have to meet them."

"Of course, you would have to meet them." She bounced some more.

"There are other options available. Shouldn't we look around some more?"

She bounced until she was practically on his lap and threw her arms around his neck. "Frank, we've seen everything from Tok to Anchorage. Wolf Creek is beautiful."

"I'll ask about it," he promised.

He didn't ask about it right away. In Frank's orderly world were priorities. Over the next few days, they spent as much time at the laundry mat as they did in unpacking. Everything was covered with dust.

The fine particles had crept into their suitcases, trunk, and boxes. It accumulated in layers in their bedding, coats, and jackets. While everything else was being cleaned, even the car received a quick scrub down, managed by keeping the engine running so the water wouldn't freeze up.

Two days before Frank was to report for work, they had their luggage unpacked and the little house ship-shape. Even two weeks of groceries lined their shelves and furnished the refrigerator. Justifiably proud of their accomplishments, they sat down to plan their remarkably chore-free evening.

"Well, here we are. We've arrived," said Frank. "And we haven't even seen the town."

Millie looked out the naked window. Curtains had not been on her necessity list and now she regretted the loss. She would have to make do with gunny sacks until she could find something better. "It's already turning dark," she sighed. "How are we going to see anything in the dark?"

"Well, ma'am," he answered formally. "That's why we have streetlamps."

They wheeled slowly into the main street of Anchorage. It looked somewhat like the Wild West, but it was the wild north. Parking lots replaced hitching posts, and dog sled mushers replaced cowboys, but the frontier atmosphere was there.

Some asphalt and concrete had been experimentally applied around the docks and up into the primary streets, but they were already expiring under adverse weather conditions.

The luxury highway that swung around the coast to the southeast and shot straight into a wilderness of hump backed mountains to the northwest was gravel, while the side roads were primarily scraped and rutted dirt trails that interlocked more by chance than by planning.

At this hour, people were getting off work and exploring the various means of entertainment, which seemed to be more prolific than the grocery and department stores. "A fool and his money are soon parted here," murmured Millie. "Bruiser would be in paradise."

Having become familiar with all manner of designing schemes for parting fools from their money during his years of service to his country, Frank hesitated before asking Millie, "Would you like to walk about?"

She nodded. She was as eager as he was to take in some of the curiosities, but her interest wasn't in the taverns, the gambling houses, and the poorly disguised establishments of ill repute, which Frank only glanced at a few times before she pulled him onwards. Behind the main avenue were several fenced in areas that could only be accessed by the rutted paths that at this time of year, were fortunately frozen solid. Two of the fenced yards showed signs of activity.

"Betting rings," surmised Frank.

"Well, let's go see what they're betting on," Millie urged.

The admission to the first ring was free. They stood against the back of the fence along with a group of other spectators in mackinaws or heavy furs. In the center of the ring was a giant dog with a wide face and powerful shoulders. He was harnessed to a sled piled high with weighted bundles. "And go," said a referee, popping a signal gun into the air. The animal groaned and scrambled at the icy ground. Inch by inch, the sled broke free from its frozen entrapment and trailed slowly behind him.

"Seven hundred fifty pounds in fifteen seconds!" Announced the referee. "Who's next?"

A St. Bernard was led into the ring. A wave of bets passed among the gamblers, the gun popped, and the dog struggled. It took the animal three seconds longer to break the ice than it had the other dog, and he didn't pull the sled quite the required distance. A murmur of disappointment past among some, although most were quite jovial about it.

They left before watching the next dog pull. "What kind of dog was that first one?" asked Millie. "It was enormous."

Frank shook his head.

"I don't know. We should ask around. They've got all kinds of dogs here, most of them husky mixes."

"It was fun. I think we should watch more of them. I like the dogs."

He grunted. "As long as you like watching them and not letting them into the house."

She had nothing to say to that primarily as they had not talked about the matter of owning pets, and pets were certainly not on the priority list at this time, but the back of her mind was already compiling objections that she would use when the timing was right.

Tonight, was not the night. Frank was already following the ragged path and streaming pedestrians connecting like the charge in an electrical current. His stride was surprisingly long for a medium-sized man, and Millie's thick legs, built more for endurance than speed, had a difficult time keeping up. She trotted beside him, mulling about dogs and how they became as inevitable a part of a family as children and medical bills.

The next ring had captured the attention of a large group of GIs', still in their army fatigues and jackets, who clustered around the entrance, placing bets. It cost a quarter to get in. It was worth it just to view the amazing sight. An oddly dressed fellow with a round frame and a large mustache was leading around by a leash and collar, a stoutly built kangaroo that seemed not at all perturbed by its audience.

"Who wants to box with Kelsey?" cried the peddler. "Ten dollars to the man who lands a punch on Kelsey the boxing kangaroo."

"I want to box with Kelsey," said Frank, removing his great coat and handing it to Millie.

"Oh, no," she protested, but he was already walking into the ring, leaving her stunned. She watched, unable to determine whether she should be anxious or angry. Anxious, probably, since Bruiser's fondness for Frank also served as a warning that she had conveniently set to one side, but that was now a full-blown illustration of Frank's lack of boundaries.

She resigned herself to watching anxiously angry. Frank had a good boxer's stance. He crouched, his fists drawn in toward his chin, his feet shifting from side to side. He tried a few experimental taps and the kangaroo jumped out of the way.

He dodged once as the kangaroo jumped at him and came up for another swing. The kangaroo was ready. It jumped simultaneously with Frank's jab at it and kicked him square in the jaw.

Frank staggered, fell to the ground, shook his head, felt his swollen jaw, then got to his feet. He mumbled to the referee, "The kangaroo wins."

A round of applause followed them as they left, leaving Frank a loser in name only. Millie was not as enthusiastic and congratulatory. "What were you thinking?" She scolded. "Look at that! You'll be checking in with your new commanding officer day after tomorrow, and you'll be showing up with a bruise the size of Rhode Island." She folded her arms and said "humph" quite loudly.

Frank laughed with glee. "He'll just figure I got offended. The guys can't help the way they look at women but that doesn't mean they get to leer at the married ones."

It was the presence of the GI's. They had intoxicated him, made him think he was back in the navy. Men who had played soldiers couldn't help themselves. They were drawn back to the game over and over. It wasn't the combat. It was the daring and the camaraderie.

"Really now, Frank!" She shoved at him only half-forcefully. "I would not take you for a cave man."

It was enough of a shove to make him stumble a few feet. He laughed again as he regained his balance. "It's your choice, really. If you want men to leer at you, I'll let them."

"No, I don't want men leering at me," she said crankily, then grumbled. "You could have broken your jaw!"

"A guy has got to prove himself around here."

They had reached their car. He stood by the door grinning, the swelling on the side of his face already mottling into several shades of blue and green.

"You're an idiot," she muttered.

Still, he opened the passenger side like a gentleman. She slid into the seat and gave him a final disapproving look.

"Oh. Put some snow on it. Cool it down."

She pulled her handkerchief from her purse, stuffed a wad of snow in it, and handed it to him, sniffing at the elegant stitching and delicate piece of linen being so wantonly abused.

"Are you going to stay mad at me?" He asked, placing the cloth against his cheek, and looking at himself in the rearview mirror.

She sulked for several seconds as she combated with the voice that scolded her for becoming attracted to a man Bruiser liked. There was always a reason for Bruiser's fondness, but then, the things that attracted him most were generally the things that attracted her.

"No, I suppose I will not. If you are in the habit of making a spectacle of yourself, I may as well get used to it."

She watched him preening in the mirror. He seemed quite satisfied with himself., until he glanced at her. He gave her a smile. With his big ears and alert brown eyes, he looked like a reticent child. "Let's eat at that restaurant right at the edge of town," he wheedled. "Our victory celebration."

She continued to look at him severely. "What are we celebrating? A kangaroo beating?"

"Our entrance. It's all about the entrance, Millie."

Five

The Hall for Veterans of Foreign Wars, conveniently shortened to the VFW hall, still smelled of freshly cut lumber and outdoor paint. It was a sight for sore eyes; generously sized, with a high roof and light bulbs attached to the naked rafters.

Millie could barely remember the last time she was in a large room. From the day their wheels first hit the Alcan, they had been confined to cubbyholes. It was the only way she could see it. They had lived out of their car for three weeks. Hotel rooms were small. The shops had narrow aisles, crammed with every assortment of goods opportunity presented. The houses were small. The buildings were partitioned into office spaces and waiting rooms.

Waiting rooms themselves, she reflected, were dreadful. They consisted of a few folding chairs and a coffee table stacked with tattered, elderly magazines dated eight months before the end of the war and splashed with photos of servicemen.

In comparison to everything else she had seen in six months of mainly living inside walls while a ferocious winter clawed at the door, the VFW hall was glorious. It was one long, solid room, with just a little of it conserved for piping, plumbing, a boiler room and a walled in toilet.

To one side of the room, several collapsible tables had been set up end to end and covered with mismatched tablecloths. Two were white lace, one a red-checkered, and another sported a print patter of bright yellow daisies. All displayed an assortment of home-made pastries, coffee, tea, Kool-Aid, disposable cups, and plastic flatware, except the one closest to the door.

It contained several piles of forms and brochures, along with two official, but cheerful looking women who encouraged random examination of their paperwork while talking privately to each other.

Millie nibbled at a cookie and took a sip of her coffee. She was supposed to be mingling, but she still hadn't developed the art of talking to a roomful of strangers. A lady drew close that she recognized, one from the Wolf Creek settlement. It had taken them longer to move into Wolf Creek than they had thought.

The hunter who had been renting the cabin decided to stay a few extra months for some fur trapping. They had not been able to transfer until the end of February and now it was just early April, not enough time to really know anyone but Solace and Betty Lou.

Solace had been her mainstay. She rose in the mornings and visited her landlady the moment Solace put the "open" sign in her window. She helped knead bread and listened to tips on pioneer housewifery. Not that she needed a great many tips. Her own life had been one of bare essentials but there were seasonal and harvesting differences and the availability of goods.

Betty Lou occupied the time Millie spent in the lodge. Betty Lou had a habit of button-holing her as soon as she came through the door, calling her "my fancy little lady friend".

She wrapped one arm around Millie's shoulders and whispered confidential secrets about the lodge visitors.

Most of the visitors were men: truck drivers, trappers, miners, burnished cheek villagers and furtive G.I.'s hoping to sneak a romance with Solace's teenage daughter, Bea.

Bea, like all teenagers, had a greater interest in candy bars and boys than she did in helping her mother in the kitchen. The murmuring sounds floating from behind the curtain separating the lodge from the workspace were routinely interrupted by clattering dishes and sharp urges to locate a bit of elbow grease.

What women Millie saw, came in with their husbands, took the tables in the back and chatted between themselves. "You've gotta come in during wash day," advised Betty Lou. "All the women come in together on wash day." To date, she had not discovered the wash day they came in. Apparently, it was a decision they chose in advance and planned accordingly.

She was only beginning to learn who was local and who were frequent visitors from Anchorage and the Matanuska Valley. "Is this your first time?" Asked the lady sympathetically.

Millie dropped the cookie on the saucer and wiped her mouth with a lacy, personal hanky. "At a meeting of veterans? Yes. What on earth do they talk about? War stories? You would think they were over and done with it."

"They are never over it," the young woman answered. "I just saw you chatting with the Mt. View huddle. Did you recognize some friends?"

"Some officer and civil service wives. Does everybody land there first?"

"Pretty much. It's a good place for getting your bearings."

Millie sidled closer to the Wolf Creek resident and whispered confidentially.

"The officer wives lord it over the civil service wives because they have the best housing and conveniences, but they don't stay long, do they? A few years, at most."

She threw back her shoulders and glanced furtively at the Mt. View group before continuing.

"Civil Service is in it for the long haul. They are jealous now because I've moved out, but I really couldn't bear it anymore. I don't like living so close to base."

"Did they insult you?"

"They snubbed me!"

The woman gave a throaty chuckle. "They do that. Beth Hughes here. You're Millie Lamar, aren't you? Solace talks about you."

"Oh, I hope nothing bad!"

"Don't be silly. Solace doesn't have an unkind word to say about anyone."

Beth was sipping her Kool Aid as though it was especially flavorful. Millie's nose, attuned to the indulgences of her brothers, sniffed rum. She stepped back a foot, not because she disliked the person, but because she disliked the smell. Beth didn't seem to notice.

"None of us enjoy living near base. Except maybe the military lifers. Some guys just like playing soldier, and their wives love them for it. We should be grateful. Without them, there wouldn't be any wars, and our husbands would be out of work." She frowned at her half-filled cup. "It's the memories, you know. The sound of the planes disturbs their sleep."

A microphone squealed from a wooden stage occupying the center portion of one wall. A thirtyish man with thinning hair and round glasses held it up. "Folk! Folk! So happy to see you here with us on this fine afternoon."

The microphone faded and he tapped it. It crackled for three loud seconds, then squealed again. With one hand jiggling in his baggy pants, he lifted the microphone, so it was even with his large red bowtie, and continued cheerfully.

"Yes, it's true! It broke forty-nine degrees today. Sun bathers drinking martinis were spotted on ice bergs as far away as the Prince William Sound. Anchorage doesn't have rats jumping ships, but I did see lemmings on Fourth Avenue building lifeboats to navigate the break-up waters."

There was light, scattered laughter and applause, which did not detour the announcer at all. "Do you know what comes with break-up? Mosquitos. A warning to newcomers here. Use the buddy system. Last year, more people were hauled away by mosquitos than were eaten by zebras."

More laughter and a few shouts of agreement, which the announcer absorbed with enthusiasm. He drew himself to his full height, which was not very tall, and strode back and forth across the stage like a professional public speaker.

"Great schedule coming up, but first, how many of you are dog mushers?" Some hands went up. "Then we have a treat. Next year, the Fur Rendezvous organizers plan to hold a dog mushing event. You can find the forms on the table to fill out, along with all kinds of other volunteer positions, so if you would like to help organize and participate in this event, please visit our two lovely ladies in the corner before leaving."

The two ladies in the corner stopped chatting with each other to smile and wave, then resumed their conversation. A few people had already started drifting toward the table full of brochures and sign-up sheets and the announcer continued hastily in case his audience thought it was all over, "speaking of events..."

A drum roll sounded from backstage, catching everyone's attention. He raised his arm with a flourish. "Here they are! Francis Lamar and the boxing kangaroo!"

"Oh, my lord!" Said Millie.

"Isn't that your husband?" Asked her new friend, tugging at her sleeve. "Frank Lamar."

Her fingers moved fretfully over her plate. "Unfortunately, yes. He has a dreadful fondness for the limelight."

Frank Lamar came out on stage in a pair of oversized boxing shorts and a loose tee shirt. He held his mitted hands up for the audience, which alternately cheered and threw wrapped pieces of candy at him. They cheered even louder as someone in a giant kangaroo costume, fitted with cartoon sized gloves, jumped out onto the stage behind him.

Beth clapped her hands together in sudden recognition. "Oh, the little clerk that tried to beat a kangaroo. That was Frank?"

"He knew he couldn't hit it. He just wanted to show off."

"Well, some people think it's scandalous. I believe the legislators have passed a law against kangaroos boxing in Anchorage."

Millie turned to her with enthusiastic agreement. "And they should! Those kangaroos can do some serious damage. I thought I was going to have to take Frank to the hospital."

Beth laughed, a free rolling, husky laugh, and patted Millie's arm.

"We must protect our good citizens from kangaroos."

The boxing match lasted much longer than the original, with both opponents hopping around and apparently knocking each other off their feet. The result was the same, however. The kangaroo landed a punch to the jaw. Frank wheeled around a few times, fell to the floor, rolled out some somersaults, then spread-eagled after flopping about a few seconds. Two jailers dressed like Keystone cops rushed up and hoisted him to his feet.

"Francis Lamar, you've been found guilty of kangaroo boxing. How do you plead?"

"The kangaroo started it!"

"Are you telling me the kangaroo took the first swing?"

"I'm telling you he had an eye on my wife and I was just giving it back to him."

"Did you know that kangaroos have cooties?" askedthe announcer to Frank's astonishment. "It's true. When the kangaroo touched you, he gave you cooties. For this reason, we sentence you to joining the Cooties with VFW post 9360. You will abide by their bi-laws, which include, but are not limited to shooting the bull, barking up the wrong tree and passing the buck."

"This is a kangaroo court!" Shouted Frank, but still accepted the vest, shirt, hat, and ring of an official Cootie.

"A Cootie!" Laughed Beth, clapping her hands. "Your husband is in the same chapter as mine. Why didn't you say so?"

"Frank doesn't tell me these things."

"Of course, he doesn't. Let me introduce you to some of the other girls. Their men have the same shortcoming's. We play it by ear, and a little spy and tell."

The ladies were of a similar age as Millie, from twenty-one to late twenties, but different shapes and sizes. Beside Beth Hughes, there were three others.

Ester Bolinder was tall, thin, dark-haired, and apparently a woman of few words. She nodded, shook hands, then returned to gravely watching the others over her teacup.

Doreen Erichman was small, with frizzy brown hair. She laughed a lot at what anyone said, although she dealt her own humor out sparingly.

Sharon Bowen was blonde, with a broad, plain face and a slightly plump but shapely body.

Beth was slightly shorter than Millie, nearly as hefty, but without the large bones. Her weight snuggled around her with fleshy upper arms and a soft, cushiony stomach.

The other Cootie wives were talking among themselves when Millie and Beth appeared. They broke off their conversation long enough to introduce themselves and welcome the newcomer into the circle before continuing, their words sealing the air around them like the bricks in a thin, invisible wall, giving her an immediate sense of belonging. The type of belonging understood best when public settings begin breaking into inclusive groups of them, us and outsiders.

She was no longer an outsider. She was an "us", as opposed to the city-oriented "them".

She stepped in closer to listen more intently.

Sharon Bowen was speaking, her blonde ponytail swinging. "That's just what I told him. You'll have to hog-tie me before I ever go down the Alcan again."

"Why on earth does Art want to take a second trip?" asked Beth sympathetically.

Sharon gave an exasperated grimace. "He wants to bring back the family furniture. I told him - I know it's been in the family over a hundred years. I know it was hauled up the wagon train trail, but it's not likely to get destroyed at your brother's house. We don't need to drag it to Alaska."

Doreen Erichman's corkscrew curls bounced with her exaggerated shudder. "Oh God. One trip up the Alcan was good enough for me. We broke down twice, had four flat tires and nearly lost the travel trailer when the hitch broke and it began rolling backward down the mountain. It was only by the greatest good fortune it hit a bridge and tipped over. A few things were damaged, but all our farm and carpentry tools were in that trailer. I swear, Alex almost had a heart attack. If we had lost it all... I really don't want to think about it. Our guardian angel was looking out for us and I'm happy with that."

"Did you drive up the Alcan?" Beth asked Millie.

Millie nodded. "We did. It was the first part of October. Winter was just behind us all the way through and caught up with us at Wolf Creek."

"Oh, my heavens," said tiny Doreen, her curls nodding vigorously. "That's just what happens around here. Winter will plop you down somewhere and you think that's the end of it, but it turns out to be just the right place. So, that's how you met Solace?"

"Yes. She promised us a cabin, but we were only able to move in last month."

The tall lady with the dour expression, sniffed and said disapprovingly, "The trappers, you know. They don't give the wildlife any peace and quiet."

"Oh, Ester," said Beth crossly. "The wildlife isn't too good at giving us peace and quiet either. We've had to battle every chicken stealing animal there is, from owls to foxes and ermine. I'm quite willing to let the trappers at a few furry pelts."

Ester shrugged as though such matters were unimportant. "Get a dog. None of the wild animals like being around dogs."

Beth whispered to Millie. "Ester and Charlie Bolinder were the first Civil Service couple to get a homestead here. They did their research. Talked with Solace and the Palmer farmers before staking their hundred sixty acres. But what to do with that much land! There is the problem. What the weeds don't choke out, the wild animals eat."

Millie's new friend fell quiet a minute, then added, "So, they raise horses. Charlie says they are too much in the shadow of the mountain for good farming."

"Do the Bolinders have a dog?"

"A husky and a German Shephard. Ester doesn't really like either one of them. She says they are too noisy."

Sharon was still complaining. "Art and I were stranded once for three days just outside of Tok. Now he wants to take another trip! Well, if we do, I'm bringing along a shovel and digging up a gooseberry bush. I want to see if I can transplant one."

"Oh, transplants won't survive," Doreen said positively, then looked with uncertainty at Ester. "Will they?"

"Our honeysuckle survived and so did the Sitka roses, but the only fruit tree to make it was the crabapple. We haven't tried any berry bushes."

Ester frowned as though trying to decide whether she had said enough or if she should give more information. "Put your transplants close to the house, in the sunniest spot. That's their best chance."

Sharon folded her arms, apparently finding the options distasteful. "Just for spite, I'm going to dig up everything I see along the Alcan that I like. If Arthur can have all his family furniture, I can have something growing in my yard besides cranberry bushes and devil's club."

"Well, my pioneering farmer, let me know when you're growing oranges," said Beth humorously. She turned her attention back to Mille.

"So, you went through a winter first! Oh my!" She fluttered her fingers against her throat, then said. "There are those who believe if you go through the worst first, you will enjoy the best that much better."

Doreen had a high, tinny sounding laugh.

"Ha! And don't we all know about the wise philosophers who say such things. They are the men who are so busy showing their bad side first in pursuit of a relationship, they forget to ever show their good side."

"To our distinct good fortune.," added Beth agreeably. "How heavily the burden lays for those who see the best first and discover upon finding the worst, that their hearts have already been invested."

"Don't be negative!" Scolded Sharon. "It hasn't been that terrible! We've been here two years," she explained to Millie. "We were already stationed at the base when the war ended. In fact, you're the first after-the-war fledging to join our little group. Have you found a piece of property yet?"

Millie took a sip of her coffee. It was already growing cold, which meant she had dallied over it too long. She took another, longer drink before answering.

"We've looked at a few pieces, but they were all close to Anchorage. We want a place further out."

Sharon of the high-placed ponytail that swung like a banner each time she turned her head, added one more cookie to her plate and turned toward tight-lipped Ester Bolinder. "Isn't there a homesite platted next to your land?"

"You'll have to ask Charles," Ester said. Her voice was icy cool, but not completely uninviting. "There are some technicalities involved. A trapper laid claim several years ago."

"There we go again," sighed Sharon, her ponytail drooping sadly. "The trappers will leave once they've trapped everything out. They don't do anything for the community.

Beth, who had defended trappers earlier, deftly changed the subject. "Speaking of Charlie, how is his ranch coming along, Ester?"

Ester was in the middle of examining a coconut confection she had placed on her saucer. She nibbled at it and brushed away the crumbs before answering. "A lot less lucrative than his civil service post. In fact, I believe the horses are eating us out of house and home. His idea was to rent them out to hunters, but Charles is a very poor hunter. I don't see how he can train his horses if he doesn't go hunting."

"Didn't he get his moose last year?"

"He shot it in the back yard!"

"Well, that's the problem," said Beth. "If he can shoot his game straight from his bedroom window, why would he want to go out into the wild? Why would anyone?"

"I'm sure that will all change soon," little Doreen soothed. "With all the building that's going on and shooting moose right in your own yard, it won't be long before there isn't a moose for a hundred miles around."

"I hope that isn't true," said Millie. "I was looking forward to a few four-legged neighbors."

Doreen patted Millie's arm reassuringly. From such a small woman, it felt awkward and amusing, liking being comforted by a young girl.

"Don't worry. If wild and furry is what you want, we have plenty of it. You might even change your tune a bit."

The voices continued cheerily, fluttering in the air like the returning birds of spring. Millie scarcely noticed when Frank put a hand on her arm, then stood back smiling, waiting to be introduced.

If Millie was lacking in her attentions, it didn't take long for the others to notice the San Bernardino man, who, having finished with his performance, had returned to wearing his traditional black slacks and white shirt. His suit jacket was thrown open and anchored back by his treacherously energetic hands, which he kept attached to his pockets.

"Oh, here's our comedian!" Beth exclaimed. "Come now, Millie. Don't be embarrassed to claim him. We could use a few more entertainers."

She blushed at this unwanted attention.

She was aware that Frank was considered a good catch. It had nothing to do with his looks, build or size, all of which were unremarkable. Nor did he exude success the way some gold miners and clever businessmen did.

He was elegant. It was in the way he held himself, the way he dressed. It was in the rich, rolling tone of his voice. It was even in the way he wrote letters. She had expected his elegance before ever receiving a photo of him and had imagined it in every shape and size, yet she still wasn't completely comfortable with the way women were drawn to him. She felt it was wise to keep him humble for this first encounter.

"Red Skelton he isn't," she said dryly. "But he does manage to keep dullness away."

Doreen giggled, whispered to Beth, who laughed out loud, then said boldly, "I'm sure he does. They all do, especially in the winter." She patted her stomach. "Am I right?"

"Am I showing?" Millie flushed. "We had really hoped to wait a year. We wanted to get settled in first."

"Lamar's always do like to get things done quickly," said Frank happily. "You can tell them to wait, but they don't often listen." He drew her close and kissed her neck. Again, Millie blushed.

The bawdy girls nudged each other and laughed boldly, except Ester, who remained as rigid as a school marm.

"And now, willy-nilly, you wish to live in Wolf Creek," Ester said crisply.

Her husband had also returned, but her response was to pointedly ignore him instead of not noticing at all.

"Not willy-nilly! Will me Millie," Frank quipped, then grinned while the women groaned at his pun. "Seriously," he said, taking the time to fill his pipe and tamp down the tobacco. "I joined the Cooties because I like the area surrounding Wolf Creek, but the final decision is Millie's."

"I thought you loved me better than that," said Charlie Bolinder. Since his wife had ignored him, he felt entitled to a few stand-up comics of his own. "You play cribbage with me every day at the office. Does your wife do that?"

Frank drew on his pipe and looked gravely at his co-worker. "I hate to disappoint you, but Millie's a better cook."

"Ah ha! Ah ha! I have caught onto you, Frank Lamar," Cried Beth a little drunkenly. "You brought your wife here because you knew we would try to woo her, which is quite right and very clever because you also knew we would never try to woo you."

"I would hope not!" interjected Sharon, slapping at Beth's arm, her ponytail swinging dangerously. "We're married women!"

Doreen's curls bounced feverishly. "That's just the point. We don't need more single men running around, keeping the area uncivilized and unsuitable for raising children. We need family men." Once again, she patted her stomach and giggled.

Sharon cleared her throat. "Let it alone, Doreen."

Sharon Bowen's eyes narrowed to secretive slits as she asked Millie in a low voice. "You two haven't been together long, have you? A whirlwind courtship, quick marriage?"

"How can you tell?" Millie whispered back.

"The look in your eyes, like you are only beginning to fall in love. I married my husband just a few days after meeting him. The war does that."

"We wrote letters to each other first."

Sharon had the mannerisms of a woman with complete confidence in her abilities. This confidence wasn't the result of foolish pride. It was built on hardships, toil, and a refusal to accept defeat. You could see it in her eyes, already starting to form lines at the corners, and the stubborn tilt of her chin.

"I met Art at a party my hometown was sponsoring for the men going overseas. He was being assigned to Kodiak. I think I fell in love with him right away, although I'm not sure. I thought it was a brave, noble thing to do, going out to defend that terrible, wild frontier. He didn't even see any fighting though. Six months later, he was assigned to constructing the Campbell Creek encampment. Art never did see any action. It breaks his heart sometimes."

"You were a camp wife?"

"It's not the worst you could be. We basically lived in a tent village, but Anchorage was that way not many years ago, so we figured it couldn't be that bad. We built trenches, sewer lines, even cabins during the war, but the war never came to us. It gave us time to learn about each other, decide what we really wanted, and what we wanted was to stay."

The rest of the group continued talking among themselves. Only Ester listened in on Millie and Sharon's conversation.

She sighed as though Sharon had said something inappropriate and lifted her head, so her aquiline nose tilted straight up. "Beth always has her mind in the gutter yet talks of the uncivilized. If you desire a post for listening to gossip, then your first stop should be Beth's doorway."

She said this loudly enough for Beth to hear and respond with her own crisp observation. "And you should know. You have planted yourself there often enough."

Ester looked coldly away from her. "That's because there is nothing else to listen to. I don't spread it. I just absorb it, like listening to the news."

"Oh stop," said Sharon. "Or Millie will think we are all perfectly awful."

"Goodness!" Millie gasped. "I don't think that at all. I think you are all very nice."

"Do you see?" Beth beamed triumphantly and linked her arm with Charlie Bolinder's and smirked. "You must show them the property before someone else notices it and files a claim."

"Frank Lamar as a neighbor?" Charlie narrowed his eyes as though the matter took careful consideration and looked calculatingly at Ester, who was still trying her best to ignore her husband. "The man will prove insufferable, but he does have a lovely wife."

Frank whistled cheerfully in the parking lot after leaving the VFW party and continued whistling as they drove all the way back to the tiny cabin at the back of the Grant property. "What do you think?" He asked as they got out of the car.

She stepped gingerly over the sloughing snow and growing mud puddles. "It was fun. Do they all work in your office?"

"Alex Erichman does. That's Doreen's husband. He works in communications. And Charlie. He's an accountant. His desk is one row over from mine. Gary Hughes and Art Bowen both work construction"

"Gary is Beth's husband?"

"Quite a character, isn't she? Gary has his hands full with her. He says the biggest reason the Japanese never invaded Campbell Creek was because they didn't want to tangle with his wife."

"But they're civil service? They aren't contracted through a company?"

"They are civil service," he agreed.

She knitted her fingers together, thinking about her encounter with the Wolf Creek women. They had a lot in common, she realized. Their husbands worked together. They were homesteaders, all close to the same age. They had just begun to raise their families.

"I should spend more time at the lodge. They have all been there at one time or another. I just haven't spoken to anyone."

"You hadn't really met anyone except Solace. I thought..." He opened the cabin door and left it open, letting the setting sun flood in from its resting place across the inlet. She knew it was one of his staged, strategic moves, but it was effective. The thawing mountains were turning deep blue, the inlet heaved with broken ice, returning birds screeched triumphantly in the fading light. "It would be good to meet the gang."

He straightened his shirt around the collar and pulled at his cuffs, lining up the cuff links perfectly. "They are going to start having Thursday night meetings at the lodge and if you're interested... if it sounds good to you, we could join them."

"What kind of meetings?"

"To make things official. To put Wolf Creek on the map." He closed the door before it became too chilly. "You wanted to help build a town. This is our chance."

He sat down on the bed and patted the spot next to him. It was the one piece of furniture they owned. When they moved into the cabin, the bed springs had collapsed, and the mattress was thin, spoiled and smelled of countless woodsmen.

They had promptly bought a new bed and Solace had shrugged as they moved out the old one, "I reckon I'll turn one of the cabins into a double. The hunters don't care much about these things."

Millie sat beside him on their new, clean, sturdy bed and waited for him to put his arms around her. He didn't. "Is something wrong?" She asked.

"No." He laced his fingers through hers, squeezing her hand lightly. "Are you falling in love with me, Millie?"

She looked into his eyes. The showman was gone, leaving only dark, sad earnest query. His large ears stood out away from his large eyes like a boy who was both guilty and innocent.

He also looked anxious, as though it had only occurred to him that his affections might not always be wanted; that maybe he had over-stepped his boundaries.

Perhaps it was her fault. It had taken time to adjust to intimacies, even more time to respond. She didn't have good guidelines on intimate behavior. Cora would have insisted all five births were unexplained miracles if she could.

Emma was more mystified than Millie, and certainly not one of her three brothers were experts on womanly advice. With only one thing on their minds when they approached women, they were the ones who taught her to be wary. Only now did it begin to dawn on her that an intimate relationship was more than acceptance, more than response.

"Yes," she answered simply.

It was as though that was all he had ever wanted to hear. He leaned toward her tentatively. She pulled his head closer, clasping her hands around his neck and kissing him earnestly. His sigh was so deep, he nearly shuddered as he scooped her up and made love to her more passionately than he had their first night in the Redwoods.

Six

April had limited advantages for viewing property. The sun was returning, with longer, warmer days, but the evenings were still chilly. During the thaw and freeze of March, long icicles formed and dripped from the outside rafters, and the run-off from melting snow formed long streams that grew wider and flowed more freely with each passing day. By April, the world was mud delicious, as Frank liked to say, borrowing attitudes from a popular poet, the icicles gone.

Millie liked the word, "break-up". It adequately described this time of year hanging in limbo between winter and spring. It was ugly. It was messy. Raw earth battled with dirty, slumping patches of snow, winning the war against winter slowly, with snow flurries and cold snaps setting the warming trend back for days at a time before resuming, just like a messy divorce.

The great advantage was the naked trees. The hillside piece had a thick cover of cottonwood and birch. In the summer, the forest would be so dense, they would be unable to get a good idea of what the property held without traipsing its entire length and width. The leafless branches allowed them to see how the top of the hill rolled gently toward the mountainous foothills bordering the back, then spread languidly on both sides into lowering slopes.

There was good drainage, and there was water. Caught at the bottom of a rocky ledge of the foothills, a bubbling spring forced its way up from the cracks in the cliff, forming a small pool before diving underground again.

It wasn't any more, or any less eye appealing than several other plots Frank had diligently shown her, beginning with the hazardous bridge crossing, and ending at the edge of the Matanuska Valley, but none of these locations had a nearby hub of ready-made neighbors and Millie had a gregarious nature.

She also had a strong sense of loyalty. Solace had been the first friend she had made upon arriving in Alaska and continued to be her favorite go-to for advice or news. Solace knew everybody in the community and half the territory. She received word from "outside" through the truck drivers.

Although Frank patiently explained the difference between news and gossip, Millie disagreed. As far as Millie was concerned, Solace's information was as valuable as reading a newspaper. It kept her up to date on the world around her.

Solace didn't even wait for Millie to enter the lodge before questioning her. She trotted busily to the cabin on her strong, stout legs and began immediately to interrogate her. "What do you think? Did you walk the entire piece?"

"I did," said Millie, pulling off her boots and straightening her clothes. "It's very close to the Bolinder homestead."

"I said it would be like that. It's nice, though. You would be close to the other civil service workers."

"You shouldn't be so quick to let so many of our kind in," Millie said lightly. She turned to watch Frank fire up the stove. "We are organizers. We will be organizing parlor games and bingo, next."

"Hear now!" Growled Frank. He dumped a couple of logs into the stove and poked at them with a stick. "The Little Theater is a good idea. We don't have any other type of entertainment. We'll have to entertain ourselves."

"Do you see? Just as I said. Your entertainment will be organized for you. By and by, we will have crosswalks and traffic lights."

Solace shook her head. "Oh, it's not going to be a town! We'll never make a town out of this. If you want a town, go to Palmer or Anchorage. We're a community."

Millie crossed her arms and watched her husband fussing over the stove. "Did you know that, Frank?"

Now that the fire was roaring adequately, Frank straightened up and held his hands close to the heat. "Charlie and I have talked about it during lunch hour."

She tapped her foot. "I'm glad you've had an hour a day to talk things over with your neighbor. It seems in return; you could give an hour a day to talking things over with me."

"You didn't want to live in a community?" asked Solace with a twinge of anxiety.

"That's not the point at all." Millie took off her wet socks and put on some dry, woolen ones. "I have to re-evaluate Frank's ambitions. I had begun to think he had illusions of grandeur at the thought of becoming a property owner and was planning to turn it into a million- dollar estate."

"Oh, now I know you're joking," said Solace, after her first intake of breath. "But she is right about one thing, Frank. You should talk to her more. She has more sense than you do."

"I didn't want to influence her decision."

Solace clucked. "So, he says. Will you be at the meeting Thursday night?"

"Yes, we will," said Millie just a little loudly, answering for them both.

"You didn't want to influence me yet talked about it every day with Charlie at work?" Millie asked after Solace had left. She joined him at the wood stove, her hands thankfully absorbing the warmth, but she kept her brows hiked high enough to let him know he needed to form some type of communication.

Explaining himself in a communicative manner was not within his field of expertise. "That's not really influencing. We were discussing. There's a lot of things to consider if you're going to help form a community. Boundaries, bylaws, social agreements. We discuss these things. I didn't think you would be interested because you hadn't made a commitment."

"I haven't made a commitment because we haven't discussed it," Millie amended. "You can't just show me a piece of land and the wives of some of your fellow employees, then say, 'yep, she wants to be a community organizer.' You've got to let me in on what it's all about."

The meeting wasn't precisely a meeting if you measured such things as an assembly of people with official capacities, taking notes and passing motions. The group that gathered, drank coffee, soda, or beer, ate potato chips and gamy tasting hamburgers, and sometimes encouraged each other to sing songs. They talked about fishing or planting or construction work.

The biggest difference between this night and any other was that the tables had been pushed together, with one in the middle, and the rest forming a solid line at each side. Plumpish Beth Hughes slid into a seat across from Millie. "We aren't formal yet, but we intend to take things in hand this year," she said.

"How do you intend to do that?" asked Millie.

Two of the railroad workers, along with Betty Lou, were trying to catch with the same hand, quarters they were popping off their biceps. There was a gold miner peddling several pair of tiny gold nugget earrings.

Gary Hughes and Art Bowen were demonstrating how they managed to clear their land with their tractors.

"We're going to vote for a president," said Beth proudly.

"Well, then," said Millie. "You need someone to take the minutes."

Beth shifted in her seat and fluffed her recently permed hair. "What do you mean?"

"Someone who takes notes of the meeting. Who was elected, the decisions that were made; that sort of thing. That's when you are formal."

"Oh." She fluffed her hair some more and twisted a lock thoughtfully with her fingers. "I'll be right back."

In the length of time it took Beth to disappear into the Grant kitchen, Ester Bolinder seized the seat next to Millie. "What is Beth getting you into?" She asked, setting her teacup on the table. She sniffed at the Coca Cola Beth had left behind. "You know she laces all her drinks, don't you?"

"She won't be putting anything into mine," said Millie cheerfully. "I have three brothers, all with the same bad intentions."

"How fortunate then that you found an abstainer. Frank does abstain, doesn't he?"

"On most occasions."

Beth returned with a legal-length notepad, gummed at the top, and a ballpoint pen. "Solace had these behind the counter." She pushed them in front of Millie. "You can be our notetaker."

"No, no," protested Millie. "That takes a vote, too. The secretary does all that."

Beth gave her an exasperated look. "You aren't thinking. If we need a secretary to take a vote, how will we ever move forward if we don't have one?"

"Ester could run."

"No, I could not!" Said Ester. "I am five months along and don't have time to be handling secretarial things. And anyway, I'm not very good at taking notes."

"Then it's decided," said Beth. She stood up and tapped a spoon on the table. "While everyone was busy jabbering away, we've decided on our secretary. She's going to take notes on all of ya, so it's best you start talking about the things we came here to discuss instead of Aunt Mary's bladder infection."

"So drunk," whispered Ester with dismay to Millie. "But at least she is bringing things about."

The group that had been milling around, suddenly sat down at the tables and looked officially business-like. "When was it put to the vote?" asked someone from a far table.

Beth continued standing. "It's coming up now, but someone has to make a note of it so it's Millie. If anyone objects, raise their hand."

Since nobody had even thought about a secretary or what secretarial skills involved, nobody raised their hand. "There you have it, Millie. Start taking notes."

This was the cue Ester needed for proper meeting procedures. "I nominate Millie Lamar for secretary."

"All those in favor, say aye," said Beth, who hadn't sat down yet. They all said "aye" before Millie could open her mouth to make a single objection. Beth and Ester looked at her expectantly and Millie made a note that she had been elected unanimously as secretary.

The vote for president was just as easy. They all wanted Charlie Bolinder. The whole idea had been Charlie's after all when they thought about it. Always talking about what they needed and how they wouldn't get anything until they were recognized as an organized community.

There were a few voices raised in favor of a township, but they couldn't outweigh the five veteran families of Wolf Creek who voted unanimously for all Charlie's suggestions.

There were all the details, such as boundaries and land use, over which none had a great deal of expertise, but all had an opinion. "There ain't much of a question over use, is it?" asked Betty Lou. "Ain't much good for prospecting and only half-good for trapping. I think it's safe to say we'll use it as best we can."

"We're thinking about public lands for schools and such," explained Solace, who was keeping a tight rein on Betty Lou's drinking habits, which led to her other less socially acceptable behaviors. "It's already been registered as suitable farmland. We just need to decide where to put what."

"Well, I'll be," said Betty Lou. "Wolf Creek keep getting fancier by the year. I hope you know what you're doing, Mr. President Charlie. We might start boundrying ourselves right out of a home."

Mr. President Charlie nodded as though glad she had brought up the subject. "That's why we are all gathered together tonight; to make sure nobody ever loses anything. We protect each other."

Frank went down to the claims office on Monday morning and paid one hundred dollars to file for his homesite. Two weeks later, he hit a snag. Word had gotten out that Frank Lamar had filed on a trapper's claim. Ted Ewing was coming to take it back.

Millie learned the news first from Solace while helping her with pastries.

"Yep, he was in here," said Solace. "Trash talking and pushing his weight around. His kind don't stay in one place very long. They don't settle down and make families. He had more than enough time to make something of that piece of land and he did nothing. Don't worry about a thing. He ain't getting it."

"But if he has a legal claim on it..."

"He doesn't, because he never lived there."

It was all Wolf Creek talked about that day. Visitors who didn't ordinarily make their appearance more than once or twice a month, found special reason to drop by for needed services.

They stuck around to listen to the heated discussion. Those who had lived in the area long enough to remember, said Ted had put the claim on the land, clear as day, and even popped some markers into place, but the most he had ever done with it was put up a canvas tent for a few days before moving on.

"He said it wasn't worth his time trapping in these woods anymore," said Betty Lou. "The best pelts are further north, but he wanted a place he could drop in that was close to Anchorage. Sort of a home away from home."

"Except he never did make a home of it, did he?" SniffedSolace loudly. "Six years he's been away and suddenly he's all interested in making a go at settling down. I gave him good trade, more than his furs were worth, but he always took what he got with him. Never stuck around long enough to share much with anyone."

"Well, no," admitted Betty Lou. "He weren't the sharing kind. Mainly, he put out for hooch and a village woman. He left a fox in a trap so long, I took pity and let it go. It was one of them box traps. The poor critter was starving. He never had a good mind as to where he left those things."

"But it were his land," said a gold prospector who was only prospecting enough to get by on a daily basis. "It ain't no matter he hasn't lived on it."

The big guns were moving in. The arguments that had been shifting back and forth all day began evaporating with the appearance of the first veteran to step in on his way home from work, Alex Erichman. Alex generally commanded the respect of the community.

He was a pencil pusher, but he was also a big man with a strong build. He built his house with his own hands and taught himself to drive a tow truck. He was always straight-forward in what he had to say, and he was being straight-forward now.

"It does matter. It's in the territorial agreement. He has to live on it before it's his."

"Maybe he was planning on living on it," said Betty Lou, who felt obligated to present an argument for the sake of an old friend.

"The Lamars were planning on it too. Even paid for the deed." Solace leaned across the counter, staring down her adversary.

Betty Lou backed away hastily. "There's no need to get hostile about it. I was just thinking it's a little sad for old Ted but if I could choose my neighbors, I suppose I'd druthers choose the Lamars."

There wasn't much hostility floating around the trading post. Solace and Zeb Grant, proprietors of this establishment everyone was fond of frequenting, joined the solid five-family block of civil service workers who made it clear which settlers they supported.

Ted Ewing's friends took their fight to the courthouse, where they demanded the deed be revoked in the name of fair play. Frank responded by arriving with his civil service friends, who also made a plaintive case.

Their testimony as landowners with neighboring lots, asserted in the entire time they had lived there, they had never seen Ted Ewing step foot on the vacant parcel. They also pointed out that the purpose of the United States Government in creating the Homestead Act was to encourage permanent settlement, not vagrancy.

This pointing out was done primarily by Charlie Bolinder, who was very pleased with his acting-attorney presence.

His statement created an enormous amount of objection from Ted, who contended Bolinder's statement by declaring the recent homesteaders could not possibly have known his reasons for filing the Wolf Creek claim.

Glancing at a paper that was apparently a guide to the things he should say, he added, "one can become tied up with other obligations and unforeseen circumstances. I don't feel I have to justify my absence, but it had never been my intention to leave it in a state of complete neglect."

He then brought forth his witnesses; several long-term residents, primarily trappers; to back his statement and agree he had filed with full intention of developing it but had fallen into several unforeseen difficulties that had hindered his efforts.

In the end, even the judge was unable to make a direct decision. He listened patiently as both sides reached their conclusion. He wrung his hands many times, then said, "the parcel is currently vacant, but has two legal claims to it. Ted Ewing, you filed seven years ago and have had plenty of time to develop it to code but have neglected to do so." He looked down at his paperwork, more to take a breath than to read the contents.

He glanced up, holding his official papers like a shield. "Now, your witnesses claim that you were on the property between 1940-1942 and that you did indeed build a structure on it, but the roof caved in the first winter…"

"An unreasonable amount of snow that year, your honor." Volunteered Ted.

"It would seem so. The roof was not repaired and there was another two- year lapse before anyone saw you again."

"Extenuating circumstances. I broke my leg in a skiing accident," he explained.

"It laid you up for two years?"

"Then there was the matter of my father's funeral. My family felt very bereaved, your honor."

"I see." The judge drew in his chin until it doubled up over his neck and laced his hands over his substantial waist. "Francis Lamar, you have filed a claim on good faith, and I am not insensitive to your desires to be close to your co-workers. I thank you for your continuing service to our country. However, I cannot deny Mr. Ewing a fair opportunity for recovering what appears to be an oversight in the land's office registry."

Having said this, he rubbed his nose, shuffled the papers together and cleared his throat. "In the spirit of the Homestead Act, which requires the owner to live on the property and develop twenty percent, I've reached this decision. Since no land has been cleared and there is no structure, the first person to clear a portion of the land and place a habitable dwelling that is not a tent, shall be awarded the parcel." He tapped his hammer. "Good luck to you both."

Only one thing occupied the minds of the pioneers who collected for the Thursday night meeting - moving the Lamars onto the property as quickly as possible. This was accomplished in a single weekend. Saturday morning, bright and early, Millie and Frank got in their car and joined the procession trundling toward the disputed claim.

It looked like a parade, with the Hughes tractor leading it. The tractor was followed by a pick-up truck carrying a plow and another with a winch attached in front. Taking up the rear was Sharon Bowen, driving the family car, Betty Lou in a battered Volkswagen, and the Lamars in their Studebaker.

The tractor carved out a driveway and the plow truck smoothed it out. Wielding their axes and chainsaws, the men shaved away the top of the hill of all unwanted trees, while the women swung machetes, clearing away the brush. The saplings were yanked out by the roots, using the winch, while the tractor scraped away the earth, leaving nothing but the raw tree stumps.

The next problem was a shelter. They stripped and stacked the logs they had cut, but it was green wood and not yet suitable for lumber. After pushing back his cap and scratching his head, Alex Erichman came up with an idea.

"I've got a military Quonset hut I plan to turn into my carpentry shop, but I haven't done anything with it yet. It's just a shell, broken glass in the windows, no door for the entry, no floor, but you can snug it up and make it work for spring."

They made it work. The next day, Alex and crew put the Quonset hut on a flatbed, hitched it to Gary Hughes' tractor, creaked up the freshly made driveway and plopped the hut down in the center of the clearing. A platform that served as a floor, was made by nailing plywood to a framework of two by sixes. Old blankets were donated to put over the windows and across the doorway, and a tin Lizzy, made from an oil barrel, served for their heat. The only furniture they had was the new bed they had bought for the cabin, but it was enough. Spring was here and Millie had very good camping skills.

The old wool army blanket fluttered in the door-less entry to the Quonset hut, revealing the troubled April sky in short frames. How its mood changed! Sometimes bringing warm showers, sometimes snow flurries. Sometimes, as though crying for days, it suddenly sat up in bed, yawned and decided to be warm and sunny. Today, it was sulking, with occasional tantrum bursts of freshly whipped up snow to show its displeasure with whatever gods or forces may be annoying it.

All that haste and noise! All that scrambling to move themselves, lock, stock, and barrel onto a piece of undeveloped land, and now; nothing. They had been living on their property for six days, cooking their meals over a campfire, piling together usable firewood, sweeping the mud away from the door, boiling water and cleaning. She had counted them. Six days, and not one time had she seen Ted Ewing step on the property. She almost believed he wouldn't, but knew it was just a trifling fancy. He had fought as hard as they had in the courts. He would be here.

An extra gust of wind shook the blanket, whipping it noisily, and Millie rubbed her arms. She had been daydreaming and the fire was burning low. She stoked it back up and poured herself a second cup of coffee. She would have to go out soon and pile more of the ground litter of sawed-off branches and splintered pieces of trees close to the entrance of the hut.

It would be their firewood until it was gone. By then, the usable logs would be stacked for lumber, and the inferior ones cut and split.

Millie liked working outdoors. She liked working with her hands, turning soil, making things grow. She liked helping to clear the land, to shape it, to give it purpose. Once the wind had died down and she no longer had an excuse for idling, Millie put on her work gloves and went outside.

It wasn't the most inspirational time of year for landscape development, nor was her immediate environment very enthusiastic about kindling utopic visions. It was rather dreary, with some of the fallen trees still tumbling this way and that, and not a single sign of virulent life.

Still, she was convinced it would look much tidier with the ground litter cleared, not to mention the cheerful usefulness it served them in the chilly evenings.

She hummed, as she often did while outdoors working, bursting occasionally into a few lines from a favorite song before bending over a particularly large branch or gathering a stack to bring back to the hut.

She was singing, and on the verge of carrying back a fine collection of stout branches that would burn for hours, when she received a strong feeling that she was not alone.

Continuing with her chore, she turned as she reached the entry way of the hut and looked in the direction of the road. He was coming up the driveway, a tall, shambling man, with a flourishing beard and red, prominent ears.

"Good day, ma'am," he said, touching his cap but not removing it. "I hope you've been doing well."

She set her bundle carefully next to the entrance. "It's been fair to middling. And you, Mr. Ewing?"

"It wouldn't bother me none to be doing better. Touch of flu going around, I believe. It kept me under the weather for days. It don't seem to have laid up you or your husband none."

"We both have fearful constitutions, Mr. Ewing. Brought on, I believe, by temperance and a healthy diet."

"I've heard as much. Of course, such energy could also be brought on by friends. You seem to have a few of them, Mrs. Lamar."

"I've been most fortunate in that respect. Did you have business you wish to discuss with me, Mr. Ewing?"

"I thought that I might. Saw the smoke coming from your chimney." He craned his head to peer inside the entry way. "I don't suppose you could spare a cup of coffee?"

Her eyes followed his and only then remembered the rifle Frank had left leaning near the entrance. "Not that I expect trouble," he had told her, showing her how to load and cock it for firing. "But it's better to be prepared than to be sorry." It appeared and disappeared now behind the flap, just inches from her hand.

Millie smiled. "It certainly is a chilly day, but it would be improper for a single man to enter the home of a married woman, especially one who is only an acquaintance. Why don't I bring a cup of coffee out for you, so we can chat and be sociable?"

"Are you going to carry that rifle with you?"

She gave him a surprised look. "Should I?"

"Well, no. That's not necessary. I don't want no trouble. I'll just stand right here and wait for you to come back outside."

Millie went inside and poured the two cups of coffee. When she returned, Ted was livening up the campfire. She handed him his cup and went back to the hut, returning with the two folding chairs. She sat across from him cordially and talked about the possibilities of a warm summer. When Frank returned home from work, the two were still talking sociably and poking sticks at the campfire.

"Good evening, Mr. Lamar," greeted Ted. "It's an hour yet before the bus leaves for town and your wife invited me to dinner."

Frank glanced at his wife, who was serenely entering the Quonset after giving him a kiss and patting his shoulder. "I'm sure she made plenty to go around. It's been unseasonably cold for April, hasn't it?"

Millie brought out the thick moose stew that had been bubbling in the Dutch Oven all day, and Ted wolfed down his portion in giant mouthfuls, his hand wrapped around his spoon like a shovel.

"Neah," he said. "That's how April is, never can decide to be a winter month or settle down to spring. It don't really happen until May. May is the big month. May is when construction starts. Everyone waits until May to build."

"Lamars aren't very good at waiting," chuckled Frank, repeating what Millie was beginning to suspect he fancied as his motto. "What about it, Ted? Do you have any plans?

Ted Ewing shook his head. "Can't say that I have. I guess you won, fair and square, Frank." He finished his plate hurriedly, wiped the remnants from his beard and checked his watch. "It was my foolishness," he said as he was leaving. "I should have gotten a good woman. They put the devil in you to do good things."

The next morning, spring came. It uncurled over the landscape like a soft, fuzzy cat. It was as deliciously fresh as nectar. Three days after its first sweet breath, tiny tufts of greenery began sprouting in the scraped earth, and life began to spread in unfurling buds.

Millie opened the flap over the entrance way of the hut to let the sun in and began tidying the walkway with stones. The ground litter was cleared, the freshly cut firewood stacked, and with the completion of each task, her spontaneous burst of joyful song became louder and more frequent.

Part II

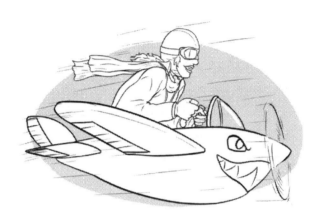

Andrea

Seven

Andy couldn't hear his voice above the gears and groaning complaints of the hydraulic shovel until he stood directly to the side of the tractor and waved his arms.

"Stop! Stop! You're digging a hole! Blame it, Andrea, can't you tell by now the soil's too soft? You're not going to hit hard pan. It's filling up with water."

She jumped down from the seat and frowned as she looked at the mess she had created. The black, loamy soil had caved on all sides, with water bubbling up from a hidden stream and spreading out in a long pool. "Jimmy marked it out."

"Jimmy was wrong and you're the eldest. I expect better of you."

She wiped her face and looked around hopefully. It seemed all the same to her. Wild grass sprouted liberally among berry bushes and wildflowers. Even with the recently downed trees, it was difficult to see what the land looked like below the greenery. "Then where?"

Pop Delaney pointed at his head and spread his mouth wide to show all his teeth when he answered. "Think. Think. Over there, where the trees are thinner, the soil is rockier. Never mind. I'll do it myself. You go help your mother."

She scowled at him stubbornly. "Mama's got plenty of help. We need to get the land cleared and the logs peeled. I can do one or the other."

"Go help Jimmy peel logs. You were digging us a swimming pool at the rate you were going."

He hitched up his overalls at the hips and swung himself into the cab of the tractor. "Cursed is the man with three daughters and only one son. You might have kept yourself married. We could use another male helping out."

"Jake is more inclined to help himself. He would have been no use to you, pop."

"I would like to have to have seen for myself."

The idling tractor growled back to life and rumbled a forty-five- degree angle away from the soggy rupture Andy had made in the ground. She watched him test the earth until he found an area of loose gravel mixed with topsoil and began scraping it down to the hard pan. It wasn't that he was any better than she was with the tractor. He just knew where to dig. She turned to join her brother.

He grinned when he saw her coming. "Did you get fired?" He asked.

"You know I did. You did that on purpose, didn't you? You knew it was wetland."

"I didn't want pop helping me with the saw. You know he drives me crazy."

"Huh." She gripped one end of the double-handled saw and pushed gently back and forth, against the blade, in rhythm with her brother.

They could feel the teeth dig in through the vibration and lifted the saw lightly and gently, so the teeth would cut and not bite and chew. It was a rhythm they had shared since childhood when they could barely raise the long-bladed tool between them and settle it over a log. Smoothly and obediently, the branches of the tree fell away, and the bark peeled back, leaving their log straight and shaved.

"You know I like driving," she said.

"I know you do, Andy. And flying. You're not the only one who wants to have fun."

"This is your sweet revenge. I should have guessed it. Sibling rivalry. It's not my fault if you're not pretty enough to find an airplane pilot."

They picked up the ends of the log and set it in the crib with several others, all clean and shaven, all straight as an arrow, all ready to be notched and assembled. Jimmy propped the heavy end of another on the work bench.

"Oh, I reckon I'm pretty enough," he said. "I just haven't found any lady pilots."

"They're around. You've gotta know where to look. I can guarantee they're not popping up behind cranberry bushes."

"Are you sure about that?" Jimmy had stopped sawing and was now looking at the grove of trees that swelled gently back and reached for the line of foothills marching steadily up the mountains.

It was an unusual sight, but at the same time, seemed quite natural. A young woman was coming toward them, cutting her own trail through the underbrush of wild berries and short willow bushes.

She was a medium-sized woman, with a wide sturdy frame and a head full of thick, dark curls, tied back loosely in a bandana. She was pretty; actually; very pleasant to look upon. Her forehead was smooth, her brows slightly arched, the faint beginnings of crow's feet lifted her eyes upward in a friendly sparkle. Her lips formed a long, perpetual smile.

If I was a man, thought Andrea, I would want to kiss those lips. They curved so invitingly, yet innocently, completely unaware of their seductive charm.

She wore the typical work clothes of the wilderness woman; a pair of dungarees and a baggy men's plaid shirt; yet she also wore a pair of nice, cotton, roll-over socks and penny loafers on her shapely ankles and feet. Such a delicate touch canceled out the robust image and left her looking like a lady experimenting with rough and tumble play.

She carried in her hands a package covered loosely with a large paper bag. From the way she handled it, the package was fragile and entailed every bit of her effort to keep it intact. "Good afternoon," she called. "Have you had lunch yet?"

Her presence was so unforeseen, that everyone stopped in the middle of what they were doing and looked in the direction of the speaker. Everyone except Owen Delaney. Still driving his tractor back and forth, trying to create a level patch of land for their foundation in the bumpy terrain, he never even looked up as the others took a few hesitant steps forward and the newcomer walked a few more steps toward them.

"The dishes were all washed and put away an hour ago," said Mama Velma, drying her hands on her apron. "We've started the makings of dinner now, but you're welcome to a cup of coffee."

"That's right neighborly of you," the lady said in happy agreement. "May I set this here?" She indicated the recently scrubbed table that was now filling up with bowls of vegetables and potatoes. Without waiting for a reply, she set the package down in a clear spot and removed the paper bag. Her revelation was a freshly baked cake spread with a thin layer of icing.

Velma's perpetually suspicious expression cleared, and she waved her hand at her charges to take a break. She didn't need to wave a second time. They practically swarmed the table as they sat down expectantly, waiting for their treat, and looking over the newcomer with curiosity.

"My name is Millie Lamar," said the young woman, not at all intimidated by five pairs of staring eyes. "I live just up the hill. You can take the driveway to it, but it's shorter through the woods."

The tractor still snarled and moaned in the background. Andrea, who had the strongest, most carrying voice, stood up and waved her arms. "Pop, get over here and meet your new neighbor!"

He looked in their direction then, but in his typical un-hurried manner, ran the tractor over the patch a couple more times, throttled it down to an idle and let it rumble a few seconds before turning off the engine.

"You've certainly been busy here," Millie said, looking around her.

"Uh, it looks like a gypsy camp," said Andrea, sitting back down.

"It's not as though you don't like it," Mama Velma reminded her and turned to Millie. "She has a gypsy soul, that one. There is no telling what will become of it but at least it inhabits the body of a hard worker."

"Idle hands are the devil's play," Millie agreed, but in a light, merry voice, as though completely unconcerned with who may or may not be idle.

108

As the older of the three women packed closely together around the table, drinking coffee and eating cake, Velma felt entitled to scold Millie for her flippancy.

"If you believe the devil isn't a hard worker, you are naïve. He is very busy, and I don't doubt there are times when my daughter aids and abets him."

Andrea gave Millie a sardonic smile. "I have a low approval rating with mama. Don't worry. I'm not really out to corrupt anyone, only myself."

"She will do that too," added Jimmy between bites of the cake. "She is determined but she makes herself useful."

Their neighbor continued to eye Andrea as though she had discovered a new friend.

They were of the same age, or close to it, certainly, and had the same stubborn stance of an independent woman.

Andy shook her head. "My family has lost all perspective of good manners. We've eaten half this kind woman's cake and haven't even made introductions."

Half-rising from the table, she pointed to each one. "Meet my mother, Velma, my father who doesn't hear very well, Owen, my brother who hears only too well, Jimmy, and my two little sisters, Anna and Carol. The baby in the cardboard box over there is my son, Ben. I'm Andrea, but my friends call me Andy."

The young woman dimpled with delight and exclaimed,"Oh! You have a baby! I do too! How old is he?"

"He'll be ten months next week."

"Little Jason is nearly eight months. We must let them play together. Is your husband at work?"

Andrea concentrated on chasing around a piece of cake. Scooping it to her lips, she lifted her face and looked steadily at the visitor. "I have no idea. I haven't seen him in three months."

"I see." Unsure whether to express sympathy or distress, Millie shook away both expressions and said cheerfully, "well, these things happen and always for a reason. I just wanted to welcome you to Wolf Creek."

She helped herself to fresh coffee from the pot placed in the center of the table. "Construction has been going on all spring, so I thought when I first heard the sounds below us, the Erichmans or the Hughes were doing some more building.

They're Civil Service employees but they're always looking around for other ways to make money. Not Frank, though. He's white collar and likes it that way."

She sipped her coffee as daintily as though she was drinking from a teacup. "I finally mentioned to Frank that there seems to be a lot of noise at the bottom of the hill. That's when he told me some new people have moved in. Can you believe it? You've been here all week and Frank only just told me we have new neighbors."

"I hope we didn't disturb you," said Andrea, not sure whether Millie was complaining about their noise or about her husband.

She set her cup down, eyes widening. "Oh heavens! Not disturbed at all! I've been wanting close neighbors. There are the Bolinders but they're nearly half a mile away. That's why I baked a cake. And to punish Frank, I left him home to take care of Jason."

Velma cleared her throat. "You entrusted your husband with the care of a seven-month- old baby?"

"Oh, not completely," she answered, shrugging with graceful ease. "He doesn't have a clue as to how to change a diaper and his only solution to when a baby cries, is to stick a bottle in its mouth. But at least I can be reassured Jason will not crawl off to join the wolves while I am away."

"I haven't seen any wolves," said Jimmy.

"I don't expect that you would. They've been hunted out mostly, except those that live higher up the mountains. Just the same, they come around now and then. If you have any dogs, they'll have at them."

"We didn't bring any pets," said Andrea quickly, knowing it was a sore spot with the family. They had given away Carol's cat, her mother's small, wire-haired terrier and Jimmy's blue-tick hound before they had left.

Owen had said it was a waste of energy and resources to carry pets up the Alcan. Although it broke their hearts, they had all agreed, except the two youngest girls, who felt the family should have been more loyal to their animals.

She added, "But if a wolf comes around, I'm sure the girls would try to adopt it."

Millie nodded as though that was the normal way of young girls. "If they're so interested, it happens there are a couple of wolf hybrids at the trading post. They attract the tourists. That's what Solace tells me. But she breeds them as well. The dog mushers like a little wolf blood in their dogs."

Velma fanned herself as though overcome with the information. "I'm not sure it's the sort of place I want my girls to visit. I suppose they have bear handlers as well."

The seasoned settler put down her coffee and stared at Mama Velma with her enthusiastic eyes.

"Oh, but you must! Everybody goes there. It's where we get our mail, do our laundry, pick up a few staples so we don't have to go to Anchorage. It's not far, only a mile up the road. You can walk it."

Having cleaned her plate of the last bite, Millie stood up and looked at her watch. It was a very nice, slim-band lady's watch that accessorized well with her gold wedding ring and was every bit as incongruous with her rumble and tumble wear as her dainty socks and slippers. "I'd better get back now. I have Jason's bowel movements timed. They are as regular as clockwork. I only wish I could say the same about myself."

"Don't forget your platter," said Andrea, leaping up and trying her best to remember the etiquette of a gracious hostess. For all her strangeness, there was something very cultivated about Millie. Something that made you want to be polite.

"Bring it back to me later," she suggested. "You still have two more pieces of cake on it. It will give you an excuse to visit me."

"Are there any boys at Wolf Creek?" chimed Carol, the older of the youngsters.

Carol had recently turned fourteen. Her blonde hair was slowly changing to ginger, with tendrils that curled around her heart-shaped face. Her chunky legs had found curves and two small, pointy breasts were pushing against her blouse. Because of her changes, she believed the only ones who understood her were boys.

Neighborly Millie studied Carol a moment, estimating her age and most probable interests. She gave Carol a pitying glance.

"Not a lot of young boys, that is boys around your age. Most of the settlers haven't been here long and are just starting their families. Solace and Zeb have two, though. One is in his late teens, the other in his twenties, but the oldest doesn't live at home anymore, only Ed."

Carol slumped extravagantly and Millie fished around for some words of cheer.

"She has a daughter just a little older than you, though. Oh, maybe fifteen or sixteen. The Grants been here the longest of any of us and started the post more than ten years ago."

Carol cheered only slightly, so Millie thought some more. "There's a railroad worker living in the bottom land who has a teenaged boy. He comes up with his dad to visit the post and stays around to visit Ed and Bea. Then there's a trapper at the lower end who married in with a Native family. He has a lot of boys. I don't even know how many, but they are not to be dismissed. He's not the usual kind of trapper. He stays in one spot. He works at odd jobs. He traps furs for his wife, and she makes them into clothing. Very respectable all the way around and he's teaching his boys to be hard workers. The oldest is around your age."

"Trappers, traders and railroad workers!" Cried Velma. "Are any of them Christian?"

"I believe they all are, although I never asked. They behave themselves. That's what's important. Oh!" Millie added as she was leaving, "I'm sorry to disappoint the girls but there aren't any bear tamers here."

Velma Delaney waited until Millie was out of earshot, then said, "there now. That's a good Irish woman. She knows how to handle her husband. You could learn a lot from her, Andrea. Jimmy and Owen can have the last two pieces of cake. The girls can lick the platter if they wash it; and I want it washed well, with plenty of soap and hot water. And when they are done..." Velma took Andy by the sleeve. "You can return it and gain a few points from your new neighbor."

Andrea didn't really know what Millie could teach her about men that her mother could not. Owen was at liberty to growl and grumble all he wanted, but he never opposed her

Ultimatum. Velma Delaney pulled ultimatums from the air as randomly as butterflies.

Not all of them were consistent. Some directly opposed each other. You knew it was an ultimatum when the threat "or else" was tacked to the end of a sentence.

Velma never clarified what "or else" signified, but it was safe to assume non-compliance meant she would pull down the fires of hell around them.

Presently, Owen was basking in his wife's benevolence, finishing off his second piece of cake with relish. If he didn't return to his tractor within ten minutes of polishing off his coffee, however, he would hear a dire ultimatum, so he did not take his privilege lightly.

"Never did cotton much to white collar men," he remarked. "But the wife seems fine."

"You don't cotton much to anyone, pop," Andrea answered. "So, I don't see how the color of his shirt is going to make a difference."

She lit a cigarette and watched Jimmy wolf down the rest of his treat. "Hurry up now," she told him. "I want to get a couple more of those logs skinned before going into town tonight."

"And the platter?" objected Velma.

"The platter can wait until tomorrow. It will be better that way. I can visit Millie while her husband's at work. Jake was supposed to fly in the rest of our things. They should be at the airport by now."

"I'm glad he came out good for something," said Velma, encouraging her husband to go back to his chores by giving him little jabs with her finger. She gathered up his plate, finished or not and added it to the stack. "Wash all the dishes," she called to the two girls who had already begun to stoke up the fire. "There's no sense in wasting water."

The girls didn't believe in wasting anything. They found a few crumbs left on the plates and had made themselves a beverage with the left-over coffee, some milk, and several spoons of sugar. Carol would become fat if she didn't take care. Anna was built like Andrea; thin, with extra- long legs and the nervous prancing of a filly.

She would fill out more slowly and she would grow impatient as she waited for her straight up and down frame to acquire bumps and curves. At eleven, she didn't care. She was more interested in tadpoles and kittens, but her day was coming more rapidly than Andrea cared to think about. Delaney girls attracted men. It wasn't their fault. It was in their genes. Once Delaney girls were equally attracted, there were always problems. Andrea could see it in Carol. It wouldn't be long before it was apparent in Anna.

"Carol wants me to buy her a bottle of fingernail polish," Andrea remarked when she and Jimmy settled once more with their long-bladed saw. "Mama's already upset because the brat gets into mine and even tries out my make-up."

"You might as well buy it for her," said Jimmy mildly. "She helps you out a lot with Ben. You should start paying her for babysitting."

"I will once I get a job. We're all living on a shoestring right now."

The saw hummed between them like a melody. It was a nice location. Small, wild animals rustled through the brush. A variety of birds called from the trees. The foothills rolled away from a long, sweeping meadow that was beginning to blush with June flowers.

June was a nice month. She had been told, in Alaska, June was the nicest month of the year. It didn't rain much in June. The days were warm, and the sun never set. "He's never going to give you a dime," remarked Jimmy. "I don't know why you don't just give up on him."

She shoved the blade toward him. "We should discuss things. That's all I'm asking."

"He abandoned you."

"We got in a fight."

He pushed back, his end whining a bit with the force.

"He left you and the baby for six weeks in that shabby Denver apartment, with no money and no food. We had to come and get you."

Andrea rammed the blade forward savagely. "Well, he told me there had been an unexpected flight change. He had a two-week lay-over in Seattle."

114

The blade stopped. "He could have wired you money. He did nothing, Andy."

She sniffed. "I guess it doesn't matter now. I'm a fallen woman. I should probably check on the trading post. If the girls get in trouble, I'll be blamed."

He grinned and mopped at his brow. "I guess I'm going to have to do something to take mama's attention off you all the time."

"Bite your tongue! Anything you do, she'll blame on me." She picked up her end of the saw again and pushed it with more kindness and less vigor.

"Then I'll have to get married. Maybe send to Colorado for Glenda Taylor. She was my childhood sweetheart. I could marry her." The saw sang lightly as it slid back.

"Didn't she get religion a few years ago?"

"It won't bother me. She rides horses. She hunts. A bit of religion won't hurt. Mama gets religion every night."

"Don't do it for me, Jimmy. You're young. Look around a while."

"I'm in no hurry, just sort of speculating on the future. What if I don't find a girl around here?"

"You don't know until you look."

"I should go into town with you."

He said it casually, never breaking the rhythm that kept the saw gently humming.

"I could use the company."

Velma didn't really have to worry about conserving water. She just didn't like dirty dishes.

A creek divided the property nearly in half as it ran toward the highway, then dropped underground. It wasn't a very large creek. They had traced it into the meadow where it disappeared again just before the timberline.

But the water was clear, sparkling, and plentiful. They made generous use of it for cooking, cleaning, and bathing. When Jimmy and Andrea wrapped up work for the day, they both heated a large pot of water and scrubbed down.

Velma seemed perturbed when she saw them in clean clothes, their hair washed and combed back, fingernails scrubbed and wearing their Sunday shoes. She crossed her arms over her chest and frowned.

"Don't go out to those Anchorage bars," she warned. "I've heard all about them. They've got gunslingers."

Andrea opened her jacket and held up her arms, rotating her eyes upward, then around. "We're not bringing six-shooters, mama. All we're going to do is pick up some crates from the airport and maybe stop by the trading post on the way home to see how it is."

Owen followed the two out to the truck, mumbling to himself. As Andrea opened the driver's door, he took her arm and said brusquely, "Don't let that boy get into any trouble."

Eight

The truck was named "Abe". Nobody knew why, except the truck legally belonged to Andrea and that was what she had named it. If she didn't give it the loving care of a woman concerned about Abe's grooming, she did look after its general health. The truck fired up on a dime and purred like a kitten. If there was a single misfire, she was under the hood, checking the fluids, points, and plugs. She wasn't a mechanic, but she was a firm believer in maintenance. The truck would run solid until it blew a gasket or cracked the engine block.

It was the first solid piece of personal property she had bought since leaving Jake. The day she had left Denver ... the day she had to eat humble pie and admit she had been abandoned by the man who had sworn he loved her... When she had to call her parents to rescue her...That was the day she had sworn to herself as the family car trundled up the road toward Aspen, that she would never again be left without a mode of transportation. She would never again rely on anyone except herself.

The truck had proven useful from the beginning. The farm, ravaged by the Depression, was in its last stages of disease. Fences and barns were patchwork affairs and even the house had given up on reconstruction. If it was falling, it was propped. If it had already fallen, it stayed where it was at. It was worth more to sell to the new generation moving in than to repair anything.

The new generation had no interest in farms, only skiing. They clustered around the town of Aspen, built their winter homes there and collected in drovesto go skiing.

If they could buy a farm thirteen miles outside of town, plop down a custom-built, two-story house, with blueprints approved and stamped by the bank, they were fine with it.

While pop Delaney negotiated for a fair bill of sale on a farm that would be plowed under and resurrected as an upper-class home with a bed and breakfast, Andrea caught a ride each day to Aspen to work at one of the ski resort's restaurants as a waitress. The pay was shamelessly modest, but the tips were good. In the four months it took them to sell off the farm and the least crucial of their belongings, Andrea had accumulated enough money to buy the truck and have a small, tidy nest egg, an egg that was now shrinking at an uncomfortable rate.

Everything along the Alcan had been expensive. Gas and food prices crept higher the further north they went. Their journey had been slowed by sleet, rain, potholes and wash outs in the dirt and gravel road, flat tires and the most enormous mountain range Andrea had ever seen.

Twice the Buick broke down, once when it overheated climbing to the top of a ridge that seemed to have no ending, and once when the alternator belt broke.

They patched the Buick as best they could, then laid over at a White Horse service station for three days while the lady was properly doctored. That's what they said about the Buick. She was a lady. She was mama's car, with thick, velvety cushions and a velvet rope behind the front seats. The lady was treated like royalty, while Abe, overloaded with a tractor, farm tools, mama Delaney's sewing machine, and various pieces of furniture, was treated like a beast of burden, but he never once broke down.

In all fairness, the lady was never meant for such a journey. She was large and bull-headed, with a great, rounded nose, and would have been able to take the entire family up the Alcan with ease, if she had not been weighed down with her own bundles of luggage attached to the top and had not been pulling a twenty-foot travel trailer, also crammed with their general needs. They had lived out of the tiny camping unit throughout the entire trip and were so grateful to raise tents and tarps for cleaning and cooking and for sleeping in the open.

Only Owen, Edna (Velma) and Ben slept in the trailer now. The rest of them lived in tents.

This was the first time she had driven the truck since unloading it at their new homestead. Abe seemed to be as happy for his liberation as she was, bouncing along the road cheerfully. She cranked the engine into third gear, watching the scenery whiz by even quicker.

"Are you sure you know where to find the airport?" asked Jimmy.

"Anchorage isn't big enough to hide an airport," Andrea answered saucily. "Pop says it's simple. There's only this road and it leads you right to it. It's directly at the beginning of town."

He rolled down his window and propped up his elbow. "Slow down, Andy. I want to see where we live, not fly by it."

She slowed. There wasn't a lot to see if you were looking for signs of development, but the scenery was nice. It was water-rich, filled with lakes and rivers. The hills tumbled over the top of each other, some falling away with a view of the inlet, others rolling back in a steady march toward the mountain range.

"I reckon it's good for hunting," he said with a note of satisfaction.

"Is that what you're thinking about?"

"There's a lot of quail around the homestead. I was thinking of hunting down a few. It would be like eating chicken."

"I got tired of eating out of cans."

"Yeah. The Alcan wasn't a lot of fun."

Anchorage was very much as Andrea had visualized it, a raw, fledging town with new shops springing up, glistening with fresh coats of paint, some squat, moldering cabins built when the land was first settled, a blend of modernization and lawlessness lurking through the streets, some dimly lit, others shining brightly. The Wild North.

The airport was brighter lit than the rest of the town. New buildings huddled up close to it as though seeking its visible warmth. In the mid-summer, with its half-hearted stab at dusk, the main offices to the airport terminal faced the wavering sunlight, drinking in its last rays that flattened dully to ochre for several twilit minutes before creeping triumphantly into the sky once more. The glass panels flared back the brilliant colors.

The saturation of light made this central hub look alive and busy at all hours, even when there was nothing more than a skeleton crew. Cessna's and cubs snuggled alongside fat cargo planes, and a whistling commercial airplane rolled down the runway, guided by flashlights and red flags. Another plane squatted, rumbling, waiting for the signal to take off.

The waiting room, however, was practically empty. There was a family of three folded into plastic seats, their seven-year-old daughter leaning against her father's knees as though she would die of boredom before they boarded their flight. There was also a group of well-dressed businessmen clustered together, clutching their brief cases, and consulting their watches.

They seemed to be waiting for a Very Important Person and would look up quickly anytime anyone walked through the "arrivals" door. They were continually disappointed for the entire airport staff casually drifted in and out on a routine basis.

"Shipping and Receiving" was a glass-enclosed office next to the long countertop partition separating the ticketing agents from the customers. "Do you want to come in with me?" asked Andrea. She was never sure how comfortable Jimmy was outside any environment that did not include animals and tractors.

Jimmy looked at the small cafeteria built into the waiting room. Only two tables were in use, one by three mechanics still in their uniforms, their faces smudged with grease, and one by a couple of teenagers eating French fries.

"I'll wait here," he said pointing at one of the empty tables.

"Get me a coke too," she called to him as he walked away. "I won't be long."

The man in the cargo office looked like he was pushing forty with very little likelihood the push had seen many good days. He glanced up hurriedly when she walked in, then down again, scrutinizing the paperwork in front of him as though nothing could be more important than locating the slightest flaw in text, the most careless abbreviation or comma.

"Can I help you?" He mumbled in a voice that said he hoped he couldn't.

Andrea sauntered up to the desk and eased one hip on it. "Good evening, Mr. Carlson, is it?" She asked, reading his name tag. "I've come to pick up a few crates. They should have arrived sometime this past week. The name's Delaney."

He sighed and rummaged through the cargo list until he found the name. "Yes. It's in bay three. I'll send someone around to pick it up."

"Thank you, Mr. Carlson. I have an extra helping hand with me. If we can drive our truck around to it, we won't need much assistance."

He scribbled on a piece of paper. "There's a kid out there who will help you. Just give him this."

She took it but continued to sit on the desk. "Did you need something more?" He asked in a pained voice.

"I was just wondering. The crates were flown in by Jake Monroe, weren't they? Could you tell me what day he arrived?"

He checked his sheet. "Day before yesterday."

"And would you know if he's flown back out? I'm his wife."

"Ah." His expression softened for a moment. "I know Jake. Sorry ma'am. He flew back out to Seattle the next day."

"I see. Is there a public phone?"

"Over there, at the corner of the waiting room."

It was one of those closed in booths with tiny, wood slat seats that weren't really designed for sitting. She set her handbag on the seat and rummaged through it until she found the little notebook containing phone numbers. She dropped in a dime and asked the operator if she could make a collect call. She waited, listening to the phone on the other line ring again and again until the operator said, "I'm sorry. No one seems to be answering that number. Should I try again?"

"Try again, please," she asked. She heard it dial. She counted the number of rings. Six...seven...eight.

"I'm sorry. Nobody is answering your call. Please try again later."

She hung up and sat down on the tiny seat, slowly putting her bag back into order.

In the cafeteria, the mechanics had left, and the table was now occupied by two dimple-cheeked stewardesses, with Jimmy on the opposing side.

She watched him flirt with them, the two cokes in front of him completely forgotten, until the girls looked at their watches, blew kisses and waggled their fingers as they disappeared through the "departures" door.

"Well," she said, joining him once they were gone. "I guess you are taking woman hunting seriously."

He leaned back in his chair, puffing out his chest proudly. "I'm getting the hang of it. We should come here more often. The girls said there's a club near here where they play live music all night on Saturdays. I've got a hankering to try it out."

She picked up her coke and drank half in one swallow. "Not tonight, Jimmy. We've got to get these crates home. They've got all mama's precious things."

"Eh, the girls won't be there tonight, anyway. They're on a flight to Hawaii."

"Lucky for them. I wouldn't mind flying to a tropical island."

"Too small. What would you do?"

"Sunbathe."

"Now that's a waste of time."

Loading the crates was easy. As soon as Andrea stepped out of the truck, the young laborers who had not been in a hurry to do much of anything, suddenly scrambled to attention.

They ushered her back to the cab, using their most polished manners, and proceeded to demonstrate their expertise in loading boxes. Not even Jimmy needed to put out much effort to help with so many volunteers.

In fact, they glanced at him with a certain amount of disdain, as though scandalized he would even think to enlist his sister's assistance and bumped against him rudely if he got too close to one of the crates. Not one of them would accept a tip. Andrea dimpled and waved as they left, and the laborers all waved back.

"I think you don't do too shabby, yourself," said Jimmy on the way home. He glanced back at the crates stacked and tied down neatly in the bed. His hands twitched in his lap a moment as he stumbled over the subject they never talked about.

"He's got no hold on you, Andy. A man like that has got no hold on what you do."

Andrea kept her eyes on the road, so as not to meet his.

"Maybe I like it like that. The times when we're together are good."

"For a while. Then he neglects you, abandons you. Fights with you. You know that's not the way it works."

"It doesn't work the same for everybody. Jimmy, you're supposed to be on my side."

"I bought you a coke."

Andrea was silent during the rest of the ride through a landscape that never slept in the summer, but rested in starts and fits, forgetting there was a realm where time was measured by the hours. As they neared the Wolf Creek trading post, she slowed.

The structure was a large wooden cabin with a row of flowers in front separated by the porch and awning at the entrance. It rested in the center of a gravel semi-circle that curved all the way behind it, puncturing its far end with a row of tiny cabins. Fifty yards in front of it were two gas pumps with round signs perched on their tops announcing their sponsoring gas company.

Several cars were parked haphazardly in the semi-circle, cozying into a favorite spot instead of parking in conscientious order. Several customers stood on the steps of the porch, drinking beverages and smoking cigarettes. The door to the post was open and from inside spilled the sound of laughter and tinny radio music.

The lodge was as multi-functional as Millie had said it would be, even from the outside. Apart from the gas pumps; a relatively new and shiny addition; a small house with a sign in the window announced there were pastries for sell.

Inside, the post reflected the transitional period of the Wolf Creek community. It continued a limited trade with the disappearing trappers, with one corner of the store piled with furs, while the main shelving units contained canned goods, dried foods, candy bars, rubber boots, gloves, and rain slickers.

A long counter held the cash register and served as a bar for visitors. They dispensed soda, beer, and coffee as refreshments, hamburgers or hotdogs and potato chips as their menu. The post had four small dining tables, all of them in use.

A sign across from the counter gave notice that you could send and receive mail. Another advertised cabin rental units, with a card tacked over it stating "occupied". To the left, next to a yellowing sheet covering a doorway, yet another sign stated, "laundry".

It was the only place in the community to have electricity. This was manufactured from a large generator housed in a box-like shelter to one side of the lodge. The owners had dispersed with the power sparingly, adding electric juice only to a few lightbulbs, a refrigerator, freezer, and the piped in hot water for laundry and showers. There was no jukebox, electric stove, fan, or heater.

The Wolf Creek crowd was friendly. Room was made for Andrea immediately at the counter, with someone even finding in the far corner, a tall, wooden stool that was supposed to be a bar stool but had been used as a ladder. It was dusted off and presented to her by one of the locals. The young man had a broadly smiling face and thin, blonde hair. He announced his name was Ed as he set the stool down with a grand flourish.

"Are you new to these parts or just passing through?" He asked, speaking directly to Andrea, ignoring Jimmy.

"We just moved here," she answered, dragging Jimmy by the arm. He had stopped to rummage through the pile of furs.

"Yep," Jimmy said, leaning against the counter next to her. "We settled in last week. Just now getting around to finding our bearings."

"Are you married?" asked Ed, a flicker of disappointment traveling over his face.

"Nope," answered Jimmy. "She's my sister."

Andrea kicked him. "And she's mean," he added.

A middle-aged woman, whose matronly appearance was emphasized by a gingham dress and a bibbed white apron, began slowly rubbing down the counter-top with a large, damp cloth.

When she reached Jimmy's elbows, she lifted them, and rubbed the space underneath them as well. "Where did you stake your claim?" she asked.

"We took up the sixty acres just below the Lamar's," Andrea explained.

"You're farmers?" The woman finished wiping down the counter, set down a beer in front of a customer, then added, "The soil is good, but it gets too much shade from the mountain to do much gardening. You'd do better with livestock."

"We thought about that," agreed Jimmy. "It's got good pastureland but not much of it stays in full sunlight."

Ed was grinning up into Andrea's face again. "Have you met the Lamars yet?"

"We've met Millie. We haven't met her husband."

Ed chortled. "Oh, no? You haven't met anyone until you've met Frank."

The woman pushed two beers in front Andrea and Jimmy.

"Here. On the house. A little welcome to the community greeting. Don't mind Ed. He's my son. He doesn't get to see many single women and gets kind of stupid around them."

She waited until they had popped open the bottles and poured the contents into glasses. "Frank is a queer one, but it takes all kinds you know. How did you meet Millie and not Frank?"

Andrea smiled at the recollection. "She was punishing him. He knew we had moved in but hadn't told her, so she punished him by bringing us a cake and making him stay behind with the baby."

"Yep, that sounds like Millie," said the woman, nodding her head with satisfaction. "She has her work cut out for her. Frank's not a bad sort, but he's not the most thoughtful sort, either. Or at least those thoughts aren't so much about others but his place in the great scheme of things. It's all difficult to explain."

"He's oblivious?"

The woman seized on the word immediately. "Yes, oblivious. They got here just in time for the first winter storm. There were white-out conditions all the way to the base, so they had to spend the night here. I told them about a cabin that was coming open, and they said they would come and look at it when the weather cleared. It cleared about a week later."

Ed buried his chin on his fists and leaned over the counter toward Andrea, perpetually grinning. The woman bumped him to one side, frowned and cleared her throat. "When the weather is good, the G.I.'s like to come visit. They take pictures of the huskies, the cabins and such and send the photos home. They call it the great Alaskan experience, even though they came in on a bus and all they did was drink hot chocolate or beer."

"The Lamars followed them out," put in Ed, who was dying to be the one to tell the story.

The woman amended him with a tired slap of her towel. "It was a Saturday. The bus always comes out on a Saturday, and it's not like a Civil Service worker has much visiting time before then. It wasn't the kind of sight we see every day. Everyone else was dressed for the weather in heavy coats and work boots. Frank got out of the car in a full suit, a long over-coat, a bowler hat and rubber boots over his shoes."

Andrea noticed that several people had stopped visiting each other, and were crowding close to the counter, listening to the woman. They all seemed to be familiar with the story yet enjoyed countless retelling.

"He went around to Millie's door and helped her out, like a gentleman, but then, he reached into the back seat and brought out a camera. He began taking a mountain of pictures; more than you can imagine. He took photos of the inlet, of the dogs, of the lodge and the mountains and forgot completely about Millie."

The woman paused long enough to refill several coffee cups. "Well," she continued when she had finished. "Millie looked at her husband leaping around, taking photos, of the GI's leering at her from the trading post, and at the pastry sign in the window of my house. She walked straight over, ordered coffee and a donut, and just stood there talking to me, comfortable as you please.

By and by, her husband realized she was missing and began looking around. The GI's pointed out where she had gone. He bounced over and asked if she had bought a donut for him. She looked at him cool as a cucumber and answered, 'buy your own.' That's Millie for you. She was punishing him even then."

"She also stood down a claim-jumper with a shotgun," said Ed cheerfully, opening a package of peanuts and shaking them into a Coca-Cola.

"She did not!" Argued the woman.

"It's just a rumor, you know. She sent a man packing who had filed on the same piece of land, but no one knows how she did it. They don't talk about it."

Ed persisted, "I suppose it's also a rumor that Betty Lou got thrown in jail again last night for running through the streets naked."

The woman's hands flew to her hair and secured a few bobby pins. "Oh, why does she do that? It really would be better if she kept her parts to herself."

Ed nudged Jimmy's elbow and winked. "She's just a giving sort of gal. Plopped a whole quarter caribou on the Davie's family porch the other day. The pappy's been off drinking instead of hunting and Betty Lou said she wasn't too inclined to see the little ones suffer because of it."

"I'm not judging her good intentions." The good woman shook her finger warningly at her boy. "I'm judging her lack of clothing. Here she is, shedding her clothes whenever she feels, even in mid-winter, mind you, and I have enough things to fret my mind without worrying about her dying of exposure."

The busy proprietor left them alone long enough to wait on some tables and go to the room hidden behind the counter by a curtain. She was obviously not alone back there. Andrea could hear some dishes thumping and clattering, and her scolding voice encouraging someone to remove some of the excess weight from her lower spine. When she returned, she was carrying a tray containing several bowls of hot chili and a basket of crackers, which she set down on a far table and began distributing with a great deal of ceremony to a group of earnestly talking men.

Returning to her place behind the counter, she set two fresh beers in front of Andrea and Jimmy. "The gentleman over there paid," she said nodding at the group.

The gentleman in question raised his glass, then returned to his discussion. "Well," said Andrea, unsure of what to say about a man who would buy her a drink, then ignore her. "That was neighborly of him."

The woman shrugged. "Civil Service employees. There's no accounting for them. The war made them a little daft in the head I think, but they bring in steady money. My name is Solace Grant, by the way, and the man over there arguing with the veterans, is my husband, Zeb. He argues with them all the time, but in the end, he goes along with whatever the veterans decide. It's better for business."

By now, Andrea had suspected her name, but was grateful for the formal introduction. "Andrea. Jimmy. Most folk call me Andy, though."

"Handy Andy," said Jimmy agreeably. "She can drive a plow straighter than I can. Does a bit of mechanics, too."

"Hum," said Solace, retying her apron. "If you're looking for work, that's easy enough. Work around here usually comes and finds you. The problem is, we've got a whole bunch of men doing manly work, and there's not much womanly work being taken up."

"I can waitress," volunteered Andrea. "And I can cut hair."

"And she draws," added Jimmy, who was always willing to champion his sister's wage- earning abilities but maintained a reserved outlook on his own lucrative skills. "You don't have a good sign if you don't mind my saying so. You wouldn't even see it unless you were looking for it. Andy could draw you a better one."

"You don't say?" Mused Solace. "You just might be truly handy, Andy." She gave a large smile, pleased with her joke. "And you, young man, what are your skills?"

"Jimmy is the best animal man and tracker you'll ever meet in your life," Andrea said boldly.

Solace muttered, "There are many who claim that distinction. We've got a good deal of hunting and fishing going on."

"Jimmy's different. Between you and me, I think Jimmy is part coyote. He knows what's under the soil, on top of the soil, and what is happening in the sky."

"He ever do prospecting? There are miners who say the same thing."

"I never had the time for it, but I'd like to try," put in Jimmy, derailing Andrea's philosophical intent. "I never put my mind to tracking gold, mainly just living, breathing things."

Solace Grant summed up his skills with a note of finality. "Like a trapper."

Jimmy disagreed. "Oh, I don't trap. Don't even hunt so much except when we need it. Down in Colorado, I tracked things that were lost, like cattle or horses, even pets, and twice I tracked a lost kid. The parents were grateful and gave us enough food for a week."

Solace stood back with her hands on the counter, her fingers tapping a coded message to herself. "You know, Jimmy," she said, drawling out the words. "I think you and your sister are going to get along with the Lamars just fine. There's not a one of you any odder than the other."

Somebody bought them another round of beer and Solace winked. "You're good for business."

Three beers were a dangerous amount after four weeks on the Alcan, but they were also a very tempting amount. It had been four weeks of listening to only their own voices, except for the occasional stop at a service station or diner. They had been a grueling four weeks, in which they had run out of things to say beyond pointing out each other's mistakes, which accumulated as one mishap after another stalled their journey.

Listening to the voices surrounding her, all eager to reveal their own characteristics, was like bathing in water after a long, uncomfortable drought.

Andrea immersed herself, not really hearing what was said, just the general melody of companionship. It was only when people began leaving that she realized the hour was late.

She hastily shook Jimmy, who had gotten into a bragging contest with Ed on how close they'd come to touching a bear. Since neither had witnesses to the credibility of their encounters, they were limited only by what their imaginations could serve.

Solace followed them out, two Dixie cups in her hands. "Some coffee," she suggested. "Before you leave. Shop's closing, but you can sit out here long as you like until your head clears."

Andrea thanked her and started to apologize, but Solace shook her head.

"I know that shell-shocked look. We all go through it when we've been alone for a while. The highway does it too."

They sat in the cab with the windows open.

Between the extra black coffee and the fresh air, their heads began clearing quickly.

"What time do you think it is?" Asked Andrea when they had regained their sensibilities.

Jimmy frowned. "It's hard to tell around here this time of year, but the sun isn't very high up. I think it's around two a.m."

"Mama's not going to like that."

"We were being sociable, weren't we? That counts."

She fired up the truck. "I hope she sees it that way."

They cruised the last half mile down the hill with the engine turned off and eased into the drive, still raw and fresh from the tractor blade. They hoped their noiselessness would keep from alerting mama Delaney, which was like hoping for spring in November. Mama Delaney didn't need any of her five senses to apprehend real and perceived delinquencies. She had an antenna that flexed like octopus arms burrowing into their most private thoughts.

She was waiting at the outside door of the trailer when they stealthily approached their tents. "I suppose you went gallivanting with those trollops and sinful businessmen of Anchorage," she scolded.

"We didn't!" Cried Jimmy jovially, "and we hardly spent any money. "We visited the trading post just like our new neighbor said we should do."

"Well," grumbled Velma. "It's a dreadful hour. I hope the two of you haven't already ruined your reputations."

"Not mine," said Jimmy. "They already have me figured out."

Andrea pulled the band loose from her ponytail and set it on the vanity stand she had fashioned for herself outside her tent. It contained a brush, a mirror and a bottle of skin lotion.

She rubbed a little lotion on before ducking into her tent. Poking her head from the flap, she said with barely concealed relish, "There is a local woman who wrestles with the fishermen and runs through the streets of Anchorage naked on a Saturday night. I'll have to put out a great deal of effort to top that."

"Oh dear, and I thought this was a Christian community," fretted Velma, shuffling off to bed.

Nine

Andrea brought back the platter the next day, as she had promised. Millie's house was so new, you could still smell the sharp scent of wood shavings, putty, and iron nails mixed together as soon as you approached the small, two-step platform that served as a porch, even though the outside siding blistered and was beginning to peel from its first winter. The siding was unpainted, the roof was tar-papered, but lacked shingles.

Millie flung open the door and beckoned the visitor inside before she had a chance to knock. "There now! Didn't I tell Frank I would be expecting company! You didn't bring Ben. More the pity, but Jason's napping, so maybe it's best. He doesn't play well with others yet. I'm trying to teach him."

"He is just a baby yet," reminded Andrea, but followed her hostess to look at the sleeping cherub. He was a cute baby; very blonde; with tight, springy curls and a round, pink face. His lashes fluttered against his cheeks.

"It's always the boys," she remarked, touching the mop of hair lightly to keep from waking the child. "They get the long eyelashes while the girls are left with practically nothing."

"That's true," said Millie. Now that she had shown off her prized possession, she turned toward the kitchen stove, poured two cups of coffee, and set them on the table, along with a plate of freshly baked cookies. "My eyelids are nearly bald, but my brother, Bruiser, has the most beautiful lashes, or at least he does over one eye. I don't know about the other one, anymore."

"What happened to the other one?" asked Andrea innocently.

"He lost it in the war. He's dreadful about it. He kept threatening to show me his empty eye socket."

Andrea shuddered. "I'm glad my brother was too young to enlist. He's such a fool, he would have been shot right away."

They talked pleasantly of their lives during the war. It seemed a rule. You talked freely about what happened while waiting for the troops to come home, but you didn't talk about the time before they left. You didn't voice the anxieties you felt once they had left. You didn't muse over how much you had lost or how hungry you had been. Everybody lost something. Everybody knew the pain of deprivation. There was nothing in it worth remembering or comparing.

When the men were gone, there were jobs. Somebody had to keep the factories running. Somebody had to manufacture clothing, sleeping bags, tents, rope, boots, weapons, ammunition, and vehicles.

The women went to work and put food on the table.

"I suppose I would go back to work if I needed to," said Millie. "Ester is looking at a career. She wants to go back to teaching but she wasn't a grade schoolteacher, which is what we need. She taught art and French. How are we going to use that when all our students are under eight?"

She sighed before Andrea, who didn't know Ester at all, could come to her defense. "I'm not interested in a career. I like being a mother. Is that bad?"

"I wouldn't say so," agreed Andrea hastily. "I hadn't even heard of all these career-minded women."

Millie, whose time in Seattle had made her quite cosmopolitan, assured her. "Oh, they are out there. Frank thinks it's good that women wish to improve their minds but isn't really keen on me going back to work. He says he provides well enough, and he does! He has all these terrible books to improve my mind with, so I suppose I don't need to go outside the home."

"Terrible?" asked Andrea, glancing at a wall containing several shelves, one carefully tacked in over the other, with small pieces of wood on each end to serve as corners. The inside walls were as stark and bare as the outside, with only half the insulation covered and only wood supports to mark the portioned rooms. The books in question were lined up obediently on the shelves, ramrod stiff. They were handsome, hard-bound books, without a paperback among them.

"Oh," said Millie. "Frank says they are classics, but they make very depressing reading. Why can't a classic be happy? I wonder why these classical writers don't commit suicide at an early age instead of living until ninety."

"Well." Andrea's curbed fingernails tapped on the table. She would like to keep them long, like Millie's, but long nails were not compatible with chopping down trees and pulling parts out from around an automobile engine. "I could use a career. I barely have two pennies to rub together."

Proving herself once and for all to be of a thoroughly objective nature, Millie cheerfully shrugged and said, "then we will march right down and talk with Solace. She's got nobody working solid in the kitchen. Her oldest boy left as soon as he turned eighteen and has done nothing but cause her grief since then. Always getting drunk at the bars and fighting. Humph. I know a few like that."

She paused for Andy's acknowledgement, for what woman didn't know a few men like that? Understanding this was one of the great ties of the Sisterhood, Andrea nodded.

Satisfied, Millie adjusted the strap of her bra under her blouse and continued, "Ed was supposed to help, but all he wants to do is pump gas and change oil. Her girl, Bea, now, only volunteers so she can sneak out and smoke cigarettes. She'll be going to school in Anchorage this fall, so she'll be out of her mama's hair. Solace is hoping an education will teach her to do something. She can't even work the cash register properly, and Ed? Ed is not to be trusted with money."

Andrea realized Millie was preparing to leave while they were talking. She covered everything on her countertop with a clean towel, took off her apron and freshened her hair. She decided Jason had taken a long enough nap and picked him up out of his crib to change his diaper and put him in a clean outfit.

"There," she said. "Shall we go?"

"I have a truck," offered Andy.

Millie paused, then answered brightly, "well, aren't you a blessing in disguise?"

"Now," she calculated as they walked the newly etched path between the Lamars and the Delaneys. "Your truck will save time we can use for visiting Solace. I am always home by four to start dinner so that it's on the table by six. Frank becomes upset if it isn't. He's a traditionalist."

"A traditional what?" asked Andy.

Millie switched her son from one hip to the other to throw up a hand. "I don't know. He hasn't explained that to me yet."

Mama Delaney had been keeping a close eye on the path in anticipation of her daughter's return. Noticing Andrea was not alone, Velma stopped juggling baby Ben on her lap, turned him over to the care of her youngest daughter, Anna and stood up.

Determined to provide an adequate friendship between her daughter and the new neighbor, mama Delaney rushed to see the child Millie was carrying and beg to hold him. Velma was able to cradle the baby for all of three seconds before Carol pried him out of her arms. She nearly jiggled him to death before passing him on to Anna, who skipped around like she had a new puppy.

"Were you going somewhere?" Velma asked sharply when she noticed Andy's general direction was toward the truck.

Andrea paused a moment. "Millie's going with me to the post. She thinks she can get me a job."

Velma mumbled to herself, then said with her lips wrapping uncertainly around each word, "well, it won't do no good dragging a baby along while petitioning for work. It's too distracting."

"Let us babysit him," begged Anna, skipping in rhythm with her plea. "He's so cute."

"He'll keep Ben occupied," said Velma hopefully, although Ben really had no limits to the things he occupied himself with, provided there were no restraints. Being nice to a citizen smaller than himself might prove a challenge. Still, Millie surrendered Jason with the faith that three pairs of eyes were better than one that would really prefer to be fully attentive to the daily gossip.

"How long have you been married?" asked Andrea as she started Abe's engine.

"Two years in September," Millie answered. "We married in the states, then came here. I have almost a year and a half at Wolf Creek now." She said it as though it was a badge of honor.

"Has it been hard?"

"The winters are hard." Her hands shuffled as though she wasn't accustomed to an empty lap. "The first winter, I had next door neighbors. I could visit when I wanted. Last winter was our first year in our new home. The post is too far to walk in the winter and Ester's house.... Well, she's Ester. You nearly need an invitation to visit her house."

"She's formal?"

Millie shrugged. "She's French. She fled to Switzerland during the war."

"That could make a person strange."

"She's French," Millie said again.

"Solace said Frank is French."

"She's right, only he's American French. It still makes him strange, though."

"That's what Solace said."

Solace recognized Andy immediately. "I see you've made friends with your neighbor," she said, leading them to a private table set strategically between the kitchen and the dining area. "Zeb, take the front!"

She sat them down and ordered coffee from her daughter, who complied quickly only because she was within easy viewing range. Officially off the clock, Solace smiled broadly and asked, "what can I do for you two ladies?"

Millie came straight to the point. "Andy needs a job and you said you needed good, hired help. Well, here you are. She even has waitressing experience."

Solace didn't even argue the point. She rubbed her chin, measured Andy's effect on the crowd the night before and told her, "Don'tlet those kids of mine slack off."

Andreas's job was to work up front three hours a day for their rush hour traffic, giving Solace time to prepare her kitchen for evening meals. The rush began at five in the afternoon when the civil service employees were coming home from work and ended at eight in the evening. The main objective of the civil service workers was picking up their mail, but they always purchased soda crackers and gas, as well.

The gas and the crackers were after-thoughts. It was logical that if they were going to stop by the post anyway, they should show their support by availing of its paid services.

It's what the Grants liked about the veterans. They had a sense of fair play. They plunked down tips for the free coffee. They paid Ed to do oil changes even though most could do it themselves. They usually stayed at the bar ten to fifteen minutes, catching up on the latest news with whoever else was around. Some bought a beer. Some bought a soda. Some just bought candy bars to take home. But they kept the wheels greased, as Solace liked to say.

Around six, the restaurant crowd began drifting in. The restaurant crowd consisted of two or three single men who regularly attended the lodge for home-cooked food, even if they did have a brief menu, an occasional young couple whose idea of a date was hamburgers and French fries, no matter where they went, and truck drivers who wheeled in with a fanfare of squealing brakes and thundering exhausts.

By seven o'clock, the rush was over. The veterans went home. Most of those who planned to eat, had placed their orders. Those who lingered were those who still craved the companionship of human voices and were reluctant to return to the silence of the wilderness.

Andrea found it leisurely work. At its peak, the rush hour never had more than ten customers at a time in the lodge. None of the customers had to wait more than five minutes for service. The rest of the time was spent in loitering, which all Wolf Creek clientele did very well.

From five to seven, she exchanged pleasantries while she rang up items, wiped down the tables and counter and took orders. She learned the names of all the regular customers and their preferences, with a pack of Camels waiting for Matt Jones and a Miller High Life for Gary Hughes as soon as they came in the door.

The hours also gave her plenty of time to spend with Millie. It was Millie who helped her piece together everyone in their relationship to each other and the community. Two days after she started work, she hiked up the path to visit Millie, this time carrying Ben.

Since it was a nice day, she plopped him in the front yard where Jason was playing inside a barrier made from fish netting. Millie was weeding the struggling beginnings of a garden.

She stopped to sit on the porch to visit when she saw Andy.

"Frank is the one who dresses like Cary Grant, am I right?" Asked Andy.

Millie nodded. "Has he spoken to you yet?"

"Not really. He comes in with a couple of other guys. They check their mail, stand around and talk with each other, then leave."

"That would be Charlie Bolinder and Alex Erichman. They all keep the same hours. You would think they had enough to talk about at work."

"Sometimes, another guy comes in when they do. He's an odd one. He bought me a beer the first night I was here and hasn't spoken to me since."

"Oh, that would be Matt Jones. He's single, you know. He has some type of life crisis he is trying to get over. We found him."

"You found him?" Asked Andrea weakly.

Millie excused herself to bring out some iced tea. "No ice in it," she laughed. "But the water from the spring is ice cold."

She sat down and arranged her summery dress over her knees. "We found him last summer. We were still living in the Quonset Hut at the time. We took the train for a weekend fishing trip to Seward. We had caught a few fish, but from shore, all you catch is salmon. Frank noticed that one of the boats had brought in a fresh catch of cod and went over to talk with the fishermen to see if he could buy some. Matt was one of the fishermen."

"Then what?" Laughed Andy. "Frank said, follow me and I will teach you to be fishers of men and Matt followed?"

Millie found Andy's humor terribly funny. She nearly fell off the porch laughing. "My advice to you. Don't say that in front of Frank. He already has enough inflated ideas about himself."

She regained her composure to continue.

"Frank learned that Matt was a heavy equipment operator and mechanic who quit his civil service job in Kodiak to join the fishing boats. It was early summer, but Matt was already

137

thinking about how to hunker down for another winter and told Frank he wished he had a mainland job. That was when Frank started talking to him about the base and how they were expanding the Elmendorf Airport as rapidly as they could.

The next thing you know, he was packing up his bags and coming home with us on the train, along with seventy pounds of cod. We used half of it to make batter-fried cod and chips for the whole community. That's what he calls it, fish and chips. He's been to England."

"During the war?"

"Maybe. He didn't say. He fit right into the community. He even knows electrical wiring, although there's not much demand for it right now. They're saying maybe within the next two years, if the community grows large enough. It's about the number of people petitioning. Be sure to add your name."

Andrea agreed she would, although it sounded suspiciously political. She had not acquired the habit of petition signing and wasn't sure if she wanted to start.

From seven to eight, she learned all the latest gossip from Solace while she piled dishes into the sink and washed them. Some of it took a news-worthy format as relationships between Russia and the United States became more strained and the territory rumbled unhappily, not ready to accept a new enemy at the door so soon after the war.

It was an uncomfortable subject with the Civil Service workers. They had sworn an allegiance to the US, but they had also sworn an oath to their community - and their community contained Russian villages - peaceful Russian villages. Villages that had no interest in Stalin or Communism or politics at all.

Andrea had plenty of opinions of her own and was given the opportunity to air them the first time she stayed after work for a community meeting. When Millie saw Andy's intentions, she beckoned her over to the tables where the homesteaders were slowly drifting in and finding places to sit.

"You've met my husband, Frank?" She asked.

Mr. Lamar answered for Andy. "Not formally." His voice was a deep rumble, kept noticeably in check. You would expect such a voice from one of the miners or railroad workers, but not from a thin, middle-sized man. "But formalities are rarely observed in this group."

She didn't know if he was complaining or stating a fact. "They aren't observed," said Matt, reaching across the table to shake her hand. "Don't let him frighten you."

Thinking she should be witty and perky, Andrea cocked her head and asked Frank, "were you trying to frighten me?"

"Of course he was," said a brittle-voiced woman, who, with a complete air of ownership, sat next to Millie. This had to be Ester. She was tall, taller even than Andy, with a long, sharp face and her hair piled high on her head. "Frank would frighten a grizzly bear, given the opportunity."

Next to her plopped the man she had learned was Charlie. Charlie was just a shade taller than she was, thick-shouldered and with box-like features.

"You're going to need to be frightening a lot of critters if your wife still plans to winter her hens."

Frank accepted the coca-colas Ed put in front of him and passed them around to the group, leaving two dollars on the tray. "She doesn't want to butcher them. I told her - we could get more in the spring, but she won't have it."

"I have laying hens and brooding hens," explained Millie calmly. "They'll lay until late September. I'm not giving up my best hens. You can have the excess roosters and the slackers."

"Do you see? Useless." It wasn't difficult to imagine that growl coming out of a grizzly.

"What are you discussing tonight?" asked Andy, turning the subject away from consumable hens.

Millie sighed. "Not much tonight. Summers get lazy. Half the members won't show. It's mainly about community hall fund raising."

"The theater is a good idea," rumbled Frank.

Ester threw back her head and sighed. "He's trying to enlist the entire community."

"We don't have enough performers," Frank insisted. "We need more."

Millie gave Andy a look that was almost pleading.

"Please say you know how to act, or dance, or sing so Frank will be happy."

Andy drew back and crossed her arms. "Certainly not. I didn't come here to make Frank happy." She saw the sad, puppyish expression on his face and softened. "But wait. My brother plays the guitar. He doesn't sing very well but he's a terrific player. He even wants to break into the clubs."

Frank's dark eyes sparkled. "A musician! You see? It will come together."

"How is the work coming along on the housing development?" Charlie asked Matt.

Matt fished in his breast pocket for his cigarettes. "They want ten new units by next spring. How big do they plan to make the new military installation?"

Charlie waved a hand. "With Truman in the lead, who knows? He's a bit blood-thirsty."

Frank cleared his throat, and Charlie added hastily, "No need to deny it, Frank. It was a mess he left behind with the bomb, and a mess he began making with all his labor laws, strapping that poor industry more than humanly decent. The only good of it all is that it keeps us in jobs."

Andrea felt she was an expert on such matters. "He made a terrible mess! We lost our farm because of him. Taxed us to death, he did. I will say, the ones who settled here even before the war ended were the smart ones. They didn't see the nightmares going on in their hometowns. Labor Union strikes, grain sellers withholding their produce. I'm amazed he was elected to a second term."

"But he's doing better now, isn't he?" asked Millie anxiously. "There must be some reason he was re-elected."

"I suppose. It was very convenient of the communists to become our enemy."

"They create a threat to the free world," grumbled Frank. "They would have been fine if they had not become so aggressive."

Matt was perplexed. He examined his cigarette suspiciously, tapped it into the ashtray and cleared his throat.

"That's what I don't understand. I've been in the Russian villages and the Native villages with Russian ties. I couldn't find any enemies. I remember when we were allies."

"That's because they live here," explained Frank. "The citizens don't want to live that way, but the communists don't give them a choice. We protect the Russians here, so they can live their own lives."

With that matter settled, they could get on with the more serious business of community development. Other members had drifted in and found seats, sharing what they would to the discussion or finding subjects of their own.

As Millie predicted, the meeting centered primarily around raising funds. Between an earlier drive that involved staging a large barbecue and serving plates at one dollar for all you could eat, and auctioning off a milk goat, they had raised seventeen dollars and eighty cents after subtracting the costs.

Club donations, which were kept in a glass jar on Solace's bar, amounted to four dollars and fifty-three cents. There was no denying they needed a serious cash cow, but inspiration was running low. Their only real resource was Frank's players.

There was a lot of practicality involved. It didn't cost the players anything except their time and whatever money they wanted to put into their own costumes. They could use the VFW Hall free of charge to stage their performance. By the time they were ready to perform in public, the community would have grown more. New people poured in each year. New people meant additional funds and additional talent. Frank used the opportunity to announce Jimmy's musical abilities as an illustration of their blossoming arts.

"Now Frank," Andy started to say, but Millie leaned toward her and shushed her.

"If you don't give him his moment, he will never forgive you. He's been trying all year to put together performing troops. They do well with skits here at the lodge, but they want musicians and dancers, all of it. If Jimmy is as good as you say, it could change things. It could give them courage."

"But I am volunteering him without asking him."

"We'll try to make him happy he volunteered."

At the end of the meeting, Matt followed Andrea out to her truck. He shoved his hands in his pocket and looked out over the inlet, finding words in the serene mountain called The Sleeping Lady, stretched over the water, arms folded across her chest.

"I'm sorry I didn't speak to you the first night. There aren't many single women here you know. It's been a long time since I talked to one."

"In some places that might be considered rude."

"Now that I've thought about it, it could be. But I didn't know what to say. I'd been planning to buy this five-acre homesite all winter. When I was sitting at the table, Frank told me where your family settled. It's right across the creek from where I was thinking of putting up a shack."

She opened the truck door and bounced up into the seat. She looked down at him, standing somewhat awkwardly, still gazing out toward the inlet. "And now you've changed your mind?"

His eyes snapped around and looked at her startled. "Oh no. I just wanted to say. It's possible you could become my neighbor. I hope you don't find that objectionable."

"Would you be a bad neighbor?"

"I would try not to be. I try to be helpful. You can ask around."

"I already did. Millie said you helped build their house."

"A lot of people did. We all got together."

"But you helped."

Then there was the matter of the field phones.

Since forming their community and establishing their boundaries, the good citizens fretted that the response time wasn't adequate for wildfires. Wildfires occurred frequently during dry spells in June or late in the autumn season.

Last year, one of the homestead families in the northwest end had lost their home, their barn, and their farm equipment to a wildfire. Starting over was a painstaking process and could only be accomplished with the assistance of others. The family rebuilt with the help of their neighbors. Most things could be replaced, but not the memories they had brought with them.

The committee had petitioned the telephone and light companies for services as soon as they received their community status, but the companies weren't impressed enough with their numbers to hurry along a schedule that meant a waiting period of one more year to pound in the power lines.

The members first met the news with a sigh of resignation, yet as weeks turned into months, the sighs turned into grumbling and the grumbling turned into demands for action.

The demand was satisfied when a collection of a dozen or so military field phones showed up at the Wolf Creek Trading Post. The next few days were spent traipsing through the woods, connecting wires so there would be a network from one house to another. As much time as they spent tracing and repairing the wires, it seemed it would have been easier to just run from one house to another, but eventually, the community had its emergency system in place, and it was satisfied.

Andrea had only been working a few weeks when the field phones were brought in and laughed when asked if the Delaney's would keep one on their property.

Matt, though, had made it sound like she would be doing the community a favor. Maybe she was. He said the line from the Grant's house to the Lamar residence was too long. They needed another respondent for passing on messages. When he put it that way, she could hardly refuse.

Matt, however, did not enlighten her on how the phones had appeared. There was only one person who could crack the veteran's code of silence, and that was Millie. Millie was able to get Frank to spill everything that went on base simply by pretending a lack of interest. The more bored she appeared, the more he tried to impress her.

When Andrea asked, Millie said, with a flourish of her brand-new teapot, "Oh, that's easy. They figure these things out at the office."

"What do they figure out at the office?"

"Their problems. Oh, Andy. You just don't know how it goes between Charlie, Frank, and Alex. I swear the three of them would have been able to plot Hitler's overthrow on their own."

Andrea pushed Millie's elbow good-naturedly, careful not to bump it so hard it disrupted the cup of tea in her hand. "No, I don't. You should tell me."

"It's like this. Frank works inventory. Charlie is an accountant. Alex is into communications. Between them, they know everything that comes into and out of the base, and what has been decommissioned."

"You mean who, don't you?"

"Oh, no. I mean 'what'. That's what they call all kinds of items scheduled for the scrap yard; 'decommissioned'. A lot of stuff, like typewriters, copiers, even radios, aren't junk at all, just outdated. Once it's been decommissioned, not all of it reaches the scrap yard. That's how we got the field telephones."

"You're scavengers!"

Millie drew back a little defensively, slapping at the air. "It's not a bad idea! The Bolinder's built their house completely from the lumber scraps they were throwing away on base. Even our house is a military discount. The army had over-ordered some prefabricated homes and sold the surplus at an auction. We paid less than its cost."

"It's a solidly made house."

"All the fellows Frank works with on base came out to help put it together. It took them three days. It's solid. Not very big, but it's solid."

There was other evidence of their scavenging. Army blankets hung in the entrance way of the two inside partitions. A military storm lantern and dark green medical kit crouched in a corner and two large, metal water containers, dark as a shadowy forest, stood under the sink.

The cabinets, Andrea noticed, had been made from wooden packing crates, and an icebox had been built into the wall using old metal grates. There was much that could be learned here; a different style of life that depended as much on the products of military surplus as it did on the products of nature.

She poured herself another cup of tea, enjoying the semi-civilized atmosphere of Millie's home. "Jimmy went out hunting spruce chicken this morning and thought you might like it if he brought back a couple for you and Frank, but now I'm thinking you prefer the domestic variety," she said, changing the subject.

"Why would you think that?" Millie was cutting thick slices of homemade bread and setting them on a plate.

"You have chickens. You'll probably butcher them in the fall," said Andy, repeating the earlier dismal conversation, but Millie had drawn a line from which she didn't intend to budge.

"Oh no I won't! Only the excess roosters. I already set the law down to Frank. I'm wintering my chickens if I have to go out and sleep with them myself."

"Get a dog."

"That's what I keep telling Frank, but he doesn't listen. Ester has two - big dogs. They keep away everything but the weasels. Now there's a lynx that started coming around in the early spring. It yowls when I go outside to use the outhouse. I'm not afraid of the lynx, but it gives off the most blood-curdling screams and it always waits until I'm settled down. Of course, that could explain some of my blockage."

Having found no more solutions to Millie's regularity than the first time it was brought up, Andrea changed the subject again by stating, "Solace wants to look at some of my artwork. If she likes it, she might have me paint a new sign for out front. She's a nice lady."

"Solace? Indeed, she is. She took me berry picking with her last summer. She paid me by the gallon for any berries I didn't keep. I should have kept more. I ran out of jelly before winter was over, but at least now I know where to look for berries. We've got to have them because fruit is so expensive. It's been six months since the last time I ate an orange. And apples! What I wouldn't do to have an apple."

Millie buttered two pieces of bread, which she now gave to the babies. "Oh, just look at them. It's one thing I miss about families. Poor Jason has no cousins to grow up with, so I do the best I can, taking him around to play with other babies."

Ben, as the older and larger of the two, had decided Jason's piece of bread looked more appetizing than his own. He bowled over the younger child, who had only recently gained a solid sitting position, taking the piece of bread and in the process, losing his own.

"It looks like Ben could use a few lessons as well," Andrea remarked, straightening out both, who rolled around like bowling pins.

Neither was distressed by the swap in pieces of bread and continued to suck at whatever they held in their soggy little hands.

"Your husband is a good carpenter," She added. Frank hadn't just tacked together his apple crates.

He had taken them apart carefully and reassembled them into tight, strong, geometrical designs that served their purposes wonderfully.

There was a variety of shelves, cabinets, and closets, all made from the same material. Even the cute little hen houses in the yard pen were fashioned from packing crates.

Millie lifted her hand in a wave of dismissal, "he says it's a hobby. They're all good at it. They all know how to build. That's why they have a hard time becoming their own business. They all have the same skills."

They were all good builders.Some, like Charlie Bolinder, never could seem to stop building.

He had built the largest house, had added stables and sheds, and now spearheaded the move to build a hall on their newly established community grounds.

"Well," said Andrea. "I think I wouldn't mind if they brought their skills our way. We've done most of our tree felling. It's just a matter of peeling and notching them, then stacking them up like Lincoln logs."

"I'll send Frank over this weekend to see what you've got going on."

Millie was as good as her word. That Saturday, just as the family had finished their breakfast, Millie traipsed through what was quickly becoming a well-worn path in the woods, hauling Frank by one arm and the baby on her hip. "Ah, good," she said. "We came at just the right time. I brought cinnamon rolls for refreshment later. And I do mean later, Frank. After a few hours of work."

Millie placed the basket of cinnamon rolls Frank had been carrying on the makeshift table and arranged a place where she could sit down while still guarding Jason.

Mama Delaney, whose first impression of Millie had not diminished, and was acquiring new degrees of warmth, hastily started another pot of coffee, then instructed the two young girls to make a playpen for the babies.

146

They dashed off, happy to be relieved from washing dishes, and gathered up several stout crates and a large quilt to build their baby fortifications.

Realizing returning to chores could be legitimately forestalled another ten minutes, Owen dawdled over his remaining half-cup of coffee while waiting a refill, and stuffed his pipe with a long, luxurious sigh.

Velma paid absolutely no attention to him at all as she stared in perplexity at Mr. Lamar. He wasn't the sort of person one would normally take seriously as an outdoors expert, but neither could you dismiss him simply because he was the kind of person people took seriously. If he said he had the formula for nuclear energy, you believed him.

He wasn't a very tall man; no more than five-foot-seven, with a thin, wiry build and small, fast-moving feet. His hair stood up like it had been electrocuted and merged with a forehead that rose so high, it appeared to travel all the way to the crown.

After sorting things out in her mind by whatever mysterious forces of logic she used, Velma tucked back a few, almost invisible, trailing ends of her hair, straightened her apron and asked, "Would you like some coffee, neighbor?"

"Yes, I would," he answered, sitting at the table with no need for further invitation. She waited until the liquid showing through the small glass knob turned brown, then poured him a cup. When he continued to look at her expectantly, she added the plate of biscuits left from breakfast to the center of the table. With a sigh of satisfaction, he picked up one, buttered it and began eating.

"Jimmy, I really appreciate those two spruce chickens you sent over," said Millie, also picking up a biscuit, but nibbling at it daintily. She nudged Frank when he reached for another. "I wanted to thank you personally."

Reminded that the reason he had been brought along was not to eat a second breakfast but to see how much he could help, Frank sat back, sipped his coffee, and cleared his throat.

"I see you've made a good start. Very good start. You've got nearly enough logs for a small cabin, but you're going to have to let them dry out. They won't be ready to use until around September."

As Frank's assessment was very much in keeping of Owen's appraisal of when they should build, pop Delaney settled back with his smoke, quite happy to acknowledge there was no need to rush on a long, June day. "There's a sight of clearing left to do, but we're readying the trees out first. I don't reckon you can help us out with that."

Owen's remark didn't bother Frank a bit as he was accustomed to being underestimated. "I can handle a chain saw. I'm not so bad with a hammer, either. We could get those tarps snugged up, so they'll be handy all year as shelter. Build up a lean-to of saplings and use the tarps as a roof."

For a reason she couldn't explain, Andrea wanted to needle her neighbor. Perhaps it was his self-assurance, perhaps his solid conformity to the other Civil Service personnel, or maybe just because he was an easy man to tease. "Oh, the military training. Where would we be without it?"

Frank rumbled in his bear voice, "Probably in dire straits."

He wasn't really listening to her, though. His sharp, black eyes, bird-like in their rapid quest, flitted past the canopy that served as shelter, to the weed-choked creek and the meadow beyond.

"What kind of farming are you planning?" He asked Owen.

Owen scratched his head, pleased with the rare opportunity to be the center of attention. "I've made up my mind to keep a bit of livestock. Andy's been talking about chickens ever since she met with your wife. Now, the wife wants a cow and I'm thinking a few pigs, but Jimmy's heart has been set on horses."

Frank puffed on his pipe. "Horses aren't very profitable around here. They take up more money to keep than they earn."

"That may be so, but Jimmy's different. If money can be made from horses, he'll make it."

"Maybe Jimmy should talk to Charlie," Millie suggested. Already looking for ways to be useful, she got up and started helping Velma with cleaning. "He's trying to quit his Civil Service job. He thought he could make money hiring out horses for hunting trips, but Charlie scarcely knows how to hunt. His wife wants him to sell them. She's mad because they couldn't go to the states this year. They spent too much money on the horses."

"Charlie has a good position," grumbled Frank. "I don't know why he wants to give it up."

Millie scolded him. "Frank, not everyone wants to marry the military. It's easier for some to get away," she explained to her general audience. "If they work construction or mechanics. But Frank has a desk job and there isn't much demand for his work in the private sector."

Frank continued to fret. "Charlie works at a desk."

Millie threw up her arms. "Charlie is one great experiment. All I'm trying to say is, Jimmy should talk with him. I believe Charlie is about ready to sell his horses."

Their idle time didn't last long. Having no idea as to the value of the horses or even how many there were, the Lamars' common ground for conversation was slipping away, and the direction turned more to the feminine side of things, with a discussion on toddler development that Frank let know by the expression on his face, he found distasteful, especially when they began exchanging tips on toilet training.

Snorting loudly, slurping the remainder of his coffee, and pocketing the last biscuits, Frank stood up, opened his tool kit, and put on a pair of work gloves. Shrugging, Jimmy rummaged around in the canopy until he had found the chainsaw and protective leggings.

Frank didn't handle a chainsaw like a lumberjack, although you couldn't say he had no chainsaw skills. He examined the tool closely - both the length and heft of the saw - as well as the tension of its bladed teeth. When he fired it up, he played with the caliber until its whine was exactly the pitch he wanted.

It took him twenty minutes to cut his notches into a tree, but when he was done and he was ready to slice through, his timber landed precisely where he wanted it to land. It took him the entire morning and most of the afternoon to fell six trees, but each one made a perfect landing.

Satisfied he had done his good deed for the day, he returned the leggings and saw to the canopy, hanging both closely together on nails so they could be located easily, and placed his gloves back in his toolbox. Millie had been filling Andrea's ears with the details of each Wolf Creek neighbor's characteristics when she noticed Frank was ready to leave.

She gathered up Jason, waved cheerily goodbye to everyone, and marched up the trail the way she'd come, one arm hooked into Frank's elbow, the other balancing Jason on her hip.

The next Saturday, they reappeared at the same hour of the morning, with Matt Jones. Velma immediately recognized him as the man who had been traipsing about in the woods just a few days ago, tracing a wire and reconnecting it.

"Mr. Jones!" She said, "our phone still isn't working. I tried it out to see if it did, but nothing happened."

Matt gave her a concerned look. "Did you crank her up?"

"Did I do what?" She gasped as though she had been delivered an obscenity.

"Did you crank up the phone?" Matt gave her the same mild smile he gave puppies and children. "You've got to give the battery a good charge, get those juices pumping. Jimmy," he said, turning to the youngster who was lurking as unobtrusively in the background as possible in the vague hope of not receiving extra duties, "bring me the phone and I'll show these ladies how it's done. You haven't messed with it yet?"

"Not this one," he said, shaking his head. "Me and Ed played around with the one at the Grants."

The field phone was bulky, heavy and took an enormous amount of arm pumping power to crank it up enough to crackle and deliver a charge. But it did work. To demonstrate, Matt rotated the handle furiously until it sparked and hummed, connecting finally with Charlie Bolinder. "Charlie, you son-of-a-gun," he shouted into the mouthpiece. "Your buckskin broke into Millie's garden again. You owe her three young cabbages."

"I'll buy her a whole bushel of cabbages once I tan that hide and sell it," a voice crackled back. "How the hell did he get out?"

Matt winked at mama Velma, who clasped her hands in close to her chest, her eyes round as quarters. "Neah, he didn't. Just testing out our new emergency network. How far were you able to signal out?"

"I got to the Rasmussen's, and they signaled the village," the voice sizzled raggedly. "That gives us a ten-mile radius."

"That'll work. Arthur Bowen is holding center-point when his wife isn't on it."

A bark of laughter blared out, distorted by the crackling connection. "If he won't stand up to Sharon, who's going to?"

Matt looked swiftly around at the women listening in expectantly on his conversation. "Nobody. She runs a gang."

"Roger that. Tell Frank to get his butt away from Mrs. Delaney's cooking and back to work."

"I heard that," said Frank, wiping away the remains of a piece of fried bread and standing up to shout. "I'm not the one who finished off the Gilman donuts in the break room."

"Only to relieve you from temptation, my friend." The voice was growing faint, the brief power surge draining.

"See? They work," said Matt with satisfaction. "But you only have a few minutes before it begins losing its charge. The phones are old. They battled it out in the trenches." He laid his hand on it briefly as though the phone was a fallen comrade.

Realizing a few more sobrieties had been given the occasion than necessary, Matt blinked, handed the instrument back to Jimmy and clapped his hands. "Shall we get to work?"

The last of the trees needed for the cabin had been felled and stripped during the week. They stretched out on the drying rack, gleaming and raw, their stumps still puncturing the ground.

"It always looks sad when you have to cut down a bunch of trees," remarked Millie, gazing at the recent destruction.

Andrea sighed as she pulled on her work gloves. "It looks like a massacre, doesn't it? Raw wounds in the earth. Trees are so giving."

"We made a pact with the Erichmans, the Grants and the Bolinders that we would never cut down more trees than were necessary. That's why we keep wooded lots."

"We'll do the same thing, I believe. I'm glad we have the meadow. It's a natural clearing."

Mama Delaney had ushered them both off when she had learned the crew would be winterizing their shelter, telling them she could handle the kitchen by herself, but the men could use a couple extra hands.

The men were currently discussing their strategy. This involved complimentary rounds of pointing to the back of their shelter, shaking the structure and woeful headshaking. During the discussion, Jimmy walked over to a sapling and whacked it down with a single stroke of his axe.

They all examined it, determined it was the right size and length and walked into the woods to hunt down their own saplings. All except Owen, who shuffled toward Andrea, mumbling a little about how he needed to do serious work, not dilly dally over a canvas circus tent all day.

"I reckon," he said. "They want you girls pulling everything out of the shelter except the heavy stuff. They've got some fancy ideas on how we can make things a bit more livable even in the winter. It ain't costing me nothing but Jimmy's time so we might as well give it a try."

"I reckon," said Andrea, drawling out the words in imitation of his own languid speech. "You should make the most of it. The place is a mess. You can't even find half your tools. You said so, yourself."

He sniffed, which wasn't to say he agreed or disagreed. "Well, the creek ain't going to get cleaned out by itself," he answered querulously. "I'm going to do some weed hacking. We'll start pulling stumps next week."

He trundled off with just a slight amount of haste as there was always the chance Mama Delaney was watching, carrying a machete and a handsaw, and looking back occasionally at the soon to be dismantled shelter.

It really was a disgraceful affair. They had put it up without a plan in their heads other than to protect their belongings from the weather. Boxes and crates had been slammed together to keep them out of the rain.

The trailer had been used as an anchor for the canvas tarps that were supported on the other side by stakes and a center pole to house their tractor. In the four weeks since they arrived, the canvas was already sagging from rains and wind and the center pole needed constant propping. And this was the good month, Andrea reflected.

Even the little girls were enthusiastic about pulling their shelter apart. They were restless. The tents they had made for themselves were dreary and wet.

They nearly piled on each other to sleep at night and had no real space in the morning to act out the daydreams of young girls. They had moved all the lighter stuff and were struggling with the heavy boxes when the men reappeared with their collection of poles.

The fellows measured a straight line from the trailer, drove six poles into the ground, five feet apart for thirty feet, then two opposing poles flush with the trailer. They added a loose lattice work of suspended poles, and a back wall of saplings, all bound tightly together with twine. Over the top of everything, they spread the tarps and tacked them into place. Andrea was reminded of the army cots, so neatly cornered and smoothed, you could flick a coin on them.

Veterans work together with military precision. When they replaced the boxes and crates, they strategically placed them to serve as a wind barrier along the back wall, and as room dividers. To the far side, was a space to snug in the tractor and hang tools, with three packing crates piled up for shelves.

The central divider created a room for Andrea and Jimmy to set up private quarters. The space around the trailer served as a patio set off with Velma's China closet, her rocking chair, and her pedal pushed sewing machine.Before they had finished, Owen wandered back from cleaning the creek to scratch his head and admire his new tool shed.

Velma showed her own pleasure by sitting down in her rocking chair, holding her Bible and humming.

Ten

On a frowsy July afternoon, when the weather brooded between overcast and a few tearful sprinkles, Andrea dropped into the trading post for her usual three hours of work. It was, as normal at that time of day, a transitional hour.

The housewives had gone home to prepare dinner, the self-employed were shuffling in to have a drink or two and discuss the threat of communism, although they were not exactly sure why it was threatening, and the civil service workers had not yet appeared to explain their cautious stance against the red menace.

The giant, Dresden Hayes, was trying to sell his jewelry. There was something whimsical and sad about it. His work was beautiful and would have fetched hundreds of dollars in Seattle, but in the wilderness and its empty pockets, he could scarcely receive more than a few expressions of admiration and promises to buy something for Christmas.

As a prospector, he looked the part; over six feet tall and weighing in at four hundred pounds. With a beard like a briar patch and arms as thick as thirty- pound pork shoulders; you could hear the clang of a pick- axe ringing against rock when you looked at him.

His appearance as an artist was incongruous with poor and starving, even without his enormous girth. He had a successful mine. He was pulling out gold and wearing it around his neck, on his wrists, on his belt buckle in shining nuggets.

But he didn't sell it raw unless he needed instant cash. For Dresden, gold had more value as a pretty metal for his art than it did as a commodity for increasing his standard of living.

Dresden didn't care about the communist threat. He had no hankering for changing anyone's opinion about anything at all unless it was for buying his merchandise. Andrea liked this about him. As much as she had pried and goaded, as many outrageous statements as she could think to make, he only laughed in merriment and said, "is that a fact, Miss Andy Delaney?"

He had once told her, "It diminishes us when we try to visualize ourselves in the great scheme of things. We become like a piece in a giant jigsaw puzzle. We lose who we are. It's better to know we are a piece, no matter how many other pieces there are, and without us, the puzzle isn't complete."

She listened to him soliciting the customers for a few minutes while she wiped down the tables. Solicitations were common at the post. Anyone with something to sell or a service to offer dropped by the post first, trusting that word of mouth would secure the best deals. When he had squeezed the last bit of interest from his audience, she turned to him.

"What do you have today?"

Dresden unwrapped a handkerchief, revealing a set of tiny figurines. "Ivory carvings. I didn't do them," he admitted. "I hired a white Eskimo."

"A white Eskimo?" She raised her brows and picked up one of the pieces. It was a walrus with protruding front teeth. "I didn't know there were any."

"Oh yes, my boy is a rarity. He even speaks with a Scottish accent."

"Extraordinary."

She picked up an unusual looking piece. It was a smiling fat man who looked very much like a Buddha, but with a high, domed head. In the belly button was a tiny gold flake.

"Ah!" Said Dresden. "You have excellent tastes. This is a Billiken, the ancient Eskimo symbol of good luck."

"Really? I had always thought the Billiken was the product of a Missouri schoolteacher."

"Remarkable, isn't it? The world works that way. Whatever is imagined has a basis in reality."

"Remind me to never get into a debate with you. It would be pointless."

Dresden spread his ringed hands over his middle and hitched up his belt.

"Of course, it would. Now, about these little charms. I've been asking ten dollars each, but for you, sweet ma'am, I will give a discount price of five dollars, because I'm thirsty."

She slapped at him playfully with her dishcloth. "Your appetites destroy your sound judgment. You would have sold me at ten, but now that you've offered it, I'll take one for five."

"You strike a hard bargain, love. Throw a beer on top and we'll call it even."

Five dollars and a beer were not bad for an ivory charm, even if Dresden did have a strange way of bargaining. She flirted with him a few more minutes before depositing it in her handbag. Giving him a kiss on the top of his head that had been washed and groomed for his appearance at the lodge, she checked the cubbyhole behind the counter for any mail addressed to the Delaney family.

A catalog for farm equipment wrapped around three advertising coupons, a form letter from the commissioner's office, a letter for Jimmy, one directed to the Delaney family from her Aunt Lisa and a third sent to her name.

For a moment, she froze. Then her hand crept to the side of the envelope, her fingers brushing gently over the return address, bittersweet and angry.

A month ago, it would have been different. A month ago, she would have run rejoicing through the door. But now... She rolled the rest of the mail back up in the catalog and set the letter on top. Two of the homesteaders came in and she barely raised her head as she waited on them.

Dresden called behind her. "Are you angry, Andy? I'll buy the next beer. I'll buy you two beers as soon as you get off work."

She shoved back her surface thoughts and threw him a smile. "Just family affairs, Dres. We all have skeletons we try to keep in the closet, eh?"

The jovial face changed expression to one of thoughtful contemplation. "And one of yours came marching out."

She lifted her chin. "Not if we can circumvent it. We had an agreement and I'm afraid my skeleton has breached it."

He stared at her, his decorated fingers dazzling as he stroked his beard.

She scrubbed down the table next to his furiously and added a newly filled catsup bottle. "It's my fault," she said. "I should have locked the door behind me."

"If you need help pushing your skeleton back in, just let me know."

The main crowd was entering, leaving Andrea with no time to for individualized attentions. She put on her cheery face, which felt frozen around the mouth, and managed to appear remarkably normal. Internally, she did not feel normal at all. The letter she had waited for was no longer welcome.

She had been happy, she realized, happier than she had ever been at any other time in her life. She didn't really understand this new Andrea and had not worked out how this could be possible, yet she had become comfortable with her and didn't really want reminders of the life she had left behind.

Then there was Matt. Every day, he had become a little more important to her. Every weekend, without fail, he would show up to put in a few hours work helping the Delaneys clear their land. He spent time with Jimmy, assisting him in shoring up the sides of the creek so it settled into a deep pool before diving underground. When she mentioned his helpfulness to Millie, her neighbor had nodded with satisfaction.

"And he won't take a dime!" Said Andy. "We tried. But he will take a meal. He even sat in on mama's Bible readings the other night."

"He's like that," said Millie. "He has to stay busy. All the veterans have to stay busy. He helped the Bolinders put in the well last fall. All he took for it was room and board."

"Does he stay with them now?"

"Neah. He doesn't stay longer than he's needed. He's been helping the Erichmans, but he'll probably be moving on. Doreen complains she wants her space."

That was the difference she supposed. Delaney women usually attracted men who needed not the ones who filled a need. She didn't need Matt. The whole farm ran splendidly without him, but he filled a want.

There were boundaries on the type of behavior a single woman could use around married men, even the husbands of her best friends.

Especially the husbands of her best friends. You were careful in using your wits and charms around them. You didn't want to appear too interested in their work or their hobbies. She liked Matt because when she was with him, she didn't have to pay attention to boundaries. They were both single. They were free to be outrageous or bold while they were together.

Perhaps it was a little more than that. Dresden was single. His wit was as sharp as a Samurai sword, and there were other single men that paraded in and out of the lodge daily, but she was attracted to Matt. As hard as she tried to keep the emotion wrapped up tight, she felt it spring out with joy every time she saw him.

Matt Jones took off his knitted cap and squashed it in his pocket as he sat down at the counter. Andrea set a pack of Camels and a cup of coffee in front of him. He tapped the pack on the polished surface, thumped the top, and pulled out two cigarettes, offering her one.

"It's quiet. You can take a break," he said.

"I told her that myself," said Dresden from his table. "She doesn't listen to me."

Andrea inhaled deeply. It was only her second cigarette of the day and felt like just what the doctor ordered. "Don't pay attention to him. He only wants to sell you ivory earrings."

Matt acknowledged Dresden by raising his coffee cup but did not invite him over. "Is that a fact? I'm told I look very striking in ivory."

He smelled of freshly turned earth and diesel fuel. The thought of earrings dangling from his ears caused a real smile. "You could always buy a pair for your sweetheart," she suggested. "That is if you have one." Her lips curved up flirtatiously.

"Maybe," he said, unable to keep a straight face, but continuing his charade. "Do you think Millie would like them?"

She gave him a playful shove. "You devil. You know she's not like that. She's had Jimmy coming around quite a bit, though. She wants him to chase off this lynx, but she won't let him shoot it. He's beaten the bushes black and blue trying to keep it away. It seems to take a perverse pleasure in waiting until she goes out to sit on the can, then start yowling."

His eyes danced with mischief. "See? I think I have a shot. Jimmy's a young guy."

"You men are all alike. Millie would no more have an affair than my mama would."

"Now there's another I've been contemplating. Do you think Owen would notice if I took her for a spin?"

"You are a mad man," she declared, stabbing out her cigarette and resuming her chores.

But he had made her feel better. He had spoken loud enough for the lodge to hear and weigh out their own chances of catching mama Delaney's eye, which would be on par with catching the eye of a velociraptor. And spotless Millie…. She would probably put a hex on any man who made inappropriate advances, and he would disappear from the face of the earth the way the scoundrel, Ted Ewing did.

The bawdy laughter lingered, deepening the ambiance of the diner. Her step was lighter, her service more personable, even some of the sparkle returned to her eyes. At the shift's end, she didn't stay and banter, however. She gathered her things, said a quick good night to Solace and left by the back door.

The raindrops had grown larger, falling closer together. Andrea sat in the cab of the truck, staring at the letter. She turned the ignition and waited for the cough and sputter of the big engine to settle to a low grumbling, but before she could pop it into gear, she heard a tap on her window. It was Matt.

"Are you alright?" He asked concernedly. "Dresden told me something you received in the mail upset you."

Her hand played with the gearshift. "Don't think about it. It's not something you can fix."

"If you need someone to talk to…"

"I don't. Matt, get out of the rain. You'll catch cold."

The truck squealed as she stomped down on the clutch and changed the gears. He jumped out of the way and remained standing in the drive watching her as she roared down the road.

The two younger sisters danced around the truck as she idled Abe a few seconds before switching off the ignition.

"Did you bring potato chips?" sang Anna, skipping on one foot, then the other. "You promised."

"I did. Here. Take the mail with you. I'm going to my tent."

"But it's early," protested Carol. "Didn't anything happen today?"

"If you mean, did I see the railroad worker's son, no I did not. Word has it, he and his dad have been spending their spare time volunteering in clearing the land for the community hall."

"They should be helping us with our house," objected Carol.

"We are already receiving a lot of help. The community hall is for everybody, so of course everyone lends a hand."

Looking at her slyly, her eyes growing long and narrow, Carol suggested, "Maybe we should too, then maybe the railroad worker's son will have time to volunteer over here."

She chased them from the front of the truck. "I think your mind is entirely too busy. I brought you chips. Go on now. You can be without me for one night."

Carol pouted, while Anna dropped her arms and turned around mournfully, saying, "ugh. Jimmy is the same way tonight. Said he wants privacy. We're going to make ourselves some private quarters."

"You should do that," she agreed as they finally retreated to the patio.

She stared at their tight military arrangement.

The central area was private only in the respect that it had been blocked off on both sides with their storage crates, and a single tarp ran down the front, partially hiding the two tents squatting side by side.

It had been enough, more than enough. It had filled her with a sense of purpose. She had begun to believe in herself. *When did I stop believing?* She wondered, and the letter in her hand seemed to stare at her accusingly.

The tarp hung two feet off the ground. On good days, they rolled it up and tied it to one of the supporting posts. On rainy or windy days, they let it drop so they would still be snug and dry without being driven into their tents. The tents were small, with room only for a pad, sleeping bag, blankets, and pillows, so they really used them just for sleeping.

It was the enclosure itself they considered their private quarters. They had moved in folding chairs, set up packing boxes for their personal items, and used a Bunsen burner for hot coffee.

Jimmy had lighted a hurricane lantern. Its glow spilled dully in an oblong shaft from under the tarp, competing with the sharp rain droplets and diffused daylight. She could see his feet stretched out from a folding chair. Maybe she would like to have someone there when she opened it. Jimmy was the best candidate. Siblings were remarkable that way. When they weren't rivaling, they were the closest friends.

She folded the letter into her pocket and picked up a paper bag containing four beers and a pack of cigarettes. "I hear you are anti-social tonight," she remarked, coming inside, and handing Jimmy one of the beers.

He accepted it gratefully. "They're driving me crazy. Carol wants me to escort her so she can go to the trading post and mama keeps pushing me to write to Glenda Taylor."

Andrea pulled around the other folding chair. "Why haven't you written to Glenda? It's not like you've been spreading yourself around to be known."

Jimmy rocked back in his chair, his beer on his knee. "I've been thinking I'd like a girl who's already broken in. An Anchorage girl, maybe. I don't think Glenda would like it here."

Andrea opened a beer for herself and took a long swallow. "Are you afraid if she doesn't, she'll talk you into moving back to Colorado?"

"Yeah. I like it here, Andy. I don't want someone as crazy as Betty Lou, but I do want someone who likes it here."

"Glenda's a Christian. She'll go where you go."

"She'll be unhappy. The women who are here just because of their husbands are unhappy. They don't want to stay."

She shuffled for the letter, then flattened it against her hip. "You should have escorted Carol to the post. At least you would be circulating."

Jimmy grunted. "There aren't any single women there except you, Betty Lou and a couple of others from the old mining camp. We should shine our shoes and hit the town."

She broke into the pack of cigarettes, lit one for herself, then tossed the rest to Jimmy. "How about this Saturday when I get off work? We could go to the Sourdough Club."

Jimmy liked the idea. They bantered a little about not being Sourdoughs yet, then Andrea said, "a letter came for me today. I want you to read it."

"It's from Jake?" She nodded.

He gave a loud sniff and turned down his mouth. "Throw it in the fire."

She drew the letter from her pocket and handed it to him. "Just tell me what it says."

He glanced over it quickly and gave it back. "You should read it yourself. It's personal. I don't read anything that begins with 'dearest'".

"Then skip through the flowery parts. What does he want?"

"He says he hopes he finds you well."

"That's nice of him."

He looked at it more closely and frowned. "It says, 'I know we didn't part under the best of circumstances, but I still think of you often and wish we could have done things better. Please don't be angry.'" He stopped to take a drag on his cigarette and polish off his beer. "Are you angry?"

Andrea handed him a refill. "I'm not sure angry is the right word. Try furious with cruel intents."

"Well, there's maybe six paragraphs of I'm sorry, then he says he's coming to town and wants to see you." He set his beer on the ground and leaned forward. "Andy, don't do it."

She took the letter from him and read through it swiftly. It did have a lot of flowery phrasing and tearful apologies, but not one word about the son he had abandoned. Not one word inquiring into the child's health or expressing a desire to see him. But he would be in town this weekend and he wanted to see her. He had written in the date and time of arrival so there would be no mistake.

"He'll be here Saturday. Just when we decided to have a night on the town. We could still do it. You could drop me off at the airport and pick me up a few hours later."

"You're letting me drive Abe?"

"Just around town. I'd come along but the Sourdough Club is no place to take a baby."

"You're bringing Ben?"

"Of course, I'm bringing Ben. That's the whole idea."

"Mama won't like it. He's one of ours now. Jake has had no part in it."

"He's the father of my child. I intend to take Ben. I want him to meet Ben."

Mama Delaney was completely opposed to sending her grandson off to meet the man whose only claim to familial relations was failure to use appropriate birth control methods.

"He has passed the point where he is entitled to anything," she scolded. "You want him to see his son? He should pay for the privilege. He should give you a proper allowance for raising him. He should be a man and provide a home."

Andrea nodded as though she was in total agreement, yet still insisted Jake should meet Ben. She said it might stimulate him more to provide for them but failed to mention Jake had not asked to see his child at all.

She hoped the baby would endear him. He was a fine, strong boy, already taking his first steps. He was handsome, with sandy-colored hair and his father's blue eyes.

The day Jake was scheduled to arrive, Andrea took off from work. It was an early evening flight, which meant perfect timing for dinner. She dressed Benjamin in knee-length trousers, a striped pull-over shirt, and his sturdy over-the-ankle shoes.

She wetted down the bit of angel fluff on top of his head and combed it into a single curl. She placed him in the truck and waited for Jimmy, who jumped in with his hair slicked back and his guitar in his hand.

"Are you going to serenade the girls?" asked Andrea, the amusement twinkling in and out of her cheeks.

"Solace was telling me they've got auditions happening for guitar players at the Sourdough Club. The band doesn't come in until nine. Before then, they let people try out their music. If the public likes it, they put money in your hat. If the Club likes it, they'll hire you for gigs. They've got a microphone, a stage, lights and everything."

She jostled him. "You're going to serenade the girls."

"I could be good at it."

"You don't sing very well."

"Maybe I'll find someone to do the singing. There's probably a lot of good singers. It's the playing that's hard. I'm a good player."

"Yes, you are," she agreed.

The letter had said he would arrive at the airport at six, but Andrea deliberately dawdled in Wolf Creek until she was nearly an hour late, knowing Jake would fret. He would probably throw a small tantrum, toss around his hat, and complain to the flight attendants, but he would wait. He would wait because right now he needed her. He had probably taken a gambling loss, or some floozy had ridden rough-shod over his ego.

He needed reassurances. He needed to feel like a king again.

She saw him before he saw her. He was leaning against the arrivals counter, trying to appear nonchalant, but stabbing his cigarette viciously at the ash tray. She surrendered the driver's seat to Jimmy, pulled Ben toward her, smoothed his clothing, and kissed him on the head.

"Time to meet your daddy, darling. Keep your smile up."

Her high heels clacked noisily on the short sidewalk and the terminal building's tile floor. He turned in the direction of the sound, the expression of annoyance smoothing out with some effort as he cranked up a smile. "I was beginning to think you weren't coming."

"My home life keeps me busy. It hasn't been that long, has it?" She asked innocently, craning her head to look at the clock. "Oh, it's nearly seven. I hope the dinner date was a standing offer. Ben is always fed dinner at six."

"Ah, this is Ben," he said, his brows furled together in a pose of serious study. "Doesn't look greatly like me, does he? He looks more like a Delaney."

Andrea disagreed. "Oh, I think he has your eyes. He's going to have your nose as well." She squeezed the sides of the baby's nose with two fingers, causing him to chortle. "And your laugh. That does sound like your laugh."

"He's big."

"He's nearly a year old. He's taken his first steps. You've missed them."

He made a good show of reticence, letting his wrist drape sadly from his propped elbow, his cigarette dripping below his fingers. He turned his head to study her. "I guess I've missed out on a lot. You look good. You look happy. I would not have thought wilderness life would suit you."

"I was probably as surprised as anyone. The locals say we arrived in the best month though, and the best of times. I might feel differently during the worst of times."

He cleared his throat noisily. "We all know what happens to you during the worst of times. You bail."

She wasn't going to let him crack her. "The thing about the weather is, it gives us winter, but it also gives us spring. Once you gave me winter, Jake, you never gave another spring."

He straightened his flight jacket, reminding her he had an important job, one that took him unavoidably away to distant places. "There you go with your silly talk again. Your words don't make sense."

He was sulking. His eyes narrowed to watch her face, to see if she felt any remorse for their months apart. She jiggled Ben, keeping her attention focused on his baby babble, encouraging it, and insisting he was saying words.

After a few seconds, Jake pretended to listen, applauded the garbled efforts then said impatiently, "Should we go then? They just opened a new restaurant a few blocks from here."

They took a taxi. Not that it mattered greatly but riding in a taxi was nice. It was romantic. The new restaurant was more accurately, seven blocks from the airport. It was in a newer part of town, verging away from the small, tight group of buildings birthed by a tent city. The freshly cultivated area had a nice view of the inlet and cunning grass and wildflower lawns in front, seeding now with late summer.

The cafeteria was nice; shiny, with lots of chrome. Miniature juke boxes sat on the tables, with a selection of country music hits.

Ben amused himself with the metal napkin holder, which fortunately contained only a half-dozen paper napkins.

He depleted the napkins immediately, tossing them out of the holder, but since it kept him busy, Andrea chose to allow it.

The food menu was all home cooking; mashed potatoes and gravy, corn on the cob, sausage and biscuits.... even beef cuts and barbecued pork ribs, which was a welcome break from wild game. She ate T-bone steak and baked potato with sour cream, pretending she was back in civilization, pretending that when she walked out the door, she would see long, even sidewalks, tall brick buildings, congested traffic, and streetlights.

They played Hank Williams and Tex Ritter on the music selection. The music tinkled around them, the tiny speaker enclosing them in the privacy of its tunes.

"I was thinking of a movie afterward," he told her. "Do you think Ben will sit through one?"

"We can find out," she said hopefully.

The theater had officially opened two years before yet was still the most talked about venue around. It was where you went when you wanted to completely escape into a world of opulence. The Wolf Creek women had gushed about it.

Lush velvet seats, thick carpeting, wall to wall mirrors and larger than life drama carved into gold-painted murals, designed to make you forget the terrible years of struggle, the pain of hunger. That made you forget they had just come out of the war that was supposed to end all wars, yet peace was still uneasy. It was all in the past. It was over. Here was the future they had been promised, in rich, royal colors, in perfume and jewels.

Andrea wanted to attend the first time she heard the Wolf Creek women talking about it. They had all been to the theater at least once. Some made movie going a once a month treat, although most were a little more conservative, keeping in mind that for the same price, they could go camping on the Kenai Peninsula, and bring home some fish.

It wasn't really Andrea's choice to be frugal. She was when it was forced upon her, but generally she preferred that others handled the serious business of providing shelter and she would bring home delicious treats, splurge on entertainment and indulge in vanities. She wanted her first time at the theater to be magical. It should have been.

The introductory cartoon kept Ben happy. He chortled and waved his plump arms, but before they had even gotten through the short documentary on war recovery, he began growing restless. She gave him her key ring to play with. The keys kept him entertained for ten minutes.

The movie playing had been the rage; a musical comedy about three soldiers on shore leave. She watched the first part with Ben squirming on her lap, tapping at her face now and then for attention and struggling to get down and play. She fed him his bottle, hoping he would go to sleep. He did not. He continued to fuss restlessly.

Twice, she took him to the lady's room to quiet him down. Twice, she returned to her seat, soothing him, while Jake, who had really been spending more attention to trying to place an arm around her shoulders and draw her close while the baby protested, then he did to the movie, finally folded his arms at the back of the neck and frowned, seeing nothing funny at all about the three skirt-chasing sailors.

She yielded to Benjamin before the movie had ended., apologizing insincerely, secretly feeling relieved she had an excuse. "I should take him home now. He's getting cranky."

Jake agreed. His face showed relief that his official visit with his son was nearing its end, but there was also a crafty gleam in his eyes. She owed him a piece of her time. He walked with her out to the curb, tucking her elbow in close to his.

"It wasn't so bad, was it? He got restless, but it wasn't so bad." Jake looked at the sky as though he expected a direct revelation from the clouds.

"He does better when he gets used to things. It was all new to him," she answered encouragingly.

The taxi pulled up and he helped her inside yet held on to the door without making a move to climb in beside her. She gave him a puzzled glance.

"You're not going back to the airport with me?"

"No. My hotel is just a block from here. Here, I'll pay for the cab." He stuffed a twenty- dollar bill into her hand, which was far more than she needed, so she supposed he was chipping in a little child support.

"It wasn't so bad," she admitted. "It could get better."

He remained at the door, unwilling to close it just yet. "Let's get used to us again, Andy. You and me. Let's learn about each other all over again. There's a night club I would like to take you to. Good music. Good dance floor. One more date. Tomorrow. You and me."

"And Ben?"

"It's a night club. I've got an idea. I don't fly out until day after tomorrow. Bring him by Monday, before I leave. We'll make a lunch date of it. He's a good eater."

It was against her better judgment, but she rationalized her decision as she always did in matters of the heart. Benjamin had not behaved well at the theater, ruining what could have been a perfect evening. She and Jake had the same right as any other couple to escape into romance.

They needed to be able to touch each other, remember what it was like to bring each other pleasure. She couldn't force Jake to become a good father. He had to do it willingly, but there was no reason they couldn't enjoy each other's company. If he loved her, eventually, he would love Benjamin. It was good sense. It would bring them together as a family.

Her timing was actually pretty good. She waited at the airport only fifteen minutes when Jimmy appeared. Perversely, Ben had chosen the terminal as a good place to fall asleep and was dozing like a lamb when the truck pulled up. She scooped him up in her arms, not waiting for Jimmy to climb out and help. She wanted to go home.

He politely asked her about her night first, but he was grinning ear to ear. Andrea knew he really wanted to talk about his. "Mine was good. It went well," she said. "Papa and son are going to end up friends. What are you smiling about? Did you get lucky?"

He broke in eagerly. "I made three dollars and I found a singer. She's a cocktail waitress for the club. The manager said he's not paying for gigs right now, but me and Tammy – that's the singer – can play for tips from the audience. Tammy says I play well."

"Good for you, Jimmy. You won't be bumming money off me all the time."

"Eh. What about it, Andy? Are you seeing him again?"

She kept her eyes on the road, one hand roaming over the gearshift of Abe, revving him simultaneously with her thoughts.

"He wants to go out with me again tomorrow night. Alone, without Ben. But it's only one night. Little by little, they'll get to know each other."

Jimmy wrapped a protective arm around Ben, asleep in his arms. "You don't really believe that. It's not going to end well. Nothing with Jake Monroe ends well."

Eleven

Everyone knew it wasn't going to end well. That was what Andrea said to Millie. "Jimmy knew it. Mama and pop knew it. They all told me it's not going to end well, but it's always about the beginning. He pulls at me like a magnet."

Millie, whose taste for adventure never exceeded her decorum, paused between counting the loops she gathered into her knitting needles to look up and ask, "do you love him?"

Andrea sighed. "I don't think that's what it is. It's like the magic carpet ride with Jake. The ticket into fantasyland. I wasn't going to fly away with him, but somehow it became easy. A few drinks, a dozen dances, a night in a luxury hotel. And then, just a flight, a short flight to Kodiak and the flight turned into three days. He did it to me again!"

"It must have been exciting." Millie awarded Andrea's confidentiality with a second cup of coffee and some delicately cut deviled ham sandwiches, then went back to her knitting, her fingertips smoothing and straightening the rows.

"It was, but after three days, I began to think of Benjamin again and how he still wasn't with us. How we really weren't being a family, just a hot pair of lovers. And it didn't seem right, and I wanted to go home."

"So, you quarreled."

"Of course, I quarreled." Andy set down her cup forcefully, nearly splashing the contents over the side. "I couldn't have done otherwise. I was with Jake for five days and he saw Benjamin for only three hours."

Millie's voice faltered and picked over her words. It was the voice she used when she really did not want to sound judgmental but was having a very difficult time remaining neutral. "Andy, how could a man possibly love you who doesn't have love for his own child?"

Andrea's green eyes flashed, and she tossed back her hair. "Did I say he loves me? He never loved me. I'm his Christmas ornament. I know it's never going to work. Jake isn't a mean man or a vicious man. He just lives in his own world. His first love is flying."

Her needles flashed furiously, reining in any careless words. "Maybe when Ben gets older, Jake will change his mind. When they're babies, they're such wobbly little things. Men see them as blobs. Frank doesn't know what to make of them at all. It's when they get older and start forming personalities – that's when the dads notice them."

"At least Frank is attempting to be a father. Millie, men like Jake aren't family men. They are successful men. They take trophy wives. They show them off at business conventions and at social events with their buddies. He wasn't planning on any extra passengers."

"Whether he was planning for it or not, now he is a father."

"No, he isn't," she said quickly. "He hated my pregnancy. Once I started to show, he wouldn't take me out anymore. He hated living in the apartment with a baby. He hated the bottles, the dirty diapers, the nightly interruptions. He hated it all and would leave me days at a time with nothing. No money, no food. He didn't even show up at the maternity ward when the baby was born. He said he had to do an emergency flight."

Andrea's fingers tapped bitterly on the table. "He bought a plane. That's where his money went. He bought his own plane. He said he wasn't going to let a snotty-nosed kid ruin his life. That's what he said, Millie."

The sandwiches sat, untouched, on the table. Millie had made them with store-bought white bread, cutting off the ends to bring out the rich taste of their filling. It would be a pity to see them go to waste. She placed two triangular pieces on Andrea's plate, encouraging her to eat.

It was the best she knew how to do. If words didn't give comfort, coffee and deviled ham sandwiches should.

Millie mulled over Frank's qualities. "He attempts as well as can be expected. He never knew his father much, either. You know how it was during the Depression. Men taking off to all parts of the country, looking for work."

"Frank's father abandoned his family?"

"Well, to hear Jocelyn Lamar say it, he did. It must have been hard for her with three girls and only one boy. No man in the house, just her young son. But Frank says it's not really so. His dad didn't abandon the family. He left it to find work."

Millie inspected the row of loops she had just finished, then picked up the count again by some mysterious talent she had for talking and keeping track of the number of loops at the same time. As though to prove this ability, she added in another color thread without missing a beat.

"The San Bernardino Valley filled up with Dust Bowl farmers looking for work. There was no work. There were too many people, too few places to put them."

"But Frank was born in San Bernardino."

"Yes, he was born there. That made it harder, seeing their fine neighborhood turn into neglected shambles. They had to sell half their property. Jocelyn wept bitterly over it. The only jobs were in fruit picking and Mr. Lamar was too proud a man for it. Wouldn't let the family do any of it, either. He said he would find better ways for them to survive, so he left."

"When he left, did he find a job?"

"He did. Not at first. He's a building engineer and there wasn't much construction going on until he hit the northwest. That's when he went to work for the government, building bridges. That's when he talked Frank into joining the youth corps. Jocelyn never forgave Mr. Lamar for that. She divorced him."

"But he sent her money!"

"Of course, he sent her money! He's a gentleman. He wanted his children to receive a proper upbringing. But he wanted her to move to Oregon where his job was at. She refused. It's why Frank eats the way he does, you know. They were a proud family. They went hungry a lot."

Andrea's hands folded and unfolded on the table. "But Frank's father was still being a father. He was still taking care of a family."

Millie's lips counted silently then stopped at a number, imprisoning a loop between her needles. "If that's what you want, then maybe you should start looking around for someone else. You can't force Jake to be what he isn't."

"It would be the sensible thing, wouldn't it? Just find someone else."

"There are a lot of nice men around. Matt's a nice guy and I'm pretty sure he likes you."

"It's because he's a nice guy I shouldn't let him get too serious."

The knitting needles halted in surprise. "Why ever not?"

Andrea groped around in her purse for her cigarettes. She sighed deeply as she brought one out and lit it. "Because I can't guarantee what happened with Jake won't happen again. I can't guarantee I wouldn't fly off with him to Kodiak or Seattle or Denver. It's the temptation. I can't get around it."

Millie's eyebrows went up, then down again as she clucked softly. "At least you're honest."

"Does it make you think less of me?"

"Why should it? You are who you are. Legally, he's still your husband. Whatever you work out is between the two of you."

Andrea watched the knitting needles construct another neat row of tight little loops, all conspiring to hold together in some design of their master's choosing. Like tiny people bowing their heads close together in prayer, stronger and more purposeful as their numbers grew larger.

"Whatever are you making?" Andrea asked. "You've been knitting all day."

Millie sighed, flopped her hand, and ate a sandwich before replying. "Oh, I'm pregnant again."

Andrea scooted her chair away from the table, feigning panic. "Oh no. Oh no, you're probably contagious. There will be a whole rash of new babies in the spring."

"Well, if we can't get more people to come in, I guess we can populate the area by ourselves."

Suddenly, Andrea felt hungry as well. It was difficult not to get excited about newcomers, even tiny ones. Especially tiny ones they could watch grow and become people in their own right. She ate rapidly, her mind filled with the sounds of gurgling babies and childish laughter. Her own problem didn't seem like a problem at all.

"They'll move in. Maybe not as fast as we would like, but it will happen. By the way, is the lynx still giving you trouble? Jimmy said he thought he saw it out in the meadow day before yesterday."

"I think it's running a circuit. Ester said she saw the lynx behind her house and that it fought with her cat. Or mated. She's not sure which."

"I'm sure they couldn't have mated."

"It's a big cat. Main Coon, I think. She says if the cat gets pregnant, she's going to sell the kittens."

"Maybe it was just another big cat."

Millie's knitting needles flew faster. "I don't like to question Ester. It's not the first time someone would claim half lynx kittens. I don't know how successful they are at selling them, though. The only real use for a cat is in chasing mice. I don't imagine we need a wild cat for that purpose."

Andrea laughed. "Knowing Ester, I'm sure she'll manage it. Does she still want Charlie to sell his horses?"

"She does. She said she is taking a vacation next year whether Charlie comes along or not, so he'd better start thinking about what to do with those horses. He's putting off until after fall hunting, though. It's the only time they bring him any money."

"I thought you said Charlie's not a good hunter."

"He's not a good hunter. He's not a good tracker. But he's Charlie! He has to try."

Andrea leaned forward, her voice a hushed whisper. "You should tell him to hire Jimmy to track. He'd probably do it for a share of the game and a chance to talk some horse business."

Millie put her knitting away to make sure the sandwiches did not get wasted, putting one on Andy's plate, another on her own. "I have a better idea. I'll talk to Frank and have him talk to Charlie. He'll listen better that way."

"See, that's Charlie's problem. He doesn't listen enough to a woman's advice."

The two boys were tugging at her skirt for a sandwich. Millie wiped their faces and give them each a triangular piece.

"We'll just have to work on him. It's a sad state of affairs, but half the men around here are like that. You have to grab them by the ears to make them listen.

They are single-minded. They want their charter. They want their community hall. They want their fire brigade, yet they have not said one word about what we are to do for our children's health and education. We must bludgeon them over the heads with it before they do anything at all."

Andrea shrugged. "The girls will be taking a bus to Anchorage this year for school."

She stopped trying to teach the boys a few social graces in their sandwich exchange to look up and say, "Andy, when Ben is six years old, do you want to send him twenty miles away on a bus in the middle of winter to go to school? It's too tender of an age."

Opposing Millie's politics was never a good idea. The men might quarrel and bicker, but as soon as Millie, Mighty Sharon, or dour Ester opened their mouths, the rest of the women fell into line and did not budge for husband or hellfire.

"Of course, you're right. Carol and Anna are big girls, and they have each other. It wouldn't set so well if they were younger."

Noticing the hour was nearly four, Andrea stood up, brushed away the crumbs of her dainty sandwiches, and located Ben under the table, playing tug-of-war with Jason over the last scrap of bread. "Before I forget," she said, pulling Ben to his feet. "The Grants overstocked their hotdogs and gave me a few packages to bring home. We're having a wienie roast tonight. Come over. Bring your appetites."

"The Grants hired you back after being gone five days?" asked Millie with surprise.

"They did. They were quite nice about it."

"Well, then. I suppose they must like you."

Andrea laughed as she was leaving. "I'm good for business."

Ben wasn't really walking well enough yet to tolerate his slow progress from Millie's yard to their own. Andrea put him up on her shoulders as soon as they reached the bottom step of the porch, carrying him as effortlessly as a backpack.

She had told Millie several times, she should carry Jason the same way; up on her shoulders so the weight would be evenly distributed; but Millie automatically hiked her baby up on her hip. Millie, though, wasn't a horseback rider. She used the same method of carrying as women did everywhere who were not bound to the rocking flow of horses. Plus, Millie's hips were ample. They were the kind of hips children hugged around like bear cubs.

Nothing went through her head concerning the un-neighborly lynx, or finding a suitable educational program for the children, but she did mull over the conversation about Jake. It was best to forget about him. He wouldn't change. She had made a mistake to go flying with him. He knew she couldn't resist, and knew once she was in the air, she was powerless. He could take her where he wanted to go for as long as he wanted.

He was such a good lover. The first night she had spent with him, they had idled the whole evening rediscovering each other's bodies and all the little things that gave them pleasure. She hadn't paid attention to the time. All she remembered in her waking moments, were the sheer green curtains fluttering against the windows, Jake getting up to bring more champagne and caviar, and occasional sounds floating in from the streets.

She was still in a haze when he had sprung out of bed and told her, "Oh God, it's late. I've got a flight in two hours."

She had protested, reminding him he had promised to see Ben.

"It's just to Kodiak and back," he wheedled. "One day trip. You can come along. We'll be back this evening and I can see Ben."

He lied. He would always lie, yet she would always believe him until it was too late.

"Why do you do that to yourself?" She asked out loud. Ben babbled. "You're right," she told him. "It is a lovely day."

Although it was getting late in the summer, with many of the wildflowers perishing and longer nights pushing their way over the horizon, it was still a wonderful time of the year. The air was warm, even a little steamy, with the persistence of clouds and occasional sprinkles. Berries were clustering together, turning bright red in the lingering sunlight.

"I should join Millie in gathering berries," she said to Ben, who gurgled back appreciably. "We'll make jellies. That should make your grandma happy. We don't have a proper kitchen yet for getting the jellies to set right. We'll make them at Millie's house."

The idea made her whistle as she entered the clearing. The idea was very tidy, very homey. Her five-day vacation made her see clearly how much she appreciated home. The very word gave her a thrill. This was home, more even than the failing farm in Colorado. It was the future. It showed promise and purpose.

Mama Delaney gave Andrea a frown when she appeared. It was still too early to be cheerful. Mama was a firm believer in long-term penitence. Andy quit whistling but the cheery plans for winter preparations still skipped through her head.

It was difficult to remain sadly remorseful as everyone at Wolf Creek had appeared happy to see her back. She felt a little guilty at abandoning such good friends, but the cheerful reunion had whisked away all thoughts of a tearful return.

The gossipers could not decide how worthy her disappearance had been of generating gossip. They didn't know Jake. They didn't know why she left him. The fact remained, he was her husband, so leaving with him for five days was not scandalous. They needed more details to relish the event properly, but details weren't coming.

Andrea decided the limbo between living apart and divorced wasn't a bad one. Maybe, it was desirable. It allowed her to visit single men liberally without getting involved. Since she was technically married, she was considered "safe" around married men. All in all, it was a comfortable arrangement.

Despite mama's censorship, the entire family was in high spirits. The campfire had been built early and now had a large bed of hot coals. As much land clearing as they had done all summer, Andrea felt there should be a campfire every evening, especially now that the nights were becoming longer and cooler.

There was a lot of ground litter, despite the amount they had stacked for winter kindling. They could build campfires until the snow fell and not get rid of it all. Once it had been picked through, the rest would be plowed under for compost.

Because there were enough hotdogs to make an impressive pile, mama had relented enough from her disapproval to make a large potato salad and open a jar of her precious pickles that she had carried all the way up the Alcan. They were going to miss mama's pickles. Millie said cucumbers didn't grow well in Alaska, except maybe in a greenhouse. Some of the valley folks were building greenhouses. Someday, cucumbers would reign supreme.

Jimmy had invited Matt Jones. It wasn't that she minded. She just wished she had known. Why she needed a warning beforehand, she couldn't explain to herself. She wished she was dressed a little differently, appeared a little less flustered with her mothering skills which were clinging to her skirt right now with sticky, mud caked hands.

"Oh my God," Andrea said, swooping Ben up and handing him to Carol. "Do me a favor and wash him up for dinner. He just spoiled my skirt. I'll have to change before the mud sets in."

She went into her tent and pulled on the slacks she had laid out for the evening. She wasn't going to rummage around in the boxes for another dress just to impress Matt. Especially considering the dress would probably be ruined before the evening was over.

Her sweater was nice, at least, and everyone said she looked good in slacks. That counted for something. She applied a small amount of lipstick and tied her hair back loosely in a ribbon. When she came back out in the open, Ben had been scrubbed clean and given a hotdog to keep him occupied while he sat in a cardboard box.

"Ah, there's my boy," she said, picking him up and kissing him. She turned to look at Matt. "Why, I think he likes you. He's offering you his hotdog."

It was true. Ben was waving his hotdog at Matt and gurgling.

178

"That's very kind of you," said Matt, pretending to take the wiener, then handing it back. "But I have one of my own. You should eat this one."

As far as Ben was concerned, Matt had lost his chance. He chowed down happily at what was left of his treat and reached out expectantly for more.

Andrea started to put him back in the box, crooning, "Just let me fix you a plate."

But Matt stopped her. "I'll hold him until you get back. He's a cute little fella."

Since Ben posed no opposition, she handed him over. The table had set out well. Matt had brought two loaves of store-bought bread to wrap around the hotdogs and Jimmy had brought beer and sodas. She cut up a hotdog and added some pieces of bread and a dab of potato salad in a bowl for Ben to paw through and returned to the campfire. Matt was sitting in one of the folding chairs, jiggling the boy on his lap.

"I think we get along well," he said.

"He's an amiable child." She picked him up and put him in his box. "Don't spoil him too much or the girls will forget their chores to keep him happy."

They had gotten down to the serious business of stabbing their hotdogs with sharpened sticks and waving them over the open fire, when Millie and Frank appeared with two large bags of marshmallows.

"Now we have a true hotdog roast," said Andrea gaily. "I can't even remember the last time I did this." She licked at the edge of her rolled up wiener. She had used too much catsup and it was oozing over the side.

"Way too long for me," agreed Millie. "I think we need to make it a tradition. One wiener roast before the end of summer."

Suddenly inspired, Frank stated, "we should have a baseball team!"

Andrea laughed. "A baseball team! Whatever brought that on?"

"Think about it." Frank had not only roasted his hotdog perfectly, but had also wrapped the bread around it, plopped it back on the stick and toasted the bread gently. It lay on his plate in perfect synchrony with the large helping of potato salad and balanced on his lap with the same refinement. "If we have a baseball team, we'll be organizing weekend games. If we have weekend games, we have to sell hotdogs."

Andrea failed to see the connection. "We're talking about roasting hotdogs over a fire."

Even though he had also used a generous amount of catsup, it dared not drip from Frank's creation. He popped half the sandwich into his mouth, chewed it and swallowed it before continuing. "We can roast anything, you know. Hotdogs, hamburgers on a grill, chicken or steak, but you've got to have hotdogs at a baseball game."

"How many players do you think you could squeeze out of two hundred residents?" pursued Matt, who had no problem following his logic. "Near half of them are miners, trappers or railroad men. Do you think they'll be interested in playing baseball?"

"We've got the Civil Service workers," said Frank. "They're solid. That makes seven. There's Jimmy. That's eight."

"I'd join the baseball team," said Millie, raising her hand.

Andrea gave it exactly three seconds of thought, then raised her hand too. "I used to play. I'm not so bad."

"Are we going to have women on our team?" asked Matt.

Frank scratched his head. "I guess so. We haven't even formed it yet and there are women on it."

Owen scoffed. "Who are we going to play against with women on the team?"

"It's not like we're forming a league. We're just having fun."

Frank added another hotdog to his stick and meticulously rotated it over the coals. The perpetual furrow between his eyes increased in the reflected flames of the fire. "The village won't care if we have women on our team. Probably not folk in the valley, either."

"Certainly not them!" Agreed Millie, whose emancipation had included a generous dose of Seattle women's libertarian life. "I'm sure the valley folk are beyond that. They probably even have their own woman's team."

"They'll just want to play," said Matt, gaining enthusiasm for the idea. "Up north, they play baseball all the time. Fairbanks has a team."

They continued to talk about baseball until their bellies were full and the babies grew sleepy. It seemed that eating campfire wieners should have diminished the memories of stadium hotdogs, yet each bite brought back the whistles and cheers, the crack of the bat slamming against a ball, the lofty sail of a home run.

Baseball! It was as much a shared memory as hungry days and anxious nights through the long Depression. It was played in the alleys and deserted lots. It was a sparkling afternoon in a park. It was a day for putting away your worries and fears. Baseball was a holiday.

The babies fell asleep in their mothers' arms and were trundled off to bed with Andrea's sisters. Velma and Owen stayed out until the first chilly winds of the evening blew in from the inlet, then retired to the trailer. Jimmy brought out his guitar and strummed a few chords.

"As we sang in the evening, by the moonlight, la-di-do-da."

"What a lovely quintet we make," said Andrea. "Jimmy, you ought to have us sing with you at the Sourdough."

He grinned. "Tammy would never have it. But you should come with us next weekend. We're playing at the Seafarer. Tammy says it's haunted."

"Nonsense," grumbled Frank. "There are no such things as ghosts."

"Really!" Andrea chided. "How can you be a religious man and not believe in ghosts? Doesn't it say something about them in the Bible?"

"Those were different times. People made up stories for the things they didn't understand."

"Betty Lou was showing me around the woods today," said Jimmy, "and she says the lowland woods are haunted. They are full of Athabascan hunters. She said they are friendly, though. They would like you, Frank, because you smoke a pipe. She told me that when you are in the woods, you should always take a pinch of tobacco out of your pouch and put it on a stone to share with the Athabascan spirits."

Andrea clapped her hands together. "There you are, Frank! You have protection. All you have to do is share your tobacco."

"Bah," he said, chewing on the stem of his pipe. "All she wants is for me to leave out some free tobacco so she can snatch it up. I'll bet she spies on everybody."

Jimmy strummed a random chord on his guitar. "Neah. She has enough to do without spying, although she does notice when people are in the lowlands. She kind of thinks of them as her own."

"She was born here," Millie said reflectively. "It must seem strange to her to see so many new people moving in."

"She says she doesn't mind. She already watched Anchorage get bigger. It's just that all those people do something to her mind and makes her want to do something wild. She's not really all that crazy, you know. She just doesn't take well to crowds."

Frank nodded as though he understood.

Millie smiled placidly. "She visits me now and then, always with some little gift; a fish, some wild herbs, once she even brought a jar of moonshine. I thanked her kindly for it but advised giving it to someone who would enjoy it more. Her cranberry wine is good, though."

During the interval in which Frank puffed on his pipe and contemplated the characteristics of the local citizenry, Jimmy cleared his throat and said, "I hear Charlie's putting together a hunting party."

"It's a waste of time and money to chip in," said Frank quickly. "Charlie doesn't know how to track."

Jimmy strummed another note, then listened to the keen, low whistle of the train thundering over the inlet. Right on time; just at midnight. It wept, long and deep, crying for a past it could never bring back, racing from the future it saw coming. "I do. I can track. I want to track for Charlie's hunting party."

"That would change things."

"Can you do it?" queried Millie. "Can you talk to Charlie?"

"I can talk to Charlie." Frank made a face. "You'll have to excuse me. Nature is calling to me."

While he was gone, Andrea asked, "Has Frank taken a scientist's world view?"

"Of course, he has," said Millie. "He's a modern man, you know. He must keep things tidied up and free of superstitions."

Andrea poked at the fire, letting the coals crackle with a loud snap. "That must be dreadfully tedious."

Frank returned from the bushes more quickly than usual and sat down as erectly as though he had a metal pole pushed up his back.

"What? No solitary contemplations?" Millie asked with surprise.

Andrea looked at his flushed face.

"Did a ghost spook you?"

Frank picked up a beer, gulped down half, and growled, "it was that damned lynx. Snuck right up behind me while I was relieving myself and started yowling."

Not even happy with his pipe, he asked for one of Matt's cigarettes and inhaled deeply before speaking again. "We're getting a dog."

Matt remained by the campfire long after Frank and Millie had gone home, and even the girls had gone to bed. All that remained were Andrea and Jimmy, who continued to strum his guitar softly and listen for missing chords.

"I wonder what kind of dog Frank will get," he remarked conversationally.

"I wonder how she does that," Andrea replied. She was still laughing to herself about the jokes that always seemed to be played on Frank, even by nature's whim. "It's almost as though the whole wilderness conspires to let Millie have her way."

"Maybe she's a witch," answered Matt teasingly.

"I've considered the possibility. She has hazel eyes."

"Ah," he said, poking at the fire. "That's always a sure sign." A smile quirked at his mouth.

"She talks to the birds," volunteered Jimmy. "Betty Lou says so."

"Betty Lou also says Ester buries frogs under the full moon." Andrea slapped at the coals, so they sparked up, and waved her fiery stick at Jimmy. "You can't believe everything Betty Lou says."

"Well, I've heard Millie talking to the birds. It's not a made-up story."

His fingers roved up and down the frets, digging for the perfect note. "Maybe she does have a power over animals."

Matt continued to laugh in soft, deep chuckles. "Would you really join a baseball team?" He finally asked Andrea directly.

"But of course, I would!" She gasped. "It's too bad we don't have a large enough community to pitch the women against the men. We'd beat your pants off."

"Here now!" Said Jimmy, putting up his guitar. "Ain't no woman beat me at baseball yet, and ain't no woman going to start."

He got to his feet, yawned, and stretched. "Well, I'm checking in." He looked at Matt as though he expected him to leave.

He didn't. He only called, "Take care of that pitching arm," as Jimmy walked to his tent.

"I'm glad you're back," Matt said after he left. "I missed you."

"It was only a few days."

"A lot of things can go around in a man's mind in a few days."

"All of them foolish, I'm sure. You should get used to it because it will probably happen again."

"You're flighty?"

"That's the best way to say it. There are things I don't resist, things I don't want to resist. Maybe they aren't good for me or maybe they just aren't good for the way people see me, which makes me wonder if it's any business of theirs at all."

"I think I can accept that."

"Can you, Matt?" She gave him a sidelong glance. He was close enough to put an arm around her or take her hand, but he stared steadily into the fire.

"Maybe it's not their business, if all it is means thinking poorly of you. I'd rather not think poorly of you, Andy. If you are flighty... or impulsive, or however you like to put it, I can accept that. Lots of people are that way. It doesn't make them less. Sometimes, it makes them more."

The hand resting on his lap began to nervously rub against his knee. "The only thing I want to know.... When you take off like that, will you always come back?"

Andy scowled as though he had asked a stupid question. "This is my home. I'm not leaving my home, my family."

A voice called sleepily from the tent, "she won't leave Millie."

Matt chuckled. "Is that true?"

She removed the ribbon from her hair and fluffed it out, laughing gaily. "Of course it is. Without me, those civil service women would eat her alive."

"Frank bought her some earrings from Dresden Hayes," continued Jimmy from the tent, determined to keep the conversation away from a serious course.

"Ivory?" asked Matt, feigning great interest.

"Gold, with jade inlay."

Matt shook his head mournfully. "I missed my chance."

Andrea waved her glowing poking stick at Matt to emphasize her warning.

"You have to be fast to get around Frank."

She let the fire play on her face long enough to soak in its heat and dismiss the coldness of her farewell to an aching marriage. It wasn't farewell. It was au revoir. Until we meet again, and each meeting would be more distant until they finally faded away.

"I'm sorry, you know, that I didn't even take a chance."

"Huh." Matt's hand rubbed his knee again, pondering her words. "I think you are the type of person who takes chances every step of the way. I can live with that. It makes you more interesting."

She shook her head, letting her hair fall and hide her expression. "Then you are in for some interesting times, Mr. Matt Jones. That's all I can tell you."

"Kiss her or go home," called Jimmy from his tent. "I'm tired of listening to all this. You sound like love-sick cows."

She tucked back her hair so he could see her, letting the thick locks run red, red like a river of fire, her smile more reserved than inviting. "You shouldn't kiss me tonight," she told him, keeping her voice husky. "I still have the smell and feel of Jake all over me."

She heard a low groan and dropped her voice lower. "Besides, busy body is listening in."

Realizing it really was late, Matt stood and stretched. Andrea followed him out to his car, a 1940 Hudson that looked weary about continuing to do service.

"Don't mind Jimmy," she said in a whisper. "He's got it bad for Tammy Buswell, the cocktail waitress, but she hasn't even let him get to first base. He can't figure her out."

"I'm not sure I'm the best guy to be giving lessons."

"I'll be the judge of that."

She gave him a quick peck before he folded himself inside the economy-inclined vehicle. "I'm sorry, really, that I can't promise anything."

"I'm not," he said. "I like you better this way."

In her tent, while brushing out her hair, she heard Jimmy call to her. "He's right about one thing, you know. It's nobody's business what you do in your privacy. You ain't hurting nobody, and Ben – Ben gets taken care of. It didn't kill mama to see you turn out this way. It won't kill anyone else."

"And you're right," Andy called back. "I can't abandon Millie. The veteran wives would smother her, and Betty Lou would teach her bad manners."

"You need her, too."

She started to sass back, then checked herself. Maybe, she did need Millie. Maybe she needed the whole Chugach. It rang like a beacon calling ships to a safe harbor. It rolled with mirth, its bell-like tones welcoming the new inhabitants. It tinkled as it rustled among the cattails, the place of many places humming to itself, tucking in the community like a mother putting her children to bed.

She finished brushing her hair and tucked herself inside the sleeping bag for the night. "You need an easier catch than Tammy Buswell."

"Neah. Don't want it. Tammy will do."

She blew out the lamp, laid back, and closed her eyes. Everything they needed was right here.

Twelve

Wolf Creek put their first baseball game together in early September. They chose a playing field on a long strip of beach by the inlet, close enough to the Native community that half a dozen people from the village wandered over with folding chairs to watch them practice.

The air had grown chilly enough that light frost crunched underfoot in the early morning but cleared by noon.

Frank had no trouble putting a team together. Enough people showed up to even run a second string. Although most of the Civil Service wives signed up, only Sharon Bowen and Beth Hughes were able to play. Doreen, Millie, and Ester would all have to wait until spring, after their babies were born. Through the unspoken, inexplicable rules of sisterhood that even caused women to synchronize their monthly cycles, the pregnancy epidemic was going around.

"Actually, I don't plan to sign up for baseball at all," said Ester with a sniff of disdain that included the can of beer Andrea held in her hand. "I can think of much better things to do with my time."

"So can I," agreed Millie, holding something squirming in her jacket. "But they aren't nearly as much fun."

"I suppose it's fun to watch," Ester conceded, leaning against the concession's table. Solace Grant had set up a booth with hotdogs in their buns, chili, soda, and beer. "It feels very modern, somehow."

"You bet it's fun," said Solace, who had seized upon the business opportunity as soon as Andrea had told her about their campfire conversation. She began remarking to everyone who came through the door how fine it would be to watch a baseball game before Frank had been able to present the idea at a meeting. That, Andy had discovered, was a typical Zeb and Solace strategy. If they liked an idea, they merely hinted at its viability until the idea had officially surfaced as a proposal. This way, it didn't seem like they had any influence at all in the decision- making process.

The decision making was working fine for her now. She frowned in annoyance at Ester, not at all intimidated by the woman reputed to eat people alive for using the wrong fork with salads. "Why don't you take a chair instead of sitting on the table? Honestly. We set a bad example for the locals."

Ester chirped a little in her throat, but did as Solace advised, "It's the fatigue that comes on.," she said, faltering for excuses. "I just wasn't thinking...Millie, whatever do you have in your coat?"

Millie unfastened the first button and a small cluster of black curls with two round eyes and a wet nose popped out.

"Oh goodness," said tiny Doreen, spontaneously cupping her hands and reaching out for it. "Is this what Frank calls a dog?"

The mop of curls yapped, then quivered all over as Doreen's small hands petted the soft fur.

"Well," said Millie, taking the chair next to Ester and arranging the little dog on her lap. "Frank said it didn't matter how big it was as long as it made noise. Baily makes noise."

Nearly as pregnant as Ester, Doreen felt the necessity to take a seat on the other side of Millie. "Has he chased off the lynx?"

The proud owner of the tiny mutt beamed. "I haven't seen it in two weeks."

"It will circle back around," said Ester positively. "The dog is too small to keep a lynx away for long."

Millie wasn't concerned. "Oh, he'll grow. He's a standard sized spaniel. He'll be able to stir up a fuss."

Ester, who cared about as much for small dogs as she did for baseball, was inclined to disagree but the players were organizing on the field, and she didn't want to miss out. She held her hands primly in her lap and looked intently ahead.

As Millie's best friend, Andrea took greater liberties. She swooped the puppy from Millie's lap, held it high and jiggled it like a baby, kissed it once on the head, then deposited it with Anna, whose eyes had been following the new plaything with agony. Unwilling to surrender her puppy privilege, Anna carried around the fur ball for others to pet before returning it to its owner.

In the meantime, Andrea dashed off to join the players. If she stayed too long with the group, there would be questions, questions she wasn't ready to answer. She didn't know why she should. Whose business was it really, that she had gone off with Jake once more, this time for three days in Hawaii? Exactly how many women would turn such an offer down from their estranged husbands? She was now sunbeam soaked for surviving the winter.

And she was free. He had quarreled with her for no better reason than that as a man, he felt entitled to greater freedom, but in the end, he had agreed.

Their marriage was over. They could part friends, and see each other cordially, or never see each other again.

Andrea was just a little breathless when she arrived at centerfield. Most of the players had already assembled and were listening to their newly appointed coach, Art Bowen. He fit the part. He was a solidly built man with a ruddy complexion and the air of a sporting man. He strode back and forth with his thumbs hitched in his belt.

"We've got three players that have agreed to come out from the village, so we have two full teams playing against each other. Since we never played together before, we don't know what each other's skills are, but this is where we are going to find out. I'm going to read you the list now of who is on each team. Choose a captain. Choose your best pitcher and let's have some fun."

She had been grouped with Matt, Frank, and Jimmy. One of the young men from the village was also on their team. "I'm playing against my brothers," he told her, grinning. He had one of those huge, infectious smiles that made you smile back.

"Does it bother you?" She asked.

"Hah! It's going to be fun! Do you see that Frank and Charlie are on different teams? That's because they want to beat each other. Great fun!" His eyes laughed with mischief.

Typical of the Athabaskans, Andrea mused, he was good-looking. He was no taller than she was, with a stocky build, a round face dark as polished cherry wood, a dimple that fled in and out of one cheek and strong, white teeth.

"You know them?"

He grinned wider. "Yeah. They come around to the village sometimes and talk to the elders. They are always asking us how we feel about this or that. They're feeling guys. We call Frank, Mr. Feeling Man. My name's Mark Henson, by the way. What's yours?"

She told him. He shoved his hands in his back pockets and looked at her knowingly. "Oh yeah. I heard about you. You've got a farm just below the trading post. Moved in this year, didn't you?"

"This will be our first winter."

She watched for his reaction. Derision, perhaps, or the same amusement he had shown for Matt and Frank. Instead, his long eyes grew thoughtful, the corners turning up with silent speculation. "It gets tough the first year. I'll come around and check on you now and then."

The challenge game was about to begin. Andrea shook hands with her new team member, cocking her head a little. "You should do that," she agreed.

Mark had been placed at first base; she was guarding third. He had a good stance, crouching with his wrists resting against his knees, hopping a little from the base and back again. With his short, powerful legs and broad chest, he would be intimidating if he wasn't constantly grinning. When he met her eye, he winked at her as though they shared a humorous secret. Andy scowled and concentrated on the game. She had enough men on her mind without adding another.

Frank Lamar had been chosen as captain, and his team had chosen Jimmy as their pitcher. Jimmy was good. He struck out two players and walked one, with another poising anxiously on second base, when Sharon Bowen, her blonde ponytail swinging, came to bat.

Mighty Sharon Bowen, who could make a legion of Roman soldiers tremble and who had been among the first camp wives to follow their husbands to Campbell Creek.

She tapped against the plate, her hips swaying, her feet planted. She raised the bat like a weapon, her eyes hidden yet burrowing from under her cap.

Nobody ever saw it coming. He pitched as he always pitched to the women, with a little leniency and no tricks. He should have pitched a curve ball or a fast ball. Her bat hit the skin so hard, the crack sounded like a pistol shot. The ball flew into an outfield that had not really expected to see action. She ran, those strong legs thundering over the bases, her teammates dashing ahead of her.

One, two, three made it over the Homeplate before the ball was retrieved and tossed back to the pitcher.

The rest of the day was like any ordinary day when a group came together to play baseball just for the enjoyment of the sport. The innings went by, the scores crept up and down, although Frank's team never could recover from that stunning first inning. Jimmy toughened up his game, trying to make it more difficult for Sharon to hit and succeeded in cooling down her performance a little, although he never could strike her out and nobody could forget the explosive sound when that plain-faced woman first swung the bat and there was nothing, absolutely nothing, that could be done to top it.

The two captains shook hands and congratulated each other on a game well-played. The final score had put Frank's team only one point behind, which wasn't bad considering their surprise encounter with mighty Sharon at the bat. "You wouldn't have been able to win if not for her," growled Frank. "We had the better pitcher."

"And we had the better batter," said Charlie gleefully. His smile fled. "What does it say about us that our best player is a woman?"

Frank jiggled his hands in his pockets. "That's easy. While we were in the trenches, the girls were playing baseball."

"It's too bad we played our game so late in the year," remarked Andrea, leaning on her bat. She hadn't played as impressive a game as Sharon, but she hadn't done too shabby, either. Mark's brother, David had been the opposing pitcher. He wasn't as lenient as Jimmy, pitching equally hard for women as for men, but Andy had learned baseball from her brother, and she had been ready. David only struck her out once.

"It will be winter soon and we won't be able to play."

As part of the team, Mark had no problem with being part of the group, adding his voice to the conversation. "Why wouldn't we be able to play in the winter? I've got a sister who would have been playing if she knew there would be girls and I've got a cousin coming down from the north next week who loves to play baseball. Her name is Iris."

Andrea accepted a soda from Matt and drank it thirstily before answering. "Pretty name," she said agreeably. "It will be fun to have more girls on the team, but once it snows.... We won't be able to play once it snows."

"Sure, we will. The snow packs. If it gets too deep, we'll just put on snowshoes."

She choked on her soda. "I can't even wear snowshoes. You've got to be joking."

"No, no, we'll play. You'll see how much fun it is. We'll invite my family from up north. They know how it's done."

His brothers were calling to him. He shook her hand once more, than turned toward them, calling for them to hold up. When he joined them, he turned his head and grinned once more at Andrea. She waved, wondering if he ever stopped smiling.

The group was slowly breaking up and wandering back toward their vehicles. The Bolinders and the Lamars were still stuck together like glue, probably conspiring over the next step in community development. They had their schemes and dreams.

It would not be surprising if they were trying to figure out how to hold a baseball game that would draw in some revenue. The land for the community hall was half-cleared and the logs stacked. Once the pilings were down, they could start construction, but there were no materials to construct.

Mama and pop Delaney had herded their troops to the car, despite Carol's protests. Some of the kids were doing field practice and she wanted to join. "No, you don't," scolded mama. "You never played a game of baseball in your life. You just want to be there because the railroad workers' kids are there. Do you know what they say about railroad workers?"

"No, mama, what do they say?"

"I don't know either, but it can't be all good. They had the Chinese working for them."

Carol pouted and flounced her skirt as she slid into the back seat. "Good heavens, mama. This isn't the nineteenth century. That happened a long time ago."

"I'm just saying you can't be too careful."

The rebellious years had begun. Carol sulked with her arms folded over her chest. Noticing Carol's mood, Anna sulked too, reasoning they must have been deprived of something. Andrea reached out her arms for Ben.

"I'll take him," she said, relieving him from his grandfather's arms. "Has he been good?"

"He's going to be a ball player," said Owen, puffing his chest out proudly. "He watched the whole game."

Jimmy was leaning against the truck, talking with Matt. He straightened up when he saw Andy coming. "I saw you with Mark Henson. Mark is right up your alley."

"Why do you say that?" She asked crossly, asserting her ownership by climbing into the cab.

"Because you told me, the only reason you dated Jake last week was because he took you places. Mark can do that too because he's a bush pilot. The whole village chipped in to help him buy his plane when he got his pilot's license."

Andrea looked at him with amazement. "How is it that you know about everybody in town?"

"Betty Lou." He held out his arms for Ben and put a baseball cap on his head. The boy grabbed it and inspected it intently. "She brings her furs to the village to make into boots and brings stuff from Anchorage she knows the girls will like, hair things and such."

Andrea's scoff equaled the sputter of the engine as she fired up Abe. "She pays them for their work in trinkets?"

"Oh no, she pays them fair and square. The girls just work better if you give them pretty things. Betty Lou said so. She said she learned that from Frank. You get better service if you tip."

Abe was rumbling and ready to roll. "It seems you know Betty Lou well enough for her to be your girlfriend."

Jimmy shook his head and rescued the cap just as Ben was tossing it to the ground. "Neah. She's too old. You haven't seen Tammy yet. She's young and pretty."

She waited impatiently and finally called, "are you coming with me, Jimmy?"

He hesitated, then placed Ben in the passenger side of the cab. "I'm going with Matt. We're going to do a bit of trout fishing."

She gave him a disappointed face, then shrugged. She didn't really feel like going fishing. "I'll have the campfire going when you get back. We'll pan fry some fish and talk about the price of wheat in China."

"What is the price of wheat in China?" He asked, still holding the door open.

"I have no idea," she answered. "That's why we should discuss it."

Home was a more comfortable place these days. They kept the tarp lean-to providing extra shelter, but the cabin had been built and the camping trailer turned over to Andrea and Jimmy. She had a real room, with a real bed, while Jimmy slept on the fold-away that turned into a table during the day. She had privacy. Mama Delaney didn't even know of her overnight trip to Fairbanks because she had left Ben with Millie. It was a deception, but she had grown tired of explaining her actions.

That was part of it, maybe all of it. Here in Wolf Creek, she didn't really have to answer to anybody. It was a youthful world, filled with young people and young ideas. The Velma's, who were such a strong voice in their own communities, were just a murmur here. You were who you chose to become.

Jimmy and Matt returned shortly after Andrea had put Ben to bed. The exciting day had worn him out and he fell asleep almost instantly.

It was a sparkling evening, turning crisp, adding enjoyment to the crackling fire. They laughed about the baseball game and the unexpected star, whose status had bounced so high, she was expected to become the next Mickey Mantle. They discussed Jimmy's musical career, promoted by a cocktail waitress and an office clerk. The fish turned golden in the sizzling pan. They fell silent in anticipation of a meal that was not hotdogs.

"I bought the land across the creek," said Matt.

Andy looked up from serving out their plates. "What took you so long?"

He juggled his plate between his knees while spearing tiny pieces of fish with a fork. "For a long time, I kept thinking, I was going back to Wisconsin. I would save money and I would go back. Make things right with the world."

"You're from Wisconsin?" asked Andrea with a note of surprise. She didn't know why this should be surprising. He had never mentioned his past at all. She had just assumed he was from the Northwest, like the Lamars and themselves. He fit in like a Northwestern man.

"I am," he answered. "I haven't been back since the war. Jobs were bad when I left. I don't think they've gotten a lot better, despite what Truman says. They were scarce, and I left family down there. I don't really know how they're doing. I don't ever hear from them, but after thinking about it a lot, I just started sending them money because I thought it would be better than burdening them more by going home and not finding a job."

"You never hear from them?"

"They write a thank you now and then to let me know they got the money, but they aren't much into writing. I expect if something worse happened that hasn't happened already, or by some miracle, they no longer needed my help, they'd let me know. So, that's how it's been with me. Sending them money and thinking I'm going to return, but I never do, and I know that I won't. And now there is another winter coming on, and it doesn't seem right somehow to keep living with married people working on their families. I've got to have my own place."

"He wants to borrow my tent," announced Jimmy. "Until he builds his shack. It won't take more than two weeks. He says it's not going to be much bigger than a shed."

Andy shrugged as she picked over her plate, removing the tiny bones. "It's your tent," she told Jimmy. "I'm not telling you what you can do with it."

She turned back to Matt. "You can leave it here under the awnings if you like. It will be a better shelter. It's getting cold out at night."

Just then, a horrendous yowl split the night, a sound so spiteful it sent shivers down the spine. The snarl boomed, then subsided. Andrea sighed. "Now we have the lynx. It's time to get a dog."

"If you ladies would let me, I'd take it down," said Jimmy.

She waved a fiery stick at him in warning. "Oh no, you don't. That's Millie's lynx. Besides, he might be the daddy of Ester's kittens."

Jimmy scoffed. "You don't really believe that do you?"

"Have you seen the size of the kittens? It's possible. Anyway, we're going to need a cat once we have a garden and livestock. Millie says the shrews have been terrible this year."

"The chicken feed attracts them."

"Mama says she wants chickens in the spring, shrews or not, so we might as well get a cat. We should probably get one of Ester's cats."

Jimmy considered the status that came from owning a half wildcat. "Guess it would do to get on the good side of the Bolinders. Charlie's hiring me to guide the hunting trip."

"Maybe he'll throw a cat into the deal."

"I'm thinking horses," he grinned.

The fire died down and so did their conversation.

Andy finally stirred and said, "I will leave you two all night to plot and scheme whatever things men come up with doing. I'm off to bed."

Within days, Matt had a skeleton structure he could move into. Within a week of the baseball game, Mark Hansen made his first call. He arrived in the morning before Andy had even gotten out of bed. Jimmy had made room for him by folding away his cot into two bench seats with a table in the middle but remained inside his sleeping bag.

Their guest carried a large cardboard box which he set on the table. Inside, there were over a dozen cans of soup and a near equal amount of beer.

"I was down at the port picking up supplies to carry out to one of the villages," he explained. "And got a good deal on the soup. I figured, why not spread the wealth around a bit? And while we are at it, we can party."

"What's the occasion?" asked Andy, wondering about beer for breakfast.

She started a pot of coffee in case her stomach said no.

Mark didn't have a problem with beer for breakfast at all. He popped one open and made Jimmy scoot over so he could sit down. "No occasion. I just like parties. Jimmy, you're really going to guide Charlie's hunting party?"

"I can track."

"Those civil service guys don't know how."

"I guess they'll learn." He waited for his coffee, then added, "We want to buy the Bolinder horses. I want to see how they perform."

"I'll tell you how they perform. Two are gun shy, one fakes a limp, one has a mean back kick and another one bites. I tracked for him last year. It was all I could do to keep the horses from running away."

"They didn't get their moose?"

"No. Gary Hughes fired a shot prematurely. Critter got clean away. I reckon he told the others to go hide. We couldn't find another."

It looked mournful to see Mark drinking by himself. After wolfing down scrambled eggs with buttered toast, Andy and Jimmy joined him.

Now that they had all shared a meal and were drinking buddies, Mark said confidentially, "Charlie does have a few fine horses. That buckskin is a stinkin' cuss, but he's got good lines on him. There are a couple of sweet-looking mares as well."

Jimmy looked worried. "Did you want to buy his horses?"

"Neah," said Mark. "He wants to sell the whole lot. I don't want them all and I don't have time to train them. They need training. That's the problem."

They drank some more in contemplation of new friends and new partners. The fading sun entered to glide faintly through the window and spotlight a small square of floor space. Mark peered at Andy almost shyly. "I heard you like to fly."

"I heard you were a pilot," she answered back.

"That's what I'm getting at," he said. "Jimmy said you know how to copilot."

"I don't have a lot of training hours in, but Jake was teaching me. Was. With winter coming in, he probably won't make many flights this way. He's like that. He doesn't really care for cold weather."

"You won't see him?"

"Probably not."

"He's full of crap, anyway," said Jimmy. "Said he would set her up with an apartment in Seattle, close to the bus lines and everything, but we all know what happened in Denver."

"It's not where I want to live," said Andy, annoyed that he took so many liberties with talking about her private affairs.

"He's just full of crap and you know it by now. That's all I'm saying."

Mark listened to the two argue, his perpetual grin flashing from brother to sister. "The reason I asked," he said, squeezing his mild voice into the pause. "I'm looking for someone who knows a bit about piloting to go out on the village run with me tomorrow. My brother usually does, but he can't make it this time. He's helping my uncle with his traps."

More than a little intrigued, Andy asked, "where are you going?"

"Up around the Tanana River. A bit chilly out there. You have to wear warmer clothing, but the people are friendly. You'll like it."

The next day was a workday, but typical of Andrea's behavior, she sent a message through Jimmy that she would not be showing up that afternoon.

Instead, she spent a very enjoyable day accompanying Mark to a remote Athabascan village that housed a substantial secondary family of his uncles, aunts, and cousins. Any thoughts Andrea may have still entertained concerning the advantages of her flying husband were now dismissed by the new possibilities. Andrea not only enjoyed her visit; she immersed herself in it, as one would enter a new country to learn a new culture.

Winter had taken more liberties in this northern region one hundred miles east of Fairbanks. It bowed over the valley spilling out from the Alaskan Range, frosting it as neatly as icing a cake. The village was close to the same size as the one that bumped shoulders with the Wolf Creek settlement and staggered in the same haphazard manner, but it was isolated. There were no nearby highways or towns, only an occasional twinkle of light to show someone lived further up the river.

The Native people had little regard for staking territory to build their homes, even less for planning streets. Homes were placed at advantage to other homes in the area who wanted a daughter or a nephew living close by. A street was any place wide enough for a vehicle or a dog sled to rush through.

The houses were built in the same squat, log cabin style as Mark's village, with plywood add-on's, mismatched windows, and four by four plank porches created from rescued military scrap lumber. The biggest difference was the lack of vehicles. Only one truck and an International Jeep idled in the common yard. Mark explained that both vehicles had been brought over in the winter. There were no roads.

The traditional clothing was the same. Heavy fur parkas and moccasins that reached to the knee, intricate beadwork sewn into their leather, as was the tendency to mix their warm, northern winter wear with American shirts, slacks, and dresses.

The Native women's clothing style was a little outdated by American terms. The moment Andrea stepped off the plane, the ladies crowded around excitedly, examining her heavy wool, knee-length coat, her cozy, soft-lined cap with fuzzy ear flaps, and her store-bought, cashmere scarf.

They scarcely paid attention to the boxes of goods hauled from the cargo doors at the back of the plane, letting the men, the youngsters, and the elders sort it out. They had other things to consider – women's fashion!

They asked her questions, showed her cut-out photos from magazines, and pointed out the differences between the magazine girls' accessories and their own. They crowded close and didn't leave even after Mark wrapped an arm around her shoulder and guided her to his grandmother's house. They simply poured into the house with him, still asking questions.

Andrea wished she had known. She felt guilty to have come so empty-handed once she had witnessed the flurry of open sharing between the community members. Not one person squabbled over the number of cereal boxes and canned goods another claimed, and often added items to a pile that seemed puny compared to the others. There was powdered milk, cocoa, and sugar, which they exclaimed over as though these simple staple items were gold, yet not one word of bickering.

"Why should there be?" chuckled Mark when she asked. "If somebody runs out of something, they'll just get it from a neighbor."

Mark's grandmother must have been a hundred years old. She was shriveled as a walnut and hid what was left of her teeth with a smile that spread over the gums. She only nodded when Mark brought in his gifts, and stood to one side of the stove, her tiny eyes demanding proper order.

The family didn't put out any of their new foods right away. They stored them, setting Andrea down to a table of their normal fare, fried fish, a pasty substance made from wild grains, and pan bread. She thought she did a good job finishing her plate, but Mark pointed out some scraps.

"Finish it all," he whispered, "or you will hurt her feelings."

She watched the others eat, finishing what was on their plates to the most microscopic crumb, and imitated them. Never had she so thoroughly cleaned her platter before, but the message in this ceremony was clear. Waste nothing.

She wanted so greatly to give, she rummaged through her handbag until she found a lipstick, a compact mirror with half a container of powdered rouge, and a manicure set she never used in favor of a larger one she kept on her dresser. She turned them over to a woman who appeared the same age as herself and assumed to be one of Mark's cousins.

The young woman was delighted, and promptly showed her treasures off to the younger girls. The grandmother's tiny eyes beamed, making Andrea wish she still had more to give.

The old woman looked critically at the bolt of dull, pin-striped fabric Mark had brought to contribute to village well-being, then at the floral print dress Andy was wearing over the top of her snow pants.

"The next time he goes picking out material for us to sew, go with him," she suggested, patting Andy's hand. "Find something more fun."

They hadn't been able to stay long. Mark wasn't fond of night-flying. The northwestern passage between the Tanana and the Matanuska Valley was meager with lights to help mark the way, and the landing strip in the lowlands had no search beams. It was when visibility was poor that Mark depended the most on his co-pilot and Andy was still a rookie.

There were groans when he said they were leaving and a lot of good-natured teasing about being nice to his new girlfriend. The girls held Andy's hand and demanded a promise from her to come back. Wisely or unwisely, she made the promise.

The low sun made their shadows look short and fat. The shadows made the young boys laugh who skipped ahead of Mark and Andy and made the squat reflections of blue snow jump around ape-like and turn cartwheels. By the cargo hold, facing away from the sun, the shadows deepened. Some men were packing two large cardboard waxed boxes into the open hold. The musty odor of wild herd animals and the pungent smell of blood clung thickly to the thin containers.

"Caribou," Mark grunted, lighting a cigarette, and relaxing with it before climbing into the cockpit. "The herds come through here so thick sometimes, you can drop them off from a lawn chair. The caribou don't run on the inlet, so my cousins send back a couple hundred pounds every time there has been a good hunt. We like caribou better than moose."

They were also carrying back an extra passenger, the cousin who was supposed to have arrived weeks earlier. Iris was small-boned, with liquid black eyes, and a straight, blue-black waterfall of hair. Like the other village girls, she was soft-faced and tender. She squeezed each one of her cousins, sisters, and aunties tearfully, promising she would stay in touch.

As soon as she had settled into the cargo hold, however, she wiped her face and began chatting excitedly with Mark.

"I would have left with you last time," she said, squatting close to the pilot's chair so she could look out at the runway. "But mama needed an extra hand with the harvest. I couldn't go while she needed me."

"You had a good harvest?"

"It wasn't bad. We put away a lot of fish and berries. Some ducks, too. I shot them myself."

Iris settled back once they were in the air and wrapped her arms around her knees. Feeling she should get to know this girl better who had basically become a family member, Andy asked, "what are you planning to do in the valley?"

She laughed. "I'm not planning to do anything in the valley. I'm going to finish out school at Anchorage and learn how to be an Anchorage girl."

"Why do you want to learn that?"

"It sounds exciting."

Andy was so enthusiastic about her trip that when she returned to work for Solace, who some time ago had resigned herself to rationalizing that having Andy come in and out was better than not having Andy at all, she told her with satisfaction in her voice, "I've made my decision. No more flying with Jake. I'm staying home this winter."

"I'm glad to hear that," said Solace, almost hopefully. "I reckon I can keep you busy this winter."

Andrea straightened her apron cheerfully and retied its big bow. "I'll be very busy! Did you know I started nurses training when I lived in Denver? Well, Jake pressured me to quit, but that's all water under the bridge now. They have a nurses training program in Anchorage because they need so many out in the bush."

She used this new word she had heard dropped now and then, with proud authority now that she knew the "bush" signified the remote locations inaccessible by road. It was a thrilling land. The only mode of transportation beside flying, was by boat or canoe in the summer and by dogsled in the winter.

She began washing dishes, her arms slathered with bubbles that floated and popped like her words. "Mark told me all about it. He said when I complete the training, I can go out in the bush whenever they need medical attention."

"Mark enlisted you."

"He did, but you have to admit, it's a wonderful idea."

"I reckon you'll still need a job while taking that training," was all Solace said.

Andrea reckoned. She plotted and schemed. Mark became a frequent visitor who occasionally took her to the villages when his brother couldn't, and sometimes took her up in the plane just so she could put in some practice hours. He also made good his word and enrolled her in nurses training although it didn't take her long to discover with household expenses and a baby to raise, she couldn't devote much time to study.

Autumn flew by to encroaching winter and the necessity of the community to do its final preparations before the hard cold set in and outdoor activities became dangerous and sometimes, foolish. Andrea introduced Iris to Carol, who brightened up at having an easily accessible friend her age, a pretty girl who attracted men, and Iris brightened at having someone to introduce her to the modern world.

Part III

Doreen

Thirteen

The scissors snipped and cut, throwing lengths of frizzy hair to the floor. "I've completely ruined it, haven't I?" asked Doreen, the tears she had been battling choking her voice.

"No, no, not completely." The hands were soothing. They rifled through her hair, massaging the scalp, and brought up one lock at a time, grooming it gently. "We've all done it at least once. To say we haven't, we'd be lying."

"Beth tried to warn me. She said not to leave the perm in too long or it will burn my hair."

Andrea had the hands of a professional hairdresser. They pleaded with her hair gently, pulling it straight from the head and clipping the frazzled ends away.

"Why did you want a perm?" She asked. "Your hair is already curly."

Doreen sighed and touched one end of her shortened hair. "Not that curly. I pin it every night."

"Well, I think you look better in short hair, anyway," said Andrea, examining her work critically. "Short hair is all the rage right now, so you look thoroughly modern." She held up a mirror for Doreen's inspection.

Doreen turned her head this way and that. It really was a cute cut. Short, but cute.

"Oh," she said suddenly, setting down the mirror. "Whatever will Alex say? He's never seen me like this."

Satisfied that her work was finished, Andrea whisked the towel from around Doreen's neck and sat down at the table.

"Really, Doreen. It's your hair. Do you tell Alex how he can cut his?"

"I do tell him he can't grow a beard," she admitted. "I don't really like beards."

"I'm sure if he insisted, you would let it be."

"Maybe. Maybe not," Doreen answered dubiously. "Men have to be taken in hand a lot. They become very foolish, and Alex is no exception."

"Did he go on the hunting trip with Charlie and company?"

Doreen fussed with the coffee cups, filling each slowly, as she debated to herself how much money she should offer Andy for the cut. She couldn't say they were close friends and just exchanging favors. She never visited Andrea. She only knew her as Solace's waitress. It was Millie who had sent Andy over after receiving the call on the field phone.

It was a good thing the men were all out hunting. They would have questioned her emergency. Making up her mind, she set the two cups on the table and pulled three crisp dollar bills from her pocket.

"Now, you take that," she said when Andy tried to push it away. "I won't be having you say no."

Andrea hesitated, then snapped open her purse and shoved the bills inside. "I shouldn't, you know," she muttered. She found her cigarettes and straightened up. Andy was one of those who exuded more confidence when she was smoking.

Doreen sat down with a sigh, relieved she had done the right thing. Alex was right, she supposed. She needed to broaden her circle, make friends with more than just the civil service wives. "Yes, Alex left with the group. Do you think they will bring something back?"

Andrea's laugh was more worldly than Doreen would have even dared to attempt. "With Jimmy along? If there is a single moose in a fifty- mile radius, Jimmy will find it. I'm glad he's not an avid hunter or there wouldn't be a single sign of wildlife on our property."

"I'm surprised you have any wildlife left on it at all, considering Ted Ewing trapped on it."

"I heard about that." Andy folded her arm, so the cigarette was away from her face, and leaned forward. "He's back, you know. I heard the railroad workers talking about him."

Doreen gave a little gasp. "He is? Here?"

"Not here." She shook her head. "Out by Knik. He's been saying a lot of stuff about Wolf Creek."

"What kind of things?" Patsy had wakened from her nap. She paddled across the kitchen floor and climbed up in her mother's lap. Like Doreen, she had wildly growing curls that had lost all sense of direction. Doreen smoothed the hair away from the child's face and gave her a cookie.

"What a pretty little girl," cried Andy. "How old is she?"

"Almost two." She gave her baby a squeeze. "I was the first to become infected."

"That's a terrible thing to say, you know. You make it sound like pregnancy is a disease."

"It upsets the men when we talk like that. That's why we do it. What did Ted have to say about Wolf Creek?"

Andy leaned back again. She was obviously enjoying herself. "Well, he says the community of Wolf Creek is uppity. All they want are civil service workers."

Doreen gasped with indignation. "That's not true! We accept all kinds. It's just that Ted isn't a nice man, Andy. Would you really want him living next door to you?"

"Of course not! It's just that you asked and I'm telling you what he said."

"It simply isn't true. Some of us don't even want to stay in the Civil Service. Alex doesn't. Charlie doesn't. Even Matt talks about becoming his own business, but the truth is, the only jobs with year-round employment and benefits are with the military. Everything else is seasonal."

Patsy was getting restless. Doreen switched her to her other knee and jiggled her. "We're lucky to have families like yours coming in. You're farmers. You know what you're doing. Honestly, none of us knew a thing when we first settled. We played it by ear."

"Then you must have good hearing," Andrea smiled. "You've done very nicely."

"It's not so much, mainly Alex's work. He loves shoving the earth around and building stone walls. He calls it landscaping."

"I think the stone walls are very nice."

Doreen shrugged. "It's an obsession of his. The veterans can't stay still. You should see the Bowens' place. They've got all kinds of things on it. Sharon says they are going to build a greenhouse. I don't know how she gets Art to agree with her ideas."

"She plays a hell of a game of baseball," observed Andrea.

Doreen gave up and put Patsy down. The toddler immediately wanted back on her lap. She gave her another cookie. Feeling slightly annoyed with Sharon, for no better reason than her instant rise to fame, Doreen said crossly, "don't get me started on Sharon. Honestly, sometimes I think she should have been born a man."

"She wears the pants in the family?"

"I didn't say that! But, you know, Art is the mild one. They work it out." She twiddled with her new haircut. "She never says so, but it was an arranged marriage. Her dad is a colonel or something and Art's dad is a wealthy man in his hometown. Mr. Bowen didn't want his son going into a war zone and Sharon's dad didn't want his daughter to remain unmarried, so they held a homecoming party and arranged for the two to meet. That's how he got commissioned in Alaska."

"They weren't in love?"

"Oh, I think they fell in love by now. They've been up and down the Alcan twice and haven't killed each other."

"Hmm." Andrea started to put her barber kit away, then stopped. "You know, I could give your little girl a quick haircut. Just a trim to tame it down a bit."

"You can do that?" Doreen ran her hand through the unruly curls on her daughter's head. "I think Alex would like that. I think he might like my haircut, as well."

"I guess we'll find out tomorrow," answered Andy with cheerful unconcern. She had Doreen set the baby on the table and started the trim. The child was surprisingly still under the hypnotic fingers, her eyes rolling upward in wondering contemplation. A few snips of fluffy baby hair and the curls turned obediently inward instead of springing out like mattress coils.

When she had finished, Andy glanced at her watch. "The day has passed so quickly! I've got one hour to get ready for work. The next time you want a perm, or a cut or anything at all, give me a call. I really like working with hair."

Doreen remained motionless at the table a few minutes, hands clasped in front of, while Patsy picked at the set of bangles on her wrists. She liked Andrea. She was sure that she did. She just didn't know how to talk with her. Andy wasn't exactly a wife and only half-way, a mother. She left her boy with his grandparents to go traipsing off all over the place. She had heard the stories. Why she even went flying with Mark Hansen. What do you say to a woman like that?

She sent Patsy off to the living room and swept up the hair clippings. She had gossiped. Uneasiness rose in her throat, tasting sour on her tongue. The things she had said about Sharon! If they came back to her, she would know to guard herself more closely around Andy, Doreen vowed to herself.

She went into the bedroom and looked at herself in the full-length mirror. Andy had really done a good job. She didn't look frowsy anymore. Maybe, with her nice pearl earrings and her new dress, fresh off her push-pedal sewing machine, she would look appealing. People might even take her seriously. Alex might take her seriously.

She cupped her hands over her tummy, just beginning to show its bubble. She knew he loved her. That wasn't the problem. Like Millie, she had only known her husband a few days before they married. Unlike Millie, she had fallen in love with Alex the first time she laid eyes on him.

He was on leave in San Diego, trying to enjoy his last few days with civilization before being sent to Alaska as part of the mainland defense corps. She didn't care where he was going – she wanted him. It was crazy. It was a whirlwind. It was months later before they realized they knew nothing about the person they had married. That was the war. It did these things to you.

She had allowed herself to become frowsy. Nobody paid much attention to frowsy women. That was all going to change.

The hunting group wasn't due back until the next day. Doreen spent the rest of the afternoon cleaning the house and scrubbing down the kitchen in preparation for their moose. She hoped they would have their moose. They had sunk twenty dollars into the trip. If Alex didn't bring meat home, he would be spending the entire winter traipsing through the woods, looking for wild game. Just because they had been soldiers, it didn't mean the men were hunters. None of them were. It was all about economics – and male pride. They were cavemen in that respect. Women go tend your gardens while we bring home the meat.

A woman was as varied in her gardening skills as a man was in hunting. Sharon had a green thumb. Everything she touched, grew for her. They probably didn't dare do otherwise. Beth was a casual gardener. Some things grew and some didn't, and her garden was always choked with weeds.

On the average, most of the women were able to grow a modest amount of produce – enough to have carrots, green beans, peas, broccoli, cauliflower, and cabbage for the winter. Just about the only thing Doreen was able to grow successfully, was potatoes.

Potatoes were easy. Just cut out the eyes and place them in the ground. Three months later, you had nice, stout potato plants. And rhubarb. The more you abused rhubarb, the better it grew, and Doreen's rhubarb was thriving. The dog dug it up twice and Alex ran over it once with the tractor, but the rhubarb still flourished. If she had shown it an ounce of loving care, it would have withered and died.

Maybe she should play it smart, like Millie, and raise chickens. How hard could it be? Sometimes Beth raised chickens, but unlike Millie, butchered all hers in the fall. She said it was too hard to keep the predators away. Or goats. She had heard goats were very hardy and produced good milk. She wondered if Andy knew anything about goats.

The next morning, she heated water, took down the round, aluminum tub, and gave both Patsy and herself a long, warm, sudsy bath. She put Patsy in her Sunday best and tied a ribbon in her hair. It was amazing how much more cooperative the fluffy brown curls were as she arranged them around the child's face. Andy was a genius with the scissors.

She tried on her new dress. It had subtle gathering at the sides of the bodice to make room for the baby as it grew. Because of the design, right now, she didn't show at all. She would have to thank Ester for giving her the pattern. Not that Ester would acknowledge her gratitude.

She would just say, "Humph, we're close to the same size. All you have to do is shorten and tuck. What is the point of a pattern if you can't use it more than once?" Ester had a whole boxful of patterns. She threw nothing away.

Sometimes, she wished she could be like Ester, resourceful and aloof. Sometimes, she wished she could be like Sharon, strong and self-possessed. Sometimes, she wished she could be anyone except Doreen. She stood up close to the mirror, applied lipstick and her tiny, pearl earrings. She didn't have to wear her hair up to show them off. That was nice, she supposed. She fidgeted with a lock of hair, tucking it behind her ear, then pulling it forward. It was short. No matter how she arranged it, her hair looked short. It would have to do.

She had run out of chores to do and was starting to pace when she heard his truck growling up the drive. He was home! She sighed with relief. As much as she tried not to worry, they were silly men. A hundred things could go wrong. She threw her arms around his neck as soon as he opened the door.

He smelled like woodsmoke, ripened berries, blood and sweat. He smelled wonderful. She pressed her nose against his neck, remembering all over again everything that had driven her wild about him. "Well," he said, a little surprised, holding her away from him to have a look at her. "Were you that positive of success?"

"I was." She swished her skirt back and forth with his hands still on her shoulders. "I heard on good authority Jimmy comes highly recommended."

"It must have been very good authority for you to get all dolled up," he observed, pulling her close again. She felt his kiss nuzzle against her newly bared neck.

"It was."

He was pushing his way inside the house without appearing to push her aside. He was hungry. When she let him by, he made a beeline for the table. She brought out the pot roast left to warm

211

in the oven and fixed him a plate. Patsy had climbed up on his lap, demanding attention.

"What happened to my wild child?" He asked. "She looks like a princess!"

Patsy giggled while he tickled her. Slowly he looked up from the child play as though noticing a difference in Doreen for the first time. "What did you do to your hair?"

She burst into tears and sat down. "It's awful, isn't it?"

He had begun eating but stopped with dismay. "No, it's not. It's nice. Just a bit short. Don't cry about it."

She dabbed at her face. "I burned it. I tried a home perm and left it in too long. It was standing up all over my head like I had been electrocuted. Andy cut it back so it would grow right."

"You had Andy come over?"

"You said I should broaden my circle of friends."

He waved his fork. "And you should. The military is sending over seven hundred personnel to base by next spring. That means we will also need more civil service workers. This community is in for a boom."

"I thought you meant with all the homesteaders."

"I did." He resumed eating. "Andy, though. Well, she's a loose woman."

"She gives good haircuts."

"I guess that counts for something."

She let him fill his belly before she asked, "how did the hunt go?"

"Good. It was good." He nodded. "We bagged two moose. I've got my quarter in the bed of the truck."

"Did you shoot one of them?"

"No." He sounded disappointed. "Frank shot the first one. Jimmy got the second."

Doreen folded her arms over her chest. "Frank did?"

"He's a crack shot," mumbled Alex.

She grimaced. "I wish there was something Frank wasn't good at."

"Mechanics. He knows nothing about mechanics."

It wouldn't do to leave their portion of the moose out in the truck bed too long. Reluctantly, Doreen took off her pretty new dress, put on a pair of bibbed overallsand helped her husband pull their hind quarter of the moose out of the back of the truck. With a heave, they plopped it into the wheelbarrow and pushed it along until they reached the back door leading into their kitchen.

Once on the table, they washed it down with warm water and salt, then began carving it into chunks.

Butchering the hind quarter of a twelve-hundred- pound moose was an all-night task. There was no need to rush, as it would only make them tired.

When she returned, Alex was ready to talk about his trip. He had drawn up the kitchen stool, so he could rest against it when his legs felt tired. He had set cushions in Doreen's chair and refreshed her bowl of wash water. Settled among the scattered sheets of waxed butcher paper and carving knives, was a six-pack of beer, their reward for preparing their winter meat.

She knew what it had been like when they set out the day before. The morning had been crisp and cool, with only a few harmless clouds. Gary Hughes had left with Alex, so his wife could have the car.

It was good for Beth, but Doreen could drive as well, and sometimes she wished her automobile experience consisted of more than helping her husband with the tow truck. Sharon was stubborn. She got what she wanted with barely a peep from Art. Beth was loud and gave Gary little choice but to occasionally comply if he didn't wish to appear as a public display of ingratitude.

If Alex had left her the car, she probably would not have had to have her hair cut. She would have driven over to Beth's house for help with the perm, but here she had been stranded with no car, no assistance, and her closest neighbor nearly three miles away. The day had been fine, crisp, and cool, like any October day when off they drove to Charlie Bolinder's homestead.

The horses had been as rumored; skittish and poorly trained. The supplier of the rumor had been Andrea Delaney. Andy had told Millie the first-hand information she had received from Mark, who was acquainted with the horses, and Millie had told Doreen. Soon, Andy would be rivaling Beth as the main listening post on the grapevine.

"Charlie insisted on riding that big buckskin," chuckled Alex. "Even though that buckskin is the oneriest cuss of all. He would snort, paw at the air, and prance stiff-legged if so much as a porcupine rustled in the brush. Charlie doesn't have much of a seat for riding horses, to begin with. He bounced up and down on the saddle so much, I thought he would develop a hernia."

He slammed the cleaver down hard on a bone to cut through it, wiped his hands and sat back for a five-minute reprieve and a beer. He took a long swallow. Alex wasn't a heavy drinker, but he was a firm believer in celebrating a job well done.

"Frank isn't much of a rider either," he reflected. "He doesn't like riding. He tries to sit ramrod straight, but he can't do it. His butt jiggles around a lot."

Neatly, delicately, Doreen trimmed a thick ribbon of fat and gristle away from a future pot roast. "He doesn't have a lot of butt to jiggle."

"No, that's what made it funny."

Alex found everything about Frank, funny. The way he fussed over his rifle, taking it apart and examining each piece of it when they reached the top of the foothills and took a dinner break. The way he slid from his horse and stalked through the muskeg as soon as they reached the back-country wilderness, doing his own scouting, his nose as sharp and pointed as the end of his rifle. Even the way he built their campfire, measuring the width and length of the sticks carefully, building a cunning teepee fed by curling bark, and lowering himself to blow on it gently and softly, so that the flame billowed into a fire. It was Frank's precision, his need for regulation, even in the high mountains of the Chugach where the only trails had been placed by the wildlife, that made Frank so funny.

Gary Hughes could ride with the ease of men from cattle country, but he had the gun-shy horse. The moment he attempted to sheathe his rifle in the saddle holster, the horse flattened his ears, rolled his eyes, and skittered sideways, snorting. Swearing, he jerked at the reins, making the matter worse. The animal circled and skittered around him, its front hooves clawing the air like weapons.

Charlie Bolinder couldn't calm the horse. He tried to assist Gary by making a dart for the saddle and clinging to it and the bridle, but all the horse did was spin around faster. It reared. It kicked. It bucked, leaving Charlie jiggling, his boots digging desperately into the earth to ground him, and Gary holding the reins with both hands, cursing and screaming about how he was going to eat horse meat for dinner.

Alex paused in his story long enough to finish his beer and resume his chore of carving the moose quarter down to manageable chunks of meat. "It's true what they say about Jimmy Delaney. He has horses in his blood. He walked right up to where the horse was pawing and bucking around, clucking, and murmuring sweet nothings. Whatever language he was speaking, the horse understood. It stopped circling and just stood there, snorting and quivering."

The horse's sides fanned in and out as Jimmy ran a hand down its neck. "Easy, sweetie. Easy fella. You're a fine boy. You're a good boy."

It waited docilely while Gary mounted. "He'll be alright now," Jimmy assured him. "Just don't shoot from his back."

Gary fumed throughout the rest of the trip. He said the gun-shy horse had spoiled things for him. He tried to trade off beasts, but nobody was willing until Jimmy agreed.

It didn't appease Gary. It made matters worse. He was sure Jimmy was a show-off who had somehow subdued the horse but couldn't possibly know as much about hunting the back country hills as a group of war veterans. They had stalked and hunted a far more terrifying enemy than an elusive moose.

They reached a desirable campsite by evening. In the summer, it would have been pleasant. It was alongside a small, crystal-clear creek with grassy banks that had withered and shrunk to bare gravel. There were blackening tree stumps, severed by nature's casual hand, providing plenty of firewood. There were moose tracks everywhere, along with piles of firm, tubular, moose turds.

They couldn't resist throwing the turds at each other. Moose turds were like enlarged capsules of goat poop, smooth and hard, nothing more really than concentrated plants. Dresden Hayes, who had come along more for enjoyment than any real interest in hunting, gathered them and put them in a burlap bag.

"What are you going to do with all those moose nuggets?" joked Alex. "Don't you get enough fertilizer for your garden with all your bull?"

"I'm thinking," said Dresden. "I'm just thinking. Tourists buy strange things."

That was Dresden Hayes for you. His mind never did follow the same avenues of thoughts as other people. Maybe that was how he found his gold mine. Only one out of ten prospectors struck it lucky in the Talkeetna's, but damned if Dresden Hayes managed to do it. There wasn't any real telling how much his mine was worth because Dresden didn't run it like a normal mining operation. He only took what he felt he needed, and what he needed never did seem all that great.

They didn't worry any longer about Dresden Hayes' strange collection, which also included some willow branches covered with lichen moss, dead, dry, wildflowers, and a few stones. His mind was no more explainable than Frank's.

Gary Hughes was the biggest problem. Unhappy throughout the trip with the poorly trained horses and using a boy barely out of his teens as a trail guide, he was now unhappy they had stopped to make camp instead of pursuing their game while there was still daylight.

"Neah," said Jimmy. "Let them get used to our smell. If we go tromping around in the woods now, they'll all just scatter, and we'll end up hunting in the dark. We could end up shooting each other."

Gary groused and threw his sleeping bag around but finally conceded to the trail guide's suggestion. Throughout the entire night and even in the wan daylight hours of morning, he complained every time he heard a twig crackle in the woods, accusing the group of lost opportunities.

Meticulously, Frank checked his watch. By eight a.m., they had finished their breakfast and washed the dishes in the creek. By nine a.m., he had everyone sorted into pairs, each with a particular moose trail to follow veering away from their camp. He made them agree they would all return to camp by three p.m. whether they found a moose or not. It wasn't sure how Frank turned into the trail boss. It was just that when Frank said to do something, people did it without thinking. Maybe it was his scowl or his thunderous voice.

"How did you get a back quarter?" asked Doreen. The hind quarters contained the tenderest cuts, the sweetest meat. They were usually the prize claim of the shooter, who was awarded first choice on the animal.

Alex grinned over his carving knife, a cigar popping from his mouth. "I lucked out. I was Frank's spotter. We made an agreement. The spotter and the shooter got the hind quarters."

"Did Gary get a hind quarter?" She asked. She couldn't help herself. Beth always shrugged off their farming skills, stating Gary was such a good hunter and fishermen, gardening wasn't that important to them. They would buy their produce from the Matanuska Valley.

Alex reached up with his blood-soaked fingers and scratched his head. "Nope. Charlie was Jimmy's spotter. Charlie took a liking to the boy. Reckon he's going to sell him the horses."

It was just one more thing that upset Gary. Alex had already agreed to be Frank's spotter while discussing the up-coming trip in the office. One thing Alex had learned in the months working with Frank. Mr. Lamar was a lunatic who could draw on anything for public amusement, even executing a swan dance on a clean plate with a knife and fork, but he wasn't a braggart. Frank said he could shoot. For Frank to say he could shoot meant he could shoot excellently.

Matt and Dresden were teaming together, leaving Gary with Art. This worked out for the best as Art was really the only one mild enough to put up with Gary's rants and accusations that his partner wasn't walking quietly enough and was scaring away all the game.

Patsy tugged at her leg. Doreen put her up on a chair and gave her a small piece of moose to wash in a bowl of salty water. "Alex, take that cigar out of your mouth and don't touch your hair while we are carving. What kind of example are you making for your child? That's good, isn't it, that Charlie is selling to the Delaneys? Ester's been wanting to see the horses go."

"I was celebrating," Alex objected, holding out his cigar. "It won't taint the moose, just give it a little smoke flavor." He set the cigar in an ashtray anyway, before continuing. "I reckon. Charlie, Frank, and Matt all seem to like them. Hell, Matt's moving in next door."

"Watch your language, Alex. We all know Matt's interest in the Delaneys. I imagine it's hard to be a man that age and still single, so I'm not judging him. What I'm thinking is that it will be nice that the horses are still in the community. If Jimmy takes good care of them, more power to him."

"Gary doesn't like him," Alex announced, wrapping the last piece of carved meat in butcher paper. "He says Jimmy is a smart aleck young whippersnapper who drinks too much and chases skirts."

"Gary should be one to judge who drinks too much?" Her voice turned up at the ends more sharply than she had intended. "Jimmy is nineteen years old, with no responsibilities. He has the right to drink and chase skirts."

"Gary doesn't think anyone has the right to be nineteen," Alex answered in a leisurely voice. "Did my thoughtful wife save some water for washing?"

"Your thoughtful wife did," Doreen answered.

While Alex bundled up the packaged meat and carried it out to the raw earth cellar to pile deep in the back where the permafrost and the new frost met, Doreen cleaned up the spots on Patsy, put her into a nightgown and tucked her into bed. She was scrubbing down at the basin when Alex returned. "All quiet on the western front?"

"She went right to sleep. She had an exciting day."

"Hmm." He buried his face deep in the water, then ran his hands through his hair.

She took a washcloth and sat on his lap, grooming him.

"You're kind of sexy this way. Three day's stubble, dirt, and blood all over you. A real barbarian. Just like the first night I met you."

"I was drunk."

"You got into a fight."

"A guy was trying to pick up on you. I had already singled you out."

"Hum." He held still as she carefully shaved him. "We were both drunk. I don't think we sobered up until we reached Anchorage."

"You seduced me."

She tried to turn her high, tinny laugh down a notch and chuckle more like Andy. "Are you sure about that? It's not the way I remember."

"How do you know when we were both drunk." He was quiet a minute. "Do you ever regret it?"

"Not for a minute, Alex."

She finished shaving him and watched as he stripped down to sponge bathe. He was pushing thirty and still had an incredible body, with large upper arms and chest, narrowed down hips and powerful thighs. He was a little hairy for some tastes, but she liked her semi-barbarian husband. "How did you ever become a pencil pusher, anyway?" She teased.

"I stole somebody else's grade stats. They think I am a genius."

Freshly washed, he scooped her up and carried her into the bedroom. "I like you best when you look like this."

"In overalls?" She laughed.

"In overalls. Or better, no clothes at all."

They made love as though for the first time. Alex said it was because he was hungry for something more than her food at the end of a three-day hunting trip, but she knew in her heart it was because she wasn't frowsy anymore. She had Andy to thank.

Fourteen

Doreen waited impatiently by the window for Sharon Bowen's car to appear. It was a nuisance not having her own transportation. It didn't seem to matter in the past. She, Sharon, and Beth were all good drivers. In the past, they would agree upon when to do their laundry for the week and one of the husbands would carpool so the women could have a vehicle for the day. It all changed when Art surrendered his car to Sharon.

Patsy tugged at her skirt, her round eyes questioning, her head tilted so high, she nearly fell over. Poor kid. She was going to be small like her mama. "Just a few more minutes," she said, more for herself than her child.

Sharon had argued Art out of the car when he bought a new truck. He had wanted to apply the sales of the car toward payments on the truck, but Sharon had said no. He could handle his truck payments perfectly fine and the convenience of owning two vehicles was worth more than the hundred dollars they would receive by selling it.

It was easy to see why Alex had gone into communications. He wasn't as easy to bend as Art. He would be prepared for an argument and devise answers ahead of time. If Alex wanted to sell their car and buy another, he would come up with a dozen practical reasons why they would need the extra hundred dollars. He would also probably give her a lecture on economics and how expensive it would be to maintain two vehicles. She knew these things. That's why she never attempted to argue with Alex.

Finally, the battered vehicle pulled into the drive. Doreen let Patsy totter out the door, then followed, tugging at two filled baskets.

"Fifteen minutes late," she remarked as she piled her laundry into the back of the station wagon.

"It's been hectic," said Sharon. She helped with the last bundle.

Doreen placed Patsy next to Sharon's little girl in the back seat. Juliana was three months younger, but she was already two inches taller than Patsy and beginning to speak. She would be tall, like her mother, and smart. She slid into the front seat and glanced over at Sharon. She looked tired. "What happened?"

Sharon shrugged as she wheeled out onto the rutted drive that served as a connection to the main road. Only the Erichman's, the Bowen's and the Hugh's lived along this drive and maintained it as they saw fit, which occurred to them in sporadic intervals.

"It's the plants. Not all of them are winter hardy. We were going to cover them all for the winter and hadn't finished it up before the frost hit. We're going to lose a few."

She hit second gear, the car whining at the savage thrust. "I told him we had to get them all covered. He kept dragging his feet. If we lose the Winesap's, oh! He will be sorry. Don't think it was easy. It wasn't easy for a minute to keep them alive."

She eased up on punishing the car. "We put them in the greenhouse with the tomatoes this morning. We never planted them in the soil. I think it's too cold for the roots. Once the crabapples take off though, we might be able to bed them better. They'll be alright. The tomatoes are alright."

Doreen gave her a surprised look. "You grew tomatoes?"

"A few. A few. They didn't quite ripen, but winter came early. We'll bring them in now and fry them. There aren't enough for canning."

Doreen sighed wistfully. "How did you get Art to agree to your whole nursery business anyway?"

Sharon smiled and scratched at her neck. Another man habit. Her hands were long and square. They were strong, clever hands, capable of mending fishing nets or swinging an axe. Doreen had heard Art say, he wouldn't go out on a boat without Sharon. It wasn't the best thing to say around navy men who teased him about it, but Art wasn't a navy man.

He was a ground pounder. Besides, Sharon probably wouldn't let him go out on a boat without her.

Sharon glanced at Doreen quickly before returning her eyes to the road and answered thoughtfully.

"It was funny, really. When we went up the Alcan last year, we grumbled and fought the whole way over Art's load of furniture and the gooseberry bush I dug up at his brother's house. You know I did say I was against it. Completely against it. I did ask permission for the bush, and for the honeysuckle bush I picked up in Seattle when we stopped to visit my cousin. I asked permission, mind you, and the plants didn't take much room at all, but we argued because the furniture was heavy and we broke down twice because of it, but he said, all I could think about was the stupid bushes."

She hit a bump, jarring the station wagon's overworked shocks. "They said they would fill that in! They've got tractors. They've trucks and snowplows. Gary, at least, has a few shovels. What's wrong with these men?"

"I guess we will have to fill it in ourselves," suggested Doreen.

"I would if the ground wasn't frozen solid. What was I saying? Oh, yes. It was funny how it happened. We stopped beside a creek in Canada because the radiator was over-heating. Turned out we had a leak from all the gravel that rattled up from underneath. He did a bubble gum fix on the leak, let the engine cool down, then turned it on and filled the radiator back up with water. We were just about to leave when Art noticed the prettiest little pine growing a short distance from the creek. It wasn't more than two feet high and as bushy as a little tree can get. It was by itself, with a row of larger trees in back. Art told me, "I want that". He dug up the little tree, put it in with my other bushes, and climbed in the car."

They had reached the end of the drive. The Wolf Creek Trading Post squatted almost directly across the road. There were only two vehicles parked in front, Andrea's truck, and a car they recognized as from the village. "Perfect day to do laundry," she said cheerfully. "Not too busy and the gossips are here."

"You quit quarreling because of a tree?" persisted Doreen.

"Yep. After that, we enjoyed the trip. We watched for things. We stopped if something caught our eye. It wasn't always plants. Sometimes, we just noticed a pretty spot to stretch our legs, even to gather a few morels or berries. I guess that's when we got the idea to start a plant nursery. To fill a gap. Art was in the Civilian Youth Corps you know - before the war began. He was in the forestry service, so he knows a lot about plants."

"I didn't know!" Said Doreen with surprise.

"Yes. Well, he has his interests, and he has his duties. Fortunately, our interests are the same."

The lodge, as they had predicted, was nearly empty. Betty Lou sat at the bar, chatting with Solace, while two Native men crouched in a corner, drinking alone. The Native men didn't even look up. Solace gave them a cheery wave and asked if they needed change. Betty Lou turned in her seat and coaxed the little girls to come closer by making herself as small as she could. The two toddlers hesitated, then took a few steps forward, fascinated by Betty Lou's many furry decorations.

"Don't worry about the girls," suggested Solace. "If they wander into the lodge, we'll keep an eye on them." Betty Lou said nothing. She was too busy playing.

Inside the laundry room was a different story. It was billowing with steam. The washing machines were clacking and turning. Millie, Ester and Andy were all sorting through clothes, dropping them into the churning machines, and chatting with each other.

"I saw it with my own two eyes," Andy was saying. "A bear as big as a house. It was attacking the villagers one by one."

"Hush," scolded Ester. "You'll frighten the children."

Andy scoffed loudly and satisfyingly. "What are you saying, Ester? Our boys are ghouls. Didn't you see them squashing the flies in the curtains?"

Before they could get into a fight, Millie intervened. "It wasn't our villages. It was the villages up north. Isn't that right, Andy?"

"It was," she admitted. "I don't think the boys know what we're saying, anyway."

"Well, there are little girls here now and their hearing is delicate," Ester announced triumphantly. "Isn't that right, Sharon?"

Ester always wanted Sharon on her side, but Doreen nodded her head vigorously as well. "Little girls get nightmares easily. They're excitable."

"Juliana isn't excitable," sniffed Sharon. "But I don't want her to be afraid of things that aren't there. You probably shouldn't tell horror stories about bears around small children."

A little disappointed by the censoring, Andy waited until the children had all been corralled together and placed in boxes to play before speaking again.

"Ted Ewing has been coming into the village. He says he wants to do trade, but do you know, he stops by and sees Mark Hansen's sixteen-year-old cousin! Now, what is an old man doing visiting a young girl?"

"He's not an old man," chided Millie. "He's only in his forties."

"He is to her! He's an old lecher is what I say."

"He hasn't done anything to her, has he?" asked Ester, a note of alarm in her voice.

"She says that he hasn't, but he brings her things. Cheap stuff from the dime store, like nail polish, make-up, and plastic bangles. Why is he buying these things for her, I wanted to know, and I told her they were cheap things. They don't mean anything, but she lets him keep coming to see her."

"What about Mark?" asked Millie. She was concentrating on running some clothes through the ringer without losing a hand. "What does he have to say about this?"

"He says it's not his place. It's Iris's brothers' place. That's her name. Iris. The one who came here from Tanana with me and Mark. The girls there are very innocent and don't get a lot of exposure from outsiders. She doesn't know about treacherous men."

Andy stabbed at the laundry in her tub viciously with a stick, making it swirl around, loosening the suds. "It's her brothers' place and her daddy's place and Mark's daddy's place to do something about it. The elders. The elders said they won't unless he hurts her."

"Well, it is inappropriate," agreed Ester. "Ted Ewing is not a man of good character."

"That's just what I told Mark," Andy said with satisfaction. "That's just what I told him. Ted Ewing is up to nothing good." She glanced at the assembly thoughtfully, then asked, "where's Beth today? She hasn't even been by the lodge."

From a pile of linen she was adding to a machine, Doreen called above the rattling noise, "Her boy is out sick with a cold. I told her not to let him go out to play in this bad weather. The temperature dropped too quickly. He wasn't acclimated."

Millie clucked and shook her head sympathetically. "Boys are difficult. They are hard to keep inside. They have too much energy. You and Sharon are lucky, Doreen, to have girls. They are much easier to handle."

"Only while they are small," put in Andy. "Once they hit their teens, they are far worse than boys."

All except Millie looked at Andy dubiously, as though someone who took care of her child half-time couldn't possibly be an expert on childcare. Millie rallied to her defense, which wasn't too surprising for Millie. She rallied to everyone's defense, but for Andy, she rallied quicker and more vigorously. There was a bond between those two that Doreen didn't quite understand. "Andy should know. She raised her younger sisters. Now, they are hitting puberty, so Andy knows."

Ester, whose strongest opinion on child-raising was that they were all unruly and needed constant supervision, picked up a freshly wrung blouse, examined it for stains, then satisfying herself it was flawless, threw it in a tub of rinse water. "I just hope Beth's boy gets well in time to make it to this week's meeting."

Andy, who rarely stuck around long enough for community meetings, asked flippantly, "what's on the agenda? A Christmas charity drive?"

Ester cleared her throat with apparent effort. "If we have a charity drive, you will be the first we will inform. I would rather be sending our donations to our villages then to Africa. I'm sure the African people can't be any less fortunate."

"I've heard the African people are far more unfortunate," said Millie. "All they eat is rice. Nothing else. And they don't have any clothes."

"But they don't need clothes," said Ester quickly. "Our villagers do."

Having settled the debate, she returned to the original question. "The Matanuska Valley is selling its old ambulance because it is buying a new one. Charlie thinks we should buy the old one. What good is an emergency telephone system if we don't have an emergency vehicle?"

Concentrating as hard as she could on scrubbing out a mud stain, Doreen asked timidly, "Has anyone looked at it?"

"Charlie and Frank have," said Ester stiffly.

Andy snorted, which caused the other women to twitter. "Our two-best mechanics! I await their diagnosis."

"Art looked at the ambulance, too." Sharon's voice could be as hard and strong as Andy's. Inexplicably, she had nearly caught up with Ester and Millie on her laundry.

"He said it requires a lot of work but it's doable."

It was neither wise nor reasonable to question Art's authority on anything, especially with Sharon present. Not even Andy, who tormented Ester more liberally than a Mexican uses salsa, had any desire for a show-down with Sharon.

They dropped the subject of the yet unseen ambulance for more interesting material. A family had staked a claim on the land just above the Grants' property.

"It's not the kind of family you were hoping for," explained Andy. "Three brothers. The youngest is seventeen. They pulled a small trailer up on the property and are building a house for their folks in the spring, but they have no wives or sisters."

"That's inconsiderate of them," grumbled Millie. "Only one woman in the whole bunch?"

"Yes," sighed Andy. "And she's mama's age. They probably won't do well together."

"But it might be nice for Solace to have an older woman around," Millie decided. "We must all seem like youngsters to her."

Sharon shrugged. "Maybe she likes it that way. We're her girls."

Andrea and company wrapped up their laundry and left in Andy's truck. Sharon finished her own pile twenty minutes before Doreen and moved toward her side, helping her pull clothes from the rinse water and wring them out.

With their heads close together, Doreen murmured, "I never thought Ester would be so friendly with Andy."

"Why wouldn't she be?" asked Sharon, picking up a filled basket and moving it to the side.

"Because of the way she lives, you know. She dates every single man in town and goes to the bars on Saturday night."

"We should be glad she dates the single men. It will make them better behaved. And she goes to the Pioneer Lounge to watch her brother play. There is no crime in any of that."

"She's technically not divorced, and she talks back to Ester. Really, Sharon, I'm surprised you're not scandalized by her behavior."

"As much as she would like it, Ester's not our nanny. I think Andy's good for her."

Fishing a pair of slacks out of the rinse water, Doreen squeezed them once more through the wringer. She sighed. "I just feel bad for Matt is all. You know he likes her, and he is as good a single man as there is."

The generator hummed loudly in the hush produced by the quiet washing machines. Sharon concentrated on smoothing a few pieces of wet linen over the pile. "If you must know the truth, Matt is married."

Doreen gasped and looked at her friend quickly. "Are you sure? How can you say that?"

"I heard him talking with Art one night. Not that I was eavesdropping, but I was upstairs, cleaning, and you know how sound carries in our house."

"Your staircase helps with that. Right in the middle of your house. He did put a nice wind to it, though."

"It has a nice wind. He is still working on the banister. I think he's trying to out-do Charlie."

Doreen scoffed. "Oh, Charlie. His staircase doesn't really wind. It just takes a forty-five turn, and his banister is standard. I saw him pick up the rough pieces at the hardware store."

They were packing up to leave, so Doreen pressed quickly, "What did Matt tell him?"

Sharon didn't answer until they were in the privacy of the car, returning home. "Actually, I overheard him several times. Matt confides in Art. They work together on the construction site, so they are close, the way Charlie is with Frank."

She skillfully dodged a hole, only to hit another, the rear end thumping loudly. Sharon's shoulders heaved and settled resignedly. "Somebody should borrow a tank to flatten out the drive. We've borrowed everything else. I don't know why we're being tortured like this."

"Sharon!" Doreen interrupted with exasperation. "You haven't told me anything!"

Tapping her gloved fingers against the steering wheel over their poorly maintained drive, Sharon continued, "Matt was married.... Years ago, I guess. Before the war. He signed with the civil service for construction in Cordova when the war ended. He went back to Wisconsin just long enough to see his family and tell his wife to pack her bags."

"His wife came with him?"

"She did but she didn't like it there. A man's gotta go where there are jobs, though."

"What happened? I thought he drifted before settling here."

"He did. She left him in Cordova. I guess she thought he would follow but he didn't. He got depressed for a while and started drinking. Quit his civil service job and got on with the fishing boats. He was docked in Seward when he met up with Frank, who was doing a little shore fishing. They talked of this and that and Frank ended up telling him they were short on heavy equipment operators in Fort Rich. You know, it's not much over a hundred miles from here to Seward. Matt got on the train with Frank and has been here ever since."

Doreen listened, feeling both dismay and pity for the mild-mannered man. "I knew he lived with the Lamars first. I just.... He never talks that much about himself. Do they have kids?"

Sharon nodded. "A boy. He would be around three now. Matt hasn't even seen him. She was pregnant when she left."

"Did he know at the time?"

"No. I don't think he would have let her leave if he had known."

The car stopped in front of the house. Sharon shifted into park and turned to face Doreen. "This was all confidential. You see, Art's a tomb. Never says much about anybody, so Matt talks to him."

"Are you trying to tell me something?" asked Doreen, cringing a little.

"No. It's just that you should learn who to trust, Doreen. Not many people know, and I think Matt would like to keep it that way, at least for the time being."

Doreen watched the car leave with mixed feelings. This was a side of Sharon she had rarely seen. Usually, she arrived with the company of Beth, who prattled lightly about anything she pleased. Sharon was testing her! If rumor of Matt's marriage began flying around Wolf Creek, Sharon would know who was to blame.

It was such an unfair thing to do because everybody gossiped. She fretted to herself as she ran a clothesline and set up the drying rack in the kitchen to dry her clothes. There was no point in hanging them outside in this weather. They would just freeze stiff as a board. Sharon probably kept her drying racks upstairs, where it was warm and airy. Alex should have built a two-story, or at least a roomy attic.

She shouldn't complain. The house was modest, but it was warm and dry. Alex was a good builder, at least as good as Charlie, maybe even Art. He was putting his building into his sheds. He needed shelters for all the tools and equipment necessary for his future business. He needed workspace to saw boards, take apart engines, sharpen blades and fortify his truck. The truck sported a winch in the front and a pulley in the back and was kept on call for pulling cars out of ditches. Nobody touched the truck except Alex.

One day, when his dream life became his real life, he would build an upstairs addition. They would make it grand and lovely, and they would have four children. They had decided this the day they settled.

She decided she would say nothing to her husband concerning this new knowledge she had obtained. She would show Sharon how mum she could be.

She remained quiet about Matt throughout the entire dinner, served in the living room on drying day. Her restraint remained intact long after the baby was put to bed. She poured over a much passed around copy of Ladies Home Journal while Alex read the newspaper.

Alex never talked much about the news unless it mentioned Eisenhower. Then he would say with satisfaction, "that's our man." She had to assume this was true. Once Eisenhower was elected, he would bring new growth to Alaska, and not just in the military. He would bring jobs in business and industry. Alex was in a position to know these things.

It wasn't until they had gone to bed, and she was in the intimacy of his embrace, that she felt her resolve melt. "Did you know Matt is married?" She asked, looking closely at his face to read his reaction.

"Uh huh," he said, sitting up against the pillows and lighting his cigar.

"You did? You didn't tell me?"

"I didn't think it was important. What's a man to do? Matt knows heavy equipment like nobody else on base. We need him here."

"But for a man to leave his wife and child," she persisted.

"He didn't leave them. They left him."

He put out his cigar after a few leisurely puffs and blew out the lamp. Doreen laid back with her hands laced across her chest, eyes open, wondering how much of a secret Matt's marriage really was and realizing she could not find out by asking questions without betraying Sharon's confidence.

"You wouldn't think," she said at last, in a voice of wonder. "A place could tear a couple apart, but it can."

Alex was half-asleep but managed to murmur, "it's this land. It chooses you. You are either married to it or you are not. If you are married to it, you can't leave it. It will call you home."

Her high-pitched laugh caught the air and she toned it down a notch.

"It's a good thing we both are married to the land, isn't it?"

He reached around and patted her hip. "It helps." He stopped patting for a moment. "A lot of things help."

That was reassuring. She looked at his turned back, his hand still on her hip, and thought, *it is reassuring.* She pressed against the warmth of his back and went to sleep.

Friday nights they played card games. Every household had its game preferences. Charlie and Ester Bolinder liked Bridge, so when they went to the Bolinders, they played Bridge. The Hughes and the Bowens liked Canasta. Oddly, when it came to table amusements, Alex's and Frank's tastes were the same. They both liked Pinocle. They were both passionate about Cribbage.

At least, Doreen found it odd, as odd as the close friendship Millie had with Andy. Outwardly, the two men were different. Alex looked the part of a woodsman. Frank wouldn't wear a wool plaid shirt unless he was chopping down trees. Alex was a man of few words, Frank a man of many, but they worked in the same office, shared the same military secrets, and enjoyed the same games. They understood each other.

Doreen and Millie did not play cribbage. When the Lamars came to visit or the Erichmans visited the Lamars, the men always set up the cribbage board first while the women pattered in the kitchen, cooking fudge, popping corn, and supervising the children's play. Jason was a big boy, but only a year-and-a-half. Patsy was nearly two, making her quicker and more agile. What he took by force, she generally retrieved through cleverness, although this did not stop frequent tantrums from both children.

Millie straightened out the current toy-sharing mishap, her face hanging half-way between resolution and defeat. "I'm trying to teach him," she apologized. "What will he do with another child in the family?"

Doreen poured the bubbling fudge into a plate to cool. "The next few months will make a huge difference, I'm sure. They begin turning into human beings."

"I'm not completely sure of that."

Washing each drooling face and hand sticky with dust and animal hair with a damp cloth, Millie sat the two children in their chairs like dress-up dolls and put a small bowl of popcorn in front of each one, sitting between them so Jason could not snatch from Patsy's stash.

"I'm afraid the bigger he gets, the more it will become like trying to control a bull in a China shop. He does play well with other boys, though."

"You want too much of a baby." Doreen pressed her finger into the fudge to see how long it would be before it had cooled off enough to cut it and set it in the middle of the table. "He's not a mean child. Ben is far more aggressive."

"Ben isn't mean, either. It's Jimmy's influence, and a bit of Mark and Owen. They think the women will coddle him, so they're trying to teach him manliness."

"Nothing against Jimmy, but he's a cocky devil to be influencing a toddler."

"Don't I know it! Why, they practically dress him like Davy Crockett, and he already has a toy rifle. Despite Frank's best efforts, with Ben as his best friend, it's doubtful Jason will grow up a complete gentleman. It's nothing to despair about," she added at Doreen's contemplative stare. "I have brothers who are not complete gentlemen, either. It's challenging to learn manners."

The fudge had cooled down sufficiently to cut it into squares. She took a couple of the end pieces and dropped them into the two nearly emptied popcorn bowls for the babies. "Mark is spending time with Ben?" asked Doreen, hoping Millie wouldn't notice how much her ears were perking at attention.

Millie was too busy making sure the chocolate made its way to the mouths of the children and not all over the table. "Quite a bit! And why shouldn't he? He has been seeing a lot of Andy, taking her out flying, so she can get in her flight hours."

"She wants to be a pilot?"

She licked her chocolatey fingers. "Not so much. She's serious about becoming a bush nurse, but she's gotta learn the ropes, like knowing how to co-pilot and meeting the villagers. It's not something you can learn all at once. They make a cute couple, really."

"But what about Matt?" Doreen asked, controlling the upward trill of her voice.

"Oh, Matt." She picked at a corner piece of fudge, sliding it into her mouth before answering. "He keeps to himself a lot these days. He had so much planned out. Not so much with Andy. People have got to understand, they are good friends but they both have good reason not to be more than that. They have things to sort out."

Now that the fudge and popcorn were ready, Doreen could sit down for a few minutes of private time and a cup of coffee. "What kind of plans? Matt never did talk much around me. He and Alex always took it out to the shed."

Millie nodded. "He can be like that. It takes sitting around a campfire with a couple of beers to make him start talking. He bought the land because he has his eye on an excavator he thinks he can buy with a good down payment. He wants to become an independent contractor. But now..." She seemed to think hard about it. "He has a problem."

"He's married," said Doreen breathlessly.

"He has always known he was married. He hasn't always known he's a father."

"Then the rumors are true?"

"If that's what they're saying, it's true. She wasn't more than two months pregnant when she ran off, but now she has sent him a letter. She wants to try again."

"She wants him to come home?"

"He won't do that, you know. His heart is already invested in the Chugach. She will have to come here."

The babies had finished their treat and were rubbing their sleepy eyes. Millie washed them down again and took both into her ample arms. "Let's put them to bed, shall we?"

Putting the babies to bed meant they could finally sit down with the men for a pinocle game. "Honestly," said Doreen lightly, putting the refreshments in the middle of the table. "I don't know how you can play cribbage all evening when you sit in an office and play all day."

"We have a tournament coming up," growled Frank. "With the military officers."

"Oh, you must not let them beat you!" Now that her evening duties were over, Doreen could feel flirty and pretty. She had tossed aside her bibbed apron to reveal her new maternity dress and the bubble of pearls around her neck. She sat down, patting at her curls.

"The military officers are good at chess," Millie said casually, shuffling the cards. "One of them beat Frank last month at an Anchorage tournament."

Frank scowled over his cards as though he thought Millie had deliberately given him the wrong ones. He rumbled in his chest. "Captain Sorenson played in Switzerland against the Russians."

"Did he beat them?" asked Doreen, her eyes wide with wonder.

He rumbled even more deeply if that was at all possible. "Nobody beats the Russians."

It became more important to concentrate on their hands. Frank took the bid, glared thunderously at Millie when he announced the suit, then fumed over his hand, finally laying down a full suit and two marriages. Whatever terrible thoughts he had harbored earlier had been forgotten.

"I heard a news flash on the radio waves today," said Alex during a lull. "Don't worry. It's not classified. It will be announced to the public tomorrow. Representative Egan is running for the territorial Senate."

"Egan?" asked Frank, raising his brows, then settling them again. "Good man. He was born here, wasn't he?"

"Valdez. Working man roots."

"Do you think he'll work well with Eisenhower?"

"Why wouldn't he? They both want the same thing. Taft's isolationist ideas are suicidal. They leave us vulnerable. This is a new and changing world. We have to be a part of it. It cost us two wars to learn that. It shouldn't cost another."

Realizing the card playing part of the night was over, Millie clapped her hands together and said, "listen to this. They talk like Egan and Eisenhower have already won and they haven't begun their campaigns."

Alex sat back in his chair and lit a cigar.

When he sat like that, Doreen noticed, he appeared to belong to the bureaucratic society he claimed no interest in. She had never seen this side before.

She hadn't seen the man behind the desk with his information channels and mounds of paperwork, staggered like chess pieces. He was the man with a line directly to the attorney general. And he shared that line directly with Frank and Charlie, who calculated costs, checked inventory, and measured their needs against the encroaching threats at the border.

To Doreen and the rest of the pioneer settlement, these threats were invisible, and dubious at best. They were peaceful. The tiny Russian towns with the domed churches were peaceful. They harbored no ill will toward anyone. Why should the Russians think poorly of them?

To the inside complex of government offices and military personnel, the threat was visible. While their own air force carried out exercises over the glaciated mountains and the massive Harding Ice Field, Russia was noisy with its own force, sweeping conspicuously close to Alaskan waters as they maneuvered the Siberian straits.

It counted in the missiles potentially aimed at their vital cities and could be launched from Russian air space. It wasn't Alex's job to understand why hostilities were building, only to relate what had been verified.

"It has begun," said Alex reassuringly. "The campaign has begun. You'll see in Monday's newspapers."

"Then there is nothing to worry about," said Millie, taking note of the late hour and rising from her seat. "If all that is needed for them to win is to campaign, we can all breathe easily. If only all problems could be solved in the same manner."

Neither Frank nor Alex seemed able to combat the flippancy Millie used when referring to anything regarding politics or religion. Frank grunted and went out to start the car while Millie gathered up the baby.

"You should really let Frank know you can dance," said Millie while he was gone. "He doesn't have enough players yet, even with Jimmy. He wants choreography."

Doreen looked up thoughtfully from clearing the card table. "Is that why he was grouchy tonight?"

"The theater group, yeah. And the politics. Now then, Mr. Alex Erichman, you should know it's not always wise to talk politics with Frank in a group of people. He doesn't like Truman. Never liked Truman. I don't think he likes Taft, either."

She left without saying more but stopped long enough to wave with one of the gloved hands supporting Jason.

"You're different around Frank than you are around Art or Gary," said Doreen after they were gone.

"How is that?" asked Alex, still sprawled in his chair.

"You're a desk sitter. It shows when you're around Frank."

"Maybe I should be careful how much time I spend around him."

"Why?" She straddled his lap and locked her fingers behind his neck. "Is it just because that's not who I saw first? The deskman?"

His smile slipped slightly, then returned. "What do you think?"

"It becomes you."

"I don't think it does. Millie's right. I shouldn't discuss politics around large groups of people. I'm not cut out for that sort of thing."

"You mean you're not a Charlie or a Frank? You're not a Gary Hughes, either."

"I'm not a bad mechanic or a shabby builder. I guess I'm close enough."

"And you've got a ham radio squirreled away in your shed that you can't use until the electricity comes through. Don't worry, Alex. I won't let anyone know you have a brain."

She remained on his lap, leaving no more of an impression than a child on his sprawling frame, while he clasped her at the waist and said thoughtfully, "You followed a dumb ass all the way to Alaska and became a camp wife because of him?"

"You never fooled me. I knew there was more to you than a guy with a radio. You do hide that guy a lot, though."

"I get tired of him. I put him out for hire. If you want him, you've got to pay."

"Then I'm out of luck. I don't have that kind of money."

They kissed and went to bed then, but afterward he turned to her and asked, "Do I really look bourgeois when I'm around Frank?"

"And Charlie," she said. "But I won't tell anyone. I like it."

Oddly, this didn't reassure him. He continued studying her, then rolled on his back, his hands across his chest. "I've always been in radio. Did I ever tell you that? My dad ran a local station when I was growing up. It wasn't much, but you know, it's how some of the big-name musicians got their start, appearing on local stations. He always thought he would strike it lucky that way, but he never did. I don't think he had that good an ear for music."

"Why does it embarrass you?"

"It doesn't! Believe me, it doesn't. We weren't any better off than anyone else, and not nearly as well off as some. For that, I'm glad. In a small town though, you don't really want to be different, and we were different. Look how quickly the military transferred me out of a war zone and into a listening post."

"I'm glad of that," she cheered, reminding him that was how they met.

"I am too. I love it here. I'm trying to tell you something though, and I don't know how to put it. I just want to be one of the guys. I don't want to stand out."

"Oh well, you're too late for that," she said as though to reassure him. "Standing out is what Chugiak men do."

Fifteen

Frank Lamar and Charlie Bolinder didn't know anything about mechanics. The community was beginning to wonder if Art Bowen did, either. The ambulance they had all chipped in to buy was so old, it used a crank to start the engine. The tires had worn down to rubber enclosures that showed no thread left at all. The steering wheel spun freely a good quarter turn before turning the tires. The only nice thing about it was the back with its padded walls and professional-looking gurney.

Doreen, Beth, and Sharon gathered as a group to look at the community's new purchase. "They might have said it hasn't been used in the last five years," said Beth sourly. She was cranky because she was still trying for a baby and Doreen was beginning to show.

As the spouse of one of the ring leaders in this dubious purchase which had landed on the Bowen property, Sharon felt it necessary to defend the decision. "Art says they can convert the crank and put in a starter switch."

"They'll have to take the whole thing apart," scoffed Beth.

"That's why they wanted it." Sharon turned to Beth and looked at her accusingly. "Gary wanted it as much as did Art and so did Matt."

Doreen nodded, conscious that her curls no longer bounced all over her head when she moved it vigorously but stayed obediently tucked close to her face. This made her want to nod more elegantly and with greater control. "It's true. I saw Gary's eyes light up."

"I saw Alex rub his hands together," Beth snipped back.

Sharon stalked around the vehicle, got up in the driver's seat, checked the amount of play in the steering wheel and tested the clutch and brakes. "We can do this, I think. All we've got to do is fire her up. It's not so different from my pop's jalopy."

"You're planning to drive it?" asked Doreen with awe.

"Sure." She looked down and beckoned at them. "Get the kids. There's plenty of room in here."

While Beth and Doreen were gathering up the three small children, Sharon was testing the hand-crank. She managed to get it to turn a little. She spit on her hands, put them in her gloves, and gave the handle a good spin. The engine muttered a little but did not fire up. "Let me give it a spin," offered Beth upon returning. "I've started up a few of these things."

Shorter and stouter, Beth still had a powerful arm. She turned the handle vigorously. The engine rumbled a few seconds longer, than died.

Sharon put her hands on her hips, staring thoughtfully, while the three toddlers peered from the back- seat window. "I have an idea. Doreen, get up in the driver's seat. As soon as you hear the ambulance start to fire up, feed it a little gas."

Doreen knew about troublesome starters. She slid into the driver's seat, put one foot on the clutch, the other on the gas, with one hand preparing to shift. The first time, she gave it too much gas, too quickly. It roared and choked, refusing to come back to life before the smoke cleared and the smell of gas evaporated.

"My fault, my fault," she apologized.

The second time, she listened for the first intense spark. She eased the gas slowly, coaxing it to feed the engine. The engine hacked, spit, and grumbled to life. Carefully, she eased the clutch, so it would idle in neutral. "We've got it girls!" She cried, forgetting they were as guilty as marauders pillaging the labor of their men.

Doreen moved over, so Sharon could climb into the driver's seat, while Beth swung in on the other side. Doreen was caught between the two larger women and suddenly quite happy she didn't take up much space.

The ambulance had rattled out of the driveway before Doreen could think much about what they were doing. She drew in her breath, feeling wild and wicked and giggling uncontrollably as the vehicle swayed haphazardly on the crude road. Not only did it have loose steering and faulty brakes, but the shock absorbers were non-existent. They felt every bump.

It was a good thing it had snowed recently. It had been the perfect snow fall for ending the cold snap. It was just warm enough to blend in with the frost, then freeze into crunchy crystals. The freshly plowed drive between the three homesites, sputtered away from the tires in listless complaint. The truck wobbled haphazardly, swaying first to the right, then to the left of their path.

The entire distance between the three homesites was two and a half miles. The Bowen property was at the far end, with the Erichman house closest to the main road. When they reached the Erichman drive, Sharon turned the ambulance around and motioned for Beth to sit at the wheel. "Your turn. Come on. I know you want to."

Beth did. She hopped out and ran around to the driver's side of the fat-nosed van as quickly as she could go. She grinned with daredevil excitement. "Hang on to your hats!"

The ambulance screeched and clattered out of the drive, the front end bouncing down and smacking repeatedly against the snow-crested earth. The toddlers in the back seat bounced against each other and chortled.

Shaking and teetering, the van roared up the mile two and a half mile stretch to the Bowen drive, made a sharp right into it, the vehicle leaning dangerously, and slammed to a stop. The entire time, the three girls whooped like cowboys. "Now, you!" Beth urged, pushing at Doreen. "You know how to drive."

"But this is insane!" She protested. However, she wanted to try it out. She waited until Sharon and Beth had settled back in, then released the clutch, letting it roll gently down the drive.

"C'mon, c'mon, don't be afraid of it," urged Beth.

Doreen shrugged her off. "I'm not afraid."

Still, she waited until they had turned the corner into the drive before giving the vehicle gas. She felt it lean lazily to the left as they turned and worked the steering wheel desperately to compensate. It had an enormous amount of play. She jerked it back and forth just to keep the van on a straight path and fought with it at every corner. The brakes were spongy. She had to pump them three times to get them to grab at the wheels, slowing their progress. Her heart was in her throat the whole time. She drove as far as Beth's house, turned around, and drove back to Sharon's.

"What do you think?" askedBeth as they jumped out. "Was it fun?"

"I want to drive it when they get the brakes and steering column fixed," Doreen admitted. "It's just a little scary until then."

"It's not scary," said Sharon scornfully. "How many cars have you helped Alex pull out of the ditch? How many broken steering columns and bent axles did you guide as Alex hauled them to the trading post garage? That's no easier than driving this bucket of bolts."

"But the kids...."

Sharon was already rounding up the kids and shooing them toward the house. "Don't be silly. That thing is an armored tank. There is not much we can do to it on this deserted little stretch of land. Even if we turned it over, the walls are padded. The kids are safer in that ambulance than they are in our cars."

She was offering them coffee and since Sharon was their transportation home, Doreen and Beth couldn't very well refuse. They sat in her kitchen, which had a semi-circular feel due to the gently winding staircase and discussed the potential of the ambulance.

"I am going to tell Art I want to be one of the drivers," said Sharon decisively. When the others looked at her with surprise, she tossed her blonde ponytail and said, "Whynot? They are going to keep the ambulance parked here. I heard the men talking. We are already the central location for the field phones because of our reception. We can bounce almost to the river," she added proudly.

"I only live half-a-mile away," Beth put in enthusiastically. She clapped her hands together and squeezed them. "I can become a driver easily. I can walk the distance."

Doreen sighed and looked about fretfully. "Oh, I don't know. The baby and all."

"You won't be carrying a baby forever and you're the next closest beside Beth. The men have to see this from a practical angle. They are all at work during the day. What if we received an emergency call during the day? We need drivers on call, day and night." Sharon slapped the end of one hand into the palm of the other to emphasize her point.

"Doreen," said Beth firmly. "If you can handle helping Alex with the tow truck, you can damn sure handle becoming an emergency driver. You are going to be a good driver even without Alex supervising you."

Doreen didn't argue but she thought a lot about Beth's words and Sharon's determination. When Alex came home that night, he went to the kitchen as he habitually did, sat down at the table, lit a cigar, and asked her about her day.

"Oh, the usual," she said casually as she laid out dinner. "Sharon picked me and Beth up for a visit. It couldn't be nearly as exciting as your day."

"Not too exciting," he said, waving his cigar around. "A new family moved into the lowlands. The head of the family showed up to work today. He's working under Gary – heavy equipment."

"What's he like?" asked Doreen, ushering Patsy to the table and sitting her down.

"Don't know yet." He waited until she was seated, bowed his head for a moment, said "amen" loudly, then continued. "I only met him during lunch break. He's kind of thin and nervous. Doesn't really look like the frontier type, but Frank doesn't look that way, either."

"It takes all kinds. That's what they are saying," Doreen remarked, correcting Patsy's table manners by giving her a fork for eating her food instead of shoveling it into her mouth with her fingers.

"Maybe. They are living out of one of those travel trailers like the Delaney's have, only they came in too late to put up a lean-to and they have four kids. It's going to be hard for them."

Doreen clucked her tongue with dismay. "Well, there's been worse. We'll just have to do what we can to help. Four kids! Are they young?"

"They're young. The oldest is ten. The rest he had after the war."

"Well, he's been very busy," said Doreen without thinking.

He gave a mock leer. "Some men think it's the best way to keep their women busy."

"I know that," she said with annoyance and squirmed in her chair. She also knew that men like that were not the kind Northwestern women accepted. They were busy enough without someone choosing their working hours for them.

She gave him a minute to relish his sense of humor. "I've been thinking, Alex. I have an idea. I've decided I want to become one of the ambulance drivers...when the van is fixed, of course."

He frowned. "How is that a good idea? You shouldn't be driving that ambulance."

She looked up with surprise. "Why not?"

"There are a lot of responsibilities involved." Believing at first that was to be the end of the discussion, he caught the truculent look on Doreen's face and added, "you'll need to take a first-aid course."

"Sharon and Beth are going to become drivers. If they can pass a first-aid exam, so can I."

Faced with the most dreaded of all arguments, the enlightened status of his coworkers' wives, Alex jabbed at his plate, then asked, "is that why you want to become a driver?"

"That's not all of it," she answered, pouting. "I'm a good driver but all I ever get to do is help you pull people out of ditches and snowbanks. I want to drive more."

Having finished his dinner, Alex pushed back his chair and folded his arms over his chest thoughtfully. "I'll get you a car. If I get you a car, will you forget about being an ambulance driver?"

Doreen did not have to think about it twice. "Okay," she agreed cheerfully. Certainly, Beth and Sharon would understand.

Beth and Sharon were not understanding, not at first. "Talk is cheap," grumbled Sharon.

"Honestly, he lives in the stone age," pouted Beth. "How do you know he'll come through?"

"If he doesn't, I'm signing up as a driver," Doreen answered firmly.

Two weeks later, Doreen had her car. She drove it proudly into Sharon's yard on a day when Beth was also visiting their end of the drive neighbor. Both young ladies dashed out the door to admire her new possession. Beth chatted excitedly, while Sharon could only whistle. The car was beautiful. It didn't matter that it was five years old. It was a Pontiac Streamliner, easily making it the most elegant car in Wolf Creek.

"I'm just a little mad," said Beth, crossing her arms. "How am I going to get Gary to buy me a car? I can't keep up with the Jones's," she sulked. "Nor the Bowens or the Erichmans. It's unfair."

Well," contended Sharon. "Art had to give me the car when he bought the truck, but my run-down jalopy isn't a Pontiac."

"Practically new," said Beth, fanning her face. "You know they didn't put these out until after the war. Look how the leather still shines."

"A ride! A ride!" demanded Sharon, wriggling her way inside. "Beth, go get the kids."

Doreen watched from the driver's side, pleased to see Beth doing something she usually was directed to do.

"You know," said Sharon while Beth was hunting down the babies, "If your husband wasn't white collar, he'd receive hell for this."

"Beth can rest easy. Neither Charlie nor Frank will buy their wives a car."

Sharon looked at her intently. "Why wouldn't they?"

"What do you think Charlie or Frank see when they look under a hood?"

"I don't know."

Doreen giggled her high-pitched laugh, then lowered it to a chuckle. "They don't know, either."

Beth was hustling the kids to the automobile, bundled up from head to toe. Patsy wriggled impatiently in the back seat, eager to be with her friends. "They can't pick up a hundred-dollar car and keep it maintained," she added. "They would have one car or the other in the shop all their time."

"What did I miss?" asked Beth, squeezing into the front seat, next to Sharon.

"Nothing important," said Sharon airily. "What did you learn about the new family?"

"The Millers?" Beth placed her hands over her purse as though it held all her little secrets. "They weren't at all prepared for our winters. Gary and Matt put up some tarps over the trailer to keep it better insulated and to give them a storm entrance. They don't have winter boots or mittens for the poor babies. They don't have enough blankets or enough food. Betty Lou gave them some packages of caribou and they were really happy about it. Where are we going?"

The snowfalls had been even; two in two weeks. It was light, dry snow that had settled unperturbed, smoothing out the landscape. It was easy to drive on. The thick crunch of the first snowfall lay just under the powder covering the road.

"I don't know," shrugged Doreen. "I thought we might go down to the lake. We haven't been there for a while."

Sharon agreed. "Why not? We should drive the car out on the ice. It must be frozen solid by now."

"Do you think so?" Doreen weighed the possibility in her mind. The boat ramp would give them easy access to the lake unless the water was low. It had rained enough during the summer to keep their own creek trickling merrily all year. There shouldn't be a problem.

There was only a three-foot drop from the cleared beach access to the lake on a gently swelling slope. The ice was thick and smooth from the freezing weather. The car drove down the clearing easily and slid a little when they hit the ice.

"Give her a spin," urged Beth.

Doreen complied, glided the vehicle fifty yards out, drifted into a half-spin and erupted into high-pitched giggles as the car skidded in several random directions before coming to a stop. Beth and Sharon roared with delight while the toddlers in the back seat clapped their hands.

"Let's skate," she suggested. "The ice is smooth and there's hardly any snow on it."

Agreeing that this was a great idea, they tumbled out to test the ice. The boots glided effortlessly as they twirled and spun.

"Look! The kids are having fun!" Called out Beth.

It was questionable how much fun the children were having. Stuck in their oversized snowsuits, they waddled out on the ice, falling on their well-padded bottoms with every third step. At least, they weren't crying, which was positive enough.

"I have an idea," said Doreen, stopping long enough in her boot-skating skills to beckon the other two women close. "Let's all get ice skates."

"I don't know how to ice skate," sulked Beth.

"You can learn. It isn't hard. Is it hard, Sharon?"

Sharon weighed the question carefully. "Not as hard as roller-skating. You just have to learn your balance."

Beth made a face.

"I don't know how to roller-skate, either."

"It doesn't matter," said Doreen. "I'll get Alex to come out and plow off this portion of the lake. We'll hold a winter picnic here. Those who have ice skates can bring their skates. We can also bring sleds and cardboard boxes to pull the kids around. We could set up a donation table for the Millers."

"No," said Beth suddenly. "I mean no about the donation table, not the picnic. The picnic is a great idea, but if we invited the Millers, wouldn't it be embarrassing for them to see a donation table set up for their benefit?"

Sharon nodded her head. "She's right. We can hold a picnic, but we should keep the donation drive private – house to house."

"We can do that now, can't we?" Said Doreen, feeling important. "We can visit the other women and see what they are willing to give."

"It will be more fun that way," agreed Beth. "We can visit each one and show off your new car." She nudged Doreen playfully.

Doing one last swoop across the ice, Sharon stopped to snatch up her little girl and zoom her sideways toward the car.

"Let's shoot for eight tomorrow morning," she told Doreen. "I'll pick up Beth and meet at your house. If we limit how long we stay at each house, we can get them all done in time to come home and fix dinner."

Pleased with their plan, they piled back into what had instantly become their favorite mode of transportation and chattered all the way home. When Alex sat down to dinner that night and asked her how her day had been, she queried, "Alex, do you still have your ice skates?"

"They are in the shed somewhere," he grunted. "Next to yours."

"I thought we had lost them."

"No. They were just packed in the wrong box."

"Let's get them out. We were at the lake today and the ice is perfect. Let's shovel it off and hold an ice-skating party. A picnic."

Instead of arguing, he chuckled softly. "I remember before we left San Diego, you insisted on buying skates and made me buy a pair. I thought it odd, this little San Diego girl preparing for a life on an Alaskan skating rink – then you told me you were originally from Lake Tahoe."

There was something nostalgic in his voice that made her shift to the pragmatic side of her life choices. "There was work in San Diego."

"For a little girl who could dance in a chorus line."

Doreen glanced at Patsy as though she could understand their conversation. Patsy was more interested in trying to scoop up all her mashed potatoes at once. She leaned across the table and dropped her voice anyway.

"Millie has been putting pressure on you. I should never have opened my mouth in front of her."

She settled back again. "Don't go telling the others. I know Frank has his talent show coming on, but I want to leave those dancing days behind."

"It's nothing to be ashamed off. You can dance. It's what caught my eye, remember?"

"I like ice skating better."

He laughed again. "Just so you don't fall on your butt. You're carrying, remember?"

Later, in the coziness of their bed, when they were their most candid with each other, he asked, "I take it your friends have forgiven you for not signing on as an ambulance driver?"

"They have," said Doreen agreeably. "Although I think Beth's a little jealous. Now, she wants a car."

"Hmm." He tucked an arm under her neck and kissed the top of her head. "Gary's had a few chances to pick up a cheap deal. There are always men leaving base. He passed them up. Too much work." He paused. "Gary is more of a driver than a mechanic. Damned good driver. He's the best bucket man on base, but he's a driver."

"Who is the best mechanic?" She asked, running a finger along his sandpaper face.

"Matt. It doesn't matter if it's a jet engine or a chainsaw motor. Matt is your mechanic. He knows machines inside and out. He knows what makes them work."

"I'm sorry I pushed him to leave," she apologized. "He helped you a lot in your garage."

"I'm not sorry. He still gives me pointers. We needed our family time." He kissed her again. "There are just too many single men here."

"You were jealous?"

"No. But men get hungry, and when they are hungry, they are not very responsible."

"Aren't you glad you have a responsible wife?"

He had buried his nose deep in her hair, inhaling the newly washed fragrance. "Yeah. One who doesn't sign up as a driver for a rickety old ambulance."

She squirmed to one side to look at him. "I thought you were working on it."

"We're working on it. We rounded up four matching tires and we've replaced the brake pads."

"The drums are going out."

"How do you know that?"

She scrambled for an answer, responding with, "Sharon told me."

Her answer satisfied him. Whatever Sharon said or did, it was Art's problem, not his. "You know," he said. "Don't do another home perm. I like what Andy did. Your hair is soft, and it smells good. You should let Andy be your hairdresser."

"Even if she's a loose woman?"

He rolled, so that he was over the top of her, kissing her more intimately. "Just don't let her influence you the way Sharon does."

Sixteen

Sharon and Beth arrived promptly at eight the next morning. They were both dressed in their Sunday outfits, with matching hats and gloves. Doreen had planned to just wear loose clothing but when she saw them out her window, marching up to her steps like school marms, she quickly went into the bedroom and changed into her new dress.

"Did you tell Alex?" twittered Beth, picking up the paper bag filled with wrapped packages of meat piled on top of five pounds of potatoes.

"I did," she sang out, hastily putting on her lipstick, "he said it was a good idea. Betty Lou drops by to visit them, and Matt brought them some eggs and milk from the valley last week, but that's been about it."

Sharon and Beth crowded each other to look at themselves in Doreen's full-length mirror. "We make quite a welcoming committee, don't you think?" asked Beth, putting down the bag to straighten her hat in the mirror.

"And we don't have time to fool around if we're going to deliver to the Miller family before dinner hour," said Sharon impatiently. "We have four places we need to stop at."

"Four?" Beth had picked the bag back up but puzzled over the number out loud.

"The Grants, the Delaney's, the Lamar's and the Bolinder's." Sharon emphasized the number with her fingers.

"Oh, the Delaney's." Beth looked uncomfortable. "I've never even been in Mrs. Delaney's home."

"Neither have I, but they have been here going on seven months. Don't you think it's time to pay her a visit?"

Beth agreed, although her agreement didn't sound extremely enthusiastic. She sulked a little when they got in the car. "She could come to the meetings to make herself more known. How do we even know she's willing to help?"

Sharon elbowed her. "Oh hush, or we are going to be exactly the type of people Ted Ewing accuses us of being?"

"Do any of us have a spotless record?" Laughed Doreen nervously. "We weren't born with silver spoons now, were we?"

This didn't pacify Beth. Stuck in the middle, she crossed her hands over her knees and sighed, "who said anything about spoons? They just seem peculiar is all. All those young girls and single men running all over the place."

"What single men?" asked Sharon. "Jimmy belongs there. Matt built a cabin next door..."

"And isn't that peculiar, all by itself? The Hansen brothers are always there, and the railroad man's son comes over!"

"Oh good heavens!" Snapped Doreen. "Rodney Pierce is sixteen years old. He goes to see Carol. What could be more natural than that?"

She was relieved when they arrived at the crossroad with the trading post. Sharon frowned and stared out the window as though some grievous fault, certainly not her own, had caused this unfamiliarity with the already-thriving farm family, her lips pressed tight.

Beth's sulkiness didn't leave her until they saw the circular drive and she cried out, "look. We won't have to make a trip to the Delaneys after all. I see Andy's truck."

Even Sharon's laugh gushed out a little quickly. "I'm sorry," she said. "It's nothing against them, but we don't know Mrs. Delaney, only Jimmy and Andy."

"And she raised Jimmy and Andy," Beth agreed with a little too much haste.

"Well, they can't be the worst neighbors in the world," said Doreen, reaching in the back seat for Patsy. "Millie hasn't complained about them."

Beth shrugged, arranged her jacket, and took her little boy's hand. "Frank and Millie. They are strange ones. They don't pick their friends like normal people. I hear Betty Lou even visits

Millie once a week and sits down to coffee and cinnamon rows just like a lady."

"They don't know any better," Sharon informed them. "I think Frank was raised a Quaker or something."

"Oh!" gasped Beth. "The poor man."

Doreen wasn't at all sure if Sharon's information was correct, or even if it was unfortunate to be a Quaker, but Frank was quirky about his friendships. Friends were the people you spent the most time with, and Frank spent the most time with Charlie Bolinder, Matt Jones, and Jimmy Delaney. Charlie, she could understand. The two were thick as thieves, and as kooky as woodpeckers. Matt, too. Matt was well-liked by everybody, but Jimmy was a kid. A bit of a wild kid. He drank. He smoked cigarettes. He spent his weekends with a cocktail waitress. She didn't find her doubts strong enough to make contradictions, however. Frank could be Hindi for all she knew.

The lodge was as busy as could be expected for an early morning in the middle of the week. Two truck drivers were eating hash browned potatoesand eggs at a corner table. One of the Phillips brothers was at the bar, drinking coffee with Dresden Hayes, who, in the winter, became practically a permanent fixture to the post. Solace's son, Ed, was leaning over the counter on the other side, listening to them talk. Solace and Andy were sitting by themselves, guarding the soda machine. The youngsters had learned to tape a string to the dime dropped into the slot, so they could retrieve their coin after getting a soda.

Grabbing some folding chairs lined against one wall, Doreen and company joined the two women at their table. Beth nudged Andy's arm. "I didn't expect to see you this early in the morning," she said, letting some of her enthusiasm for the surprise creep into her voice.

Andrea arched her brows. Beth had always been careful not to add much warmth to her welcome, which made her instantly suspicious. "Well," Andy said, taking out a cigarette. "Mama is on a rampage this morning. She found condoms in Jimmy's clothes when she was sorting laundry. For once, her wrath isn't aimed at me, so I thought I would get out of there before she found a reason to make it my fault."

"Now then, you can't be too careful with cocktail waitresses," said Beth. Her boy wanted a soda. "No," she told him. "It's too early." He started to whine, and she sent him off with a pat on his rump.

Andy laughed. "I think he's just hopeful. Mark thinks Jimmy is still a virgin. He has a plan to take care of that. He is visiting some cousins up north and he wants to take Jimmy with him. He says he knows the girls will love him because he has blue eyes."

"Andrea!" Beth waved her hand in front of her face as though scandalized, yet even Sharon muffled a chuckle.

Andy crossed her long legs and took a drag from her cigarette. "Eh? A little honesty never hurt nobody. Maybe once Jimmy learns how to perform, he'll have better luck with Tammy." Sharon's chuckle stopped and the three gave each other uneasy looks. It was one thing to be married and talk about your husbands, but girls did not set their teenaged brothers up with village girls.

Or, at least, if they did, they would not be talking about it.

And that is why it's so difficult to be friends with Andy, thought Doreen to herself. *How can I possibly pretend this is acceptable? She might as well boast that she was sending him to a brothel to teach him how to become a man.*

Solace only cackled gaily, which was what you could expect of a trading post owner who kept company with the likes of gold miners, trappers, and Betty Lou. Sharon was the first to regain her composure.

"We're really so glad we ran into you here," she said, in that clipped, practical voice that was a Sharon trademark. "We're on a mission and we thought the Delaney family could help."

Andy pushed her chair from the table with exaggerated noise. "I already told Frank - Jimmy will play his guitar for the variety show and Tammy has agreed to sing," she said this while tapping her cigarette furiously into the ashtray. She waved it in the air. "He is not going to get me up on a stage."

"It isn't about that!" Sharon turned to thank Ed, who in a rare act of gentlemanly thoughtfulness, had brought them all coffee. "No. It's about the new family – not the brothers."

She added when Andy looked anxiously at the Phillips' brother talking with Hayes.

"The Millers. The ones who moved into the lowlands with four kids. They didn't come prepared, and they don't have enough food to make it through the winter. We're on a house-to-house mission to help them."

"Oh, I want to help!" Cried Andy. "What can I do?"

"Maybe you could introduce us to Mrs. Delaney," suggested Doreen. "We were going to ask each family for a food donation."

Andrea's eyes widened.

"Not today. Believe me, you do not want to see her today. The way you three are dressed, she will think it's a church group come a-calling. She will bring out the Bible and lead all of you in prayers. She will be without mercy! I'll take care of our donation." Looking around, she brightened up and said enthusiastically, "I will take care of a few others, as well."

Getting up from the table without listening to another word, she went straight up to the truck drivers and began her spiel. They frowned at her, then glanced at the group of women watching expectantly. They reached into their pockets and pulled out their wallets, each handing her a dollar bill. She waved the two bucks triumphantly, then marched over to the counter.

Doreen fixed her gaze at the moose head on the wall across from her. She remembered when she used to lean like that over a man's shoulders, enticing him to drink more, to buy more, to dance more, to keep the party going so the money would flow into the cash registers and into her blouse. She shouldn't be ashamed. She had just been a chorus line dancer whose sideline job was helping military men to part from their paycheck. Still, it was an uncomfortable reminder. Maybe that's what bothered her about Andy. If she had not found Alex, she could still be waiting tables and dancing in a chorus line. Women weren't scarce in San Diego, nor were they scarce in Las Vegas. If anything, they over-ran the two cities.

Beth nudged Solace and asked in a stage whisper, "which one of the Phillips brothers is that?"

The proprietress, who had been keeping a careful eye on Zeb and his inability to find work beyond adding more firewood to the stove and arranging a chair close to it, glanced over at the counter, and grunted.

"That's the oldest one, Hank. These boys are a bit touched in the head if you ask me. They claimed the whole mountainside out back because they thought there was gold on it. Dresden's been telling him, there ain't no gold in this pile of rocks, but Hank only shrugs. He says, let the young uns chip away at it all they want. He's got other plans."

Doreen's interest returned to the table. Beth and Sharon were also leaning forward expectantly. "What plans?" She asked.

Solace spread her hands. "He didn't say."

Three pairs of disappointed eyes dropped to the table, mulling over the mysterious Phillips brothers who came without wives or farming skills, only an ungrounded belief that one hundred sixty acres of rock and gravel would somehow be of value.

Unable to restrain themselves any longer, all four women turned to watch Andy beguile her neighbors. She used greater familiarity than she had with the truck drivers. She sat on the bar stool next to Hayes and slid across the seat until her thigh was pressed against his over-flowing hip. She put her hand on his arm to talk across him to the oldest Phillips brother.

Hank Phillips listened with his head half-cocked. When Andy had finished, he set his cowboy styled hat back a little and reached in his pocket. Instead of doing the same, however, Dresden patted his immaculate bulk and called for Ed. The boy hurried over, disappointed he had not yet had his fill of gossip.

"I've got a hankering for that big box of cornflakes," Dresden said in a booming voice. "A half-dozen candy bars, and...." The Phillips brother whispered in his ear. "A pound of bacon. Make those two pounds of bacon."

While Ed hurried to package the items, Sharon leaned over and whispered, "bacon! That was a good idea. They can flavor their beans and have grease besides. Maybe the Phillips brothers aren't so bad. They know their survival skills."

Solace scoffed. "Not so much, I think. They bought that land thinking they'll find gold. Ain't no gold in the Chugach. It's all in the rivers."

"It's true," agreed Sharon. "Nobody ever found gold in the foothills. It's all been in the rivers. Reason tells you, it's gotta come down from somewhere, but it hasn't been found here."

Solace was unconcerned. "I guess they will find out soon enough. What do you suppose they will do when they discover there ain't none? Their side of the mountain doesn't even have enough topsoil to do diddly squat."

"Well, you said the big un there has plans," Beth coaxed. "They must be up to something."

"Adventurers I'd say." Solace got up herself to refill their coffee. On the way, she thumped Zeb on his back. He had fallen asleep on his chair by the fire, his head curling toward his lap. He straightened up, looked around and said, "I'll be right with you, Dres," before settling into a more comfortable position.

She plunked the cups down and watched Ed carefully as he filled the prospector's order. "They've been up and down the coast. Real seafarers. The youngest comes in all the time with wild stories. Says his brother wants to go to Japan."

"What would he do in Japan?" asked Doreen curiously.

"Buy stuff, I guess, to sell over here. The boy said you could buy silk and Japanese China for cheap."

"Japanese China," calculated Sharon thoughtfully. "Not so nice as bone China, but it has a sweet ring."

"Wouldn't that be a pleasant thing?" Solace mused. "We could hold fancy parties and click our China cups together to make them ring. We would be the bells of Chugiak."

"I'm sure I would look lovely in silk," said Beth jovially.

"Every woman looks good in silk," said Andy, returning to the table. She plopped in a chair and handed the money she had collected over to Doreen. "Seven dollars and Dresden's order. How did I do?"

"You did great!" Said Doreen, trying to keep her high-pitched giggle from rising too far in her throat.

Satisfied she was going to get no more work out of her husband, Solace prepared to return to the kitchen. Tying back her apron, she said, "let me put together a package before you girls take off."

She wasn't gone long. Five minutes later, she returned with the package Dresden had ordered, as well as a bag containing sugar, coffee, and unsweetened cocoa. "We will spoil them!" said Sharon happily as she looked inside.

Solace added two scratchy, wool blankets to the pile. "Zeb will scream about it, but we are going to keep the poor babies warm. You tell Millie to give up some of her eggs. They won't last much longer before they'll go bad."

"Well, the chickens aren't laying anymore for the winter," said Andy, helping to carry the donations as each member of the group had a child in hand. "She's doing her best to make the eggs last."

"That's what I'm saying. The eggs will spoil. Tell her to let go of a few and start buying eggs at the grocery store like the rest of us."

As they placed the groceries and blankets in the trunk of the car, Andy told them to follow her to her house. "I won't bother mama none. I'll just go out to the cellar and pick up a few things."

The fresh, new homestead glistened in the early day. The cabin had been built in a natural clearing, the soil too thin for anything except weeds and Bermuda grass. A wide drive spilled out on both sides of it, scraped clean by their tractor. To one side of the drive, close to the main road, was an assortment of logs, a partially built shed and Andy's trailer.

Andy's set-up reminded Doreen of a military camp. A giant canvas tarp was hung from the trailer to two solid posts dug deep into the earth. Two more posts were propped in the center to give the tarp, stretched as tightly as the cover of a drum, adequate drainage. Wooden crates were stacked to serve as both a partition and shelves. The tractor squatted at the far end, better sheltered than the car out front or Andy's truck, Abe.

"I slept here all summer," said Andy, pointing to the blank space between the trailer and the partition. Now we use it for our patio."

"Let me guess," said Beth, appraising the precision of the arrangement. "Frank and Matt's work."

"Mostly Matt's." Andy waited while Doreen opened the trunk. "Frank came over sometimes on a Saturday. He likes mama's cooking."

Beth was chewing gum. She popped it as she asked, "doesn't he like Millie's cooking?"

Andy chuckled.

"He likes everybody's cooking. He was raised in the San Bernardino Valley, you know. They got hit hard."

"I thought he was raised in Kansas."

"That too. He had tuberculosis as a kid."

"Oh, dear," murmured Doreen with dismay. "Tuberculosis and a Quaker."

Ignoring the comment directed at Frank's unfortunate childhood, Andy slinked around to the side of the house and opened the shelter door to a cellar. She disappeared a few minutes and returned with a half-filled cardboard box.

"This is mostly spruce chickens. Mama has done the same thing as Millie. She won't kill her hens, even though they haven't been setting as nice. All we have are a few scrawny roosters in the cellar, so Jimmy's been out hunting spruce chickens. I swear," she said, as she put her bag in the trunk and shook the snow from her gloves. "This spring, I'm buying meat chickens and freezing all of them if I have to go out and wring their necks myself."

She followed Doreen to the driver's door and looked in the back seat. Ben had tagged along and peeked out from behind her. She whistled appreciatively at the plush interior. "I want to come with you. You have plenty of room. The kids hardly take up a corner."

"Of course, you can come!" Doreen batted her eyelashes as though she had planned to ask Andy to ride with them all along.

With only three small children occupying it, the back seat looked somewhat empty. Andy shoved Ben inside and jumped in behind him.

Doreen hadn't been to Millie's house since it was built. They had finally put up the clapboard siding that shone from its new coat of paint, but the house remained without shingles.

The snow stuck in black crystals to the tar paper. It wasn't as roomy as Doreen's house, nor did it have the graceful design of Sharon's house, but it was solidly built and warm. The furnishings were plain, enhanced only by Millie and Frank's craftsmanship.

Millie bustled frantically in her kitchen when she saw them. "If I had known there would be company, I would have been more prepared. Sit down! Sit down. I'll bring a crate from the bedroom to sit on. It's no problem."

She disappeared before anything could be said and arrived again with a stout wooden box in her hands.

"Millie don't bother with the coffee," ordered Andy. "We've been drinking coffee all morning at the trading post and we're all coffeed out."

"Oh, did something terrible happen?" She drew the box up concernedly and straddled it.

"No, no," laughed Beth. "Relax Millie. We're just here on a charity drive."

"Charity!" Millie managed to look at ease perched on a packing crate. She crossed her ankles tucked inside the enclosure and gripped the box on each side. "I haven't done that in a long time, not since I left Seattle."

"There hasn't been opportunity until now," said Sharon, sounding almost nostalgic. "It's the new family in the lowland. They don't have a thing."

"Broke as a Nevada gambler," Beth told her, nudging Doreen as the most likely person to understand her joke. "And they're civil service, you know. Rick Miller works on Gary's crew."

"Of course, we would help them even if they weren't civil service," put in Doreen quickly before Andy could make one of her caustic remarks. "It's just how we know about things."

She watched Millie's eyes grow thoughtful as she calculated what she should give up. "Solace said to let go of some of your eggs. They will spoil."

"Oh, but Frank!" She gasped, then exhaled slowly. "It's true my eggs won't stay good much longer. The chickens stopped setting last month. I was thinking of pickling them..." Her fingers drummed against the side of the box. "Never mind. I can spare a dozen."

"Come with us!" Cried Andy at Millie's back as she started into her pantry.

"Should I?" She turned around with several jars of jelly and canned salmon in her hands. "I haven't even met the Millers yet. I do want to be a good neighbor."

"That is one thing you never have to worry about," Andy told her, tucking her arm into Millie's. "There's lots of room, isn't there, Doreen?"

Doreen nodded her head vigorously enough to set her curls bobbing. She was a little jealous. She had been one of the first to befriend Millie and Andy acted like Millie was her own, personal companion.

Andy's taking Millie away from us, Doreen fretted to herself. *We must start visiting more with her.*

Still with her arm locked in Millie's, Andy accompanied her as she took off her apron and called for Jason. She took over then helping the boy into his jacket while Millie quickly slipped into a dress and applied a little lipstick. She also found a matching pair of gloves and a hat for their excursion.

"Am I to be the only one in slacks?" Laughed Andy, shrugging as though she didn't care. She ushered the three boys out the door, who had immediately begun a contest of stepping on each other's toes, but with the expansive wilderness in front of them, made a beeline to the car, shoving and pushing each other once they cleared the porch. When they saw the little girls toddling after them, they turned and stuck out their tongues.

"Look at that," sighed Andy. "They aren't even two yet and they are already macho. I think the men encourage them too much."

Doreen had never seen Ben before, only heard of his robust reputation. He was a big, blonde boy, handsome the way all Delaney's were, with bright, cunning eyes.

He was more aggressive than softer-eyed Jason, who held his own through the sheer sturdy build of his bone structure. Beth's boy, Cody, was more accustomed to girls and hesitated, yet seeing that to be one of the guys he had to behave like them, pushed Sharon's daughter, who pushed him back.

The two fell on the ground, crying, while the other two boys scuffled with each other. Millie got in the middle of it, piling the boys into the car and getting in behind them. She picked up Jason. "What have I told you about bullying?" She scolded.

Andrea sat Ben on her lap and admonished him as well, but a little more half-heartedly.

After giving time for Millie to settle the other three children between her and Andrea and admire the deep chocolate leather interior of the vehicle, the group set off for Ester's house.

Ester appeared as flustered as Millie had been, which gratified Doreen a little. Ester was intimidating. She was spotless in her housekeeping, flawless in her décor.

The story was that Ester was originally from France and had fled to Switzerland during the war. Everything she owned had a Swiss/French touch. It was in her porcelain dinnerware, it was in her ceramics and small, framed paintings. It was in her mahogany China closet and matching oval dining table. Ester came from money, but this was what was left of it; a few pieces of furniture, some dishes and ornaments, a house built from lumber scraps and a one-hundred-sixty-acre homestead.

She was already wearing a dress and she already had a tray with teacups and a matching pot in the middle of the dining table. Her arrangement, apparently prepared on a daily basis, sat on a white, crocheted doily. She insisted they sit down and drink tea. Since it was now nearly midday, she also set out a tin of imported English biscuits.

"Don't say no," she insisted, pushing the tin toward Doreen. "Charlie's sister sends them two or three times a year."

"Charlie is English?" asked Doreen with surprise.

She looked insulted. "I will say he is not! He is Swedish, but his sister has been in England for the last four years."

"Nothing wrong with being English," Doreen mumbled.

"There is not," agreed Ester, settling down with her tea. "It's just that you asked, and now I have told you he is not. He fought at Normandy; you know."

Normandy had not been a good place to be, but from what Millie had told Doreen, neither had Okinawa. Both places had been a bloody mess. She was glad Alex had spent only a short time in Europe before being transferred to the fledging military base in Alaska. When he received his orders, she had checked out with him, never regretting it for a day. She was going nowhere in San Diego.

She could be anything she wanted to be in Wolf Creek, except an ambulance driver. Even that was negotiable if her heart was set on it, which it wasn't.

With Ester, one always used decorum. If none of the husbands had seen the same action as Charlie, it certainly wasn't the women's fault. It wasn't like they had dragged their men's heels out of the fire. Well, maybe Sharon did, but that was neither here nor there and never to be discussed.

She cleared her throat. "We came to see if you would like to help the Miller family. We've got quite a few things together, but they could use a little more."

About to raise her teacup to her lips with an elegant lift of her pinkie finger, Ester froze with her hand still delicately posed, and asked severely, "Why didn't you say something?"

She looked at her well-stocked shelves thoughtfully. "It's a good thing we buy everything in bulk. I'll fill up some canning jars with staples."

"Solace already denoted sugar and cocoa," blurted Beth as though they were the two most vital items.

"Okay," said Ester carefully.

The four women waited while Ester made her deliberations. She went through all her kitchen cabinets and moved on to the pantry, finding odds and ends she thought the family could use. She collected several empty quart jars and filled them with beans, rice, flour, and found a small container to fill with salt. Almost as an afterthought, she added six, juicy oranges.

"Oh, don't look at me like that," she said when she noticed the round eyes of the others. "Charlie went down to the docks the other day to pick up some oats in bulk and saw these crates of oranges that were being put up for general sales. You have to buy a whole crate, though, so he did."

The eyes remained accusing. "I was going to share them anyway," she added crossly. "There's enough here for everyone to have one, but you have to share with the kids. Charlie was thinking of fresh orange juice, so I need to save some."

She gave them each a precious orange. Doreen peeled hers back carefully, even sucking the juice from the peelings. Oranges! Sweetly bursting with the sunshine that had been robbed from their homes during the long, dark hours of winter.

She separated a slice for Patsy and looked around for her, spotting her near the living room. Ester's boy had joined the three others in ostracizing the girls. They sat on the first step of the staircase and kicked out with their feet every time the outnumbered little ladies drew near. Juliana was making faces at them, and Patsy was starting to cry. Doreen called her over and handed her the treat.

Deciding if these crusaders were going straight to the Miller's house from the Bolinder homestead, the children needed more nourishment than an English biscuit and a couple of orange slices, Ester cut some roast beef and gave them each a little. "I suppose you will want to be going now," she said, pretending hard not to look sad.

"You're coming with us!" Said Andy brightly. "We're the welcoming committee. You have to be on it!"

"No, I can't," she protested. "There isn't enough room."

"Sure there is!" Somehow, it had turned into Andy's party. She was beckoning the wayward boys and gathering the coats. "The kids are just babies. We can hold them on our laps."

Still, Ester hesitated. "Denny will squirm."

"Let him squirm. You know our boys have been getting too wild. They need a bit of discipline."

She was pushing Ester out the door before she could raise any more objections. "It's a Pontiac, Ester. Just look at it. I know you want to ride in it."

"Oh!" Ester stopped short when she saw it. "It is beautiful. It must have been a town car. There's not a dent on it."

"Belonged to a lieutenant general," Doreen explained proudly. "He ordered it new when he was first stationed here. He's been transferred to Panama."

"See there," said Sharon, sounding slightly jealous. "That's the advantage of a desk job. You get to know all the upper brass."

"But they are awful people, aren't they, Doreen?" asked Ester, climbing into the back and stabbing at Doreen's shoulder.

"I haven't really met them," she apologized. "I think they wouldn't come out to visit in our community. I think it wouldn't do. We don't even have running water."

Ester settled back in the seat. "Well, Charlie doesn't like them. He says they are a lot of stuffed shirts."

"Frank says the same thing," agreed Millie. "And he says they don't know good music."

Ester murmured with her hand to her throat, "poor taste in music is abominable. Not that I mind Jimmy's country twang. It's very cute, but your station in life carries certain expectancies. A man who buys a Pontiac should not have poor taste in music."

Doreen glanced in the rearview view to see if they were ready. Knowing Jason and Ben's displeasure in being separated, Millie was holding both on her ample lap. Ester sat next to her, with Denny leaning toward Ben to pat at his face, and Cody, who sucked at his thumb.

Andy sat on the far end, holding Patsy. Sharon's girl, Juliana, taller than any except Ben and more apparently a two-year-old, sat squeezed between Ester and Andy, and peered into Andy's face speculatively.

Perhaps there was something in the unperturbed face that reminded Juliana of her mother because after a few minutes, she reached over and began examining the collection of bracelets sliding over the top of Andy's hand.

The drive into the lowland was more rugged than even the single, plowed earth lane connecting the Erichman's, the Hughes and the Bowen's properties. It snaked worriedly down a long, steep hill, the sharp turns and dips a failed effort to ease the rapid descent.

Unlike the upper ridge of Wolf Creek, filled with a variety of conifers, the lowlands contained only cottonwood, birch, and scrubby-looking willow. The hills that marked the ridge were simple, gentle swells in the lowland. Icy and hollow in the winter, the lowlands flooded in summer's hard rain.

The Miller trailer squatted in a hollow. The walkway was as raw as polished glass, the tell-tale sign of water-overflow, frozen by winter's hand.

Hannah Miller appeared terrified to see the troop of six women, most of whom were in their Sunday best, pile out of the shiny, brick-red car, each hauling a small child by the hand. She stuck her head outside her trailer door, shut it tight, then peered out again, as though expecting they would be gone.

When she saw that they were waiting an invitation, she said grudgingly, "We ain't set up for company yet, but you're welcome to come in and sit a spell if you'd like. I can't offer you much."

The women looked at each other. They hadn't chosen a spokesperson and had no idea what to say. This didn't bother Millie at all as she generally spoke out whenever she had the itch for it. She stepped out front, her hand extended, the same open, friendly smile on her face Doreen had seen the first time she had met with the Wolf Creek women at the VFW Post.

"I'm Millie Lamar, from just up the road. We're your neighbors and we just wanted to welcome you to the neighborhood."

"Well, that's right nice of you," she said. Her voice was soft. She offered a thin, limp hand and opened the door wider. "If you can find a place to sit down, just take it."

Millie continued to smile as she retrieved the small, lifeless hand in her own and shook it industriously. "Well, we would, but we brought some house- warming gifts we would like to give you first."

Recognizing her cue, Doreen opened the trunk of her car and started handing out the bags of groceries. Millie led the procession into the house, still talking with Hannah, probably filling her in on everything that had happened in the community from the first day the Grants opened their trading post.

Barely aware there was anyone else, Hannah sat down at the folding table across from Millie and let the others find anyway they liked to be comfortable. Ester found a chair. Andy perched on the countertop. Sharon leaned with her back to the doorpost. Beth and Doreen stood looking at each other, the bags of groceries piled at their feet.

Eventually, Hannah began to speak. A little tearfully, while dabbing at her eyes, she told them, "This was our last hope. Rick can drive heavy equipment. He learnt it in the army. But when he got home, he couldn't find no jobs worth having. They would last a few months and he was out of work again, always out of work. Then he saw the ad for heavy equipment operators in Alaska, so he told me, that's where we're going. Alaska or bust."

"That's what they say now when they go up the Alcan," said Andy. "We got here in June. Every other car along the way had Alaska or bust written in the dirt on the back windows of their cars."

"We busted," said Hannah. "More than once. We ran out of money in Alberta and spent three weeks helping ranchers move their barbed wire for the fall. We broke down near Edmonton. Hadn't even made it to the mountains. Another month working side jobs to get the car fixed and keep moving. We broke down again, just short of Tok. Some nice people took us into their home, helped Rick get the car fixed and gave us some food and gas money. That's how we made it here. We didn't mean to come busting in during the winter like this, with nothing to our name."

"But you made it," said Millie, squeezing the poor, limp hands that seemed to be permanently captured in Millie's strong ones. "What we brought isn't so much, but it will help you get through the winter.

While they were talking, Hannah's children crept from the single bedroom of the trailer and crowded around the doorway, gaping at their strange company. There were three boys and a girl. They were all tow-headed, long boned, and thin. Although the youngest was approximately the same age as the six toddlers, he looked at them as disdainfully as did his siblings, who judged the babies as being too young to play with. This was agreeable to the toddlers, who clung to their mothers' knees.

Doreen glanced around at her surroundings. The trailer had a musty odor, as though it had not been thoroughly cleaned and aired very often, if ever at all. Ragged blankets draped over the windows. Laundry piled up in one corner. A small oil burner was rumbling away, but the trailer still felt cold. A steady draft rose from the floor and crept in at the corners of the thinly insulated shelter.The family was in for a bad winter. They would need support.

"It's always hard the first year," she said. "We lived out by Campbell Creek our first winter: in tents! It was a mess. The military thought the Japanese would be coming up the inlet any day and the army was working frantically on a defense post."

She chuckled. "The Japanese never did come, thank goodness, or we would have been in the line of fire."

Hannah's pale blue eyes turned round as dimes. "Your husband brought you to a military camp?"

The tone of the timid voice made all the women giggle, covering Doreen's high-pitched laugh. "Hey, we married two weeks before he shipped. I wasn't about to let go of him. He couldn't have kept me away with a Billy club."

"I didn't let Art go to Kodiak without me," said Sharon lazily. She was still leaning against the doorpost, with Juliana wrapped around her legs. She rested a hand on the child's head, smoothing the already carefully groomed hair. "Our deal was, I'll marry you if you take me with you."

"Good heavens!" Hannah squeaked. "Can you do that?"

Doreen nodded. "Quite a few women did. We were called camp wives. When our husbands got stationed in Alaska, we picked up and came along. Most of us hadn't been married long, but you know what they say...."

"If you're settling in Alaska, bring your woman with you," The veteran wives said in unison.

"The camps would have been a pigsty without us," sniffed Sharon. "The women did most of the laundry, the cooking, clearing ground litter. We were entitled to set a few rules."

"Of course we set our own rules," said Millie. She pressed the seven dollars the group had gathered into Hannah's hand. "We work just as hard as the men. Why shouldn't we have just as much say-so as the men?"

"It just doesn't work that way where I come from," said Hannah softly.

"Well, it should!" Said Ester forcefully. "Do you think I would have followed Charlie into the wilderness without a few rules?"

"Ester is French," whispered Millie.

If possible, Hannah's eyes grew wider, and her mouth dropped open. She stared at Ester as though examining a new species of human, which by Doreen's calculations, wasn't far from the truth. "Didn't you lose the war?" She asked uncertainly.

Ester's icy stare examined the ceiling. "I gained a country."

The group wasn't quite as boisterous on the way home as they had been on the way to the Miller homestead. They were all thinking of the thin edge of survival that was a familiar companion by now; an unwelcome one that left its reminders of how painful it was to be cold and hungry, with no knowledge of where the next meal was coming from.

"We should knit mittens and hats for the kids," said Millie. "They'll catch their death of the cold without them."

Beth had been unusually silent, but she spoke up now. "Rick is Gary's co-worker. We should have visited them by now. I'm going to make sure we do that, so we can keep an eye on them. The kids don't look like they're doing that well."

"Don't let that type fool you," said Ester knowingly. "They're skinny little runts but tough as nails. Still, they look cold. I think I will make them a nice Afghan to wrap in."

"Did anyone invite them to the picnic?" asked Sharon.

Nobody answered.

"I'll get Gary to tell them," Beth promised.

One by one, Doreen dropped the women off at their homes. "I just can't believe it," fretted Beth once there was only Sharon and Doreen in the car. "The way Andy invited herself along. And invited Millie and Ester like it was her car. Why didn't you say something, Doreen?"

Doreen waited for Beth to get out of the car before answering. "Because it was fun."

"It was, you know," said Sharon as Doreen drove to the final stop. "Andy's fun. So what if she flirts with all the single men? They are single!"

"Except Matt."

"His wife is an idiot. She should never have left him. Matt's clay, Doreen. He's clay. His heart is on his sleeve. Andy sees it."

"Then why doesn't she stick with him and be done with it?"

"Because she is fascinated by men who are already molded. And because she doesn't want to be in the way when his wife comes back."

"She's coming back?"

"Why do you think she wrote him?"

It was difficult to hold back on saying anything until after Alex had asked her, "how was your day?" but she managed by fixing a very elaborate dinner, complete with butter, biscuits, and blueberry pie. Browning the pie to perfection absorbed her attention so much, Alex was already sitting, waiting expectantly, before she had it out of the oven, and had breathlessly served their meal.

"How was your day?" he asked finally, after she had seated herself and said a short grace.

As soon as she opened her mouth, the words poured out, one spilling over the top of another so excitedly, she barely gave herself a chance to breathe.

"They all went with you?" he chuckled. "Five other women and their kids?"

"Yes," she said, twiddling with a necklace she had forgotten to remove when she returned home.

"You must have scared that poor lady half to death!"

"We did," she admitted.

"You probably shouldn't have given her the seven dollars. You probably should have bought more groceries from Solace with it."

She frowned. "Why is that?"

"Because Rick drinks. He'll just use the money to drink."

"Maybe he won't. Maybe she won't even tell him about it."

"With you women to influence her, she probably won't."

Seventeen

The cold, clear weather remained for the next two weeks, creating perfect conditions for the ice-skating party. Because the snowfalls had been light, it had been easy to scrape off a large patch of clear ice, giving the most ambitious speed skaters room to practice their sport, as well as clean, unchipped ice for figure skaters.

Apart from the adolescent sons and daughters of the railroad workers, trappers and villagers who grew up in the wilderness, very few people in the community owned skates. Most were out with sleds, pulling around each other, or skating in their boots. Solace had brought along her two hybrid huskies, which she tied to a genuine dogsled for the children. They piled up, four and five at a time, and screamed with pleasure as the dogs trotted across the ice, pulling their cargo.

Millie was in a new pair of skates, trying them out with short-stroked caution. Her husband circled around her a few times, then skated off to join the more confident skaters who were drawing impressive figure eights with their blades and demonstrating a few backstrokes. Undeterred, Millie continued laboriously wobbling forward, barely lifting either foot, her eyes watching the ground ahead of her.

Beth had borrowed a pair of skates for ten minutes, then got back into her boots. "You go torture yourselves," she told the others. "I'm taking up sledding."

Hannah was huddled close to the oil barrel that served as their fire pit. The piled-up wood inside the barrel snarled and popped, yet still she shivered.

Her children huddled close to her, except the ten-year-old, who sat on a bank looking sullenly at the other children playing. Her husband had wobbled off on second-hand skates to join the handful of men who were not sure of their bladed footing, which included Gary, Art, and the railroad worker, Joe Pierce. They stayed close to a bank in a pretense of nonchalance.

Doreen skated to the barrel, her blades crunching in the snow. "Why don't you put your children on the sled? Solace will be careful."

Hannah nodded woefully at her oldest son. "It's Wally. He don't want to ride on the sled. He says it's for babies. If he won't go, the others won't, either."

"Maybe he would rather skate," Doreen suggested. "He should use the pair Beth was wearing. Her feet aren't very much bigger than his."

She muttered it wouldn't do much good but followed Doreen to see what her son would say. He was still sullen. "I can't put those skates on. They are white."

Doreen tried to laugh about it. "So what?"

"They are girls' skates. I can't go out in girls' skates."

She still encouraged him. "Just pull your pant legs over the top. Nobody will notice."

He looked doubtful. "Do you see any other boys close to here?" She answered herself. "No. They are all chasing each other around out in the middle of the lake. You can't join them unless you learn to skate. If I see you learning in these, I will make sure you get some boys' skates."

Recognizing her as one of their recent benefactors, thereby capable of doing anything Santa Claus could do, Wally asked her hesitantly, "you'll get me black skates?"

"I'll get you black skates," she promised.

It wasn't an empty promise. It would be easy. Andy said she picked up two pairs of used youth skates in the valley for fifty cents a pair. Kids grew out of their skates. All it took was for one family to break down and buy a new pair, for the size to be passed around to a dozen kids before they were too rusted out to ever glide again. Valley people kept their kids in skates. It was inter-generational. The Chugach could do the same.

Doreen remained close to the firepit long enough to watch Wally tentatively put on his first pair of skates and wobble out to the ice, and for Hannah to place her other three children on Solace's sled before shooting off to the lake center where figure skating was in progress.

Doreen knew dance. It was in her blood. It was in her small frame, her limber joints. She didn't need any more music than the sounds of nature when she skated, and those sounds became a dance. She became lost in it - the circling, the pirouette, the graceful, swanlike movements that came from being lifted an inch off the ground, with metal sliding against ice, more rapidly and gracefully than could ever be done on stockinged feet and a wood floor.

She wasn't even sure when she first noticed Frank skating beside her. It seemed one minute, she was skating alone, the next, he was there; and appeared to have been there all along. He was a capable skater – light on his feet, but with no real technique. When he saw he had her attention, he said in his deep, rumbling voice, "I see you do have talent."

"I'm not going to ice skate on your stage," she warned, taking a turn on the ice, and skating backward so she could face him.

"You have rhythm."

"Frank, you're not the only one to have been raised rubbing shoulders with movie stars. I grew up near Lake Tahoe."

His ears perked under his bowler hat that provided very little cover except to the top of his head. "A performer?"

"No." She executed a few small circles. "I grew up with skates is all. Pop was a retailer, but there wasn't much retail during the war. His business was going bust. I joined a chorus line at a nightclub in San Diego. I never would have made it past auditions in Vegas, just like I never would have made it to Hollywood."

"You dance." He made it a statement.

"Frank, you're baiting me."

"Of course I am. I need more performers."

She slowed down to skate beside Frank as they glided back to the main party.

"It's a life I wanted to forget about. When I put on my first pair of skates, I wanted to become a professional skater. I think it could have happened. War changes things, you know? Next thing I knew, I was dancing in a chorus line to help keep the business afloat. I like to dance. I do. But not like that. Not to make men drink and forget who they are."

Much to her astonishment, he laughed quite hardily. "Doreen! Doreen! This is family entertainment!" He caught his breath and added, "Ester is in charge of choreography."

"Ester! Ester! What does she know about dance?"

He had done a fair Fred Astaire imitation, raising one leg to pivot in a circle but nearly lost his balance before completion, and zigged a few steps before falling in with her again. "There. You see? That's why we need you."

She looked at him speculatively. "Do you really think it will work? Putting together performing troops to raise community funds?"

"Of course, it will work," he said forcefully. "We have a good relationship with the valley. We'll do performances for them and charge admission."

"What about Anchorage?"

He winced. "Tough audience, but we'll see."

At least he thought they were talented enough for the valley. That was some consolation. It also put things in a different perspective. They weren't competing for stardom on a territorial scale. They were simply offering homesteaders some good rural entertainment. She should have known. It was part of what made Frank such a strange fellow. Everything about him was urban culture, yet his heart was rural.

He glided away to join Millie without waiting for a definitive answer. His wife was still teetering close to the bank, absorbed in conquering this new sport. He wrapped one arm around her back to help her skate, pushing out in long, deliberate strokes, making it easier for her hesitant feet to follow.

Frank was a good teacher, Doreen reflected. Charlie whizzed past, intent on impressing nobody but Charlie. He did a half-turn and waved. Doreen waved back.

Ester! Really, Ester! Ester's rigid figure sliced across the lake like a mechanical soldier, with neither style nor grace, only rhythmic precision. She was a month further along than Doreen, but with her straight up and down body that had one long stomach from bosom to legs, she didn't show at all.

Ester taking a free hand with the choreography wouldn't do. It wouldn't do at all. Ester would put the chorus line in gunny sacks with cardboard cut-outs for animal ears. Something would have to be done to keep Ester under control.

Somebody had the foresight to bring a few army blankets for the cold and inactive members. One of the blankets had found its way around Hannah's shoulders. She sat in a folding chair next to Beth, more animated in her self-expression than Doreen had seen her since they first met. Perhaps it was relief that her son had taken an interest in something other than controlling his younger siblings. He was still out on the ice, slowly making headway with his newfound skills. Surprised at their freedom, the younger children were exploring the territory around them.

When she drew closer, she saw that both Beth and Hannah were holding dixie cups of Kool-Aid, which explained much of their newfound camaraderie. Doreen took off her skates and slid on her boots, joining the two with her skates tied together and slung over one shoulder.

"Ah, and you need to keep those blades clean and shiny," said Hannah. "You cut a bit of a figure out there."

Her eyes were bright, her cheeks flushed. Doreen shrugged as she stretched by the barrel listening to her wet boots sizzle. "It's just to have fun, you know. Anyone could do it with practice."

Beth snorted loudly in a most unladylike manner. "Easy for you to say. I weigh a hundred-seventy pounds. No matter how much I practiced, I would still look like an elephant."

Skinny Hannah slapped at her with her ineffective hands. "Don't talk about yourself that way! That's terrible. Anyway, where I come from, a well-fed woman has a successful husband."

"Where are you from?" asked Doreen.

"Little Rock, Arkansas."

"Oh, my. You have come a long way."

Beth's attention had been diverted during the conversation. "Good gracious!" She almost screeched. "Is that Ester out there?"

Doreen's gaze followed Beth's finger. "Yes, she is. I didn't think miss party pooper was going to do anything except roast hotdogs."

"She poops parties?" asked Hannah.

"Shh," warned Beth. "That's gossiping. Why are you mad at Ester?"

Doreen hugged her jacket closer and shoved her hands inside the sleeves. "I'm not mad at her. She just doesn't qualify to be a dance instructor."

Beth nearly fell out of her chair, laughing. "He got to you! Frank got to you! Look. He's even got Art playing the piano. It's bad. We meet at the VFW hall and their piano is out of tune, but it's a fun place to practice."

"Art plays the piano?Damn. He's as strange as Frank or Charlie."

She didn't feel comfortable as the only sober woman in the small circle. She wished Sharon would join them. Sharon had found a tiny pair of training skates for Juliana and was guiding her around, the tiny hands raised and clutched to Sharon's fingers. Juliana would probably be winning championships by the time she was five. Her mother would make sure of it. Not that she disagreed with a well-guided upbringing, but babies should be allowed to be babies.

Somehow, she had lost Alex. He had begun lagging long before she found the unblemished sheet of ice to fly around in a trance. He had left her to her solo flight, to her dance. He had given her privacy and time to shake hands with her memories.

They should take a vacation soon. It had been a long time since she last saw her family. When she and Alex married, they took a quick trip to Lake Tahoe to meet her parents. Times were hard then. They didn't even show any embarrassment when Doreen gave them the hundred dollars she had saved, telling them she didn't need it anymore because she was going to Alaska. They only sniffled and tucked it away.

She could have used the money on the Alcan, but she didn't care. The family was doing better now. The business wasn't completely out of debt, but it was recovering. They hadn't lost it. Alex had never said a word about it. Her family was his family, and his family was an unseen force, like God. He had no siblings and his communications with his father, set behind a battery of blinking dials and measurements, were like a priest in holy communion.

Her eyes located him near the left shore where they fished in summer because of its swampy bank. It's where the fish liked to be, among the tangled roots and branches of fallen trees. He was probably trying to figure out where the fish would be when the ice melted in the spring. Matt and Jimmy were assisting him, walking more than gliding on their skates, poking at a branch captured and frozen in the water, as though they expected trout to pop out.

Knowing where Alex was always made her feel more confident. She let her gaze shift to the small children who were still delighted with being pushed around in boxes or on a dog sled. Betty Lou had joined them. She was waddling on her knees, her arms tucked in at the elbows, squawking like a duck.

She looked more like a furry penguin. The kids squealed and jumped at her until she rolled around on the ice with them. It was difficult to tell whether Betty Lou or the children were having the most fun.

"Oh, now, this is really going to upset somebody's mama if it gets back to her and that's no gossip," said Doreen, pointing to the group of adolescents skating close together. Among them was Carol, who appeared perfectly normal. However, the one partnering with her as they zigged and zagged over the frozen surface, was the youngest Phillips brother.

Beth sucked in her breath. "Should someone tell Andy?"

The three women scanned the skating crowd simultaneously. "Is that Andy?" asked Hannah innocently. A grave length of army green blanket dripping from an arm directed their attention to the farthest end of the cleared section. A young man and woman waltzed in unison, hands crossed in front and locked together. The low sun caught the top of the woman's head, brightening it to polished copper.

"That might not be good either," said Beth.

Doreen looked down at her feet. "Maybe it's none of our business."

There was a lull. A few seconds later, Hannah leaned toward her and whispered, "I didn't tell Rick about the seven dollars."

Doreen straightened. "What?"

"The seven dollars. I never told him. Usually, I do, but you see we didn't hardly have no underwear left. That ain't so bad for the boys, but it's a disgrace for girls. You know that it is. Rick don't understand these things, so I went and bought underwear without him ever knowing it. I told Matt what I wanted when he came out, and he took me to the valley. I wouldn't want no trouble on him. I didn't tell Rick."

Hannah was learning! Whether appropriate or not, Doreen felt a small exaltation, a tiny victory.

Ester returned just then, as unperturbed as though she had taken a leisurely garden stroll instead of sprinting six miles on skates. She heard Hannah's last words as she pulled up a chair and began removing her blades.

"What didn't you tell him?" She asked.

Hannah explained a second time. "Huh." Ester pulled off her gloves and set them over her feet, close to the hot barrel. "A gentleman does not deprive his wife of her necessities."

"It's gentlemen we have here, have we?" asked Hannah, her words slurring slightly. "It's something I been wondering about. How can they be war veterans when they don't cotton to fighting?"

"Hush, now," said Beth. "It wasn't easy for any of them. Ester, tell Hannah why Charlie never stops building things. First, a gigantic house, then stables and a barn. Didn't he say he's putting another building on the corner lot?"

"He can't stop building," said Ester, glaring at Beth coldly. "Things get on his mind. He's got to work them out. It's no difference with Alex and his stone walls or Frank and his apple crates. They've got to build back what they destroyed. They are gentlemen, Hannah. We don't expect any less than that because what we have to give them has value."

The babies had become exhausted with their play. The boxes they had scooted around in were now lined up close to the fire and cushioned with bedding. The toddlers were set in their little boxed nests and given warm food and hot chocolate. Too tired and too hungry to do anything else, they munched happily and smeared their faces with brown liquid.

Betty Lou and Sharon had also returned. Sharon placed Juliana in a box with Patsy, who immediately offered her half-eaten sandwich, and Betty Lou sprawled out on the ground, kicking her feet toward the barrel.

"Merciful heavens," she panted. "I ain't been with so many cubs in all my born days." She patted her stomach. "I think I could get used to it."

Seeing a possible ally in Betty Lou, Hannah drunkenly persisted. "It's just in some parts, you see, it ain't proper for a woman to push a man around. Call him gentleman all you want but if he don't put up a fight, he's a pussy."

"Pushed them around!" Ester repeated indignantly. She folded her arms over her chest. "There's no pushing Charlie. He's stubborn as a mule. But, if he can be stubborn, I can be stubborn back."

"Yeah," agreed Beth, whose husband was as sandpapery as a lumber jack, and had no desire to be overpowered by him, but who never allowed him to intimidate her, either. "What's good for the goose is good for the gander, I always say."

Amazed at this conversation, Betty Lou had rolled over on her side to study the newcomer with a mixture of wonder and consternation. "There ain't no need to be insulting your company, Mrs. Miller. We north women, we see things differently. Ain't a one of these fine ladies that can't split a log or push a car out of a ditch. No siree."

Warming up to the subject, she sat up and fumbled around in one of her numerous fur pouches, bringing out a bag of tobacco. "Truth is, ain't nothing a man can do that a Chugiak woman can't, and that's a fact. I'm going on thirty-six years old now and I ain't never depended on a man for nothing. My daddy wouldn't allow it. Said it was the nature of a man to be a beast."

Rolling a pregnant-looking cigarette, she popped it in her mouth and lit it. "Now, my daddy weren't no modern man and didn't see the cities growing up all over the place like I do. I figured out there be two kinds of men, good uns and bad uns. The bad uns, they fight and drink and cuss and them's the ones my daddy was talking about. The good uns, they go about minding their own business and making families. It don't matter if they're fancy. Sometimes, fancy can go a long ways. Speaking of which, there's my favorite fancy friends."

Having straightened Hannah out on the subject of husbands and their roles, Betty Lou stumbled sluggishly to her feet and lumbered off to meet the Lamars, who were just coming back from the rink. Millie had learned in the twenty minutes her husband had synchronized his stride with hers, how to skate almost gracefully.

They were all returning to the warmth of the fire. As often happened in mixed company, the men drifted to one side of the barrel, while the women monopolized the other end. This did not stop the flow of the women's conversation, only dropped its level of sound a notch as they continued to make comments about those still out on the ice.

The men started out that way. Their voices were low murmurs that drifted inandout of an arena, silent except the light, high chorus of their feminine companions, the whistle of a low wind rustling the frozen cattails and the occasional screech of a passing raven. But as they stood close together, leaving the chairs to the women, they began to drink. A few had been drinking leisurely all day, but now began in earnest. With each new beer passed around, they became louder.

Under their tone, the women bent closer, their shawls muffling the sound of their voices. Ester tested her gloves, found them sufficiently warm, and placed them back on her hands. "Charlie says he will play Santa Claus for the children this year."

"Charlie?" Beth scoffed. "He's too skinny."

"We can fatten him up with pillows." Ester sounded hurt.

Beth huffed and refilled her Kool-Aid. "Why doesn't Dresden play Santa? He's got the right size."

A snappy, youthful voice skipped through the airwaves, temporarily over-riding the huddled women. "I'm telling you just what the Hansens told me. General Eisenhower went to

Kodiak." It was Jimmy, a little excited from his beverage. "He was thanking all the Native people for defending the Island."

Lately, the name "Eisenhower" had been on all the men's lips, even the ones that had been too young to go to war when the Great Man led. Doreen kicked out with her feet restlessly. You would almost think Eisenhower was a Messiah.

"We asked Dresden," she said irritably. "He said he would if he can wear caribou antlers and an Eskimo mask."

Beth spilled her drink laughing. "That's too funny!"

"No, it's not!" Snapped Ester. "A joke is a joke, but we are not going to let Dresden scare the little ones half to death."

It was like a chorus of flutes and trombones, the lilting voices on one side growing higher, on the other deeper and more insistent. A voice rose above the rest, like the triumphant entrance of an oboe. "Damned commies. String them up, I say."

"Ever meet a communist, Rick?" Frank's voice was deep and carrying.

"Not a live one," Rick whipped back. He was drunker than the others. Charlie, Frank and Alex were practically tee-total's, enjoying the buzz associated with comrades-in-arms more than the beer, drinking only enough for the ambience. Jimmy and Matt were not bashful, but drank slowly, enjoying their all-day high, but Rick was careening through the alcohol-induced spell without barriers.

He saw the order of rank that was no longer rank and no longer counted outside the workplace. They were military no longer. They were veterans, and each was equal to the other. He was exhilarated by it.

"Bet not a one of you hit boots to the ground. Construction workers, medics, radio specialists. Out there with your pea shooters. It was infantry that did the dirty work. Infantry!"

They were trying to ignore him with inside office jokes. Jimmy, having no idea what communists were or if a ground-pounder was the real definition of military, had wandered off to badger his sisters.

One by one, the women trailed off in their conversation as the thundering retorts of the men overpowered theirs. Gary wasn't far behind Rick in his disorder.

Weaving on slack legs in half-buckled boots, he tapped at Alex's chest and said, "You did the rest of us a bad turn when you bought Doreen that car. Now Beth wants one."

"Don't get Beth a car. Then Millie will want to learn to drive," grumbled Frank.

"Why did you teach your wife to drive, anyway?" Demanded Rick.

Alex spread his hands. "I didn't. I think she was born driving."

"Same with Beth," agreed Gary. "I've known her all my life. I think she was raised on a tractor. It don't really seem right somehow not to get her a car, but she's getting her first aid certification. She sure wants to drive that ambulance."

"I'll let you know the next time an officer is leaving the country," promised Alex. "I was going to buy the car anyway. It was too good a deal. At least, I kept Doreen from signing up as an ambulance driver."

Gary groaned and tossed his empty beer bottle in the garbage bag, refreshing himself with a full one. "If I pull the same thing with Beth, Sharon is going to give me hell. You're lucky you don't live as close to her as I do."

Rick gave a long, derisive laugh. He was too loud. The sound ricocheted across the lake, startling a covey of quail. "You're afraid of your women! What will they do? Slap you down?"

With each statement of the men who remained unconscious of the ominously quiet fairer sex, Sharon's eyes had flashed a little brighter, Ester's a little sharper, and Doreen's a little darker and smoldering. In one swift movement, Sharon stood up and strode the four steps it took to stand in front of the unfortunate Rick Miller.

"I'll slap you down."

It was a traumatic moment for Rick Miller. Raised within the circle of quieter, more reticent women following the rules of good housekeeping as laid down by the men, he had never encountered a woman who would look him in the eye before from a height of two inches taller and a weight of thirty pounds heavier to confront him.

Not just any woman, either. She was a woman who could drive a nail home with two sharp strokes of a hammer, who could cleave through a moose bone, a woman who could slam a baseball into left field. She was Mighty Sharon, the Rock.

Behind her stood Beth, shorter but just as impressive in her muscular development and Doreen, who was small but nimble. As though to clarify their intentions, all the other feminine faces had turned toward him, including the thoroughly amused, butt-scratching Betty Lou.

He saw that none of his friends, or what he had assumed to be his friends, were going to intervene, least of all Sharon's husband. "Now," Rick said with a false chuckle, "Ain't no need to get riled up. We're just making men jokes. It ain't like you women never say shite about us."

After staring at him intently for several seconds, Sharon walked away. Rick found another beer to drink and dropped his voice considerably the next time he spoke. "We was just playing around. She wouldn't really slap me, would she?"

Gary placed a hand on Rick's shoulder. "Now you know what you're up against."

Doreen was a little bit miffed by the incident all the way home. "You were going to buy me the car, anyway?"

Alex grinned. "It was a good deal, and I didn't even have to ask if we should buy it."

Once again, he had outwitted her. It really wasn't a wonder he worked in communications. He could sell toilet water and convince you it was an antiseptic.

In late December, the snow fell, one deep snowfall after another. It lay so thick and heavy; the entire world was glossed over. Even the trees bowed, crushed under the weight of the falling snow.

Christmas was the community's last real celebration. The new year came in silently, the homesteaders buried in their homes, the drives, and roads indistinguishable in the pale half-light. For five days, it snowed relentlessly. Each day, after work, Alex attached the snowplow to the truck, cleared the snow from the drive to the road, and all around the trading post. On the sixth day, the snow stopped, and the plow trucks from around the settlement came out in earnest, clearing the road from the valley to Anchorage.

Because he was busy, he was happy. Alex went stir-crazy in the winter. It was too cold to remain in the shed or garage for long. He had no small handcrafts like some of the other men and his reading library was small. He was a big man, a strong man, and he liked to move around a lot. The winter inhibited him.

Mid-winter was the worst time. When the dry weather moved back in, the temperatures plummeted. You could not breathe in it without the air being snatched from your lungs. To go out in it, you wore layers and layers of clothing, from head to toe.

Alex hated those bitter, Arctic days. He fretted for things to do. One Saturday morning, after the temperature had finally crept its way back up to zero degrees Fahrenheit, Alex sprang out of bed and announced to his wife, "I'm going rabbit hunting."

"It's too cold," said Doreen crossly.

"Oh, no," he argued. "It's perfect. It warmed up."

There was nothing she could say to persuade him to change his mind. While they argued, she cooked him an extra-large breakfast, packed him a lunch and filled his thermos with coffee. In that length of time it took to prepare, the temperature went up another five degrees and Alex became very hopeful. "Do you see? The cold spell broke. You'll be sunbathing on the deck by the time I get back."

Doreen gave him a bitter smile and patted his face. "I think you're being foolish. You just want to show up Gary and Art. You think I don't know about the pissing contest you had over who bagged the most ptarmigan? It seems you could give the wildlife a rest now and then."

"You gave my favorite part of the moose to the Millers."

"One rump roast! The rest was all scraps."

"I'm craving a rabbit stew."

He was silly and foolish and that is what had attracted her. She watched him track through the unblemished snow, puncturing it with marine-blue prints. He followed the bluff that sheltered the rolling landscape from the brisk western winds, shrinking to a tiny black spot that disappeared into the trees.

Alex was a northwestern man, a sophisticated man from Eugene. For those who did not know the significance, Doreen was happy to fill in. Eugene was a small university town in the heartland of Oregon, where the French had traded and the pioneers had settled, blushing with shame later for their part in the history of Native American conflict.

They were a part of the pioneer heritage that, upon arriving in Alaska and settling alongside indigenous villages, vowed they could do better. They would not repeat the bitterness of intolerance and discrimination.

This set Alex apart from the farmers and lumbermen who made up much of the rural northwest. He was well-educated. His father was a radio announcer. Alex took to radio like a fish takes to water. The military snapped him up faster than he could say, "jack rabbit", but the military had been kind.

He only did one tour before they began preparing him for Alaska. It was the best thing that could ever happen to him. One year of war duty had nearly snapped him.

The day started out well. The temperature rose another five degrees. The sky turned pale blue and pastel pink. Doreen felt cheerful enough to sit down at her pedal-powered sewing machine to fashion a new flour-sack dress for Patsy. The flower sacks were pretty this year, tiny blue floral prints against a yellow background.

As the unspectacular sun set, five hours later, a breeze sprang up. The breeze turned into a light wind. The wind began to moan, the sound swelling as it rolled in from the north. In minutes, it was roaring. It howled across the land with inexplicable fury, shaking the snow-laden trees, and wrenching free their frozen branches. It threw the powdery snow high in the air, twisting and swirling it, blowing it in every direction.

Doreen watched out the window uneasily. He was out there, in the storm, with nothing but a flashlight to guide him home. She opened the curtains wide and set the lanterns next to the panes to send out extra light. She paced the floor, her stomach churning. She counted the minutes, then the hours. By dinner hour, he still had not returned.

She fed Patsy listlessly and readied her for bed. She held her daughter longer than normal, allowing her to fall fast asleep in her arms before tucking her in. He built himself a shelter, she reassured herself. Nobody can see in these conditions. The wind died down late in the evening.

She thought, *good. Now he can find his way home.*

She laid on the couch thinking she would nap, but she did not nap. The thoughts raced through her head, all the possibilities as to what could have happened. Finally, she could bear it no longer. She picked up the field phone and called Solace, her mind racing so much, she could not find her tongue. As soon as she heard the warm, familiar voice, she felt calmed enough to shakily whimper out her fears.

The early morning was velvet black when the search party began gathering. There were soon so many flashlights and storm lanterns, the yard lit up like a corner of Anchorage. Gary and Art were the first to arrive. Art put an arm around Doreen's shoulders and squeezed awkwardly. "We'll find him. You know how it is out there. He probably got turned around and stumbled upon Betty Lou's cabin. I'll bet she's feeding him fish soup and crackers right now."

Trying to find his own words of comfort, Gary added, "The girls will be along shortly. They are waiting for the kids to wake up and have their breakfast."

Art stammered a few unintelligible words and scraped one boot against the side of the other. Gary kept his hands shoved in his pockets, studying the ceiling as though he had found something remarkable in the wood pattern.

During these few unproductive seconds, Doreen fretted silently over Patsy, wondering how long it would take for the child's slumbering little mind to realize there was a commotion and rouse from its sleep.

Believing they had appropriately delivered their moral support, the two men went out to the yard and wandered around, looking for tracks. Doreen stood on the front porch in her boots and jacket, watching them. Finding no clues in the recently groomed snow, Art trudged reluctantly back to the porch, Gary close behind him.

They had no sooner begun to confer with Doreen, when the yellow glare of another pair of headlights flashed into the yard, lighting it up for brief moments before switching off with the sound of a dying engine. Three new arrivals stood in the half-light of the lanterns.

"Why is he here?" asked Gary belligerently and gesturing toward the vehicle.

The light caught more of their features: Frank, Matt, and Jimmy: ruddy under the lanterns, dark as phantoms in the shadows.

"He's a good tracker," answered Doreen.

A disgusted flush swept over his face. "Jimmy? He got lucky. That's all. He's never even been in service."

That was Gary's great objection to the friendship that had sprung up between his civil service friends and Jimmy. It wasn't like Jimmy had deliberately chosen a date to be born that put him safely out of the reach of military discipline. It wasn't like the military even needed him. The only real reason why the military was so valuable here was that it gave people jobs, and Jimmy was already capable of earning an income in the wilderness.

Doreen didn't care how Gary felt. Jimmy was already sweeping his flashlight in a wide arc and squatting to study the ground reflectively. Art squatted beside him. "No tracks. We looked everywhere. No tracks."

Jimmy continued to examine the terrain thoughtfully, his flashlight peering from the drive to the tangle of trees in the distance before approaching Doreen. "Did you see the direction your husband went?"

She pointed in the direction of the bluff that just began its long rise in the clearing. "He went out there and disappeared in the trees."

He slapped his furry mitts together before slipping them on his hands. "Good. That's good. That ridge runs all the way to the inlet. There could be some prints."

Whether Gary liked it or not, Jimmy was leading the search party. The troops followed him toward the bluff, swinging their lamps, and calling Alex's name. Doreen held her lantern high to shine out on the slowly disappearing team.

The sky was slowing turning from indigo to violet, with a thin, ruddy streak filling the horizon. Jimmy stooped, studied something, and took a few steps further, his body crouched. It's where Alex would have gone. The bluff gave shelter. The brush, shocked to stiff, brown and gold shafts in the winter, gave rabbits something to feed on. As the group disappeared into the woods, a cold, lonely wind swept over her, and she shivered.

Another vehicle flashed its lights into the parking lot and rumbled to a stop. Not even the dusky morning could completely hide the copper sheen of Andy's bright hair that sprang to life with the slightest light reflection. She strode like she was behind a plow, her long legs covering space quickly without hurrying.

"What are you doing standing outside here like that? It's not going to make things happen quicker."

"They found tracks," whispered Doreen. Her voice sounded faint and hollow.

"That's good," said Andy encouragingly. "Come inside now. There's not much you can do except wait."

She let Andy lead her through the door and sit her down at the table. As a firm believer in the philosophy that you lose your guest status and become a family member the second time you visit a home, Andy rummaged freely through the kitchen until she found the coffee and a box of hot cereal.

"When was the last time you ate?" She asked, rattling things around on the stove.

Doreen rested her head in one hand. "I don't know. Lunch, I guess. I wasn't worried at lunch."

"You can't let men ruin your appetite. You'll dry up and blow away. Alex is a big guy. He can take care of himself. The first time I saw him, I thought he was a lumberjack."

A few gulping breaths, then Doreen warbled over her coffee, "he likes the look. I think he wishes he had gone into construction. His job is really high-pressure."

"Why doesn't he switch?"

"One dayhe'll quit when he can afford his own business. At least, that's what he says, but they need him right now. There aren't that many people who can do what he can do. It's not just his job. It's his security clearance."

"Huh." Andy set a bowl of steaming oatmeal in front of her. "Eat. If you won't do it for yourself, think of the baby. You're eating for two."

"I can't think of the baby right now," said Doreen, taking the spoon and twirling it in the bowl.

"Well, I think you can!" Andy scolded. "I've never taken you for a selfish woman before, but that's a very selfish thing to say. Nothing that has happened is the baby's fault."

She choked down a few mouthfuls. "Well, there's no lumps in it."

"I make the good stuff. Patsy's waking up."

The morning became a blur. The sluggish dawn was as drained and colorless as Doreen felt. The snow was a blue ribbon with long, black shadows. The flashlights spread out in the distance, bobbing and growing fainter until they disappeared in the half-light.

Sharon and Beth arrived in Sharon's station wagon. Beth wasn't extremely helpful. She screeched in a loud voice about the idiotic things that occurred to men. Men never learned. They could live in the wilderness for ten years and they never learned. Sharon put her to work folding blankets in preparation for Alex's return.

The baseball champion set a plate of fudge on the table. "How are you holding up?"

Doreen tested a piece. The fudge was good comfort food, much better than oatmeal.

She cried a bit, wiped her eyes with her handkerchief and blew her nose. "I don't know why they can't keep their competition down to chess and cribbage."

"You know why," said Sharon. "They say they like brains, but they really like brawn."

Andy, who had been busy cleaning up and preparing for the next meal, called from the sink, "even Art?"

Art was a bit of a mystery. Art was round-headed and wore glasses. He walked funny, as though uncertain of his footing. He rarely spoke.

"Especially Art," said Sharon energetically. "He didn't have to go into construction. He could have chosen teaching. Big toys make boys feel bigger."

Sharon said things like this all the time about Art, but nobody really knew the truth since Art never did the talking. He knew how to handle machines, though. His landscaping was the best around, and apparently, he was a good engineer, or he would not be designing an airport. Nobody complained about him, which was as good as saying he knew his job.

Realizing her outburst had done nothing to assist Doreen's state of mind, Beth stacked the folded blankets on the couch, and searched in the coat closet for Patsy's box of toys. The three babies had reached full toddler status. They chased around a ball together and tumbled half-way constructed walls of blocks. They tormented the cat whenever they could coax it out of hiding.

The clock ticked so loudly, it drilled into her brain with sharp, relentless taps. The piercing sound drove her deeper into the dark unknown, the pain increasing with each tap. She couldn't understand how the world could keep moving around her when she sat, suspended in a timeless void.

Charlie arrived, stamping the snow from his boots, and apologizing for his tardiness as he set a casserole dish on the table. "Ester said you would probably be clustered with women. She and Millie will come over later."

She couldn't explain what came over her. Before he had finished his apology, she rushed to him and sobbed with relief when she felt the enveloping shelter of his arms lending her the strength she did not feel. This was Charlie, after all, the one who had fought at Normandy. He had survived the worst there was to see. He had returned from hell, rescuing the lambs. Wherever there was Charlie, things would be alright. He could part the seas if necessary. He could bring water to the desert.

"Yep," he said, holding her, that incredible fortitude of his washing over her as water being drawn from a bottomless well. "It's not always easy being brave."

He let her get it all out, not at all awkward, his stoic arms steadily embracing her.

"We're going to find him, you know," he said encouragingly when her tears subsided. "Alex is well-seasoned. It will take more than a snowstorm to bring him down."

He guided her back to the table and gave her a fresh cup of coffee, sitting her down firmly. "I'm going to follow the tracks of the other men now. They may need my help."

"Take one of the blankets with you," she pleaded, still clinging to him.

He patted her arm and placed her hands around the coffee cup. "Of course."

He took the one from the top and folded it over his arm. He no longer needed his flashlight, but he slipped it through his belt loop. There was no knowing how long he would be.

Twenty minutes later, he was running back toward the house, with Gary two hundred yards behind him. They were both waving frantically and had begun shouting as soon as their voices were close enough to faintly carry.

"Blankets, quick!" He shouted at the women streaming out to the porch. "And someone get Frank's first-aid kit. Alex is hurt."

"Where is it?" asked Sharon, running half-way down the steps to confront him. "The first aid kit?"

"Frank put it in the ambulance." He stamped impatiently, waiting for the blankets.

With no other thought in mind than that her husband was out there in the woods, injured, Doreen flew into the yard in nothing more than her nightclothes, robe, and slippers. "Take me to him! Now!"

Gary had caught up. Snatching the blankets, he turned and ran with them, leaving Charlie to mediate on his behalf. He watched the fleeting figure, calculating how long it would take to catch up with him, before deciding the important aspects were now covered. He took Doreen by the shoulders and told her sternly, "Notlike that you won't. It's still a good walk and you're not dressed."

He guided her gently back toward the house, his arm hooked into hers. "Get into some clothes. Put on your boots. By the time you're ready, he'll be back."

"Ready for what?" She asked, not caring that her voice was high-pitched.

He paused at the house entryway, his eyes boring into hers, commanding clear thoughts and practicality. "Frank thinks he has a broken ankle."

"But he's alive? He's alive! Oh God, he's alive."

Clear and practical were wise but required a great deal of resolve. The low roar in her ears colored the world in hues of red and black. Her thoughts were racing so fast, she couldn't keep up with them. Alex was alive. He was hurt. Oh, what had the fool done – shot himself in the foot?

She fumbled into her maternity dress, which seemed to grow more worn and tired by the day. After a moment of indecision, she slipped on a pair of long-john's and covered her feet with thick, wool socks. Charlie had said to put on her boots. She ran numbly to the kitchen to locate her boots, jumbled together with the boots of the children.

She realized, at the door, as she struggled into her coat and hat, the only other adult in the house was Andy. Beth and Charlie were running toward the rescue team. Sharon had vanished. Doreen hesitated. Andy looked up from a game she was playing with the children and their blocks and smiled.

"Go after him. Don't worry about the kids. I've got them."

The children, well-acquainted with each other, were certainly not worried about her. Doreen dashed outside, braced against the cold morning air, and struggled up the now clearly defined path toward the bluff. She had not gotten far when she saw the team come out of the woods, a blanket stretched between them. Whatever was in that bundle was completely covered, yet occasionally mumbled out a curse or an insult.

"Alex!" She cried loudly, recognizing the voice.

Small movements rippled through the blanket stretcher, and the grumbling voice floated muffled through the heavy covers, "now I'm in trouble."

They didn't stop their forward march to let her see him, but the sound of his voice had been reassuring and the continued shifting within his cocoon a vigorous statement that he was not yet close to his deathbed. She followed in the lead, taking up a portion of the blanket that cradled his head and scolding him as they walked.

The ambulance and the group of rescuers arrived in the yard at the same time. The back door opened, and the gurney set on the ground just as the search team stepped into the clearing, so smoothly synchronizedit looked orchestrated. The ambulance driver, bundled from head to toe, grabbed the metal stretcher and raced to meet the team with it as soon as they appeared.

Transferring Alex from the blanket to the gurney was the easy part. The hard part was keeping him there. As soon as he saw the destination of his new ride, he sat half-way up, groaning and slapping at the hands that held him back. "Just a blamed minute. You're taking me to the hospital, and you don't even know if I need it?"

"You need it," said Frank loudly. "You need it. We cut away your boot. There could be a fracture."

"Bah," he spat. "Fix it, Frank. Pop it back in place. Wrap it up. Give me a penicillin shot. I saw what you've got in that kit."

The veterans always worked with purpose. Loud noises didn't distract them. During their argument, the gurney had already arrived at the back of the ambulance and was being lifted inside. "You've got four puncture wounds from the trap," grunted Frank. "You need a tetanus shot as well."

"Then do it. You've got a tetanus shot in your witch's kit, don't you?"

Frank squatted inside the ambulance and lent an arm for Doreen to climb in with them. "No, I do not. I'll clean up the holes along the way, you stubborn old fool, to keep gangrene from settling in, but I'm not going to treat you and take the blame if you have to take three months out of work because your leg didn't heal right."

"Bah." Alex spat, then noticed his wife watching him quietly. "Doreen!" He demanded, "tell him I don't need a damned doctor. Just clean up the holes, give me a penicillin shot and set the ankle. He knows how to do it, Doreen. Tell him."

She folded her arms across her chest. "You've done enough foolishness for one day, Alex. I don't want to hear any more from you. If Frank says you need a doctor, you're going to a doctor. You're wasting time, boys. Let's go."

The back door slammed closed, and someone tapped the glass on the driver's side. With a sputter and a roar, the ambulance lurched then careened nearly sideways around the corner of the drive. Alex lifted his head, then lay back again. The warmth, after so many hours of frozen exposure, was making him drowsy.

"I knew it was a bad idea to get an ambulance," he mumbled as they swayed down the road. "Now a man can't spend a decent time at home mending. He's gotta go to a doctor."

He fretted between the chills and the warm invitation of sleep. Frank brought out a pint of whiskey, only two fingers low. "Here. Take a good swallow of this. I'm going to clean out those holes now."

Alex didn't argue. He swallowed long and deep.

The alcohol had an almost immediate effect. A deep flush swept over his face, then eased into blushing rouge. He relaxed and began shivering only in intervals, as though reminded of the ordeal that was quickly distancing itself.

When Alex appeared to be asleep, Frank peeled back the blanket from his ankle. Doreen stifled a cry. The entire foot was swollen with angry blue and green mottling. Just below the calf were four jagged puncture wounds, closing tight and oozing thinned drops of blood through the openings.

Frank was a knowledgeable, if not very gentle medic. Telling Doreen to keep the foot held straight, he poured a bottle of rubbing alcohol over the holes.

"Sadist," mumbled Alex sleepily.

He wasn't finished. Pinching each wound between his thumb and index finger, he squeezed until it bled clean, red blood. Alex screamed, thrashed, and demanded another drink from the bottle. Doreen gave it to him. He groaned and lay back, dozing more easily this time, the chills gone, the throbbing eased by the bandages Frank wrapped around his ankle.

"What happened?" Doreen asked when it became apparent Alex was resting peacefully.

Frank leaned against the side of the van and drew out his pipe. "Wolf trap. He was on his way home from hunting when he stepped in the trap. He managed to pry himself loose, but his ankle. You saw how it is."

"Is it badly broken?"

He let three small clouds of smoke float to the top of the van like smoke signals. "I don't know. The puncture marks add to the swelling. I'm not a doctor, but I don't think it's too bad. I think he just aggravated it from using it too much."

"He tried to make it home?"

"He used his rifle as a crutch. He said he was making headway until the wind came. He was snow blinded and couldn't go any further. He dug out a snow cave and waited it out. Once the wind died, he tried walking home again. Jimmy saw him first, hobbling along with two rabbits slung over his shoulder, leaning on his rifle."

"He got two rabbits?"

"He did. Jimmy brought them back for you."

"He is a good kid, isn't he?"

"He's probably got them skinned out and in the cellar by now."

Alex opened his eyes again when they stopped at the hospital doors. "Who was driving this thing?" He asked.

"Sharon," they told him simultaneously.

Alex groaned. "I knew it was being driven like a bat out of hell."

Sharon appeared at the back to help with the gurney. "That's because the brakes are still floppy."

The emergency door burst open, and the professionals poured out, taking over their rescue operation. The three Wolf Creek residents followed briskly behind, asking questions and giving their own observations until the "authorized personnel" door closed firmly on them. They wandered into the soft-lit waiting room and settled on the couch unhappily.

Frank sat on the edge of his seat, his hands between his knees. After a few minutes, he went to the vending machine and came back with three cups of poorly mixed hot chocolate. Having something in his hands seemed to ease him. He sat back more comfortably and crossed his legs.

Sharon made faces when she drank from her cup, although she cradled it closely, rotating it thoughtfully in her hands. She reached over and rubbed Doreen's expanding belly. "How's the baby doing?"

Doreen leaned back, giving her bulge more prominence. "He's kicking a bit hard, so I suppose he's upset, but nothing to be alarmed about."

Sharon smiled. "So, you think it might be a boy?"

"I think it's a boy." Doreen moved Sharon's hand so she could feel the kick. "I'm carrying him differently. More pressed against my back. It's a boy. What about you?" she asked. "Are you and Art thinking about another?"

Sharon straightened back up and took a drink of her watery chocolate. "We're thinking about it. We don't want Juliana to grow up an only child."

"Then you shouldn't wait too long," advised Frank. "It's better when they have siblings close to their ages so they can grow up together."

Doreen nodded her head vigorously. She had heard the same things.

Several hours later, the examining doctor returned with his metal clipboard and a pen behind his ear that showed his serious demeanor. "Your husband was lucky," he told Doreen. "It was a simple fracture. No complications. We were most worried about the puncture wounds, but they were cleaned out pretty good."

Doreen stole a glance at Frank. He was preening. So that was why Millie was always getting after him. She stole another glance at Sharon. She was smiling.

The vague noise of a clearing throat.

"We gave him a tetanus shot and antibiotics. There shouldn't be any problems. We wanted to keep him for observation overnight, but he insists on going home." The doctor shook his head. "I don't know why he's awake. After what happened, he should be sleeping like a log."

"Because he's Alex," said Doreen. "He's a stubborn old man in a young man's body."

They took him home in the ambulance, but this time, Frank drove.

Eighteen

The incredible, magic hands massaged her scalp, relaxing tension she didn't even know she had. The scissors could snip-snip all they wanted as long as these hands soothed away her worries and stress. Alex had not been the best of patients.

Once he had slept off the trauma of his harrowing experience, he ranted about being kept like an invalid. He was ungrateful toward Sharon. He was ungrateful toward Frank. He was ungrateful toward the doctor who put him in a cast that limited movement.

He was even ungrateful toward Jimmy for being a hero and finding him. "I would have made it home on my own sooner or later," he growled.

It was ego, all ego, she knew. Men of both brawn and brain were supposed to be invulnerable. They didn't make mistakes. They weren't foolish and impulsive. Alex had been all of it. Mixed with cabin fever, he was miserable.

His attitude improved once he was cleared for returning to work. For the past week, Frank had picked him up, waiting patiently in his car while Alex hobbled out, knowing if he tried to assist his injured friend, Alex would get mad.

A small curl fluttered to the floor. Doreen's hand crept to her head to test where it had been, experimentally. Andy pushed it away. "Don't worry. I'm not cutting your hair short."

She felt that she owed Andy. When they returned home the evening of Alex's accident, the only car in the yard apart from their own vehicles, was Andy's truck. Frank and Sharon carried Alex inside on the gurney, with Doreen leading the way.

The lamps were softly lit, the kitchen ship-shape. Tin foil wrapped dishes, crinkling at the edges, abundantly decorated the dining room table.

Andy opened the porch door ahead of Doreen, her eyes wide, her russet hair tied in a scarf with the loose ends tucked in.

"Beth had to go home," she apologized in a stage whisper, "She said she would take Patsy with her, but I told her I would babysit. Little girls are never a problem," she added wistfully.

"Maybe your next one will be a girl," Doreen had said.

"Maybe," she said as though blessings never really came her way.

Between the four of them, it had been easy to transfer Alex to the bed and tuck him in, although at that moment, an elephant probably would not have disturbed him.

No sooner had they reached the general vicinity of Wolf Creek, when Alex gave a contented sigh, as though he knew exactly where he was at, and fell asleep. He did not stir when they pulled him out of the back and laid him out on the gurney. He did not even mumble as they brought the gurney into the house and heaved him onto the bed. Doreen tucked the blanket around his neck, and he snored peacefully.

"I'd better get home," said Sharon, giving Doreen a peck on the cheek. "Art is probably worried."

Andy led the way out of the room, carrying a kerosene lamp. "I told him Juliana could spend the night, but your husband took her home anyway."

Sharon's face flickered in the lanternlight, deepening the round cheeks, bringing out her strong, square jaw. "She's young for spending the night at others. But thank you."

Frank left directly behind her without saying anything, neither requiring nor desiring gratitude. The house that had been in turmoil just a few hours before, was silent.

The voice came from behind her. "I can spend the night if you would like."

It startled her for a second. She had almost forgotten Andy was there. Doreen started to decline than reconsidered. She was incredibly tired, completely drained. Between Alex and Patsy, she would have her hands full in the morning.

"Thank you," she had told her, then asked, "Do you think you can come over in a few weeks – after Alex has gone back to work – and give me a hair trim? It's starting to bounce around again, but I don't want you cutting it while he is home. He will only drive the two of us crazy."

She had agreed.

A few more curls fell to the floor. Doreen picked up the hand mirror to check on the progress of her clip. "What's the news, Andy?"

"Oh, Alex's accident is still on the top of the list. It will be a while before someone tops it, but I will tell you, that terrible Ted Ewing is still hanging out at the village. I told Mark, that man is up to no good. The elders should make him leave, but he doesn't listen to me."

"What has Ted done?"

"He's still courting a sixteen-year-old girl and last week he took her dancing in Anchorage."

Doreen clicked her tongue against the roof of her mouth at such disgraceful behavior. "There are laws concerning these things."

The scissors snapped at the air angrily. "Only if you take the matter to the law. If the family doesn't take it to the law, nothing's going to be done."

"It's a terrible pity. He's old enough to be her father."

"That's what I say, but now Mark thinks she might want a blue-eyed baby."

Doreen shuddered with disgust, then reconsidered. It was, after all, a village affair. They did things differently. She shouldn't be one to criticize. She had seen old lechers before, hooking up with girls so young, they were still growing an upper chest. It was what money can do. She had learned not to look too hard because even in the gutters, you can see a reflection.

"Not everyone sees things the same way. What if he marries her? It happens all the time. Old men with teenage brides."

Andy scoffed and another feathery curl fell to the floor. "Ted get married? Not a fat chance! He's playing with the poor child. If she has a kid, he'll ditch her. Break her heart, that's what he plans to do."

Doreen felt it best to change the subject. "Wasn't Mark going to take Jimmy north?"

Andrea chuckled. "They haven't gone yet. Jimmy's chomping at the bit. Tammy hasn't given it up and he can't think of anything else."

"Don't you think you're teaching him bad habits?"

"What bad habits? If you mean like Ted, it's not the same at all. Jimmy's a lamb and the girls he'll be seeing are experienced women. They will take pleasure in enlightening him."

Noticing Doreen still looked distressed, she added patiently, "It's something I noticed when I began visiting the bush. It's in all the villages, really, but they don't worry about what women do as much as here. If she likes blue-eyed men or runs off with moonshiners, well, that's just the way it is. No use quarreling about it."

"It just doesn't seem right to me. I've heard how village women can be, and I'm not faulting them. They were raised differently, but I also know about women's professions. A cocktail waitress? Is she playing with him?"

"Could be," Andrea answered agreeably. "Or she could be playing for keeps. She's a smart one and Jimmy is like the new driven snow. I would have taught him more about women but what he needs to know, a sister can't teach him."

"It's better he learns on his own, anyway. You can't mollycoddle him. Is Tammy as good a singer as he says she is?"

Andy finished the clip and stepped back to study the results. "You've never been to the Pioneer Lounge, have you?"

"No," she mumbled, keeping her head down while Andy brushed off the loose hair and whisked away the towel. "We don't drink much."

"Frank and Millie don't either, but it doesn't stop them from coming by for fun. The music is good and there's a nice dance floor. Millie cuts a fine step. I'll bet you can, too."

"Not at seven months pregnant," she laughed.

"No," Andy said, sitting down to light a cigarette. "Millie isn't dancing right now, either. She just taps her feet. She's due next month."

"She was the first to infect us!" Doreen hurried into the bedroom to look in her full-length mirror.

Andy had done something that made her hair look flatter on top and longer at the curly ends. It was very modern. She twirled carefully to take in her swollen belly. The baby was still high. Two months. She had two more months.

She returned to the kitchen patting her hair. "I like it."

Andy tapped an ash into the tray. "I'm infected too."

"Oh no." Doreen sat down and looked across the table sympathetically. "What will you do?"

"Not sure yet."

"Is it Matt's?" Doreen asked in a low voice.

"No." She poured herself a cup of coffee. "It's either Jake's or Mark's."

"Goodness."

"I'll probably marry Mark. He says he doesn't care who the kid's dad is."

"Does Jake know?"

Andy squashed her half-smoked cigarette viciously in the ash tray and lit another. "I just received my divorce papers in my hot little hands last week. Do you really think I'm going to tell Jake?"

"What about Matt?" Doreen blurted.

"What about Matt? His wife is giving him another chance. She's coming back up this spring."

She poured a cup of coffee so she could sit down and visit. "I'm sorry, Andy."

"Why? Oh, there's mama. She'll moan and groan, but secretly she will be pleased. Nothing makes her happier than knowing the world is being supplied with Delaneys."

"What about you? And if you marry Mark?"

"What of it? I'll still be here, just at the village."

She had brought Ben this time. The big-headed boy didn't know how to play with girls. He kept snatching Patsy's hair bow and throwing it across the floor. Andy retrieved the bow for the third time and popped Ben on the butt, telling him to behave.

She caught Doreen's sympathetic look just as she was straightening up, and swept off her blouse, which had picked up some remnants from Ben's last peanut butter sandwich.

Resuming her sophisticated pose, with her legs crossed, then crossed one more time at the ankles, a feat only the long-legged could perform, she sighed and said, "look. It's one more kid, that's all. It doesn't change me. I'm where I want to be, maybe for the first time in my life. That's what's important."

Noticing the hour, Andy got ready to leave. She gathered her instruments like a surgeon, fixing each one in its slipper.

"About your question concerning Tammy." She snapped her case shut and brushed it off. "She's good, but not that good. Her voice isn't strong enough. It doesn't carry, but she's all he's got. It's part of why he joined the performing troops. He wants to find a good singer."

"Oh my, what does Tammy say about that?"

Andy shrugged. "She doesn't care. She's only singing to help Jimmy. It's not a career for her. She says she does just fine waitressing."

Doreen put a five- dollar bill on the table. "That's too much," said Andy, pushing it back.

Doreen held two fingers on the bill, sliding it slowly across again. "No, it's not. You've been a lifesaver. Take it, Andy."

She pocketed it hesitantly. "I shouldn't, you know. It's too much, but Carol will be needing a new dress for the spring prom and spring isn't that far ahead. Oh," she said as though the mention of spring reminded her of something. "Frank really wants you to try out for the performing troops."

"He is a devil. Alex says Frank half-killed him."

Andy pulled Ben to his feet before he could do any more damage to Patsy's belongings and began stuffing him in a snowsuit. "Half-way isn't bad. I'm sure you were tempted to do some extra damage, yourself. Anyway, Frank is sure you are hiding your abilities."

"I'm waiting for the balloon to pop to make my commitment."

"If you can dance, they really do need a couple more girls on the chorus line. They've got Millie. There are two girls from the Pioneer Lounge who said they would dance. And Ester has taken over the lead."

"Heavens! Ester? Can you imagine her dancing?"

"You've got to rescue the poor girls, Doreen. Millie will never say anything against her, and the Lounge girls will just do as they are told. They only agreed because they like Frank and

Millie. They make good customers. But there is the matter of having someone there who knows what they're doing."

"Frank put you up to this, didn't he?"

"No, Millie did. She said Ester's ideas are awful."

"How am I supposed to change this? I've never stood up to Ester."

"Because Frank says you are a professional choreographer. You're the authority."

"Oh, the devil!"

"You didn't know that about him?"

Now that they were leaving, Ben wanted to spend more time with Patsy. Doreen held the door open while Andy dragged the toddler through, screaming and kicking out with his feet.

Maybe little girls were easier. Cody played well with girls because he was always around Patsy and Juliana. The three children together weren't as much of a handful as Ben by himself.

During the two weeks that Alex had been laid up, she could hardly wait for him to go back to work. The first few days had been fine. The women from Wolf Creek visited in the mornings, families dropped by in the evenings. They carried casserole dishes, fruit Jell-O salads and desserts. She didn't have to cook. Patsy remained entertained. Alex slipped in and out of consciousness, groggy with pain pills and his harrowing ordeal.

The novelty wore off. The morning visits turned into sporadic ones with Alex in the background complaining about interfering women and quacks that fancied themselves medics. Evening visits grew shorter, then disappeared altogether.

Doreen began to crave the free and easy discussions with her friends without the eavesdropping of male company. Today was the first day since the accident she had been able to speak with unguarded pleasure of anything and everything that came to her mind.

As impatient as she had been for Alex to go to work, she found herself just as impatient for him to come home. She washed and peeled potatoes, her mind picking over the news. It had been established that Andy gossiped freely. However, Andy had become her friend. It was a matter of sorting out what could and could not be repeated.

Certainly, the news concerning Ted Ewing was critical information. The crude and callous fellow was most likely the one who had set the wolf trap. It wouldn't be Betty Lou's handiwork. Betty Lou refused to hunt wolves and her traps for smaller animals were all box traps.

The Natives preferred to use snares, teaching their children during their early years how to make and set them, never exposing them to the vicious metal jaws of cruelty. Only Ted was low life enough to go skulking around in heavy winter snow, setting steel-toothed traps in the populated Wolf Creek area.

Ester was safe to talk about. Everyone knew about Ester's inhibitions. It wasn't gossip. It was straight-up news, and it did make her feel better about participating in the chorus line.

It was probably safe to talk about Jimmy. Andy didn't seem to mind having Jimmy's affairs talked about. Jimmy had a reputation. The stories about him only enhanced his youthful, musical life: his charisma. That's the word Andy had used. Doreen liked it. Jimmy had charisma. Unsullied by the war, eyes soft and guileless, fingers like Andy's; filled with their own magic, coaxing music from nylon strings.

Doreen traced their conversation carefully. They had said nothing about Beth or Sharon. That was a home run. To even mention their names was enough to start a rumor. To maintain the balance, she must not say anything about Andy or Matt to the other girls. The only way to keep the words from spilling out accidentally to indiscreet sourceswas to channel them to the one person she could trust – her husband.

There was only one thing different in their new routine. With Frank picking up Alex for work each morning and driving him home each afternoon, the two had become thick as thieves. The accident couldn't be what brought them together. Alex was still miffed that Frank had not tried out his medical expertise, circumventing all the fuss of a hospital visit.

Yet the routine had been the same for over a week. The two sat in Frank's car, spending a good ten minutes chatting conspiratorially with each other before Alex came inside, that mesmerized look of office talks still on his face.

It was a small thing, not worth developing a grievance, but today Doreen was impatient.

She stuck her face to the windowpane and watched while shifting her weight from one hip to the other, as Alex opened the Studebaker's door, then continued his apparently all-important conversation. Finally, the crutches came out, then a foot. Unfolding himself slowly, Alex leaned on the crutches, his plaster-cast foot raised, talked vigorously another three minutes (Doreen was checking her watch), waved goodbye and hobbled to the house.

Before she could say a word, Alex had already slammed the door shut and was nearly bellowing in the most excited voice used since announcing D-Day. "Guess who came by our workplace today?"

Having no idea who could possibly find interest in their dull little cubby-holes stuck on an underdeveloped military base, Doreen lifted her shoulders and spread her hands.

He hobbled into the living room and threw himself down on the couch, propping his leg on the coffee table. "William Egan, that's who!" he answered, still unable to contain his volume.

The three second answer completely deflated her Delaney news. William Egan was the most important person in the world! Well, maybe only in Alaska, but it was close enough. It's not often one got to rub shoulders with a territorial representative running for Senator.

Her hand crept up to twist one of the curls of her new haircut. "Why?"

His eyes glowed with that old fervor he showed when they first talked of building a community. "Because he wants help with his campaign! He spoke with us; everyone in the office; and asked for volunteers."

"What did you tell him?" she asked, forgetting completely now about Andy's dilemma and Matt's soon-to-arrive wife.

"We told him we would! Of course we would! He's coming for dinner next Sunday evening at the Bolinder place. We're invited and so are the Lamars."

"The Hughes and the Bowen's?"

Something fleeting passed over his eyes. He shifted his gaze to bring out a cigar and light it. "It's just a small private gathering. We're on the committee, Doreen. He'll be meeting with the community the following Friday at the trading post. Everyone will have a chance to talk with him."

She rung her hands. Alex didn't understand these things, but first the car and now this. "But whatever am I going to tell Beth and Sharon, and why does it have to be at Charlie's house? If it was here, I'd invite all my friends." Her voice wound into its high-pitched whine.

The blue cloud of smoke was gathering furiously around his face, partially obscuring it and adding its own heightened cloud of authority. "It's not a big party, Doreen. It's politics. Charlie's been here the longest and his house…"

She interrupted. "Is full of fancy French furnishings. I get it, Alex. She even has an inside water pump."

She went into the kitchen to set out dinner. He called after her. "You don't get it. The others aren't on the committee. That's all there is to it."

Seeing he wasn't getting off the couch, she fixed a plate, fretting. "Well, Beth isn't going to forgive me. First, making friends with Andy and now going to a special dinner at the Bolinders. I'm losing my best friend."

"You can't let Beth control your opinions, Doreen."

She couldn't let Beth control them. She couldn't let Sharon. Apparently, the only one who had a say in her opinions was Alex.

"She doesn't like politics anyway."

She was suddenly angry. She was angry he had upset her snug little world. She was angry he had made her worry. She was angry that he seemed to be in control of every little thing, and she was only his dutiful lieutenant.

"I just don't know you anymore," she cried with exasperation. "What is happening to you?"

He didn't answer immediately. He finished eating slowly and deliberately, taking his time to thoroughly chew each bit. "I don't know what you're talking about."

"Yes, you do. You haven't really been the same since the accident. You've been bad-tempered, rude. You've chased half our friends away and now you're going to dump the rest of them to rub shoulders with politicians. That's everything you never wanted to be, Alex."

"No! It's not like that!" He made a face, then wiped his hand over his mouth, so that he appeared expressionless. "It's.... I will tell you, Doreen. But don't hate me for it. You see, I'm a coward. I've been trying to tell you and I'm so cowardly, I couldn't."

She laughed hollowly, almost mockingly. "You're not a coward, Alex."

"Just hear me out. During the war, I never wanted to kill someone. When I was sent overseas, it was all I could think about, how I didn't want to shoot anybody. Just the thought of it would make me nauseous, you know. And here I was, in some strange little place outside Versailles that maybe had been a town once but there wasn't much left but battered fields."

He rubbed his nose, sniffed, and she brought him a beer. This was the first time he had ever talked about it, the first time he had ever talked about those eleven short months in Europe that must have been for him, an eternity.

"I was a field operator. I was supposed to keep those radios going. And I did. I crawled around, snapping back together lines, pirating parts from a half-blown radio to jack up another. It was crazy. I didn't have to pick up a rifle often, just protect that radio."

He had been hunkering down in a trench, trying to touch bases with the commander. The radio kept fading out, so he scrambled in his tool kit for a screw driver to nudge a spark from the lagging connection. He sensed, rather than noticed someone standing not far from him and looked up.

"He was a German soldier. A young guy." He laughed. "They always are, but we were young too. How old was I? Nineteen? Twenty? The same age is Jimmy.

He raised his rifle. I raised my gun. I closed my eyes and I shot. I didn't aim. I just closed my eyes and fired. And I kept them closed until one of the troops – I don't know who – tapped me on the shoulder and said, 'we're moving out.' I never looked. I don't know if I killed anyone, but I never wanted to."

"By the grace of God," whispered Doreen, hoping they were words of comfort.

"That's what I wanted to know! Did God grace me, or am I just a coward who got lucky? Maybe the kid took pity on me, this big man huddled on the ground, crying like a baby, his eyes squeezed closed, and he just walked away. I was too cowardly to even look!"

"Alex! Alex!" She sat on his lap and took his face in her hands.

He held her wrists. "Don't pity me. I've had enough of pitying myself. I'm done with it. Every year, when the hard winter comes and there's nothing to keep my mind occupied, I feel it come back – all the doubts, all the fears, all the darkness."

The darkness was overwhelming. It swallowed things even as you were trying to hold them and etch them in your memory forever. It was selective in what it left you with – only the most painful encounters, only the torments of your own twisted conscience.

It was so merciless, it laid out its blackened days in frozen silence, so that each labored breath was a rasping reminder of your isolation. Instead of seeking comfort in the warmth of a fire and the tinkling, bell-like laughter of his wife and companion, Alex's mind followed the dark, turbulent summons, yearning to confront them and put them to rest.

On a morning when it seemed the frozen spell was loosening its grip, Alex sprang from bed, positive this was the day he would prove to himself he was as competent as any of the veterans, as rugged as any pioneer.

It was an excellent day for hunting. The break in the cold weather had brought the hungry woods animals out of hiding and there were clear fox, squirrel, and rabbit tracks, as well as an occasional sliding dip through the snow where an owl had swooped in to snag its prey. They punctuated the diamond-bright cover with ocean-blue patterns.

Alex felt his spirits rise. All he needed was space. The walls contained things – undesirable thoughts, dark, secretive corners, scents and sounds that should have disappeared ages ago. The walls inhibited your thoughts, made them go around and around in circles. They channeled noise, the worst kind of noise – anger, envy, suspicion, accusations, and – Crack!

The snowshoe rabbit stretched out in his line of sight, and he fired a perfect shot just to the side of its shoulder, hitting its heart. It leapt, did a back flip, and laid still. That was one. He pursued a little further into the brush for one more.

The rabbits must have had a good summer. Their tracks were everywhere. Fifteen minutes later, Alex had taken down another, and decided to do a loop and head back home after a little lunch. They still weren't getting enough sunlight to stay out long, and winter evenings could be treacherous. Not that there were any predators willing to tackle a man with a gun, but nature herself was out to get you, with tricky gullies and holes camouflaged by the dark and snow.

He had almost finished his loop, with the trail he had made earlier, glittering not far ahead, when he heard, rather than felt, a sharp snap. He looked up and swiftly around before he looked down. When he lowered his head, he saw the splash of red drops pooling up around his boot and studied it with wonder.

He picked up a handful of bright red snow, puzzled as to where it had come from, and in one searing blast that raced from his foot to his brain so fast, it felt it would explode, he realized his leg had been caught in the brutal metal trap used for hunting wolves and coyotes.

He tugged at his pant leg. It pulled up frayed and bloodied. "Okay," he muttered to nobody. "It's not that bad. It bit through the boot, not the bare leg. I've just gotta open it."

Opening it was easier said than done. It wasn't as large as a bear trap, but large enough to snap a human bone. In sub-zero temperatures, the teeth gripped rigidly together.

Alex drew out his thick-handled hunting knife and shoved it between the metal jaws, so they could not snap solidly closed again, and began prying them apart. Twice, his hands slipped, and the teeth pinched tighter, causing him to howl with pain, but through sheer willpower, he finally heard the satisfying click as he opened the trap completely.

He eased his foot out, the swollen veins pulsing and heaving fiery blood. His boot felt too small, too painfully tight. He loosened the laces and packed snow inside. The pulsing ebbed - the pain eased.

"Well God," he said, using his rifle butt to pull himself up. "That was a good one. That took me by surprise. I don't suppose you're of a mind to tell me what it's all about."

The wolf trap was still wide open, its teeth glaring under the lowering sun. Alex picked up a stout branch that had been blown loose by the wind and slammed it hard against the centralized middle, so that the trap leapt into the air and sprang shut again.

"You already wasted an hour of my time. You don't need to be trapping anyone else for a while."

An hour of precious daylight wasted and two miles to go with a bum leg. It was throbbing the way a toothache would, sometimes just a background pain, sometimes washing over him in fiery waves, squeezing the breath from his lungs and nauseating him so much, he gasped and crumpled to the side of the trail, waiting for the flames to pass.

The sky began to thicken, turning ocher and deep gray when the wind sprang up. At first, he thought it was the change from afternoon to evening that was often accompanied by a cold, brisk wind. Then he heard the sound you never want to hear if you are alone in the wilderness. The wind moaned from somewhere far away, sobbing its lonely transport, gaining speed as it swept over the inlet.

Screeching with fury, it touched down over the tidal flats, then after rolling the ice and snow in a giant carpet, and raking the shivering trees with vicious claws, it shook out its winter bedding.

The snow and ice billowed and whined, drunk with their storm-filled lives. He fought it – the clawing fingers, the ice and snow pelting his face like stones – struggling to move forward in a world where the separation between air and solid ground had become undefined.

He sank repeatedly to his hips in snow cover. He couldn't find his trail. Between the storm and the darkening evening, he could see nothing at all except the furious evening. He patted around until he found he found a small dip with an overhanging tree. It was facing leeward, offering shelter against the wind.

He dug inside, almost to raw ground, and packed the snow around him. He wasn't in pain anymore. He was numb, which wasn't good news, either. If frostbite set in…."Doreen's going to kill me!" He raged.

The storm didn't care. Removing the scarf that Doreen insisted he always wear when out in sub-zero temperatures, he wrapped it carefully around his injured foot. Doreen wouldn't be happy about the ruined scarf, but she would be unhappier if he was a cripple.

"I went out looking for God," he said, wrapping up his story.

She knew the rest. As soon as there had been light enough to see, he had followed the fledging hill until it joined the collection of others marching up the familiar gully.

He had not even begun to climb when he saw first Jimmy, then Frank and Art, their figures appearing in layers as they topped the highest hill. He didn't try to go any further. He just let them come for him. "I ended up only worrying about what you were going to say."

"You didn't find any answers?"

"I think I did."

He waited until after she had put Patsy to bed and could give him her full attention before continuing. "I think I found my place. I think I know who I am."

She was still trying to sort out what he had told her earlier about his months in France. "You're not a coward. You didn't have a choice, and you don't even know if you killed someone or not. It doesn't matter one way or the other. It was war."

"There's going to be another war."

Her smile slipped, along with the optimism she had been bolstering in her mind, "a war with Russia?"

He fished a cigar from his breast pocket and rolled it between his fingers. "Let's hope not. A war with Russia would lead to another world war. Nobody wants to see that happen again. No. It's Korea. The communists are trying to take over the country. We can't let that happen."

"Is it any of our business what Korea decides?"

"Yes, it is," he answered swiftly. "The Korean government is asking for our help, and frankly, we can't afford to allow communism to keep advancing into the Asian countries. Once it takes over Asia, it will take over the Mideast. Once they do that, they will sweep over all of Europe. Where would that leave us? Where would it leave our allies?"

"I don't know," she whispered, suddenly frightened.

"Without freedom," he said firmly. "Without freedom."

He smoked grimly, watching the imperfect smoke rings wander delicately above his head. "Eisenhower is right. We need to build a strong military complex. The Russians are stock-piling weapons. We would be foolish to turn a blind eye to it."

"I thought we wanted to leave Alaska out of these war games."

"We can't. We are too strategic a location. And that's the change, Doreen. I realized when I was stuck out in the storm that we can't protect the community by ourselves. We need government. We need a safety net. I have a duty and I can't run from it. I have a family now. I want my children to grow up happy and thriving. We must control Alaska's direction. We can't leave it wide open for anyone who wants to exploit it. That's why I have to get involved."

"And not Gary?"

"Gary has a luxury I don't have. He can listen to the news or not. He can choose what to read. My job is to relay the news as soon as it occurs, but not just any news. The messages between international leaders. The reports from ambassadors and spies. I'm the fly in the corner, listening in on conversations. Gary likes accident report and police scandals."

"So, you've joined Charlie and Frank's political band-wagon."

"We need Egan. We need a strong, territorial government."

This simple truth concerning the Hughes and their lack of concern for worldly affairs made the upcoming dinner far more palatable, and even something Doreen could justifiably look forward to. After all, it wasn't as though everyone had been invited except the Hughes. Only the men from the office would be there. Only the committee men.

There was no doubt Alex was a committee man. He attended all the meetings. He filed paperwork and calculated numbers. We wore a tie to work.

You couldn't say that about Gary or Art or Matt. They were on-hands men. They checked the proposals of committee men and did what was necessary to realize the end goal. You didn't have workers without committee men, as without them, there was no direction and you didn't have committee men without workers, for the workers were the ones that got things done.

Doreen set Patsy at the table with her plate and took her own into the living room, posing as daintily as possible, hoping Alex would notice her new hairdo. "Andy told me Matt's wife is coming back," she said, patting at her hair.

He was still to absorbed in his plate and his own news. "Yeah," he grunted.

"You knew?"

"I just found out today."

"Oh." She dawdled over her plate. "Did you also know Andy is going to have another baby?"

She was gratified to see a flicker of surprise pass over his face. He rubbed his nose, wiping away the look, and asked, "Is it Matt's?"

"She says it isn't."

"She doesn't need to lie about it. He'll do the right thing by her."

"He doesn't have to think about it. She might be marrying Mark."

He put down his knife and fork and stared at her. "He's a Native."

"I think most of us are aware of that."

He ate a few more bites. "Did you do something to your hair?"

She tugged at the relaxed curls. "Andy."

"Oh. It looks nice. I suppose it doesn't make a difference. Andrea could do worse. Mark's a good man."

Their evening meal over, Doreen began stacking the dishes in the sink. "Andy also said Frank still wants me to join the performing troops.

A full-work day under his belt, his belly satisfied with the evening meal, Alex was feeling expansive. He pushed his chair back, reached inside the cold storage cabinet built into the wall under the counter, and brought out a beer.

"You should," he said, waving it around. "Beth and Gary joined. You'll be friends with her again. Not only that, but Representative Egan also said he wants a seat in the front row on our opening night."

A high-pitched giggle erupted from her throat that she smothered between her hands as it reached her mouth.

"Goodness gracious, but Alex. What about the baby?"

"Frank said they won't be ready until spring. He's still recruiting, I think. You won't even have to do tryouts. Just come to practice. By spring, you'll be back in shape."

"Do you really think we can raise money for the community with the performing troops?"

"Frank thinks we can."

"Frank sees talent in a potato," she laughed, although her thoughts were rapidly exploring other directions. It could be fun. It could raise money to build their community hall. If that were the case, she would be shirking her duty not to join the troops.

She found it even easier to justify her new-found interest in the stage after their dinner with the Bolinders. As much as they gossiped about Ester, the vanquisher of all carefree delights knew how to create atmosphere. The table was flawlessly set from the centerpiece to the cutlery, with an unblemished linen tablecloth and five courses, excluding dessert, one of those pudding-like dishes sitting on top of what tasted like caramelized brandy. Ester called it flan. Alex ate it in four bites. Doreen copied Ester and Millie, nibbling at it in tiny pieces. Frank ate it with his pinky raised.

It didn't seem Representative Egan spoke a lot, just very earnestly. His eyes crinkled when he talked and his hands touched at the fingertips, then spread outward, as though trying to encompass the ambitions of the entire territory.

As few people as there were, it still wasn't easy. Trappers and miners wanted one thing; homesteaders wanted another. The military wanted construction workers. Construction workers wanted Union jobs and independent contracts. Businesses wanted permits.Conservationists wanted environmental protection laws.

Doreen began to believe in Egan, not because he favored one side over another, but because he was conscious and aware of all the issues and the difficulties in navigating through them.

He would leave nobody by the wayside if he could help it. This she began to believe whole-heartedly before the evening was over.

She told this to Alex on the way home.

"Egan has magnetism."

"He was born here, you know. Out in Valdez. A real up-by-the-bootstraps man. A lumberjack."

"No wonder you like him."

"There's a lot of money to be had in Alaska, Doreen. More than most people realize. They think gold. They think furs. Both are half-emptied out already and don't fetch diddly-squat on the market. There's more. So much more."

"Like what?"

Alex grimaced. "Damned cast. I'll be glad when it comes off. Watch the road, Doreen. All I'm saying is, I've seen the geological surveys. You wouldn't want them in the hands of a greedy man."

Unenlightened as to what resources needed protecting, but agreeable that their community needed healthy growth, Doreen settled into what she discovered to be the very pleasant role of serving on the campaign committee. It meant frequent weekend visits to the Bolinder house, with the Lamars also in attendance. It meant long discussions and taking notes. It meant elegant bowls of nuts and mints, dressing in fine clothes and meeting guests from Anchorage. It also meant a full commitment to the Little Theater that would be staging its first performance with a celebrity in the audience.

Part IV

Beth

Nineteen

Wedging herself into the narrow bench seat between the wall and the table, Beth leaned back and said, "I don't mind not being invited to the Bolinders. Me and Ester never got along much anyway. She's always looking down her long nose at me just because I drink a little. What's wrong with that, I say? It's not like I get stupid about it."

"Nothing's wrong with that," said Hannah in her soft, timid voice.

She looked at Beth with her wide eyes and handed her a beer.

Beth waited until Hannah sat across from her, then popped both beers open with her Swiss Army knife. She placed the knife back in her pocket.

"It's Doreen. Ever since Jimmy Delaney found Alex during the search, Doreen has been glued to Andy like she is her best friend. Gary said it wasn't that amazing. Jimmy just took the most logical direction and found a few prints. It's the prompt attention that saved his life. I wonder, has she even thanked Sharon?"

The wide eyes looked at Beth reproachfully. "You haven't been to see Sharon?"

"I have, but you know, Sharon is a tomb. She doesn't tell you about nothing."

"Well." Hannah drew herself up and swept back a few dim strands of hair that had gotten in her face. "She was here a few days ago, dropping off some sweaters she and Millie made. That is, she and her husband and that sweet little girl."

The bitterness of the last few weeks welled up in Beth's throat with each swallow. "Juliana? I don't know why her mother is raising her so proper out here in the middle of the wilderness, but Sharon says they may even buy a piano later down the line. Can you imagine someone buying their kid a piano? It must cost a million dollars."

Hannah gasped and raised her brows. "Rick moaned and groaned about giving the boys a football. But it was Christmas, you know, so he finally did."

Beth glanced at the kids playing on the meager floor. Most of the toys had been donated. She recognized a few. Still, there really was a football, closely guarded by the eldest.

"We can't deprive them. There's natural things they expect out of life. Boys have their trucks and football. Girls have their dolls and party dresses. That's the way of things, no matter where you are. But buying a piano....There's only some that would think it's the way of things."

"Do the white-collar workers make a lot of money?"

Beth scoffed and lit a cigarette. Noticing a look on Hannah's face that was much like a puppy waiting politely for a treat, she shook another from her pack and offered it. Hannah took it and sat back with her legs crossed, dangling the cigarette like a starlet in an all-star restaurant.

Beth let two expert smoke rings rise to the ceiling, impressing Hannah, who had developed no real smoking skills at all. "No, they don't make any more money than we do. It's all in your ratings. Hell, Art isn't even white collar. He's a construction engineer. I guess it don't make him completely blue collar but he ain't white collar, either. He's got an inheritance. It ain't much, but it gives them plenty of money to fall back on. It's a good thing, too, because that plant nursery won't be paying off any time soon."

Hannah leaned over her chair to shoo a toddler from under the table. She straightened and resumed her practiced smoking position. "Rick said we should invest in something practical that makes money right away."

"Like what?"

"He's thinking pigs."

"They do a lot of rooting."

"There's a lot to be rooted."

"Could be." Beth contemplated her beer. "Watch them around the birch trees. If they pull out the roots of one, wham. A whole line of birch will fall over."

"Then I better tell Rick before he goes chopping any of them."

"The birch? Yeah. Not the pigs, I hope." Beth frowned at the painting on the wall behind Hannah's head. It wasn't a real painting, just a cheap representation of a bullfighter made to look like it had the rough surface of a real painting. It bothered her somehow. It was incongruous with sled dogs and fur parkas.

"Doreen says she's going to raise goats this year. She can't grow anything on her land except potatoes. She doesn't have enough good topsoil is what it is. Half this area is rock and gravel. The rest is black silt so rich if you don't find something to mix it with, the plants can't grow. Ain't much you can tell Doreen about these things, though. Especially not now that she's putting on airs."

Hannah crossed one arm across her chest to clasp the arm holding up her cigarette. "You miss Doreen."

"Hah!" Spat Beth. "I do not miss Doreen. "Do you know, she even has Andy's sister come over every other Saturday night to babysit so she and Alex can go out on the town? Can you imagine it? That girl... What's her name? Carol! She's a boy chaser. You know what that means."

When Hannah gave her a blank look, Beth explained. "I'll bet she has boys over when Doreen and Alex are gone."

"Do you think?" asked Hannah, taking this all in as though it was extraordinary news.

"Well, I don't know for sure. It's not like I spy on them, but I'll tell you this. I have half a mind to leave the performing troops."

Hannah gave her a shocked look. "You wouldn't!"

Beth slumped suddenly. "No, I wouldn't. I made a promise and I'm keeping it. But now, Doreen has started coming to practice. She can't do anything. She's about as round as she is tall right now, but it's seeing her there. I do miss her."

"Then why don't you visit her?"

Beth looked at her beer sourly, then at her son, who was tentatively trying to make friends with Hannah's only girl. The girl was around the same age as Cody and around the same size, but she shrank away as though he was older and stronger.

"She's too busy to come see me in her big, fancy car. Why should I go to see her? The only reason I have a car today is because Gary agreed to let me use it once a week while he goes to work with Art. I'm not going to waste my time going to visit someone who doesn't come to see me."

"Well, that's still nice. That Gary lets you use the car, that is. Rick would never allow it. Not that I know how to drive anyway." Hannah laughed self-consciously.

"Hmm." Beth shrugged aside Hannah's words with a wave of her hand. "It wasn't like he went down without a fight. He had every reason he needed the car, mainly because Art never puts in overtime and Gary likes to put in an extra hour or two a day. But I told him, with spring coming in, I needed the car to go out to the valley and pick up the things we need for planting. We're planting this year."

"I wish Rick could get overtime. We need the extra money."

"When the snow melts. There will be lots of overtime when the snow melts."

"You know," said Hannah, clearing her throat. "Gary is Rick's foreman. Gary could get him extra work."

Beth dropped her head and studied her fingernails intently. It was an unspoken rule between them. Beth never interfered with her husband's job. "I can ask him," she finally said grudgingly.

She looked at her watch. "How time flies! I've got to go into the valley and pick up the new rototiller. Don't forget, Friday night, Canasta. It will be good for the kids. It will give them a whole extra room to play in."

"We don't have much room here," sniffed Hannah wistfully. "They like getting out."

"Don't worry about it none. The first winter is always the hardest. By next summer, you'll be sitting pretty. Mark my word."

The beer had affected her more than she cared to admit. It was too early in the day to be drinking, yet she had wanted to.

She had craved being in that humble trailer, with no rules, no obligations. Sharon would have called it, "slumming it." Damn Sharon.

She didn't drive into the valley right away. She stopped by the river, sluggishly oozing into the inlet, bloated with ice that had begun to crack and heave with the early thaw. She rolled down the window to let the salty wind sting her face.

She had lied about Juliana getting a piano. It was for Art. He knew how to play. Their practices had been at the VFW hall, which recently had acquired an old, slightly out of tune and somewhat tinny sounding piano. It worked for Art, though. Somehow, he managed to squeeze out enough harmonious sounds for them to resemble performing artists. The harmony, it was hoped, would get better with the Palmer auditorium's well-maintained piano, or with a great deal of practice among the participants.

Juliana would probably learn to play, though. She was a child prodigy or something. She was already potty trained and speaking short sentences. She drew squiggly things on paper instead of scribbling all over the page.

"Mama?" asked Cody, tugging at her. She glanced down. He had been making "vroom" noises with his toy truck but now his face was questioning. She rolled the window half-way as a compromise and patted his hand. He continued playing.

Cody was a good boy. He didn't talk much but he was the only one in the group who played well with girls. He was nice. That counted for something. She felt sorry for Millie. She just had a girl and Ester had another boy. That left little Nancy only Patsy and a prodigy to play with, and they would both be two years older. The poor thing. If Doreen didn't have another girl, the newcomer would grow up with the worst gang of toddler bullies in town.

She didn't want to think about Doreen. Doreen had a new circle of friends. She had moved up the ladder with her fancy new car and had started rubbing shoulders with politicians. Whoever would have thought it? Frank and Charlie ate politics for breakfast, but she had always believed Alex was a regular guy once he left the office.

He never talked about weird things like the growing Communist threat or who would be running for president in a country that now seemed so far away it hardly seemed important who was sitting behind the desk. They were here. With or without US help, they would survive. The military wasn't leaving. She was sure of that. Not while they wrung their hands over Russia. But now, here was Alex, snapping to attention and running around with as much political fever as Charlie and Frank, and there was Doreen, right behind him.

The air was moist, disguising the handful of salty tears that trickled down her face. She found a handkerchief in her coat pocket and dried herself, rolling the window up at the same time. She felt better now. She knew what the problem was. She needed to have another baby. There were too many boys. They needed more girls. She knew her second one would be a girl. She could feel it.

She drove back out to the road, feeling refreshed. She did get to meet Representative Egan at the Wolf Creek meeting. She even shook hands with him and sort of listened to his answer after asking about getting a school in their district. He looked like a regular guy, not too tall, with a round face and a round bend to his shoulders, but he talked like a politician. All she wanted was an answer in number of years and she received a full campaign speech on demographic dynamics. There wasn't one of them who gave a simple yes or no, but he did have a nice voice, the kind you believed, like a teacher who talked about things way over your head yet was kind enough not to expect you to understand.

She stopped at a diner to buy coffee and a hamburger to split with Cody. The coffee made her feel sharp and alert. By the time they finished the hamburger, she was sober.

The rototiller was much larger than she had thought it would be. They were barely able to get it into the trunk of the car. One wheel skidded dangerously close to the edge and the handlebars stuck out triumphantly. They solved the problem by roping down the trunk and tying a small red piece of cloth to the handlebars.

Gary was right. The rototiller was a good investment, maybe a better deal than Doreen's Pontiac. Not only would they be able to punch out their garden quickly, but they could also rent it out to the rest of the community and get their money back before spring was over.

Beth was suddenly inspired about her garden. She would show the rest how it was done. She wouldn't have any of Sharon's fancy plants and shrubs, but she could grow a hell of a crop full of winter vegetables. She would be the weed puller of the year. She would grow cabbages so big, just one would fill the back of a truck. She would grow green beans fifteen inches long.

Beth was in a much better mood when Gary got home. Her life had regained purpose. She would grow enough vegetables to keep the entire community happy and she would have a little girl to play with the poor prodigy, Juliana, Patsy, and Millie's new daughter, Nancy. Maybe her daughter would also be a prodigy. What a contribution she would make!

She was in such an excellent mood that she brought the round, aluminum tub off the wall, filled it with warm, scented water and took a scrunched-up tub bath. When she was finished, she put on a clean dress and red lipstick.

She had his slippers and a beer waiting for him when he came home. He slumped in his armchair, one of their first pieces of furniture, already growing old and tired, dingy with the dirt and grime he brought in with him from long hours on the big machines. He groaned and put up his feet on the milking stool they used as a footrest. He grumbled, "They're already bringing in more military personnel and we haven't half-finished the new landing strip."

"Why don't you let your team put in some overtime?" She asked, tucking a pillow under his feet.

He opened his beer and took a long swallow, smacking his lips and burping before answering. "We've been running the plows hard all winter. Broken hoses and belts, blown radiators, cracked engine blocks. Do you know what happens when you have a cracked engine block?"

"You put in a new engine."

"Yeah." He set down his half-finished beer and fished for a cigarette. "Anyone wants overtime needs to talk to Matt. He's been up to his elbows all winter repairing the equipment."

She sat on the sofa, her feet tucked under her, and leaned forward. "Rick needs some overtime work."

Gary grunted. "Rick dented a plow blade the other day. Warped it good. Reckon we can eventually straighten it out, but in the meantime, we're out one truck until we find another plow. You got dinner ready?"

She nodded. "Rabbit stew. Do you want it in here or at the table?"

"I'll eat in here. Put the boy up to the table, though. He might as well learn some manners."

"He should eat by himself?"

"Why not? It's not like he needs supervision. He knows what he's doing."

She brought two bowls of thick stew into the living room and set them on the end table. Cody seemed unconcerned with eating alone, taking advantage of the lack of supervision to handle the food with his fingers. Beth didn't correct him. "I invited the Millers over for Friday night Canasta."

"Why did you do that? What happened to Saturday night with the Bowens?"

"Nothing happened to Saturday night with the Bowens. Can't we have more than one night a week that we go visiting or have visitors?"

"I reckon there's nothing wrong with it, especially if they're coming here. We won't have to go anywhere." He picked at the stew. "Did we run out of moose?"

"Nearly. I saved a little, but it won't last out the spring."

"How much did you give the Millers?" He didn't wait for her to answer. "I know you feel bad about them. We all do, but Rick Miller works for me. A lot of his bad luck is his fault."

"Like the dented plow?"

"I suppose it could happen to anyone. We're pushing ice. What does a guy from Arkansas know about ice?"

She stretched across the arm of the couch to adjust the kerosene lamp, which had grown dim. The brighter beam spilled over the front of her dress, lighting the swells over the dark vee of her blouse opening. "They've gotta have the time to settle in, Gary. They weren't assigned here. They came on their own, without knowing a thing."

She returned to eating but his eyes remained fixed on the curve of her neck ducking under a laced collar. "I suppose it's hard," he agreed.

He had discovered his moral compass often needed correcting by his wife's more accurate instruments and did little to oppose them. Typical of so many of the pioneers, he believed women belonged to a superior species with far more wisdom to discern right from wrong than men have. If they said something was true, it must be true.

Satisfied he had acquired the correct attitude concerning life with the Millers, she asked, "where are they going to put all the new military?"

He shrugged. "Don't know. It's not my problem. Art told them we wouldn't be able to resume construction until spring. Brass doesn't listen. It gives orders and expects them carried out. Well, guess what? We're civilians. We're not military. We don't try to do the impossible, only the improbable."

After she had put Cody to bed, dazed with a bath he had not seen coming, (but one cannot waste heated bath water after all) she brought out the bottle of gin and prepared two hot toddies. They sipped them together until they both felt warm and relaxed. Gary quietly contemplated going to bed, but Beth had better ideas than falling asleep in the same mystified daze as Cody.

While Gary rumbled about the bedroom, not at all concerned with his toiletry, but desirous of finding the automobile magazine that had just come in the mail, and leafing through it, dreaming of larger and more impressive cars than Doreen's Pontiac, Beth retired to the bathroom.

She slipped into the negligee she saved only for special occasions. It was silky and kind to large figures. It had a tropical floral print and a low-necked, black lace bodice. It was the only thing she had that made her feel sexy. As she rubbed rose water over her shoulders and neck, she thought to herself, *I can do this.*

Beth took a lot of pride in her relationship with Gary. Unlike Doreen, who married after a whirlwind affair, Millie, who received her proposal through a letter or Sharon, *whose marriage had been one of convenience,* she reminded herself with emphasis, Beth had married her childhood sweetheart.

They had done everything the proper way. They got to know each other and helda big church wedding with all their family members and friends. She knew the meaning of every breath Gary took. Did he know the meaning of hers? She was determined to find out.

He was still flipping through his magazine when she returned, happy to have found it under the bed. She turned the lamp so low; it barely produced a whimper. He frowned.

"I was still reading," he said, without looking up.

"I don't want to read," she said in what she hoped was a seductive voice. It came out sounding like she was catching a cold.

This time he did look up. She stood next to the lamp, the light rosy against her silken nightgown. "Did I miss our anniversary?" he worried.

"No. It's not until next month." Unsure of how to proceed, she sat on the edge of the bed and sank a hand into his hair. Gary kept his hair short. It was spiky under her fingers. "It seems silly to waste perfectly good nightclothes. I've only worn this gown five times. Should I really just save it for our anniversary?"

"Well, I like it on you."

"We could buy another when it wears out." She leaned closer to him, so the silky material brushed against his arms.

His eyes widened in surprise. "Why, Mrs. Hughes, are you coming on to me?"

She pulled up his tee shirt and stroked the curling hairs trailing down to his navel. "Is it working?"

"A little," he said with a pleased smile, folding his arms above his head.

She kissed him and let her hand travel further down. She heard him suck in his breath. "And now?"

"What do you want? A new car?"

"A baby."

He pulled her down on top of him with an urgency matched only by her own. Maybe it was the hot toddies. Maybe it was the rose water and slippery negligee that had been worn only once a year. They made love passionately and joyfully. It was free and exploratory. It was exuberant. It was everything their years of knowing each other should have been.

Afterward, when Gary had gone to sleep, she stared at the ceiling and wondered, *what was different?* They had made love like the first weeks they had been together. It wasn't just the light perfume or negligee. It wasn't something she had said.

It was something she had done.

She had never before made the first move.

Well, why not? She scolded herself roundly.

There's no harm in a woman letting her man know she wants him. I'll bet Andy does it all the time. It was indecent of Andy. Three men, for heaven's sake.

Twenty

Spring came in its leisurely manner and the Big Event loomed near. It was even bigger now that everyone knew Representative Egan would be coming. Everyone wanted to get on stage. They had three more chorus line volunteers and a librarian who claimed to be a psychic. Her act was funny and involved planting members of their acting troop in the audience to ask her questions.

Even Dresden Hayes volunteered to recite Robert Service poetry and Gordon Phillips planned to play a saw.

Beth was beginning to like the Phillips brothers, at least she liked Gordon. Hank left for Japan with the first warming trends of March, without anyone learning so much as his opinion on the communist menace.

Brad was too young to be a real human being yet. He drank with the men when he could shoulder his way his way into a conversation. When he couldn't, he sauntered outside with a beer and waited for the teenaged crowd to cluster around him. They always did. Brad was the popular guy around the youngsters.

Gordon involved himself. That's what Beth noticed about him. He was only a year or two older than Jimmy, which meant he had also missed the draft, but he had signed up with the Youth Corps and served two years, so he was respected.

There were other differences between Jimmy and Gordon. Gordon was a thinker and a listener. He began attending community meetings on a regular basis and signed up for their volunteer fire department. Already, he had his own field phone and was taking the first-aid courses for ambulance services.

The warming spring sun found its way into a small window, recently bared to bring in the natural light. As Beth and the experienced veterans knew would happen, the melting snow swamped the area around the poorly perched Miller trailer, cracking open to reveal raw, bubbling earth and water.

The walkway from the car to the house had been impossible to navigate without rubber bootsand the drive itselfwas six inches deep in mud. Tree branches had been cut and crossed over watery potholes sinking deeply into frosty sludge.

There were no roots to hold the earth down in the ripped clearing Rick had made with his truck and plow. The saturated ground, washing out where the land reared in uneven bumps, gathered, and flowed freely into the dips and spread thickly over flat earth.

The rocks, scraped clear of their thick soil layer at the top of each bump, clinked together, chuckling with the roar of each vehicle grinding over them. Instead of flattening, each vehicle that passed over it, sank the crude driveway deeper, with mud banks welling up on each side and boulders displaying their jagged teeth.

It was a good thing the Millers had a small trailer. It wouldn't be hard to move it to higher ground once the land dried and they could build a proper foundation. Finishing her appraisal of the Phillips brothers, Beth took a few sips of the almost tasteless coffee and set the cup away from her.

"Anyway," she told Hannah, trying to keep her voice cool enough to prevent a whine in her tone. "I hope Frank remembers Gary and I were among the first to join the performing troops, long before anyone knew we would be performing in front of a celebrity."

Groping under the table until she found her purse, she shifted it to her lap and began rummaging the contents. She pulled out a compact mirror and patted her nose.

"It seems to me Doreen has taken up a sense of her own importance. The very first night she showed up, nearly as big around as she was tall, she began taking over the choreography. Bumped Ester right out of her place. I can tell you. I never saw Ester look so astonished."

Putting the compact back, she snapped the purse shut and tried the coffee again. It had not improved. She shrugged.

"Maybe it did come out for the best. Ester is a poor dancer and Doreen does seem to know what she was talking about, but between you and me, I can't help feeling the only reason Doreen joined the performing group was because of Rep. Egan."

"Is Rep. Egan an important man?" asked Hannah. She was ignorant in these things. Important men to her were the ones she had seen in the movies.

"He could well be," said Beth with an air of authority. "With the elections. We're voting for him."

"Oh. I don't know that Rick votes for much of anybody. He ain't never talked to me about it. He voted for Truman though, then got sorry about it. I don't know what to think."

"That happens to everybody. Not that it matters much up here. The best we can do is send someone to Washington that's looking out for us."

"I see." Hannah tapped her fingers on the table. "Nobody but you have come to visit in a month. I think everyone has forgotten about me." She sniffed a little. "Do you want a beer?"

The coffee was terrible. It tasted like reused grounds. "Yes, I would," Beth replied. "I need something to wet my tonsils. Things around here are so busy. Sharonisworking in her greenhouses. Charlie is building something. Who knows what? Doreen has been Her Royal Highness ever since she had the baby."

Hannah opened the two beers over the sink and brought them to the table. "She had her baby? What was it?"

"Doreen had her baby in March. It was a boy, just as I suspected. You should see her at practice. She and Millie and Ester march in like royalty, carrying their babies as heirs to the crown. Of course, they are all cute, just weeks apart and still in the soft-boned stage, with tiny fists that wave in the air without acknowledging their owner." She smoothed back a pang of jealousy with the palm of her hand.

"What I want to know is, what will Nancy do around so many boys? Andso rough and tumble. Not at all like Cody."

Hannah looked at her beer. "I have a little girl," she said as though she was offering up her child to the common good.

"Yes, you do," Beth agreed, glancing at Polly, who wasn't much distinguishable from the boys. She wore the same ragged clothes, played in solitude with the same ragged toys, no sounds bubbling from her lips, her wheat-colored hair falling in her face. "A very lovely girl."

"She's a quiet one but she gives us grief. She don't come when she's called and she don't do what she's told."

"Well, two-year-old's," said Beth, shrugging. "They get like that. As I was explaining, though, Ester and Doreen got into a big fight. Ester didn't want the dancers to kick their legs so high for the can-can number and Doreen told her that's crazy. Can-can dancers kick their legs. All dancers kick their legs, she said, and they can't dance if they can't do some kicking."

Hannah gasped and tapped her throat with her fist, nearly choking on her beer. She could not imagine anyone arguing with Ester. "Was Ester mad?"

"A little at first, but when Doreen came back all skinny and showed them how she danced, Ester simmered down. She's French you know."

Hannah said, "I see," as though she did, even while trying to grasp the true significance of being French.

"Anyway." Beth drew two cigarettes from her pack and tossed one to Hannah. "Frank put Ester in charge of costuming, and I think she likes it better. That woman can't dance, Hannah. There's not a bone in her body that's got rhythm."

Hannah whispered, "is that gossip?"

"No," Beth told her, saluting her beer to Hannah's. "It's the gospel truth but don't spread it around. Nobody wants to be quoted as the one who said Ester's got no rhythm."

Hannah seemed to find this bit of information far more pleasurable than learning who would be on stage or that Representative Egan would be watching the Wolf Creek Players. "And Jimmy Delaney's girlfriend," she pressed. "Is she really a good singer?"

Beth said, "Hah!" loudly, followed by a satisfying belch. "Don't get me wrong. She's a pretty girl and she dazzles a dude's eyes when she's up there on the stage. But her voice is kind of weak. It doesn't carry. Millie sings better. I've heard her, but Millie won't sing solo. She'll only sing and dance in the chorus line."

"I've heard you sing, Beth. You're pretty good."

She tossed her shoulders as though it didn't matter. "I can't sing so high, but I hit all the right notes and my voice carries. It carries real good. I'm an alto or a tenor or something like that. Frank told me about it."

"I don't know what I am," said Hannah wistfully. "I think a Catholic."

Beth gave her another salute. "Well, they sing too."

Cody began to whine, reminding Beth of the hour.

"I do have to go home. We have rehearsal tonight and every night for the next five days. I'm running ragged. You and Rick really ought to come to the opening and bring the kids. It will be good for them."

Hannah said that she would, but who knew really. The only way to get the Millers to go anywhere was to drag them by the hair. Well, Beth decided she had done her good deed for the day. She was watching out for the Millers even though the rest of the community was running around like peacocks.

It wasn't a good evening. Confiding in Hannah had not helped her mood that was rapidly becoming more irritable. She burned the meatloaf they were to have for dinner. She fumed over the costume Ester had designed for her, saying it made her look like a daffodil.

"I can't go on stage like this," she told Gary tearfully.

"Then put on overalls," he told her. "You're Betsy from Pike. You can wear what you please."

She didn't want to wear overalls and resigned herself to the yellow polka-dot dress. She would look like a giant, dancing flower. What could be more impressive?

The evening didn't get any better. The VFW Hall felt cold and hostile. Their voices echoed in the near-empty room. The furnace wasn't working correctly, adding a grumbling background to their music.

It got on Beth's nerves. She screamed at Art that he was playing in the wrong key, although it was impossible to tell what key was being played on a tone-deaf piano. Her clogs weren't right. They double clacked. Gary fumed he had worked on her clogs for two days to get them to clack correctly.

She wasn't the only one at her wits' end. Ester was grinding down her molars because the can-can dancers' bloomers didn't quite cover the tops of their mesh stockings.

Andy's little sister, Anna, who was going to do some rodeo tricks, got tangled in her rope and burst into tears. Dresden Hayes got drunk and fell off his chair. Frank threw down his director's script three times and went into a corner to sulk. Millie had to bring him out.

Gary was grinding some molars, or at least a few gears on their sedan as they drove home. "Well, that was a fiasco," he said as they rumbled into the drive.

Beth said nothing. She was suddenly nauseated. She bolted out of the car and dashed around to the puddling side of the house vomiting.

The steps came thickly through the slush. A shadow bent in the evening. Gary held up a flashlight, Cody just behind him, the silhouette of his little face gaping with wonder.

"Just how much have you had to drink?" His voice sounded like the rumble of the engine.

Already, the world was righting itself. It was just a short, dizzy spell. Beth patted her face with the melting snow, then wiped it with her sleeve. "Not that much, really. Only two beers in the entire day."

His anger turned to suspicion as he helped her to her feet. "Are you pregnant?"

"Pregnant?" Why hadn't she thought of that? She had been so busy she had let the days slip. She placed one hand over her stomach. It did feel more solid, not just the soft pouch she was accustomed to carrying around.

She counted back the days in her head to the last time she had menstruated. "Oh, my God!" Her hand flew from her stomach to her mouth. "I'm nearly three months along!"

She grasped his arm with both her hands, her thoughts racing on this astonishing discovery, while Cody plodded along behind them, finding some large and satisfying puddles to wade through. He was soaking wet from his knees down by the time they reached the porch.

Not even bothering to scold him, Beth stripped Cody of his garments and placed him in a dry pair of pajamas.

"Go to bed now. It's late. And consider yourself lucky if you don't catch cold."

"What's wrong with me?" She asked, turning to Gary. "How could I not have noticed? I'm losing my mothering instinct!"

He folded his arms across his chest, studied her a moment, then grunted. "It's all there. You've just been busy mothering Hannah and cubs."

The next two evenings of rehearsals brought their own disasters. The entire cast had the jitters. Tammy had decided, for an unspoken reason, that Jimmy had broken her heart and cried each time she sang.

In a fit of jealousy, one of the can-can dancers tripped up another, causing her to sprain her ankle. Fortunately, it was a light enough sprain to perform on opening night.

The evening before dress rehearsal, Frank became so depressed, he stood with his arms folded, his back to the stage and smoked his pipe. Not even Millie was able to appease him. She pleaded and he simply tilted his head and blew smoke rings at the ceiling.

It was at that point that Betty Lou walked in. "Well, I'm ready to perform," she said, walking right up to the stage.

"You can't perform," said Frank, turning his head ninety degrees but leaving it tilted. "You haven't practiced."

"I been practicing all my life. You just ain't seen my gifts yet," she answered proudly. "Anyways, I don't see nobody else practicing. They're just sitting on their butts complaining."

"We had a quarrel," said Ester stiffly. "It's over now."

The others agreed. It was over now. "Then iffen you don't mind, I'll just watch to see how it comes out," offered Betty Lou.

With an audience of one, they were better focused, not to mention just a little ashamed of themselves. They went through their routines as flawlessly as could be expected in a room with a kinky piano and a bellowing furnace.

Betty Lou was a marvelous audience. She clapped, stamped, and whistled, however, she still felt should be squeezed into one of the skits. She was finally told she could work backstage on the props. Although it meant working with Ester, Betty Lou felt sufficiently enlightened to handle the task.

The performing troops went out to the valley for the dress rehearsal to accustom themselves to the stage and a properly tuned piano.

They were as nervous as lemmings at the edge of a cliff.Despite an empty auditorium, it felt like the whole world was watching. Nearly everyone appeared at least an hour earlier than scheduled to do a few warm-up practices.

Art had even taken the day off from work so he could familiarize himself with keys that did notplunkor stick.

When Beth arrived, two hours early, Ester was already examining the costumes and sets, fretting to herself, Anna was determinedly whipping around her rope, and two of the chorus girls were quarreling with another about being out of step.

Beth and Gary used the quarrel to instruct Art to take their number from the top. They tried it out, worked on their clogs, then tried it out once more. Not wishing to appear frivolous, the chorus line united and wheedled the piano player into one more attempt at a previously failed dance number.

Frank arrived with his typical punctuality; fifteen minutes early. Millie had once said she had never seen Frank arrive late for anything. If they could have scheduled an exact time for their children to arrive, he would have demanded they come fifteen minutes early. The invisible audience turned with expectancy as he walked through the door.

Beth felt her stomach muscles tighten and her heart hammer against her chest. This was their last chance to get it right.

Even Ester held her breath and stood motionless by the rack of costumes. The curtains rippled back in shushed awe. With an opening whistle, Frank scampered across the stage in a bowler hat and cane.

Close behind him pranced Charlie with a Billy club and a big yellow star on his chest. The piano tinkled merrily. The skirts of the chorus line flashed and danced. They performed without a mishap. The timing was excellent. Only once, as the curtains closed for each act, did they open with Betty Lou still moving around the props.

At first, Frank said nothing about their performance. He was still brooding over their disastrous week. He kept his head bowed as he took center stage, refusing eye contact with his troops. They sighed and shifted uneasily, wondering what they had done wrong.

"Do you know what they are going to say about Chugiak people when they see us up there on the stage? Do you?"

He demanded his brows furrowed together. The players hung their head and looked at their hands.

"They are going to say," he said warningly, "They will say…. That's the best damned variety show I've ever seen!"

Gary whistled a sigh of relief through his teeth. The chorus girls squealed while they jumped up and down. Tammy burst into tears and cried on Jimmy's shoulders. When the group prepared to leave, they cheered and hustled out the doors as though they had been to a pep rally for a baseball game. It was the same euphoria and expectancy.

They went home and celebrated. The next day, after breakfast, Beth found it appropriate to celebrate a little more. An hour before they were to leave for the valley, she handed Gary a beer and drank a gin with Kool Aid. "I just need to loosen up a little," she told him.

Beth wasn't the only one loosening up. When they arrived at the auditorium, they discovered a few of their players were finding courage in a bottle. Dresden was rinsing his mouth with vodka, explaining he was gargling. Tammy was crying again, and Jimmy was comforting her with a metal flask.

Betty Lou was also carrying a flask, which she giggled over as she watched Ester abuse Dresden for drinking. Her crafty eyes lit up when she saw Beth, and hastily beckoned her to her conspiratorial corner.

"She'll get after Dresden good, but she won't go after a Delaney. No siree. She won't come after me, neither. Do you know why?"

Beth shook her head and accepted the drink offered.

"No, why?"

Betty Lou wriggled to make herself more comfortable on the three-legged milk stool intended for a prop.

"I don't know why, either. I was hoping you would know."

She stuffed the flask inside her clothes and rubbed her nose with the back of her hand.

"There now. Gotta fix up the stage. You just stay there, Miss Daisy Chain. I'll be right back."

The warm glow from Betty Lou's finely distilled moonshine left Beth wanting a little more. She tasted it on her lips as she watched Betty Lou change the set, then deliberately go behind one of the props and wait. When the curtains opened for the expectant audience, she came out and waved.

The audience tittered. The two girls running out from left and right stage in black spangled swimsuits fluffed out with crinoline had no ideas as to what was happening behind them.

They assumed their perky entrance had caused viewer enthusiasm and brightened their glittery appearance even more, emphasizing the shake of their fannies as they placed the two cards that together, announced, "Act One".

This upset Ester dreadfully. Frank was having too much fun being chased by Charlie around the stage as they announced each new act to notice any misbehavior backstage, but Ester's sharp, bright eyes saw it all. She began scolding everyone in sight she suspected of having a nip, except, as Betty Lou pointed out, Jimmy Delaney and herself.

The can-can girls were lining up. Betty Lou gave Beth another taste of her spirits. "I don't know why," she said confidentially. "You ain't up there with them frilly dancers, Daisy Chain. You're as good, if not better than any of them. Show me that clod hopping again."

"Clogging," amended Beth.

The two began clogging. They didn't really think about where they were going, just looking at their feet. The whistles and cheers coming primarily from the male members of the audience, suddenly turned to roaring laughter. Beth looked up. They were dancing with the can-can girls.

No sooner did she realize this, then Ester had them both by the back of their collars and was marching them off the set. A round of applause followed them.

Whatever scalding words of enduring shame she had in store for them were quickly cut short by Frank's appearance.

"That was great! That was great!" He said, pumping Betty Lou's hand and patting Beth on the shoulder. "I wish you had let me know a little sooner. It was a bit of a surprise, but that was great. That's the spirit."

Ester's long mouth clamped together and turned down. "You're on after this next act," she snipped at Beth. "See if you can detach yourself from your furry companion."

"Yada, yada," said Betty Lou. "C'mon now, Daisy Chain. Your hubby is waiting."

Gary was waiting and looking a little thunderous. When did he become such a wet blanket? Beth laughed as she took his arm and clacked her shoes, urging him to clack his. "Not yet," he whispered. "Wait until we go out."

She gave his arm a squeeze and turned her head, mouthing the words, "sourpuss" to Betty Lou. Betty Lou chuckled and took another swig from her flask.

Having demonstrated his ability to yodel, the railroad man's son was leaving the stage and the curtains were closing. He received a hardy round of applause and a few sighs from the teenaged girls.

A goat cart, a caged chicken and a few other props were being dragged out to change the set. Frank started his spiel. "As the wagon wheels crossed the desert, there were many that expired by the wayside. One such...."

"Halt!" Cried Charlie with a shrill whistle. "Arrest this man! He's stealing an act!"

As they scampered across the stage, the piano tinkled, and the curtains opened. "With a doodle-lang fall, did-ay doodle-lang fall."

Their clogs were clattering. In time, out of time, all together with a skip and a circle-your-partner. Beth's voice was unleashed. "They broke out the whiskey and Betsy got tight!"

She crashed into the goat cart. She turned over the cage, setting the rooster loose. She rolled on the floor, yipping, "down on the sand she lay rolling about" and remained while her husband looked on in ghastly surprise.

A stomp on the stage and a new voice roared out, "Betsy, get up, you'll get sand in your eyes!"

It was worthy to note that this was the only song Betty Lou really knew, but she was enthusiastic about it. She pulled Beth to her feet as though she was light as a feather and stomped her fur covered feet in time to the music. "Doodle-lang fall, di-di-all. Do-lang fall, did-ay."

The duet became a threesome, and the threesome brought a flurry of devotion. The audience screamed. They stood up in their seats. They thundered so loudly, they nearly brought down the auditorium. Sweet Betsy from Pike was the smash hit of the evening.

Beth was as drunk on success as she was on the nips she had taken from Betty Lou's flask. She saw each act come and go from backstage, felt the rush as the players prepared, joined in the girlish giggling, and jumped up and down with each roar of approval from the audience, but she felt, her act had been the best. She knew it had been, even if Jimmy's guitar had made half the women swoon in their seats and openly melt. Tammy had a weak voice, and it was only the guitar people heard.

She knew she was the best when they held their celebration party afterward. They used one of the back rooms of the auditorium. It had been adequately prepared for moderate success, although this was a wild success. There were balloons and cake and ice cream for the kids and champagne for the adults.

There were cheers and congratulations. Oh! Were there cheers!Beth thought they were all for her. She raised her arms high like a champion. She pulled Dresden from his chair and danced with him. She danced with Frank. She danced with Charlie. Unaware of the scene going on around her, she suddenly realized she was dancing with Representative Egan. She stopped for a second, uncertain.

"Show me how to do that clog again," he urged.

She didn't need much encouragement. The drunken night was magnificently alive and applauding her name with every exalted breath. She clacked her shoes and he imitated her, failing only twice to keep in step. She held up his hand and announced loudly, "Our future Senator!"

If only the glorious party had not ended with a crash. Her crash. Her words, spoken in carelessness.

Maybe it was all true. Maybe she had gotten carried away and had a little too much to drink. She didn't remember much after the Important Man left, only that she cheered, danced. and sang a little louder, a little more exuberantly than the rest. She believed she bragged.

They all thought it was funny when she talked about how she was fifty-pound beets and rutabagas and that her little girl- she knew in that secret communication between infant and mother that she had a girl - would pop out playing a piano. But then, Beth told Doreen…

Yes, she could remember it now. She told Doreen…

Representative Egan liked her best. He had taken a drink with her. He had danced with her.

And she had told Doreen, "Shove that up your fancy patootie."

Gary had taken her home silently, grimly. He wasn't nice about it. He had let the unfortunate car express his disapproval, revving it impatiently while waiting for it to warm up, shifting gears noisily, finding every rough patch in the road to rattle through. She slept most of the way.

When they reached the doorstep, he shook her roughly. Her head felt loose. She tried to keep it from wobbling, then closed her eyes again. She heard him get out of the vehicle, slamming the door so hard it made her shudder.

Cody cried from the back seat. The back door opened.

Gary cursed, then said, "c'mon, Cody." Some sniffling. A slight shuffling, then the back door slammed, and the car shuddered.

There were a few moments of blessed silence, in which she was slipping off once more into nirvana, when the door on her side abruptly opened. She would have tumbled to the ground if he had not caught her by the arm. "Get out!" He commanded.

Her legs barely allowed her to stand. He wrapped an arm around her back, propelling her forward. She made it to the porch steps and threw up.

He waited while she crouched on her knees, the whole evening, with all its crazy, chaotic performances, spewing out her throat while the night sky sparkled dizzily above. He waited as bits and pieces of the evening came back to her and she realized she had been an ass.

She had made a spectacle of herself. She crawled to a patch of nearly melted snow and rubbed it over her face. It stung and felt alive and clean at the same time.

He helped her to her feet, muttering about "crazy, damned women", and led her into the house. Walking made her dizzy again. She made it to the kitchen and plopped down in a chair, her stomach swelling and heaving. "Here," he said, giving her a bucket to vomit into. She threw up the rest of her evening's disgusting exhibition, laid her head on the table and cried.

She didn't know how long she sat there sniffling, the tabletop as comfortable as a pillow, but it was long enough for Gary to bring a warm bowl of water and a hot cup of coffee. He made her drink the coffee first, then wiped away her face with a wet towel.

"I fucked up," she said, her mouth no longer censoring her language.

He grunted. "It won't be the first time. Do you remember when you were sixteen and stumbled into the 4th of July fireworks display just as they were set to go off?"

"Yeah," she said ruefully. "Fucked up the whole display. I got a few burns from it, as well."

"You were lucky. It could have been worse."

"It could have, couldn't it?" She sniffed and tried to hold her head up on its own. It crash-landed against her neck explosively, the falling debris of the evening settling into dust. She held it in her hands, groaning.

"How am I ever going to face the others?" The tears start to fall again.

He wiped them away. "Nearly everyone there was drinking. It was a celebration. Frank and Charlie were playing bull and bullfighter with a tablecloth. It will all be forgotten tomorrow."

"Doreen won't forget."

He poured a glass of milk and dropped in a raw egg, scrambling them together.

"Drink this. It will line your stomach."

339

She made a face, but she obeyed. He set down a package of saltine crackers, and she began nibbling at them. She wasn't hungry, but they covered the taste of the egg and milk.

"You know," he said hesitantly. "You really shouldn't drink so much. Not with the baby."

She cradled her stomach remorsefully. She could have said it was Betty Lou's fault. She could have said she had caved to temptation, but she knew the truth. She had been weak. She had always been weak. Alcohol gave her a courage she didn't have on her own.

"I don't want to lose her."

"You lost two others before Cody was born, remember?"

Closing her eyes on the tears, she whispered, "I don't know why I do it."

"You were the wildest girl in Chippewa County. The toughest, too. That's how I knew you were the one for me."

She sniffed. He was beginning to make her feel better. That was one of the best qualities of their marriage. They always had each other's back.

Gary was a drinker too, but he kept it under control. He wouldn't drink during the day, not as a heavy equipment foreman. Mistakes could be fatal.

It was why he was so hard on Rick. It wasn't so much about his homelife, although Rick's homelife left much to be desired. What a man did in his home was his own business, but you don't climb into the big machines with alcohol on your breath. That was Gary's rule.

"Charlie sold his horses to Jimmy."

Now that her head was clear, she was remembering parts of the evening before she got drunk.

He nodded and sat down across from her. "So I heard."

"Are you canceling out on this year's hunting trip?"

He made a face before scoffing deeply from his throat.

"Probably not. We need our game."

"Jimmy's a good kid."

He was being the good husband now, bringing her coffee and lighting her cigarette.

He lit another for himself, studying the glowing end earnestly and blowing out the smoke as a random thought.

"I reckon he knows what he's doing when it comes down to horses. He partnered up with Mark Hansen's brother, Dave. Dave is as good a horseman as you'll ever see."

She swirled the remains of her coffee around in her cup. "Did we do well, Gary? I mean, did we raise enough money?"

"We made enough to buy the lumber. We can begin building the community hall as soon as the ground thaws. Now, little lady, it's off to bed."

"Little lady," she chuckled.

She slept in late the next morning and was awakened to a rumbling sound that was too light to be the tractor. She wrapped a bathrobe around her waist, slid into her boots without tying them and went outside. It was a beautiful morning. It had warmed up so much during the night, that the only patches of snow left were in deep shadow.

Gary was out in the field, trying out the new rototiller. She waded through boggy soil until she was close enough for him to hear. "I thought I was going to try it out first."

He finished the row he was tilling, then idled the machine. "I wanted to see how much backbone you have to put behind it before turning it over to you." He took off his cap and wiped his brow. "Ground's still too wet and frosty for you yet. I don't want you pushing that hard."

She scoffed. "I've broken frozen soil before."

"Not now!" He snapped. The anger he had controlled the evening before flitted across his face and stole into his voice. "Not while you're pregnant!"

"You're afraid." Somehow, this amazed her. She had always thought men didn't really care that much about babies at all. They were just a happenstance of marriage that became tolerable once they learned to walk.

He shouted. "Yes, I am afraid!" He throttled the rototiller back up and shoved it viciously through the earth. It muttered and growled, tearing the smooth field into clumps. "I don't want to go through it again."

He pushed the machine ahead viciously, as though his life depended on it. It whined and grumbled, chewing the earth, spitting it out behind. He was deliberately exhausting himself.

Beth waited until he had cut through another row and returned to her. "I'm not going to lose this baby."

He leaned against the handlebars, catching his breath. "How do you know that? You lost two! How many more will you lose before you can't have any more?"

"I was young and did a lot of stupid things."

"Exactly. No more stupid things, Beth. Not things that risk the baby. No more pushing around heavy equipment. No more lifting heavy weight. You can plant your crops. Pull your weeds. But no heavy stuff, and no drinking."

"A beer in the evening when you come home."

"A beer is good." He turned off the rototiller and wiped his hands with a bandana, an indication he was ready for breakfast. "One beer. I'm not really mad about what you said last night."

"To Doreen?"

"Yeah. They don't have no call to dump us like that. When they ask to rent the rototiller, I'm going to charge them double what I charge everyone else."

"They'll find out."

Spring slid in rapidly over the next two weeks. Within four days, Gary had the garden plot tilled and the manure plowed in. For the next week it sat drying in the strengthening sun.

Gary was right. Half the community wanted to rent his tiller. The Lamars asked for it. The Bolinders and the Rasmussens asked for it. Even Solace drove over in her 1940's heavy-bottomed car and checked on it.

"We always hand plowed a garden in the past," she said. "But it gets wearisome with the years. I reckon we can start doing things the easier way."

Beth had her seeds planted before Sharon and crowed to her abouther early success.

"I've got three rows of garden peas. Gary loves his garden peas, and two rows of carrots, along with everything else that can grow. Some seedlings have already come up!"

342

Sharon wasn't sufficiently impressed. "We ordered some gladiolas that are supposed to do well in cold weather, but we'll see. I started them in the green house. I've got pansies coming up, too. I'll give you some to transplant when they get a little bigger. It's still a bit cold for them."

Beth glanced toward the double row of greenhouses. To the side of one was the neatly plowed vegetable garden, with its straight, hoed rows. It was a little fresher than Beth's and a little wetter, but in a few days, it would be ready for seeds.

"I haven't heard from Doreen for a while," said Beth. "Isn't she planting a garden?"

Sharon had been drawing Beth toward one of the greenhouses. "Oh, Doreen has given up on gardening. She says she just can't do it. They bought goats."

"Why did she do that?"

Sharon looked surprised that Beth should ask.

"Two kids, you know. She said half the paycheck was going down in milk. Maybe you can barter out some of your vegetables for milk this fall."

"Are the goats already milking?"

"They drop their babies in February."

They had stopped by a bed in the greenhouse filled with tiny pansies just beginning to spread their leaves. "You have a lot," Beth observed.

Sharon looked at them proudly. "Most of them are already spoken for. Millie wants half a dozen. Ester wants eight. Doreen wants a few. You've got good soil and sunlight. I'll give you a few just to make them happy."

Back in the yard, Cody and Juliana were playing together. Lord, that girl was getting tall. She didn't have her father's genes except in the prettiness of her face, emphasized by a short, straight nose and full, curving lips.

Sharon's features were bland. Her face was broad, with a short, ski-run nose that thickened at the base and a cleft chin. Only her smile was the same as Juliana's. When Sharon smiled, which wasn't often, she was beautiful.

The children stamped exaggeratedly up and down, twirled around, and fell to the ground, rolling. They stood up, linked arms, and did it again.

Slowly, Beth realized the children were clogging. They were imitating her dance! She flushed and looked down.

"It looks like I left an impression."

"Are you still wringing your hands over that? Good heavens, Beth. Do you think the kids know any difference between your clowning around and Frank's clowning around? Do you think the audience did? I'll tell you something. Frank was pleased as punch. He said you and Betty Lou were spontaneous. He likes spontaneous."

"Didn't he know I was drunk?"

"I think he lets Ester worry about such things. They give her greater pleasure."

"Art really does play a good piano."

"I know he does, but I'll tell him you said so."

Beth felt better after leaving, even if her friend had failed to be impressed with Beth's toil. At least Sharon wasn't critical of her first public performance. She even said their rendition of Sweet Betsy from Pike was good because now the kids were interested in the stage. "They don't know drunk. They know imagination."

You would almost think Sharon was a schoolteacher, who she wasn't, Beth well knew. Just one of those girls whose daddy was a big fish in a small town. Beth knew everything about Sharon, but she kept it to herself because Sharon kept everything about Beth to herself.

They had been closer once, before the community grew so large, before it was about raising families and not just survival.

They had been camp wives. They had washed their clothes in boiling water, stained their hands with berries, blistered them with wood and fire.

The men dug holes, chopped down trees, and listened in on naked wire communications. Back then, it was just Sharon, Doreen, and Beth, three women casting their eyes on the thick inlet waters, the slumbering mountains, and finding their souls irretrievably caught in this boundless freedom, this wilderness that proclaimed it would never be tamed.

Sharon didn't mind drinking back then. She used to say she liked anything that made her life easier.

Then came tee-totaling Ester. Beth dug viciously into the still-damp earth with her trowel, muttering over the indignity of her demotion from Beth, the life of the party, to Beth who drank too much.

When did the French stop drinking? She had heard, the French start giving their kids wine as soon as they were weaned from the baby bottle. Beth bet there were a dozen bottles of French wine hidden under the Bolinder's kitchen sink. Ester was just too cheap to share.

She put up with it. Ester was married to Charlie and Charlie was an organizer. He got things done. Without Charlie, they wouldn't be a community, just a group of homesteaders who had drifted away from Anchorage. There wouldn't be the volunteer fire and ambulance service or the community hall. Hell, there wouldn't even beFrank Lamar and they wouldn't have performing troops.

She wouldn't say it, but she thought the performing troops were the best thing to happen to the community. It set them apart, made them unique, entertained the children.

The troops made her feel she was part of something. She had always known she had a good voice. She had sung solos in her hometown, but this was different. She had sung then just to show off, laughing in her throat while she did it, knowing her voice might have a deeper range than the average woman's vocals, but its depths were powerful and rolling with song. She had laughed because they couldn't do it. She could, and she didn't care. Becoming a celebrity had never been on her agenda.

The difference was, now she cared. She hadn't really wanted to crash her own performance, even if the song was silly and the drunkenly belted lyrics were suitable. What she really wanted...

She moved on hesitantly to the radishes, brushing away a web on slender weeds. She wanted respect. She didn't want to be a clown. She wanted her voice to make music, real music. Beth scoffed to herself and wiped her brow with the back of her gardening glove. She didn't even know how to read notes and had never had formal voice lessons. How were people going to take her seriously?

Beth was so absorbed in her thoughts; she didn't realize she had visitors until she noticed two squat shadows wavering over the work in front of her. Shielding the sun from her eyes with her hand, she squinted upwards.

At first, they were just two bluish blobs, outlined by golden rays. The two blobs flickered and gained form as they squatted beside her, light dividing into colors, colors into details and shadows.

"Jimmy Delaney," she grunted. "What gives me the pleasure of your company?"

"Just being neighborly," he said quickly. His nervous hands crept along the ground, pulling unwanted growth away from her newly dug holes. His fingers were quick and smart, like his sister's. They slid through the fresh earth, finding the slender roots of newly awakened grass, and digging them loose.

"Been to Betty Lou's to talk about trapping that beaver dam that's been choking up Ship Creek, but she don't want nothing to do with it. She said where the beavers are, there's good fishing."

Beth shrugged. "She never gets concerned unless it's Wolf Creek. And she won't raid a beaver dam for its pelts. She says if you do that there won't be any more beavers and Betty Lou believes in long-term investments."

"Yep. That's what she told me."

Unsure how to continue, he glanced at his companion, Tammy. Her hands did not offer to nurture the new plants but wandered to her long hair and twirled a ringlet. She offered Beth one of her toothy stage smiles, meant to dazzle her audience into musical submission.

"We had something we'd like to talk to you about," she said in that tinkling voice that just wouldn't carry.

Groaning with a little more effort than necessary to come to her feet, Beth sighed and brushed off her apron, slid her work gloves into her pockets, and scanned the field for Cody. He was at the far end, poking a stick at a drying mud puddle. She called and beckoned to him, then turned back to her unexpected company.

"Well, come inside then where we can be comfortable. Gonna have to bring this fella in. He's at the wandering age."

She wasn't sure about Delaney protocol. The Delaneys weren't high society like Ester, but neither were they openly casual like the Millers. Nor did Jimmy Delaney seem sure of his own sense of good manners. He hesitated in the doorway, one hand on Tammy's arm, who was willing to walk right in and plop down on the couch.

She gestured to them to make themselves comfortable in the living room and reached into the cold box for iced tea. She felt flustered and embarrassed. She didn't know why.

Gary had built a fine house, with two bedrooms and wood interior. They had a woodstove that was the envy of the whole community. It was huge. They could cook and bake on it and keep the whole house warm. Additionally, he had built in a stone fireplace they could open or close. He had done this piece by piece, every smooth corner, every polished surface, every rounded and sanded piece of trim. She was proud of his work.

Yet, as she handed each of her guests a glass of tea, her hand trembled. She sat on the edge of her chair and gave them a plastic smile. "What can I do for you?"

Tammy twisted a blue bandana in her hands. Beth really wanted to like the girl, but she was flashier than the type of woman who usually settled and made babies. Her hair was unnaturally blonde, especially in a climate that darkened all but the fairest shades. Her blouse glittered with sequins. It seemed strange to see a glittering blouse in full daylight. She wore tight denim pants rolled halfway up the calves and a pair of boots with a swirled design on the sides. She wore make-up, but Beth was good at looking underneath the paint. Tammy was at least twenty-four, if she was a day. Jimmy was only twenty. He really was a lamb.

Tammy tried to begin. She sighed and lolled her head, leaned forward and said, "It's like this, and it don't come easy for me, but I wanted to ask you.... I think you should know.... There are a couple of places where Jimmy could get gigs..." She sniffled and wiped at her nose, then under her eyes, careful not to smear her mascara.

Folding her hands neatly in her lap, she squeezed them together tightly, and continued. "It's not that I'm a bad singer,

understand. They said I was good. I hit all the right notes...I hit
them all..."

She broke down and began wailing into her bandana.

"She can't sing loud enough," blurted Jimmy. "You can
blast the cannonballs out of a battleship! I mean, it's loud but it's
still singing. It's not shouting or anything."

"I suppose I should take that as a compliment," Beth
answered uncertainly.

"It is," said Jimmy, barely able to lift his voice above
Tammy's heart-broken sobs. "It almost sounds like a man's
voice, you know. It's that strong. I'm a country guitar player and
I need a country singer."

"We could be a duet," said Tammy, trying to make it sound
like there was nothing she desired more. "You could take the
lead and I would back you up with the girl sounds."

All at once, she felt she knew what it must be like to be
Gary, to have people come to you, asking for favors that resulted
in a drawn-out decision-making process

. When Jimmy offered her a cigarette, she accepted it by
reaching over languidly and tapping it on the coffee table several
times before lighting it. She refused his assistance, lighting it
with her own silver-colored Zippo, a gift from her husband last
Christmas.

She inhaled deeply and watched the smoke rings she had
proudly learned to make, counting each one floating to the
ceiling like airy frosted donuts.

"You want me to sing with you," she said faintly.

"Well, now," agreed Jimmy. "That's what it amounts to. If
we land the radio show, it pays good and it's a guaranteed once-
a-week check. We just need to play three more houses and go
through auditions. It wouldn't take much of your time, just
Friday and Saturday nights."

Beth took another drag of her cigarette and watched the
smoke lazily roll. "Because I sound like a man," she continued,
almost mournfully.

Tammy stopped dabbing at her face long enough to stare at
Beth wide-eyed.

"Oh, not like a man! Like one of those woman jazz singers. They never sing softly, just belt it out. That's how Jimmy's manager wants me to sing his songs, but I can't do it."

"His manager?"

"Kind of," said Jimmy. "He just makes suggestions, but he's never been wrong. He said he could get me a gig at the crab festival, and he did. They had a big, open-air stage. But that's when he told me Tammy's voice doesn't carry enough. I need a louder singer."

Without ice, the iced tea was beginning to grow warm. Beth took a long swallow without answering. Discovering there was a fellow male among their company, Cody tottered off to find his favorite truck, and brought it to Jimmy for his inspection.

He admired the toy, complimenting the stout, free-spinning wheels and looked up at Beth bashfully from where he was stooped next to the boy.

"I know you don't need money, what with Gary's job and all. Construction foremen are worth their weight in gold. Matt told me all about it."

"But it's good pin money," broke in Tammy. "Even Doreen is making pin money selling milk."

"I'll have to talk to Gary about it." Finishing her tea and tamping out her cigarette, she offered them a smile. "We can't be disrupting our weekends without talking about it first."

"No, of course not," mumbled Jimmy, still examining Cody's toy. "And I know Gary didn't think highly of me in the past, and he didn't like me buying the Bolinder horses, but I'm trying to change it. We're holding an auction this weekend to let a few of the horses go and to show off the new foals. There will be a lot of Valley folk, but the Bolinders and the Lamars will be there. We'd like you to come as well."

"You should," urged Tammy, rising. She placed a hand on Cody's head. The long, red fingernails seemed predatory, causing Beth to breathe and sigh with relief when Cody ducked free from her grasp. "It would be good for Cody to play with other boys. All he has to play with around here are girls."

Beth waited until they left, then returned to her gardening. There really wasn't much to do beyond transplanting the flowers Sharon had given her.

She muttered to herself for several minutes while she mulled over this inexplicable turn of events. Not only was she considering becoming friends with the most scandalous family in Wolf Creek: she was weighing the possibilities of a musical partnership!

Gary would never stand for it. She was certain. Andy Delaney had no shame. Jimmy Delaney had no respect for his elders, and Tammy was a cocktail waitress. How could they possibly align themselves with such scandalous people?

The Lamars were friends with the Delaneys. Her trowel tapped thoughtfully, snugging in a warm spot for her pansies. Of course, that was how the Lamars were, but it was peculiar. Andy and Millie were like sisters, even if they were as different as night and day. They were practically inseparable when Andy wasn't flying off to the villages.

The most peculiar part, though, was Ester Bolinder also liked Andy, at least as much as Ester liked anyone. They visited each other! Ester even gave the Delaney's one of her wildcat kittens for free. And now...Beth lined up one more rock alongside the flowerbed to keep it secure and rose heavily to her feet. She stood up, scratched her head, and said out loud, "ifthis don't beat all!"

Twenty -One

Sometimes, it's all about whose unhappiness is greater. Gary was unhappy about becoming friends with the Delaneys, but Beth convinced him she would be unhappier if she didn't take a shot at a music career. This was a powerful point in her favor. Gary was her greatest fan. He fumed and fretted a little, measured out other possibilities that didn't go farther than the unpaid performances of the Little Theater group, then finally agreed she could be Jimmy's lead singer provided her name was included in the billing.

"Beth Hughes and Jimmy Delaney, that's what it should say," he said, holding his hands in the air as though there was a signboard between them. "Or Beth and Jimmy."

"What about Tammy?"

"Too many names. She's just there for decoration."

He questioned the necessity of attending the Delaneys' party. This required a different tactic.

"Oh," she sighed, opening a beer for him, and setting it on the table where the scraps of their dinner still floundered in sad rejection.Having stuck to her vow of only one beer a day, she sat across from him and rested her arms on the table edge. "When was the last time we went to a rodeo?"

"In Wisconsin. Your brother liked bull-riding."

"He did. I liked the horses."

He belched informatively. "All girls like horses."

"I never really had a good look at the horses the Bolinders kept. They were always at the far end of the property."

He belched again. He had a remarkable ability for driving all stomach bubbles into his throat on command.

"They're horses. Some look nice. He's got a good-looking buckskin and an Appaloosa mare in the mix, and it's quite a mix."

Beth cleaned up the scraps to make their conversational table setting look more appealing. "Well," she said, taking off her apron and returning. "Ester says there is one with Arabian blood."

He snorted so hard; he sprayed a little beer. "Ester thinks that mutt she picked up is a toy poodle!"

"Well, he looks like a toy poodle," said Beth defensively.

He rested one arm across his chest and sulked. "Just because it looks like a toy poodle, doesn't mean it is a toy poodle. It's gotta have papers to be a toy poodle. Ester doesn't have anything with papers except her travel visa. I don't know why she has three dogs, anyway."

"She doesn't like the other two. They are Charlie's dogs. Ives is her dog."

"That is the most ridiculous name I ever heard."

She drew a few circles on the table with her fingertip. Her nails were neatly curved and painted cherry red. She appeared absorbed in their movement. "The Bolinders are transferring the horses to the Delaneys this weekend."

He tossed her a cigarette and lit one for himself, leaning back to watch the smoke rings. "Good for them."

She clacked at the table surface with her nails, bringing back his attention. "They are having a party. We're invited."

His eyes remained fixed on the clacking nails. "To the Delaneys?"

"It will be good for Cody to play with other boys."

"Hah! Andy's oversized kid? He'll probably grow up to be a thug."

She finally lit her cigarette and let the end grow bright red before exhaling a cloud of smoke. "There will be other boys - Millie's and Ester's. Do you want our son to grow up a sissy?"

Gary's composure crumpled in an instant. He sat straight up in his chair, slammed down his beer, and shouted, "A sissy! Never a sissy! Absolutely not. I will not hear of my boy becoming a sissy."

Cody, who had been mildly listening, not understanding much beyond horses and his own name, jumped back a foot from where he had been standing by his father's chair, and hurried into the living room to hide behind the couch.

"Now look what you have done!" Beth scolded, completely offended. "You have scared the daylights out of him, and he has no idea why. If that isn't reason enough to put him with other boys, I don't know what is."

Faced with the unfathomable possibility that his son could grow up timid and weak, Gary thundered around the yard for two hours, found a fallen tree to quarrel with and begin chopping into firewood, then stomping back to the houses, met Beth in the kitchen and announced, "Alright. We'll go to the Delaneys' party."

Beth smiled and prepared for the weekend. Unwittingly, without planning, Cody had aided and abetted his mother.

Spring was amazingly cooperative that year. By Saturday, the leaves were beginning to bud on the trees, leaving a flurry of tight, green dewdrops hanging suspended from the branches. The wild grasses had started shooting up in tufts, springing wherever the soil was warmest. The marbled sky fitted over the Alaska Range to the Chugach like a crystal cap.

Beth dressed Cody in his first pair of bib overalls. He was finally potty-trained and got to wear big-boy pants. He was growing lanky like his father, with sandy-colored hair that would turn the same warm-brown shade as his father when he grew older, and blue-grey eyes that puzzled over his place in the scheme of things.

She put the cowboy hat on his head, the one his dad had given him for Christmas, and helped him strap on his toy guns. "Horsies," she said, hoping he would repeat back. "We're going to see horsies."

"Bye-bye," he answered, waving at the door.

She had not been to the Delaney property since their rescue mission to the Millers. It shaped up nicely in the spring. Owen had begun scraping the earth with his tractor as soon as the snow melted, and it now lay raw and drying. A brand-new fence had been built around it and staked off into partitions. There was also a hastily built barn for the horses. The new construction was as fresh as the spring air.

The cabin had been built well off the road, close to the foothills. In the spring, the area in front spread out to a wide arena, slowly blanketing with grass. There were vehicles parked as randomly as though they were visiting the trading post.

Gary found a spot that didn't seem to block anyone's ability to get in or out. He stood next to the car a few seconds, hat in his hands, as though he was trying to get his bearings.

"I ain't ever been here," he admitted. "Just to see Matt once or twice, over there in that little place."

Her eyes traveled to where he pointed. Apart from the precious, white Birch and a thick row of conifers running alongside the road to give privacy to their homestead, the land had been cleared to the meadow and the now-visible, creek. On the other side of the creek was a small structure with a steeply pointed roof. The meadow spread across the creek and rambled behind the tiny cabin.

"Why didn't he make it bigger?" asked Beth.

Gary shrugged and opened a beer to feel comfortable. "He was planning on just him. I don't think he wants to put more work into it right now on account he's been saving to buy an excavator. Or a backhoe. They've got a backhoe going for a good bargain on an Anchorage lot."

The party seemed to have been split into three groups. One group clumped together at a vantage point behind the corral, where they nodded at various horses and talked among themselves. This group consisted of Jimmy, Tammy and what appeared to be some people from the Valley.

A second group consisted of the Hansen brothers, a girl from the village, Frank, Charlie, and Matt. The Hansens leaned against a truck, drinking beer, while the girl sat on the hood, laughing at something Charlie said and snapping chewing gum.

"I'm going that way," said Gary, pointing at the truck.

Holding onto his mother's skirts at first, Cody's bright eyes caught a streak of another toddler running across the yard. "Horsies," he said. Letting go, he chased after Jason.

The third group was gathered around Velma's outdoor dining area. The Delaneys really could put out a spread.

They had a barbecue grill stacked high with grilling chicken, caribou ribs and hamburgers. A pot of beans boiled over an open fire. The plywood table was covered with salads, casseroles, and deserts, all neatly covered and under close watch by Velma.

Andy looked up from setting out tableware and beckoned Beth over. The third group was a committee of women; Velma, Andy, Millie, and Ester. There were no Bowens or Erichmans among the assembled.

Just how much this relieved Beth gave her guilt pangs, but she shrugged them aside. If Doreen and her fancy car, and Sharon and her piano thought they were too good for the Delaney celebration, it was their loss. That they had not been invited never crossed her mind.

Ester stalked about with her infant as though expecting someone to do bodily harm if she didn't remain on alert.

"You can relax and sit down now," Andy told her. "The wild Indians have all been chased away."

She took a seat next to Millie, who had just plunged a bottle into her baby's mouth. "It's not that," she said, glancing at the infant girl with a little jealousy, then tending her own precious cargo. "The horses attract bears. That's why we keep dogs. You should get a dog."

"Are you offering me your dogs?"

"No!" Said Ester. "Charlie would never allow it. Besides, he is thinking of getting geese."

"Geese!" Cried Millie. "They aren't the friendliest creatures on the planet."

"No, they are not," said Ester, as though this suited her just fine. "But Charlie must have his animals. He can't bear to be without them."

Millie looked sulkily in the direction of her husband, who was sharing a story with the Hansen brothers and didn't appear at all interested in the horses. "I wish Frank would be a little bit that way. He can barely tolerate Baily. He only likes the cat."

Baily put his feet up on Beth's lap hopefully as she sat down. "If we don't get anything to eat, you don't," she told him. The dog snuffled away, disappointed.

"I heard you've been keeping an eye on the Miller family."

Without appearing to have done a thing, one of Millie's hands had slipped inside a platter and removed a cookie. She nibbled at it, throwing a few crumbs to her dog. "How have they been doing?"

Beth sniffed at the spoiled behavior of Millie and dog who had committed their transgressions under Velma's nose. "They're getting by. We're going to have to pull the trailer to high ground with the tractor. It sank six inches into the mud."

"Oh dear." She polished off her cookie and licked her fingers. "They set that trailer on frozen ground. It was bound to sink come spring."

Beth sighed and wondered if she could summon the audacity to help herself to a cookie. As a first-time guest, it didn't seem wise, so she helped herself to coffee instead. "They didn't know any better."

"He is a brute, that one," said Ester positively. "I think he hits her."

Millie drew back and clutched at her throat at such a scandalous statement. "He wouldn't!" She drew her breath in sharply. "Does he?"

Ester had finally decided to make herself useful. Taking a stack of disposable cups, she filled four with Kool-Aid and brought them back to the table. "I saw some bruises on her neck the last time we visited, and they weren't hickies, Millie. I know the difference."

Andy had been paying more attention to the flight of the toddlers, streaming toward the corral with Anna behind them, calling to Ben a wide assortment of astonishing names. Andy's eyes seemed to leave a green trail as they flashed back and fixed on Ester.

"Well, they still could have been from something else."

"And what kind of accident leaves bruises on the side of the neck? She even tried to cover them up," Ester sniffed. "But she was drinking, and her scarf slipped, so I saw them." She gave Beth a significant nod.

Beth took a deliberate swallow of her coffee and watched Ester fret over the Kool-Aid meant for the four hell-bound toddlers. "She hasn't said anything to me. Maybe she doesn't want to talk about it."

The conversation still had not sufficiently absorbed Andy's attention. "I swear," she murmured, her eyes returning to the corral. "The boys are turning into Huns. They will be burning down towns and villages before long."

Beth didn't doubt it. The children's survival appeared eminent. The savage little tribe had scattered in four directions, but Anna's devotion was only toward one. Overtaking Ben, she tried to wrestle something out of his hands. He struggled and kicked at her with both feet. He did not stop squirming away from her until she grabbed him by the ankles and turned him upside down.

A cascade of screams and several words one would not think belonged in a toddler's mouth, came tumbling out, along with whatever it was he was trying to keep from Anna. She scooped up her trinket quickly, marching past her elven tormenters who gazed up at her innocently.

The boys grouped back together to plot further mischief. Even Cody tottered close and squatted next to Jason, a jolly enough boy who didn't mind sharing his space. It was good for Cody to have other boys to play with. She began to wonder why she hadn't started bringing him to play before now. All she had thought about was how outnumbered the girls were. It wouldn't be bad if she had a boy. They could end up with a Little League Baseball team.

A horse was being trotted around, a big red gelding with black mane and tail. One of the valley men stroked his beard. Dave Hansen made a hand signal close to his hip. The girl on the hood of the truck shook her head.

"That damned girl is holding out for the Appaloosa," grumbled Andy "I knew it."

"Who is she?" asked Millie curiously.

"One of Mark's cousins. The one who is signing up for the baseball team. She'll show Sharon a few things."

"Is that the one who is seeing Ted Ewing?" She whispered.

"No. That's another cousin. They have them all over the place. I would not be surprised if they were related to every Athabascan in the territory. I wanted that Appaloosa. Now I think Jimmy's going to let it go to the village. Damned shame."

Tammy led out a sorrel. It was a sweet, docile thing. The girl on the truck leaned forward, but a valley person named a price and she leaned back again, popping her gum.

"So, they're really getting hitched," mused Beth. "How many wedding bells will be ringing?"

"Not so many and not so soon," answered Andy. "They're going to wait until Jimmy builds a shack and has some money aside. That sort of thing isn't going to happen overnight, but he bought her a ring. Had Dresden design it. It's eighteen karat gold, with a half-karat diamond."

"It must have been very expensive."

"It is, but Jimmy's gonna work part of it off at Dresden's mine. I took her for a gold digger, but she's got Jimmy doing the digging. He ain't never going to get rich, not Jimmy, but maybe she doesn't care, after all. There's no denying she likes horses."

"But yours," pressed Beth. "What about you and Mark?"

"Oh, that." Andy rubbed her slightly developed mound. "I kind of like not being married. I was thinking of trying it out a little longer."

She stood up and began uncovering the dishes, smoothing out the tin foil and folding it into a neat, even stack. "Anyway," she said, somewhat loudly, so all might hear whó chose to do so, "Marrying Mark means I would be living in the village. I am not living in the village as long as that foul man, Ted Ewing, is still around."

Her voice carried in the wrong direction for Mark to catch it, but Millie and Ester heard it well. Millie's mouth opened in a wide "O" and Ester scowled and tapped one foot.

"What?" Ester asked sharply. "Did that scoundrel come back?"

Velma was busy running back and forth from her house, bringing out her best China and ceramic tableware. "Mama! Whatever are you doing?"

Andy cried instead of answering. She took away the assortment of plates her mother had set on the table and replaced them with a package of paper plates.

"We'll lose half our dishes if we put these out," she scolded.

"I don't want the French thinking we live like heathens," Velma Delaney whispered back, but too loudly not to be overheard.

"I don't mind paper plates," said Ester, pretending she ate from them all the time. "My goodness. Just look at how many people are here. Who would want to clean up after them? Of course, I would use paper plates."

"That's not what I heard," said Velma in a stage whisper to Beth. "China tea service, English biscuits, holding dinners for big wigs."

"Well," said Beth, who was familiar with the tea parties if not dinners with big wigs, and had no intention of turning against Ester, "Charlie is the president of the community meetings. That's sort of like being the mayor. And Frank is vice-president."

Velma looked sadly at her best dishes, which must be retained for more formal gatherings. "Well, I don't much trust politicians. What have they ever done for us?"

Andy sighed. "They gave us one hundred and twenty acres, mama."

She huffed loudly and tried to give the paper plates a satisfying rattle. "After we lost the farm. They stole it out from under us, they did, and now we're in the cold north."

"It was a broken-down farm that hadn't made money in years and Aspen isn't much warmer than here." Andy directed her remark more at her audience than her mother.

"It didn't make money because the government stole all the money," Velma muttered, but she simmered down enough to pour herself a cup of coffee.

On the Delaney homestead, you did not have to call people to dinner. As soon as the food was exposed, they automatically began migrating toward it, using the senses of animals in the wild. The first to arrive were the little boys, who peered up at the full table anxiously, as though afraid there was not enough to go around. Ester gave them their Kool-Aid and said not to spill it, so they did.

It was nice they had begun eating half-way like humans. They had their own miniature table, chairs, and individual plates. They still ate largely with their fingers, but they didn't drool, and they didn't snatch each other's food. It meant they didn't have to be so closely supervised anymore when they were eating.

She knew Gary's footsteps and dark, broad shadow without looking up. "Did you find a horse you wanted?"

Gary sat heavily beside her; his plate filled high. He sniffed at her coffee. "I guess not one with a kick."

"Nope." Beth laced her fingers in front of her. "I haven't had a drink all day."

"Then we should take care of that," giggled Tammy. Positive she was the most attractive woman on the homestead, she flashed her professional celebrity smile at the group of men collected around her, more interested in the feast than her Western outfits pants and fringed shirt. She wriggled into a spot across from Beth and plopped down a beer.

Beth felt her throat grow thirsty, but she slid the beer toward Gary. He put an arm around her shoulders and grabbed the bottle by the neck. "We'll share it."

He took a long swallow, handed the beer to Beth, and asked Tammy, "I don't know your accent. Where are you from?"

Tammy beamed at the attention but corrected him. "I don't have an accent. I'm from Bakersfield."

"Why can't you have an accent if you're from Bakersfield?"

"Because Bakersfield is in California," rumbled Frank. "You can't have an accent if you are from California."

"Why ever can't you?" asked Millie indignantly.

Frank patted at his lips with a napkin before answering. "Because Californians don't have accents. They speak correctly."

"I'm sure not all of them do," she mumbled, still unhappy with the role Hollywood played in fashioning American speech, then brightened. "So, Miss Tammy. How did you end up here?"

Tammy answered with her mouth full, which was a little astonishing to the pioneering women who grew up on proper table manners. "Waitressing. Seriously. I waited tables all the way from Bakersfield to Anchorage. I spent three months in Seattle, saving money, before I had enough to fly to Anchorage."

"My," said Millie, trying to ignore the improper etiquette by blinking rapidly several times. "Why did you do that?"

Still unaware of her breach in good manners, Tammy continued to chew her food as she talked and waved around a forked piece of caribou. "Because I wanted to. Have you ever been to Bakersfield?"

Beth felt her head shaking along with the other women, who all dropped their eyes so they wouldn't witness this crass behavior. Dropping her fork and resting her right arm loosely on the table, she gestured with the other holding the bright diamond ring. Beth's head reluctantly rose at the sunbeam sparkle and followed the jeweled hand, transfixed.

"It's an oil town," she said, finally swallowing her food. "If you aren't an oil man, you are nothing. My pop wasn't an oil man, just a guy with a dirt farm and a job driving a dump truck. We were nothing."

Tammy was pleased to notice she had the attention of half the people at the table. Waving her magic ring once again, she took a swallow of beer and continued.

"Bakersfield is hot, dry and hilly. There's nothing to do except ride horses and shoot rattlesnakes. We collect the tails and wear them around our necks." She reached inside the collar of her fringed, checkered shirt, and pulled up a leather string with half-a-dozen rattlesnake tails hanging from it.

Jimmy grinned proudly, Andrea chuckled, and Ester covered her mouth to keep from exposing its open gape. Instead of drawing back in horror, Millie reached over the table to examine the rattles with fascination.

"You must be a good marksman," she said, then sat back to alternatively feed Baily and nurture her baby. "But there are no snakes here to kill."

Unconcerned about the lack of her favorite prey, Tammy tucked the tails back inside her blouse and announced, "I'm going with Jimmy on the hunting trips. I've already got a favorite horse. I'll be working with it all summer."

Gary had been listening with quiet interest, but now threw down his fork. "You're going with Jimmy on the hunting trips? That's a terrible idea!"

Beth half-twisted in her seat to look at him.

"And why is that?"

He attacked his potato salad savagely. "Because if we have one woman going hunting, all of you will want to go hunting."

"I was thinking of going hunting after the baby is born," said Andy. "I've got a favorite horse, too."

"I could go by next year," said Millie. "I don't hunt, but I can be the camp cook. You men always come back starving."

Gary looked at Beth as though it was all her fault. "Do you see? I suppose you want to go hunting, too."

"Well, not until next year. I'm pregnant."

The afternoon was growing late. The valley folk left shortly after settling their business, demolishing most of the caribou ribs, first. The villagers remained, but never sat down at the table. They filled their plates and found some nice stumps or boulders to sit on, talking between themselves. They tossed Baily enough scraps that the dog completely abandoned all begging efforts and simply waited for food to fall.

Baily ate so much and became so lethargic, he did not even get up and wag his tail gratefully at the benefactors when they stood to leave, as he was generally prone to do as an animal with a strategic mind and accomplished social graces. He snoozed with half-closed lids, as the Hansen brothers made their rounds to thank and shake hands with their hosts, rolling to expose his belly when Mark reached down to scratch him.

It was only after it became apparent the Hansens were returning to their truck that Andy leaped out of her chair and hurried to catch up and put an arm around Mark's waist.

"Your cousin got the Appaloosa, didn't she?" Andy asked accusingly. "You'd better take good care of it."

He kissed her openly, in front of Matt and everyone else to see. "You'll have to talk to Vicky about it. It's hers now." The cousin, strolling a few feet ahead, turned to smile a little wickedly and wave at Andy.

Andy remained a gracious hostess. She walked through the sun speckled yard with her guests, her back curved in a pregnant walk even though she was barely showing. Just beyond the dining area, the four boys were slugging it out with long sticks. Their sword play was turning violent as they bashed each other on the head and poked each other's round, little tummies.

Andrea broke away from her engagement with Mark long enough to disentangle the toddlers, capturing Ben, who was always the ringleader.

"How many times have I told you?" She said with exasperation. "Play cops and robbers. Then you can shoot each other without killing each other." She demonstrated.

Ben stomped his feet and threw down the stick. "Fine," she said. "Play ball."

She tossed a rubber ball at him. He threw it angrily and Jason caught it, waddling off with it, grinning happily. She had turned around to rejoin Mark, her arm tucked unconcernedly in his, when Cody in a fit of toddler rebellion, whacked her with his sword-playing stick across the bottom.

Indignantly, Andrea wheeled around, ready to tongue whip her aggressor into submission, then hesitated when she saw her tormenter. He looked up at her, his lower lip trembling, then threw down the stick and ran away.

"Oh my God! Oh my God!" Beth warbled with dismay, bolting to her feet. "Cody!"

It did not help that the villagers were laughing so hard, they were falling against the trees. "Mr. Feeling Man!" shouted Mark to Frank. "Looks like there is going to be a job to do with that one!"

"That wasn't my boy," Frank argued.

Mark shrugged as his troops climbed into the truck. There were five of them, total. Two were thirtyish looking young men with a touch of grey to their hair, who had done little more throughout the day than smoke, drink, eat, and fold their arms to observe the party in action. All but Mark and Dave jumped into the bed.

Mark stood by the door of the driver's seat and called back. "You're the tribal leader, aren't ya? You and Charlie. Yep. You've got your work cut out for you."

Beth still stood, rigid as a stone, unsure how to handle her son's transgressions. When Andy returned, she took one look at Beth's face and laughed. "Relax, will ya?" She said, sitting back down. "He's a baby! He just wasn't ready to stop playing swords."

"Terrible two's. Treacherous three's," agreed Millie. "He just grew into phase two."

Since Andy was sitting and everyone appeared unconcerned, Beth eased herself back into her seat. "Maybe I do want a girl. Someone who can play with Millie's girl. To think, Doreen had a boy this time. I'm carrying high. I carried Cody against my back."

Andy nodded wisely. "Boys do that. They like to snuggle against your back."

Now that the party had dwindled to a small social group of mixed company, the conversation slid away from babies and marriages to the general interests of men. Charlie reminded everyone there would be a work party for building the community hall in late May. Owen grumbled that the project better not take Jimmy away from his own tasks too long. Jimmy grumbled that he had horses to train and a weekend job.

Frank wanted to talk about the next salmon run. Fishing had been poor the last few years, causing them to speculate on other fish to fill their freezer. "We should probably rent a boat," he suggested, "and fish for cod."

Renting a boat was a solution both Matt and Frank came around to every year. Both were so comfortable with the sea; they swore they could feel the tidal movement under them although they lived five miles offshore. The problem was, they needed at least two other people to pitch in for deep sea voyaging. There weren't that many among them with a fondness for open water. Most were landlubbers and proud of it.

"I'll go if I can put together enough money in time," offered Jimmy.

His fiancé groomed back her long hair with the fingers of one hand and used the other to pinch him. "How often have you been out on a boat?"

Jimmy rubbed his ribs where she had attacked him, answering sulkily. "A couple of times. I don't get seasick. I just think about fish."

Finding room in his stomach for another corn fritter, Gary popped one in his mouth and growled, "there ain't no need to go all the way down to the peninsula. Betty Lou catches all her fish right here on the inlet."

"They don't taste as good as ocean fish," said Millie, siding with her husband.

"I hate it when Charlie goes deep sea fishing," said Ester. "The house stinks for a week."

Charlie was unapologetic. "You ate that rockfish quickly enough."

Ester had found a piece of white bread to torture. She held it between her bony fingers, twisting off pieces and finding only the tiniest crumbs worth chewing. "Rock fish is a delicacy," she explained.

The elder Delaneys yawned and said they were going to bed. The children were so worn out, they were nearly comatose. They draped their heads across their mothers' laps, their eyelids heavy, their mouths half-open. Beth stroked Cody's silky brow. It was damp with sweat from crawling through the bushes near the creek. It smelled milky sweet.

"We should be going home now," she suggested to Gary. "We've got some planting to do tomorrow."

Gary found no reason for argument. He picked up Cody, half on the ground and half on Beth's knees, hoisted the child up over his shoulders and stood. "I can't believe you let Sharon talk you into buying two lilac bushes," he grunted, since he could find no grievance with the party.

Beth glanced at the sharp-eared company, and placed one hand at his elbow, helping to move him along. "She says if we take care of them, they'll do fine."

It was a nice beginning to what promised to be a good summer. The dusky sky brooded, the shadows of evening flitting, as the sun cleared a path over the mountains. The car eased into their yard as though reluctant to break the silence.

Beth lifted herself slowly from the passenger side, feeling the weight of eating all evening, and trudged toward the house, her feet thudding dully, her back aching. She collapsed on the couch. Her ankles were swollen. She took off her shoes and rested her feet on the milk stool. She was only mildly aware that Gary had taken the boy into his room and put him to bed.

She became more aware when he sat next to her and put a beer in her hand. "You did good. Half a beer. I think you deserve another."

She sat up straight and took a generous swallow. She wasn't really all that worn out, she realized. Just her feet. She didn't know why she had shoved them into those ridiculous patent leather shoes when she could have been wearing a comfortable pair of loafers. Ester was the only other woman who had worn dressy shoes, but then, Ester's feet were so long and narrow, she could put a sledding hill under them and not feel it.

"It was a good day, but I didn't find a horse I wanted."

"I thought about the Appaloosa," he murmured. He leaned against her with one arm across the back of the couch. "They wanted too much money for it. Maybe when the mares foal, we'll buy a pony for the kids."

"Cody said horsey today."

He drew in a deep breath and let it out slowly. "Do you see what he did today? Do you see what he did?" He gave the loud laugh he had restrained all evening. "Nobody is going to call my boy a sissy."

Twenty-Two

The lodge visitors were spilling right out the door during the next community meeting. It wasn't just the energy of those who had successfully pulled off the fund-raising entertainment, and now drew together to discuss the next event. There were newcomers. There was the Phillips family and the Miller family. There was a family who had moved in on the north side of the river. There were two more railroad workers.

Since they were providing labor and talent, the teenagers felt entitled to stand by the open door of the lodge and listen in on the meeting. Occasionally, they delivered an opinion, but mainly they smoked cigarettes and talked among themselves.

Most of the newcomers left soon after adjournment, including the Millers, but the Phillips brothers did not. Gordon embedded himself as securely as though he had been attending the meetings for years, flanked by Dresden Hayes and Matt Jones. Brad had abandoned the doorway to join Ed in peering inside the hood of a car and contemplating an engine.

They hadn't had an after-meeting like this in – Beth couldn't remember how long. Ever since they had incorporated the boundaries, the talk had been about raising funds. They talked so much about this, that by the end of the night, they were exhausted and had nothing left to say about anything else.

There was a new atmosphere. They had done it! The Little Theater had earned them $223.75. It was enough to buy the lumber to build the entire shell for their hall, plus wire it for when the electric company came through. There was a lot of talk about the electric company these days.

Folks said, as fast as Wolf Creek was growing, they could get their poles by next spring. Everyone had signed up except Betty Lou. She said she didn't need no damned lightening juice snaking through her cabin.

Solace said she wanted a juke box, the prettiest one in the whole territory. "Zeb never leave me to buy one before," she said. "On account of they take too much electricity, but we're going to light this place up like a Christmas tree when the power comes through."

Gary was rumbling in his best voice with Frank and Charlie. It bothered him that though he was a larger man, his voice was not as deep and resonant as Frank's. He practiced his deep growl in public but rarely used it at home.

"Charlie, what are you building out front of your place?"

Beth leaned forward so she could hear, along with several others, who paused with their drinks in their hands and turned to gaze. They were all curious as to what Charlie was building next. Millie once told her, Charlie was so anxious for people to move in, he was building a whole town on his property, and if they didn't come, he would drag them over. Beth could believe it.

"Just a lot of tinkering and thinking right now," said Charlie. "Zeb keeps talking about how he doesn't want to run the store part of things anymore. He just wants to run a diner. And we've got the money from the horses now. I'm thinking of an investment."

Ester coughed politely and raised her coffee cup as though it was a teacup. "We have already agreed on what we are invested in. We are taking a vacation next spring."

"We will take a vacation," agreed Charlie. "But you don't use investment money for vacation money. You save for vacation. You invest on investments."

Ester turned to Beth and Millie, satisfied the men weren't worth talking to. "He wants a store."

She brought her baby to her shoulder and juggled him as though he had whimpered, although he hadn't made a sound.

"What will he do with a store? He has a job."

"But if Zeb closes his store, we have to go all the way out to Anchorage to buy everything," said Millie, glancing accusingly toward Solace.

368

After such a large gathering, Solace didn't have much time to sit with her friends and defend her business decisions. She noticed Millie's glance, and waved but continued wiping down the counter, which had become quite cluttered in the aftermath of the meeting.

Beth felt obligated to come to Solace's defense. "The trappers don't come around the way they used to and there isn't such a demand for furs anymore, either. Some people are downright opposed to them, so the Grants sit on a lot of inventory. They are ready for an all-cash business and the diner makes the best money."

"Then it's a pity," said Millie, looking at Ester woefully. "We could really use a store in this area."

Ester sniffled into her sleeve and Charlie beamed.

Breaking away from his private conversation with Gordon, Dresden made an announcement in a baritone voice that carried quite well when he wished it to and could probably even compete with Frank for dramatic impact.

"I'm thinking of opening a shop. A shop, not a store. There's a nice piece of land about two miles up the road that I keep looking at. Competition is healthy and I think I could compete with Hank's Japanese shop."

"Oh now," said Gordon, who had apparently been hashing the whole thing out. "We won't really be competing. Japanese products and Alaskan gold. They are two different things. But it will be great for tourism."

"That's the way I see it." Having finished clearing off the counter, Solace slapped it one more time with her towel and picked up the coffee pot to refill the empty cups. "With a gold shop and a Japanese shop and a diner, heck. We'll be bringing in tourists left and right."

"And a store," added Charlie. "They've got to have a place to buy their candy bars and potato chips."

Dresden was pleased with his reception.

He brought out his pipe, a minimal occurrence, filled it carefully and took two puffs before setting it down.

"It won't really be a gold shop. It will be a jewelry shop. It's for my jewelry."

"You make very nice jewelry," said Millie. If Beth didn't know any better, she would think Millie was flirting with him.

She leaned toward him and smiled, showing her best profile. Only then did Beth notice that under those neatly tucked curls, Millie was wearing a pair of gold earrings with jade settings that looked suspiciously like the workmanship of Dresden Hayes.

Dresden reached for the plump curved wrist resting on the tabletop, examining it. "When are you going to replace that plain gold band with one of my own? It doesn't do you justice, Millie. I recommend jade inlay. It will bring out your eyes."

Not to be outdone, Ester turned in her seat so the bracelet she was wearing on the wrist that held up her baby was clearly visible. "Well, my watch has sentimental value. It's Swiss made, you know, but I am looking forward to collecting more charms. This one is so darling."

It was darling. The tiny charm was a gold pan with the miniature figure of a prospector squatting in the middle of it.

Beth whispered furiously to Gary. "Why haven't you bought me any gifts from Dresden?"

On the verge of biting into Solace's famous rhubarb pie, Gary set it down meekly. "I didn't know you like his work."

"Well, it's gold," she replied sulkily. "Of course I like it."

Her eyes swept over the lodge, trying to calculate who else might be wearing Dresden's jewelry. Andy was wearing earrings of ivory and gold. Mark Hansen wore a belt buckle with jade and gold inlay.

Beth began to feel impoverished. She had gold, but none of it was the work of Dresden Hayes. "I want one of his watch bands for Christmas," she added in a low voice. "I just know Millie is going to get one."

For no other reason than to change the subject, Gary called loudly. "Say, Matt. When is your wife coming?"

Now that the meeting was over, Matt was basking in his neutrality at the far end of the table. He had been tentatively flirting with Andy, who was openly flirting with everyone, but he answered in a self-conscious tone. "Two weeks. She is supposed to arrive at the airport two weeks from now."

Reminded that he was married, Matt shoved his stocking cap on his head, turned up his collar and prepared to leave. Feeling sympathy for his discomfort, Beth said, "I guess you'll be happy to see your boy,"

"I will be," he agreed, stopping at the cash register to pay his bill.

Millie didn't appear to notice Matt's change in mood, only that he is leaving. "And Ben is big for his age, so your boy will fit right in even if he is older. Luke, is it?"

He nodded, keeping his head down. "Matthew Luke Jones, Jr. She calls him Luke to keep us separated."

She waited until his back had disappeared out the door, then sighed into her open hands. "The poor man. He is so lonely. He craves family. It's the hardest thing really, to have no sisters or brothers or cousins to turn to."

"Or mothers, or fathers, or grandchildren," mourned Ester. "The Delaneys were smart. They carved out the entire family with a trowel and plopped it in the middle of Wolf Creek."

"I'm glad I didn't bring my entire family with me," said Beth. "All we ever did was quarrel."

"We did too," agreed Millie. "But now I miss them."

Frank interrupted the conversation to remind her, "Bruiser said he was coming up."

"Bruiser." Millie gave a laugh that implied everyone had a Bruiser somewhere in the family. "He says things. Don't rely on him though to come through because he doesn't always. He just talks. Anyway."

She played with her baby to make her chuckle.

"Bruiser won't come for the family. He'll come to stir things up. It's just sad the children won't have cousins to grow up with because cousins are usually best friends. That's why I think it's important for the boys to grow up together."

"What I know," said Ester. "Is that the three boys are out to kill each other. You are better off where you are at, Beth. Your boy is distanced from the others and much better behaved."

Beth raised her brows doubtfully.

"It wasn't one of your boys that ambushed Andy from behind. Seriously, Millie. Have you thought about how poor

Nancy is going to defend herself against so many boys? And with another one coming, no less!"

"Andy will have a girl," said Millie positively. "We used the string and button test yesterday. It swung in a circle. It's a girl. If the button at the end of the string had swung back and forth, it would have been a boy, but it's a girl."

"That's not how it works," said Frank irritably.

"You have no idea how it works," retorted Millie. "Men. They are so interested in a woman's body functions they would dissect one like a frog if they could get away with it."

"Eww," said Beth.

"Well, it's true. The very idea that they could know more about us than we do."

That men knew nothing about the physiology of women was a common truth they all held dear. There were a few mumbles from Frank about the ignorance of the masses, while Charlie found something interesting in the patterned tablecloth and Dresden stroked his beard, deeming that words were unwise.

Finding the moment a good time to say good night, Gary patted his wife's shoulder and captured his son, who had just realized they were about to leave, and bolted toward the kitchen.

In the spring, that short duration between break-up's remnants of snow and ice, and the blossoming of summer, it was pleasant to visit with Sharon. The half-mile drive by what was loosely termed a road, was shortened by almost a third if you walked through the woods. It was also more interesting.

The clearing of the Hughes property dwindled to a fine point that trailed into a groove of slender, tall birch, splattered with grey-green leaves. There was little brush. The birch was selfish. It shared the water source only with each other, passing it along through their roots. Only a soft, molting leaf mat covered the earth, along with some freshly springing berry bushes and wildflowers that only required moisture to survive.

The Bowen property was almost completely open and faced the inlet. When you burst into the clearing from the woods, your immediate view was a yawning slope, a pencil line of grey water, and Susitna Mountain, the Sleeping Lady, beyond. Square in the middle of this image was the Bowen house. It was so carefully positioned that the home squeezed every bit of sunlight possible from the sky, even in the winter when daylight lasted no more than a few hours.

The Bowens were building a new greenhouse and had missed the last two community meetings. The greenhouse was finished now, gleaming with new glass, and they had no good reasons left not to get involved with the next step in development. It seemed everyone was getting a little uppity these days, one way or another. You would think they were Hollywood movie stars instead of dirt farmers.

Well, Sharon needed to catch up on the latest gossip. It didn't matter who you were, there was no use pretending you didn't want to know what was happening with your neighbors. Beth hurried along, Cody just ahead, confident of the path and where it was taking them.

She was, as could be predicted, puttering around in her new greenhouse, Juliana right beside her in a child-sized gardening apron, diligently filling in pots with soil. As soon as she saw Cody, Juliana dropped her trowel and ran after him.

"Well," sighed Sharon, hands on her hips. "There goes my work force."

"There are child labor laws," said Beth, glancing a little enviously at Sharon's already sprouting plants.

Sharon also glanced at her tidy rows, all embedded in little, square pots, industriously trying to keep up with her standards for thriving, productive plants. She tweaked off a few brown leaves from one and tapped the soil in firmer. "I'm not laboring her. I'm teaching her. There's a difference."

"I suppose I should start teaching Cody a few things," agreed Beth. "He watered my African Violets with his milk the other day. He thought if milk was good for him, it must be good for violets. Killed them right off, it did. Fortunately, Millie was separating hers out and gave me a new plant. I guess he learned one thing. Don't water your plants with milk."

"Oh, little boys," said Sharon with a huff. "I heard Ester gave Ben a whacking for peeing on her Elephant Ear plant."

"My goodness!" Answered Beth. "That must have made Andy mad."

"Nope." Sharon removed her work gloves and began migrating toward the house, Beth following with her ears perked. "When she learned what Ben had done, she gave him another whacking."

"Gracious. He probably thought peeing on her plant was no different than peeing in the bushes."

"He knew better, he did. He's a Delaney. They do as they please even when they know better."

Still brimming with things to say, Beth started to elaborate on the Delaney party, but Sharon cut her short with news of her own. "Well, Art did it. He ordered a piano. I know it's his inheritance money, but don't you think I should have said something to say about it? I get greenhouses. He gets a piano!"

"But Sharon," said Beth in confusion. "I thought that was what you wanted."

Oblivious to the comment, Sharon knelt in front of the cold box and poured out two glasses of sweetened tea.

"That's only the half of it!" She said, placing the glasses on the kitchen table and sitting down. "I saw him sign some papers at the dockyard and got suspicious. Sure enough, he was ordering a piano. I asked why he hadn't said something. He said he wanted it to be a surprise. Well...."

Sharon hung over her glass as though delivering the most terrible news in the world. "The surprise wasn't for me. He's ordering it for the community hall."

Every bit of news Beth had to share seemed paltry at this point. Shamefully, instead of feeling consternation, she experienced a slight explosion of joy. Holding the happy passion in, she responded carefully. "That's a generous donation."

"I will say it is," Sharon sniffed. "How is Juliana to practice on a piano located three miles away?"

"That's not so far. You have a car." Despite all her best efforts, Beth could not drum up any real sense of dismay. "Think how jealous Ester will be. The Council will buy a brass engrained plaque with Art's name on it and tack it to the piano. He will be immortal."

Sharon suddenly laughed, that beautiful smile she rarely showed spreading across her face. "I was just yanking your chain. Not about the piano, but about being mad. I wanted to see how you would react. Don't be mad. I knew what Art was planning all along."

Beth had reached a critical point in her life where it was becoming impossible to remain angry with any of her friends and was relieved to discover she did not have to place Art among the anger instigators. "Good heavens, no," she said. "It's wonderful news. The players will be jumping for joy. We just can't have a theater without a piano."

"That's just what I told Art." Pleased with her joke, Sharon doodled with one finger on the table. "Did you talk with Doreen?"

"No," Beth admitted, dropping her head. "She was at the meetings, but I didn't talk with her. I keep feeling like I should apologize, but I don't want to."

"A lot of buts. I don't think she cares if you apologize. She misses you."

"She knows where I live. She's the one with a car, not me."

Sharon's square hands rubbed against each other with dismissal. "I think it's silly, is all. You two have been best friends for years." She changed the subject matter abruptly. "Didn't the Phillips brothers say they were sending for their parents?"

"Oh, not right away. They say they have to build a house first. Mrs. Phillips wants a house before she comes. It's all very peculiar. I can understand sending their grown sons, but why those two men were entrusted with the care of the youngest, I'll never know. Solace says he's going to grow up just like her oldest boy - always drinking, fighting, and getting into trouble. She had to bail Percy out of jail five times this past winter."

"What did they expect giving him a name like that? Percy. It sounds like someone who carries around a purse."

Beth had been playing with the pack of cigarettes on the table, wondering if she should light one. Sharon's answer made her feel justified. She shook one out of the pack. "Whose side are you on, anyway? I don't know what's got into you, Sharon. You know it's been a heartbreak for Solace, and now she has Bea to worry about. Bea drops everything she's doing to run out into the yard every time Brad Phillips appears. Solace says she can't get a lick of work out of the girl."

Sharon laughed and knocked the cigarettes from Beth's hands. "You don't need those. You're pregnant. Solace never could get any work out of that girl. That's why she has Andy. It doesn't matter that she doesn't show up half the time. A half-time worker is better than no worker at all."

Beth retrieved her cigarette and lit it determinedly.

"It's smoke or drink. I've been trying not to drink, but it's been harder than I thought it would be. Anyway, Mark Hansen says his cousin will kick your ass at baseball. She's signing up for the year."

"Is that so?" She didn't look at all distressed. "Mark seems to be right cocky these days."

"Well, it will all be interesting to watch." Beth checked her time. "I'd better go home now. I've got a roast to put in the oven. Don't forget – Saturday, the work party for the new hall. Come early and bring lots of food."

It was true she needed a cigarette to keep from drinking. She stopped half-way up the trail, to lean against a tree and light one. Things were getting tight. Half the women in the community neither smoked nor drank. Sharon used to, before she got pregnant with Juliana. They used to spend hours together, drinking gin tonics and smoking cigarettes. Now she was as uppity as the rest.

Beth took a long draw, the nicotine unwinding the tension nerve by nerve. So easy to be uppity when you have an inheritance or work at a desk job. Those desk workers didn't even have to drive the Alcan for a vacation if they waited three years. If they waited three years for each vacation, they could fly out for free. Construction workers didn't get these benefits. She was just going to have to spend more time with Andy and Hannah. They didn't get so judgmental.

When she returned to her house, she rummaged deep in the trunk that saved their most precious belongings until she found a small bottle of schnapps.

She took one swift swallow and shoved it back in the folds of her best linen tablecloth. Gary would never notice.

The hammers ring and the chainsaws buzz in the summer. The sounds echo through the narrow corridor between the mountains and the inlet, blending with the screeches of the owls and the seagulls. Wolf Creek comes to life. This summer, Wolf Creek's life centered around building the community hall.

The Hughes were running late. So many vehicles had showed up, they crowded the side of the road, and teetered sideways down an embankment. Every kid in the neighborhood must have been out there, plus half-a-dozen from the village, running joyously across the expansive field, the first to lose its winter snow, the first to dry, scraped down to thin topsoil and given a generous spread of pea gravel. The older ones, ranging from ten to eighteen, had claimed the driest, evenest corner for a baseball field. They didn't have enough to make a team, but there were enough to put in some practice.

While Cody trotted off to join the other toddlers who were being firmly controlled by Ester, Beth watched the game in progress. The two youngest Delaney girls had joined in. The oldest didn't really know how to play. She couldn't pitch. She couldn't swing a bat. She burst into giggles with each strike. At the end of her turn, she joined the older boys in the lineup, chatting gaily and shrugging off her lack of baseball skills.

The younger one was different. Tall for her age, with extra-long legs and a scowl on her ginger-framed face, Anna meant serious business. The pitcher, the oldest son of Gene Brewer, the trapper who married a Native girl and settled down just outside the village, threw gently for the younger kids. Anna popped the ball twice, giving it a glancing blow each time, then hit it hard enough to run to first base. It wasn't just Mark's cousin who would soon be giving Sharon competition!

The Brewer boy, the railroad man's boy and Brad Phillips played until they heard the boards being hammered in place, then abandoned the game. Carol pouted and looked around for something to do. She finally joined Solace's daughter, who was helping by sitting on the boards, keeping them still while the men sawed them.

There was always something to do if you looked around. There were buckets of water, boxes of nails, levels, squares, ladders, measuring tapes and rulers to carry.

There were tables to be set and food to be kept warm. There was holding things still and keeping things aligned. There were the children, always the children, bless them, to be watched.

Not that the toddlers gave any real trouble, yet. Somebody had thought to build them a sand box with sparkling, fresh sand. This kept them well-occupied, other than the occasional theft of a toy another child wanted.

It was the older children. Even ten-year-old Wally Miller sneaked into the woods to smoke and swear, a very young age to be influenced by the likes of Brad Phillips. It wasn't really her problem, she supposed, but it was obvious Carol Delaney and Bea Grant were sneaking into the woods too, and God knows what they were doing while they were out there.

She didn't want to be the one supervising the older children. Ester's brittle eyes would find them soon enough. Beth could hammer a straight nail, a fact she was proud of and that entitled her to do men's work. So could Sharon and Andy. They were pounding into place the floorboards stretched over the foundation. The steady tap-tap of the hammer was relaxing.

She fell into the rhythm, her mind digging down to talk with the tiny life growing inside her.

Just you wait, she promised her unborn child. *By the time you are walking, we will have swing sets and monkey bars. We will have teachers and chalk boards. You'll have friends. It won't be such a wilderness any longer.*

Tap-tap. Another board snugged into place. "Did you hear?" asked Andy, driving down nails beside her. "Ted Ewing got a seventeen-year-old pregnant out in Knik. Now, he's hiding somewhere near the village."

"Where near the village?" asked Beth between strokes.

"Well, nobody rightly knows, but they know he's around. They've seen him too much in the same spot headed out of town."

"He's lurking out in the woods?"

"Somewhere out there. Probably down on the inlet. There are some good hiding spots along the beach."

She stopped hammering to wipe her brow. The late May sun seemed to have been shining in the same spot for hours.

"What about that cousin of Mark's? The one that's been dating him. What's she got to say about all this?"

"Iris swears she hasn't seen him, but she sneaks off sometimes and is gone for days."

Andy didn't miss a beat. As soon as she tapped one board down, she slid another into place, her hammer beating away at anything that might trouble her. She would tap her worries down. Nail them tight so they wouldn't bother her.

Beth muttered to herself. She didn't like this. She didn't like this at all, raising her unborn daughter in a place where lechers were molesting teenage girls. That wasn't the community they agreed to build. She banged a nail too hard, sliding it sideways and cursed as she withdrew it to straighten it.

"Hey," said Sharon. "Let's take a break. The tables are ready."

One table had been set apart from the others that still carried their mysterious treasures under wraps. A white plastic tablecloth covered it, further separating from the identically set checker-cloth tables, lined on each side with chairs, with a stack of plates and cutlery in the middle.

The solitary table held the refreshments; of which there seemed a never-ending supply of coffee, hot water for tea, Kool-Aid, donuts, and cookies. Hannah was standing close guard to make sure the kids didn't stuff themselves with too many sugary treats before dinner.

She looked funny in guard duty, tall and skinny, pale as a ghost, yet she somehow managed to look intimidating enough for anyone under twelve. Beth poured a cup of coffee and placed two cookies on a paper plate.

"What? No Kool-Aid?" Hannah asked in a high, nervous voice.

Beth added one more cookie in case she wasn't satisfied with just two. "I haven't had a drink since the night of the variety show. Well, a beer now and then with Gary, but you know." She patted her stomach.

"Oh." Hannah sounded almost disappointed. "Nobody comes to see me anymore," she mumbled.

Beth felt a twinge of guilt. She had been working hard, planting her crops, and remaining busy in general, so she wouldn't have to think of that awful hunger that tugged at her, a hunger she had never truly curbed since she was fourteen.

"It's the season, Hannah. Our spring doesn't wait on anyone. Get the seeds in by late May, or it's too late. We don't mean nothing by it. Why haven't you been coming over on Friday nights?"

"Rick's been wanting to go out on the town on Friday nights. Now that Wally has turned eleven, we've got him babysitting for a few hours while we're gone."

"You don't think that's a little young?" asked Sharon with some concern.

"Oh no. Rick says eleven is a good age to learn responsibilities. They all listen to Wally, you know. There ain't one of those kids that will get out of line with Wally around."

Without stating any more opinions on the appropriate babysitting age, Sharon glanced around at their troops. Most were working. A few had taken a break. Jimmy had appeared with two horses and was giving kids horseback rides.

"I think it's time to go hammer some nails," she said. She picked up her cup and plate of cookies. Andy and Beth followed suit, stepping in line as Sharon led the way back to the unfinished floor.

"You can join us if you like," invited Beth, turning.

Hannah beamed, poured herself a cup of coffee and trotted after them. "But who's going to watch the refreshment stand?" She asked anxiously.

Beth shrugged. "Eh. Let the kids have at it a few minutes. They'll run all that extra energy off, anyway. We're on break. You're on break. Besides, what do you think will happen if Ester sees them overloading?"

"What do you think will happen if Ester finds I deserted my station?" quipped Hannah back in a voice that was half-joking, half-fearful.

At least, they were all laughing together. They perched on one end of the half-constructed floor, swinging their feet over the edge.

Almost directly in front of them, Charlie and Frank were measuring and cutting the boards needed for the framework, worrying over the slightest lack of uniformity.

It was a good thing they weren't framers, or the community would be marrying off their grandchildren before the hall had any windows or doors.

"So, Andy," said Beth, bringing the subject around to the main topic of conversation that had been rumbling through Wolf Creek. "Did Matt's wife show up?"

Andy nodded. "She arrived Thursday. That's his boy out there with the catcher's mitt."

Some kids were still playing baseball, although the size of the team had dwindled considerably. The primary members were Wally Miller, the two youngest trapper's boys, a Native boy who was apparently the trapper boys' cousin, Anna, and a boy who did not appear to be more than four years old, but hung on to his mitt ferociously, expecting a ball to hit it any second.

"Kind of looks like Matt," Beth mused.

"Kind of doesn't," said Andy. "He looks like his mother. If you saw her, you would agree."

Sharon scanned the faces of the women attending the kitchen. "She didn't come?"

Finishing her donut, Andy licked off her fingers before wiping them with a napkin, "she says she don't take to crowds too much. She comes around and visits with mama. Doesn't truck much with me or Jimmy."

Considering all the going on between Andy and Matt, that didn't really sound too surprising. The wife was bound to catch on. She probably knew the first time she saw Andy. You can't hide these things from women. Most likely it was why she began writing to Matt. She knew he was slipping away. She woke from a dream and felt it.

"Has she been to visit Millie?" Beth asked.

"Hah. It's more like Millie went to visit her. You know how Millie is. She just loves having neighbors, but Sarah didn't return the call." Andy spat on the ground in a most unladylike manner.

"Well, it's a very short period of time to be making judgments," Sharon remarked, brushing cookie crumbs away from her briskly. "Give her time to warm up to the place."

"I am thinking the place needs time to warm up to you." Hannah's voice slid softly over her words, and she laughed like a young girl. "It's a fact it can get downright unpleasant."

"It's a fact it can," agreed Sharon. "And not just in winter. The weather doesn't really give you a moment of peace and quiet."

Andy sighed and tucked back a lock of hair that had escaped her bandana. "Well, it's a pity she didn't go with us fishing. Millie and Frank did. We went to Seward and caught a dozen salmon in two days. It rained the whole time, but that's Seward for you. We thought once about settling there, but mama isn't completely agreeable with the ocean. She says she has sacrificed enough by living on the inlet."

"We didn't even have to go to the ocean," Hannah murmured. "We caught five reds on the Susitna River."

Sharon pounced on the words as though she had discovered new prey. "The Susitna? You fished the Little Su? How did you learn about it? I thought it was supposed to be one of the best kept secrets in the valley."

She shrugged. "Ain't no valley folk told us about it. It were one of the trappers. Name is Ted Something or Other. He comes and visits with Rick here and there to have a few drinks and pass the time of day."

"Ted Ewing?" asked Andy sharply. Her intense dislike for a man she had never met could only be explained by her loyalty to Millie and her fondness for Mark Hansen's family. Whipping around the words like a barracuda, she snarled, "That man is no good. You should not allow him to come around you or your children."

Hannah made a little face that would have been deprecating if she had found the courage to express herself in such manner. "I've heard the talk. I want to say, he ain't all bad. He taught us a bit about hunting and fishing that ain't much the Arkansas way and he gets right jolly when he's sitting and talking with Rick."

Andy, who never had a problem with deprecation, said a few words that did not normally come out of the mouth of a young lady and asked harshly, "Then you would be knowing they have a quarrel with him out there in Knik? He ran off and left a girl pregnant."

Hannah was unimpressed. "Well, she weren't one of you fancy girls. Her pappy is a miner and her mama is a Native."

It wasn't wise to make this type of statement in front of Andy. Her copper tones turned so coppery, she looked like she would spontaneously combust. It was even more of a mistake to say such words in front of Sharon.

Sharon didn't often have strong opinions, but when she formed one, she was immovable. Sharon didn't care if a girl was fancy as Ester or as wild as Betty Lou. If a man found her good enough to get in her pants, she was good enough for him to do the right thing by if he left a package. This was probably why Sharon had never said anything bad about Andy and her tragic affair with her husband.

"How would you feel," asked Sharon angrily, "if your daughter turned sixteen and a forty-five-year-old man got her pregnant?"

"Ain't nobody going to want Polly," Hannah murmured, her eyes fixed on the ground. "She's retarded."

Sharon gasped. "How can you say that? She doesn't look retarded to me!"

"She's three-years-old and she ain't talking," Hannah snapped. "She's retarded."

Beth stirred uncomfortably. She could feel the hostility building inside Andy and Sharon as they stared at pallid Hannah, who kept her eyes on the ground, realizing somehow, somewhere, she had said the wrong thing.

You would think Andy would understand but she didn't. She came from a different type of farm background; the pioneers who had trudged up the Oregon Trail, their Bibles, their satchels, their primers, their bottles of ink and stacks of paper kept among their greatest treasures. Come fire, come high water, they would not slack in teaching their children reading, writing and arithmetic. They were gentleman farmers, brought to their knees by the Great Depression but still clinging to education.

She would talk to Hannah later. Or maybe, she would invite over Millie and the two of them would talk with Hannah. Millie was good at these things. The next time she wheedled the car off Gary, she would pick up Hannah and take her to see Millie. That would do it.

She cleared her throat. "I suppose break is over girls, and just in time. Ester has discovered the refreshment table unattended."

Beth couldn't suppress a giggle as she watched Hannah scramble like a tardy schoolgirl back to her post and wilt under

Ester's stern gaze. It took a moment, but Sharon finally chuckled, then Andy.

"We'll straighten her out," Beth promised. "If we can't, we can always turn her over to Ester."

"I don't like it one bit, though," Andy continued to mutter, beating her hostilities into the head of a nail. "A man like Ewing lurking around in our woods. It's not decent."

"That little girl is not retarded," grumbled Sharon, beating out her own hostilities. "Look at the way she plays. She doesn't sit by herself and stare at the sand. She makes sandcastles with the other kids and pushes along toy trucks."

"Then why won't she talk?" Asked Beth, missing the nail and cursing to herself.

Sharon drove in another nail. She hammered like a professional. One tap to set the nail straight. A second blow to drive it home. "Maybe she doesn't want to," she said.

The floor was finished and the framework up for their community hall by late afternoon. The siding and the roof would come later, in bits and pieces as members squeezed in the time. Large canvas tarps were tacked over the top in case the rain came before the roof was finished. With a final tap to hold them in place, the community called it good.

It was the moment they were waiting for. The covered dishes were uncovered, the beans that had been boiling all day were set out with fresh cornbread, the top of a barbecue grill fashioned from an oil drum, was opened to display the mouth-watering pile of caribou ribs, grilled salmon, and roasted game hen. Once again, nobody had given up their chickens and once again, Jimmy had filled the demand with spruce chickens.

Gary was in a good mood. He had rented out his rototiller to four different neighbors, paying him back half the money on his investment and had busted out a garden for a co-worker in Muldoon, adding another twenty dollars to his net worth.

Ester and Millie had ambushed him almost as soon as he had knocked off work for the day to harass him into preparing a plot in front of the community hall where they could plant flowers. He made them no promises, but they knew he would do it. Sometime over the summer, he would till a patch of land, run a mix of good topsoil and manure through it, and carefully border it in with rocks.

The women would finish the job and next spring, the patch in front of their hall would be festive with flowers.

He ate so much, she began to wonder if he was competing with Frank and Charlie as to who could put away the most food, but when he sat back, rubbing the extra amount he had packed into his usually flat stomach with one hand, the other am around the back of her chair, she saw the most satisfied look on his face she had seen in a long time.

"It's nice to feel appreciated," he said, apparently to no one in particular.

She chuckled and laced her hand in his. "You haven't felt rejected, have you?"

"No, no. It's not that." He was silent a moment, watching the musicians prepare for a hoe-down. "If I buy you a car, will you make friends with Doreen again?"

"Who says we're not friends?" She asked uneasily.

"You don't hang out with her anymore."

"It's still a little embarrassing. I should apologize, I know, but I don't want to."

"Hum. We're not really political people, you know."

She considered the truthfulness of the statement, which was a bit undeniable. The most political thing Gary had ever done was put on a uniform. Once he had been able to take it off, he abandoned all thought of who ran the country. He supposed it was enough of a handful to run without his meddling.

"It's just," she said, "I never thought Alex was political."

Gary guffawed a bit loudly. "Of course Alex is political! He works in communications! All those boys working in an office have to be political. The bosses breathing down their necks are the government."

He shook two cigarettes from a pack and handed her one. The musicians were practicing their chords with a great deal of discordance. The dancers sat poised at the tables, waiting for the signal. "Did you want to dance?"

She shook her head. "The baby is tired. She didn't like the hammering much and she's just now settling down."

"She didn't like the noise, eh? We construction workers have it better, really. We don't have to answer to Uncle Sam. Anywhere you go, we're needed. The military bitches at us, but they need us more than we need them. What would they do if we suddenly stopped building the extra housing units for the twelve hundred men who are currently living in army tents? They don't have anything without builders."

"I'm sure she will understand that when she's born."

"Soon enough."

The caller was using a bullhorn. After giving the band time to warm up with a good Hank Williams tune, he strolled in front of them and called out the square dance number. "Everybody grab your partner. We're going to start with something easy. A little Virginia Reel."

Beth didn't dance, but she did clap her hands and tap her feet. Music had come to Wolf Creek. They had Frank and Jimmy to thank for it. Frank found the talent. Jimmy, with his guitar and his swagger, drew it to their festivities. Soon they would have a whole band of their own.

"Swing your partners up and down the middle."

The dancers jiggled. They skipped and twirled, and daisy chained. Her feet wanted to follow but the tiny being resting in her belly wanted nothing more than the lulling sounds of the gay festivities. She wrapped her hands around it reassuringly. "That doesn't seem proper, Andy and Matt partnering up for the square dance," she whispered to Gary.

Gary mused, his arm still around Beth's shoulders. "I can't say why not. They were already seeing each other before Matt's wife came. She was gone long enough for them to divorce. Four years is a big stretch of waiting."

"And there's his boy just watching."

"So? There's a bunch of people up there dancing."

The feet clattered on the new floorboards. Beth found Gary's free hand again and pulled it around, so it was resting with hers on her stomach. "We put down a good, solid floor, didn't we?"

The baby kicked under his hand, and he laughed. "You did. Damned good floor. You women built a good foundation."

Tired out from his long day at play, Cody curled up in the chair next to his mother and laid his head on her lap. She put her sweater around him to guard against the evening chill. "Ted Ewing's been visiting the Millers," she whispered.

She felt the hand on her shoulder tense, then relax with an effort. "I reckon we can't be telling folk whose company they can keep," he answered, grinding his words.

The evening was winding down. The festivities had come to an end. The dancers were staggering back to their seats, fanning their faces, and chatting at each other excitedly. It was so cheerful, Beth wished she could imprint every last detail forever in her mind. Even Doreen, bouncing and refreshed with her baby weight gone, became an intricate part of the memory.

"Trouble is brewing on the horizon," she told him. "With Ted Ewing around, trouble is brewing."

He didn't disagree. He gathered up Cody and slung him over his shoulder. "Let's go home."

Twenty-Three

It was shaping into a good summer, neither too little, nor too much rain, the plants growing rapidly under the midnight sun. Already, the radishes and carrots were coming up, some nearly ready to pull. Of all the summer chores, Beth enjoyed her time in the garden best. The baby liked it. She could feel her tiny passenger curled between her hips as she squatted, pulling weeds, and humming to herself. The baby rocked gently and contentedly in her sac.

Cody liked it. Beth was in a fixed spot where he could run and play while she kept an eye on him. He realized his greater freedom from her relaxed supervision came from trust and rejoiced in it, never wandering out of sight. She bent over her lettuces. Cutworms were getting into them! She cursed to herself as she tried to remember the remedy for getting rid of cutworms. She would have to ask Sharon. Mrs. Big Head knew everything about plants.

She was so absorbed in hunting down cutworms, she didn't notice at first that somebody was cutting through her backwoods trail. Only when the sound of footsteps scrambling rapidly over the hard earth registered on her brain that she realized someone was coming toward her, raggedly disturbing the air.

She looked up, not especially alarmed, only curious as to who could be so frantic. She thought at first, it was Betty Lou having one of her fits, but instead of drunken staggering in oversized clothes, the figure scrambled with purpose and direction. The runner was wearing shorts and a mud-splattered blouse, the inlet clay on it turning chalky gray. Her wild hair tumbled in thick russet curls. The scene didn't make sense.

Delaneys were many things, but they never panicked.

"Carol?" Beth asked uncertainly.

The girl veered from her course toward the road and stumbled toward Beth's voice. She ran like an animal, crouching with her arms pummeling in front of her to give more speed. When she reached the garden, she skidded several feet and stopped, her chest heaving. She squeezed her hands between her knees while she caught her breath and looked at Beth imploringly.

"You have to help me," the Delaney girl begged, her words spilling out in a rush. "It's Iris. He hurt her. He hurt her bad."

"Wait. Hold it." Beth groaned and stood up, adjusting the baby so she could walk comfortably. "You are going too fast. Tell me what happened."

Carol Delaney struggled to regain her composure the way she had been taught. Her ragged breath whooshed in and out, slowing with each exhale. The panicked blue eyes calmed, although her lips still quivered.

"It's Iris. She's got a shack on the inlet not far from your house. I get there by cutting through the woods, but you'll have to take the long way around if you're driving."

"Okay, okay."

The girl wasn't really making much sense. Her words were hurried and gave no helpful information other than the shortest way to Iris's hide-away, but she had said enough to give Beth a few suspicions. She called to Cody and led Carol to her house.

"What seems to be the problem?"

She was a Delaney after all. Stopping for a moment, she looked at Beth fiercely and retorted, "there's no seeming about it. Iris is hurt. You're one of those emergency people. Call the ambulance."

The poor child was near hysteria. Her teeth chattered and she trembled uncontrollably. Delaney or not, Beth was her senior. She led Carol to a chair and handed her a glass of water.

She sat down tentatively but drank greedily and cried at the same time.

Beth drew up a chair close to her and leaned forward. "What happened, Carol? I need to know."

She avoided looking Beth directly in the face and mumbled into her glass. "It was Ted Ewing. He beat Iris and hurt her bad. Call the ambulance, Mrs. Hughes."

Carol's sense of urgency was beginning to infect her. It wasn't like a Delaney to panic. It wasn't like Carol Delaney to ask for help, her clothes all dirty and ragged, her face streaked with tears. A few small twigs still clung to her hair, and Beth automatically picked them loose.

Carol waved her hand away. "Don't worry about me. It's Iris. She needs you."

Feeling a small degree of irritation at being addressed so bluntly by a young girl, Beth snatched her hand back and almost answered sharply.

Instead, she searched the girl's face, untidy with fear and urgency, and a second uneasy surge overwhelmed her. Despite her age, Carol was mature.

Even her younger sister, Anna, spoke with the same grave maturity. This, more than anything, was what made Delaneys hard to accept. They were older than their years.

Understanding she should take Carol's words seriously, Beth hurried through the house until she had hunted down the field phone and cranked it up. It rang several times then faintly, she heard Doreen's mild voice say, "Hello?"

"Doreen?" Beth flinched a little.

She hadn't really made up with her friend yet. "I tried to get Sharon, but she didn't pick up."

A moment of silence between the hiss and snaps of the irregular reception. "She's gone for the day. I think she went out to the valley."

Beth pressed her lips together and glanced at Carol. The tears were streaming from her eyes, a soundless "please" repeatedly tumbling from her mouth. "I need the ambulance, Doreen. Come pick me up."

Doreen didn't ask questions. That had always been one of her best qualities. If a matter was so urgent, the word "need" was used instead of "want", Doreen trusted the messenger.

"Right away," she promised and hung up.

While they waited, Beth gave Carol a wet cloth to wipe her face. "Why did he hurt her?" She asked.

Carol sobbed into the washcloth and blew her nose. "I don't know. I went to visit Iris, but when I got there, she was all bloodied and bruised. She was crying and in a lot of pain. She said Ted had hurt her, but she didn't say why."

There weren't many more words Beth could wring out of Carol before Doreen arrived. Most of what she said was repetitious and squeezed in between shuddering sobs. It took no more than a few minutes for Doreen's shiny automobile appeared in the driveway, but in those few minutes, Beth had already packed a change of clothes for Cody, and was waiting in the yard with him, along with a still-quivering Carol.

"Solace picked up when I picked up," Doreen said on the way to the Bowen house. "She's going to want to know what it's all about."

The wheels were flying faster than Beth had ever seen the mousy Doreen drive her Pontiac. Beth was impressed. She was putting her mousehood on a shelf.

She braced one hand against the dashboard and answered, "It's that young Hansen girl Ted Ewing has been bothering. Carol says he beat her up."

She kept both hands on the wheel, her eyes darting straight ahead, but her words still bounced sharply. "Didn't I say he was no good? He's the ones who been putting out the traps, sure as anything."

The Pontiac screeched into the Bowen yard, dust raising a banner behind it. The ambulance was parked in a two-sided shelter with a pointed roof, loosely referred to as a garage.

"She's down on the inlet if anyone asks," said Beth, opening the door and preparing to leave. "Carol, give Doreen directions, so she can call for help."

Carol sat deathly still in the back seat of Doreen's car. "Come on," Beth told her, gesturing. "You're going to have to show me where Iris is."

"Don't tell Andy," Carol pleaded. She crept out of the car reluctantly and stood next to Beth with her head down. "Or don't let her know right away. She's going to kill me. Oh cripes. Why does that man have to be such a creep?"

Cody and Patsy were babbling together, probably filling each other in on all they had done during the time they had been apart. Beth hung at the door a few seconds.

"Take care of my boy."

Doreen nodded. She was already taking charge of the nursery. She passed several plastic toys into the back seat for the toddlers and tucked the blanket more securely around her baby. Her calm eyes smiled, and Beth knew she had been forgiven.

She waved at Cody, who waved back, then continued playing. "I'll be back as soon as I can."

It didn't take much to get the engine going anymore. It still used a crank to spark, but it caught easily, the whole vehicle rumbling so violently, the engine looked like it would fall apart. Carol swung into the passenger's side of the van fretting, twisting her hair, and staring out the window.

The shack Carol indicated was less than a mile away if you cut through the woods from the Hughes property, but the road to it connected to the village road, which swung around to travel along the inlet, giving them a full three miles by vehicle. The last mile was beach road, uneven, rocky on one side, slippery with clay on the other, riddled with gouged out holes that filled with water during high tide and ebbed slowly when the tide was low. The ambulance bounced and bucked like a wild creature.

"All this time and they still haven't put in new shocks," muttered Beth. "If your friend doesn't have any broken bones, she'll have them by the time we get back on the main road."

Carol gave a small, straggled gasp. "What if she does have broken bones? Beth, are you a medic?"

She wasn't really. Beth had taken the first aid course to qualify as an ambulance driver, but she didn't have the knack for it, like Frank. She wouldn't be able to tell a broken bone from a sprain and was completely incapable of setting a bone or of returning a joint to its socket. She could clean and wipe with alcohol swabs, squeeze a gash together and tape it to stop bleeding, but all that internal stuff was an entirely different matter. She found herself praying Ted Ewing had not beaten-up Iris too badly.

With more bravado than she felt, she answered, "We'll work it out."

The shack was located on a small bluff surrounded by trees. It blended so well with the landscape you would have to know where to look to find it. The only trail to it was on the beach. When people were on the beach, they didn't look at the ugly bluff with its over-hang of water-soaked brush, tumbling, salt-covered rocks, and a collection of thorny bushes that produced tiny, defeated berries.

They looked at the ocean and the march of the mountain range beyond it. They looked at the explosions of wild flowers that fanned out toward the mud flats. If they had looked toward the bluff, all they would have seen was the unbroken wilderness crowding close to the banks.

Carol was anxious to lead the way, but Beth insisted they open the back of the van first and bring out the gurney and medical kit. "It would be stupid to go in empty-handed and have to need them," she reminded the girl.

Carol nodded her head up and down, teeth chattering. "That's right. That's right."

It was so dark inside, with only a weak filtering of sunlight penetrating the entrance and the woods surrounding it. So dark and small, with only a pot-belly stove and a mattress on the floor. Beth blinked to adjust her eyes. A shadow in the corner of the scanty bed, containing a blanket and a pillow, rustled and shrank, squeezing itself into a ball.

"Iris?" Carol's voice behind her sounded ghostly. "Iris, it's okay. She's here to help."

The shadow turned around and allowed a beam of sunlight to touch her. Iris was a pretty girl, with sleek black hair hanging to her waist and eyes that tilted slightly at the ends, emphasizing the dark pools in the center.

She wasn't quite as pretty today. One side of her face was bruised and swelling, the fawn-like eye disappearing behind the discolored lids. An angry red line dripped down the middle of her berry-stained mouth, oozing crimson tears. She was clutching her left arm, although she seemed to be in pain all over. She rocked back and forth, whimpering.

Beth stood at the doorpost, clinging to an extra moment of sanity before going inside. She hadn't expected vertigo.

393

She hadn't expected to panic. Carol's critical gaze came back to her. She wouldn't let her down.

These were young girlsa full twelve years younger than she was. She had a responsibility to them. She took a deep breath, stepped over to the mattress and squatted down next to the victim resting her belly between her knees.

"How are you feeling?" She asked, pulling back the undamaged eyelid and looking into the eye. She didn't know exactly what she was doing but she had seen doctors do it and felt it was the best way to calm her patient.

"He doesn't want me anymore," was all Iris said and began whimpering again.

Carol could move quickly. You wouldn't think so. She looked soft, with a tendency to become heavy-set. She looked like the kind who stayed home and played princess of the castle, although Beth knew for a fact there were no castles or other escapes from harsh reality in the Delaney home.

She had the gurney lined up with the side of the bed and the medical kit open before Beth could completely gather her wits.

It was true that Frank kept it well stocked. There were advantages to working inventory. She bet that man had his finger in every pie.

The two girls continued to look at her expectantly. "Let me see your arm," she urged Iris.

She didn't want to show her. She didn't want to move at all, but slowly and painfully, the injured girl loosened her grip and let it slip below her elbow. Beth pulled back the blouse. Just below the shoulder, the arm was a sickly, mottled color. She sucked in her breath. "Okay. We'll put it in a sling."

She rummaged through the packaged supplies until she found a large, plastic-wrapped piece of gauze with a paper drawing inside showing how to make a sling. She looked at the instructions dubiously. Carol twiddled a curly lock and stabbed with her finger at the individual steps but didn't appear enlightened, either.

"Do you need some help?"

It was the most damnable relief to hear a familiar voice call from the doorway. It was a good John Wayne imitation, but a decidedly feminine voice, even if it was deep-throated.

Beth looked up in frustration, a somewhat lethal looking sling flopping from her hands. "Do you know how to make one of these damned things?"

Andy moved away from the door, which provided the most viable means of light, and walked briskly into the room, pushing Carol to one side, and taking over the medical kit. "I got here as fast as I could."

"Did Doreen call you?" asked Carol timidly.

Andy frowned as though she had caught her sister in the middle of a burglary. "She called everybody. I picked up Ester along the way."

Reluctantly, Beth glanced once more toward the entrance. Ester stood just outside the door as though uncertain as to whether she wanted to come in. Deciding it was her duty, she strolled the few steps across the floor and shooed everybody away from Iris except Andy.

Ester was many things, but timidity wasn't among them. She capped one long, bony hand under Iris's elbow and poked at the edges of the inflamed area, causing the girl to wince although she did not cry out. Ester sniffed. "Could be broken."

Andy agreed but said it only with her eyes. She did have a way with young girls, probably because of her sisters.

She cradled the girl's back and asked if she could move her arm at all. Iris lifted it a little to show her she could but not without pain.

"Alright honey," she soothed. "We're going to wrap it up. Not tight, just enough to make you feel a bit better, eh? Then we're going to put it in a sling."

Ester had the gauze folded into a sling before Andy had finished wrapping Iris's arm. She wasn't satisfied with just the upper arm itself, but generously wrapped around and up over the shoulder, fussing about the degree of swelling, and finally lifting the generously but lightly bound arm into a sling. "There now. Do you see?" Andy stood back to look at the work. "We're professionals."

Carol spewed a short, nervous laugh. Ester was not so easily amused. She asked crisply, "Do you have any other injuries we should know about?"

Iris stared at the ground. "Can you walk?" Ester persisted.

She shook her head.

"He kicked her in the stomach!" blurted out Carol. "She told me so. He kicked her in the stomach until she thought she would die!"

"He was drunk!" protested Iris, gritting her teeth with the effort. "He didn't know what he was doing."

"Show them!" Carol's voice became as demanding as her sister's. "Show them what the bastard did."

Wilting under the Delaney stare, Iris pulled up her blouse. There were lumpy red splotches traveling up her ribs, turning yellow and blue with bruising. Even Ester's face crumpled, and though her mouth tried vainly to remain still and straight, it quivered at the corners. "Broken ribs?"

Andrea didn't want to touch them. "Maybe. We need more bandages."

"Frank is going to blow a gasket," muttered Carol, handing over the last two rolls of wrapping. "We're using all his bandages."

"They aren't Frank's," Andy scolded back. "They belong to whoever needs them. If he's a whiney baby, we'll buy more."

Sniffing her agreement and mumbling something about Charlie having as many resources as Frank, Ester held up Iris's blouse while Andy completed the job of mummifying the girl's upper torso.

Muttering the entire time, Andy barked out instructions for the other volunteers. "I think there can't be too much bandaging for this job. She's going to need a lot of cushioning on that wretched beach road. Speaking of which, Carol, use that blanket and pillow to create extra cushioning in the gurney. We'll have to carry her out."

Ester pursed her lips together. "You're about to pop," she fumed. "And Beth is pregnant as well. Neither one of you is supposed to lift more than twenty-five pounds."

Beth scoffed. "There are four of us and she can't weigh more than a hundred pounds. That's twenty-five pounds apiece."

Ester finally did allow Beth and Andy to help with the gurney, although she warned them, she and Carol would carry the heaviest part of the load. Beth didn't see how Ester could control this until she saw the strategy.

She put Carol at the foot and herself at the head of the gurney, giving Beth and Andy no choice except to prop up the middle, which didn't need much support.

Iris was light as a feather.Carol started to follow Ester as she climbed into the back of the van with Iris, but Andy held her back. "Oh no, young lady. You're riding with me. You have some explaining to do."

Beth cranked the ambulance and waited until Andy had pulled back out to the road, giving the other vehicle clearance, then matching its speed as the van barreled back to the main thoroughfare. Beth pushed the gas for all it was worth, flashing the lights and sounding the bells as the van drew closer to Anchorage.

Twenty-five miles at breath-taking speed, the bells of Chugiak ringing their warning. The sparse traffic made a wide berth for the screeching ambulance and the blue truck that followed it carrying two wild-eyed, red-headed women inside.

The ambulance roared in front of the emergency entrance, bells clanging, with the truck thundering behind it, Andy leaning long and heavily on the horn, blasting the announcement of their arrival. Every attendant in the hospital must have come pouring out at the racket. To their credit, they showed more astonishment with the antiquated ambulance than they did the volunteer emergency team.

Beth eased from the driver's seat, letting her baby bump settle before taking the required steps to reach the rescue scene. Ester had already burst through the back doors of the van and was ordering around two young medics who leapt to obey her commands. Even though she was in a more advanced state of pregnancy than Beth, Andrea sprang from the running board of her truck and strode across the parking lot, Carol just ahead of her. The bright hair streamed in the breeze like banners.

They were quarreling as they left the truck but settled down to walk in unison as the procession swept through the glass, swinging doors.

Beth didn't like hospitals. She didn't like the antiseptic smell. She didn't like the horrible uniforms medical personnel wore, somehow hiding the human under the sterile garments. She especially didn't like the way they simply took over, whisking the patient away before you even had a chance to say, "I'll see you soon."

She didn't like waiting at hospitals. The chairs were small and slippery. The coffee and hot chocolate came from vending machines. She stood in the hallway, between the lobby and the neatly arranged set of plastic chairs called the waiting room. Ester had already taken a seat, holding herself up primly. Andy and Carol glared at each other sullenly.

Andy broke off her staring contest to glance over at Beth in her discomfort. "You and Ester can go home if you want. We will stay until we find out how Iris is doing."

Ester folded her wrists over her knees. "It's not a problem. I'll just give Charlie a call at work. He can come get me later if Beth wants to go home."

Beth stalked halfway into the waiting room. "Did I say I wanted to go home? Maybe you think I care less about her than you do? I'll tell you now, I care about everyone here, so there."

She felt her lip tremble and sniffed. "What I need is a cigarette. I'm going outside."

"So do I," said Andy.

She marched purposefully toward the door, Carol tagging behind, saying, "I want one too."

Ester gave a "humph", and played with the telephone on the small, circular table next to her chair. "I don't smoke but I could use some fresh air. I'm going to give Charlie a call first. I'll tell him to let Gary know you drove the ambulance."

"Why don't you call the newspapers while you are at it," Beth mumbled under her breath, but left Ester to her pleasures.

She would call and tell Charlie how she and Andy had given the Hansen girl emergency treatment and mention that Beth drove the ambulance as an afterthought. Or maybe not. Beth didn't really know the kind of things Ester told Charlie.

She lit up her first cigarette of the day, well, since the morning. The morning didn't even seem real anymore, just part of a dream world she had lived in a long time. A world where nothing bad really happened. A world that tasted like coffee and sunshine and milky-sweet baby kisses. It was a fragile world. It took only one person to shatter it.

Leaning against a wall, Andy continued her dispute with Carol, who also leaned with her arms folded and a sandal covered foot kicking at a clod of earth.

"What were you doing down on the inlet?" Andy asked as she fumbled around in a long-strapped, leather purse.

"I already said," Carol answered sulkily. "I was visiting Iris."

She finally found her cigarettes and shook one out. "Since when have you become friends with Iris Hansen?"

Carol sighed. "A long time now, Andy. You never notice my friends. I have Iris and Bea and..."

"The railroad man's son?"

"Yes, him too. He has a name. Rodney Pierce. And the trapper's oldest son, Eugene Brewer, like his father, but they call his father Gene. We all meet down at the inlet."

"You knew that Iris was seeing Ted Ewing!"

All the airs, all the defenses, seemed to go out of Carol at once. She sagged against the wall silently.

Andy continued bitterly.

"And you never told anybody where she was at even though you knew people were looking for her?"

"She wanted her privacy!"

She began to cry again but wiped at her tears defiantly. "Can I have a cigarette now?"

Andy handed her a cigarette. "What are we going to tell mama?"

"That I'm almost sixteen years old and have a right to a life of my own."

"And look where that life has gotten you."

Another voice, more strident, broke in. "Well, just think. If Carol had not been friends with Iris, who would have come to her rescue?" Having finished her conversation with Charlie, Ester had strolled briskly out, discovering to her delight, she had an opening for antagonizing her greatest opponent.

Feeling sorry for the poor girl who had really been remarkably brave, Beth added her agreement. "It's not the kids who are a problem. It's that terrible man preying on kids. Something needs to be done."

Carol mumbled, "I thought he was a bad man, but Iris said she loved him. She was unhappy because her cousins didn't want him around anymore. They said Ewing has no respect."

"And he doesn't!" interjected Beth vehemently. "Look what he has done to that innocent child. I'm so worried now he will take out his vengeance on Millie."

She looked up almost shyly and gave Beth a half-smile. "You don't have to worry about Millie. Ted's scared of her. He thinks she might be a witch."

"Hah," said Andy. "And well she might be. Ted is lucky she hasn't turned him into a toad." Ester tilted her long nose and cleared her throat.

A small café close to the hospital sent out its homey collection of aromas. The women knew they had a long wait ahead of them. Even Carol understood the village girl's injuries were serious. Beth shoved her hands in her pockets and turned to inhale the inviting smells. "We might as well get a bite to eat."

The others didn't need any prodding. The café looked pleasant enough, with frilly curtains in the windows and round tables. They filled up on soup and crackers. The soup was comforting. Made with barley, it had tiny pieces of real beef and fresh-cut carrots and onions. Beth slurped at hers noisily. After watching a second, Carol copied her.

"Is Charlie coming for you?" Beth asked Ester between bites.

Ester didn't consider slurping socially acceptable. She raised each spoonful carefully and blew gently over the top. "He's not," Ester answered primly. "He's going straight home so Millie can have a break. She's got the kids."

Slurp and breathe. Pots rattled mechanically in the kitchen. Carol leaned with her elbow on the table and gave Beth a confidential look. "You know I babysit at nights when couples want to go out. I don't charge so much, either."

"No more babysitting for you," said Andy loudly. "Leave it for Anna. She's old enough."

Carol started to argue again, but Andy overrode her. "I've been talking with Solace. You're to start putting a few hours a day at the lodge."

"I'm going to be waitressing?"

Andy huffed. "Washing dishes. You've got to earn waitressing."

"But I will be working at the lodge!"

"I need some way to keep track of you."

Andy got up and walked to the counter to pay the tab. Ester glided behind in that strange, noiseless walk she often used in public places, and pressed down a five-dollar bill on the register.

"I've got this one. Buy her a pack of smokes or whatever it is you do to reward her."

On the way back to the hospital, Carol tucked her arm in Beth's, so that the two lagged behind the others. She put her mouth close to Beth's ear and whispered. "Did you hear what Mrs. Bolinder said? Smokes! I will have to tell the gang to be careful how loud they talk. Mrs. Bolinder has radar ears!"

It felt strange to have a young fan. It hadn't really been that long since she was fifteen years old. Just ten years. Alright, Beth admitted to herself. Thirteen years. Nearly half a life- time, but not so long. She had never pictured herself this way, but it was pleasant, like having a younger cousin who looked up to you.

Beth squeezed the arm interlocked in hers. "You're learning."

There was still no word concerning Iris. The women resigned themselves to flopping in the uncomfortable chairs and thumbing through outdated magazines.

They had gotten no further than showing each other a few wistful photos of fashionable haircuts and clothing styles, now two years old and already more modern than anything they sported, when a rush of air and a clatter of boots announced the opening of the entrance door. Beth looked up in the same second Andy jumped to her feet.

The Hansen brothers thundered into the lobby, the turbulent air swirling in behind them a flurry of motion in the still hospital corridors. "Where is she?" Demanded Mark, directing his hostility at the receptionist. She looked up with a pale, nervous face, aghast the rules of silence had been disturbed.

Andy shook his arm, trying to quiet him. He turned from the receptionist long enough to glare at her. "Where is she?" He asked again accusingly.

The disturbance alerted the medical examiner, who appeared suddenly on the other side of the automatically locking emergency treatment doors.

He was a modern-age type of guy, not much out of his twenties, with square, black glasses set halfway down his nose and a non-military haircut that left plenty of hair on top and close cropping on the side. He didn't even carry the classic clipboard in front of him, only a small notepad and a ballpoint pen. He scurried some mysterious, examining notes into his pad, then looked up, smiling diplomatically.

"Are you family?" he asked, tilting his head a little to look into Mark's eyes.

Mark crossed his arms over his chest and bellowed, "I'm her cousin!"

If the examiner's intention was to subtly separate the Hansen Brothers to speak to them privately, he was sadly mistaken. Recognizing the classic strategy, the group of Wolf Creek women congregated around him, penning him in to wait expectantly for his diagnosis.

Pressing his lips together, desirous of being both professional and diplomatic, the medical man tapped his pad with his ballpoint pen as he appraised the unlikely diversity of the Hansen family. Surrendering to the collective will, he put his pad and pen away and folded his hands.

"She stabilized. She'll be fine." He gave his attention directly to Mark. "Her arm isn't broken. It was dislocated. He grabbed her by the wrist and twisted it around behind her back." The doctor demonstrated cautiously on Mark, using no pressure, as though his smaller frame could do actual damage to a Hansen brother's blocky body. Mark grunted his understanding.

Satisfied he had correctly communicated the process by which Mark's cousin had been disabled, he congratulated the women on their timely rescue operation. "She has two broken ribs, both on the right side."

"He kicked her in the stomach," blurted Carol.

The glasses caught the artificial lighting and blinked. "Can you tell us who the attacker was, young lady?" asked the examiner hopefully.

Carol's eyes turned round while she gazed at him silently. The doctor grimaced and sighed loudly. "She won't tell us, either. I'm filing a report in case she changes her mind and presses charges, but the Highway Patrol can't do a thing if she won't say who assaulted her."

He looked hopefully from one member of the rather large audience to another, but they all seemed to have lost their tongues. Even Ester appeared to have found something interesting in the shape of her fingernails. Mark scowled at the smaller man. "Can we see her now?"

The examiner wasn't easily intimidated. Although disappointed he hadn't been able to glean more information concerning Iris's assault, he stroked his chin while considering.

"Only two people and for just a few minutes. She's still very groggy. It was touch and go for a while."

Mark looked at the doctor incredulously. "For two broken ribs?"

"For the baby. We almost lost it. She's a fighter, though. The baby's safe."

"What baby?" Mark's voice was small and harsh.

It was the classic glasses blink, which the doctor finished by placing his finger to the center bridge of the frame and pushing them back up on his nose. He hesitated and cleared his throat. "She's four months along. She didn't tell you?"

Obviously, she had not. The Hansens flashed their black eyes at each other, communicating a language only they understood. Taking the smallest of the three by the collar, Mark propelled him to the front and took the doctor by the arm. "Me and him. This one is her brother."

There wasn't really a reason for staying longer, yet they remained, clustered around Dave Hansen, who stood in mournful solitude, offering him their silent sympathy. Mark's visit didn't last long. Within fifteen minutes, he had barreled his way back through the emergency doors and thundered into the lobby. Without a word, he beckoned to Dave that they were leaving.

He didn't so much as say hello to Andy. Raising her shoulders and giving her company a wide-eyed look, she hurried after him, calling his name.

He stopped in his steady stride to wheel around and face her savagely. "She forgives him, Andy! She forgives him! We don't forgive him. Not this time."

If she had not seen it, Beth would never have believed she could see Andy frightened. Shaking her hand off his arm, Mark stomped through the exit and into the parking lot without looking back. She ran after him, calling his name, but her calls were useless. The Hansens formed a solid wall with their turned backs. When they reached their vehicle, they piled in, their faces tight with intention.

Holding her swollen stomach with both hands, Andy rushed to catch up with them. Carol tagged behind, throwing around her arms and shrieking that the world had gone insane, until Andy turned and shoved her toward the truck. Carol got in obediently, put her feet up on the dashboard, and shook out a cigarette from her new pack.

Beth watched with amazement. She must be missing something. She had seen angry men before. Gary was angry half the time, and Rick Miller was perpetually angry, but there was something in Mark Hansen's wrath that frightened Andrea Delaney. She had heard before that the worst tempers were in mild mannered men.

Mark was an easy-going man. Beth wondered what Andy thought he would do now that his anger was aroused.

She watched through the glass at the drama taking place in the parking lot. Andy was still trying to stop them as they climbed into their own truck, a half-ton with wooden side rails.

She stood outside the driver's window as they fired the beast up, then watched with her hands on her hips as they roared out of the parking lot. Stamping her foot, she flicked them off with her middle finger raised rudely, then stormed to her own truck and slammed the door.

Carol took her feet off the dash and sat up straight, her half-smoked cigarette dangling. They looked at each other once, then Andy was roaring down the road, chasing after the larger vehicle. Beth turned to Ester. "I guess you're with me."

The drive home was far quieter than the drive in, with no screeching tires, clanging bells, or frantic blares from the horn.

The only sound beside the unmuffled rumble of the engine was the ragged breathing of the two women, slowly subsiding to what sounded like soft sobs.

"The beast has found us," said Ester finally.

Beth swallowed and kept her attention on the changing gears. "Don't be so dramatic, Ester. It doesn't suit you."

"I wonder what Andy thinks Mark is going to do," Beth said casually for conversation.

"It's not what she thinks Mark might do," answered Ester, arranging herself primly. "It's what the village will do when he returns with the news. They warned Ted not to hurt her."

The town limits slid by, the marching foothills of the Chugach overtaking the scenery. Ester's long fingers knotted and twisted over each other.

"It really was terrible in France," she said.

Her words startled Beth. Most of the women were willing to share their stories of what they had done during the war, but Ester had always been silent. She never talked about occupied France. It was a forbidden subject. Her little book of horrors never opened for public viewing. Beth groped on the dashboard for her pack of Camels. Ester found them and lit a cigarette for her, her face drawn inward, her lips tight.

"Do you want one?" asked Beth, trying to adjust to this new side of Ester.

She shook her head. "No. I never did take them up, but my father smoked. I used to light them up for him when he was driving."

"You keep a lot of things to yourself," remarked Beth.

Ester looked out the window, her hands twisting over her purse. "There's no point in it. It's over. Everything is gone. If I don't keep my past to myself, what do I have?"

"Nice furniture?" asked Beth, trying weakly to make a joke.

Ester gave a tight smile to acknowledge the attempt. She sighed and rolled the window half-way down, letting the breeze loosen a little of her carefully placed hair.

"We got out in time but not really. The monsters don't let you forget them. It's not enough for them to take your home, to take your family, to destroy your life. They must humiliate. They

405

must make you..." She stopped. "Why are you asking me these questions?"

"I haven't asked you anything," said Beth in surprise.

She crossed her arms, squeezing her purse against her middle. "You were always asking. Your eyes were always asking. And now you know."

The foothills marched by like soldiers, an occasional house peering shyly from the trees in front of them. A low-flying plane whined overhead, echoing a distant memory. Beth understood. "Charlie was your savior."

"Charlie fought at Normandy," was all she would answer.

She supposed, that's all anybody had to say. How would they ever forget Normandy and the bold advance into Nazi territory? How would they ever stop counting the dead? How would they get on except by making families, going fishing, and constantly building and building? Charlie fought at Normandy. Charlie saw the beginning of the end.

She dropped Ester off at her house. During the drive, Ester had gathered herself together in small bits and pieces, holding herself more upright as they passed the Wolf Creek lodge and arranging her expression into its usual, disapproving serenity. She descended from the ambulance and walked toward the house with her back ramrod straight.

Charlie stepped down from the porch to lead her inside. Beth couldn't tell if she was crying or had said anything at all, but when he reached for her, she slumped. He held her closely as he brought her in, hovering over her so protectively, he looked like he was sheltering her from a storm although the drowsy evening was clear.

At the steps, she bowed and bent like a willow in the wind and buried her head in his shirt. Beth waited until the door closed before driving off. She no longer wanted to know what Ester had gone through during the war. She began to suspect she knew.

Beth supposed it wouldn't hurt anything to drive the ambulance home and have Gary take it to the Bowen homesite later. She couldn't see what difference it would make since they were all first responders. She was dead tired. All she wanted to do was curl up on the couch and hold her own child close.

She wasn't sure what type of greeting she would receive. After all, pregnant women did not normally barrel around in rickety vans on rescue missions. He would probably say something about her foolishness.

Doreen's Pontiac was still there. The cooking smells wafted around her as soon as Beth stepped out of the van. Thank goodness for Doreen. Gary was a nincompoop in the kitchen.

She took six steps, the front door burst open, and Gary swept her into his arms. He held her tight a few minutes. "I'm sorry," she mumbled. "I didn't mean to…"

"You did good," he said, kissing the top of her head, then her cheeks, then her lips. "You are an angel."

He led her inside where it was warm and safe, where arguments never became physical, where violence was out of the question. And though she was hugged and patted on the back, it wasn't until Doreen squeezed her in an embrace that she began to cry. She held to Doreen as she would a sister.

Her neighbor felt like a sister, a smaller one. She bent a little to draw her closer. She pressed against Doreen's softness, and felt those gentle little hands soothe the ache that squeezed hard against the small of her back. She released long, aching sobs and Doreen gathered them up and held them in, the way sisters do, the way they clean and tidy all the terrible pain that was transferred to them.

In one keening wail, Beth told her, "He tried to kill her baby! He beat her and tried to kill her baby."

Twenty-Four

Trauma has no effect on summer. It rolls out its days as it pleases, bringing sun, rain, flood, and draught without a moment of concern for outside opinion. It would have suited Beth just fine if the skies had pulled down and drenched them in a sullen summer-long downpour, but they did not. They continued with their even distribution, neither drenching the summer plants beyond repair nor scorching the fragile blooms.

Since the weather would not cooperate, Beth cooperated with the weather. She began taking pleasure again in the products of her labor and quit worrying about a child molester lurking in their woods.

Ted Ewing hadn't been heard from in over four weeks. Nobody seemed to know where he'd disappeared to, but nobody seriously inquired. It was Ewing's habit to disappear for months, even years at a time.

Iris was released from the hospital but would not return to the village. She moved into one of the cabins at the Wolf Creek lodge and supported herself by helping Solace in the kitchen and by laundering the bedding from the small collection of cabins. Beth saw her a few times. Iris's face was always pale and unhappy. She appeared to be wasting away even though her wounds were healing.

It was because of the baby, the other women said. The baby was still anxious and had not settled down completely. But Carol, Beth's new-found friend, said privately that Iris was grieving. She could not accept that Ted had voluntarily left her and believed her cousins had done something to chase him away.

"She thinks he would have owned up sooner or later to being a dad," said Carol. "But he got two girls pregnant at the same time. It doesn't look likely to me."

It didn't look likely to Beth, either. Ted Ewing was not a man of conscience, nor did he have regard for community standards. She believed as much as anybody in the right to choose your own livelihood, but she did not believe in choosing a life that harmed others. Whatever the Hansens had done to send Ted Ewing away, he deserved it. Iris needed to accept that he was a bad man before granting him forgiveness.

It was one of those tawdry late-summer days of over-blossoming flowers, hanging heavy in the muggy, overcast air, ripening berries wafting sticky-sweet fragrances, the poignant waiting period between spring planting and gathering.

Beth put on her new maternity dress, ordered from Sears and Roebucks, still crisp with starch. It was less conservative than the jumper Doreen had worn until it became shapeless and faded. It had trailing blue and green flowers on a pastel background. The bodice was scooped, with puffy sleeves and pink ribbon edging. She added a flower-shaped brooch with an amethyst in the middle and a set of different colored bangles.

Millie was holding a tea party. Their new tradition had begun sporadically with Ester on the day on their charity drive. This inspired Velma Delaney, who felt knowledgeable about the French and French traditions, to hold one as well, even inviting Solace, but not Beth, Doreen, or Sharon. Solace reciprocated by holding a party of her own, inviting all the same women, including Beth, Doreen, and Sharon, plus one more: Betty Lou. It was generally understood that Velma had declined all tea party invitations since then.

Millie was including everybody, even those who would probably not show, such as Hannah Miller, Sarah Jones, and Iris Hansen. It was a special day for Millie. Unlike most of the settlers, the Lamars had liquidated nearly all their belongings, bringing with them only the most essential items when they went up the Alcan.

They had carried on the back of their automobile, no heirloom furniture, no hundred-year-old Bone China, no precious ornamental keepsakes.

They started with nothing, except a bank account. Millie Lamar had just purchased her first tea set.

Because the party was at Millie's, it was an important affair. Not that she had an impressive house. Compared to the men who had carved their homes with their own hands and patient care, her home was plain. It was starkly utilitarian, with an unfinished inside. The fortunate aspect was the kitchen, dining, and living area were all one large room, making it easy for large congregations to gather.

You didn't turn down invitations to visit Millie. It wasn't just because she was likeable with a personality that embraced everyone. It was because you wanted her to like you. If she didn't, there must be something terribly wrong with you - something that couldn't be repaired.

A horn beeped in the yard and Beth quickly slid into her high-heeled shoes and took Cody by the hand. "Are you ready to play with the boys?"

"Boys!" he shouted, jumping up and down.

She hurried out and placed him in the backseat with Juliana. "Boys!" he shouted again, pointing at his playmate.

"Well," said Sharon from the driver's side. "He's talking."

Millie had pushed the table into the living area, so the seating arrangement was a circle around it that included the couch, Millie's rocking chair, Frank's armchair, four matching kitchen chairs and a tall stool that was generally used as Jason's high chair. Currently, it was being occupied by Doreen, who enjoyed the perspective of sitting in the highest chair in the house, as well as the only one small enough to sit in it comfortably.

Solace had come and was enjoying the rare luxury of relaxing on the couch. Hannah, surprisingly, had accepted the invitation after Doreen said she would provide transportation. She sat on the other side of Solace, shrinking as much into the corner as possible and casting furtive glances at the other occupant as though in some obscure manner she might offend the older woman.

"I saved you the rocking chair!" Said Millie, pulling Beth into the room and guiding her through the seating arrangement. "My, look at you! You look almost ready to pop!"

Beth sat down and looked jealously at Andy, who was also about to pop but carried it more like a speed bump in the road. Andy had taken Frank's armchair, which had deeper cushions and a wider seat than the rocker. Still, Millie had made the rocking chair accommodating. It was deep with her hand-knitted pillows and a knitted afghan thrown over the back. Beth poured a cup of tea, put some cookies on the edge of the plate and sat back to rock her tiny passenger.

"Oh, pansies!" Said Ester, examining the pattern on the cup. "How quaint." She held up the saucer to scrutinize the gold English Royal Crown stamp. "Ah, but you have good taste in china."

This was a cue for the others to lift their cups and examine the pattern and stamp. Quaint or not, the pansies made a pleasing design with their deep velvet colors.

"That sure is nice," agreed Hannah. "I got a few pieces of china I picked up for free when we filled up at the gas station. It had a pretty rosebud pattern. 'Course, the boys broke it all by now."

"Oh dear," said Ester, fanning herself.

"Ain't that right nice!" bellowed Betty Lou, slapping her leg. Incredibly, Betty Lou had also been invited, which explained the absence of Velma more clearly.

Solace was unconcerned about shrinking Hannah but kept her watchful eye on Betty Lou. "I'll have you mind your manners while you are here," Solace warned her. "No spitting. No rummaging through Frank's books. No playing around with Millie's new China."

"I ain't touching nothing!" Betty Lou protested. "I'll just have some of them cookies and drink from my own flask."

She had done what she promised, never touching the delicate table arrangement, but filling her pockets with cookies and sitting back in one of the chairs, listening cheerfully to the conversation and sometimes adding a few enthusiastic comments.

She popped another cookie in her mouth and gave Hannah a friendly nod. "Imagine giving out that pretty tableware for free. All I ever drank from in my born days was a tin cup."

"About English china," Ester began, but Betty Lou waved her off.

"It's probably not as good as 'Merican. I hear don't nothing come better than 'Merican made."

Seeing there was nothing she could do to further the cultural education of either Hannah or Betty Lou, Ester turned her attention to Andrea, who was sprawled out so much she looked like a balloon with sticks. "Honestly, when are you going to have that baby?"

Andy rubbed her tight, round belly contentedly. "Any day now. She's gone quiet. She's ready to come."

"You really think it's a girl?" Ester asked, putting down her cup and wiping at her mouth.

"Oh, it's a girl. Millie had a dream, didn't you, Millie? She dreamed this was the year of the girls."

"I didn't have a girl," said Doreen, who didn't seem to mind.

"That's because you already have a girl," said Andy practically.

"Well, I didn't either," Ester reminded her.

This didn't influence Andy's reasoning. "My dear," she said from the king of armchairs, "that's because you and Charlie don't know how to do things right."

For reasons known only to herself, this angered Ester. She stood up and told Andy bitterly, "You're so mean!"

Startled by her abrupt outburst, Baily who had been hiding under the couch ever since he realized the invasion of visitors was accompanied by small children, scurried out with the full ferocity of his species, unleashing all his pent-up emotions over this matronly occupancy.

"Oh for Pete's sake!" Ester snapped. "As many times as I've been over, you're going to bark at me again?"

The dog froze in mid-air, dropped his stump of a tail, and slid under Andy's chair. "Oh, I see whose side you're on," sniffed Ester, settling back down and picking up her teacup. "Charlie says we might adopt a girl."

"Whose girl will you adopt?" asked Andy, whose mission in life seemed to be poking fun at the Bolinders and Frank Lamar.

"An orphan, of course. There are children in the north who are orphaned."

Millie set out a tray of clever, checkerboard cookies made with chocolate and vanilla squares. They must have taken her hours to prepare. "There are orphans in the north," she agreed. "Tuberculous is very bad and it's affecting many of the young parents. It was in the newspaper," she added.

"I never read the news," admitted Doreen. "I read the funnies and do the crossword puzzle."

"And the advice column," agreed Beth.

"Well, I read the newspaper," said Sharon. "Sometimes. Provided it is local news. I really don't care what happens down in the states."

"Can't argue with that," agreed Andy. "It's too far away. It's like a different country."

"Well," said Solace, stretching herself divinely on the couch, crunching Hannah further into her corner. "Isn't that what you all were looking for? You wanted a place to start different. We got different for ya."

Millie passed some peanut butter sandwiches around to the toddlers, then came back to the table. "We've got different and now we have a problem."

Solace reached for a checkerboard cookie. "You mean Ted Ewing. Nobody's seen him in weeks."

"That's a fact!" said Betty Lou from her no-longer-isolated corner. Juliana and Patsy had discovered their favorite, fur-covered playmate and were squirming all over her lap, examining her many pouches.

Fortunately, she had tucked away her flask in her breast pocket and what the children were pulling out was an assortment of stones, tiny plastic toys left deserted along the wayside, bubble gum wrappers, and bottle caps. They examined each item as seriously as scientists. Betty Lou shifted in her chair to make her lap more accommodating for the little girls.

"He can't be a problem iffen he ain't around to make one. He's gone. Ain't nobody heard from 'im."

"No?" Millie arranged herself so her nicely tailored dress and tasteful, ruby-red earrings were more noticeable. They were garnets, of course, but still tasteful. "Think about what you're saying. How do you suppose it will be in seven or eight years, when those two little girls are growing up and pretty, if we still have a Ted Ewing around? Do you want them to grow up in fear? We have to settle it."

As she had never taken into consideration that little girls grow into big girls, and rather quickly, Betty Lou gave the two toddlers an agonized look. "I reckon his kind shouldn't be considered welcome."

Andrea struggled up into an upright sitting position from her throne chair and rested her arms on her knees. "Ted Ewing's not coming back. That's what Mark told me."

Millie was not so easily convinced. She had never spoken ill about Ewing, even though he had tried to steal their land claim, but she drew a hard line on abusing the innocent. Such sins placed them in her book of the unforgiven. She asked sullenly, "how can he be so sure?"

When Andy wanted to make an emphatic statement without using the exact words, she placed her emphasis on body language by leaning forward intently. "I looked him in the eye more than a week after it happened and asked him why Iris didn't want to come home. I said, you did something to Ted Ewing, didn't you?"

"And?" Encouraged Millie.

Andy took her time to tap her cigarette into an ashtray and take a long sip of tea. There was not one peep from the entire group of ladies assembled around the table as they stopped whatever they were doing to wait an answer. Even the activity of the children seemed to be suspended.

"Well," she said. "He told me there was a village decision."

When Millie's mouth pursed, her lips formed a heart-shape. When Ester's pursed, her lips disappeared. Ester cleared her throat. "If it was a village decision, I guess it's not for us to say."

Although the other women carefully tried to drop the subject, Hannah failed to see the significance of the words. "Why would a village decision stop Ted? Ain't much of anything stopped him yet."

Betty Lou scooted her chair closer to the couch, so she could pat Hannah on the shoulder. Although it was meant to be a comforting pat for this newcomer who knew so little about their culture, Hannah shrank so deeply into the couch, she looked like a rabbit peaking from its burrow.

"It's like this," she explained in her slow, deep drawl. "Iffen the villagers make a decision, best not to ask no questions. It's been done. Ted Ewing been done." A low moan trailed with her last sentence.

"Is that why Iris won't return to her brothers?" asked Millie.

Andy sighed. "She says it's not fair. She forgave him."

Beth snorted. She had heard about village girls' devotion toward their lovers and felt they were sometimes unwise in their choices – such as falling for manipulative, self-interested men with shiny baubles. They still hadn't figured out there are men who never give their hearts away. "Maybe she should try forgiving the village." said Beth dryly.

Solace found Beth's statement slightly objectionable. "We can't go making judgments on the villagers and we can't be making judgments on those who come out of the village. If Iris wants a place in the community, she's got one. We've got the Rasmussens and the Brewers, and they are all mixed up with the villagers. It won't hurt us to have a few more."

Doreen wiggled on her stool, happy to have some news to share. "That oldest Brewer boy is a good kid. Alex tells me he just graduated in the spring and already took a good job at the auto parts store. The boy's smart. He knows exactly what to look up."

"Eh," said Solace. "He only spent four years in my back yard, helping to tear apart engines. I reckon he should have some sense by now. He's already wanting to try his wings, that one. He asked about renting a cabin this winter when the hunters leave."

To those who had grown up on farms with brothers who had no inclination for leaving them, except active military duty, this seemed slightly scandalous. After some murmuring, Millie asked, "he's wanting to move out of the home already?"

"That's what he says. There's a lot of Brewer kids. I reckon he wants to make room for the ones that are crowded."

The conversation stalled as the group attempted to remember other news-worthy items. Not having had much to contribute to the Ted Ewing incident, which had found her missing in action at the most critical time, Sharon spoke up with some hope of a receptive audience. "In case anyone is interested, the community hall is finished. Art and Gary moved in the wood stove and the piano last night."

The added stimulus was satisfying. After their initial ground-breaking party, work on the community hall had been sporadic, squeezed into the hours the settlers had available between chores, accomplished through individual efforts. "Is it insulated?" asked Ester.

"Nope," Sharon answered. "It's going to be cold in there this winter but at least the shell is complete. We ran out of funds."

Millie looked at the positive side. "That will do until the hard winter.'

Sharon nodded. "That's what we figured. We can still hold meetings at the lodge until it gets too cold. Not so many people come out that time of year, anyway."

She picked up one of Millie's checkerboard cookies and nibbled at it delicately. Sharon always looked a bit strange when she behaved femininely, but she did it with polish, wiping the crumbs away and dabbing at her mouth with her napkin. "I suppose we will have to hold another fund raiser."

"Frank wants to perform a play." Millie said these things about Frank as matter-of-factly as announcing the dinner hour and with the same expectancy that everyone would come to the table and accept whatever the meal offered.

Beth groaned. "I'm not learning Shakespeare."

Andrea unleashed a loud "Hah! Knowing Frank, he will find something absolutely ridiculous. You have nothing to be afraid of, Beth. If it's Shakespeare, it's Taming of the Shrew."

"It's true," agreed Millie. "He wants to do one of those evil landlord plays with a poor, frail woman victim and, of course, a champion."

"No champion ever saved me from a landlord," grumbled Hannah. "When the landlord said, 'get up and move out', we got up and moved out, no question about it."

"That there," said Betty Lou, her arm stretched on the back of the couch still intended to be reassuringly, although it was in vain, "is why you moved to Alaska and made yer own home. Ain't nobody can tell you to leave."

The checkerboard cookies were delicious, rich, dark chocolate with sweet vanilla. Beth found herself eating more than she should. The doctor had said to watch her weight. She had been watching it but how much could you seriously watch when you have a growing baby inside you? She felt hungry all the time and the little cookies couldn't be that bad. They weren't more than two inches square.

As each person ran out of newsworthy items to relate, the conversation dwindled away. Solace sighed. "As pleasant as it's been ladies, I need to get back to the store. Zeb will be holding a drinking contest with all his friends if I don't get back soon to keep an eye on things. That man has given me every gray hair in my head."

She wasn't alarmingly gray headed for a woman in her forties, but knowing Zeb, Solace's statement was probably justified.

Doreen jumped down from her stool. "I'd better go to. Alex hates it when dinner is late. Hannah, are you coming with me?"

"Oh," said Ester, getting out of her seat. "If you're going my way, you can drop me off at my house. It will save the walk. I can't keep up with Denny anymore."

Hannah unfolded herself slowly from her corner and edged around Solace, keeping her eyes down. "Yes, ma'am," she murmured. She began collecting kids from various hiding places but stopped to whisper to Beth. "Just what do they mean by the village made a decision?"

Beth stopped rocking contentedly to whisper back, "It just means just like Betty Lou said. Ted Ewing is done for. He won't ever be coming back."

"Rick thinks it's wrong and all, to be so mad about Mr. Ewing, but he don't want to lose his job and he don't want to get on the bad side of everybody seeing they have been so nice to us, but he don't understand it. That's the truth."

Beth noticed Sharon was also preparing to leave. She patted Hannah's arm before lifting herself out of the rocking chair with a few grunts. "Like we were all saying, we do things differently here. Iris is from the village, so it was a village problem. The village took care of its problem. There ain't anymore to it."

Millie had begun clearing away some of the dishes. She looked up when she saw Beth beside her, stacking a few plates, and smiled. "We've all got to rush to our kitchens, except Andy and Betty Lou. Sometimes, I think they are the smart ones."

Neither Andy nor Betty Lou showed any inclination at all to leave the comfort of their surroundings. They chatted with each other on the merits of young Eugene Brewer and a few other developing members of the community, all of whom were of interest to Andy, considering her wayward younger sister.

"They kind of live by their own rules, don't they?" Beth mused. "The men. I don't know how they do it. It doesn't matter how big a lunch you pack for them. They are bottomless pits. If they had a restaurant right in the middle of the work zone, the men would still come home starving."

Realizing the assembly was breaking up, Cody had taken up a position behind the armchair. He had no interest in leaving the other boys. He clung to the chair and screamed. Beth waddled over with his sweater, and crouched down, her big belly popping out between her knees. She tried pulling him out with one hand, while the other gripped the arm of the chair for support. He thrashed and cried harder, screeching, "Boys!"

A bony-fingered hand that disavowed any sign of nonsense snatched the garment from Beth's hands and a voice rising above it ordered sternly, "Cody, get into your sweater this instant." Cody stopped crying and looked up at the interloper. Ester stood over him, her face unsmiling, formidable enough to scare a gold miner into submission. Meekly, he allowed her to help him into his sweater.

Beth groaned and tried to struggle to her feet. Sharon caught her and pulled her upright. "I think your squatting days are over for the next month or so," she remarked.

She smiled wryly and kneaded the small of her back. "I got all the vegetables in, at least. We had a bumper crop."

"You worked hard." There was a note of curiosity in Sharon's remark.

Beth grimaced. "I quit drinking. I had to stay busy, or I would go crazy."

That beaming smile flashed once, quickly, across her face. "You already are crazy." Picking up her sweater and purse, she called loudly to the other women as they were leaving, "Who's doing the next tea party?"

"I am!" Waved Doreen, jumping to make herself better noticed. "I'll send out notices next week."

The late summer folded in on itself, pining for the endless hours of sunlight. There was so much to be put away before winter. Each year it was the same. They spent their entire summer preparing, the entire winter, hunkered down.

Now there were new people, some maybe as ignorant of survival as the Millers. It wasn't their fault. You couldn't judge a person based on where they were from or what they knew. Still, it would be better for the community overall if not too many walked in empty-handed. Beth had felt Hannah's strain during the winter as though it were her own. Well, it was time for Hannah Miller to start standing on her own now and maybe start teaching somebody else the ropes.

Sharon agreed. After dropping Beth off after the tea party, she told her it was time she stopped spreading herself so thin. "You've got your own family to worry about," she said, her voice mildly scolding. "You can't be taking on one with four kids. Gary is Rick's boss, not his father."

She knew that. Lord knows, she had been trying, but when it came to Hannah Miller, there was always a problem. If one kid was sick, they were all sick. If one needed a new pair of shoes, they all had broken-down shoes. When their leaking roof was fixed, a windstorm tore down their lean-to. They cleared the wrong areas, planted in the wrong spots and too late in the season, and did not know how to build a cellar. Bless them, it wasn't really their fault, but if Rick Miller would just listen to advice first instead of going ahead and doing as he pleased, to discover what he pleased didn't bring good results.

She sighed when she waved goodbye, barely concealing a pained look that traveled across her face.

Beth filled the canning pot and started the first jars boiling. Her ankles were swelling again. She hobbled uncomfortably to finish dinner preparations before collapsing on the couch and putting her feet up.

Cody patted at her legs, wanting to play. She gave him some garden peas to open. They should have planted more peas. Cody and Gary loved them raw and had been raiding the row of peas ever since they began forming pods. They didn't have enough to can. They would just have to eat them fresh. Instead of opening them, Cody chewed on them happily, pods and all.

She was still sitting when Gary came home. She half-rose, then settled back again. "The dinner is ready," she said. "Could you just turn the stove off and fix a plate? My feet are killing me."

Always a casual eater, Gary pattered around in the kitchen, clattering plates, opening drawers, and dropping silverware. Eventually, he returned with two large plates and one small one, which he set on the coffee table for Cody. "I turned the jars off. They were boiling."

"I think I ate too many cookies at Millie's house," she said, picking at the food. "My appetite is spoiled."

"Do you want a beer?"

She nodded. A beer would be nice. It would help her relax. Her feet throbbed. Her back ached. A beer helped a lot. She drowsed.

The next morning she discovered she had been left on the couch to sleep. Her legs were drawn up and a blanket snugged in around her. She sat up to start breakfast. Gary was already in the kitchen, slopping coffee all over the stove and trying his best to clean it up before she woke.

"I forgot to turn it down when it started perking," he apologized. "Then it started bubbling and just made a mess."

She picked up a towel and began cleaning up. "You should have waked me."

He sat down expectantly while she heated a skillet for bacon and eggs. "You looked too tired. You never looked that tired with Cody," he added anxiously.

Her feet still throbbed and her lower back ached. She sat down heavily. "I don't carry her the same. She pushes on my ribs a lot. Solace thinks she might be breach. She knows how to give one of those massages where you turn the baby around so it's pointing in the right direction."

"You're not letting Solace do her voodoo stuff on our baby," Gary muttered. "What does the doctor say?"

"All he cares about is my weight. He nags me all the time about it."

"Huh. Did you tell him I like big women?"

"I did. He wasn't impressed. Since when do doctors busy themselves with a woman's weight, anyway? It seems indecent to me."

"Just keep your feet up today," he advised. "You don't have anything to prove to anyone. Hell, you'll be feeding the whole community vegetables all winter."

It was a tempting idea. She set down his plate. "How did Rick do with his pigs? I forgot to ask Hannah about it."

"Not bad. The sow dropped eight piglets. He'll be slaughtering them in October."

"It will help them out a bit, now, won't it? Are you buying a pig?"

"I thought I'd buy a nice ham and some salt pork. Hannah knows how to make salt pork."

"I haven't had ham in a while. It will be a nice break."

When he left for work, she thought about the upcoming holidays and how nice it would be to hold them in the big, new hall, and have a splendid ham at the feast. The image was so appealing, she kept it in her head while she fed Cody and went about her morning chores.

It was true. There wasn't so much to do now except wait. She could pick berries, she supposed but the activity didn't really sound appealing, not with two gigantic ankles.

It wasn't just Hannah's woes that filled her mind. She could not stop thinking about Iris. She could not stop thinking about those soulful eyes, too mild to understand how anyone could be willfully brutal.

Iris awoke something more than the thin edge of danger they had accepted by living in the wilderness.

She reminded them of the vulnerability they all had as women. Their greatest predator was their own species.

Gary was a good man. He never backed down from a fight, but he never hit a woman. Neither did the other men in the First Families, not even the irascible Delaneys. Most likely, among the Delaneys, it was the opposite problem. She couldn't imagine a Delaney woman backing down. Nor Millie Lamar, she added to herself. Millie was the only woman in town Ted Ewing had been afraid of. Beth wondered what it took to make men fear her. It wasn't ferocity. Next to Doreen, Millie was the least ferocious person Beth knew.

Iris had exposed their weakness as women. She had exposed it and Beth had felt the fear crawl inside. The woods were lonely, the empty spaces yawned with cravings. The children played at the edge of the woods. Someday, it would call to them. Someday, they would become a part of the wilds.

She could only hope the wild men did not come to them, the predators of sweet innocence. The image of Iris would not leave her, tiny, battered body pressed against a wall, her eyes cornered and trapped, the trust she held for all things living, beaten out of her. It wasn't tolerable. None of it felt tolerable.

The uneasy feelings rumbled. She didn't like being afraid. She had never felt afraid before because she had never felt powerless. She was surrounded by protection: her man, the familial bonds, the closely-knit community.

Even during the war, she hadn't been afraid for herself, only of losing a loved one. She was afraid for herself now, or not really for herself, but for the child she was carrying. For all the children growing up who did not know that some adults should not be trusted. Those adults would trickle in, invade the community, regardless of their vigilance. As hard as she tried to remember how she had learned to sidestep the users and abusers, she couldn't.

Maybe it was because she had started drinking so early in life. Maybe the drinking was so she wouldn't remember she had only been thirteen when she tried her first beer. There wasn't a "why" to it. She liked it. It loosened her up, made her funnier and bolder. She was popular in school with her big, belting voice and her willingness to try anything daring.

Nothing seemed wrong about it, and she had Gary. She always had Gary. It had been like a knife ripping through her heart when he confronted her on becoming an alcoholic.

She hadn't meant to start drinking again. She only wanted something to take the edge off her nerves. She could see the scene so vividly in her head; the way he had towered over the young girl and struck her again and again, twisting her arm behind her back so she would feel greater pain. The picture of what he had done was written all over the child's body. And the eyes... Beth could not forget the eyes of innocence shattered, of love hanging by a lifeline that had been cut off at the boat.

She began having nightmares. Sometimes, she was Iris. Sometimes, her unborn child was Iris. Sometimes, she dreamed of recklessly driving the ambulance to a hospital that always remained far away, her heart pounding, her lips dry with desperation. She bought a pint and took a sip. She was grateful for the instant relief.

Each day, she took another small sip. They were all small. She was sure of it. She just stopped counting how often she sipped after it became twice a day. She hadn't had a sip all day. She needed something for the pain. Her feet were dreadfully swollen. Why had she crammed them into high-heeled shoes? Her doctor had told her, "Wear only flat, comfortable shoes. With your weight and your condition, your blood circulation gets cut off too easily."

He had pressed her puffy ankles to demonstrate. "Do you see how much water you are holding? This can be dangerous for your health and that of the baby."

"Couldn't you just give me those pills that get rid of water?" She had asked half humorously.

"No, I cannot," he had answered with a serious gaze. "Cut down on your salt. Cut down on your sugar."

Exhausted with proving his manliness to three other toddling boys, Cody threw himself down on the couch as soon as he returned home and fell asleep. There was time before Gary came home, time to relax and nurse her aching feet.

She pattered guiltily into her bedroom and opened the linen trunk. The bottle was there, under the crisp pile of carefully folded towels and sheets.

She checked the contents critically. Christ. She had drunk over half of it. She would have to slow down, or Gary would find out. One sip. That's all. She just needed one sip.

She took a deep breath as the pain subsided in her head and the throbbing in her feet ebbed. One more little sip, and she put the bottle away. What did the doctor know, anyway?

He told her not to eat salt. He told her not to eat sugar. He told her to watch her weight. He told her to keep her feet up at least two hours a day, as though she could remain idle that long with all her chores.

She should have taken her shoes off when she was at Millie's house. Why hadn't she done it? What did it matter? The doctor was a pervert. She was sure of it. Why else would he care if she had a little belly fat?

The entire community equally shared a guilt because they equally shared a secret. Ted Ewing was done for. He got what he deserved and there was no point in talking about it. It probably didn't make them law-abiding with the law, but they were law-abiding among themselves. Justice had been served.

"We won't let it happen again," she said to the empty room, and from the uneasy recesses of her mind, she spoke the words that had been kept silent to the listening walls. "Not even if it's Rick Miller beating his wife and kids."

It had only been two sips of Jack Daniel. Why did she feel so strange? Everything was dark and fuzzy, like a poorly taken photo. It must have been the long day stuffed in tight shoes. Her feet didn't hurt anymore, though. They were numb. She felt numb all over. She needed a nap. She needed Cody. He was all that was real.

She tried to rise, then gave it up. She would crawl. She would crawl to the couch and take Cody into her arms. She would protect him. She curled up around him and pulled him close, inhaling the soft baby smell of his hair. He mumbled and snuggled closer.

She was shaken awake.

"Oh!" She said, sitting up with a start. "Did I fall asleep again?"

"You did." Gary looked at her with concern. "You're sleeping a lot."

"Cody!"

"He's alright. He was asleep next to you when I came home. No dinner tonight?"

"I'm sorry." She rubbed her head, trying to clear it. Everything seemed distorted, like she was drunk, but she had only taken a swallow and that was hours ago. "There are leftovers in the cold box. I'll heat them up."

"I can do it. You've probably got an entire banquet in there."

"Just about." She sat back again, wondering about her exhaustion.

She went to bed early, still feeling foggy. The dinner didn't sit well. Gary had heated it thoroughly enough, but the beans boiled in her stomach, and she could still taste the sauce from the potato scallops clinging to the back of her throat like chalk. She closed her eyes, waiting for the cool night air to soothe them and for the room to settle.

She roused long enough from an uneasy sleep that included disembodied voices babbling over nothing of great consequence, and swirling colors of red, yellow, and blue popping from bubbles, to notice when Gary came to bed. She curled up close and laid her head on his chest. The rhythmic thumping carried her into a deeper, dreamless sleep.

The first sound she heard was a clock ticking. It was unusually noisy, becoming more persistent with each second. A voice whispered that seemed to come from both inside and outside her, "*We're running out of time.*"

She jolted awake. The sleepy sun was gazing through the window, dust motes dancing in the burnished rays. The clock ticked away the seconds loudly. "Gary!" He slumbered in oblivious bliss.

Something dark and aching crawled up and down her spine and she sat up, pressing her back against the headboard. She shook his shoulder. "Gary, wake up. Something's wrong."

He scrambled out of the covers, his face reflecting the alarm in her voice. "What? What? Are you in pain?"

"Call the ambulance. She's coming, Gary. She's coming now."

He hopped half-way into his pants and struggled to pull them up by the suspenders. "It's not time!" He fretted, tucking his tee shirt in sideways, his big hands working frantically to finish dressing. "She's three weeks early!"

She doubled over as flames ripped from her lower back and burrowed into the soft sanctuary between her thighs. The pain was like an ocean's roar, rearing up and crashing into her intestines, hot and biting, low and aching at the same time. It howled its rampage, then subsided. "I don't care how early she is. She's coming."

Not really dressed, his tee shirt slopping over his pants, his work shirt flapping like wings behind him, Gary found the field phone and slammed it down on the table. She watched from the bedroom doorway. He cranked the phone so hard it was a wonder the spark didn't catch the house on fire.

"Art!" He screamed into his end, when the crackling stopped, and a sleepy voice picked up. "Art, bring the ambulance around. Beth is having her baby!"

It was a most uncommon view of her husband, scrambling, bumbling, hopping up and down as he shoved first one foot into a boot, then another. It would have been comical except as soon as she found enough breath to laugh, another pain began to well up, gently at first, then pressing in its intensity. She was being ripped apart from the inside out. The scream she had suppressed the first time, shattered the air so loudly, Cody sat up in his crib and cried.

"Two minutes apart," mumbled Gary. "Oh God, two minutes apart! Jesus! Lord! I need your help!"

She quit remembering anything clearly with the third spasm. She heard Art come in, stamping his feet, and muttering something about coffee. She was conscious of being carried out on a gurney through wave after wave of dark nausea.

She vaguely saw Sharon's worried face looking down at her. The colors were bleeding away. She was a grey shadow with yellow glints in her hair. Sharon faded out. The inside of the ambulance faded out.

The ride, rocking, wheeling, leaning into the curves and bouncing straight again, weaved in and out with the pain.

The darkness was a blessing. It was thick, black, and velvety. It cushioned her. It cooled the burning sensations between her eyes, inside her head, down the curving arch of her spine. It was warm and friendly. She wrapped the darkness around her like a cloak, her eyes sinking back in her head, back into the forgetful, cool depths.

"That was close."

Beth blinked and opened her eyes at the unfamiliar voice and stared at an unfamiliar, immaculately white ceiling, framed by immaculately pale-blue walls. She found a few remnants of her voice and asked hoarsely, "where am I?"

A crisply manicured head with black-framed glasses loomed over her face, studied her intently and sat back. Her eyes focused more as they tracked him.

"Where do you think you are?" he asked, sitting in a chair, holding a notepad in front of him.

The clues were obvious. The white medical jacket, the stethoscope around his neck, the IV bottle over her bed, the box of tissues. "A hospital room," she answered, gathering her words. She studied him studying her and scribbling notes. He looked familiar. "I remember you. Are you one of those woman doctor specialists?"

"An obstetrician? Yes. I see your cognitive functions are returning. How do you feel?"

"Like holy shit."

She attempted to sit up and he touched her chest in wordless advice to lie back down. "How long was I out?"

"Three days."

She sucked in her breath, then a fear so horrible, she could barely contemplate it roared through her brain.

"My baby! Where's my baby?" She clutched her stomach, gone empty and soft.

He had a reassuring voice. He was too young for it to be practiced, so it had to be natural. "Your baby is alright. It's a girl. A little light – five pounds, four ounces, but normal for an eight- month pregnancy."

The hard knot of fear melted, replaced by a small burst of joy. "I knew it was a girl. When can I see her?"

He slid his chair so close to the bed, his knees touched the side of it. She knew what that meant. He was about to say something serious. She braced herself, her heart beating rapidly. "Beth, did your doctor ever talk to you about gestational diabetes? You were seeing a doctor, right?"

She let her breath out. "I went to him a few times. He said it was something a lot of women get, and they return to normal after the baby is born."

"They do, most of the time. You went into what is commonly called diabetic shock. It happens when your body can't create enough insulin, causing your blood sugar to go up. There were some complications. It was a difficult birth and the baby needed treatment for jaundice. I want to schedule regular visits for both you and your child. I don't think you'll need insulin, but I want to make sure."

"I gave my child diabetes?"

"No, we can't say that. I just want to keep a check on her to make sure, and you too, Mrs. Hughes."

She was glad she wasn't sitting up. She wanted to shrink deeper into the pillows, fall into them like a deep, dark hole. But the hole was cold now, not nearly as warm, or comfortable as it was before. She felt hot tears sting her eyes and closed them.

The chair scraped and feet shuffled as the doctor stood to leave. "I'll let your husband know you're awake."

Beth didn't respond. She turned her head to the wall and listened until the door clicked shut.

"What have I done to myself?" She accused her silent mind bitterly. *"What have I done to my baby?"* A long, quaking sob escaped her lips. "What's wrong with me?"

Twenty-Five

The frost crunched across the Lamar drive and framed the sides of the house. A candle glowed from behind a pumpkin made from construction paper, setting off a window. Hard to believe winter was moving in and the holidays were upon them. Beth had let the days slip by in her guilt and despair one by one.

She could not breathe during the week-long ordeal when she had been officially released from the hospital, but little Greta had not. Her arms had ached to hold her baby and tell her over and over she was sorry.

As Gary put it, she had lucked out. Greta's blood sugar stabilized. She began gaining weight, so that by the time she arrived home, she was rosy and plump. Greta wasn't the one Gary began worrying about, however. It was Beth. Beth didn't want to go visiting anymore. Beth no longer burst into robust song or made jokes about Ester. She didn't make jokes at all.

Gary thought she needed cheering up, so he bought her a car. It was a modest car, at least ten years old, with sour-faced heavy grillwork in front, and a squat, rounded body, but it had a good engine and a recently built-in radio.

When the weather conditions were right, she could tune in to two stations. She had only driven it once – to the Wolf Creek trading post. Solace had given the car the admiration it deserved, and a free ginger ale to Cody.

"You don't seem your usual, chipper self," Solace had observed.

"I'm not," Beth had answered honestly. "I didn't do right by my kid, and it bothers me, you know. It eats away at me. It's my fault she came early. It's my fault she almost caught diabetes."

"Can you catch diabetes?" Solace asked with surprise.

"I guess you can," said Beth, declining the donut that was offered, her near-death experience still fresh in her mind. "Greta almost caught it because of me. That's what the doctor said."

Solace scratched her head in puzzlement. "I never really did understand about these things. You should talk to Andy about it since she's studying to be a nurse."

Beth looked restlessly at her black coffee and ordered two pieces of thin toast with oleomargarine from Bea, who took her order with a lackadaisical pen, then trudged back to her conversation with the youngest Phillips brother.

"That girl," said Solace. "I can't get a lick of real work out of her unless Andy is around, especially with Carol eager to take her job. I've a good mind to hire Carol on and make Bea help Iris with the laundry."

"Didn't Andy just have her baby?" asked Beth.

"That she did, the same day you had yours. Your little girl has a birthday twin."

"Well, it was inconsiderate of her. She could have had the baby the day before or the day after. How do we even know the two kids will like each other?"

Solace snapped her fingers to make Bea hurry with the toast. She frowned at Beth. "Does it matter?"

"It certainly does!" She bit crisply into a slice of toast. The bread was homemade, the oleomargarine melted like butter. She convinced herself it was better than a donut.

"Two girls born on the same day, the same year, in the same community. What are the odds for that? Do you think they will get to enjoy separate birthday parties? Heavens, no! They will always be grouped together. They will be obligated to be like blood sisters. If they don't like each other..." Her voice trailed. "Anyway, I don't want to see Andy. All she'll do is prattle on about fate."

Solace tapped her fingers on the enameled table. "What about Millie? Frank has all those books and I know she reads them because she always has something to say about them."

"Even his medical books?"

"Especially his medical books! She calls diabetes a hereditary disease and she's all about hereditary stuff."

So, the next day, bright and early, she had taken it upon herself to visit Millie. She hesitated before shifting the gears into "park" and turning off the ignition. She had never paid Millie an individual social call before, but then, she had never had her own car before.

It was silly to feel timid. You didn't need an invitation to visit Millie. She had good manners, but she wasn't formal, like Ester. You practically needed an appointment to visit Ester. Even Betty Lou popped into Millie's house as she pleased.

Gathering her resolution, she opened the door and coaxed Cody out of the car. "Boys?" He asked skeptically.

"One boy," she said, taking his hand. "Jason."

"Jessen!" He shouted, releasing himself from her and running toward the porch steps. He banged on the door ahead of her. "Jessen. Open up."

Millie never looked surprised at having visitors, only pleased. "You brought your little bundle," she said, taking the baby immediately and peeking under the blanket, while Beth took off her coat. "And you had a girl, just as you promised, to play with Nancy. With three girls so close in age, they will probably be the terror of the neighborhood."

Without knowing exactly how it had happened, Beth found herself deposited in Frank's coveted armchair. It really was comfortable, with plush arms and a deep seat. Next to it, on an end table, was Frank's pipe stand and an ash tray. Behind it, was his library full of books. It was the kind of chair you sat in for reading or ponderous meditation.

"Won't Iris be having a baby soon? What if she has a girl?"

"She's got three months left. She's due in late December. Andy says it's a girl. She did the button test."

Beth fussed in her chair feeling somehow deprived. "Why didn't Andy do the button test on any of us?"

Everybody knew about the button test but only a few women could conclude one accurately. The test was simple. You threaded a large button with a string and formed a loop at the other end to hold between your thumb and forefinger.

You let the button hover eight inches above the pregnant woman's stomach. If the button swung back and forth, it was a boy. If it swung in a circle, it was a girl.

If you had already formulated a hunch as to the baby's sex in your mind, the test won't work correctly because your impulses would influence the swaying of the string. Being able to do an accurate button test was almost as accomplished as palm reading.

"Nobody asked her to do it," Millie said shrugging. "I guess we were all satisfied with our dreams. Iris, though. She likes to gather evidence. Carol told her Andy does button tests, so Iris asked for one."

Believing Beth had come visiting to catch up on the community's activities, Millie launched into an account of all that had happened over the last month and a half.

"We've used the community hall three times now. Twice for meetings, once for a bingo game. Charlie thinks we could make money off bingo games. The place was packed! You should have seen it! Problem is, I don't think we'll be able to use the hall much more this winter. It's getting too cold. We lit up the woodstove for the last meeting and it was still a bit drafty. Some were talking about a Thanksgiving dinner, but you know it can be freezing in November. I don't think it will happen, but we are holding a Halloween party for the kids. Frank and Matt have already started building some props. I told him not to make things too scary, but you know how men are. They will probably traumatize the poor kids for life."

"It's terrible," murmured Beth sadly. "I didn't even realize how close to Halloween we are until I pulled into your drive. I haven't made Cody a costume, made Halloween treats, or anything."

"After baby blues?" suggested Millie, setting a cup of coffee on the end table.

"No," said Beth, retrieving the cup. "It's worse than that. I could have lost my baby through my own carelessness."

Millie pressed her lips together before answering. "You never told anyone you had gestational diabetes."

"I don't even know what the hell it means," Beth said bitterly. "All I was told was I had to go on a diet. No sugar, no salt, no alcohol. I thought he was just a doctor who didn't like fat, sloppy drunks, but I swear, I hardly drank at all. Just a sip or two from the bottle. That was it. And he said the diabetes would go away when the baby was born!"

"So, he didn't really explain anything to you, just told you what to do."

"You could say that."

"I could say that. It wasn't the drinking, Beth. It was the sugar. Alcohol was just a catalyst because it turns to sugar. I have a brother with diabetes."

Millie explained in words Beth could understand. She hadn't known about the treacherous pancreas and its job in building insulin.

She still didn't quite understand it, but she at least knew now it had to do with a body part that didn't always work properly, and when it didn't, needed careful dietary supervision. It made her feel better. If the doctor had sat down and explained things the way Millie had done, she would have known better. It wasn't enough to be told not to do something. She needed to know why.

Ignorance wasn't really bliss, not when it nearly kills you. She had spent her life avoiding studious subjects and skimmed through formal education by learning her basics and not much of anything else. She would have to change. She had children now.

Millie's pep talk made her realize something else. She had a condition. Having a condition was like being an elite member of society. While Sharon and Millie dieted religiously to keep their full figures from overfilling, Beth had to diet. She needed fresh fruits. Suddenly, her home had apples, oranges, grapes, or cherries in it on nearly a daily basis. The others nibbled at their pastries and watched her jealously as she ate her expensive fare.

Beth had to wear comfortable shoes. Her necessity caused a fashion trend among the tea-partying ladies. They no longer wanted to wear high heels to their private gatherings. They enjoyed their flat shoes with dresses so much, they even began showing up in public in their casual footwear.

She was doted on. She was always given the most comfortable seat, pillows, and even a footstool when available. When she went to the lodge, nearly every man there stood up to offer her his chair.

Their consideration was so endearing, Beth didn't have the heart to tell them being a borderline diabetic didn't mean she was fragile and would break into pieces if she didn't sit down.

As predicted, Halloween marked the last time they would be able to use the community hall comfortably. There had only been a couple of light, dry snowfalls that mingled with the hoarfrost. The ground crunched loudly underfoot, startling a few non-migratory birds that screamed in objection as they soared toward the inlet.

Cody drew in a deep breath and let it out again, laughing at the billowing white cloud. "Look mama. I'm smoking."

He was wearing his cowboy outfit. All he wanted to be these days was a cowboy. His dad encouraged him. Along with his boots, hat, and guns, he wore a fringed shirt, a vest, and a shiny, silver star on his chest. He didn't like his eye mask, so wore it on his forehead. He strutted in his best imitation of a cowboy with his legs bowed from riding horses. He forgot to pretend to be anything as soon as they walked through the community hall door.

It wasn't sure how much had been set up for the kids, and how much for the parents. The hall was lavishly decorated with the materials and stage props generally reserved for the Little Theater. There were scary booths with black construction paper cats, webs, plastic spiders, a cauldron, ghosts, and cackling witches.

Ester watched with her sharp, narrow eyes, measuring the authenticity of fearful expressions with authentically fearful screams. "I told them not to make things too scary for the kids," she muttered. "If one of them starts crying, I'm going to beat the living daylights out of Frank Lamar."

Most of her suspicions were groundless. The children were rushing around so much on cookies and Kool-Aid, they would not have been fearful if King Kong had burst through the walls.

They knew the two cackling witches were Andrea and Millie, and that the "bloody drink" they were inviting them to taste was hot apple cider. They knew the spook who dared them to bob for apples was really Doreen.

Of course it was Frank Lamar who managed to genuinely scare them.

At the far end of the room, unnoticed at first with so many other enticements, was a casket propped upright against the wall. Bored with all the other tricks and lures meant to startle and make your skin crawl, Wally Miller, the oldest Miller boy, felt this lonely, dreary coffin was worth investigating. He called to his side all the younger boys who boasted they were brave enough to crack open the lid.

The coffin was large, had been built from scraps of plywood, but painted cleverly enough to look old, moldy, and heavy. A large chain was wrapped around it with a lock keeping it in place, but the lock was open and dangling loosely.

Wally pushed his sister, Dolly, in front of him. Timidly, she touched the lock, then lifted it from its place. The chains sagged, the single ties twisting into a snagged grin.

She jumped back, quivering.

The fascination of the Miller gang drew the rest of the children. One by one, they stopped what they were doing and gravitated toward the shadowy corner of the hall with its mysterious coffin. Nobody said they couldn't touch it, which of itself, was suspicious. The quiet surrounding it was suspicious; no cackling calls, no ghostly whispers beckoning them over. It was dreary, earth-stained, laced with cobwebs, as though it had been there forever.

The village children were the boldest. Gathered in a tight cluster, three young boys stepped forward. They examined the lid with their small, prying fingers, finally slipping them over the lip to open the coffin a crack. Nothing happened.

They opened the lid wider. It creaked, causing the girls and half the boys to leap back. Still, not a sound came from the morbid enclosure. Taking a deep, collective breath, the three village boys flung the coffin lid open.

It was a ghastly sight, a terrible sight for young eyes. A white corpse, turning green and moldy, in ragged clothes and countless bandages, stood rigidly within the box. The hair was matted and thickly clumped with blood that stained the bandaged face. The telling blood, combined with black-baked gore and mud, traveled down his wrapped arms and body - dried and caked - ending at his boots. The eyes were closed.

Stifling their gasps of alarm, the children stepped back, but continued to stare in round-eyed fascination at the mummified remains. The remains suddenly opened its eyes more widely than their own, its mouth dropping, showing black, decayed teeth. It raised its arms, the hands hanging limply.

The kids screamed and scattered, homing in on their mothers with the unhesitant accuracy of lambs sensing danger.

Even Wally Miller joined his younger siblings in their quest for motherly shelter. "Do you see? Do you see?" Ester told Hannah when she saw the brood coming. "I told Frank not to scare them too badly! Does he ever listen? Oh no. Not for a minute. Now, the children will never enjoy another Halloween. They will be too terrified."

Millie and Beth, whose toddlers were too young to be anything but indifferent toward caskets and walking dead men, still agreed. The children would follow the example of the older ones. If they were frightened of the macabre, the younger kids would be frightened, too, and it would be all Frank's fault for getting carried away with his make-up.

Armed with their scalding words, the three women prepared to corner the culprit, when Wally, with a shout that could be heard by all but the deaf, "That was the best scary thing I ever saw! That was fun."

The kids were all savages after all. Maybe it was for the best. Maybe that was what they needed to survive in the wilderness. Frank was forgiven but still cautioned to make his Halloween attire less frightening in the future. Wally Miller's enthusiasm wasn't exactly the universal stamp of approval for child entertainment.

By mid-November, the deep winter had set in, and the idea of a big Thanksgiving dinner at the community hall was scrapped for individual plans and a spread at the trading post for those who didn't have plans.

The clock began clicking for the biggest holiday of all, the day after the Thanksgiving dinner tables had been cleared and the leftovers stored or eaten. The pioneers didn't go into shopping frenzies. They handcrafted so many of their items over the course of months, buying only a few special gifts for each other, and wish list toys for the kids.

However, there were a lot of preparations with foods and decorations, which the women felt were best accomplished in the presence of others. Their end of the month tea party became a planning committee for Christmas activities. It also brought up an issue: what to do about Iris.

The tenacious child had still refused to go home. Her due date was approaching, and she had gotten so large that Solace stopped using her in the laundry room and found other small jobs for her to do for bread and board. She remained wan-faced and withdrawn. She wouldn't even talk to her best friend Carol, which caused Carol to grieve.

Solace mourned about this. Andy grumbled bitterly. Millie said with that crushing resolution that gave no real room for argument, "we need to include Iris in our group, even if we have to draw her in the way we did Hannah."

The corners of Hannah's mouth turned up with quivering uncertainty, while she puzzled over whether she had been complimented or criticized.

Beth, who felt Hannah's circumstances were entirely different, crossed her arms in objection. "She's only sixteen. This is a woman's group."

Millie punctured a fluffed-out kernel of popcorn with a needle and slid it down a thread. "She's going to be a mother. That makes her a woman."

"Ain't she putting the kid up for adoption?" asked Hannah.

Realizing she had once again said something inappropriate, she put down the popcorn she was threading and twisted her hair.

"Rick said it would be the best thing, seeing as how the kid ain't got no father and she won't go back to the village. How can she raise a kid by herself in a white man's town when she isn't white?"

"Ah," said Andy with relish, lighting a cigarette. "That is exactly why we need to include Iris in our woman's circle. How can any single woman with a child live in a white man's world without womanly support?"

"Or any man's world," roared Betty Lou, slapping her knee as though she had made a good joke, without realizing she had made a good point.

The conversation thickened and rambled in various directions that somehow managed to twine holidays and the tribulations of women together. In the end, before they left to continue their feverish preparations for a spirited Christmas at home, they arrived at a strategy for drawing Iris into their group.

They would throw a baby shower for her. They had all been so busy having babies of their own in close sequence, they had neglected showering each other. Iris was different. No husband, no family, no funds of her own, they could shower her with everything that caught their eyes. Even though her due date was late December, they scheduled the shower for early February so they could have time to recover before the next party.

The holidays were the bright spot of cheer in the dark night that occupied December and January. Iris' baby girl arrived January second. By then, the community was so exhausted, the news of her arrival barely made a ripple. The only thing Beth said was, "We knew it was a girl."

Solace said it was a pity. Iris still refused to allow her family to see her. Unwilling to disrespect her wishes, they hung around her cabin door in twos and threes, huddled and shivering against the cold, hoping she would change her mind.

"She's not in a good place," mourned Solace. "She's pining away."

The sun begins returning at the end of December, Beth reminded herself. *We are over the hump.* It didn't feel that way. What difference did two minutes a day of returning light make in a darkness that folded over them for nineteen hours and lifted for a few leaden, dusky hours with no daylight at all? The darkest day and the day of returning sunlight clicked together, hand in hand, with no notice that one was any greater than the other.

January swelled and roared in with full fury, turning the world crackling white and bristling with long, black shadows. It rattled the tops of the trees and climbed into their windows, frosting the sills, and crept up the doors and into corners.

There was little to do except huddle in blankets and feed the fire. Beth tried to keep her mind occupied with memories of good times, but those memories included warm, sunny days, family picnics and family outings. More and more, she remembered family.

438

She had never really believed she would miss them. Families argue. Families disagree on everything. Families push each other aside on the way to the top spot in their hierarchy. Family members were as important as the amount of money they made.This is what she tried to hold on to when her mind turned to family, but it was all crumbling quickly in the memories of the good times. She craved it - all of it. She craved the closeness, the warmth, the private conversations between siblings.

January marched on, one dark day after another, and all the happiness she had mustered for the holidays, trickled away in yearning. The woodstove cooled down and she opened the stove door to feed it more wood. It squeaked on its iron hinges, reminding her of Frank's coffin scare.

It was fortunate the toddlers had not gathered around, as they had been far more interested in the free treats. If Frank had scared the little tykes, they really would have had to beat the living daylights out of him. Since the Ewing incident, none of the women had felt very tolerant toward the shenanigans of men.

She had brought Greta's cradle into the living room to keep her warm. Four months old now, the baby entertained herself by playing with her hands or attempting to roll over. Beth called it the safe age. They had passed the vulnerable stage of the first six weeks, thickening and solidifying, but did not yet have the muscles to sit up or crawl.

Cody sat on a blanket close to the fireplace, playing with his toy trucks. He wouldn't wear his shoes, but he would wear the lace-up moccasins Betty Lou had given him for his birthday. He liked them almost as much as he liked his cowboy boots.

She shook off her lethargy to prepare the evening's meal. She and Gary had gone through changes since the baby was born. Dinner was served at the table. She was teaching Cody proper manners and felt the best way to teach them was to use them. This was what Sharon kept saying and Juliana... She stifled the thought. Greta had a high, square brow and a shock of short hair standing on top of her head – she looked just like her father. Greta was going to grow up to be a pistol.

They even said prayers, which was strange at first, but was getting easier. It wasn't much, just a small note of thanks for the blessings they had received, because for the first time they understood they had received blessings.

The cold weather had made them all lethargic. Greta kicked in her basket but did little to try leaving her downy comfort. Cody didn't even look up when she moved into the kitchen. She should do more baking. It would warm the house better. She caught herself. Nothing would warm the house better. It had been fifteen below zero out for days.

She had just finished setting out the plates when Gary came home. Their timing was becoming impeccable. She brought out the main course, a roasted wild duck, and set it in the middle of the table. Jimmy had taken Gary duck hunting last fall and now Gary wanted a bird dog. A spaniel would be nice, but she had a feeling he wanted a Labrador Retriever.

All the men wanted labs and those busy dogs were always breaking loose and running all over the place, mixing up perfectly good pedigrees with their genes. Not that there were a lot of pedigrees in Wolf Creek, but of the ones that were, the owners became distressed when their lovely huskies or German Shepherds produced coal black puppies. And what if one got hold of a tiny dog? They were scoundrels, those labs.

She knew something was bothering Gary before he had finished prayers. His words were too curt and didn't truly sound thankful. He began eating as soon as his plate was served without saying a word.

She broke the silence. "Something troubling you, dear?"

"Humph." He scowled at his fork. "I did it. I gave Rick his walking orders."

Her own fork clattered to the table, and she picked it up with a start and a mumbled apology. "Gary, how could you? They'll never make it through the winter."

Gary pushed against the table, the chair scraping loudly, its complaint a sharp bark as he thudded back into it. "He came to work drunk! And it wasn't the first time. What was I supposed to do? He's running heavy equipment, not kiddie cars."

"But Hannah, and the kids...."

"It's gonna be alright. I didn't really fire him. I just told him not show his face again until he sobered up. I'm putting him in a dump truck when he does."

"You're demoting him?"

"Damned right I am. He's too risky to be put on a shovel."

His confession gave him a returning appetite. He attacked his meal in a respectable manner, showing great appreciation for the flavor, and drew the pot over for a second helping.

"He pissed me off, Beth. He really pissed me off this time. He came in late. He was stumbling all over the place. He started screaming about how he was going to give his little girl away because he couldn't afford to keep her."

"She has been getting a lot of ear infections."

"Yes, well, they had to take her into the hospital the other day because of a ruptured eardrum. The doctor said those infections had been building a long time. They don't think she'll ever be able to hear much."

"She'll be deaf?"

"Not completely, I guess. Just sort of. He said he can't raise up a deaf person."

"He wouldn't really do that, would he? Give away his own child?"

"Not if he wants to work for me."

This was, said Gary, the end of the line for people like Rick Miller. Alaska was their last hope. If they didn't make it here, they were not going to make it anywhere. The Chugach never asked much from anyone, only that they behaved decently toward others.

Gary never asked for much from his team. Only that they showed up in time for work, followed the safety rules and did a good day's labor. Rick Miller couldn't have gotten a better foreman. All he had to do was apply himself, and never give up. The Chugach had no room for quitters.

Beth was able to rationalize Gary's decision throughout the night and over the next two days. The third day, when Gary came home, he announced Rick had sobered up and gone back to work. It should have been the end of it, but it wasn't, at least not in Beth's mind.

She brooded over the neglected child, just a little older than Cody and about the dark, terrifying days Hannah must be going through. She could not keep them out of her mind.

The longer she brooded, the more she felt her own walls closing in on her. The smaller and darker the room became. She began pacing; slowly at first, then faster and faster. Finally, she cried out loud, "I can't take it anymore!"

Bleak, unforgiving January. Bleak, empty days when your only company is the ghosts of the past wailing their frenzied complaints. It couldn't be tolerated.

Numbly, without thinking, she wrapped the baby in her warmest bunting and a thick baby blanket.

They had buried their first unborn child in the January cold. Not really buried, just whisked away with nothing but the memory that at one time, a tiny heart had beat close to hers.

It wasn't to be tolerated. Somewhere there was warmth. Somewhere there was laughter. With no real destination in mind, she began stuffing Cody into his snowsuit, muttering to herself about the nasty effects January had on already perverse men.

"Bye-bye?" Cody asked innocently, while she jerked angrily at the buttons.

Bye-bye. Where would they go bye-bye? Her frantic thoughts stumbled over the question.

"We're going to Sharon's house," she said. Her words came out hoarsely. In her ears, they sounded maniacal, but she still could not stop herself. She had to get out.

The January air crouched, hurtling itself at them as they struggled toward the short cut between the two houses. Beth shifted the baby inside her coat and wrapped the wool shawl more closely over the top. The circling wind still tugged at the ends pulled together around her neck. Cody gripped at her thigh-length coat, terrified of the wind's velocity, whimpering softly, and stumbling as he fought against its pull.

While she walked, she scolded and justified herself in turns, convinced she was both crazy and restless. She needed the walk and she needed female company.

She was jeopardizing the safety of the children.

Bah. It was only a short distance. It kept them tough. You can't live a sheltered life in Alaska.

It was irresponsible and reckless.

"It was necessary!" she shouted at the rattling, mocking trees.

By the time she reached Sharon's house, she was especially convinced of her craziness, but she was there and there was nothing more she could do about it except bang on the door.

She heard the latch lift and waited as the thick home-made door creaked open and Sharon's head appeared.

When she saw who was on the other side, Sharon swung the door wider and chattered with alarm.

"Beth! Why didn't you call me? I would have come to get you. You shouldn't be out in this cold."

Shivering uncontrollably, Beth kicked off her boots and strolled over to Sharon's fireplace, looking into the coals as though there, she could find some answers. "I need a drink," she said, jiggling her baby. "I really, really need a drink."

"Beth," said Sharon uncomfortably, but could find no more words to say. She helped her friend out of her coat and pushed an armchair in front of the fireplace for her to sit in.

Still noncommittal, she knelt and began removing Cody from his snowsuit. Beth stared at her. "Do you remember, before we had kids, we used to meet up in the morning and have coffee with brandy? I could sure use a cup of coffee with a spot of brandy right now."

"Those were different times," Sharon murmured.

"They took the edge off. They were hard times, and they took the edge off. These are still hard times."

Beth edged closer to the open fire, her teeth chattering. Fireplaces had their advantages. The flames were like warriors driving back the cold and loneliness, snapping their defiance at the frozen air.

"I didn't really drink much while I was pregnant, and I haven't had a drink at all since the baby was born. Millie said, even without alcohol, I could have gone into diabetic shock and had the baby early. It's about the sugar."

Sharon finished unpeeling Cody and sent him in Juliana's direction, where he quickly forgot the trauma of the inhospitable hike and began playing.

443

She pattered into the kitchen and poured two cups of coffee. She stirred the two cups thoughtfully, then reached high in the cupboard and pulled out a bottle of brandy. She added a few drops to each cup. "For old time's sake," she saluted.

It was just enough alcohol to blaze a warm trail down her throat and loosen her vocal cords. She didn't crave the drink. She didn't suck it down greedily. She needed the drink. Her words had felt tight for weeks, curled into a ball, unable to express themselves.

When Sharon asked, "Now, what's the problem?" her words tumbled out in a torrent, all that she had gone through, the weeks of worry over their fragile new member, her feelings of guilt.

"And just when everything settles down and I feel okay again, something else happens. I can't take it anymore. It's just one thing after another. It never stops."

She looked despairingly at her diminished drink. Oddly, she did not want another. She pressed her lips together. "I have a big mouth. I'm a show-off. I flip people off and I guess it makes it look like I don't care."

"But you do care," said Sharon gently. "Maybe a little too much. You care so much, it hurts you. Other peoples' problems hurt you."

"I do care," she agreed. She fiddled with the cup without lifting it. "Every time there is a crisis, we women cling together. We console each other. The men, bless them, they try, but they have other things on their minds. It's us, the women, who look out for each other's needs."

The words that had been locked up so long would not stop.

"Do you know, Gary has taken to giving prayers each night at the dinner table. He thinks the baby and I were saved by divine intervention."

"You had a close call," said Sharon gently.

"I had a close call. And it occurred to me, while I was lying on that hospital bed, we're out there without a rudder. We need something more, Sharon, for all of us."

"What do you suggest?"

"I don't know."

Sharon poked at the logs in the fire, moving them closer together for a stronger flame.

The Bowens didn't have a large, stone fireplace like the Hughes. It was more of a built-in stove with a large iron grate that could be swung to one side for adding more wood. It was efficient but not nearly as beautiful as Gary's handiwork.

The fire should hold answers. Flames had structure. They were stronger when thrust close together. They died out if they weren't fed. They had been flames once, so fierce they made the mountains roar. When their flames began to die out, the men and women of the community had drawn closer together. But now....

"We need something to feed the flames," Beth said suddenly.

Sharon gave a half-smile. "Are you still cold? I have plenty of firewood."

"Not those flames. Our flames, Sharon. Before we lose something and forget who we are."

"I don't think I'm following you."

"You can't say we've stepped right every inch of the way. We make decisions we regret because we can't take them back. Those regretful decisions are like putting water on a flame or separating it out, so nothing feeds it. It's going to die one way or another. I won't say water has been put on our flames, but there is nothing feeding them. They get dimmer with each hardship."

It was difficult to tell how much Sharon's practical mind followed Beth's colorful description. In case there truly wasn't enough fuel to feed it, she added another log to the fire and watched the flames leap around merrily.

"Are you still worried about the Millers?"

Beth kept her eyes fixed on the billowing fire. "Not just the Millers. We're spread thin. Ester is a sadder, lonelier person than you can imagine. She won't talk about it because it still haunts her, the way the war still haunts Charlie. It hurt to see that side of her. Then there is Sarah Jones, who cries alone and never leaves her house, and..."

She hesitated, before adding, "There is Iris. How do we keep their flames going, Sharon, as well as our own?"

It was a piece of truth none of them could escape. The isolation wore on you, drew away portions of yourself in layers. You had to dig deeply to find the hard metal core that defined you. That core isn't always iron, copper, or gold.

445

It could be something fragile and disappointing. It could be bent, warped, and filled with impurities. It needed fire to remold, temper, and refine it. The isolation, the dark days, the icy winds, left you raw and ready to be molded.

"Let's go to the lodge for lunch." Sharon turned the logs once more and closed the grate. "We can stop by and pick up Doreen and shoot over to grab Millie and Ester. Let's have a luncheon."

At first, Beth felt cross. "How is that going to help anything?" Yet Sharon still smiled, and she reflected. A luncheon would brighten their day. A luncheon would bring a few other heads together. Everyone was tired of January and its dark, motionless days. A luncheon was just what they needed.

It didn't take long to round up the girls. They didn't even bother to change out of their house clothes, just took off their aprons and bundled their children. Their voices chirped like birds. They flourished their Dresden designed jewelry, of which Beth now also owned a piece, a lovely gold watchband with tiny gold nuggets on each side, collected around diamond chips. It was tasteful and kept her in vogue with the main clique.

The lodge was practically empty, which wasn't really surprising this time of year. Few ventured far from their own hearth unless it was necessary. They waited out the darkness and the cold in solitude.

It was so unusual to have a large party walk through the door this time of year, that their boots rang louder as they kicked them against the steps to knock off the snow and the warm air that rushed out when they opened the door, seemed more pent up and urgent to escape.

Solace was both surprised and pleased to see them, as was Andy. The two women were sitting at the nicest table, near the middle of the room, closest to the warmth of the kitchen and the pot-bellied wood stove heating the lodge. They immediately pushed two tables together for closer intimacy.

"What brings you out on this perfectly dreadful day?" asked Andy, bringing the coffee pot and a trayful of cups.

"The fact that it is perfectly dreadful and horrid," Millie answered, freeing her son from his snowsuit, so he could jump up on the bar stools and spin around. "Please tell me it's a chili day."

"It's a chili day!" She agreed. "And there's clam chowder."

"Clam chowder please," said Ester. "Chili gives me heartburn."

Solace grumbled under her breath, then told her, "You certainly ate enough of it at the baseball games."

"And I suffered every single night."

A pen slid across a pad, then clicked loudly as Andy finished taking their orders. "Everything makes you suffer, Ester. Tonight, you will lie in your bed and think about all those poor clams that got ripped out of their beds and you will suffer. You can't avoid it."

Ester sniffed loudly and rubbed her long nose as she watched the swaying skirt of her antagonist return to the kitchen. "I don't know why she has to be like that. You would think Andy might have some respect for people who have a condition." She looked pointedly at Beth and arched her brows. "Indigestion is a condition, you know."

Feeling magnanimous, as nobody had a condition as markedly delicate as her own, Beth nodded gently. "Absolutely," she said. "A very disagreeable one."

The mothers were busy peeling back the wraps around their babies, so they could be displayed properly on their laps.

Ester's number two son was growing up as strapping as his brother. He was in the crawling stage now and put out a great deal of effort to slide down from his mother's lap. He wasn't a pretty boy, but he was cute, with a round face, blown-out cheeks, and a perpetual frown.

Doreen's baby was pretty. He had his mother's delicate features and fluffy curls. He was still in the sitting stage but reached for everything on the table while still clinging to his mother's hair.

Millie's girl was a little wobbly yet stayed secure enough with her mother's arm around her waist.

She was also a pretty baby, with Frank's fierce, dark eyes and her mother's cupid-bow mouth.

"The doctor said Nancy has a condition. She can't drink cow's milk. It makes her sick. We're putting her on goat's milk this week."

The bowls of soup were already being passed around, steaming hot, waiting for the lonely truck driver or railroad worker to come in out of the weather for a while and warm up. "Oh, you would not!" Andy scolded, finishing her task, and sitting down to join the ladies. "Goats don't have enough cream for butter. You are the only one around who makes butter. What would mama do without your butter?"

Millie sighed. "It can't be helped. I can't do much more breast feeding and Nancy throws up everything but goat's milk."

Andy had made herself a hamburger. Beth looked at it wistfully but ate her chowder. Her doctor would approve her choice, she was sure. She was still being pampered. Solace gave her a free peach. That peach must have cost a fortune! The golden juice ran sweetly down her chin, and she licked at it, savoring each drop.

"You can't ignore a condition," she said with the voice of experience.

Still not eating, Andy opened a pack of potato chips and shook them on her plate. Beth's eyes grew more longing.

"You know what it is," said Andy, crunching down on a chip and directing her words at Millie. "It's your Indian blood. They don't drink cow's milk well. A lot of the Natives don't tolerate it, either."

"It didn't bother my blood," said Millie.

"Well, it doesn't bother everyone but when it does, they've got Indian in them."

Ester scoffed. "Honestly, Andy. I don't know where you get your information."

She waved a potato chip in Ester's face. "I'm almost a practicing nurse and I spend a lot of time in the villages. I should know. Anyway, none of the Hansens cotton much to milk. Iris says she doesn't think much about it because they nurse their babies until they are kind of big and if they want some milk, they have a few goats. But they like butter, you know. They all like butter. I guess we will have to buy a cow and give Millie the cream to make butter. Is everybody going to start having conditions?"

"It's vogue," said Doreen, who had been studying conditions herself after her mother sent a letter announcing she had osteoporosis. "I saw it in a magazine. Women are coming out with all kinds of conditions, especially the movie stars."

Andy finally began eating her burger. "It's the men again, always becoming experts on a woman's body. I'll bet those male doctors got paid a million bucks to find a condition to give their celebrity patients. Half of them have anemia. Can you imagine being that wealthy and having anemia? Their conditions are a bit strange."

"Well, ours are quite genuine," Ester answered. "Women are complex organisms. I read magazines, too. Anything can upset our balance. It's a plain fact."

"Speaking of Iris," said Millie. "How is she doing?"

Andy sighed. "She is moping. Between her mopes and Sarah's mopes, I'm going up a wall. I don't know which is worse. Sarah wringing her hands because she can't find a way to be happy or Iris angry at the world because she forgave a worthless old lecher."

"Good heavens!" Said Millie.

"No, it's something more now. Iris isn't really angry anymore. But she's heartbroken and I'm not the one that can mend it."

"It's been a hard winter," said Beth. Realizing she had an opening for the real purpose of their meeting, she sought to explain the despairing break-down of her early morning, the snap they had all felt occasionally. That moment when you became fed up with all the crap in the world being thrown your way and shouted, "Enough!" The words wouldn't arrange themselves in correct order. "Gary ... oh Sharon, I don't think I can say it."

"You're not blaming Gary," objected Sharon. "It has nothing to do with Gary. It has everything to do with Rick. Rick showed up at work drunk. Rick had the choice to shape up or ship out. Rick said those hideous things about his daughter."

The damned tears that kept finding their way out for several months now, trickled down Beth's cheeks. She brushed them away with annoyance.

"It's just awful. Rick has been demoted. Gary says he doesn't trust him around a bucket. He's driving a dump truck."

Solace hadn't been interested much in eating, but she was greatly absorbed in the conversation.

"A dump truck ain't so bad!"

Beth gave her a bitter smile. "It is if you are a heavy equipment operator. They don't make the same amount of money, and well.... Caterpillars are bigger toys."

She pursed her lips, her business-like fingers tapping the table. Finally, she reached over and squeezed Beth's hands. "You can't take on the whole Miller family, Beth. They aren't your responsibility. You can't carry them around on your back like that. It's not fair to Gary. It's not fair to your children."

"And what's fair to Hannah?" Beth interrupted. "What's fair to her daughter?"The lump in her throat made it too difficult for Beth to speak.

Sharon answered for her. "Rick said he wanted to give her away to Ester."

"He was drunk," said Beth quickly. "He was saying things, but the truth is, she's had these ear infections and now she has a ruptured eardrum. The doctors think she may lose her hearing, or part of it."

"But..." protested Ester. "There are operations."

"That's just it," said Beth. "They don't have the money for the operations. They don't have the money to pay the hospital bill they have."

Ester's hands fluttered about like startled birds. "I'm sure there are resources. The GI Bill or some other. We should look into them."

If her words were meant to comfort Beth, she failed. She had been stumbling for weeks, for months now, and nobody had seen it. It wasn't about solving immediate problems. It was the hardships that built on them, one after another, with no reprieve. They piled like bricks on the women's collective backs, and nobody noticed.

"Yes, there! Do you see? We're always looking out for each other. Then there is Iris and there is Sarah and Andy looks out for them."

Her voice lifted, flirted with the hysterical ledge. "We keep taking on more responsibilities." Beth was openly crying now. She had never felt so emotional.

"Today," she said, recomposing herself and attempting to speak lightly. "I wanted to scream. I got up this morning and all I could think about was running wild through the brush. Doing a Betty Lou. It made me understand a little more about her, but I can't be like Betty Lou. I can't strip off my clothes and dash through the woods. I have children and I have a husband who deserves better."

Appearing neither surprised nor scandalized, Millie shifted the baby in her lap and gave her a cracker. "God knows, I've thought about it."

"I'll join you," offered Andy gleefully.

Ester huffed and fanned her face. "I hope you would abstain."

"It's cabin fever," said Solace, drawing on the wisdom of her years and experiences. "It happens to all of us. It's worst when you get it in the winter instead of early spring because you can't go out and work it off."

Beth dabbed at her eyes. They were trying to make her feel better. Even the strongest women had weak moments. She knew that. She had lost count of the number of times they had fallen and gotten back to their feet. Those maddening episodes were inevitable.

"It's not just cabin fever. It was worse than that. It was..." She ran a hand nervously through her hair thinking about it. "It was hopelessness. I've never felt that way before. I'm going on six years here and I've never felt that way."

Ester looked at her soup bowl as though something about the design pleased her. "It's taking on too much all at once. It buries you."

"But we do have to watch over those in need," said Millie reluctantly. "There is always someone in need and we can't just let them suffer."

Letting others suffer was out of the question. Suffering had a habit of creeping into your own life, even when you thought you were secure. The very thought of suffering made them all dab depressively at their food and wring their paper napkins.

451

"Well, what should we do?" asked Ester crisply. "It's not as though our husbands have time to get involved in these matters. Why, we can barely get them to plan our children's education."

"We need a preacher." The words blurted unexpectedly from Doreen's mouth.

"A preacher?" asked Andy thinly.

"Hah!" spat Ester with satisfaction, deciding her bowl of clam chowder was tasty and deserved proper attention. "I've said that all along. We need a preacher, someone who will be our moral compass."

Sharon's prodigy trotted over on lengthening legs already losing their toddler shape and climbed into her mother's lap. Lisping in a soft baby voice that barely carried beyond Sharon's ears, she explained the injuries to her doll caused by careless Ben. Sharon comforted the doll's head and gave Juliana a sip of tea. Saying "Thank you," the child pattered off to share more confidences with Patsy.

"I don't think there's anything wrong with our moral compass," Sharon corrected in her most precise voice. "We don't need a preacher. We need a pastor. Someone who will guide us."

The others agreed, adding their views of the ideal spiritual leader, but Beth remained bitter. "How do we find a pastor when we don't even have a church?"

Doreen already had an answer.

"We'll use the community hall."

Part V

Solace

Twenty-Six

Zeb always did say one day Wolf Creek would be booming. It was difficult to imagine in the first years – before the war – before Japan boldly invaded the Aleutians and Kodiak became a prime military post and there was nothing to Wolf Creek except a few miners, trappers, truck drivers, and villagers. She had always believed the area would become more settled. She hadn't contemplated the way it became settled. She had assumed there would be farmers slowly moving in, increased production, railroad lines, fishermen and lumber men. She had not imagined military personnel and the people hired by the military.

It was strange at first, but Solace had a practical mind and Zeb some sound business sense when he wasn't drinking. The G.I.'s pouring out of Anchorage, looking for something to write home about, brought a dependable income to the trading post. They paid cash for everything. The Grants no longer had to fret over the shaky credit of trappers and miners.

Everything changed with the first homesteaders enticed by Civil Service jobs and cheap land. They brought wives. They brought families. They brought steady income. Wolf Creek was no longer a stop-over for fancy-free wanderers and lonely woods people. It was a gathering place for dreamers, and they had so many dreams!

They brought what she had craved the most, the company of other women. She had not realized the greatness of the craving until she had begun to quench her thirst. The utter deliciousness of it all after being deprived so many years.

Before the Civil Service wives, there had been the village women, but they were shy and sometimes said nothing at all for hours. They came in with their husbands, their brothers, and cousins, and sometimes three or four women together, willing to trade their handcrafts for flour and sugar. They were friendly but didn't lounge for hours gossiping with Solace, and gossip was a treasured commodity.

Betty Lou had been her only real friend for so long, the years blurred. She had watched Betty Lou grow from a wild teenager to an even wilder young woman pushing middle-age.

The woodswoman's own father had been surprised Betty Lou had not had a child by age twenty, but it happened that some women couldn't and apparently, Betty Lou was one of them. It might be for the best. Solace had never seen another woman raised so much like a man and Betty Lou would probably have as few ideas on how to raise a child as Dresden Hayes did.

She had forgotten what it was like to be around a group of women all talking about womanly things and making plans for their husbands so their husbands wouldn't have to carry the burden. It was so long ago it didn't feel real anymore. Only the solitude of the deep mountains felt real; until the homesteading women came.

First it was the Bolinders, with strange Ester, tight as an overwound watch, suspecting every price change was treason to the struggling settlers. Then there were the Erichmans, the Bowens and the Hughes, popping up like mushrooms and spreading out their agenda.

Solace was all for progress. Her oldest son hadn't done so well with wilderness life and had run away to Anchorage as soon as he was able to stand on his own two feet. He knew how to work. The problem was, he also knew how to fight and get in trouble.

Ed wasn't such a problem. Ed was simple minded. He was the same age as Jimmy, but instead of gravitating toward the older men and their mature conversations, he dropped back and made friends with teens several years younger than himself. Jimmy no longer hung with him much, seeing him as juvenile, but if Ed was never really going to grow up, he was reliable. She could put her mind to rest about Ed. He wasn't going anywhere and wasn't doing anything to greatly astonish people.

It was Bea she worried about. Before the Delaney's came, Bea had no real friends. She was a plump girl with a pasty complexion, but for military personnel, a long way from home and feeling lonely, she seemed ripe for the pickings.

Solace had been on edge trying to explain to the guileless girl the difference between honorable and dishonorable intentions before Bea met Carol.

Carol was a little more worldly wise than Solace would have liked for a young girl to be, but that was the Delaney girls for you. They learned young and drew their own conclusions from their experiences. Carol quickly taught Bea which men were creeps and which were desirable neighborhood boys. She even teased Bea over the girl's infatuation with Bradly Phillips, who was of appropriate age but a bit flashy and wild living.

Progress had brought development, stability. Progress also brought change. The old ways of the wild people clashed with the new ways of the settlers, and when the dust cleared, the new ways brought their own threats to community harmony.

Change was inevitable. It just never occurred to Solace that Beth Hughes would be the instrument that heralded change. Ester, yes. Ester had a lot of fancy ideas of how people should behave and would have enlisted her own rules and regulations if she had been allowed, but one thing both the old and the new community had in common was that they didn't have a great deal of appetite for rules and regulations. Even the civil service workers skirted the rules as much as was available for the greater enterprise of creating homes.

Even Millie, with her aptitude for developing friendly situations, would have been less surprising. It was Beth who stood up at the next meeting and proposed that the community look for a pastor. Most of the members did not want to appear anti-religion and discussed this prospect somewhat seriously among themselves, but a few who saw the old ways were quickly fading, grumbled, and asked, "Why do we need a preacher?"

"He could officiate at weddings," said Andy, who wasn't religious and had much to say about church-clinging people yet had ultimately caved to the social pressure of her gender to present a unified front.

Andy was beginning to see the practical applications of having a preacher, even though she wasn't sure a man of the cloth could lift her own burden of humane duties.

Hannah hadn't been at their emergency gathering, but that didn't mean she had missed the beat of woman unification, even if her passions were a bit out of alignment with their overall sentiments. She lifted her weather-stained hands, shouted a few hallelujahs, and even sobbed a little.

Ester disapproved equally of religious outbursts and atheism. She raised her haughty French brows and informed the group in her icy, solid voice that invited no opposition.

"We need one in time of crisis. Think about all we've recently been through."

"And the children," reminded Millie. "We can't neglect the children." Fearing the others might misunderstand and believe she was going to press educational matters for perhaps the seventh time that year, she added, "The church is like a giant tarp reaching over the entire community and giving it shelter. We tend to take care of each other first. Jobs, building our homes, growing food. The church takes care of the children first. It's the grandfather with a hundred children."

Beth made the motion again and Ester seconded it. Before there could be further discussion, all the women said, "Aye", jabbing their men so they echoed the agreement and the motion passed.

Finding a preacher to their specifications wasn't as easy as a general agreement that they needed one. They ascribed to no denomination. Some had no idea what a denomination was, just that they were sure they grew up with a Christian religion. Some weren't even sure of that.

The Rasmussen kids had a Jewish dad and a Native Eastern Orthodox mother.

Sometimes, they attended the tiny Orthodox church in the village, sometimes the even tinier temple in Anchorage. Most of the time, they spent their Sundays the way the rest of the homesteaders did with fishing trips and picnics in the summer, and indoor board games and quiet family time in the winter.

Andy had said she was a spiritualist.

Solace wasn't completely sure what that meant, other than that Andy had ESP and liked to join chants. That was fine with Solace. She always felt the best way to survive in the wilderness was with some extrasensory perception and chanting was a favored pastime among many of the villagers. She couldn't say they were any worse for it and many seemed satisfied afterward.

Then there were the Lamars, as peculiar in their religious beliefs as they were about everything else. She had heard they were Quakers and had always thought that was a Christian religion, but Millie had said, "I don't know. I guess we believe in a little of everything. Except Frank disagrees with some things. I'm not sure I disagree with any of it."

Andy had said that sounded to her like Quakers. "That's how they are," she had assured Solace knowledgeably.

They had no church, no hymnals, only a hall that hadn't been used in over a month and a piano that was probably frozen solid by now. A social worker who would lead them in prayers would have been just as viable as a pastor, but a pastor was what they wanted.

It was not to be assumed pastors, preachers, ministers, or whatever you wanted to call them, were in short supply. They had their specifics. You couldn't just say you believed there was a creator and had a notion to find someone who would represent them to the Grand Assembly.

They wanted affirmed believers signing up to their registry. They wanted an already built church with a sign in front announcing who they were, or at least the land for building one. They wanted specifics.

Astonishingly, after a great deal of diligence on part of Ester with her eloquence and Millie with her typewriter, they found one. He was a young circuit preacher who had been doing missionary work at four different churches in the valley, visiting each church once a month. Recently, one of the churches had found a full-time pastor, leaving him with an empty slot.

The circuit preacher who had turned one of his founding parishes over to a full-time resident introduced himself as Rev. Brighton. He met with the church planning committee, which consisted of Ester, Millie, and Beth, in his office at the missionary headquarters in Anchorage.

"It was a lovely office," said Ester. "It had green carpeting and stuffed bottom chairs, a telephone with two calls waiting buttons, a typewriter, and a mimeograph machine. He is so modern."

Beth was not concerned with aesthetics, only results. "We let him know we are a troubled community. We will need more than once a month church service. He said we should see how things go. Can you imagine? We weren't interviewing him. He was interviewing us!"

"He has a nice voice," Millie said hopefully. "Maybe we can convince him we are needy enough to deserve his attention."

Reverend Brighton was willing to include Wolf Creek in his circuit provided they used the Methodist hymnals.

He explained that this was because he liked singing hymns during his services and the songs in the Methodist hymnal were the only ones he knew.

The news that he would be holding his first service at the community hall swept through the community like wildfire. There was a sudden explosion of neighbors stopping by the trading post for gas, on their way to Montgomery Wards in Anchorage to shop for new clothing. There was some criticism about the hymnal choice, but with their exposure to the Little Theater, they all understood the importance of familiar music.

Preparations had gone on for days, stacking firewood outside, bringing furnishings inside, including a hand-made pulpit, embroidered alter cloths, and a set of candle sticks. The community hall was thawed and dusted several times over, yet still the walls were thick with frost.

Solace readied herself for the first church service she had sat down and listened to in over fifteen years. The women had all bought new Sunday dresses, although there was little chance those dresses would be seen. The weather never improved during the entire month of January and with the first week of February, hovered at minus twenty degrees. They wouldn't be unbundling their scarves, let alone their coats and sweaters.

It seemed strange to put out a sign on the lodge on a Sunday saying they would be closed three hours for church, but when Solace looked at the sign, carefully painted by Bea the night before, she felt pleased to be part of the change.

Just as the family piled into the car, Betty Lou showed up saying she didn't really know what the hullabaloo was all about but if they were going to have a pastor, she guessed she should find out.

Betty Lou wasn't wearing a Sunday dress, but she showed signs of having passed a wet cloth over her face and neck and was wearing clothing that smelled faintly of a recent wash, which was an improvement over her everyday wear.

They arrived early to help warm up the hall and prepare it for Sunday services. Gene Brewer with his numerous sons were already there, chunking out split logs from the back of a truck. It was as cold inside as it was outdoors. The frost had laid claim on everything. It crept up the walls, clung to the ceiling, bristled in layers over the sparse furniture.

"Oh, doggy!" exclaimed Betty Lou. "Your preacher is going to freeze his buns off." She ran out the door and came quickly back inside with her arms loaded with firewood. One of the older Brewer boys had beaten her to the stove. He crouched next to it, ready to light a large pile of kindling. She pushed him away roughly and tore into his firewood structure. "What are you trying to do? This ain't a Tin Lizzy. She's solid iron. You've gotta break her into the cold slowly."

She made a small teepee out of twigs and paper and blew on it gently. The Brewer boy got restless. "We've got an hour to warm this place up and it's colder than..."

"Don't be committing profanities in the House of God," Betty Lou scolded, quickly breaking in. "Ain't no doubt what it's colder than but we start this lady slowly or she'll crack wide open."

"This isn't a House of God," said the boy sullenly. "It's a community hall."

Solace left Betty Lou and the Brewer boy to squabble over the proper way to heat a cast-iron stove so she could arrange the refreshment table. Somehow, over the last few years, she had evolved into the main table setter for the community's events.

There was a practicality involved. She was the one with the easiest access to tablecloths, paper napkins and throw-away service ware. She also appreciated the desire of the women to demonstrate their baking skills, disguised as sympathy for the lengthy hours Solace already spent in the kitchen and a desire to relieve her baking duties a little.

It wasn't that hard to double the recipe for her sweet bread and contribute pastries, but there are times when stepping down for others is a blessing and a kindness. The other women got to show off their handiwork, and it kept her own in that special realm of professional, paid-for services.

Betty Lou satisfied herself the stove was warm enough to start adding serious fuel without the metal splitting apart at its seams. "There now. Give it fifteen minutes."

She looked critically at Solace, still placidly smoothing out the tablecloths and arranging plastic spoons.

"You don't need to start in working right away. You've got Ed and Bea helping you and a whole squad of Brewer kids. Sit down a bit and warm your hands."

It was inviting. The fire had started chuckling cheerfully and giving a warm ring of heat. Solace pulled up a metal folding chair and sat down. The metal was stiff and icy cold but warmed quickly when placed close to the stove.

"Ed!" She scolded when she saw her boy also about to also make himself comfortable by the fire. "Go bring in the cannisters of fresh water. They'll freeze out in the trunk."

"They'll still freeze in here," he predicted. "The floor ain't got no skirting. It's gonna stay colder than an ice box."

"Then set the cans up on the table! It's gonna get dryer than a bone in here and we'll need water."

"Can't make coffee without water," Betty Lou reminded him, throwing in another log. "Tell them boys to bring me some more of them logs. They should be as good at carrying as they are at chunking."

He groaned as he left, tormented with the thought of lifting two ten-gallon metal cannisters of water from the automobile trunk and in prodding the Brewer boys into more action.

"I don't know how we're going to do this," said Solace with dismay, suddenly struck by the degree of their commitment. "It doesn't look like a church at all."

The place was beginning to warm. The heat caused a halo and turned the frost into rivulets that evaporated within minutes. The walls though, were thin as the veils of an Arabian dancer.

They hissed back against the heat with violent tremors of icy vapor. It was also true what Ed said, who may be simple but still knew how to build, without skirtingthe floor would remain cold. The biggest fireplace in the world would not be able to prevent the low-laying wind traveling merrily under it.

There was nothing there except a stage, a piano and some military issue folding chairs and tables. The cans were also military issue. They were the ten-gallon metal containers painted army green and stacked carefully under the sinks of every household. The military provided the little necessities of life.

The Brewer boys burst through the door, boots dragging in snow, their arms loaded with wood. "There's someone else coming in," announced one of them. "An old blue truck."

That sounded like Andy! Solace half-rose from the chair, her lethargy shaken, and applied herself to looking busy. She filled the giant percolator and the tea kettle, setting them on top of the stove. When Andy stomped inside, she turned around as though surprised.

"Andy! I never dreamed I'd see you arrive forty-five minutes early for a church service!"

Making a big fuss about the cold, Andy stormed over to the glowing iron stove and stretched her hands over it.

"Blame it on those unscrupulous rascals, Matt and Frank. They got me into this."

Looking around as though annoyed, Andy crooked a finger.

"Brewer boys. Ed. Go out to the truck and bring those things in that I've got in back. Be careful about it or Charlie Bolinder will have your hides! I brought Kool-Aid," she added, turning to Solace.

"Beth doesn't drink Kool-Aid anymore," said Solace, bringing out one of the two pitchers she had carried in a cardboard box.

"The kids do, and they drink it straight. There is a mountain of kids now, Solace, including Betty Lou."

"She's drinking that sweet tasting stuff with them, is she?"

"She is, and so is Ed. He likes it almost as much as he does soda pop."

The boys were hauling in Charlie Bolinder's contribution: two new-to-them church pews that had been re-sanded and revarnished. These two pews, stained as deep a color as their hand-fashioned pulpit and alter table, seemed to add a legitimacy to their worshipful intentions the other items lacked standing on their own.

Without the pews, the pulpit was just a podium and the alter table was just a short-legged table. The pews completed the arrangement, creating a small island of religious sincerity, a sanctuary for prayer and meditation.

After several minutes of quiet contemplation and admiration regarding their handiwork, which consisted only of arranging the pews a short distance apart, perfectly lined up with the stage and set precisely six feet back, they were prodded into reminders of their unfinished chores. Noisily, with relish, they snapped the folding chairs into place, crisp and groaning with the brittle cold.

"Is Iris coming to church?" asked Andy, keeping a supervisory eye on the boys' progress.

"She is. The oldest Brewer boy is going to pick her up. I told him we could drive back to get her in time for church, but she insisted the Brewers were fine. I reckon now she has a mixed- race child, she wants to be with mixed race people."

"I said all along we ought to mix things up more. The Brewers and the Rasmussens have the right idea."

The heat radius was increasing pleasantly, allowing Solace to push back her seat and stretch her legs comfortably. "I guess you were trying for that, too."

"I was trying," admitted Andy. "I guess Jake tried harder. It doesn't matter. I'm not marrying anyone, maybe never again."

"Oh hush," said Solace, slapping at her. "Don't sound so dramatic. Remember where you're at! You just made a few bad choices is all."

Andy stood up and studied their seating arrangement anxiously. "The Hansen brothers are coming, too. About half the village is coming. We aren't going to have enough chairs."

It didn't look like enough to Solace either, not even with their new pews. "We've got a few benches stashed in the garage we've been meaning to donate. I'll send Zeb after them."

She found him, as she had expected, lounging next to the Brewers' truck, chatting idly with the senior Mr. Brewer, whose secret to uniformly raising six boys to be helpful and diligent had not been revealed, and was even now wordlessly correcting the five-year-old who was leaving a trail of kindling behind him as he carried a bundle to the hall.

Gene Brewer had a lazy, warm voice that melted the winter frost attempting to capture it. "No need to send off Zeb. Eugene is goin' that way to pick up Iris. He might as well do it all in one trip. Just send Ed along to show where the benches are at."

Men looked out for the interest of men as stolidly as women looked out for each other. Zeb beamed a tobacco-stained smile and walked away with Mr. Brewer, who had surrendered the keys to the truck to his son. It was their day of rest. If there was work to be done, the women and children could do it.

The hall began to fill by nine-thirty, with the Lamars and Bolinders arriving first and claiming one of the two pews. By a quarter to ten, the seats were full. The adolescents squeezed onto the benches in the back, while the younger children dashed up front carrying blankets and their snowsuits to make multi-colored birds' nests on the floor. The villagers filed in as a single unit, giving the women the last remaining seats, with the men standing in the back, arms folded across their chests. It was the largest gathering the community had ever seen.

The Grants were given the honor of sitting in the other pew, along with Betty Lou, who giggled and jumped up every few minutes to check on their iron stove.

She was finally imprisoned by Iris who sat next to her and Eugene Brewer, Jr. who sat at the end of the pew and promised to keep the fire fed. At precisely ten a.m., the door burst open one last time and the pastor walked in.

Nobody knew what to expect. Preachers come in all shapes and sizes. Solace half expected a young man with prematurely thinning hair and a thickening middle. Andy had said she thought he would be small and nervous. Betty Lou believed he would look like Jesus.

He was tall and lanky, with grave, dark eyes, appearing sort of like Abe Lincoln without a beard. He wore a worsted greatcoat and black, wool scarf, which he removed at the door and hung on the coat rack with a restrained show of ceremony, revealing to his respectful audience that under the greatcoat, he wore the robes and clerical collar of his profession. What he did not remove were his heavy winter boots that worried and disrupted the clean straight drop of his trouser legs. They clumped when he walked, his majestic robe rippled vainly its attempt to cover them.

Hesitant music, growing stronger and more confident as the new minister to their wounded souls proceeded up the center aisle, tinkled from the piano. The reverend stepped up to the stage and turned to face his audience. A triumphant cord rang out, a burst of joy as Art Bowen's fingers recognized a familiar song and sang without waiting for the pastor or anyone else to join in. "All things bright and beautiful!"

Not to be outdone by his enthusiastic music director, the preacher belted out alongside him, "All creatures great and small…"

"Fancy that," whispered Betty Lou to Solace. "That song be in the Bible. I heard that song before at the Knik River mining camp and never knew it was in the Good Book."

"This isn't a Bible, it's a hymnal," Solace whispered back.

Betty Lou peeked at the opened page. "It's got Japanese words in it."

Solace nudged her. "Those aren't Japanese words. They're musical notes. Either sing or be quiet now."

Betty Lou chose to sing, although she was more comfortable with the line, "…Made them all" than she was with any other and sang it emphatically at the end of each chorus.

It was understandable that Reverend William Brighton wanted songs he knew how to sing. He had a marvelous voice, rich and rolling, inviting you to sing along. His words were clear, his notes precisely targeted. Although the accompaniment was staggered, with some of the congregation joining in on the song later than others, by the time the chorus came around a second time, nearly everybody was singing.

Once he dispensed with all the formality of songs and prayers, the reverend didn't look quite as confident with his mission. During the silent prayer, the children had decided the floor was too cold to sit on and moved their blankets and coats to the stage, where they now sat cross-legged and arranged around the preacher.

Certainly, he must have heard their muted shuffle as they climbed up and gathered around him, and felt them brushing his feet as they squirmed, but said nothing during the silent prayer and only looked at them perplexedly when the quiet meditation had finished.

"Well," he said after a long moment. "Let the little children come onto me, although I'm not sure I'm the reason for them being here."

Observing that it seemed perfectly natural to his cong-regation for the children to be sharing space with the pastor, the revered minister loosened his collar, which was becoming uncomfortably warm and half-way unzipped his clerical robe, revealing a black suit and white shirt underneath, before beginning his sermon.

He shuffled through his notes, frowned, then shuffled again. He cleared his throat and reached for the water glass, drinking down half of it. The congregation huddled in their coats, below the dry Sierra heat that baked the rafters and dropped a phenomenal ten degrees for every foot underneath them. The floor snapped with frost. The rafters groaned with heat. Tall Rev. Brighton stood between them.

"I heard..." he began. His voice cracked, forcing him to pause and finish off the waterglass.

Attentive Betty Lou, under the spell of this marvelously attired gentleman, leapt from her seat and wrestled with a water container to bring him back a whole pitcher of water. "It's right torturous, Mr. Reverend, standing up there like that," she crooned in her most genteel voice. "We ain't finished with things yet. You could sit down if you like, it will make things easier."

He thanked her but declined to sit down. He declined to make things easier for himself. He drank a little more water for good measure and tried again.

"I heard a voice in the wilderness calling. That is the line I usually begin with for inspiring recruits engaged in missionary work. When I would say those words, I would paint an image of people in far-away places who had never heard the word of God. The One God. Our Creator. But the truth is, everybody has heard the word of God. They use different names. They belong to different religions. And just as a neighbor may appear one way to you and another way to your sister or brother, God appears differently to all of us."

He looked at the packed community hall that had come not because of a fondness for Protestants, but with a simple desire to worship together. It wasn't the kind of congregation you might normally see.

There were Natives, half-Natives and whites all sitting loosely together, except for the Hansen family, who always stood in back, their arms folded over their chests like guardians of the north. There were trappers in their furs and railroad workers in their bibbed overalls. There were farmers and construction workers awkwardly decked out for Sunday. There were civil service employees in their pressed black and white suits, and civil service employee wives in their store catalog dresses. They were all sitting patiently, waiting for the sermon, their feet tugging at the ends of their blankets for more warmth.

"As many places as I've been, I've never heard before a voice in the wilderness calling to me. This is the truth. When we create a mission, we look at a map and say, 'That place needs one.' Not one village, not one town has called me up and asked, 'Will you help us build a church?' We just assumed they needed our help."

His throat was drying out. He stepped down from the stage a moment to drink another full glass of water. He unzipped his clerical robe and let it flap loosely around him. He unbuttoned his collar. "You are a church," he said, somewhat replenished, yet still a little hoarse. "I don't have to tell you to love your neighbor. You already do. You love your neighbors so much, you are willing to worship with them, regardless of their own beliefs. I can't teach you what you already know."

Betty Lou whooped loudly, and Hannah broke out with a new hallelujah. Ester looked down her nose at Hannah, and Solace jabbed viciously at Betty Lou. "You don't whoop in church."

"But he said a good thing, didn't he?"

"You still don't whoop in church."

Betty Lou sulked only for a moment. Noticing Hannah had not received an open rebuke, she resorted to hallelujah. Since it was acceptable in some churches, Solace let it go.

With all of Hannah's and Betty Lou's hallelujahs, it was difficult to concentrate on the rest of the service. The rest didn't matter so much, anyway.

Pastor Brighton had heard the voice in the wilderness calling and agreed to answer it, no matter what the need. Even more remarkable, he had completed a full service during the worst cold spell of the winter in an uninsulated, unfinished building that had never been designed to be a church.

Any casual observer looking in on the Wolf Creek Experiment would have found it inexplicable that a preacher would agree to drive over thirty miles in below zero weather, give a sermon without preaching, in a building that hadn't been completed and wasn't even a church, to a congregation with no defined faith. Yet there he was, wilting like a lily, removing even his robe eventually and conducting the finale of the service with a burst of song in a voice definitive enough to inspire the most discordant choir.

He didn't know what their needs were yet. He didn't know about the terrible Ted Ewing secret, or Iris's cold-hearted lack of forgiveness toward her family. He didn't know about Rick Miller's mean streak or Sarah Jones's depression. They were sinners, all of them, committing sins of omission, turning blind eyes on the victims, unwilling to judge, or be judged.

Reverend Brighton didn't know that. He didn't even talk about hell or damnation, only what good people could do together. In some ways, he sounded a little like Charlie and a little like Frank, enough so that Solace began to have suspicions. Maybe he wasn't really a Methodist at all, but a Quaker, maybe even Amish. He looked like he could be Amish.

Solace's suspicions were reinforced after the service. Barricading the door so he could not escape, the front-runners of the drive for spiriting a preacher into their midst, crowded around the unfortunate man, to bribe him with coffee and fresh pastries. Not everyone was of the mind he was the answer to their prayers. Seeking the companionship of someone as mature and wise as herself, Velma Delaney shuffled by the folding chairs until she was standing next to Solace, and confided in a low voice, "I don't think he can be my preacher. He has the wrong Bible."

As far as Solace could tell, Rev. Brighton used a Bible that appeared no different than any other. She waited until she was able to corner Andy before asking about irregularities in Bibles and which was the correct one to use.

"I don't know." Andy expertly scooped up her son as he flew by her and began cramming him into his snowsuit. "Mama's Bible is as old as the Gutenberg and twice as cumbersome. She may even have the stone tablets hidden away somewhere in that pirate's chest she lugs around. C'mon, Carol. Mama says you can't walk home. It's too cold."

Andy told her she would probably not return to church either. "It's nothing to do with the preacher or his Bible. I just don't stand much on formalities. There are some that need him and I'm willing to help out, but between him and mama, it's probably as much religion as I can take."

The Delaneys were the first to leave, followed by most of the villagers. The Hansen family stayed. It became clear to everyone present the Hansen brothers were trying to corner Iris into acknowledging them.

"Do you believe," asked Mark Hansen once he finally had a chance to shoulder a path through the homesteaders that crowded around the new pastor, "that if a man removes his sister from another man who has done his sister harm, he is doing the right thing?"

The good reverend wasn't a chechako trying out his wings. He was familiar with the bush and the tricky language of the villagers. He sensed right away he was being set-up for his first judgment call on family matters. He hedged like an attorney and asked, "You mean hold her against her will?"

"She's not being held against her will!" objected younger brother, David Hansen, vehemently. "She goes where she wants! We mean, what if you removed the harm from her."

"Did you?" asked the pastor uneasily.

It wasn't clear if the Hansens intended to answer, and as it turned out, it wasn't necessary. For reasons of her own, perhaps a softening of the heart, Iris unveiled the face of the baby she had tightly wrapped, for the Hansen family to see her, and said, "Tell aunty I named her Stephanie, after her."

Villagers were strange.

There wasn't an outpouring of emotion, words scrabbling hastily over each other, tears pouring down their faces, as they embraced and reunited. None of that. The Hansen family gazed at the baby that Iris had not surrendered to be held, nodded with satisfaction, and left the church that was rapidly transforming back into a community hall.

Ed whistled as he noisily stacked folding chairs.

The Brewer boys carefully hauled the podium, altar table, candle sticks and pews to one corner of the room and covered them with sheets.

Ester gave a nervous laugh and said in her shrill voice, "Do you see, Rev. Brighton? You have already handled one problem. Iris hasn't talked with her family in months."

"They were there," mumbled Iris. She retreated without further explanation, shrinking back to join the teenagers who had not yet gone home.

Poor girl. Even among the kids her own age, she looked out of place. The others were still in school. They were dreaming their romances, planning their careers. Iris was an unwed mother with no romance left and no real career in her plans.

Feeling a twinge of sadness, Solace rounded up Zeb and Ed, letting them know it was time to leave. Neither had been filled with the holy fire but they were both having fun socializing and felt no real motivation for returning to lodge duties. She prodded them into inspiration anyway and invited Iris to return with them.

"I can take her home," said Eugene Brewer instantly. "Your car is already crowded."

Iris disagreed. "I can fit. It's not much. Three in front. Three in back. The baby doesn't even count."

"Pa won't mind a quick trip."

She shook her head. It wasn't even explainable how Mr. Brewer crammed all those kids into the cab of his truck, yet here was the oldest son telling her the Grants' vehicle would be crowded. It wasn't as roomy as Sharon's station wagon or Doreen's fancy car, but six people wasn't an unreasonable number, even with the amount of space Betty Lou and Zeb always felt they should have for themselves.

Although Betty Lou and Ed had plenty to say regarding the pastor in particular and the church in general, neither with the profound voice of experience, Iris was silent on the way home.

Only as they were getting out of the car, did she turn to Solace and say, "I want my aunty to see my baby. I want her to visit me. I miss her."

When Andy clocked into work the next day, Solace asked, "How many aunties does Iris have?"

"At least half-a-dozen," she answered airily. "You know how they are. Everyone is an auntie, a maw, or a cousin."

"Well, you'd better ask Mark. We will have to make more invitations for Iris's baby shower. She wants her aunty."

Twenty-Seven

Things never do go exactly as planned. For all the pomp and ceremony they gave out for their new preacher, he could only visit them once a month. This was discovered by the general assembly on the day of Iris's baby shower.

Every woman in the community must have come, including all of Iris's aunties from the village, of which there were many. It was a good thing they had decided to hold her baby shower at the lodge, for it required every chair and table in the diner, including the counter and bar stools.

Most were of the inclination that if Rev. Brighton stuck around, he could cure every ailment they had been inflicted with, beginning with patching relationships between Iris and her family. Iris was happy to see her aunties, yet still had no intentions of returning to the village.

She wouldn't tell them why. She didn't have an explanation for anybody, although she did like all the baby things she received. Some of the little dresses were store bought, and she cherished the glossy tags between her fingers, even trying one of the matching bonnets on herself.

Since this was a subject that had been delivered to Rev. Brighton's field of expertise, none of the women pressed her on her decision to remain in Wolf Creek.

They turned the conversation lightly toward babies and future expectations of child growth, and of the inevitable tide of new settlers that cropped up each spring. Wolf Creek must have over two hundred people…

"Three hundred and counting," said Doreen, whose husband was in communications and could keep track of these things.

With March around the corner, the weather had improved. "I reckon Rev. Brighton won't be so bothered by hot ceilings and cold floors this time around," said Betty Lou with the satisfaction of someone who had personally taken a hand in improving weather conditions.

That's when Ester chose to announce the probable scarcity of their preacher. "He can only come once a month. It will be the middle of March before we see him again."

Betty Lou stood, propped a foot up on her chair, and asked with complete indignation, "What kind of preacher is that? How is he going to help us out if he only comes here once a month? We've already got stage performers."

"He is shirking his civic duties," agreed Beth bitterly. "We haven't even told him our problems yet and he's running away from them."

Ester argued over the top of them. "It's not like that. He's still doing missionary work and has three churches in the valley to attend to. One will be getting their own pastor soon, then he will have just us and two other churches."

Beth, who had invested a great deal of her time spearheading the hunt for a preacher, was still not satisfied. "If all his churches are from here to the valley, wouldn't it be easier on him to move to Wolf Creek?"

Ester wriggled uncomfortably and gave baby Lee a sip of her sweetened tea before answering. "Well, no, he can't. He needs electricity for his mimeograph machine. Every pastor has to have a mimeograph machine. How else would they print out programs and notices?" She added gruffly, "I already told him he could stay in our spare room."

"But he can! He can have all the office equipment he wants," exclaimed Millie, who had been holding back her own news with a great deal of effort. "The electric company is putting in their poles this spring. We'll all have electricity by the fall."

It was amazing that Millie had been able to go that long without blurting out the most important news in Wolf Creek since the end of the war, but now it was out, and she basked in the astonishment and exclamations that ricocheted like bullets from one mouth to another. All dubious inquirers were assured the news had come straight from Frank Lamar.

One did not question Frank Lamar's information any more than one questioned Alex or Charlie.

A few days later, Matt verified it. As part of his effort to be his own business, Matt began advertising his willingness to wire houses. "You know how it will go," sniffed Andy. "Half the people he does the wiring for won't pay him. They will come up with every excuse as to why they don't have the money for his services and of course, he won't press them. He won't even ask. It's a shame to take advantage of a man like that."

Solace attempted to be sympathetic, but her own mind was soaring in a hundred different directions. Electricity! They would no longer have to depend on the miserly use of the generator powering only the most important functions. The lodge would be lit with brightly colored lights in the winter. They would buy air dryers for the laundry mat, and a walk-in refrigerator and freezer. They would buy a jukebox! Solace always did want a jukebox.

"Well," she said between folding and kneading her bread dough. "That is why I made Zeb place a limit on credit. There are people who borrow more than they can pay back. Matt is a blessing, but he has more heart than brains. He can't stand to see people deprived, but his own family gets deprived because of it. I reckon Sarah hasn't done much better with her depression."

"We all thought we would get the preacher's help with that. I don't think he's going to do her much good when she won't even go to the services." Andy stopped cutting potatoes and carrots long enough to place her hands on her hips and sniff loudly.

"That's what I'm saying," agreed Solace. "Iris's depression hasn't gotten any better, either. It's not going to do any good at all having a once-a-month preacher."

Maybe they were being a bit hard on the preacher. He had only appeared one time and had performed a minor miracle. Maybe they were rushing things too much. March came, and Rev. Brighton returned for another two hours of administrating to the heart-weary and discouraged. It wasn't quite as populated as it had been the first time.

True to her word, Velma Delaney had not attended. Relieved of the obligation, Andy didn't either, although Jimmy came, dragged in by Tammy, who had recently found religion, and his two younger sisters who viewed every gathering as a good time to visit with the boys.

Now that they had permission to visit Iris, the Hansen brothers didn't come either, although the aunties did. Rick Miller didn't appear either, but Hannah called Beth on the field phone at the last minute to pick her up, along with the four kids. It seemed a shame that Rick Miller hadn't come, since he was one of those in need. Solace was a bit more than half-inclined to believe the gossip concerning his abuses, as Hannah was a pitiful-looking thing, afraid of her own shadow.

It seemed the ones who needed guidance the most were the ones who didn't come to church. Maybe it wasn't about soul-saving but about good people needing support.

Whatever her thoughts, or anyone else's for that matter, Ester had determined the community that needed Rev. Brighton's services the most was the area between the two big rivers they called Chugiak, the place of many places. With that remarkable ability she had for button-holing people, she pinned the good pastor into the corner by the coffee and pastries, where he was continuously bribed with dainty breakfast treats while she explained their dire situation and need for a full-time pastor.

Ester would have made a good businesswoman. She could haggle the fur coat off a polar bear. Before he was allowed to escape her clutches, he had come to an agreement that he would begin holding services in Wolf Creek twice a month and move into one of the Bolinders' spare rooms as soon as the electricity came through.

In April, there was a temporary change in the plans. A tuberculosis epidemic was sweeping through the northern villages from Point Hope to Kotzebue and inland toward Noorvik and Selawik. They would not see Rev. Brighton all summer. His missionary work came first. Andy was upset because she felt as an almost practicing nurse with bush experience, she should be part of the crew administering aid to the remote villages, but she hadn't been invited.

Not even Mark Hansen was willing to spend the summer in the far north when so many of the villages within his circumference needed help. Tuberculosis was taking another swing at all the villages. It was just that in the far north, where testing and medical facilities were scarce, it was more prevalent.

The ladies who had slaved in their kitchens and bought new dresses to charm and retain their pastor were upset because they no longer had a good excuse for dressing up and making fancy treats.

Betty Lou was upset because she had just experienced her first three church services, and with the help of Hannah Miller, was getting her hallelujahs down pat.

Jimmy Delaney was upset because Tammy had told him she wanted the new preacher to marry them as soon as the community built a church. He was worried the pastor would not come back, or that a church would never get built without him.

Reverend Brighton had not expected so much unhappiness from his congregation when he announced plans to spend the summer north among the inflicted. It's possible his youthful mind had never visualized beyond a humble servant of the church, taking his orders from the higher hierarchy of ordained ministers, bishops, and official church directors. In his sub-conscious, there was certainly a vague idea that one day he would have a parish of his own, guided by the wisdom of his experience.

It's possible Reverend Brighton had spent his entire life among administrative rule, yet here was a congregation that had designed its own rule book and he couldn't help – he surely couldn't help but wonder whose rule book was correct.

He had a change of heart. He didn't give up his plans to visit the medically afflicted in early May, but he did commit himself to treating the spiritually afflicted within the suffering community. Three days after the disappointing church service, he showed up at the lodge and sat at the corner table generally used by Solace and Andy.

The table had the strategic advantage of being exactly at the curtained doorway between the kitchen and the dining area. From there, the two women could observe the entire diner, as well as counter and cash register. Also, if they were working in the kitchen, the sharp-eyed women knew immediately if someone took their table.

Usually, the only ones who sat at Solace's table were women who trotted over for a friendly visit. This was the first time a man had sat down in her chair. She looked up immediately from the round of beef she was chopping and made a clacking sound behind her teeth to get Andy's attention.

Andy was criticizing a cheese omelet that refused to remain neatly wrapped when she transferred it to a platter. She tucked in the ends, turned it over to Iris, who was on active duty until Bea came home from school, and turned around.

She peered puzzled at the figure just behind the fluttering curtain. "Isn't that Reverend Brighton?"

Solace dipped her hands in a bowl of water then wiped them on her apron. "That was just what I was going to ask. It sure appears to be him."

Andy took off her apron and straightened her skirt. "Maybe he has come to ask me to accompany him as a nurse after all."

Capturing a few escaping curls and fastening them cruelly with a bobby pin, she swayed busily toward the curtain divider and flipped it back to sit across from the surprise visitor.

"I have a busy schedule, but I can clear it up all with a little time. Give me two weeks to notify the nursing school and arrange babysitting for the kids. And I will have to find a fill-in to help Solace. I think Millie is looking for a summer job."

Rev. Brighton held up his hand and laughed. "I'm not trying to recruit you, Mrs. Delaney."

"Andy," She corrected.

"Andy. I appreciate your offer, but our volunteers are all paying their own airfare and lodging."

Disappointment flickered over her face. "Is it expensive?"

"I think so."

Realizing she probably would not lose her most valued employee after all, Solace filled three cups with coffee and claimed the last advantageous seat, the one that put her back to the kitchen but allowed her to watch the diner.

"How will you afford it?" she asked.

"My salary takes care of it. It brings me to what I really wanted to discuss. I'm not a fully ordained minister yet. This errand of mercy will help me complete my missionary studies.

I'm obligated to follow the path set for me and that includes completing my circuit missions in the Valley. I'm obligated."

He drank coffee as though indulging in a delicious sin. Remembering his fondness for pastries, Solace offered a donut on a plate, which he accepted eagerly.

"There is another obligation," he said, breaking the donut in half and dunking the larger portion into his coffee. "One that isn't on my study list. One that isn't ordained. I have an obligation to extend mercy wherever it is needed. You want something of me. All of you do, but you haven't really told me what it is."

"We suffer," explained Solace. "We pine away without thinking. All the hard times, all the disappointments build up in us, and it's not that we fall. It's like Beth says. Our flame starts going out. It starts dying."

"We have a lot of sufferers," agreed Andy. "There is Sarah Jones suffering and some will tell you I caused it, but I don't believe it's the case. I think Sarah Jones suffered a long time before coming here."

They checked them off on their fingers. The suffering of Hannah, Iris, and Ester. "And Beth," added Solace. "She probably suffers worst of any of them, but she won't tell you. None of them will. You have to make them open up."

"What about you, Andy?" he asked. "Do you suffer?"

Andy laughed that hard brittle laugh that was too old and too wise for a young woman. "I'm a Delaney. Of course I suffer. But there is no cure for Delaney suffering. It is our fate and our curse."

"Don't believe the rumors that Andy is a fallen woman," warned Solace. "She didn't fall from grace. She teaches how to gracefully move on from bad relationships."

Andy casually lit a cigarette and blew the smoke at the ceiling. "We only fall if we are dragged down. That's the problem here. There are some that are getting dragged down and when they fall, they bring others down with them. We don't get to hurt by ourselves, Rev. Brighton. We all hurt together."

Reverend Brighton listened to Andy and Solace explain the woes of the community as seriously as though he had gone to a temple and asked the advice of deities.

At the end of two hours, he looked at his watch and thanked them for an informative discussion.

A few days later, Beth came to the lodge beaming as Reverend Brighton had spent an entire morning with her and had joined her for lunch. "Maybe I was wrong about him," she said. "After all, we've gone this long without a preacher. I think we can last three months longer."

Ester looked so full of self-importance after Reverend Brighton's visit to her door, Solace was sure she would burst. She chattered excitedly from a bar stool, over hot tea, and saltine crackers. "I showed him all the rooms we have in the house. He said there were enough to start an orphanage. That was our idea, we said, to shelter homeless children, but most of the ones around here already have a home. He promised to let me know if he finds any children we can adopt."

Iris said Rev. Brighton had a lot of feeling. Hannah thought Reverend Brighton would be her family's salvation. Everybody on their list of women in crisis came to the lodge to talk about his visits except Sarah Jones. Sarah remained in her neglected shack of a house, keeping her experiences to herself.

The thoughtful reverend had stopped by to visit Millie, although nobody could imagine what Millie suffered beyond a brother who broke his promises, irregular bowels, and a flamboyant husband. She apparently suffered all of them cheerfully with the assumption God was as much of a prankster as Bruiser and as melodramatic as Frank.

"What did you tell him?" Ester demanded, her ears twitching as she attuned her fine radar.

"We talked of this and that." Millie answered as casually as though Jimmy Delaney had dropped by to see if she had any chores that required assistance. "He asked about Betty Lou and if she needed counseling for her naked habits. I told him not to worry about Betty Lou. I believe she was born with an angel of god on her shoulder."

"No!" groaned Ester. "There is something seriously wrong with her impulses. She could die from exposure."

"If Betty Lou had a death wish, she would be dead by now," Millie replied with brittle practicality. "She only strips in public places."

"That's a fact," agreed Solace. "She's two years shy of forty. If she was going to change her impulses, she would have done it by now. What else did you talk with the preacher about?"

Millie found something delightful about little Nancy's chin and waggled it repeatedly between her fingers. "He asked if he was the right person for our community. I told him he was asking the wrong question. He should ask himself if our community was the right place for him."

Ester slumped and held her head in her hands despairingly, "you said all the wrong things! Of course he is right for our community. The way you say it gives him a choice."

"I told him the truth! We all made our choices. The place didn't grab us up and say we had to stay here. We chose the place because the community was right for us."

"If he chooses to leave us, it's all your fault and I will never forgive you," wept Ester.

Millie didn't have to ask for forgiveness. A week before his scheduled leave to far northern realms of Alaska, Reverend Brighton moved all his belongings into two rooms of the Bolinders' shambling house. One was for his bedroom, the other room served as his office. Ester was quickly elevated to the most important woman in town.

In April, while the snow was still thick and slushy, Charlie Bolinder fired up his tractor and began clearing the land at the far corner of his homestead. When asked what he was doing, he answered, "This is where we're going to build the church." It was an agreeable choice. The area around the Bolinders was developing quickly, mainly due to his own inventiveness. When an extra-large house, sheds, and a barn weren't enough to satisfy his building cravings, he added a squat log building out front, which was mainly a community gossip post but was gradually becoming a store.

This was fine with the Grants, who had not been happy with the store side of their business for a while. Most of the staple food products they sold had been trades with the trappers for furs. The furs had been piling up in recent years as favors began turning to desires for hard cash.

It was easy to blame the civil service workers for this, but it was the way of the world and modernization. Solace didn't believe in standing in the way of modernization. Those that did got left behind. They became as archaic as miners still working the gold banks of ghost towns and the trappers who never settled down long enough to build a home.

What bothered her was the modernization of the youngsters. They were smoking and drinking before they were sixteen. They had their own music and their own language. They avoided adult supervision at every opportunity imaginable, disappearing without a trace when they saw adults coming. It could only mean trouble. Iris was proof but the only lesson they had learned from her misfortune was not to fool around with older men.

She supposed she should be grateful. Bea wasn't getting any wiser as she got older. The only thing that held her back from making a complete fool of herself was the cynicism of Carol Delaney. Carol was wiser than she should be for her years. Not that it was surprising.

Delaney women seemed to grow up with an instinct for the waywardness of men. Even Anna, shooting up straight as a reed and who seemed to be in love with nothing except horses, had that look in her eyes that said nobody fooled her. Solace supposed there was no wrongness or rightness about it, but it was disconcerting to see so much adult awareness in young girls.

At least Carol was a good worker. Her occasional winter help turned into practically full-time employment as winter loosened its grip and the shut-in populace once more gravitated toward social functions and public places.

She was fast. She could bus the tables and wash a sink load of dishes in half the time it took Bea. Her skills at the register were almost as good as Andy's.

The main problem with Carol was, she was a teenager and behaved exactly like the other teenagers when she was with them. She smoked and drank. She packed eight to a car for rides with Brad Phillips, who drove recklessly. Everything that Carol did, Bea did too.

Like today. Winter was shrinking away, leaving only a few traces of its rampage. Change was coming. It was whispered on every pair of lips, and the community stirred like seeds waiting to burst forth from the soil and flourish.

The teens were all crowded around a partly gutted car. Eugene Brewer and Ed were buried deeply under the hood, only their butts and legs apparent as they loosened the engine block. Brad Phillips stood with an arm around the oldest Rasmussen girl's shoulders, giving advice without lifting a finger except to hold his beer. Bea stood unhappily on the other side, hoping for a wrap from his other arm.

The freshening day fluttered around the youngsters like the few uncertain butterflies circling in surprise they had waked so soon. Bea was thickening out. Her arms were like unbaked rolls of bread and her hips spread broadly under her gathered skirt. However, her face was pleasant, heart-shaped, with rosy cheeks and a modestly small nose. It wouldn't be long before one of the other boys noticed her. Hopefully, it would be one of the nicer ones, like the Brewer boys or the railroad worker's son. Brad Phillips was a skirt chaser, but Bea didn't see it. Carol did. She flirted with Brad, but no more than she did the other boys.

Carol had watched her weight more carefully over the winter, or more accurately, sharp-eyed Andy had kept an eye on it, criticizing every bite the poor child put in her mouth. Thwarted in its attempts to grow fat, Carol's figure rolled out in voluptuous carves that should not be on a sixteen-year-old girl. She threw back her mountainous red hair when she talked, conscious it made an impression on others.

Solace left the tablespace where she was dicing vegetables to shuffle over to the patch of sunlight and call out to the yard, "break's over girls. Get back to finishing your chores."

Andrea lived by her own schedule which changed as often as the wind. Clearing the last of the debris from the breakfast crowd and placing Bea and Carol back on detail, she brought over two fresh beers and sat across from Solace.

"Salud," she said.

"Ester isn't here," answered Solace, popping open the beers. "You don't have to use French."

"I think that was Spanish. At least, that's what Gordon said, but who knows? When you get people speaking a lot of different languages in a small area, it gets all mixed up."

"It's no wonder they went to war. They didn't know how to talk to each other."

"Yep. It's a crying shame."

Eugene Brewer looked up once as Iris drifted away to do laundry, then returned to pulling the engine block from under the hood.

"If I could offer a decent living wage, I'd have that boy mechanicking for us," Solace said mournfully. "He and Ed go way back, but it's always been Eugene who figured things out. He's got that kind of head that puts things together. As it is, the best thing I can do is let him rent one of the cabins for the favors he does around here. I ain't going to say he puts in work hours, but I make note of what he's done and take it off in rent."

The grill screamed as Carol ran a large metal spatula over it and Andy raised her voice to speak above it. "He's moving out of the house kind of young, isn't he?"

"He's eighteen and graduating in May. They've got a sight full of young-uns, and I have no doubt they ain't finished having them yet. The youngest is four."

"He wants a cabin because he's trying to get Iris to marry him." Carol stopped torturing the grill to empty the filled ashtray and whisk away the crumpled paper napkins on Solace's and Andy's table. "And you won't have to worry about him not being able to pay rent much longer. The Anchorage auto parts store is planning to hire him full-time as soon as school's out."

"Well," said Solace, completely surprised at the audacity of the youngsters in keeping her out of the loop. "And what does Iris say about it?"

Carol lifted a shoulder and let it drop as fluently as the way she scooped up the invisible air and scattered it. "She likes him well enough. She says Ted Ewing is haunting her though and won't let her get into a relationship."

"There now," said Solace bitterly. "That would be just like Ted Ewing. Won't even leave a poor girl in peace when he's passed on."

It was the girls' job to clean out the cabins before the next guests arrived. They hurried through their kitchen chores and dashed out to spruce up the cabins as the one who finished first got to waitress while the other washed dishes.

This worked very well, especially now that Iris could be considered a contender for the limited paying jobs available to teenage girls.

"It looks like Millie got her wish," said Andy above the crackle of hot grease. "She wanted more girls. We got a bumper crop of girls being born and more girls coming in. It would do well for the youngsters to take their time about marrying."

It seemed so. Girls were everywhere these days. One of the new homestead families had two teenage daughters who were already popping up at the lodge whenever they got the chance, only to be hustled home again as soon as they were located.

"I was seventeen when me and Zeb hitched," said Solace. "Not that I'm recommending it to anyone. Those were different days. Modern girls give themselves a chance to grow up a bit and look around. At least they do in these parts. Never saw as many cantankerous women with opportunities to marry that don't want to get it done. Now there's a lady journalist moved in who says she ain't interested in marrying at all. As in, she's never going to do it. Can you beat that?"

"Is that a fact?" asked Andy. Her attention had been obediently fixed on the hamburgers she was frying, but she looked up long enough to illustrate her degree of interest.

"That's a fact," said Solace, delighted she had learned something first. "You should have seen her at the community meeting. Oh, no. You should have seen Frank. A journalist! He fell all over himself trying to impress her."

Andy's brows raised despite her best efforts to remain neutral. "What about Millie?"

"You know how she is. She told me she had come to accept that Frank loved the stage and there is nothing she could do about it. A good stage needs a good journalist, that's what she said. It's about publicity."

"Why would a lady journalist want to live here?" asked Andy, sliding her burgers on to buns and arranging them on plates.

Solace shrugged. "Why wouldn't she? Even lady journalists have got to live somewhere."

Carol returned just before the dinner rush, her face flushed from hurrying through her menial labor. Andy sniffed, unimpressed. "About time one of you arrived."

Andy sent Carol off to wait on two young men in a corner. They were among the newcomers Solace had learned to recognize. They had been at the lodge during lunch hour every day that week, dripping with the sweat of outdoor labor. They weren't railroad workers or miners. They were too clean. They weren't fishermen. They carried with them, the sharp scent of the forest, but the closest lumberjacks were in Girdwood.

Carol approached the table the way she did all apparently unattached young men, swishing her skirt and laughing the deep-throated, Delaney laugh. The girl would end up in trouble, sure as anything.

"Good thing Anna isn't growing up as fast as Carol," Solace commented.

A customer approached and the cash register clattered, dinged excitedly, then slammed shut. "Humph," said Andy. "Have you seen her lately? She's nearly as tall as I am and as straight as a string bean. All she wants to do is play baseball."

"Well, at least she's not interested in boys."

"Not in that sense. She just wants to be better than them."

"The best way to be. She'll be happier for it."

Realizing she had been beaten at the cabin cleaning task, Bea returned slowly and sullenly back to the lodge and began washing dishes. Solace hurried her along with a few bodily threats, then turned back to Andy, who was studying the orders.

"Anyway," said Solace. "The lady journalist said she's going to start a newspaper. She's got all her printing machines. She said she used to print cards and such in Fairbanks, but she got tired of their winters. Forty below it gets, she says! It's so blamed cold you don't even feel it until you come inside and discover you're frostbitten. She has selected for a warmer climate."

"It's not exactly sunny California here," grumbled Andy. "That last cold spell lasted unreasonably long."

"Alaska always is unreasonable."

Solace didn't receive a chance to answer the caustic statement.

Carol finished serving the two young men and had spent a little time visiting with them while Andy and Solace were talking.

"Guess what?" The younger Delaney exclaimed. "You will never guess what," she announced, sliding into the chair normally used by the older women who hung around for a visit. She arranged herself as though she belonged there, even pouring a cup of coffee.

If Andy wasn't still busy over the stove, she would have yanked the girl to her feet. Instead she called crossly, "I'm guessing you're still not too big to smack your bottom."

Carol stuck out her tongue but remained glued to the chair.

"Do you know what kind of job those two guys have that have been coming in here all week?"

Since the occupation of the two young men had been in the speculative stage since they first appeared, Andy and Solace waited expectantly. Even Bea drifted closer, wiping her hands on a towel, and standing just far enough back not to appear idle. Carol preened and sipped at her coffee.

"I will tell you. They are linemen for the electric company. They are running the powerlines."

"Oh my God," said Andy, leaving her station with an unconcerned drop of her spatula. "I have to talk to them."

Solace followed, just to listen, but the men were already getting up to leave. They assured her everyone would have power before the summer was over, but no, they could not rush ahead of some clients to put up poles for others. Just like their field phones, which were supposed to be a secret, they needed to run the poles progressively.

It was a nice try. Andy was trying to get them to do Wolf Creek first, but the power plant was close to Knik. The lines would run north to south, not jump in the middle and go where they pleased. Andy made a few disappointed faces, which were more skilled than Carol's, and extracted a promise they would notify her as soon as they reached the Wolf Creek vicinity.

When Andy returned to the kitchen, she chatted about what she would do when the powerlines were in place. She would buy a radio and listen to the news. "I don't believe just because Ester said something was to be, it would be," said Andy.

Solace studied her tabletop for wisdom. "Well," she said, reaching for more carrots and lining them in a row, "she said Eisenhower would become president and by golly, he did. She said Egan is going to be the territorial senator and it looks like the race is on his side."

The grease was too hot. It roared its complaints. Andy turned the burner down. "Danged gas stoves. They sneak up on you."She waited until the stove cooled before speaking again. "It doesn't mean she has control over events. She is married to a government man, and she knew something. The government men know everything."

Solace was beginning to realize that. Government men knew who the enemies were before anyone else, even in countries she never heard of. They knew how to move people around, make towns bigger or smaller for reasons of their own. They knew what a piece of land had on top of it, under it and how much it was worth.

Solace supposed government men were necessary. Look what they had done. She had neighbors who were women, most of them married and supplying children for the lonely settlement. She had dreamed of this. Even the women from the village had come in rarely during the early years, cautious of the truck-drivers and military men who might bring them grief. It changed with the pioneers.

The pioneers wanted to be friends with the villagers. Some, like the Rasmussens and the Brewers intermarried with the villagers, which was fine by her. She never did take much to people who made baseless judgements and didn't want that kind settling in Chugiak. She hadn't been born here, like Betty Lou, but she saw the land in much the same way. It was her home and the people who lived and loved here were her family.

When Andy and Carol finished for the day, the lodge had quieted down. Everybody who was anybody knew the power-lines were coming through, as well as a few who weren't anybody at all.

Dresden Hayes was impressed enough to say, "I've been thinking about opening a shop somewhere close to Anchorage. I think this area might be the right place."

Zeb was shooting darts with some military personnel who had thought they could impress him, saving his best shots for just before money was passed around. The sly devil, chortling all the time and pretending he was half-drunk when he was generally stone-cold sober. Solace made sure of that.

She indicated to him she was going to take a walk-about to see how well the girls had cleaned the cabins, leaving Bea in front of the register with stern warnings concerning free beer for the Phillips' boy.

Bea widened her eyes and pretended innocence, but Solace knew better. She had been following her daughter's exploits all winter, always in the shadow of Carol, but because of this shadow, receiving second-hand radiance.

Carol was a flirt. Her interest in the boys flitted from one to another. You never really knew who she was interested in. Maybe none of them at all. Maybe she had a secret boyfriend in Mountain View, the school twenty miles away the Chugiak students were shuttled to on a bus each day. Carol was very much a mind-your-own-business type of person.

Not Bea. Bea carried her heart on her sleeve. She raved over her heroes, went sparkly eyed over her infatuations.

Like Carol, she pretended interest in all the young fellows who clustered around them, but her eyes remained fastened to one: Brad Phillips.

Bea would get her heart broken but there was nothing Solace could do. Girls had to learn these things on their own. Besides, the Phillips' brothers were next-door neighbors. The only way to keep Bea away was to keep her under lock and key, which Solace had considered doing.

These evening excursions to check on the girls' handiwork were really an excuse to get away from the lodge a while. It had become too noisy, too intense, a low roar that began in the early afternoon and accelerated in pace and volume which each passing hour, until the wan early morning sent a drained population nodding home.

Andy had worried, as she always did about anything that represented change, that the Wolf Creek Trading Post would suffer once the community hall was built, but Andy hadn't been there in the early days.

She didn't realize the meetings were because of Wolf Creek, not the other way around. The churning, the wondering, the ideas that had been expressed once were expressed again with new appreciation.

The second wave of settlement was following the trail of the first wave and Wolf Creek was the stepping off point. Nobody ever stopped coming to the post. They simply added the community hall in with their circuits.

Solace opened the door to the first cabin and checked inside. It smelled of bleach and laundry soap. This had to be Carol's work.

She practically worshipped bleach. The bed was made, and a clean, white towel lay over a chair. The curtains were drawn. Solace opened them, then the window. Hunters would keel over and die with this much antiseptic.

Carol's other rooms were treated the same way. Bea's interpretation of cleaning was different. Bea had swept and dusted but declined to use cleaning agents.

Still, she paid scrupulous attention to the windowsills, tiny bed tables, and spiked coat rack, dusting them to a dull gleam. It was good enough for Solace.

Tomorrow, she would have them switch cabins, which should please everyone to know that their units had been both scrubbed and dusted.

She continued down the neatly brushed and stone bordered path to the last cabin. Hanging from the rafters were pots with sleepy plants contemplating their future development. The nearly finished bench swing sat on the floor of the sheltered porch, waiting its finishing touches.

Despite the homey appearance, there was sadness here. The heart that lived here had never mended. It waited like the greening plants, its tender buds still only a dream within the design.

It was snuggled close enough to the mountain shelf, pockets of melting snow gleamed in the background. It was isolated, a trailing afterthought in an explosion of woodworked development. Iris would be at home. She had left the group supervising Ed's and Eugene's mechanical project at the same time as Carol and Bea, returning to the back of the lodge to hang out the freshly washed linen. It was flapping on the line now, a little thrilled at the warm breeze that had sprung up during April's waning days.

She knocked twice, but seeing the door ajar, went inside. Iris even had plants indoors. She hung them from the easterly facing window, away from the cutting view of the mountains. The bed and slumping sofa were covered with woven blankets.

She was reading a magazine, her baby cradled in her lap when Solace came in but set her reading material aside immediately.

"Do you ever look at these things, Mrs. Grant? The pictures. Do you think women look like that? Down there in the States?"

Solace glanced at the magazine. It was one of several Millie routinely brought to the post to be passed around by whoever might be interested. Millie like women's magazines. Apparently, a lot of the other homesteaders did too. Solace never really understood their interest.

"I guess some of them do, in the big cities like New York and L.A. They didn't look like that where I came from. Leastwise, not that I can recollect." What she recollected was a childhood with deep Vermont winters not much different than the ones she experienced now. There were differences, she knew, but they had faded from memory long ago.

Iris continued flipping loosely through the magazine. "He told me he was going to show it to me, you know. He promised me. I don't guess I will ever see it now."

"He wasn't ever going to do that, Iris."

"I forgave him, though. I forgave him, but it didn't matter, did it?"

Solace sat on the bed, waiting. She had been through this before. Village girls, these golden-brown blossoms, with eyes like does, they gave their hearts completely. They forgave all.

Iris passed a hand over her child's head, transferring all the love she had meant to pour into a man. "She has his eyes, doesn't she? Blue like the deepest part of a lake. Eugene says he doesn't mind. The Brewers didn't have anything to do with it. That's why I agreed to marry him."

The surprise was enough to cause her to jolt and the bedsprings to creak. It was the first time Iris had talked about marrying, and the first time she had admitted to knowing anything about what had happened to Ted Ewing. "Your brothers love you, Iris."

"I know that, but I forgave him. I told my brothers. I told Mark I forgave him."

"Would you have forgiven him if the baby had died?"

The hand that had been caressing the tiny head, hovered, and cradled over it. "I guess not."

She moved a little to get more comfortable on the couch. "I visited with Sarah Jones the other day. I wasn't actually planningon it, but I was walking down to see Andy and she wasn't home. I thought, I could go see Millie, but then I saw that little house Matt built and I decided to visit Mrs. Jones. Nobody ever goes and visits her," she added sadly.

"She doesn't do much visiting, either." Solace scratched at her arm, uncomfortable with talking about someone she didn't know. "Matt's been with us for, oh, going on three years, and we've always been able to count on him lending a helping hand. It's not our place to be prying into people's lives if they don't want us in them."

"She is embarrassed, you know, and unhappy."

"Because of Matt and Andy?"

Iris nodded, innocent sympathy welling in her eyes.

Didn't they break off their relationship?"

"But she knows, and Mark said he thinks Andy's still in love with Matt although she won't say it."

"Iris, a woman cannot leave a man for four years, carrying away his unborn child and come back thinking everything is going to be the same as it was."

"She told me she didn't know she was pregnant at the time. She wasn't even two months along."

"Why didn't she contact him when she found out?"

"She said she tried, but he moved around a lot after she left him."

"That's true, that's true," agreed Solace. "It weren't until Frank met up with him that he settled down. Well, Iris. If you and I could figure these things out, we wouldn't much be needing a pastor, would we? Except the marrying and burying part."

She smiled shyly. "I think Pastor Brighton is nice. He's another feeling man, like Frank. In the village, they call him Tall Feeling Man."

Solace couldn't prevent the chuckle that rose in her throat. "Frank is Feeling Man. Pastor Brighton is Tall Feeling Man. What do you call Charlie?"

A ray of sunlight found its way to the sofa, lighting up Iris's face and the enormous grin she couldn't resist displaying. "We call him Charlie No Horses."

Solace prepared to leave, unable to decide whether she had successfully cheered up Iris or if Iris had successfully cheered her. Setting her baby carefully in a woven basinet, Iris scrambled to her feet. "There is something I want you to do for me."

She picked up a cardboard box, bound and tied neatly with a string. "I was given so many things for my baby and she has outgrown some of her clothes already. I'm thinning them out. I want to send this north, to my cousins."

She shifted from one foot to another while Solace looked at the package dubiously. It had no address, return address or postal stamps. "I know," Iris explained. "Andy is still flying out with Mark when he bush pilots. Give the package to Andy. She'll know what to do."

When Solace returned to the lodge, the dart game was still going on although the players were markedly more erratic. Betty Lou was passed out on a table, drunk. Ed, Bea, and Brad were huddled together, drinking beer and smoking cigarettes like they were grown-ups. Bea quickly began wiping down the counter when she saw her mother coming and Ed picked up a broom.

"Last call," she warned. "Closing in fifteen minutes."

Having been marvelously outplayed by Zeb Grant, the military men grudgingly paid their bill and somehow managed to navigate their way to their vehicle, their feet stumbling over invisible obstacles. Once inside, they collapsed, heads lolling against the seats, and there they stayed. Brad tossed a dollar bill on the counter, looked at Ed's broom as though it was a contaminated object, then told him, "I'll see ya tomorrow," without once looking in Bea's direction. Ed nodded and gave a lazy salute.

"I'm checking the beer inventory," warned Solace, shooting an angry look toward Zeb, who was supposed to have been keeping an eye on his offspring. Zeb stopped counting his money long enough to glare thunderously at his children and tell them to start paying attention to their mother.

"All the beers were paid for," said Bea sulkily. "You can check the register."

Ed nodded his head vigorously. Ed was too simple to lie. Still, Solace felt dissatisfied with her daughter's performance. "Don't drink beer in the lodge. You're underage."

Bea sniffed. "Carol drinks beer."

"Not in the lodge," Solace repeated emphatically. "If I see either of you girls drinking in the lodge, I'll fire you."

Bea began closing the bar, slamming things around sulkily. "Why is it you let Ed drink in the lodge after he turned sixteen, but not me?"

"Because I'm trying to teach you to be a lady and Ed is, well... he's just Ed. There ain't no hope of him putting on a gentleman's clothing or learning manners."

"Or moving out of the house like our brother."

"There's no need to bring up Percy. The only time we hear from him is when he needs money. For the few brains the good Lord gave Ed, at least he gives a helping hand. Matt says he's shaping up to a good mechanic."

"Brad says it's because Eugene helps him. He couldn't do it by himself."

"You shouldn't listen to everything Brad has to say. What kind of brothers are they, traipsing all over the countryside, looking for gold, taking ships to the Orient? It's disgraceful."

"Their ma and pa are moving here in July. They almost have the house built."

"What on earth are they going to do with that rocky hillside?"

Handing the receipts and register over to her mother, Bea took off her apron and put on a sweater. "They don't know yet. Brad says they are entrepreneurs."

She sauntered out, leaving Solace alone with the lodge. Having discovered the floor didn't need much sweeping, Ed had slipped out with his dad. The two were probably sitting at home now, drinking and celebrating Zeb's winnings.

At least she didn't have to worry about Ed. He could never become a con man because he would elaborate on how he planned to con you before trying it out. And he wasn't mean. There had never been a mean bone in Ed's body.

She may never be able to brag about his achievements, but neither would she have to live with his failures. Unlike Percy, who needed bailing out of jail every six months.

Solace checked the receipts against the cash and counted the beers in reserve. It all balanced out. Either Brad had paid, or Bea had learned to use her feminine wiles against the G.I.'s, who had been growing drunker by the minute. Solace suspected the latter.

She also suspected Brad had put her up to it as Bea didn't have the gumption to do it on her own. Until this year, she would not have even known how to do it. She had Carol to thank for that. Maybe it was just as well. Bea was a plain girl. She needed to learn how to make herself appealing.

Putting the proceeds in a leather pouch that she tucked under her arm, Solace blew out the last lamp, threw an army blanket over Betty Lou, who snuffed loudly before turning over, and closed the lodge.

The military men were just waking up. She handed them a large cup of coffee. They were waving at her and passing the coffee around when she walked away. She sat on her porch step, pulling her shawl tightly around her in objection to the cool, late spring breeze. Five minutes later, the engine started in the parking lot below her and an automobile roared off, blowing smoke. "You need an oil change," she muttered, getting up and going inside.

Zeb was alone in the living room. "Was it a good day?"

"Yes," she mumbled. "Did Bea go to bed?"

"She did. You shouldn't be so hard on her."

"She's growing up. Do you know what word she used tonight? Entrepreneurs! What are they teaching the young people in school these days? We never talked like that."

"We didn't get a chance to, I think. People didn't speak fancy where we came from."

"We've got a big streak of fancy around here these days," Solace mused. "Journalists and artists and actors and French people. We could fill up a whole bucket with fancy."

"If you want Bea to grow up a lady and marry a fine-speaking man, she's going to need all those fancy words and education."

"I want her to grow up a lady who marries a plain-speaking man!"

"Well," said Zeb, reaching over to pat her hand. "That all remains to be seen, doesn't it? It's time to quit clipping her wings, Solace."

Solace agreed with him and followed him to the bedroom. But as she was slipping her nightgown over her head, she asked fitfully, "Why does it have to be Brad Phillips? Why can't it be someone nice, like the railroad boy?"

A few days later, she was reminded she should always be careful of what she wished for. Bea and Carol sped through their chores at an astonishing rate, and were spruced and ready to leave the lodge by seven p.m. "What are you girls doing on a week night?"Solace asked, surprised with their lively appearance.

Bea giggled behind her freshly rouged cheeks. "Out to the Eklutna Dam. That's where the powerline guys are camped."

Carol's eyes flashed excitedly. "Iris made some pan-fried bread and Eugene said he would bring it to them. He invited Iris to come along but she didn't want to, so he invited us."

"Well, that was nice of Iris," Solace answered with uncertainty.

Carol handed Solace a handful of bills and loose change. "They already asked Eugene earlier if he would bring by some sodas and beer because they can't be lugging that stuff around while on the job, so Iris made some pan bread for a snack. Here's the money. We need a case of beer and a case of soda."

Solace peered out the window. Eugene's battered truck was in the parking lot. There was Ed but no Bradly sitting next to him. If she couldn't trust Eugene, she couldn't trust any of the youngsters.

She filled the girls' order and watched as the truck drove away with a merry chug from the tailpipe.

"I will have to ask Zeb," she murmured at the window.

"But I think powerline men and railroad men are about the same. Let's hope, anyway."

They weren't supposed to grow up. That was the heart of it. They were supposed to stay young and dependent forever.

Twenty-Eight

As soon as the weather turned warm, Millie walked to the lodge each day between the hours of one to three to visit with Andy and Solace, so they could relax during the lull with coffee and gossip.

She hauled her two children in a large, toy wagon with wooden slats on the sides. The wagon was technically a Christmas gift to Jason, but Millie was a practical woman. In the summer, she used his toy wagon as a baby carrier and in the winter, she used his nice runner sled. How she kept those two children inside their carrier while she traveled was anyone's guess but knowing Millie, they probably learned to stay inside by trial and error. Millie was a champion of hands-on experiences.

You always knew when Millie was bringing news by the lipless smile she thought was her poker-face and the twinkling in her eyes. Hazel eyes, Ted Ewing had said. Treacherous eyes, he had told Solace. They changed with her mood. They changed with the weather. They changed with the clothing she wore. Andy said they were nature's eyes. Solace wondered at times about this relationship with Andy and Millie and why Andy had named her daughter, Hazel. Hazel didn't have hazel eyes. She had blue eyes like her mother's.

Jason leaped out of the wagon before Millie had pulled it through the door and ran for the bar stools. The boy was going to self-inflict brain damage as much as he spun around. He also had a cast-iron stomach. Believing nobody was looking, he shook the mustard bottle until it splattered some thick yellow drops on the table, and cleaned them up with his fingers, licking them with relish. Solace ignored his transgressions. Boys eat everything.

Millie was dressed for summer weather, in sherbet green with eyelet lace. She even wore a perky new white sun bonnet and a pair of kid gloves. She folded her kid gloves and crunched them into her purse. "You will never guess what Charlie has been building."

"His new store?" Suggested Andy.

"That, too. He put in the foundation, but he hasn't started building it yet. No. He has started building a church."

Solace sputtered in her coffee. "Now that's just crazy! Weren't he and Ester going on vacation this year?"

"They are," said Millie, arranging her fashionable purse in her lap. "But as soon as Pastor Brighton left, he began building the church."

"Is he building a church or going on vacation?" asked Andy impatiently.

"Both." Nancy was climbing out of the wagon on her own. Millie gave her a saltine cracker to keep her busy. "He has started building the church, but he wants the community to finish it while they are gone."

"We can't do that." Andy shoved back her chair and sulked. "We've gotta have Charlie! Nothing gets done without Charlie."

"My goodness," chided Millie. "It's not like he's going to be gone forever. We can survive six weeks without Charlie."

Solace looked woefully out the kitchen window, which showed nothing unusual, only Ed still worrying over an engine. "No pastor. No Charlie. That's a bad sign for our summer."

Bea and Carol were running off to the Eklutna Dam every chance they got, sometimes with deliveries, other times, simply because boys were there, and the girls never overlooked an opportunity. Andy said at least they would be able to keep tabs on the powerline progress.

Bea didn't talk about the progress. She talked about a lady that brought the linemen sandwiches every day and helped them with camp chores. "They even named a waterfall after her," she told Solace.

"Can they do that?" asked Solace with amazement. "Can the power company just look at a mountain or a waterfall and decide, we'll name this after so and so?"

"I guess they did," shrugged Bea. "They named it 'Barbara Falls.'"

Solace didn't consider herself a prophet, but some things can be felt before they are seen. The builders pitched in to help Charlie build his church on the far corner of his property, nearly completing it before he left and adding leisurely finishing touches while he was gone. Tammy visited the lodge a few times, fretting over how long it would take for them to be married with both the pastor and their best man gone.

It all seemed completely normal, but there was a feel in the air of things to come.

The first of the bad luck struck the trading post. May had moved in with a mixture of rain and sunny weather. The trees were greening slowly. The creek was roaring with winter's break up. Brad Phillips sat heavily down in a bar stool and looked at Solace accusingly. "There was something wrong with the stew you served last night, Mrs. Grant. It gave me food poisoning."

Suspecting the worst of all attributes and intentions in this impertinent neighbor, Solace bridled with indignation. "There certainly was not. I've never cooked a sour meal in twenty years of running this post. That's more years than you are old, young man. You had too much to drink. I'm not responsible for your hangover's."

"It wasn't a hangover. No ma'am. Gordon has been as sick as I am, and he wasn't drinking last night."

He did look rather green at the gills. She floundered for possibilities. "Maybe you're coming down with something. You should stay in your own place, so you don't spread it. We're just coming out of winter. People don't want to start getting sick."

He doubted he had a contagious condition, but for the sake of not stirring an argument, agreed it was too early to know what caused his ailment and he would go home until he improved.

Solace believed this to be the end of it, but just to be on the safe side, dumped all the left-over food from the night before, and began scrubbing the kitchen thoroughly. She was behind on the baking schedule when Andy came in. Solace put her immediately to work, telling her Zeb would handle the front.

By noon, Zeb began feeling ill. Several of the customers who came in complained of stomach pain. Not all those who were ill had eaten at the lodge the night before. Not all those who had eaten at the lodge were ill.

Andy was fine, as were Carol and Matt, all of whom habitually ate Solace's preparations. But Solace's entire family became ill, and Solace wasn't feeling like a spring filly. Her stomach boiled disagreeably. She spent half her time in the outhouse, smoking cigarettes to cover the smell and groaning every five minutes as new gasses found a way to collect and bubble in her intestines.

The Grant family was so ill, Andy even enlisted Jimmy to help out for a few days and had long-legged Anna running around doing errands. The girl had all the wild beauty of Andy and the independent mind of Sharon. She would become a terrifying adversary when she grew up.

Maybe it was just as well. Something told Solace the Ewing incident had created more of an impact on impressionable young Anna than it had on Carol. Anna would be wise to that type of man. Solace chuckled to herself as she watched Anna streak across the parking lot to bring back some more medications from Frank's extensive medicine cabinet, her colt-like legs covered in rolled-up jeans. What was she thinking? Anna would be wise to every type of man. She would probably marry a scientist or a schoolteacher.

She must be feeling better to find her humor. She returned to the lodge and sat down to a sandwich and a glass of water. An hour later, her stomach was churning again.

The gastric attacks on the various community members did not lessen, and in some cases, grew severe enough to have the victim groaning at home in pain. This eliminated all possibility of food poisoning, as this type of suffering was usually contained within twenty-four hours. As a contagious disease, it also came into doubt, as exposure didn't necessarily mean you would get sick. As they pondered over a common denominator, it finally occurred to Zeb, "it's the water! There must be a carcass upriver."

When Frank stopped by for his mail that afternoon, Zeb cornered him.

"I think we've got a rash of beaver fever going on, doc."

"Giardiasis," grunted Frank. "What makes you think so?"

"Because the only ones who have gotten sick are the ones who drink their water from the creek. You have your own water. The Delaneys have their own water. So do the homesteads across the road. But other people don't. They get their water from here and the water is what is making us sick."

Frank fingered his tie, staring at the far wall, contemplating his business suit, which did not collaborate well with thrashing through the brush. "I'll pick up Matt and come out after dinner. We'll find the culprit."

He did as he promised. Shortly after dinner hour, dressed far more suitably for rock climbing than he had earlier that day, he showed up at the creek with Matt and Jimmy. The snow had melted except in short chunks along the water's edge half-way up the hill, then began stretching in thinned ice bridges.

Millie had come along to keep Solace company, or her own self company while the men explored the upper reaches of the tumbling river. She settled at the counter, letting her children play on the bar stools. Even the little girl was learning, pulling herself up so her belly was leaning over the stool, and swinging back and forth with one pointed foot.

"Well," she said, accepting the cup of coffee Solace offered. "The church is nearly finished. All it needs is a coat of paint and don't you know, Ester and Charlie are on vacation. I would have thought they would wish to see its completion before they left. After all, it was Charlie's idea."

"What isn't Charlie's idea?" asked Solace testily. The Lamars had brought water from their homesite, but her stomach was still complaining. She added the powdered magnesium Frank had given her to a glass of Lamar water and drank it down.

"Sometimes I think even the trading post was Charlie's idea. He dreamed up the Chugach, put the trading post in the middle and started building. Me and Zeb, we just popped up all at once and there never was anything before Charlie."

"You are in a fine mood!" Millie sniffled, then turned sympathetic. "It must have been hard with the entire lodge sick all week."

Sympathy was exactly what Solace wanted. She brought out a handkerchief and blew her nose. "It has been a nightmare and that Phillips' kid accusing me of food poisoning. The very idea. I will never feed his mouth again."

"He's just a boy. They get like that. Smart alecks. Think they know everything. My brothers, oh! The mouths they have. We can't always judge them by what comes out of their vocal cords. Their brains aren't attached."

"It's my girl I worry about."

"And rightfully. Bea's a good girl. I've seen the way she cares for old man Rawlings when he's in his cups. Nobody else pays him much notice but she always makes sure he's fed and goes out in proper clothing for the weather. That's a sweet girl for you, Solace."

"I try to raise them up right. Old man Rawlings ain't never done harm to anyone. He's just broken-down and tired out. The years can do that to you."

The magnesium was having its effect. Solace excused herself a few minutes and returned, feeling relieved. "Wasn't your brother coming for a visit this year?"

It was Millie's turn to take out a handkerchief and dab at her eyes. "Bruiser. I should know better than to depend on him for anything. He wrote me. He can't come out this year. He says he doesn't have the money. Four years and he's not doing better."

"Prosperity hasn't caught up with everyone yet," murmured Solace, who felt her own prosperity was the greatest it had ever been, despite contaminated drinking water.

"It hasn't caught up with anyone," said Millie bitterly. "I know this much. Next year, we're taking a vacation. I know Frank qualifies for free air flight now and we're going to take it. If there is one thing I've learned from the other civil service women, you've got to put your foot down or the men will wander off to do as they please. We have vacations coming and we're taking them."

"Now see, Millie. That's a bit of prosperity. Me and Zeb would have to save up for years and years for that kind of vacation."

"Well," she said, twisting a curl. "The pay isn't as good as the benefits, so we would be wise to use our benefits. Certainly, Ester uses hers. She even has the benefits of a pastor."

Solace realized she should never have brought up the subject of Millie's brother. It was causing her to feel sorry for herself. She chortled. "How is he Ester's pastor? I thought he belonged to everyone."

"That may be so, but now they have the hymnals, and they have a church. They want more than monthly services. Ester won't allow him to get away, even if she has to chain him to the pulpit." She dabbed again at her eyes, her disappointment threatening to overtake her.

"We need him.," said Solace. "He's been helping Iris. She likes him."

She finished her moment of self-pity and put her hanky away. "How is Iris?"

"She's better." Solace found herself nibbling at the packets of saltine crackers. "I think she's over Ted. She says she loves Eugene now."

"It would be a bit pitiful for her to marry him if she didn't love him, or at least believe she could learn to love him."

"Well, she hasn't said she would, but she could do worse." As soon as Solace said the words, she flushed. The worst Iris could have done they would rather not think about.

With the beaver fever epidemic - Solace didn't care much for Frank's big words that were impossible to pronounce - there had been fewer people coming to the lodge. Partly because so many of the residents were ill and partly because there was still a great deal of uncertainty among the general populace as to the cause of the disease. Since the entire Grant family was indisposed, leaving the post's management almost entirely in Andy's hands, this was agreeable with Solace. It was empty while the three waited, other than a few customers who bought gas, soda pop or beer and nothing more.

They were losing the last of the sunlight, the sky stained by the radiance that had hopefully groped at the clouds to stay afloat, when the three men returned. They were covered with mud from head to toe. They walked briskly across the floor, holding their hands in front of them until they reached the fat-bellied wood stove. Jimmy cackled as he warmed his hands over the iron grate. "Good thing we found it when we did," he cried out enthusiastically. "Another few days, it would have rotted all over the place."

Hearing his voice, Andy came in from the kitchen, wiping her hands. "You found something."

"Yeah," Jimmy grinned. "A dead moose. It had been upstream all winter, then started thawing out. Got caught in the branches of a fallen tree. It was starting to come apart."

Frank cleared his throat. "I don't think the ladies wish to listen to the gory details."

Jimmy grabbed a chair and scooted it close to the stove. "Sure they do. These women have cast iron stomachs."

Solace's stomach gurgled and she opened a can of ginger ale. "I'm okay. Just getting things settled down."

"Yeah," said Jimmy happily. "As it was, we had to climb down a bluff. When we reached the dead moose, Matt began yanking on a front leg and it started pulling loose. He yelled, 'Holy mother of...' well, I won't tell you all he said, but the three of us had to get down in the river and boost it up on the bank. It was thawing out good, too, you know. Another few days... phew, what a mess."

Their smell verified their story. As the three men basked in the heat of the stove, a rank, decaying scent floated up from their steaming clothing.

"But you got the whole thing out?" asked Andy.

Frank groped around in his jacket until he found his half-filled pipe. Surrounding himself with a cloud of smoke that smelled far more pleasant than his garments, he confirmed. "We got it all out. It didn't break up. We brought it high enough up the bank that it won't contaminate any longer, but I still wouldn't drink the water for a few weeks."

"We probably won't drink it again ever," said Solace crossly. "I keep telling Zeb, we should put in a well. It's safer that way. He doesn't listen. It's all about expense."

"We should put up a 'no drinking' sign," suggested Andy.

Solace nodded but fretted. "It will be so hard for those who get their water from here. They are going to need a new water source."

"They can still use it for cleaning and bathing if they boil it," said Millie helpfully.

Solace wasn't mollified. "It just looks so bad for the lodge. We have bad water." She sniffed back her tears.

All that they could do about it had been done.

Solace closed the lodge and left it closed for the next three days, so her family could begin to mend and so Andy could get some rest. Strange one, that Andy. She was the hardest worker Solace had ever seen, yet she wasn't dependable. She would be gone without explanation, sometimes for two weeks at a time, then show back up like nothing had happened. It was always because she caught a flight somewhere; it didn't matter where. She was addicted to flying. She wasn't dependable but when the chips were down, there was Andy, picking them up.

Gradually, her customers returned. The Grants couldn't be blamed. It was just one of those things that happened. It was only because the creek was so fast moving that it hadn't happened before now. The only difference now was that the Grants had to haul their fresh water from the Delaneys in military cannisters. Some of the customers swore the Delaney water was better tasting. Spring water always did taste better.

They could have spring water if they would dig a well. The whole mountain shelf was full of water. She began to pressure Zeb, especially when she heard other homesteaders talk about digging wells. "The Bolinders have a well," she mourned, as though she had been deprived her whole life. "They even have a water pump inside, so they don't have to carry water."

"We aren't such that we can keep up with the Bolinders," grumbled Zeb. "Them that have inheritances. We inherited a bag of rocks."

"The Erichmans have a well. It has an outdoor pump, but they have a well."

Zeb rattled his newspaper and brought it close to his face as thought he had found something interesting to read. "How the hell did he dig himself a well? He's no heavy equipment operator."

"Neither is Charlie. He hired a professional. Alex hired Matt and rented the backhoe."

"That's still a lot of money, Solace, and they've gotta know where to dig. How many attempts did Matt make before he found water, eh? I'm not saying the man doesn't know what he's doing. I'm just saying it isn't cheap. It can take days to find the right spot and dig a good well. All that time, you're renting equipment and hiring a man to run it."

"I heard Millie say Frank knows how to witch water, and that's how the Erichmans' well was dug."

"Frank does? I thought he didn't believe in these things."

"He doesn't. He's very unhappy about it."

"Dangest thing I ever heard." He rattled his paper some more in the assumption the conversation was over.

"The Hughes are planning to have a well put in. They don't have inheritance money."

"Gary works construction. He knows all the right people."

"He's using Matt. They all say he's the best heavy equipment man around."

Zeb put his newspaper down on the table very carefully and sighed. "Solace, I know you look at the receipts and this has been the best year we've ever had. The cabins are full. The laundry mat is bringing us money. We sell lots of beer, soda, and hamburgers. The gas don't help us much. We've still got to haul it out from Anchorage, but it draws customers. What I'm saying is, it looks good, but it ain't that good. We can get the electricity and the new dryers and the kitchen gadgetry you want, or we can get a well. I don't see how we can do both."

"So, we'll be hauling water from the Delaney's for who knows how long?"

"Do you have a better idea?"

She drew her mouth down to show her complete dissatisfaction and set about doing her chores. It was her laundry day. On Mondays, she closed the laundry mat to the public, so she could do the family laundry and wash the bedding and linen from the cabins. She gathered the freshly washed sheets and carried them out to the line. Usually, she had Iris hang out the laundry but on nice days, she liked to do it herself.

While hanging the sheets, she saw the strangest thing. Gordon and Brad Phillips were hopping over the rocks leading down from their property, with Frank in front, holding something with both hands, his jacket tails flapping in the breeze. She whistled to Ed, who was bent over an automobile. "What is going on over there?"

He glanced toward the Phillips' brothers then straightened. He jumped several feet forward, then looked again. He reminded her of a rabbit venturing cautiously into a field.

He hopped again and beckoned to her. "You should watch. I never seen nothin' like it. Frank has got a stick, see, and he's got it out in front of him. It looks about like a sling shot. He'll stand in one spot and the stick will get all jittery and the brothers will shout and put down a little red flag, then he'll move on until he starts getting jittery again."

"He's witching!" gasped Solace.

Ed's ears perked with interest. "He is? I've gotta watch that."

Since Ed had already begun ambling in the direction of the flagged hillside, Solace felt it her obligation to follow. They picked a pathway across the ridge and inched down the rocky slope where Frank was sniffing out water with his witching stick. What he held was a thick, green sapling with the bark peeled away from the pointed end.

He grappled with the vee shaped handlebars at the other end as though fighting it. What was peculiar, as she drew closer and was able to observe the phenomena in detail, was that Frank was doing his best to point the stick upward, while the pointed end insisted on arching down. It was like he had caught a fish on the invisible string of a fishing pole.

"Right there," said Frank. "Put your last flag right there."

He was standing over a short cliff with a solid, almost smooth, rock wall. This cliff erupted only around seventy feet off the main road from a generous deposit of gravel and dirt. How deep that cliff boulder sank was anyone's guess. It supported an entire network of hilly rock cropping. It was a stop sign, telling the road to go around.

Gordon scrambled down the embankment to the side of the cliff, loose pebbles clattering behind him. He circled around until he was facing the cliff wall, which towered about three feet over his head. He ran his hands along it and looked up toward the long line of flags marching toward the mountain. He became especially interested in one of the cracks. He dug at it a bit with his fingernails, then took out his snap-blade and began scraping away the moss and dirt.

He called to his brother. They both tested the small, natural hole inside the crack where the boulder had split, leaving one side to lean against the other. Frank also inspected their findings. "It's in there," said Gordon. "We're gonna tap it right here."

Unable to overcome her curiosity, Solace picked her way down the embankment to stand beside the men. "Exactly what are you going to tap?" She asked.

"Water. There's a creek that goes underground near that foothill where you see the first flag. We followed it all the way here. It's what caused this boulder to crack. There's water behind it." He showed her the dirt sample he had pulled out with his blade. It was damp.

"How are you going to get to it?" she asked, looking dubiously at the tiny hole. It was already beginning to seep with moisture, so she didn't doubt his word.

"We're going to slam a pipe into it," said Brad casually.

The words were simple. Driving a pipe into the rock face by hand was not so simple. The Phillips' brothers enlisted the help of Dresden Hayes. It was the first time Solace had seen the big man doing physical labor. His shirt fluttering fluidly behind him, he dug at the hole with a pickaxe, then a heavy, wedged hammer. Beating, grinding, battering with axes, wedges, and hammers, the four men managed within four hours, to create a four-inch-wide hole that tunneled six inches into the cliff face. Solace shook her head, clucked to herself, and assumed the young men would put to rest the idea of drilling through four feet of rock.

She was wrong. Early the next day, while working in the kitchen, she glanced out the open back door and saw that the Phillips brothers were back at work. Dresden felt he had already served his active duty, but he was there to supervise three more volunteers: Jimmy, Eugene, and Ed. Solace thought about calling Ed back to work but decided to watch instead.

The brothers had with them, a long, stout galvanized steel pipe, which they were now trying to shove in the hole. Not being able to get much past the lip, they with-drew the pipe to make the surrounding area deeper and wider. This time, the pipe would remain in the hole provided someone held it there.

Brad and Ed volunteered, bracing their feet against the hillside, and gripping the pipe with both hands. They nodded at Gordon, who was not only the oldest, but the most physically developed among them. He readied himself with his hands wrapped tightly around the handle of his sledgehammer. His buttons strained to hold together against his chest. His neck muscles grew their own set of muscles. As he held the sledgehammer high, his shirt sleeves flattened and pulled against his arms.

He swung. The impact seemed to reverberate through the entire hillside, ending in a shudder. The boys yelled but held the pipe steady. He swung again, the metal howling against stone. All day and into the late afternoon, they labored, each strike a belligerent bellow that echoed through the mountain range and boomed over the inlet.

At lunchtime, Solace made the group sandwiches and sweetened iced tea. Bea and Carol were doing their best to appear busy but cast long, wistful looks at the youthful laborers. Not wishing to appear as though she had a soft spot for the girls, Solace thrust the refreshments rudely into their hands and pushed them out the door, warning them not to dawdle too long.

She watched them skip over the freshening earth, responding greenly to spring. Solace had a poorly kept secret. She was a romantic. Nothing pleased her more than watching young people fall in love during the spring. As much as it pained her to see her baby girl growing up, nothing made her happier than seeing her daughter coming out of her shell and becoming a woman.

"They ain't seventeen yet," observed Betty Lou behind her back.

Solace wiped at her face with her apron, pretending she had food smudges. "I know, but some of them start early. It's a fact of nature."

Betty Lou screwed up her face as she studied the ceiling. "I reckon so. I might have been eleven or twelve when I started thinking these things."

Solace gave her a surprised look. "Betty Lou, you didn't."

"I'm not saying I did. Just the thinking on things, you know. A girl begins to wonder. 'Course, if she gets too curious, she don't wonder long. That's another of them nature facts."

"Betty Lou, I've known you a long time. You've had some good men. Why didn't you keep any of them?"

"I should say I had some good men. Had some bad uns too. I still visit the good ones now and then. We have some great drinking times, getting wild and nekkid. You just let the bad uns go. They waste your time. No point in it."

"When did you figure that out, Betty Lou?"

"Maybe a year or two ago. Blame, Solace! What you talking about me for? I just come to tell you Anna's here and wants a pound of brown sugar and a box of corn flakes for her mama. And her mama says, the brown sugar better not be hard."

Betty Lou continued to look insulted, even after Solace, who knew never to pry into the wild woman's life, apologized. Using the moment Solace turned to assist Anna, Betty Lou stalked out the door and meandered over to the pipe fitting crew. Solace fingered through the sacks of brown sugar, checking for the softest contents. She placed the two items Mrs. Delaney had ordered in a bag and watched as Anna carefully counted out the amount, down to the last penny. The girl was tall enough to look Solace straight in the eye, which was a little discerning when the face appeared no more than thirteen.

The girl didn't look in the direction of a single male as she left, but she did glance at the gathering by the cliff. Not seeing anyone of interest, she unhitched a horse from the log fence, mounted it and began trotting home. It was going to take one energetic fellow to impress Anna.

When the crew came in, one at a time, tiredly, for a rest, she gave them free cokes when they ordered hamburgers. Even though she had no faith in their project, it pleased her to see the youngsters working together. They even withstood the jokes that spontaneously sprang up from the customers who had stayed to observe their progress.

Most of the jokes centered around the Phillips' brothers looking for black gold since the yellow gold didn't pan out. Ed, who was used to being teased on a daily basis and cackling it off through some internal knowledge mechanism of his own, giggled more than usual and kept reassuring his mother, "just wait. They'll be surprised"

It was in the early evening, just as the Wolf Creek settlement began to lose interest in their new neighbor's steel-driving efforts, that a shout sprang up from the laboring boys.

Solace was as urgent to see the new development as the others. She barely took time to untie her apron before running up the highway to the rock face.

She could scarcely believe her eyes. The determined team had managed to drive that pipe in so that only three feet of it extended from the hole. From this jutting metal tube, poured a clearing stream of mud and water. "See? See?" Said Gordon excitedly. "I knew that creek was inside there. There's your public water. Fresh as a daisy."

Whatever ill will anybody had harbored toward the Phillips' brothers, ended that day. Even Brad's youthful fondness for adult habits and pastimes was forgiven.

There was still some speculation as to the qualities of the oldest brother, Hank, who had run off on a mysterious expedition to a country that had only recently been their enemy, but these speculations were censored by the watchful woman's society who reminded the general public they lived in the place of many places.

What they said to each other in private was a different matter because after all, the Phillips brothers had admitted they were entrepreneurs and there was something sly about the word.

Twenty-Nine

Trouble always comes in threes. The community had barely settled down to its new water access when another threat rose on the horizon. The children were all getting chicken pox. It began in the valley and swept quickly into the village and Wolf Creek. Every child that had not been exposed to chicken pox before, had it, from the babies to the teenagers.

The chicken pox was raging at the Delaney household. Not only were both Andy's children sick, but so was Sarah's boy and so was Anna. Carol had already been exposed but Bea had not. The poor girl woke to the most hideous red bumps with yellow, pussy centers. They looked especially blistering on her pale skin, adding livid color to what generally had little color at all. She screamed that her life was ruined and covered her head with a pillow. It took several days to convince her she was not going to die, and she would not be permanently scarred.

If Andy appeared at work looking haggard, Solace felt more haggard. "I believe the older kids suffer more with it," she sighed mournfully. "Bea hasn't gotten out of bed in three days."

Andy nodded. "They suffer. The older they are, the more they suffer because they have forgotten how to get through it. When they are little ones, like the boys, all they've really known is the suffering."

She dropped a coin into the soda machine and brought out a coke, turning it in her hand before continuing. "When they are babies, they swallow too much air, they get gas, their stomachs get bloated. They get constipated or poop everywhere and get diaper rash. When they teethe, their bodies hurt. Chicken pox is just one more thing they figure they have to suffer through. It's not so much to them. It barely slows them down."

Solace mopped her head with a towel, then threw it aside for the laundry bin. It wasn't especially hot, but it was sticky. The slumbering air soaked into you until you were as sticky and lethargic as the crumbling day. "How about Anna? She's in her teens now. She must be suffering."

Andy guzzled down half her soda and looked at the bright green bottle offering greater refreshment than spring water. "That girl eats oats every day for breakfast. She's half-horse. She goes to the spring, puts her feet in the pool and stays there all day, drawing water up wherever she itches. She'll come out of this without a blemish."

"Bea scratches. I told her it would leave scars if she scratched too hard, but she's not listening. I've a mind to clip her nails."

Andy wasn't worried about Bea scratching. She worried about the babies. "They are the ones you have to watch," she mourned. "Their temperatures go up too fast. I had to spend the whole night with Millie night before last. Nancy's temperature had gone up to a hundred three. We put her in a baking soda bath to cool her down, then wrapped her up tight and fed her chicken soup. The fever broke about four in the morning. And then, Hazel got sick but that's when mama took over. She's got a bond with Hazel she never had for her daughters."

"It's a good thing you're getting all that nurse's training. Are you almost through?"

"I've got another year if I want to be a registered nurse."

"A registered one! Are you going fancy like the rest of the woman's society?"

"It irritates Ester."

"It seems strange with her gone. She got out before the chicken pox hit."

"Oh," said Andy, stretching, yawning, and generally enjoying the reprieve. "If there is an epidemic here, you can be assured there is one in the lower forty-eight. It probably spread here from the new people coming into Anchorage. I'll bet Ester made sure her son was exposed, so she could have it done and over with and enjoy her vacation."

"It would not hurt for them to come back, I would think. Iris has gone off saying we've been cursed, and I haven't been able to talk it out of her head."

"It could be we're cursed. I wouldn't say that we weren't. There are some powerfully bad things going on right now. But maybe Charlie isn't the one who can lift it. Iris's people know about these things. If there is cursing involved, they can usually spot it."

"Hum," said Solace, finding a good excuse to get out of the kitchen. "We should pay a visit to Iris. We can get Carol to take over a while. With all the sicknesses and all the usual fishing, not to mention a few vacations, there ain't much of anybody in here."

"How is her baby?" asked Andy anxiously.

"You know how it is. Those tiny babies still nursing never do get chicken pox the first time around."

Carol was happy to be placed in charge for an hour or two while Solace and Andy visited Iris. Without the competition, Carol had been doing her best to prove her waitressing capabilities, hoping she would shine out in exemplary duty when Bea came back to work.

The girl deserved a raise, but if she gave her one, Solace would have to do the same for Bea, who still needed a nudge now and then with a cattle prod. She would just have to give Carol a bonus. That was fair.

With only one admonishment to not drink beer with the boys, the two set on their way. "I don't know why the civil service think they need vacations all the time," grumbled Solace. "Most of us do without them. Pampered government pets, that's what they are."

"Believe me," said Andy, with a stride so long, it was difficult for Solace to keep up. "If I was married to one of those civil service men, I would want a vacation, too. They get disgustingly grim and morbid. They talk about the government all day long and who is going to save them and who is going to start another bloody war. They never have enough of it, you know."

"Well, it is their livelihood."

"And they carry it home, laying it on their wives, but keep their terrible little secrets. The women deserve every bit of their vacation whether the men do or not."

Iris was sitting on her newly assembled bench swing, cradling her baby. She was looking better. Her plants were opening, promising lively color, but she hadn't truly opened. Shelooked wan. Her eyes slid unhappily away. She still would not visit with her brothers.

They talked with her a little about the niceness of the day and how June could be a better month, but Iris shook her head. "It's not the weather that's cursing us this year. It's something else."

"Now then," said Solace reasonably. "The children's illnesses come through all the time. It's not a curse that brings them. It's all the busy going here and there. And the beaver fever – what creek hasn't had a dead animal in it now and then? It's the way things are."

"It won't stop happening with that," insisted Iris stubbornly.

With a strong ulterior motive for visiting the girl, Andy cleared her throat and said as gently as she could, "You really ought to visit your cousins, or let them visit you."

Her eyes grew large and glimmering with astonishment. "That is the worst thing I could do! It's Ted Ewing. He put a curse on us. He's angry that I'm marrying Eugene. He'll be even angrier if I see my cousins."

"They miss you."

"And I'm sorry for that but we have to live with this until we get it straightened out. Maybe the pastor will help."

"Pastors don't perform exorcisms," said Andy, making herself comfortable on the steps.

"Then what good are they except for marriages?"

"They perform baptisms," suggested Solace.

"There you go," said Andy. "They've got their uses. I don't reckon we'd be building a church if they didn't."

"He might curse the church," said Iris worriedly.

"He won't curse the church!" Declared Andy emphatically, then settled down. "Millie would never allow it."

"Then we need Millie," said Iris, whose mind remained on one solid track. "He always was afraid of her."

Both women sighed, realizing only a good summer would convince Iris they had not been cursed.

The summer refused to cooperate. Productivity was good. Plants were growing vigorously. Baby goats were bleating, chicks were cheeping, small furry animals rustled in the brush. On a pleasant June day, a sudden thunderstorm rolled in, carrying a few frenzied streaks of lightening. One of these streaks hit the Rasmussen barn. The burning barn caused a wildfire.

The field telephones buzzed. Trucks began pulling into Wolf Creek, loaded down with containers for putting out the fire. The women formed an automatic brigade, filling buckets and passing them down the line to the waiting trucks. All day, the volunteers battled the wildfire. They beat at the burning brush with towels soaked in water. They dug trenches by hand and with tractors. The Anchorage fire department came out and hosed down the crisply sizzling trees.

By late evening, sixty acres of land had burned away but the fire was out. Tiredly, the volunteer firefighters went home, their throats raw with smoke, their arms rubbery from beating out flames and carrying buckets of water. The fire had encroached so closely, it had scorched one side of the house, but they had saved most of their livestock and belongings.

This time, Solace and Andy began to take the curse seriously. They talked with Millie first, cornering her the next time she visited the lodge. "Why, I don't know anything about removing curses," Millie told them innocently.

"Don't worry about that," Andy assured her. "Iris has it all figured out, but she thinks you need to be there."

Millie didn't take long to mull it over. "Frank wouldn't approve."

"Why would you tell Frank?"

"I wouldn't. He's such a wet blanket about these things."

"We also need Beth, Doreen and Sharon," Solace reminded Andy.

Millie gave Solace a puzzled look. "Do we need that many people to perform an exorcism?"

"It's not really an exorcism," Andy explained. "You need a priest for that. We're holding a séance to summon Ted Ewing's spirit."

"Do we need to do that?" asked Millie in alarm.

Solace nodded her agreement with Andy. "We do to put his spirit at rest."

It wasn't that easy to convince the others. Doreen was nervous about provoking spirits. "We're not provoking them," said Solace. "We're un-provoking them. Iris has a plan."

Beth was hesitant at first but became worried that the curse might somehow affect her garden, which was growing even better this year than the last. If it meant placating a spirit, it was better to be safe than sorry.

Sharon said it was the most ridiculous thing she had ever heard. "But what if it's true?" Asked Beth anxiously. "What if he destroys the plants in your greenhouses? He could send a worm or a bug or a hailstorm!"

Without declaring that Ted Ewing was dead, they all began to worry about the restful state of his spirit. Even if he was alive, well, but two thousand miles away, it was better that he harbored no ill will at all than to wish a string of calamities on Wolf Creek. It was better to confront their grievances than to suppress them and risk further reprisal. The group finally pressured Sharon into joining them.

It wasn't the biggest secret they had ever kept. There were a surprisingly large number of outsiders involved – including Bea, Carol, Zeb, Eugene, and Ed. They all wanted in on the séance. "You can attend the burying ceremony later," Solace said, admonishing them to go about their chores and mind their own business.

"There is going to be a burying?" asked Ed eagerly.

Solace assured him, "There's going to be a burying, and I don't want one blabbermouth among you, including Ed. We don't want the spirit to wander around willy-nilly, visiting who it pleases."

Andy cemented Ed's silence. "If you open your mouth, Ted's spirit will jump inside you and take control of you for the rest of your life."

"I ain't saying a word," he promised.

Ed spent the rest of the day and the next, tight-lipped, pushing along his broom like he was deaf and dumb, all the way to the hour the women agreed to meet. When he saw first Andy's truck, then Doreen's Pontiac pull into the lodge parking lot, he was tearing down yet another vehicle in the back of the parking lot. As the women hustled passed him on their way to Iris's cabin, he reached up and ran his fingers over his lips like he was zipping them shut.

Solace was busy giving last minute instructions to Bea and Carol when she noticed the other women arriving at the lodge. "I want you to keep a special eye on Zeb to make sure he doesn't come sniffing around the cabin. If the spirit sees him and his buddies, sure enough it's with them it will be wanting to hang out and we can't be having it. It's a very wrong-telling spirit."

She turned the spatula over to Bea with faith her daughter had learned some cooking skills, and bustled after them, stopping only long enough to give Ed a warning look. He glanced at his mother, then bent his head industrially under the hood of the car, twisting a wrench. That's what he was best for, loosening up the parts. It took Eugene to put them back together correctly.

The room smelled of burnt sage and brewing leatherleaf tea. Iris had been preparing for them. The furniture had all been pulled back, leaving a wide, clear, central space. All her rugs had been moved to the space, and several blankets, woven Native style, spread over the top of them. She had also moved all her pillows and cushions to this space and had arranged them in a circle.

Solace was neither very familiar, nor comfortable with floor sitting. She felt envious of Doreen, who sat cross-legged easily and spread her skirt around her like a showroom doll. Millie experimented with several positions and finally sat with her knees tucked to one side. Sharon plopped down as though floor sitting was part of her daily life. Beth couldn't be appeased until the couch had been pulled close enough to prop her back. Solace thought this was a fine idea and joined her on the other end.

Andy was wearing some type of silky black and red robe that looked something like a kimono. She sat with Iris on one side of her and Millie on the other. With her bright hair and painted nails, she looked like she could summon the dead. "I suppose I should read your tea leaves first," she said, once they had all gathered around. "It's what I'm best at."

"Oh, ugh," said Beth. "We have to drink leatherleaf tea?"

Millie took a sip, making only a light grimace. "I make sure the whole family gets a round of this every spring. It purges your stomach."

"I thought we had been purged enough," grumbled Solace, but recognized the wisdom. The best way to clean out all the winter germs was to drink leatherleaf tea in the spring. It wasn't really any more bitter than green tea, just sharper.

Sharon looked at her cup suspiciously. "Why do we have to have our tea leaves read?"

Andy passed her hand over her cup in a gesture that could easily invoke mysterious energies. The steam rose and wrapped around her fingers like vaporous playthings. "I have to know if the spirit harbors any resentments against any of you. It can be dangerous if it does."

Doreen stared at her cup, aghast at what it might reveal. Beth shrugged and said, "Bottoms up." Solace hesitated, curious, yet dreading the answer. Not that she was afraid of evil spirits, but Andy might read into her future and Solace questioned the wisdom of learning what lay ahead.

She drank her tea down quickly and showed Andy her empty cup. "What's the verdict?"

Andy wriggled inside her kimono, making herself more comfortable. She passed a hand over the cup and gazed deeply. "You're fine. Nobody wishes you harm."

Solace huffed and crossed her arms. "I would hope not. It wouldn't be to anyone's benefit." She screwed her eyes shut, then peaked at her cup again. "I don't suppose you could tell me about the lodge."

"It won't be a trading post anymore. You turn it into a diner and it's successful."

Solace speculated long and hard. "Are you sure about that or is it just you and me wanting?"

"It's in the leaves." If the leaves said so, it must be true.

Completely forgetting the main purpose of the tea leaf reading, the others immediately demanded to know their future.

Their seer told Sharon she would have another baby in two years, a little boy, but if they didn't remove the curse, he would be born weak. Sharon frowned and cleared her throat but said nothing.

Doreen could barely stand Andy's gaze into her tea leaves. She squeezed herself into a ball and squeaked, "If Ester was here, she would be so mad."

"Ester's not here and we will not say a word of this to Ester," scolded Sharon severely. "Cough it up, Andy. What do her tea leaves say?"

Doreen shuddered while Andy cleared her voice. "I don't know if you consider it the curse or not, but you're going to have a lot of children. Your next pregnancy, you will bear twins."

"Oh, twins!" Gasped Millie excitedly. "You are so lucky. I want twins. Do I have twins?"

"We should probably lift the curse pretty quickly," Doreen squeaked. "I wouldn't mind the twins, but I don't know how many other kids I'm willing to pump out."

Beth grew impatient. She scooted around on the floor, waving her cup, and demanding, "what does mine say?"

"Oh, Beth," said Andy with dismay. "You and Millie have the most to worry about. The darkness is trying to come through your doors."

"Oh, yeah?" Beth answered belligerently. "Let it try. I'll show it a thing or two."

A cloud passed under the sun, temporarily darkening the room, and the girls glanced at each other with quick alarm. Doreen slid along the floor, huddling close to Sharon.

"Alright," said Millie. "Now that we know it's there, how do we get rid of it?"

"We summon it," said Iris, as though it was a simple task. "Then we catch it in this basket."

She got up long enough to pick a small, tightly woven reed basket from the couch. The sides and snugly fitted lid had a stained violet zig-zag pattern, with a red rose sewn into the center of the lid. It was oval-shaped, around ten inches long and five inches high. She opened the basket and showed a pint bottle of Jim Beam. "He will come for this," she said.

The door suddenly burst open, and the assembled seance screamed in alarm.

Betty Lou stepped one foot into the room, then jumped one step back. "What in tarnation? Did I grow a beard?"

Millie pressed her clenched hands against her chest. "Dear Lord, I thought we had raised the dead."

With a sigh of shameless relief, Solace quickly beckoned Betty Lou into the room, ordering her to close the door behind her.

"What cha got goin'?" Betty Lou asked, plopping down next to Doreen, causing her to shrink closer to Sharon. "I seen your fancy car out at the post and figured you had to be somewhere and since Andy and Solace disappeared, figured it had to be here. Is this one of them Woman's Society Meetings? I told you before, I'm grooming up to be one of them society women."

Andy had started throwing some shiny, little plastic sticks around and mumbling to herself. "Something like that," she said, looking up from her deliberations. "We're trying to get rid of a curse cast by an evil spirit."

Betty Lou reached over for the bottle of Jim Beam. "Well, this ought to do," she said.

"No, no," said Iris, taking it away, and placing the bottle back in the basket. "We can't capture him that way. He'll just drink with us and deceive us. We have to make him crave his drink."

Andy threw her sticks a few more times and groaned with agony. Her face turned pale, almost bluish. She hardly seemed like Andy at all, but an old croon whose hand raked across the curtain between the past and the future. "He's with us," She whispered in a shivery voice. "He became angry when Millie and Beth defied him." She spread her arms out, her kimono dripping bloody red. "It's Ted Ewing's ghost. He's come back to haunt us."

"Well, that nasty, ill-mannered, bad-natured critter," said Betty Lou with complete indignation. "What is he doing, picking on innocent women? He wants to wrestle with me, there ain't a man alive what beat me and there ain't a ghost can do it either!"

The teacups rattled perceptibly in their saucers and the curtains fluttered at the windows.

"What a nasty draft!" said Millie.

Doreen whimpered.

Betty Lou took note. "That's the game you want to play, eh? I'm telling you, Iris, you're doing this wrong, just getting him riled up. All you smokers, crack out your cigarettes."

Sharon groaned. "Leave me out."

"Oh no," said Betty Lou. "We have to invite him. You don't have to smoke a whole one. Just a puff or two. You too, Millie. We gotta be sociable with him."

She got everybody to smoke a little, even if it half-killed them. Millie hacked up a substantial portion of her lungs and Sharon looked ready to pass out, but nobody else had a problem with smoking. Andy even waved her cigarette around as though it had been her idea all along.

The smoke swirled and wafted; tobacco with sage, steamed leatherleaf still adding its lingering sharp scent. Something palpable seemed to be waiting, something that was complete only when the group concentrated on its presence. Solace inhaled and released the plume slowly, as much for relaxation as for watching the smoke drift lazily and mingle with the thickening haze in the room.

The non-smokers were turning greenish. Betty Lou encouraged them to try a little harder while she reached into one of her numerous pouches and brought out a tobacco pouch of her own. She rolled herself a cigarette, then added the pouch to the basket. "I think Millie is going to get sick," Solace whispered.

"Now don't you go doing that," Betty Lou scolded. "It ain't like you have to smoke the whole pack, just enough to invite him to join us. He just ain't that much for tea and cookies."

"This is the most awful séance I've ever been to," said Millie tearfully.

Andrea looked up from her meditations that seemed centered primarily on manipulating the wisping smoke with her hands. "You've been to a séance before?"

"Well, no," admitted Millie. "But I'm sure most don't require that we smoke and drink."

"That's because most ain't for miners or trappers," Betty Lou told her boisterously. She reached for the bottle in the basket and Iris slapped her hands.

"Now don't be getting riled girl," Betty Lou argued. "I know what I'm doing. Ain't no spirit more restless than a miner's spirit, 'cause he's always lookin' for gold. Had to put a few of them to rest. Yes siree."

She took the bottle, despite Iris's objections, opened it, and poured a little at the bottom of the basket. "There you are my friend. Come and get it." She tilted the bottle, took a long swallow, sighed with satisfaction, and passed it to Iris, who took a small sip before handing it to Solace. Solace took a single nip and capped it, knowing how sensitive most of the Woman's Society were to day drinking.

Betty Lou looked critically at the half-finished bottle, then deciding it would do, tossed it in the basket.

Afterwards, everyone swore they saw it, although Solace still had a hard time believing it when she brought back the memory. The basket on the floor shifted, rocked a little back and forth, and elevated two inches before Iris slammed the lid down on it, swift as a frog catching a fly, and wrapped it in a cloth. "I have it!" She said triumphantly. "I have the spirit."

Doreen slowly wiggled out from under the protection of Sharon and leaned toward Andy. "Is it true? Is it captured?"

Andy lit the sage back up that had dwindled to a pitiful, thin trail of smoke, and fanned it vigorously, so it glowed. "He is caught. I'm purifying the air now."

"Eugene and I will be burying the basket tonight," said Iris as though announcing a funeral.

Agreeing enthusiastically, Betty Lou added, "Me and Solace will join you, won't we?"

It had never been Solace's habit to stand in the way of a person's religious beliefs, especially their views of the afterlife, since the most logical course through the unknown was to fill in the blanks where logic and reason left them. Her years in the wilderness had taught her a belief in a primal power that wasn't completely impersonal.

Sometimes, it was amazingly benevolent, such as with village children who became lost in the woods and could have been killed by a hundred different predators or by the forces of nature itself but were miraculously found unharmed several days later. Or the fire that turned away from Tok just as it lapped at the town's edges. You filled in the gaps because there was something bigger and more far-reaching than you were.

They went to bury the basket as though it contained the body of Ted Ewing himself, even though there was no proof he had died. He had disappeared before, only to turn up at the most surprising times and could do so again as though nothing had ever happened during the interval.

Solace supposed Ewing could have a vengeful enough spirit, even alive, to rain down a curse. They had taken something from him. They had taken the life he had grown accustomed to living, the rights he had assumed he had because he had always had them. He had sinned, but a man like Ted Ewing might not think like that.

It was time to pacify him, just in case. It was a precaution, like washing your hands. The band that stood around the burial site consisted of Eugene, Iris, Betty Lou, Ed, and Solace. Zeb wanted to come, but Solace made him take care of the post, promising him he could sit by the vanguard all evening once she returned. It wouldn't be quite the same, but it wouldn't bother Zeb too much since he didn't often get a chance to drink alone with a spirit buddy.

They stood in a solemn circle as the basket was lowered into the ground, still shrouded in its cloth, and gently covered with dirt. Eugene was the first to sit. He crossed his legs, Indian style, and patted the mound. "Probably shouldn't mark it."

Betty Lou squatted beside him. "Nope. He wouldn't cotton to it anyway. Just leave some tobacco now and then."

"Gotta have the tobacco."

"Yep."

"Well," said Eugene, getting on with the ceremony. "I want you to know, Spirit Ewing, you don't have a reason to quarrel with me and Iris. You broke her and threw her away, but I took what you threw as trash because to me, it was a treasure. And I am going to be so bold as to thank you for that. I'll have a wife.

I'll have a beautiful daughter. You gave them up. They are mine now, but I won't ever speak poorly of you if you promise never to harm them. Deal?"

He took a long drink and poured some alcohol on the burial site to seal his end of the bargain.

"I guess you never quarreled with me," said Ed, sitting down and scratching himself. "But we don't have enough pretty girls to be messing with them like that. Be nice to them, so they don't go live somewhere else. That's all I'm saying." He took a drink, then poured half his beer on the mound to show his sincerity.

"I forgave you and I still forgive you," said Iris simply. She took a short drink from Eugene's bottle and added the equivalent to the site.

Still squatting, Betty Lou hitched her thumbs in her suspenders and said loudly, "Here's how it's going to be. I'll make sure you never get thirsty and smoke with ya on a regular basis, but if you ever mess with those dear ladies again, you will never get the taste of another drop of liquor or enjoy good company. Am I clear?" She dropped to her fanny and waved a beer. "I thought so." She drank half and poured the traditional half on the ground.

It was Solace's turn. She folded her arms and scowled, trying to decide how hospitable she should be to a treacherous spirit.

"Now you've heard from everyone, Mr. Spirit Ewing. There's no need to keep up your curse, because it won't do you any good, only make people think more poorly of you. You've got a peaceful resting place. You'll be getting regular visitors paying their respects. You can't ask for better than that, all things considered. Zeb will be coming along shortly, but he'll say the same as me. Those are our girls. Leave them alone and we'll all get along fine." She took a quick nip from a bottle of schnapps she was fond of carrying around and allowed a few drops for the spirit. They had all made their peace. Only time would tell if Ewing had lifted his curse.

Although they had agreed not to talk about their séance with the men, Solace felt Zeb was an exception. If they were

525

capturing spirits and burying them in the Grants' backyard, Zeb ought to know.

She was disappointed in his reaction, which she felt should have been more respectful of their abilities to communicate on the astral plains. That was how Andy had explained it and she was pleased to have memorized the phrase. He was skeptical. "Andy just told you what you wanted to hear."

She sat down next to him on the steps of their porch and spread her skirt, so it draped between her knees. "And if Sharon has a baby within two years?"

He grumbled and put down the wooden sled dog he was whittling for Iris's baby. He was doing a good job other than the head was disproportionately large for the body. It was possible the toy would frighten little Stephanie. "Those society women are popping out babies like puppies. Of course, she'll have another baby within two years."

"And if Doreen has twins?"

"She won't now if the curse is broken, will she? That's what Andy will say. And if Doreen does have twins, she will say they weren't able to lift the curse in time to keep it from happening."

"What about the cups rattling and the basket lifting off the floor?"

He snorted. "We probably had a minor earthquake that you never would have noticed if not for your tea party."

"Did you feel an earthquake?"

"How can I with the dadblamed generator rumbling all the time? I'll be glad when the powerlines come through and a man can get enough quiet time to think."

"This is what I know," said Solace in the tone of voice that prevented argument. "There was something powerful strange in the room. We all felt it. It doesn't matter what other folk think it might be, hysterical women or imagination. Iris caught an unhappy spirit, and it is our duty to put it to rest."

Zeb was agreeable to laying Ewing's spirit to rest. As far as he was concerned, the spirit was captured because they believed it was captured, making it so. He was quite happy to have a spot in the woods where he could drink and commune with nature and not be criticized for it. The location soon became his private sanctuary. He kept the ground dampened, and the air livened with opinions he rarely expressed to his customers.

Considering Zeb's attitudes, Solace realized the wisdom in ruling out men from the spiritual gatherings. They simply did not understand, and their skepticism could have destroyed the benefits the women received by addressing these malicious blows against community members.

Iris changed almost overnight. She was like someone who had just been released from prison. She blinked at the dazzling sunlight. Her startled eyes swept over the horizon, realizing its expanse. She began coming to the lodge during Bea and Carol's lunch hour to eat with them and did her laundry when they did theirs. When the young folk gathered outside the lodge to talk, she joined them, linking her arm through Eugene's, the way young couples did when they were in groups. She allowed her family back into her life.

Andy brought the first four Hansen family members over, crowded into her old blue truck with the name, "Abe" painted across the tailgate. They were Iris's mother, the baby's namesake aunt and two sisters. That evening, Mark and Dave Hansen visited, along with several cousins. After that, there was rarely an hour of the day or night when there was not two or three Hansens visiting the Brewer cabin.

June rolled into July and there were no more outbreaks of diseases, no fires, floods, or other routine disasters, just warm, slumbering days under partly cloudy skies and frequent drizzles.

A normal summer. A summer of productivity. A summer of absorbing new faces into the community. A summer incomplete only because it waited breathlessly for the march of the powerlines and for their pastor and the Bolinders to return.

Thirty

The lodge was being renovated. Zeb put a big painted sign in the window facing the highway, saying, "lodge under repair", but it only discouraged the truck drivers, G.I.'s and newcomers. Dresden Hayes continued to drop in four days a week and stay until it occurred to him he should be conducting business elsewhere. The homesteaders continued to drop in after work to pick up their mail and stay for coffee or beer.

Without Ester to manage their tea parties, the woman's society wandered in twice a week, always on the same day and usually at the same hour. Solace swore to Zeb they could tear the lodge to the ground and people would still feel they had the right to pull up a chair and have a conversation on the premises.

Not that she really minded. It was comfortable seeing only the old, familiar faces. She needed time to adjust to the new world coming to them and could do it best among people she knew and trusted. There were many considerations. As the Phillips brothers had promised, their parents moved in, just days before the electricity was to be installed. Matt wired their house for them as soon as it was insulated.

It wasn't a standard log cabin. The Phillips brothers had used two-sided logs, scraped the interior smooth, stuck insulation between the cracks, then put sheetrock over the top of Matt's wiring. It was bright inside, even without lights.

Matt was working on the lodge wiring now. They had cleared the area around the back wall of the laundry room where they planned to put in the dryers and marked the space for each one with chalk. Their connections wouldn't be neatly tucked inside a wall.

They would be on thick, black rubber coated ropes, draped along the sides like Christmas garlands. Except the ceiling lights. They were paneling them with long, tubular florescent lighting. Andy said it would make the lodge look more like a diner.

They were also getting rid of the fur pelts. It didn't seem much point anymore. They didn't move among the local population. The only ones who truly had a use for them could trap their own furs. Some had been gathering dust for years.

Nor were there many trappers left. The rich population of ermine, mink and marten were thinning out as homesteaders moved in and changed the environment. The remaining trappers were taking their furs to Anchorage where they could get a solid price, instead of trade.

The Grants had found a furrier who would take the whole lot. Solace still felt she could get a better price if they could sell the furs individually, but Zeb said it just wasn't practical anymore. At Andy's advice, they would continue to trade with the villagers for their handcrafts, however. She said the display of beaded jewelry and moccasins added class.

Scraping two cheese sandwiches off the grill and landing them on plates alongside two bowls of tomato soup, Andy picked up her preparations and set them down on the table. "There you are, Miss Millie, Miss Doreen."

As the last two to place an order, Andy felt entitled to sit down and prop her chin on her elbows. "So, Miss Doreen, where have you been keeping your hubby the last couple of weeks? He hasn't been in much."

Doreen made a sour face and waved her hand. "I haven't been keeping him anywhere. He's got it in his head now that the electricity is coming through to set up his ham radio. Why won't a regular radio do, I asked him. He said it's not the same. He can listen to the whole world on a ham radio. Now, that is exactly what he does all day at work. Why does he want to take his work home with him? Does he think he can change the world just by listening in on it?"

"So he can feel miserable," said Millie positively. "Frank does the same thing. Not that he has a ham radio or talks about what he does, and I have no idea what the world is saying, but I receive plenty of details on the latest chess tournament."

"Don't mention chess!" cried Doreen with alarm.

Millie expressed equal alarm. "Oh no. Did they lose against the military again?"

Doreen nodded and Millie dunked her sandwich in her soup fitfully. "I don't know why they go up against the military brass. They never win."

Doreen shrugged. "As you said, so they can be miserable."

Andy lifted her head from her hands and waved at the air. "I'm sorry I brought it up. Solace, have you seen Mrs. Phillips yet?"

Solace slapped lazily at the table with her towel. "No, I haven't. It's only been a couple of days. I hear she is a seamstress."

"A seamstress?" objected Doreen. "We all know how to sew."

Millie could sew as well as anyone, but she liked fine clothes. She liked dressing suitably to match Frank's bowler hat and dark, wool suits. She fingered the ribbing of her crisp, store-bought dress and contemplated the worthiness of having her clothes fashioned by hand. "I would hate to discourage enterprise. Anyone can raise chickens, but not all of us do."

"Not all of us are successful at wintering brooding hens," said Andy. "You've got the bird talk in you. But what you're saying is true. We can all make a beef stew, but we still like to go out to eat sometimes."

"Well," said Solace. "I just don't know why entrepreneurs would invest in one-hundred-sixty acres of rocky hillside though."

Andy shrugged. "It's a homestead. All they've got to invest is their backbones. They didn't even spend much money on building the house."

This clarified matters quite well for Solace, who began to see she was also an entrepreneur within a business enterprise. If they sold their business, even a portion of it, as they had done with the furs, they couldn't spend the money. They had to reinvest it in a new business.

Although she had felt jealous at first, seeing her matronly position as the oldest woman in their little society threatened as the surrogate mother to the younger crowd, she now looked forward to another woman her age managing a business. That their wealth could be determined only by the success of the business was an even greater consolation. She and Zeb had been moderately successful even if their dwelling was humble.

"We got a letter from the pastor yesterday," announced Millie. "He's returning the second week of August."

"That's soon," squealed Doreen. "Is he going to hold a service in the new church as soon as he gets here?"

Millie rummaged through the purse on her lap and pulled out the letter. "He didn't say," she answered, spreading her hands. "He did ask if the Bolinder house is open if he returns before they do."

"Is it?" asked Solace.

Millie watched the passed around letter with sharp, careful eyes. "Of course it is!" she said once the missive had been safely returned to her purse. "They left the house open so I could feed and water their dogs and cats. I'm glad they took the little dog with them. It always nips at my ankles."

"It doesn't like Baily," said Andy.

Baily lifted his head from the floor and hopefully eyed a piece of uneaten sandwich. Millie gave it to him and scratched his neck. "Well, that's just too bad. Baily seems attached to me no matter what I do to keep him home."

Their meditations were interrupted by a clatter of hooves outside the lodge entrance. Through the large bay window facing the drive, the women saw a tan horse with black tail and mane and a yet unclear rider rapidly approaching, the mare's stiff-legged gait stirring dust clouds behind it. Believing a rampaging moose invasion had occurred, Baily yelped frantically until the door burst open and Anna strode in. The dog wriggled from nose to rump then, crawling to her apologetically when he realized his mistake. She spent three seconds reaching down to rub him all over, then stood.

"Guess what!" she said, planting herself in front of the table. "The powerlines are coming through."

Andy sneered at her little sister. "We know they're coming through. We've been knowing that for weeks."

"I mean they are coming through now!" Anna stamped a cowboy booted foot. "I saw the linemen working!"

She rushed around excitedly until Andy offered her a soda. She guzzled down half, wiped her face with the back of her hand and explained. "Earlier today, I heard these sounds coming from the Bolinder property. Really busy sounds, machinery and hammers, everything. I thought at first, the Bolinders had come back so I jumped on my filly and rode out to see them. It wasn't the Bolinders! It was the linemen, putting in power poles! Mrs. Lamar, they were almost to your house!"

"Oh gracious! Oh goodness!" They twittered and fluttered around like pigeons interrupted in their roost. Doreen and Millie grabbed up their purses and their children. Solace took off her apron and tossed it on the table. Andy threw hers on the seat of her truck and beeped at Solace. "Get in." The Pontiac was already leaving. Anna sat on her proud horse and led the charge but was soon left behind. She would not put her horse in a lather just to show off.

When they arrived at the Bolinder property, they saw that the electrical company had already set their poles halfway into Lamar land. They exited their vehicles as a single unit and tripped down the newly plowed powerline path to where four men had stabilized a pole. They stared in awe at the two heavily paneled company trucks and the giant spools of cable strung out on the ground waiting to be strung from pole to pole and filled with live energy.

"Ladies!" Two of the men broke from their task to come toward them. Solace recognized them as the young fellows who came in regularly for lunch. "Please ladies. This is a work zone. You're not even wearing hard hats."

"Is it dangerous?" Squeaked Doreen, clasping her hands at her chest.

"It is. It is," said one, gesturing they should take a step back. "We're putting in the transformers now. They handle the juice," he said at their blank faces.

"Are we getting our electricity tonight?" asked Millie eagerly.

"How long until it reaches Wolf Creek?" asked Solace at the same time.

"We should have your entire community wired up within three days. Then we turn the juice on. If you're on the contract and your house is wired, you'll be connected."

"We're all wired up," they sang out together, their voices tumbling over each other.

Even though they kept their distance, they continued watching for several minutes. It wasn't until the boys busted out of Doreen's car and came running toward them, Baily joyously taking the lead, that Doreen and Millie decided it was time to go home. Doreen left in her Pontiac, and Millie wandered down the now very shortened path to her house.

"I've got my contract," said Andy. "And they put a pole square in the middle of my yard, but mama wouldn't sign. She said she didn't need no damned electricity. Well, I wanted it and my trailer's getting it."

"Our whole place is gonna be lit up like a Christmas tree," gloated Solace. "We're running it into all the cabins. We got a big, new neon sign to put in the window instead of the little one. At night, you'll think we're a city."

"Just when the nights are returning." They walked slowly back to Andy's truck. "You don't think you'll miss something until you no longer have it."

"It's why we bought that big ole generator," said Solace. "Folk were craving a bit of comfort that was more than just a warm place with a good meal. This way they could listen to a bit of radio, wash clothes, read by a light that didn't need pumping every fifteen minutes. We needed it for the refrigerator and freezer, too. Can't run a good business without them. I'll be glad to see the generator put to rest now. It's noisy, breaks down and guzzles more fuel than it's worth."

It was an ordinary day. The sky was overcast but the air was warm. The fireweed had climbed over five feet high and was preparing to bloom. The insects were droning, the sparrows were darting. Yet a curtain seemed to have lifted from this ordinary day, the way the last flimsy drapes are drawn back on a theatrical performance. Everything appeared brighter, the forest sounds more melodious, the heady scents of summer, sweeter.

They returned to the lodge and sat in the truck staring at the landmark's final days of renovation, chiseling it into their memories. By next week, it would no longer be a trading post. It would a well-lighted diner with red-leather booths, a juke box, and a colorful neon sign beckoning in the customers.

They would still have their convenience store selling staples and delivering mail. They would rent their cabins to hunters and fishermen. They would continue with their laundry service, but the diner would be prominent.

Andy breathed out a long sigh, as though narrowly escaping a collision. "All we have to do now is wait for the pastor and the Bolinders to come back to know if the curse is broken."

Solace took a little nip from her bottle and handed it to Andy. "Seems like if the curse wasn't broken, it would have done something by now. It had plenty of opportunity."

Andy belched as she swallowed and handed it back with satisfaction. "It was a powerful summoning. Betty Lou knew what she was doing."

"Hmm." Another small nip to bind the blissful companionship of womanly dreams. "Betty Lou has a lot of experience with these things. She had to put her pappy to rest, you know."

"What happened to her pappy?" asked Andy, accepting a second round.

"He was a miner, like she says. He was always making accusations, always thinking someone was stealing his gold, when the truth be told, he drank it away. He made one accusation too many and he ended up in the ground."

"When was that?"

"Hmm. About twelve years ago."

"What happened to the other guy?"

"He went mad, he did. Began seeing things, hearing things that weren't there. He put up a terrific yowling one night and streaked through the woods like a holy terror was after him. That's when Betty Lou realized it was time to put her pappy at rest. It was the first time she'd tried such things on her own, but she had seen others do it, so she felt she was up to it.

Turns out, she was a complete natural. The day she summoned her pappy, the sky turned black. There was a moan that came up right from the bowels of the earth that shook the trees and toppled three cabins. She put a little nugget of gold in his basket along with a bottle of whiskey, and his spirit jumped right into it. He's been right cordial these days, never gives a bit of trouble. He's got his gold and his whiskey. It's all he ever wanted."

Feeling her blissful companionship as much as Solace, Andy propped one elbow up on the steering wheel and observed sadly, "Nobody has ever thanked Betty Lou for the things she has done."

"I don't think she ever expects it."

"Maybe so. We should give her a birthday party."

"She doesn't even know when she was born."

"So? We make up a date and give her a party. It's the most decent thing we could do."

"I reckon it is. She never had a mammy to do these things for her. She died when Betty Lou was no higher than a tadpole to your knee. Everyone should have a birthday party at least once in their life."

"Things are sure going to be different with electricity," said Andy, making no move to get out of the truck.

"They sure are," agreed Solace, passing the bottle again. They sat together and drank and talked about things to come.

Zeb was confident the curse had been lifted. "After all," he had said, "If it wasn't, one of the poles would have fallen on the linemen by now."

Since Zeb had been skeptical of the séance, Solace only said, "humph. It's still to be seen." Andy's words of caution remained in her ears. She wasn't going to let her guard down until the Bolinders returned. There was no point in tempting cantankerous spirits.

Solace could barely sleep that night as cascading thoughts crowded in her head, dancing like forest fairies. They spun and hurried, bumping into each other, exploding in vibrant colors. Three days before the electricity was turned on! Oh!

The things she hadn't thought about and now realized they needed with their shiny new lights in place, red-leather bench seats at the tables, things properly raised people like Ester would never overlook. She needed aluminum napkin holders, easy-wipe, plastic-coated tablecloths, a dozen small, matching flower vases, toothpick holders, and look-alike salt and pepper shakers.

The next morning, they went shopping with Solace's list penned down on an ordering pad. She went to three different stores to find everything, with Zeb and Ed tagging along meekly, wringing their hands, and grumbling as they shoved the packages wherever they found empty space in the back of the car.

Solace stood back to admire her collection of items. They shone like party favors in the cellophane wraps, all bundled up and overflowing the back seat and trunk.

It made Solace feel guilty instead of giddy. It was like a party, and she couldn't go back to the girls empty-handed. She looked at the waitress uniforms, with their aprons and cute little caps. They were expensive, and the girls probably wouldn't be that excited to have clearly designed clothing for work. Maybe just caps and aprons. She checked the prices and did some re-figuring. Maybe just aprons, she amended, but the figures didn't look appetizing there, either.

Her thoughts juggled around, trying to come up with a way to put the girls in perky, matching waitresses' aprons. Perhaps Mrs. Phillips would be interested in striking up an agreement for sewing five new aprons, three for the girls, the other two for herself and Andrea.

Now, there was an interesting business proposition. How much would it cost to have Mrs. Phillips sew uniforms for her girls? Her thoughts grew grander as her pocketbook, lost in a world of unending profits, became a magic purse where money reappeared as quickly as it had been depleted.

Happy that she had worked out the practical aspects of neighborly cooperation, Solace wandered into the five-and-dime store and bought rose water for Carol, hair barrettes for Iris, and a new lipstick for Bea. It was a subtle shade, not too dark, just something to bring her color out. They were good girls. They deserved an occasional reward.

Zeb was behaving mysteriously and smirked all the way home. When she asked what the devil had gotten into him, he answered, "Nothing much", yet smirked even more. The second day, Zeb told her, "Blame it. I've got to go to Anchorage and buy some more coils."

"What kind of coils?" she asked.

"Oh, just the kind you need when you get electricity. With all our washing machines, dryers, and refrigerators, we need a lot of coils." He hitched up his suspenders and put on his crumpled felt hat. "I'm going to have to take the truck. Gonna need to bring Ed along as well, to lift all them coils."

This seemed strange to Solace but having no idea as to the number and size of coils needed for electricity, chose not to argue, just to watch suspiciously as father and son trundled out to the road. She asked Andy about electrical coils. Andy wasn't sure either but agreed a lodge with so many electrical needs probably used a lot of coils.

Impatiently, the two women and three girls finished sprucing up the diner for its grand opening, setting all the shiny, new accessories into place, scrubbing down the countertop and sweeping out the corners one last time, and filling the vases with water and wildflowers. That was the fun part. The wildflowers were everywhere. They crowded the edges of the pathway. They sprouted colorful announcements from the hill across the road. They lined along the cabins and even enthusiastically decorated the insides of tires tossed outside the garage.

The girls liked their gifts. Each one of them wore a pair of the barrettes Solace had given Iris, had matching color lipstick on their mouths, and smelled of rose water. She felt they looked like fairies or wood sprites gathering flowers.

It was late when they had finished with their flower arrangements, and even later when Zeb came home. "Where's the truck?" she asked, puzzled.

"Well, that's just the thing," said Zeb, scratching his head and looking at the new diner with approval. "The Phillips were needing extra coils, seeing as how Mrs. Phillips will be running her sewing machine night and day, so we picked up some for them, too. It's going to take some time for them to unload their coils, so I left the truck at their place."

Zeb sure was behaving suspiciously but grilling him did no good. She turned to Ed, who had become remarkably adept over the years at covering for his pop, but never could keep from giggling when he lied. "It was a powerful amount of coils," he said, chortling and slapping his knee between words. "Why they filled the whole back of the pickup truck!"

They were lying their heads off. She knew it, but the peculiar part was, all her staff agreed there was a great need for coils at the diner. She went to bed that night feeling she was the only person in the community who did not know the extensive need for coils when you are using an enormous amount of electricity.

Because she spent a restless night bothered and battered by the gaps in her knowledge concerning modernization, Solace overslept. Even more astonishing, instead of taking advantage of the error in her normally precise internal clock and sleeping in with her, Zeb was already up.

In fact, she discovered as she checked into the other bedrooms, Ed and Bea were also up and had already left the house. Now she was genuinely suspicious. Her family did not normally appear for active duty early in the morning and never before Solace was up and about.

Muttering and banging things around, she dressed, then reconsidered her clothing. It was opening day at the diner. She should look nicer. She glanced inside her closet speculatively. She couldn't wear her Sunday dress. The blue flower print she wore to watch the Wolf Creek players perform their variety show in the valley would do. Why, it was the one she wore when she met Rep. Egan, so it must be lucky. And Zeb always said blue was a good color for her.

Zeb....Zeb....She remembered once more, Zeb was acting suspicious. She bet he bought a new pool table. The more she thought about it, the more positive she became. It explained everything. Of course, even the girls would cover for him if he bought a pool table. She applied her lipstick, threatening to turn it into a bright red gash, but controlling herself at the last minute. She looked at the red blot on her tissue. Oh, he would have hell to pay when she caught up with him. She didn't care if it meant making a scene at the opening.

The day was fair to middling, but a fair, neutral day didn't set with her very well. Her shoes crunched loudly against the gravel as she crossed the driveway, and she announced her entrance by pushing the door against the wall with a thud. The cabin walls were heavier than the door, which caused the door panel to cry out in pain and swing a few inches forward.

For the rest of the day, Solace thanked heaven for inspiring her to use the front door and directly confront the offensive item instead of going through the kitchen door she normally used, and button-holing Zeb and Ed with her vindications.

As soon as she opened the entrance door, she saw it in the most prominent corner of the diner. It was red and silver, matching the leather upholstery and aluminum napkin holders, and though it slept, its white, labeled face looked inviting.

"A jukebox!" She whispered in awe. "You bought a jukebox!"

"Ain't many songs in it yet," said Zeb. "But we figured we could ask people to write down the songs they like, and we'll fill it up with more records."

Ed was also feeling knowledgeable. "It's good business. You've gotta drop a dime each time you want to hear a song. Three songs for a quarter, so you want to fill it up with the songs everyone likes. That's what the sales guy told us."

The girls assured her it was very good for business, but it wasn't an aspect Solace had considered. All she knew wasshe had always wanted a jukebox and now she had one.

At exactly three in the afternoon, just as the linemen promised, the electricity came on. The neon sign flashed brightly the "open" announcement in the window. The dual refrigerators, freezer, and soda machine, suspended from duty while they switched from the generator to a powerline, made a familiar, collective hum. The florescent lights hesitated, blinked, then glowed warmly. The entire lodge looked brighter, more festive. Red leather and chrome gleamed everywhere. "It looks," thought Solace to herself, "like a diner."

It took Solace no more than half an hour to discover what it was like to run a diner with a juke box and an open floor space instead of a lodge piled high with merchandise and dependent on the occasional guitar-picking singer.

Her youthful employees shoved each other as they poured over the song titles on the juke box and searched inside their pockets for dimes and quarters. They danced. At least, the kids called it dancing although it wasn't like anything she had ever seen. Times change and the music changes with it, just like fashions and inventions.

Since the electricity had come on spontaneously to all the hooked-up community at once, there wasn't a giant rush to her grand opening. Each home needed to first savor this amenity they had lacked for so long. It felt like a miracle! The Phillips were her first customers. To elaborate, the entire family arrived, minus Hank Phillips who was still sailing the Orient.

Mr. Phillips looked like an older version of Gordon. He had the same bulky shoulders, square jaw, and narrowed, quick eyes, crowned by a head of thick, unruly hair. Brad Phillips had gained his fair looks from his mother. Mrs. Phillips was a handsome woman, with her hair swept dramatically into a smooth roll at the back of her head, her eyebrows as neatly arched as wing tips, her eyes round and clear.

She was stylish and more up-to-date in her stylishness than Millie. She wore the muted colors of maturity, a light-tan skirt and jacket with brown trim. Gordon escorted the two older Phillips to a booth, but Brad had lost interest in family protocol as soon as he stepped through the door. He sauntered straight to the juke box and hung over it as though it was his own.

"How do I look?" asked Solace quickly, turning to Andy.

Andy glanced at her with surprise. "Near as I can tell, you look just fine. Are you expecting the President of the United States or something?"

"It occurs to me, I haven't been keeping myself up. I might look a little dowdy." She found the mirror used to view the back of the room and studied herself critically. "I look a bit dowdy," she said firmly.

Carol had already left the new amusement to pick up her pad and wait on the Phillips' family, while Bea deployed specialty skills on the youngest Phillips' brother, still lurking over the jukebox and jiggling his change.

"I'd try the tender cuts," suggested Carol. "It's not really steak. That's why we call them tender cuts. It's caribou, but it's really good."

Mrs. Phillips patted at her hair and tucked a straight end into her twist. Even her earrings matched her suit, stubby, gold-colored shell shapes with embedded tiger eye. "Gordon tells me," She said, beaming at her middle son, "That Solace Grant makes the best potato salad. Do your tender cuts come with potato salad?"

"Potato salad or mashed potatoes and gravy," said Solace, pulling up a folding chair. "I've been wondering when best to make your acquaintance."

"Rosemary." The lady turned in her seat and held out a hand. When Solace took it, she was surprised at the strong shake and looked down long enough to notice they were not pampered hands. They were calloused and knotted at the knuckles. "You've had a business to run, and I've had unpacking to do. Today seemed like a good day for visiting. It's your grand reopening and I'm tired of cooking. I do not recommend a house full of boys for anyone who doesn't really like to stay in the kitchen."

Solace had meant to ask her about so many things, like how she could let a seventeen-year-old boy run wild in Alaska. How terrible it must be to have someone sailing on boats like a pirate, going God knows where, and doing who knows what, yet Rosemary Phillips didn't seem to be concerned with any of it. For years they had run a lumber mill, she explained. Made good money off it, but Stewart didn't want to work anymore. He was ready for retirement and the boys had no interest in the mill, so they sold it.

"It's all up to the boys now to decide what to do with their lives. I can't be making their decisions for them now that they're grown. Brad now, he's a bit wild and doesn't have a good business head, but he'll go along with his brothers. They've got ideas. Maybe they will succeed. Maybe they won't, but I'm not the one to tell them they can't try."

Rosemary Phillips had answered all Solace's questions before she had time to ask them, leaving her to marvel at her new neighbor's self-assurance. It was possible Mrs. Phillips was a fountain of wisdom. She certainly fit the role. The lines drawing back from her eyes and crinkling her brow were studious ones. Her tastefully reddened lips rolled over her words as though each was so precious it needed savoring.

The lodge was beginning to fill. Bea had cornered two young military men and was wheedling them into dropping change into the jukebox. Now that the Phillips family no longer required her attendance, Carol was encouraging the coin dropping by dancing with another young man, if you could call it dancing. They flew around the room furiously, swirling and ducking through each other's arms. Only Iris was waiting tables. Solace excused herself to put things back in order.

In the short time it had taken to put the girls back to work, Millie and Frank had come in and taken the table next to the Phillips's booth. Solace hurried back, not wishing to miss a word of conversation and arrived in the moment Millie asked, "When are you opening your shop?"

"Well," said Mrs. Phillips, removing her jacket and tucking a napkin under her chin before she began eating. "I have some fabrics coming in and hadn't thought about opening until they arrive. The fall colors, you know. We will be wanting them by the end of summer."

"Of course we will," said Millie as though she knew these things. "And how perfect could that be with our preacher returning in August? That is why I'm asking. I want a new dress for our first Sunday at the new church. A fall color will do." She sighed and turned her head with a drop of melancholy. "Our winters come so early."

"They certainly do," said Solace eagerly but her voice trailed as she realized she really could not sit and visit any longer. A disturbance in the kitchen told her somebody had upset Andy. She excused herself once more.

Andy had a back-up of orders. Carol was frantically trying to help but had burned herself with the spatula. Pushing the girl aside, Solace took over the stove and Andy took over filling plates.

It was a busy night, the busiest they had had all summer. The stove sizzled, the coffee cups piled, the swinging doors swung in a perpetual swing. The voices pitched feverishly as the newly electrified group shouted and greeted each other and speculated on what they would buy to plug into the wonderful commodity. They were all buying radios and refrigerators. The women wanted electric sewing machines. The men wanted electric record players.

It was the day they had all been waiting for, yet still Solace felt a small nudge of dissatisfaction.

As they prepared for bed that night, Zeb scratched himself inside his long john underwear and smiled at the evening's revenue. Solace wrung her hands and looked down.

"What are you looking so down at the mouth for?" Zeb asked gruffly. "I thought you would be happy."

"I am happy," she said quickly. "I am. The diner looks perfect. It's just..." She looked out the window, then back at Zeb. "I need a new dress for going to church."

Thirty-One

Every time Rosemary Phillips visited the diner, Solace paid a return visit to the Phillips residence. It was more than the courtesy of next-door-neighbors, although Solace couldn't even remember the last time she had a neighbor the same age as herself and within easy walking distance – a neighbor whose house she could see from her back yard. It made her understand and appreciate the luxurious, sisterly relationship Andy and Millie had for each other, although a sisterly relationship wasn't what she sought.

Rosemary was a businesswoman like herself. She had successfully helped the growth and sales of one business venture and was now attempting another. This mindset alone created a special bond between them. Furthermore, Rosemary had raised three children, just like Solace.

They all had their quirks but the remarkable thing about Rosemary's children was their cooperative spirit between each other. Even Brad had helped pound in the pipe that delivered clean water to all who needed it, and Brad had continued to show teamwork in building the Phillips family house and Rosemary's modest shop. They were a collective that never once thought of holding each other back. Solace felt maybe there was something she could learn from them. She had never really given up on wayward Percy and hoped someday to bring him back to the family fold.

As Rosemary's new friend, Solace was the first to learn about the new fabrics and patterns when they came in. Rosemary had it all, from lace and featherweight chiffons to deep velvets.

She had fluffy eyelet and thick brocade trim, rickrack, tassels, and fringe. Solace fingered through everything and poured over the patterns, unable to imagine how to choose the right pattern with the right fabric for a modern, church woman appearance.

"Plaids are fashionable this year," suggested Rosemary, showing Solace a wool blend.

"Oh, blues and greens," said Solace in dismay. "Millie says blues and green clash."

"Nonsense." Solace whisked away the bolt of cloth clinging dutifully to its flat, oblong box, and brought out a pale linen fabric with large, intersecting squares in light greens and blues. "These blues and greens complement each other. It's all in color variation."

The variation was certainly nice. "What if Millie chooses plaid?"

"Millie won't choose plaid," said Rosemary confidently. "She's too large a woman to look good in plaid. I suspect she will go with calico."

The calicos looked youthful, not at all for the mature businesswoman she had in mind. Would a polka-dot dress work? They looked so carefree and lovely. Maybe a suit similar to Rosemary's? That wouldn't do at all. She liked the dress with the wing-capped sleeves. It would look nice in polka-dots, and it looked professional with its belted waist and full skirt.

"Well," she said, finally determining her choices. "Reverend Brighton returned from up north yesterday. He moved right into the Bolinder house."

"Without the Bolinders being there?" asked Rosemary, raising her brows.

"It was all arranged," explained Solace. "He has a key. Don't you know that as soon as Millie found out – she has been taking care of the animals, you know – and told Andy about it, Andy told Jimmy and Jimmy told Tammy. She came right down from Anchorage to talk with the Reverend on this very morning!"

"Hmm," said Rosemary, putting the rolls of cloth and trim back on their shelves. "Without even giving him a day of rest? What is her hurry?"

"She wants to be the first married in the new church and she doesn't want Iris and Eugene beating her to it."

"What difference does it make?"

Solace nodded her head fervently. "That's what I want to know, but Tammy seems to think it makes a difference. I don't think Eugene and Iris really care. They just want to get married."

Rosemary placed the pattern Solace had picked out, along with the fabric and trim, on her sewing table, and looked up, puzzled. "Why don't they just go to a justice of the peace then?"

Solace gave an insider's chuckle in response, happy to share her superior knowledge of the community's inhabitants. "They both want the preacher to marry them. But here is the difference between Iris and Tammy. Iris doesn't want to get married until the Bolinders are back."

"I see," said Rosemary, staring at her table, and in that orderly collection of measuring tapes, measurement guides, straight pins, scissors, tightly rolled sewing thread, she did seem to see what Solace saw.

Solace wasn't the only one who thought Tammy was being selfish. As the word spread around, most of the community thought her hasty plans to hold the first church wedding were inappropriate considering it would be another two weeks before they held their first service in a real church. Even Andy felt indignant, although not because of the church.

"Sure he told them he wouldn't be able to conduct their wedding until the first of September, but Solace..." Andy put down the butcher knife and waved a bloody hand. "What if the Bolinders aren't back by then? How could she possibly hold a wedding without the Bolinders?"

"I ask myself that night and day," said Solace. "When all is said and done, it's the Bolinders' church. Why, we barely got the paint job done by the time the pastor returned. There's not much this community would be without Charlie, even if he is Charlie No Horses."

"Well, Iris is one of us. She understands these things." Andy's butcher knife targeted an awkwardly cut chunk of meat and trimmed it into slices. "Put that in your stroganoff. It's too tender for stew meat. Tammy's going to take time. She's attracted to glamor."

"I don't suppose it will take more than a year or two for Tammy to realize there is nothing truly glamorous about Wolf Creek."

"Don't be too sure and it's not just about Jimmy, even if he has been getting star billing at the Pioneer Lounge," she said, cramming the information in quickly. "Oh no. We've got acting troops and now we have a lady journalist. It's always better to be a big frog in a little pond than a little frog in a big one. We have a few big frogs in a little pond," she added with satisfaction.

"But Charlie...."

"Charlie isn't a frog. He's a builder. That isn't glamorous."

Despite the criticisms of the community, the invitations for the wedding came out one week after Reverend Brighton's return. Solace huffed over a bowl of eggs, beating them into oblivion, while Andy threatened the bubbling deep fat fryer with a mound of potatoes.

"She sent them out. She did," raged Andy while the fryer popped angrily over the potatoes. She gave it a good shake, upsetting the boiling fat further. "She couldn't wait for the Bolinders to come back. Oh no! She couldn't wait for that!"

Solace looked down at her eggs. They seemed to have been beaten into submission. She poured them out over the griddle. "It certainly put a strain on Mrs. Phillips! The only two church dresses she could make were mine and Millie's because now she'll be making Tammy's wedding dress."

With her potatoes crackling under fat, Andy paused long enough to light a cigarette. "They aren't opening the church if the Bolinders aren't there, are they?"

"It's a week and a half yet. The Bolinders could still make it in time."

"And if they don't."

Solace folded her eggs carefully over making sure they were appropriately scrambled without turning into tiny clumps. "The pastor's got a schedule, Andy. If he doesn't do it on schedule, he's gotta wait until next month."

"Oh fiddle," said Andy, giving the fryer another hard shake. "It's all the Bolinders' fault. They said six weeks. It's been nearly eight weeks."

"Things happen on the Alcan. They could have broken down somewhere."

"Why didn't they just fly?" mumbled Andy. "They could have just flown. They had to take that stupid station wagon."

Andy was in an ill mood all morning, as was everyone else. The Bolinders' absence was growing too lengthy. Ed wanted to set out in the car to look for them on the highway, but even Zeb told him it was a ridiculous idea. "If something happened to Charlie Bolinder, his office would know, and his office would tell Frank. There's no point looking for him, Ed, if we don't know where he's at."

Still, Zeb looked worried and rubbed his scratchy chin. Betty Lou sighed and protested every two hours that it wasn't right to go partying in their new church when the Bolinders weren't there, then accepted another beer to keep her quiet. The lunch hour came with a dispirited shuffle falling away to an early afternoon slumber. Solace and Andy sat together at a table facing the unpaved road and looked out at the crumbling late summer.

"It's time to start picking the garden patch clean," murmured Andy.

Solace nodded. "And the berries. The berries are ripe." She twisted a napkin in her hand, then said, "why Andy. Look at that. Anna's riding over. I wonder what your mama wants this time."

There was something different about the way Anna rode. Usually, she didn't ride at a fast clip, and always took her time to hitch her horse, pat it down, and give it a handful of oats. This time, she flung herself off, barely took time to tie the reins, and marched with her long-legged stride toward the diner.

"Is your mama ill or what?" asked Solace with alarm.

"Anna doesn't look worried. She looks..." Before Andy could finish, the girl burst through the door, her eyes shining like falling water.

"They're back!" Anna cried triumphantly. "The Bolinders are back. I saw them when I was out riding. They just drove up in their station wagon about twenty minutes ago, and they've got something really big and heavy wrapped up on top."

The news of the Bolinders' return hit Anna's listeners like an electrical jolt. It was like the day the lights came on. The listless lodge sparked with energy.

Her chair scraped across the floor as Andy bounced up and flung her hands in the air. Zeb slapped his knee while Betty Lou said, "well, I'll be damned."

What customers there were, suddenly had things to do. They slammed on their hats, paid their bills, and hustled outside, clamoring and gesturing.

"I reckon I'll mosey down that way," said Betty Lou, scratching at her ribs and looking hopefully at Andy.

Andy looked calculatingly at Solace. "We're not going to get any more customers today except the military men. It wouldn't hurt to turn things over to Zeb a few hours. We've got the girls in back."

"I reckon we can close early," mumbled Solace, not completely trusting the cash register with anyone but herself.

"I can watch the blamed restaurant," said Zeb fitfully. "You've got more girls behind the counter than we know what to do with half the time. "Go find out what took the Bolinders so long."

Perceiving a ready-made ride, Betty Lou linked arms with Solace and Andy, remarking on the splendid weather for visiting and noting that Anna hadn't even waited, but had leapt back on her horse, probably to visit her returned neighbors.

They had barely reached Andy's truck before Ed caught up with them. "I want to go. I want to see what Charlie has on the top of his car." He swung into the bed of ole Abe with Betty Lou, who had already made herself at home.

"You can sit up front with us," offered Andy.

"Nope," said Ed, folding his arms and making himself comfortable.

Slamming the truck into gear, Andy observed, "He's as bad as the villagers. None of them ever want to ride up front."

Solace settled her sweater around the shoulders. "It ain't that so much. He doesn't want to sit up front with women unless he's driving. He thinks it's beneath his dignity."

"I didn't know Ed can drive," muttered Andy.

Solace nudged her. "Not very well."

The Bolinders had not been back much more than an hour, yet already a fair-sized crowd was gathered on their property.

It occurred to a few to pick up a box or piece of luggage from the depleting but still over-loaded station wagon, and carry it to the Bolinders' front door, but most were absorbed in idling and asking questions. The one unanswered question was, what was on top of the car?

Whatever it was, it was monstrous. It was as tall as the car, but squatter in appearance. It perched on a sled made from two long 2x4s and thick plywood and was wrapped round and round with rope.

It was obviously turning into a party. Millie had brought a gallon jar of iced tea from her place. The pastor had whipped up a gallon of Kool Aid for the kids. Several of the men had brought their own choice of beverages.

The most neighborly thing to do was locate Ester to make sure she wasn't burdening herself with hospitality chores. They should not have worried. Ester had rounded up Ed and Betty Lou as soon as they hopped out of the truck, charging them with the task of carrying a heavy leather and brass-bound trunk to her house.

"Did you buy out an entire town?" asked Solace, admiring the chaotic assortment of bags and boxes spilled out over the lawn.

"It's Charlie! It's Charlie!" Ester exploded. "Men always criticize women for their shopping habits, but we are not impulsive. We don't just walk in and buy the first thing we see. A barbeque grill! He bought a barbecue grill! I asked, why do we need a grill? We can make our own. He said, this is a portable grill! A man was selling them from the back of his car. Of course, Charlie had to have one!"

Solace scratched her head, trying to make sense. "Why doesn't he just bring along the oven rack when you go camping, and put it over the rocks? That's portable enough."

"Don't you think I told him that? Oh, no! He wouldn't listen. It's a new invention that hasn't been sold in stores yet."

Andy strolled impatiently around the car and the circle of men admiring the bulk on top. "Well, where is it? Let me see it!" she demanded.

Ester peered into the back of the car. There wasn't much left. Most of the cargo had been hauled out to the lawn, revealing only a few tools, a pull strap, and a strange looking item against the wheel well of the back end. "There it is!" she said triumphantly, beckoning for her two lackeys. From the way Ed snapped to attention, she suspected he was being bribed, either by Charlie or Frank, although certainly not Ester.

They had barely begun to pull out the legs of the unwieldly contraption when Charlie bounded over to halt them. "My grill! Guys, come over and have a look at this. You've never seen anything like it."

He finished pulling out the strange-looking device himself. The fold-out legs supported a bulbous container with an air vent at the top. When he opened the lid, they could see a form-fitted grate covering the bottom half. The men marveled at the engineering, which was really just a miniature version of their oil barrel grills, while Ester tapped her foot and looked exasperated.

"Do you see?" she said bitterly to Millie, who had wandered over to give them iced tea, but now stared at the contraption in amazement. "They'll buy anything that's new, whether they need it or not."

"Well," sputtered Millie. "It looks nice, and you won't need a truck to haul it."

"I don't want to lug that thing around every time we go camping," quarreled Ester. "It's unsightly. What's wrong with a campfire, I'd like to know? And it's not even sold in stores! That's how much faith the stores have in it."

"Charlie likes supporting entrepreneurs," said Solace, relishing her command over her new word. "Look at the way men gawk at it. I reckon it will be something that catches on."

"Did you get anything for yourself?" Pressed Andy.

"For myself?" asked Ester bitterly. "What could I get for myself? He buys new battery cables, one of them electric record players and a garden hose. Why? I ask him. You can order them in Anchorage. 'Because they are cheaper here,' he tells me. So, what do I buy for myself that can be fitted into his junk pile? I'll tell you what I bought, a bottle of Este Lauder and a pair of elbow-length gloves for when we go to the 4th Avenue theater."

"But Este Lauder," fluttered Millie. "It's expensive."

"Of course it's expensive! I spent three years smelling like horse manure. I deserve something for my suffering."

"Did you buy nylon stockings?"

"A couple of pair. For going to church only. They're delicate."

"I was going to buy some from the department store," said Andy sadly. "But the luxury tax is shocking! You should have brought us back nail polish. It's twice the price here as it is in the states."

Ester frowned then stamped her foot, looking offended in the manner only Ester could look, with her nose high in the air, her tea glass suspended at shoulder height. "You just ruin everything, Andy. Now I will have to tell you. I did. There was a lady selling nail polish in a kit. Twenty bottles for five dollars! You won't find prices like that in the stores. I'm giving everyone a bottle, then I'm keeping the rest."

"I want two," protested Millie instantly. "I'm nearly out."

"Me too," said Andy. "Cooking is hard on the nails."

"But the others..." began Ester.

"The others aren't here," pointed out Solace. "I don't wear polish and neither does Betty Lou. You can give them our bottles."

"I'll show you right after the unveiling. But Charlie isn't going to unveil until everything is brought inside."

Solace looked skeptically at the help that was still more interested in Charlie's new-fangled grill than in clearing the lawn of baggage. "What's the unveiling?"

"Well," she said. "I'm not going to let you spoil all the surprises. You just have to wait."

One of the reasons men need women is they would always get sidetracked from their duties without feminine reminders. "Just give me a moment," said Solace, excusing herself. Singling out Ed, she invited him in a loud voice to get the lead out, with a ferocious gaze that included anyone brave enough to look into her eyes. It was a reasonable suggestion that reminded their male company there was still work for them to do.

The mystery package was good motivation. It remained shrouded even as a few tightly bundled items were untied and removed from around it to be added to the luggage going inside the house. Ed scrambled, crowding two or three pieces under his arms at a time. Betty Lou, however, had gotten sidetracked watching a toddler tug at a suitcase nearly as tall as himself.

"Gracious, is that Denny? Come here, you rascal. You shot up like a beanpole this summer. Did you catch polio?"

"What is the matter with you?" gasped Solace with alarm. "It wasn't polio that went through here. It was chicken pox. Are you willing to give Ester a heart attack?"

"Who has polio?" asked Ester, who had left the house to witness the progress of the work detail.

Solace glared at Betty Lou. "Nobody has polio. The kids all caught chicken pox this summer."

"Oh," shrugged Ester. "Denny caught it in Seattle. It was good he got it right away, so we could enjoy the rest of our vacation."

Solace sighed with relief. It was as Andy had said. Ester was unchanged. Charlie Bolinder was still Charlie Bolinder, a living, animated village. The chaos of the last few months settled into place as quietly as the packed boxes and cases were swept away and piled into the Bolinder living room. Order had returned to the Universe.

The station wagon emptied out, the yard swept clear, nearly the entire community gathered at attention, Charlie finally untied the ropes securing the canvas tarps. He peeled them back like the unveiling of a new monument to glory. It was a monument to glory. It was a bell - a giant, cast iron bell, designed to ring its cries of triumph over hill and valley. It squatted, thick and majestic on its plywood throne, its sound silenced by the wadding inside its lip.

There was a moment of speechless awe.

There wasn't another bell around this large for twenty miles in either direction, for good reason. Their size and weight made them formidable, expensive transport items. Now, Chugiak stood out with a distinction few could boast. It had a genuine, four-foot -tall iron bell.

"How the devil did you get it up the Alcan?" asked Frank, who showed more interest in the strategic framework Charlie had used to box his bell into place on top of the station wagon, than in the bell itself. "It must weigh seven to eight hundred pounds."

Karla Fetrow

Charlie patted his handiwork cheerfully. "Heavier bells, sweeter tones. It's all in weight distribution, Frank. Oh, I had a few bad spots climbing those sharp upgrades and snaky curves. Riding top-heavy isn't as easy as it looks, but Penelope here has a lot of heart." He gave Frank a wink. "You should give your automobiles names, Frank. They will serve you better that way and last longer."

Frank hmphed at this clear insult to his stand against superstition. "Gonna start trading mine in every five years for a new car. I don't have the time or know-how for keeping one up."

That was the fancy thinking of people like Millie and Frank. It wasn't their fault. It was city-thinking, but that thinking influenced the community more than they realized. Now there were entrepreneurs talking about putting in shops for jewelry, custom-made clothing, and Japanese things. It was a good thing when the electricity came, the diner had put in a jukebox. It was good to keep up with the times, even when the times were baffling.

Mechanics, Solace reckoned, never would lose out on work, even with people like Frank buying cars every five years, for the simple fact that there weren't many men like Frank. Frank didn't understand that a car was an artificial life, with lungs, a heart, and a tiny brain wrapped up in the starter box. That's why he didn't have a feel for vehicles the way mechanics' men did. For most drivers, there was a communion, an acknowledgement with this artificial life, just not with Frank.

It hardly even seemed right to remove the bell from its perch, cribbed in the way it was. It was a testimony to the unwavering will of Charlie Bolinder. Four men shouldering the four posts of the crib, were still shouldering two hundred pounds apiece. You had to respect that and the loyal automobile that had brought it here on two thousand miles of unpaved road with potholes, washouts, and buckling frost heaves. Two thousand miles climbing altitudes five hundred feet at a time until you were in blinding, maddening heights that squeezed your heart apart in their explosive fury.

It took six men to lift the bell's platform enough to slide it along the top of the car without scraping it and set the bell gently on the cement blocks hastily carried over and arranged to hold it.

Solace crowded as close as the others to touch it. It felt smooth and rough at the same time.

It was smooth with the almost chrome-like polish that had been given it, rough with the density of iron. It looked like the liberty bell to her, except it had no crack, nothing to damage the song that came from its throat.

Although she stayed no more than an hour after the bell's unveiling to listen to the Bolinders' stateside experiences, the lodge was already buzzing about the bell when she returned home. It was no longer just about the first service to be held in their new church. Tammy's wedding plans were elevated to a matter of importance comparable to Christmas. The glorious events would be heralded in by a bell! The new decade that had begun so slowly, was shining bright now with new energy, new people, and a sparkling, beautiful bell.

The next morning, instead of sweeping the lodge or tinkering with a truck that had been sitting in the yard so long grass was pushing up around its wheelbase, Ed brushed off his work cap, took up his denim jacket and prepared to walk to the Bolinders' homestead.

"Why do you think you can go bothering them the day after they got back?" scolded Solace. "They've got enough to do without you hanging around all day asking questions."

"Ho ho!" chortled Ed. "I've got man work to do. Yes siree. That bell's gotta be suspended and we gotta put a roof over the top to keep the rain out. Charlie Bolinder said so. He's got me and Jimmy helping him out."

Off he sauntered to do his man work that would pay him five dollars a day if he didn't get any lofty sentiments about volunteering.

Fearing even her simple-minded son was developing independence, Solace fretted while she punched down the dough for pastries, sure that somehow, Charlie Bolinder was at fault. Why, he even took it upon himself to teach Ed how to read a mechanic's manual last winter. Now the boy was stuffed full of his own importance. It was important, she supposed, that he could now name the parts he pulled off the automobile engines.

It didn't seem like much of anyone was working that day. Carol came in an hour late and Andy didn't come in at all. "Where's your sister?" grumbled Solace.

"It's her day off," Carol reminded her. "She says she's coming around later to pick you up for a visit with Ester."

"I don't have time to visit Ester," she snapped, although it wasn't true. It was a slow day. Those who weren't putting things away for the winter were visiting the Bolinders to gawk at the bell. By two in the afternoon, the place was nearly dead. Solace began tidying up the diner restlessly, refilling the flower vases and cleaning out corners that had not yet had a chance to gather dust. By the time Andy appeared, Solace had forgotten her glum mood of the morning and wanted nothing more than to go visiting. After all, Ester did promise them nail polish. If Millie or Andy wanted two bottles, they could take Betty Lou's. She wanted to give hers to Bea.

Millie was already at the Bolinder home when the two arrived. Ester waved them inside peevishly and sulked, "I've been waiting all day for you to come."

"Unlike some people, I have a schedule to keep," said Solace, letting Ester know by the tone of her voice that she was still hurt over their long vacation.

Ester was trying to show Ben she was happy to see him, but he squirmed out of her hug and ran in the direction of his playmates. She straightened. "Well, the car broke down twice if you must know. Charlie notified work and they gave him an extra two weeks. Frank could have opened his mouth and put everyone at ease."

"Hear now," objected Millie. "Frank isn't the one who gave Charlie the extra two weeks. You're just mad because he isn't getting paid for those weeks."

Andy was already helping herself to a cup of tea. Pouring some of the beverage in another cup for Solace, she sat down and crossed her long legs, crossing them once more at the ankles. "Did everybody wake up on the wrong side of the bed? You invited us, Ester. Why are you attacking us?"

Finding a box of cookies that had survived the road trip, Ester shook them onto a plate and set them on the table. "I'm not attacking. I told Charlie we were overloaded but he didn't listen.

We had to spend six days in Whitehorse waiting on repairs! Then there were two in Edmonton and another three out in the middle of nowhere when we had a flat tire and had run out of spares. We waited overnight for someone to come along and haul us to the next service station, thirty miles away. In the long run, it would have been cheaper to just order that damned barbeque grill."

"I'm sure the barbeque grill isn't what weighed you down," said Millie.

"You're missing my point! You're missing it. We could have left half that stuff behind and carried just the bell and some changes of clothing, but Charlie wouldn't have it. He had to find a way to cram everything into the car. It's a station wagon, he said. We don't even need the back seat. He never thought about the weight, though, until we were half-way up the mountains. It will be a miracle if the car makes it through another year."

The monumental setback their trip had cost them welled up in Ester's eyes and she dabbed at them before regaining her composure. "We can't complain. Not really. We were visiting Charlie's cousin in Iowa and found out their church was selling their bell because they were buying a new one. They sold it to us for seventy-five dollars, which is a very good price for such a big bell. It has a nice ring, too. Nothing wrong with it at all."

Millie gasped in amazement. "Why did they sell it?"

"They are buying a bigger bell. It's a big church."

Now that she had vented her woes, Ester brought out the box of fabulously colored nail polish. "I thought I should let you girls choose first," she said. She ran a hand over the tight twist of hair at the back of her head, and mumbled, "since you're my best friends."

"Hey now," said Andy. "Don't get all weepy on us. Whatever the favor is you want us to do, we'll probably do it."

Ester removed her hand from her hair and twisted it with the other in front of her. "It's not a big favor. It's really not. It's something we can do while drinking tea and visiting."

"I hope you didn't pick up a bushel of snap beans," said Millie. "Our snap beans went wild this year. I don't care if I never see another one in my life."

"No, it isn't snap beans or any other food." Ester stood up and said almost despairingly, "Here. I'll show you."

She left the kitchen for a few seconds and returned dragging a large cardboard box along the floor. The box bulged at the sides and was dented in at the top from whatever had been placed on it. The box was so full that whatever had been placed on top did not leave a large dent, just crinkles where tape had been strapped over the folds.

"It was Reverend Brighton's idea, really," she said, kicking at the box. "The people at the church who sold us the bell, gave us this box of clothes to give to the orphans. The box took half the space in the back end of the station wagon! But we crammed it in for the orphans, you know, even though we don't know any orphaned kids."

She looked at the giant box as if opening it would release all the plagues of humanity. "I showed it to Reverend Brighton, and he said the box is too big! There's only one orphanage and that's in Seward, and they don't want to bring any more used clothing because they have plenty. They are carrying blankets, winter gear, books and toys this year. We carried that box two thousand miles for nothing!"

"Not for nothing!" Objected Millie. "There are plenty of needy children. Does it matter if they aren't orphans?"

"That's just what Rev. Brighton said! He said our new church should create its own charity service. We should go through the box and sort things out. There are a lot of needy children in the Chugach. And you know how those donation boxes are. Half what you see in them is only fit for rags. We could cut up the ragged ones for quilt pieces."

Ragged or nice, clothes were clothes, and very few women could resist looking at clothing. Ester slid a knife edge down the center of the tape where it held the folds together and peeled back the flaps. "That is a lot of clothes," she remarked.

The clothes had all been washed and neatly folded, the smell of laundry detergent wafting crisply as soon as the box was opened.

"These clothes don't look so bad," said Andy, holding up a garment. "These overalls would fit Ben. He's always busting out the seat of his pants," she added, laying the bibbed overalls to one side.

"Are you keeping them?" asked Solace, who had been sorting the clothes by gender and size.

"Well, sure," she answered, keeping her fingertips on the item to show she felt no guilt. "I'm needy. I'm a single mom with two kids, a house, and a truck to keep up, and six months left of nursing school. It's not like Ben's close enough to Jimmy's age to get his hand-me-downs. What should I do? Let Ben go bare-assed?"

"Language, Andy," hissed Ester.

"The kids aren't listening. All they care about is the bell. Oh, and look at this little dress, Solace. It will be perfect on baby Stephanie."

"Stephanie qualifies as needy," agreed Ester. "She's half-orphan. Eugene will be a stepdaddy, and Lord knows, as young as they are, her mommy and daddy will need all the help they can get."

"And the Millers," Millie reminded them. "They are definitely needy. Four kids, and only one is a girl. She wears the same hand-me-downs as her brother. She's going on five now, isn't she? About the same age as Ben. She needs some girl's clothes."

"But she's not nearly so large as Ben!" cried Andy, objecting to the stack of frilly, girlish clothing Millie was setting aside. "And get the even sizes. They are made for thinner kids. Dolly is thin."

"They are all nearly new," said Solace with wonder. "Some don't look like they were worn more than two or three times."

"Oh, it's the truth," said Ester, beginning to grow weepy again. "Before going to the church, we had to buy Lee a new set of clothes so we wouldn't be embarrassed in church. Even then..." She dabbed at her eyes with the terrible realization of how clothing deprived their children had been. "We looked humble, you know, among so many wealthy people."

She blew her nose and diligently dived into the box and placed a pile on her lap. She had sighed noisily as she found well-made boy's slacks and button-up shirts in her oldest son's size but sorted them dutifully on the table. Suddenly she gasped as she held up a boy's gray, pinstriped suit. "Oh no! That's it! I'm not giving this to the poor. Look at these things. The poor will be dressed better than our own kids. This isn't tolerable. It's a thirty-dollar suit. Denny deserves it. We were squeezed like sardines all the way home, thanks to this box."

She set it aside, along with several other items she had initially stacked unhappily in the general pile of toddler clothing. "Millie," she said. "You haven't picked out anything for your kids. You should take a few pieces. There's a mountain here."

Millie tilted her head to one side as she fondled the thick wool of a Scandinavian sweater. The sweater was red, with an aurora design rippling across the chest and cuffs. With his pale, fluffy hair and apple cheeks, Jason looked good in red.

"Frank would never approve," she said, setting the sweater down, and smoothing out the soft, electrified fibers. "He doesn't like to accept charity. He hardly approves of the clothing his sisters send me from time to time, but he just doesn't understand you can get clothes so much cheaper and there is so much more to choose from than we get here."

"Don't tell him," Andy advised, nudging her. "If he asks, say Ben outgrew them before he had a chance to break them in. There's some truth to it. I buy all his clothes two sizes too large because he grows so fast."

"Maybe," she agreed, still smoothing out the sweater, then adding a Shirley Temple style pinafore and a pair of Buster Brown pants. She gazed at the three items that would have been formidably priced if she had bought them new at the store. "What about Doreen, Beth, and Sharon? Won't they feel bad if we left them out?"

"Well, we're doing all the work," sniffed Ester. "They can pick out some things if they help with the work."

Millie looked at their half-finished task thoughtfully. "I have a better idea! Let's rummage sale them! They are all nice and clean. We can put some on hangers and some on tables, so they all look attractive."

It was an interesting proposal. If they distributed the clothes, they would have to hunt down the needy homes to deliver their care packages. As many as there were, they would probably have to send some to the northern villages, and it did seem a pity that the village poor would then be better dressed than the pioneers making the deliveries.

The debate continued as they neared the end of the box, continuing to find treasures that were hard to ignore.

It was all about the children.

As much as they scraped for the benefit of the children, their clothing was still the scraps of their labor. Babies grew rapidly and became small children before you knew it. It was impossible to keep up with their needs. Flour sacks were made into dresses, and men's worn-out jeans were cut down of all their usable parts for britches. You mended and patched, and never once thought about how your children were growing shabbier. Poor Ester. Her humiliation still shone in her eyes.

If they held a rummage sale, all they would have to do is display the clothing and people could pick out what they liked. Even the poorest could buy a full wardrobe if they kept their prices low. And they would be happier because they were all contributing to charity.

"What would we use the donation money for?" Solace asked finally. "It doesn't sound right that it would go into the community funds."

They agreed. It wouldn't be right. Community funds were for community projects and none of those projects included a poor fund.

"That's just what we will do," said Millie. "We'll create a poor fund for emergency situations."

Andy surrendered to the profound reasoning, but asked reluctantly, "Does that mean we have to put the stuff back we kept for ourselves?"

"No," decided Millie swiftly. "We'll each put a dollar in the donation box for the clothes we selected, except Ester. Ester brought them and she had to suffer for it. She can have anything she wants from the box."

It was a good plan but there was still a minor hitch. Solace looked at the pile of clothing they had been sorting out for the Miller family. It had grown substantially by the time they had come to the end of the box.

"Should we put these things back too, and let Hannah pick out what she wants at the rummage sale?"

Andy scoffed and enfolded the stack of children's wear as though guarding the crown jewels. "Oh no we don't! You should know Rick by now. Hannah will be lucky if Rick gives her fifty cents to spend at the rummage sale."

It was late afternoon by the time they had finished sorting the mountain of clothes. Solace apologized, as there was still so much left to be done, but she had a diner to run and was feeling uneasy about leaving the girls alone with the evening crowd.

"You worry too much," laughed Andy on the way back. "Now that Iris is getting married, she's been behaving like a grown-up. You should see her at the register. You would have to knock her silly before she would commit a mistake. Carol doesn't like Iris showing her up and knows she won't be distracted by G.I.'s, so she's doing everything she can to become the better waitress. You should put Bea in the kitchen, Solace, not just for washing dishes, but for cooking. She's better at it than the other girls."

It was much as Andy had said. Carol and Iris were out front, handling the waitressing tasks with ease, while Bea was in the kitchen, desperately trying to keep up with the hamburger orders. Since putting in the jukebox, it was nearly always about hamburgers.

Zeb was no use at all. Having found a new group of fresh-faced military boys, he was enticing them into his wicked, too-drunk-to-throw dart game. There was no point in telling a man what he was allowed and not allowed to do.

They don't pay attention to allowances, and very little to words of discouragement. Solace gave him a dark glance as she passed into the kitchen to let him know she knew what he was up to, and took over for Bea, telling her to send in Iris for washing the dishes. She wasn't punishing Iris. She wanted to measure up the girl's skills first-hand and see if she had become as attentive as Andy said.

Iris was efficient. She did everything quickly, with a minimum of energy. After washing the dishes, she helped with cutting and splicing, and even attended the deep fat fryer. At the end of the night, Solace sent Bea and Carol home with their tips, but asked Iris to sit down with her.

"I want you to be secondary supervisor under Andy. Andy will probably leave us once she finishes her nursing training, and I want to spend more time in the bakery, so I'm giving you a raise in the hopes you will stay with us."

The dear girl blushed as she accepted her new position.

"I never thought beyond working for you, maw. Me and Eugene want to find a close by piece of land for setting up our homesite. We're thinking across the way from the Erichman's place. Then it would be within walking distance. He's got a future, they say, because he's so smart, but I like working here and he knows that."

"When are you going to hold your wedding?" asked Solace, handing Iris the new playsets for Stephanie and explaining how she got them.

Iris examined the festive garments approvingly. "She has nearly outgrown everything." She folded them into her lap. "Next month, I think. We talked about it with Reverend Brighton. He's got a lot to handle with Tammy's wedding. I believe she invited everybody, even the President of the United States! We don't want a lot of hoopla. We're not getting married in the church. We want to get married in the diner and just invite our friends and family."

Solace laughed. "If you invite your friends and family to the diner, it will be a lot of hoopla. Why did you wait for the pastor then, if you don't want to marry in the church? Why didn't you just use a justice of the peace?"

Iris shook her head vigorously. "Oh no, we couldn't do that. Rev. Brighton isn't an any old body justice of the peace. He is our pastor. He's tall feeling man."

"I see," said Solace. In a moment of clarity, she did see. They were proud to be called the Place of Many Places. Somehow, they had thought it meant that people of diverse backgrounds living together meant tolerance for individual differences. Now she realized it was more than that. It was a change in views as cultures began blending. It was the creation of a new culture. She saw it in Andy and Mark. She saw it in Iris and Eugene. They were the shape of Chugiak's future, not truly European, not truly Native either, but an incorporation of both.

"We will be proud to host your wedding… daughter."

Epilog

August comes wetly. The sun is too weak to dry up the rain but warm enough for the leaves and grass to glisten greenly on a sunlit day. The sun is waning. Now, the hours of darkness stretched from ten in the evening to seven in the morning and were growing longer with each day.

Goodbye summer. Hello autumn, crisply waiting around the corner. Your golden days are waiting to burst out in glorious attire for a few short weeks before winter shreds your garments and lays you down in a featherbed of snow.

The sun fluttered over the dress laid out on the bed. She had ultimately chosen the blue and green plaid. Millie would not approve. Solace held it up, then slipped it on, studying the way the skirt fell away from the hip then spread out like a bell, leaving her long ankles and pointy shoes as the clapper. The skirt swished back and forth, creating its own music. Who cared what Millie approved of? Maybe next year, she would wear orange. Nobody ever wore orange. Orange with a purple hat. She bet that would get tongues wagging.

Zeb didn't want to wear his new suit. He liked the old one better. "You will wear it!" she scolded. "It's a fifty-dollar suit. This old thing has been patched and mended a hundred times, and the sleeves are frayed. Plus, it's a brown tweed. Nobody wears brown tweed anymore. Do you want the Bolinder's four-year-old to show you up?"

"Ain't nobody told me we had to start going all formal once we got a church," he grumbled. "Who used all the hot water last night? I had to reset the boiler."

"It was Betty Lou. She stayed in the showers so long, I believe she shed twenty pounds of dirt."

He shuffled into his new suit, twisting, wriggling, and trying to find fault with the fitting. It fit just fine. "Did she buy a dress, too?"

He was surprised enough to pause in his half-dressed state. She shook her head. "Neah. She bought a new set of buckskins. She's excited. This is the first real church she's ever gone to, and she's been practicing her hallelujahs all week."

Zeb snorted. "Does she think God Almighty is going to descend on his throne if she gets her hallelujahs just right?"

The smell of coffee wafted thickly into the room. The kids were up. She could hear them in the kitchen, making breakfast. Solace arched her brows as she prepared to join them. "You never know, Zeb. Sometimes, I think Betty Lou knows more about God than any of us."

Unwilling to allow her the last word, he called after her, "Maybe you have to if you're going to live alone in the woods."

It was only Ed. Bea was preening in front of the full-length mirror at the end of the hall. The youngster was as slicked down as a seal, fixing scrambled eggs in his slacks and tee-shirt. "I've gotta get around early, maw," he said, almost apologetically. "I've got an important job to do. Maybe one of the most important jobs there is to do on a Sunday, other than being the preacher."

He gave his eggs a flip and slid them onto a plate. Solace looked at the amazing fluff and golden yellow of his dish. The boy could cook! Why was she using him as a grease monkey and a broom pusher? The new light she had seen in Iris spread out over Ed. He suddenly seemed more mature. If he didn't think in the same way she did, it didn't mean he was wrong. This new understanding endeared him to her. She smiled. "What job would that be?"

He sat proud in his chair, his chest swelling. "I'm the bellringer."

He was wearing Percy's suit, the one her oldest boy had worn when he graduated from high school. Percy left it behind when he left home. He didn't need itwith the type of work he was doing. Sometimes, he worked at the docks unloading crates. Sometimes, he worked as a bar bouncer. Most of the time, he simply worked the streets, unloading the unwary.

Percy's suit was nearly new. She had been so proud of him when he graduated, but he had changed. He was no longer interested in their wilderness settlement. He wanted the lights, the noise, the excitement of the city. He left them. He scorned them. He thought they were fools, squeezing a dollar for a few extra pennies. They no longer talked about Percy, but the vacancy he left behind still hurt, still mourned for the future they had prepared for him and that he had rejected.

The suit was a little too big for Ed. The pant legs folded over his shoes. The shoulders stood like wings floating over Ed's narrower shoulders. But when he looked in the hallway mirror to straighten his tie and put on his bowler hat – a present from Frank – he filled the suit better than Percy ever had.

"You and pa should walk to the church," he suggested. "Charlie said you can hear the bell all the way to Wolf Creek. If you ride in your car, it won't be the same."

Solace began preparing her own breakfast, adding enough eggs and bacon to prepare Zeb's as well. "Won't that make us late for church?"

He was leaving. He paused a minute at the door and said, "nope. I get to start ringing the bell fifteen minutes before church begins. I stop ringing it five minutes before the service starts, so if it stops ringing before you get there, you'll know you're late."

"It only takes fifteen minutes to walk from here."

"Yep. You'll get to hear the bell all the way."

He sauntered off, hands in his pockets, whistling a tune. Ed wasn't really a boy anymore. He was still simple. He was direct and outspoken. He didn't always choose his words with wisdom, but he was right-thinking and honest. He was becoming a man.

"I'm walking to church."

Bea's voice came from behind her. Solace turned and saw her, fully dressed, eating a piece of buttered bread. "This is all I'm having for breakfast," she said, as though Solace had invited her to the table. "I'm on a diet and exercise program. Look at this dress! I could barely get into it."

It did look like a tight fit. The fabric strained into close-packed wrinkles around her fleshy arms and waist. "I'll ask Mrs. Phillips to make you some new dresses unless you want to make them yourself. I don't have time to sew."

"I don't want new dresses. I want to fit into the ones I have. If I'm going to have a new anything, it has to be a poodle skirt. I am dying for a poodle skirt."

"Give Zeb time to eat his breakfast and we'll walk with you."

Bea looked at her mother with alarm. "Oh no! I don't want you walking with me. I'm walking with Brad."

Solace answered back irritably, "I don't know why you spend so much time with Brad. He's not the marrying type. He will only bring you heartache."

"Mother! I don't want to marry him!" She finished her bread and licked her fingers. "I'm almost eighteen and I've never had a date! I just want to know what it's like to have a boyfriend or two before I marry. I just want to know what it's like."

So, that's the way it was when you had children. You molded and shaped them but, in the end, they shaped themselves. It was the modern way of doing things. Women liked to look at their options. They weren't as set on marrying as they had been in the past. Some even chose careers, like that lady journalist, or couldn't decide on just one man, like Andy. Maybe the war changed them. They discovered so many things they could do while the men were gone, when men had become a choice, not a necessity.

Bea was gone before Solace had any words for her. "The children are grown up." She didn't know if she was talking to Zeb, who had finally resigned himself to his church-going clothes and had sat down at the table, or to herself.

"They don't look in any hurry to move out," he observed. "What's this I hear about walking?"

Mrs. Phillips had gone out, her hand tucked around her husband's elbow. Her pink-trimmed burgundy skirt lifted and fluttered with the breeze. Iris and Eugene were just behind them.

Her arms wrapped around her baby, Iris's hip tapped rhythmically against Eugene's, while her long skirt swung back and forth like a bell.

"We are walking. It's probably our last good day of summer. We might as well make the most of it."

"You're the blamedest woman," he said, but didn't argue and didn't really seem perturbed.

Gussied up in his new suit, he was as handsome as the day they married. If Solace had been the sort to always speak her sentiments freely, she would have told Zeb so, but she wasn't. Instead, she showed her approval by patting his forearm.

Surprised at the parade of festive humans tripping down a normally quiet street, a den of rabbits foraging for their last sweet taste of clover close to the side of the road, watched them swinging by. A flock of trumpeter swans flew overhead, their cries ringing in summer's end. A lone butterfly rested on a tree branch, breathing heavily in and out the cool, damp air, waiting for the sun to warm.

Clang! The first bell tone bounced over the hills and rolled over the inlet flatlands.

Clang! Clang! The sounds echoed, the tones changing with each new ring, until throughout the hilly town, it seemed a hundred bells were ringing together. They crested the highest bend and Solace could see them – the couples and lovers and friends. The children growing up strongly together, their toddler legs growing sturdier, their faces absorbed with the wonder of that is life.

The women of Chugiak were all bells. Frank, his mind always on the fancy and lofty linguistics of phrase turns, had said it first. It was true. They were the wilderness voices crying out in sorrow, ringing with both despair and joy. They were the bells in the tower that guided the ships at night.

Clang! Clang! Clang! Clang! The happy music of the bell filled the sky. They had climbed out of the dust and poverty of social collapse, had caught a glimpse of the world's end in a billowing mushroom cloud, yet dared to dream.

They dared believe they could do things differently, care more, give more to others. They were a small group, with only the mountains and the ocean to protect them, but it was enough to hang on to, enough to make them hope their changes would be the changes that influenced the world.

They gathered that day in a church of their own making, their only unification, a belief in a higher power and faith in the future. They gathered under a pastor who was searching as much as they were for an understanding of their spirituality and their place within the universe. They followed their hearts beyond the logic of reason and didn't look back.

The bell chimed its last ring, but the music continued to resonate. It echoed through the mountainous channels. It was the bravest sound in the world – the sound of triumph. They would commune. Some would pray, some would shout for joy, all would sing. They would dream, and in those dreams, make plans. In those shared plans, they would find ways to make the dreams come true, for they were the builders.

Rev. Brighton began his service, his voice bright and springy with the new day. It didn't matter what his words were, his congregation was inspired by him. He could have talked about growing pineapples. They wouldn't have cared.

Solace heard his words drift in and out of her thoughts. He was relating his experiences in the remote region of the far north, the inevitable mosquito swarms, the crisp sun that blazed all summer but cooled down far too quickly when autumn made its appearance. He reflected on children with tuberculosis. You dig deep inside at times like this and question the wisdom of your Maker. Funny, though, Solace thought, she had never questioned her Maker's wisdom. She couldn't explain why He put out a disease like tuberculosis, diabetes, or cancer, although she suspected most sufferings were by human design.

Whoever was at fault, Rev. Brighton did get one thing right. Where there is human suffering, you need to reach out a hand. If you can't do it by yourself, then someone will take your other hand, and another, until you have a bridge to bring the sufferers out of the mire.

Millie had told Rev. Brighton to ask himself if the community was right for him. She was also right. The blueprint had been drawn, the foundation laid, the structure was taking place. Only someone who appreciated the design of the community could become a part of it, could be the helping hand that reached out and pulled people out of their despairing troubles.

Rev. Brighton added to them, strengthening their firm foundation, but he wasn't the end of their building, only the beginning of their vision. The town would grow larger, the people more varied, but they were ready. They had their bridge.

"Hallelujah!" shouted Betty Lou, interrupting the pastor's sermon.

"Hallelujah!" agreed Hannah, jumping up and down in her bench.

"Praise the Lord," said Rev. Brighton gently.

It didn't matter if they shouted hallelujah, danced, shouted, beat a drum, or prayed silently. It was all for the same purpose, the purpose of giving thanks, the purpose of showing joy for what they had been given. The shadow of the war to end all wars was flickering behind them, slowly fading, and the threat of other wars loomed ahead, yet they would not be afraid. What they had built was an idea and ideas don't die. They wait for the spring to nourish them, the summer to blossom, the autumn to throw their seeds, and the winter to strengthen their roots.

It was doubtful much of anybody in the congregation questioned the Lord's wisdom. The Lord's wisdom had shaped them, filled them with the same hunger, had offered the same refreshing water to quench their thirst. The Lord's wisdom had drawn them together. If the Lord created transmittable diseases that affected young, old, and everyone between, there must be wisdom in that as well.

Maybe it was to remind them how vitally they were all connected. Maybe it was to make that handclasp stronger, the bridge wider and sturdier. The congregation didn't question the Lord's wisdom, only humankind's ability to understand it.

The pastor had a new hymn he wanted his followers to learn. It had a catchy tune, but they stumbled over the first stanzas, contemplating the power of the words.

"Come oh thou traveler unknown whom still I hold but cannot see

My company before is gone and I am left alone with thee"

That was the winter, a cold and lingering traveler. He seized you in the night and wrestled from you the shadows where you kept your darkest memories, your deepest fears, playing them back to you in slow panorama so you would never forget.

The unfamiliar song faltered on stumbling lips, picking up supporters in startled pieces, and dying again to a low murmur of puzzled concern for analogies beyond their understanding, but in the last verse, Beth got it. Beth of the magnificent vocal cords and a poet's instincts, belted the song's significance in rolling bell tones.

"Tis love! Tis love! Thou died for me
I hear thy whisper in my heart."

The congregation heard it. They understood. They stood solidly for the last lines, the voices singing joyfully, "Pure Universal Love Thou art".

With the end of the service, the congregation filed out to enjoy the last good day of summer. They blinked in the warming sun and admired their handiwork. They had both a community hall and a sturdy church, but they weren't finished building.

Putting his hands on his hips, Charlie Bolinder studied the undeveloped land across the road from the church. They had already designated the area as community property, as it was adjutant to the hall, even though it was choice land for habitation. It was set within a crown of gently rolling hills, with thin dirt and a voluptuous spread of gravel fanning towards the road.

"That would be a good place to build a school," Charlie mused.

Andy, who had sworn she would no longer attend the church, but had come anyway, scoffed as she lit a cigarette. "Of course you would think so. It's right across the street from your house and that new store you're working on."

"It's sensible," said Frank, taking Charlie's side. "There won't be much to do in clearing and leveling it. We can get all our gravel fill straight from the hillside. There's water. There's a lake just beyond the first hill and plenty of underground springs."

Andy wasn't impressed. "The one thing this community doesn't lack is water. We're just pieces of land floating on top of falling water."

"It's smack in the center of Chugiak," Solace pointed out. "Right between the village and the river."

Andy had no better place in mind for public structures, so she sniffed. "A school would mean we need teachers. Where will we put the teachers? I don't think they want to homestead."

"I'll build apartments," said Charlie. "Then they can walk to school."

"I should have guessed." Andy rolled her eyes and tucked an arm through Solace's. "Didn't I tell you? Charlie plans to build a town all by himself."

Solace chuckled and patted the snugged in arm. "There are more than one kind of builder. You could put up a hundred buildings but that doesn't mean people will come. When you have helped create a community.... Then you know you are a builder. When the people come."

They would come. Solace could feel it in the dancing voices chatting about their fishing trips, their winter preparations, and the upcoming weddings. She could see it in the leveling land, cleared from brush, smoothed for cabins and roads. She could hear it as a faraway background noise of awakening thoughts attracted to an idea.

The idea was Chugiak, the place of many places, where unity is created through diversity. They would come and see the handiwork of the builders. The community wasn't right for everyone. Many would leave, but those who stayed would follow the example of the builders, their voices ringing like bells as the mixed culture they had created becomes their society's culture.

The builders had laid a solid foundation, built on a rock. It was a haven in a protected cove, with a bell to guide the weary. Solace couldn't visualize what their new culture would be, just as a real estate agent doesn't know how the buyer will decorate the rooms of an empty house.

She only knew it was a well-designed house that could easily accommodate new additions. She knew there were storms ahead because storms are inevitable, but their foundation would hold. Their idea would hold because ideas don't die. They are planted like seeds and nurtured by thoughts. They grow when they have good builders and Chugiak's builders were very good.

"And Frank will be his collaborator. Charlie will build the houses and Frank will bring the people, singing and dancing."

"Like the Pied Piper."

"Pretty much."

Frank and Millie had gathered their children and paid their respects to the pastor, shaking his hand and congratulating him on an inspiring service.

It seemed fitting, somehow, that the Lamars should lead the parade of worshipers who had walked from Wolf Creek and were now returning home. The russet sun beamed down, painting the heads of the dapper man and equally dapper woman. Jason scrambled beside him on still-chubby legs, and Nancy clung at the hip of her mother. They were the pipers who drew in the crowd.

The hills were rolling like an ocean. The bell clanged twice, three times, the youngsters pushing each other to make it ring because nobody had said they couldn't. The sound of the bell was like the song of the Chugach, like the beacon and low moan of a lighthouse, calling the lost ships to come home, come home. On an ordinary day, a young couple reached across half the world to tell each other of a common dream. They had an idea that had occurred only to a few coming out of that war to end all wars.

They wouldn't just start over. They would do something different. Like this handful of others, they weren't sure how they would do things differently.

It took the Chugach to teach them. It took the place of many places, which the homesteaders understood was more than a place with a diverse landscape, with meadows and lakes, rivers and swamps, roaring cliffs and gentle hillsides. It was a place where diverse people could come together and learn from each other. It was a blending of people and cultures.

The war didn't end all wars. Already, the great division between the East and the West were stocking their weapons. The imperialistic fear had been replaced by the fear of communism. But on that day, when the church bell rang over the hills of Chugiak for the first time, there was no fear. Native villages rested peacefully alongside Russian villages. European immigrants built alongside American migrants.

The dream was becoming an idea. They were clay shaped by the tides and the seasons. They would learn. They would adapt to all cultures for creating the best culture possible. With each step Millie and Frank Lamar took on their way home, this blending of all races and all walks of life becoming more firmly embedded in the soul of Wolf Creek. The idea would take a long time to mature but the idea had taken roots in the fertile grounds of the Chugach.

Made in the USA
Middletown, DE
18 October 2022